THREE LOVES

THREE LOVES

by

A. J. CRONIN

LONDON
VICTOR GOLLANCZ LTD
1979

First published 1932
25th impression 1979

ISBN 0 575 00069 4

Printed in Great Britain at
The Camelot Press Ltd, Southampton

CONTENTS

BOOK I

I

WHEN she had finished dressing, Lucy went to her bedroom window, but there was still no sign of Frank. And absently she stood behind the long lace curtain, letting her eyes mirror the white stretch of road which followed the estuary shore towards the town, nearly a mile away.

The road was empty except for old man Bowie and his mongrel dog: the one baking the rheumatism from his aged bones upon the low wall outside his little boatyard, the other asleep with head between licked paws, stretched flat on the sun-warmed pavement. For the sun was glorious that August afternoon: spangling across the firth in dancing sequins, touching Ardfillan with a shimmering glow, making of Port Doran's roofs and tall chimneys, across the water, a city glittering and mysterious. Even this prim roadway before her drew in the splendour of the sunshine, and the neat houses which flanked it lost their ineffable precision in that glorious welter of golden light.

She knew it now so well, this view: the glistening water caught within the arms of the sweeping bay, the woods of the promontory of Ardmore shaded to coolness by a blue haze, the rifts of the western mountains tumbled in abundant majesty across the pale curtain of the sky: but to-day, transfigured, it bore an elusive quality of loveliness which somehow uplifted her. The season, too, holding for all its heat the first faint hint of autumn: one wayward leaf rustling on the path, the wrack more saline on the shore, a distant cawing of rooks inland: how she loved it! The Autumn! She sighed from sheer happiness.

Her gaze, shielded against the glare, travelling across the road to Bowie's boatyard, picked up the figure of her son playing aboard the *Eagle*, helping or hindering Dave as he worked on the deck of the tiny launch moored to the grey-stone slip. More likely hindering, she thought, severely stifling all maternal fondness.

Half smiling to herself, she turned and paused before the oak wardrobe, now confronting her image in the glass with the natural instinctive seriousness of a woman before a mirror.

She was not tall—" a little bit of a thing," her brother Richard had tolerantly named her—but beneath her muslin dress her neat form was outlined with a youthful grace. Ridiculously youthful and untried she seemed: looking, as Frank—escaping in an unexpected moment of appreciation his habitual reserve—had consciously suggested, more like sixteen than twenty-six. Her face was small, open, and alert: tending, indeed, towards a natural animation, a vivid quality of eagerness; her skin was fresh and, marked now by the warm print of the sunny summer, wore a delicate bloom. Her eyes, widely spaced, were blue: an opaque blue, reticulated by darker threads which meshed little sparkling points of light; singularly candid and unconcealed. Her mouth had an upward turn, the long line of her neck and chin a smooth round curve, her whole expression a frankness, something constant, vivid, warm in its sincerity.

She raised a hand to her dark brown hair, regarded herself only for a moment, then, folding the plain cotton dress she had worn during the day, she placed it in the bottom drawer of the wardrobe and, making a last swift inspection of the room to ensure its order, noting the shining linoleum, the exactitude of the antimacassar upon the fluted rocker, the smooth hang of the white bed-mat, she gave a neat movement of satisfaction with her head, swung round, and went downstairs.

To-day she was later than usual—Friday was her baking day—but the clean smell of her polished, spotless house—a mingling odour of beeswax, soap, and turpentine, incense to the nostrils of a house-proud woman—rose up to justify her tardy dressing.

A due and modest pride was hers in the immaculate perfection of her house: the small, detached habitation—by courtesy a villa—situated so pleasantly on the outskirts of Ardfillan. She liked her house did Lucy, liked also to see it shine! And now, within her kitchen, she turned towards the open door of her scullery, said enquiringly:

" Finished up yet, Netta? "

" Just this minute, Mrs. Moore," came the answer, muffled through lips which clasped a hairpin, from Netta, the maid, now achieving a belated toilet at the small square mirror above the copper.

" Mr. Moore will be home any minute now," continued Lucy reflectively. " I heard the train go down. If I were you, I'd slip in the eggs. Four."

" Yes, Mrs. Moore "—this rather indulgently!

" And careful when you poach them, Netta. A little vinegar in the water—to firm them. Don't forget now."

" Indeed *no*, Mrs. Moore."

The lips, no longer constrained, protested the impossibility of such omission, and in a moment Netta herself supported the declaration by an emphatic appearance through the scullery door.

She was a rangy girl of seventeen—willing, touchy, reticent, and amiable; yet through her amiability she betrayed already the self-determination of her race. Knowing by hereditary instinct her worth, and the worth of her sturdy stock, she would not, despite her willingness to work, admit to serve. No coercion would have drawn the words " Sir " or " Madam " from her ruddy, independent cheeks, but, instead, she maintained a presupposed equity towards her employers by addressing them in civil yet unservile terms as Mr. and Mrs. Moore. Upon some occasions, indeed, a faint superiority tinged her immature manner, as though, conscious of the atrocious doctrinal peculiarity of the Moores, she balanced heavily against it the consideration of her own worth and orthodoxy.

Now, however, she smiled, and said consciously:

" I'm longer dressing since I've started putting my hair up."

" You're longer," thought Lucy, " since Dave Bowie started looking at you."

Aloud she said:

" It's nice. Does Dave like it that way? "

Netta tossed her high-piled head in answer—what maidenly coquetry and tender yearnings did not this brusque sign express?—and tapped an egg sharply against the pot rim.

" Him! " said she; and that was all. But she blushed violently towards the vinegar bottle.

Standing a moment watching the girl's movements, Lucy concealed a smile. She had, suddenly, a realisation of her own happiness, a ridiculous contentment mingling with a pleasant feeling of achievement, that personal coolness and tidiness following her dressing, a sense of having earned this present leisure. She loved always this moment, which usage had not staled, of Frank's return from the city: she, dressed and ready, her work done, her house immaculate, awaiting him; it gave her unfailingly a little thrill of warm expectancy. Turning, she went through the narrow lobby, opened the front door, sauntered along the pebbled pathway. The small square green, with its plot of calceolarias, lobelias, and geraniums—a combination in that year of the Diamond Jubilee admittedly the last word of horticultural artistry—bloomed effulgently under her appraising eye. Delicately she plucked an impudent weed which harassed the more voluptuous of the geraniums; delicately she cast it from her. Then, walking to the front gate, she swung it open.

Now there was movement in the road, a quick scatter of sounding movement, and, looking up, Lucy saw her son coming towards her, his shadow trotting gaily beside him as he raced along.

" Mother! " he exclaimed immediately, with an air of great tidings. " I've been working on the *Eagle* with Dave."

" No! " she exclaimed, displaying an adequate amount of incredulity.

" Yes," he affirmed, with all the enthusiasm of eight years for the momentous, " and he let me splice a rope."

" Gracious! What next! " she murmured, thinking about the freckles upon his nose. The nose was frankly snub, and the freckles merely points of pigment. There were also, she freely admitted to herself, other noses and other freckles; but for her the combination of this nose and these freckles was irresistible!

A well-set-up boy for his age, she often thought—" refined " was perhaps the word—brown-haired, and with his father's light brown eyes. Other boys? Most assuredly they had their virtues, but not— not quite like Peter!

" Can I go and play marbles? " he was asking ingenuously.

" Marbles? " she repeated, with real incredulity. " Where did you get marbles? "

He grinned at her, showing the gaps between his growing teeth, and his grin ravished her; then he lowered his eyelashes, which had, it seemed to her, an exquisite darkness against the fruit-like freshness of his cheek.

" Well," he said meditatively, kicking the toe of his boot against the wall, " they just began playing to-day, so I borrowed two from a boy. Then I played him, you see, and I won—then I paid him back, you see. You see how it happened, mother? "

" Oh, I see," she returned, controlling her lips. He put his hands behind his back, threw out his stomach, and straddled slightly to look at her the better.

" It was quite fair, wasn't it? " he suggested, with his eyes at different levels. " That's how it's done—at least, how I did it. I've got fifteen for my jug." He had lately begged from her a metal-lidded jug wherein, with miserly intensity, he hoarded all his minor treasures. " And if you let me play, I might win more."

" Well," she considered, with a judicial air which took all sting from her refusal. " I think we'll have tea first, anyway. Your father'll be home any minute."

" Ah! " he said profoundly, with the air of having received her confidence; then he reflected openly: " I wonder if he'll bring me anything. Might, you know! "

" Run in, anyway, and wash your hands." To prove that she could be severe with him for his good, she added: " They're a perfect disgrace."

" Well, you see," he explained, examining his dark knuckles and the lines on his sweat-stained palms, " if you work on the *Eagle*. And that splice—whew! " He paused, and, beginning suddenly to whistle, turned and made off along the path.

As the boy entered the house, her gaze detached itself and fell again upon the road to the town, expectant of the appearance of her husband. A moment later, indeed, he swung into sight, slouching carelessly along towards her. It was so like him, this leisured gait, that, involuntarily, she made a slight sound, half affection, half impatience, with her tongue; and suddenly, with instinctive association, there came to her a realisation of the fitness of her marriage.

" Yes, indeed," she meditated, tacitly affirming their suitability towards each other. " It's as well I took Frank in hand." And, dwelling upon the happiness, the rare success of their present state, her thoughts leaped back through the years to the pre-ordained occasion of their meeting. What was that name again? Yes, " The Kyle "— owned by the Misses Roy. Never would she forget that name, nor Miss Sarah Roy, the managing sister who didn't cook, presiding, all jet front and trained eye, at the head of the " liberal table "—the phrase was Miss Sarah's from her advertisement in the *Catholic Trumpeter*; " patronised by the clergy and the cream of the laity," ran the rest.

Yes, " The Kyle " was irreproachably genteel, or Richard and Eva would never have gone. Richard had always been a stickler, punctilious, even in those early days of his married life before he had made his way in the law; besides, he *would* have things right for his Eva. Hadn't mattered about her, of course; she had been simply taken—an extraordinary mark of brotherly patronage. Or had it been to look after Charlie, the baby? Eva, following her confinement, was languishing—not strong!

Richard and she had never got on really well—some curious incompatibility, or was it similarity, of temper—though, left together as they had been, they ought to have agreed. And when young Moore had started to pay her attention——!

At the recollection she almost smiled: Frank, on his fortnight's holiday, ill at ease, careless or ignorant of the precise gentilities of the table, altogether in the wrong galley; " a butter and egg man " —Richard's phrase—" making up to her! "

Ridiculous to have met your husband at a boarding-house—and at Ardbeg, of all places! Not very dignified; rather—rather commonplace. And yet Frank and she, drawn together by the very opposites of their qualities—drawn irresistibly together—there had been no getting away from it. Both of them rather flushed, that lovely languid afternoon—just such an afternoon as this, when the dry larch needles in the Craigmore wood were warm to her moist palms, and the resin-oozing pines exhaled a heavy, heady scent. Beneath them the sweep of the bay; around, the hum of insects in the bracken; within her a happiness, rushing, ardent, soft. Not so backward then as at table, young Moore!

But Richard had been severe, inimical, holding to ridicule her association with a petty commercial traveller. Yes, though Moore professed, with some indifference, their own creed, Richard had disliked him: a nobody, he said, the product of Irish parents expatriated by the famine; peasants, he suspected, driven out by the failure of two potato crops, when turnips were thrown to the starving people, and the empty cart piled up with the corpses that lay upon the roadside. They came to Scotland, these Irish, to beget their prolific progeny, a mongrel breed: supplying chiefly the navvy and the labourer, or, in its higher flights, the bookmaker and the publican; a race unwanted, and uncouth.

Not a pleasant picture for Richard, proud of his Scottish birth and his good Murray blood, who later, at Eva's whim, had linked his pedigree to a Jacobite strain.

Well, the issue had been plain, the upshot swift: Richard and she had disagreed in this, as in most things; as if she would, indeed, let anyone control her choice. They had simply walked off, had Frank and she, that day nine years ago.

That was why she was here, waiting at this gate, conscious of her happiness, aware quite firmly and unashamedly of her love for him.

He came nearer. She waved her arm—a restrained wave, no doubt, but nevertheless a wave; an action differing openly from the unobtrusive conduct of the age. In that year when the red flag still moved cautiously upon the public highway, normal wives did not greet their partners in matrimony in this immodest fashion. To wave the arm was not becoming! And he too, by an answering upraising of his hand, confirmed the act, established the certainty of misdemeanour.

" Hallo! " she challenged, smiling long before he reached her.

" Hallo, yourself! "

He was a tall, loosely built man of thirty, not well dressed, with a relaxed carriage amounting to a stoop. His hair was light brown, his colour tending to be florid, his eyes a peculiar limpid shade of hazel, his teeth of an arresting whiteness. Some quality about him— his lounging air, the slackness of his gait, an indifference in his eye, mingling with an odd reserve—stamped him with a curious individuality, as though indolently he weighed the universe and found it worthy merely of mistrustful irony.

" You're late," said she briskly, noting with satisfaction, more for him than for herself, that the moodiness which so often clouded his brow was absent. " I thought you'd missed the 4.30."

" Moore misses nothing," he returned amiably, " except his prayers. You trust him. F. J. Moore! "

" Did you forget my d'oyleys? " she enquired, as they went up the path together, and the form of her question was significant.

He looked at her sideways less confidently, and rubbed his cheek slowly with his hand.

" That's too bad of you, Frank," she reproached him. It was so like him to forget. And he had said specifically he would be passing Gow's to-day. Gow's—acknowledged in the Moore family as the paragon of emporia in Glasgow: if it came from Gow's it was good. Everything in the villa, from the cottage piano to the cullender, had been provided at one time or another in return for ready money by the almost omnipotent Mr. Gow.

" A tin of sardines," he answered slowly. " I could bring you that next Friday—to make up for it." Her lips twitched; yet, really, she had wanted those d'oyleys; and he had forgotten all week. But that was like him: he would forget anything—her birthday, Peter's, even his own—yes, more than once he had confessed to an ignorance of that momentous date.

" Quite meatless," he assured her gravely. " Supplied to all the confraternities. My dear brother Edward recommends them. Not a sin in a tin."

She shook her head, laughed in spite of herself.

" Is that how you are to-night? " said she.

They went into the small dining-room, which lay between the parlour and the kitchen in the straight sequence of rooms on the ground floor of the house—no complexity about the architecture of the " villa "!—and here, when Peter had tugged the bell-handle at his mother's request, the three sat in to tea.

" And what's been doing to-day? " said Moore, after Netta had made her bustling entry, like a breeze, and taken her independent departure. " How many murders since this morning? "

" Things just as usual," she returned calmly, passing him the toast. " Except that your son appears to be hoarding marbles now."

Moore's eyes dwelt for a moment on the grinning boy.

" Solid Shylock, that one is," he murmured towards his egg.

" And I met Miss Hocking in town this morning," went on Lucy.

He eyed her over the rim of his cup—he had habitually a stooping position at table—and said with an agreeably derisive air:

" Pinkie, darling! And what had she got to say for herself? "

Conscious of his mood, she shook her head agreeably, non-committally, without deigning to reply.

" Funny thing," he persisted, " I can't get the length of her foot nohow. Too la-de-dah, is Pinkie." In an affected voice he intoned: " Hoity-toity. Heaven's almoighty. I belave she's crazy." He drank the last of his tea, added with significant emphasis: " the less we mix with them here the sooner. It's the place I like——"

" Now you're ridiculous, Frank—as usual," she rejoined tranquilly.

At this moment the knocker rapped smartly upon the front door, causing Peter to exclaim:

" Post! " and at a nod from his mother, to slide from his chair and run into the hall. He came back with a letter, exclaiming with a responsible air of triumph: " It's for you, mother! "

Lucy took the letter, examined the square envelope, the writing of the address, the postmark blurred over the red stamp, with scrutinising brows and distant, slightly tilted head. Then she slit open the envelope carefully with her knife.

" I thought so," she remarked placidly.

A faintly petulant air spread over Moore's face; he took a quill toothpick from his vest pocket and, reclining in his chair, watched her slowly read the letter.

" From Edward, I suppose," he said satirically, before she had finished, thinking of their most regular correspondent. " What is his reverence after now? Is it the state of our souls or the state of his liver? "

But she did not answer; indeed, with silent, moving lips and intent eyes, she did not hear him: always when Lucy read her absorption was complete.

" Well," he persisted, " has Miss O'Regan got the mumps, or what is it? "

At this association of ideas—he knew Uncle Edward's house-keeper, and he knew also from sad experience about mumps—Peter let out a short giggle. But the letter was not from Edward.

" It's from Anna," said Lucy at last, laying down the note and looking up with a pleased expression. " She's coming. Joe'll drive her over from Levenford next Thursday."

" Anna! " exclaimed Moore, in a moody, completely altered voice; he threw down the letter, which he had briefly scanned. " Anna coming! What—why on earth did you ask her? "

She frowned at his manner—and before the boy, too.

" You forget that she's your cousin," she exclaimed. " It's simply common decency—hospitality—to have her over for a week."

" Hospitality! A lot of fuss about nothing, you mean."

" My dear Frank," she argued, with unanswerable logic, " was it a lot of fuss when Anna and her father gave you hospitality when you had to go to Belfast? And for more than three months, too."

" It was for business I was over—that's why I had to stay with them," he answered restlessly. " I tell you I don't want to be bothered with Anna."

" Well, I'll be bothered with her," she replied, maintaining her calm even in the face of his supreme unreason. " Remember that I've never even seen Anna. I want to know her."

" Know her be hanged," he cried resentfully. " I don't want her in my house, or, for that matter, I don't want any of the rest of the gang "—thus he characterised his relations.

She frowned. Yes, this was a side of him—this desire, so antagonistic to her own friendly instinct, to avoid people, to keep separate, detached even from his own relations—which always irked her. With an involuntary spurt of her lively temper, she said indignantly:

" Good gracious! What harm will it do us to have Anna over? You're always running down your friends—your own brothers even. You sneer at Edward because he's a priest, and Joe doesn't please you because he's a publican. And now Anna! "

" The priest and the publican," he echoed moodily. " A pretty pair. What did they ever do for me, or for anybody else? And I tell you again I don't want Anna here."

" Why don't you want her to come? "

" I just don't want her here."

" Are you perfect yourself, that you can afford to take up that attitude? "

" You should know. You married me, didn't you? " he countered sulkily.

She bit her lower lip, which quivered indignantly, conscious of this cloud pressed down into the small sunlit room—simply because a postman had knocked at their door with a letter from his cousin. And really, what had she done? To invite this cousin, Anna Galton, to spend a few days with them. Was that an unpardonable crime? Anna, " born and brought up " in Levenford, had left ten years ago for Ireland with her father, who, a partner of Lennox & Galton—Frank's own firm—had then settled in Belfast to take charge of the exportation end of the business. Now old Galton was dead, and Anna, returning to arrange with Lennox upon the matter of the settlement of the estate, had not unnaturally taken thought to visit her relatives. Surely it was reasonable after those years, that long, protracted absence! Already she had been with Joe a fortnight at Levenford; she would probably go on to Edward at Port Doran; what, then, was more inevitable than that she should come here to Ardfillan? It was an act of social decency. It was more than that: for, when Frank had been obliged to go to Belfast five years ago, to take charge of the agency on account of old Galton's illness—it was the first attack of that angina which finally carried him away—he had been admirably looked after by his cousin for over three months. A great relief it had been to her, this sense of Frank's security, when, knowing him, knowing how easily he could be imposed on, she had dreaded damp beds, bad food, indifferent hotels—those evils which might arise from his separation from her. And yet, here was Frank, protesting against this hospitality which she proffered in return. The very thought roused her indignation; but with an effort she compressed her lips, stifled the angry words that lay ready upon her tongue.

For a moment there was silence; then Moore got up slowly, with a slightly shamed air; he pulled the inevitable green cardboard packet from his pocket, lighted a cigarette. His boots on the dyed sheepskin, his shoulder against the marble mantelpiece, he inhaled a puff, watching her self-consciously out of the corner of his eye.

" Bit of a rush we had to-day," he said at length, rather sheepishly.

It was actually an apology. She smiled openly, renewing at once the normal current of feeling between them, and, tacitly avoiding the subject of contention, she declared:

" I'll have something to say to Mr. Lennox about that one of these days. Soon, too! "

" What do you mean ? " he asked, surprised.

" You'll see! " And she gave that competent little nod. " I'm going to ask him to supper next week."

Without replying, he stared at her as she rose and began to clear the table, then insensibly his gaze drifted through the window. The tide was out, and on the hard dry sand some children were playing. Rounders! Peter had slipped out to join them, and in the cool of the evening lent to the proceedings a swift foot and a thin but penetrating voice. Moore watched idly: what was he doing with a son? Used to play rounders himself when he was a kid; and now——! Funny how things came along—just happened! And Anna coming—it was an unpleasant thought. He didn't want her in his home. Lovely evening it was, though. Might go out and cut the grass. Then he thought he wouldn't. To-morrow, perhaps. To-morrow—it was a great word with Moore. Idly, he sat down on the horsehair sofa by the window; out came the green packet; he lighted another cigarette, let the smoke down his nostrils. Watching the glowing tip of his cigarette, he remarked:

" Lennox is going ahead with that idea."

She paused in her clearing of the table, contemplating the information, which already she had studied intimately. The fact was that his firm—it was the same firm of eight years ago, with Lennox now the sole proprietor—in business as importers of Irish produce, had decided to extend their interest to the importation from Holland of the new synthetic commodity: margarine. Odious word! More odious substance! Yet Lucy did not demean the issue by dwelling upon the vileness of this new butter substitute. Enough that with the march of progress Lennox proposed extending his small business. She favoured the extension because she had her ambition for Frank in this direction. It was time that he too advanced, and she would be at the bottom of that advancement.

His present position she did not often define—perhaps because she did not care to define it; sufficient to say that Frank was " with " Lennox & Galton: a pleasant implication of trust and indispensability, and with quite a comfortable wage. Yet, for all her loyal euphemism, coldly described his post was merely that of a petty commercial traveller. It was not right. It was not just! She desired for him something better, something altogether more important than that. Ardently she desired him to " get on," and already in her eager mind she had formulated her project. She had spoken to Frank of this project, yet she knew he was evading the issue under the pretence of considering it. " Of course I'll see about it. Give us time," she heard him reply; or, with an assumption of great candour: " I'll speak to L. to-morrow." But he had not seen about it; nor, she was sure, had he even mentioned it to Lennox, despite his frequent assertion that he " had the measure of the old man's foot." That was like Frank: how often had she chafed at his vacillation. But now, with a contemplative eye upon him, she said:

" Perhaps that's going to be the making of us, Frank. Not that I think much of the stuff "—she concealed her eagerness with a shade of satire—" nothing like butter. I wouldn't have it in my house."

" It's a clever idea though—and cheap." He could adduce no more articulate arguments for its success. " And Lennox is pretty wide. I believe I could sell it for him." He yawned. " I'd like to die rich—if they don't hang me first. Might combine the two. Millionaire's last speech from the dock. ' Dearly beloved brethren, I am an innocent man. Never done nothing but tear my scapulars.' "

He relapsed into silence, staring out of the window towards the beach where Netta, who had gone to call Peter at the hour of his bedtime, was now in the last act of that nightly pantomime, chasing the boy wildly to the gate.

At the scutter of footsteps upon the pebbled path, Lucy went out of the room, carrying the loaded tray. Moore sat still; said good night to his son, who came in, presenting a face still effervescent beneath its perspiration; then he waited. It came to him easily, this waiting, and somehow epitomised his character. He appeared always to be awaiting something—a little nervously, a little moodily, as though in effect he had the premonition of some disaster which would one day come upon him. It was this tendency in him which caused Lucy sometimes to shake her head questioningly, failing, in her own boundless energy, to comprehend fully his outlook. Often she wished him brisker, less indifferent to the minor details of existence. There was, indeed, as little doubt of Moore's indolence as of his moodiness, his scepticism, his weakness—altogether he was a queer fish; yet for all that he was not without his accomplishments. He could, for example, pare the skin from an apple intact, in one long pellicle of wafer thinness; he could make a willow whistle to perfection; he could discover mussels on the Ardmore shore and roast them there to tempt an anchorite. In his management of a toothpick —the quill had a meditative protrusion from his lips—he was unrivalled. He had, too, at times a curious humour. When people commented, as they often did, on his really exquisite teeth, he would say seriously: " That's because I cleaned them on turnips when I was young." Or, again, who but Moore, accompanied by his wife in her best Sunday clothes, would have stopped a stone's throw from his own house and gravely demanded of old Bowie to be directed to that house?

" Excuse me, Mr. Bowie," he had said politely, seriously, " can you tell me where Mr. Moore lives? " When the stupefied old man, he was seventy and of an apoplectic tendency, had raised a palsied pointing finger, Moore had acknowledged his information with the same punctilious gravity.

" Thank you, Mr. Bowie. Will you accept this? " And, pulling a match-box from his pocket, he had rewarded the stricken ancient with a single match. Then, his head in the air, he had strolled away whistling " Boyne Water." Lucy had been furious. Yet that, somehow, was Moore.

But he was seldom so gay; at other times he had frightful fits of melancholy, when he would crouch over the fire sitting absolutely motionless, his lower lip protruding, in a brooding misery, his dark eyes staring fixedly into the leaping flames.

He had, moreover, little gift for friendship, and that only in the oddest quarters: the rabbit-catcher of the Gielston Woods, a roadmender who cracked his heap of stones along towards the Point; that same old Bowie, whom he named the Ancient Mariner and to whom he often threatened to teach the art of knitting. He knew nothing about knitting—but that again was Moore. F. J. Moore, idler, dreamer, maker of willow whistles, upon whom there seemed always that indefinable melancholy presage of disaster, that presage which often made him moodily to say: " It's a bad end I'll come to. If they don't make a lord of me, they'll hang me. Sure."

But now, as he sat at ease, Lucy had returned. Briskly she took up her ribbon embroidery—a black satin cushion-cover with floral and bow design—and seated herself companionably beside him on the sofa.

" Well," she demanded pleasantly, " what's in the paper? You might at least let your poor wife know what the news is to-night."

Half-heartedly he picked up his evening paper, skimming through the news: the sheets made a continual rustle as he turned from one page to another, then back again, looking for something of less than superficial interest. Occasionally he read out an item, adding his comments, which were invariably wisely sceptical. " Believe it if you like," his attitude said, or, " You know what they say in the papers "; but he heard willingly—indeed, he openly invited—her opinion. Moreover, at her request he read aloud a short article pertaining to the current fashions in feminine attire: interested in dress was Lucy—perhaps, as he averred at times, unduly so: and she listened attentively, desisted even from her sewing, nodding her head once or twice in appreciative agreement.

At length the paper was exhausted: he let it drop in a crumpled heap.

" Take up a book," she suggested, after a few moments, biting off an end of silk and threading her needle.

But he hadn't much taste for books: liked a weekly paper occasionally. *Photo-bits* he used to read; not that he cared much for it; you could get a stray joke for a customer, there, odd times! But Lucy had put her foot down firmly after that day Peter had run to her with a number, enquiring about " the ladies with stuffed legs." So he put his hands behind his head and leaned back on the smooth horsehair.

" It's easier doing nothing," he replied. " I'll take it quiet for a bit." He sat watching her whilst gradually the dusk crept into the room, and in his face, with the growing darkness, there kindled slowly a warm consciousness of her nearness to him. At last she gave a little exclamation.

" I can't see," she cried, smiling at him—and her smile was fascinating in that shadowy room. " I'll have to light the lamp."

" What," he said meaningly, " would we be wanting with the lamp? "

" To sew by, of course."

" Ah! you've done enough sewing for to-night."

His hand, stretched out to detain her, slipped round her shoulders, drawing her close. The cushion-cover, so richly wrought, fell unheeded from her lap; passive and contented she lay against him. Yes, she was contented. She did not deny her happiness; nor did she lack a modest confidence towards the future. And she was, ah! yes, she was so fond of Frank. For a few moments they lay thus whilst the last faint streak of twilight slipped softly from the room. Then gradually she felt his hand slip under the bodice of her dress, move gently, caressingly. It was a sign—a little sign they had. Her bosom rose and fell warmly against his side, and, unseen, she smiled again: she had known this mood of his! But it was so like Frank to turn to her here, unexpectedly, in this spontaneous fashion. And she murmured, provocatively, her breath upon his face:

" You'll have to behave, you know, when Anna's here! "

He made as though to speak; but he did not. And then he had no chance to speak, for all at once she pressed her warm lips against his cheeks.

" I love you, Frank," she whispered. " You know I do."

ON the following Thursday at half-past five the wagonette driven by Joe from Levenford, containing Joseph himself, his sister Polly, Anna and Anna's luggage, drew up opposite the house with a flourish. The flourish was because Joe on the box was imperative, justifiable, magnificent. And now, swinging down his bulk, he ensured the tired nag's comfort by a benignant pat upon its steaming flank and a clicking sound of approbation with his tongue. His air towards the horse was largely professional. Joe was, indeed, professional towards everything; nothing big Joe didn't know! A marvellous omniscience in one who read nothing, signed his name with difficulty, and misused the Queen's English with affable contempt. In his own idiom, everything " came easy " to Joe; and little wonder; he was—again the idiom—such a " good fella." True, he was a publican; he sold spirits; he was even, in a quiet way, something of a bookmaker. But what of that? He had been known, very decently, to protect his customers from their own vicious instincts by a judicious blending of his wares with honest Scottish water; and as for the ' gee-gees "—well, there was a certain nobility in this connection with the turf, and at this moment it was manifest how much Joe loved a spanking bit of horseflesh. But now, a thumb in one armhole, his head thrown back, he called out affably to the others:

" Aloft there! Down you get. And leave the trunk. Frankie'll take that in. Holy St. Bridget! That dust has gave me a thirst."

Then, with permissible swagger, he advanced up the path; it was as though his bearing said: Let all who deny the Irishman's right to invade and acquire Scotland gaze upon the figure of Joseph Moore and be confounded.

He was big—not so much tall as bulky, the honourable full-bellied bigness of the publican—and he had all the big man's heartiness. Benevolent geniality glistened out of his small black eyes that were set deeply, currants in the suet of his smooth pale face; his nostrils were comfortably wide, and little tufts of hair stuck out of them; his teeth, which he showed when he parted his broad, blue-stippled upper lip, glistened also strong and regular, part of his ivory skull. Upon his round and close-cropped head, that narrowed at the top, his billycock sat at a knowing tilt; his short tan dustcoat fell rakishly apart; and his boots, befitting his blue suit, were a beautiful shade of ochre. Altogether he was a grand figure of a man, not young, of course—his age was fifty—but his spirit—ah, Joe's spirit was eternal. Something of that spirit could be gathered from his brawny heartiness; but there were incidents, numerous historic incidents, which testified more fully to Joe's capacity and the essential magnificence of his marrow. That occasion, for example, when he had blandly retailed to a drunken riveter, who had rashly sworn once and for all to taste champagne, a bottle of ginger ale; that other when, having purchased a parrot warranted to sing, he had found the bird songless and caused it instantly to be stuffed; and that when, invited to an ecclesiastical banquet, he had starved himself for two long days beforehand—astounding self-denial—to do more justice to the sumptuous repast.

That was Joe, inimitable, and as he proceeded up the path, behind him came his sister Polly—two years younger—waddling a little, as was excusable from her girth and the manifest importance of her petticoats. She was not as tall as Joe, but she was fatter, so fat that she had an almost sagging look which diminished, apparently, her stature. With her round chins beneath her full red face, her heavy breasts—twin obscenities—her pendent stomach, even her ankles flowing in slack folds over her half-buttoned gaping boots, she had the air as though the force of gravity acting upon her adiposity strove continually to weigh her downwards. Even her hair was a little down her back. Her dress was rich, and, though it might oppress the eye, at least " there was money in it." As for its colours, they had the virtue of pleasing Polly. Over all she wore a loose fur cape, out of season—" for the drive, you know "—and now she panted.

Arrived upon the doorstep, Polly drew breath whilst Joe announced their advent by a series of boisterous pulls upon the bell. A sight to do the heart good, this pair, so reassuring, so full of the comfortable zest of living. As Netta swung open the door, he took Polly by the arm, exclaiming gallantly:

" Intil the house with you. Wha' d'ye mean by standing like a pig with its eye on the butcher? "

" I can't walk through you, can I now? " said Polly, answering his badinage like some faithful back-chat comedian. It was clear she loved Joe; that admiration mingled freely with her sisterly affection. For five years now she had been his housekeeper, and in those years immeasurable adulation had gushed from her generous bosom towards him.

He gave her a playful push by way of recompense, then, turning genially, he cried:

" Anna! Come along, guyrl! What are you stuck there for? " And in the same jovial second he was in the hall, pumping Lucy's hand—he always made a fuss of her on the rare occasions that they met—staging a mock encounter of fisticuffs with Peter, calling out loudly for his brother.

" Frankie! Let's have a swatch at you, Frankie boy."

He was a fine fellow, was Big Joe Moore—in his own phrase: " By God he was an' all."

" Frank'll be down in a minute," said Lucy quickly. She had with difficulty induced him to go upstairs to shave and change his suit; and, her wrapper that moment discarded, she was a little warm and flurried from her own exertions in the kitchen. " I'm delighted to see you," she declared openly. " But, Anna—where's Anna? "; and her bright eye slipped over Joe's shoulder eagerly.

" Anna! " shouted Joe again, and, removing his hat, he hung it up on the back of his head.

Anna advanced, though not assuredly at his bidding, with a negligent air, her manner passive and composed. She was dark and tall, her dress quiet, her figure good, her age under thirty, her face pale, contained, with large, dark, almost stolid brown eyes. Those eyes had a drooping, indifferent look, her lip, protruding, a vague fullness, her whole expression, half-smiling, half-disdainful, a curious ambiguity at once defensive and averse.

" So you're Anna," said Lucy, smiling and offering her hand " I'm glad—glad you've come."

" Thanks," said Anna pleasantly. Her voice was quiet, surprisingly refined. Anna's whole appearance, considering her origin and her background, gave Lucy a sudden unexpected pleasure. I'll like her, she thought instinctively. I *am* glad I invited her.

" And I'm not sorry to be quit of her," broke in Polly, with a jocular shake of her plumes—ostrich feathers of a purple hue were in her hat. " Deed and I'm not. She's been keeping my brother Joe off his work this last fortnight. An' him a decent man with a starvin' sister on his hands."

Peter, arrayed in his kilt, as all occasions of company demanded, let out a sudden laugh, then blushed vividly; he had been previously grounded in the adage that he be seen but not heard.

" Good! Good! " cried Joe, slapping his haunch. " We're all aboard for Mullingar "; and he took the boy's arm as they moved into the dining-room—now arranged elegantly for the amenities of " high tea." Imposing sight. Lucy's best was on that table: her finest napery, her brightest cutlery, the silver biscuit-barrel that had been her mother's—Richard had wanted that barrel and hadn't had it!—even her " hand-painted " wedding china, preserved miraculously intact throughout the years. And there was choice food upon the table; cold meat, pancakes, scones, a promising ham; and the crochet mat beside the epergne gave promise of a hot dish to come. Unquestionably the preparation of this repast had cost Lucy trouble. It was a fact, moreover, that the tone of those familiar assemblies rasped at times her sense of strict decorum. But this, in her decided way, she put briskly to one side. These were Frank's people, and she had her social instincts towards them. A sense of social obligation.

Meanwhile Joe had fixed the table with an eloquent eye.

" Bedam! I could do with a tightener," said he agreeably, pulling down his waistcoat, and patting his paunch with sympathetic understanding. " Me and Polly and Anna left early."

Here Polly, making leisurely but intimate inspection of the photographs, fingering the ornaments and the china on the stand, addressed the air:

" Shook the hunger out of me, you did, with your scorching. And me not well. Wind round the heart," she explained to Lucy with an air of exclusive ownership towards the affliction. Polly had indeed proprietary rights, or at least an option, on several of the more harrowing morbidities. " Like a stone it is! Hard and heavy as a lump. Then ' ffflute,' up it comes with a rush! It'll finish me some day."

" What's come of that brother of mine? " cried Joe, sniffing impatiently. " Where is he—seeing a man about a dog? "

Almost at that moment Frank came into the room, wearing that conscious, troubled look, the result of his effort to appear natural and at ease.

" How is the body, boy? " roared Joe at once.

Frank nodded without enthusiasm, then opposite Anna he paused awkwardly and hesitated; his best suit sat upon him stiffly.

" You're back again then, Anna," said he.

" Well, that's pretty plain, Frank," she answered, with her elusive smile. " You'd think you didn't know me now."

" I'd have known you all right," he said, in his constrained voice. " You're not the least changed since I was over there."

" That's good," she replied evenly. She had a pleasant composure, her striking feature a capacity for stillness.

" Mr. Lennox may come in later," said Lucy, breaking in upon the short succeeding silence. " But we'll not wait. He said he'd be after tea."

They sat down to the meal in the utmost harmony, Netta appearing briskly with a steaming ashet, Lucy, a little flushed from her pouring, eagerly attentive to the needs of her guests.

" I hope you're going to enjoy your visit," she remarked, leaning companionably towards Anna. " Peter's arranged a picnic for you. And we've been invited to spend a day with Edward at Port Doran. But perhaps you're going to stay there later? "

" No," said Anna reflectively, " I don't think I'll stay there."

" Never cared much, did you, Anna, for Ned? " panted Polly through her toast.

" Ned," said Anna, gently considering the Rev. Fr. Moore. " He's as nice a priest as you'd meet anywhere."

" Order, order, Anna," cried Joe, masticating jocularly, perceiving perhaps a tinge of irony where none had been intended. " Respect the cloth! Honour the fambly! "

" And that was a nice housekeeper he had—Miss O'Regan," she

went on, unperturbed. " She looked after him like his guardian angel. A kind woman! "

There was nothing to laugh at in the words; nevertheless, Joe grinned; Polly gave a little snigger; even Frank smiled.

Lucy did not understand. Her flush deepened, and she looked at Anna, touched for a moment by something of that subtle quantity in the other's air. But the moment passed. Anna met her gaze mildly and said:

" I don't see the fun of it either."

" Holy Mother! " broke in Joe, with that touch of brogue he assumed in moments of emotion, " these eggs eat tasty as a turkey's. I'll have a couple more, Lucy. And some of that cold meat."

Polly thrust herself forward, passing her brother's plate obsequiously.

" I'm pleased to see you sharp set, Joe," said she. Turning to Lucy, she smiled, taking care to avoid dislodging her teeth—a beautiful set with which Joe had recently endowed her; and she added:

" ' Give the men their food ' is my motto. Every man's heart is in his middle. And there' nothin' makes blood like underdone meat. That's the stuff to stick to your ribs. Stops a decline." She paused, folded her arms composedly across her stomach. " God's truth, that is." Polly had, indeed, a profound belief in the Deity's veracity For a woman of sickly habit she had great conviction, pinning her faith in Providence and the enema pipe.

" And how's the butter business, young fella? " asked Joe, licking the yolk from his knife, his question touching lightly upon the occupation of his brother.

" Well, it's good," answered Frank briefly, " but it's none the better for your asking."

Joe nodded his well-shorn skull amiably.

" Do you know," said Polly again, her mind running, as usual, on matters of pathology. " Do you know what they're doin' with butter now? I heard the other day about a woman that took a chance on one of them new-fangled sanatorium places, and they did nothin' but feed her on butter. Pounds and pounds of fresh butter she ate. They filled her with it till she sweated fat. Sure, she got that sick of it one mornin' she flung the whole screed out of the window and, as God's my Maker, it landed full flush on the top of the principal doctor. She died a couple of months later, rest her soul. I believe he kilt her out of spite. I'm beginning to fancy me own lungs is touched."

" Ah! kiss me hand! " was Joe's gracious comment. " And King Billie's toe! It's your brain that's touched." Rattling down his knife and fork, he swivelled his round head on its thick neck with an easy heartiness.

26

" That was a great feed altogether. D'ye hear that, Frankie boy? It's a treat of a wife you've got! "

" Thanks for the information," said the other in a stiff voice. " I didn't ask for it."

But Joe would take no offence.

" You're welcome, boy—welcome. As a poor old widower I envy you. And never mind the Ten Commandments. My poor Katie, rest her soul, couldn't have raised a feed like that to save herself from purgatory."

Lucy moved restlessly. These family gatherings, though she admitted their familiar tone, went usually with an easy swing once Frank's reserve had been dissolved. But now Frank's reserve had not been dissolved; she was conscious of that constraint of his persisting, despite her efforts to dispel it; and she was not accustomed to see her efforts go for naught. Frowning a little, her manner briskly imperious, she addressed him over the yellow chrysanthemums in the epergne.

" Come along now, Frank. You're not looking after your cousin. Pass her the shortbread."

" He's doing fine," said Anna with a smile. " He just hasn't got over the shock of seeing me again! "

" Shock, indeed! " said Lucy, reproachfully regarding Frank as he glumly advanced the plate of shortbread. Then, turning to Anna with determined compensatory amiability, she demanded:

" Were you glad to get back to Levenford? "

" I was and I wasn't," said Anna impartially.

" She means," said Polly briefly, " that she hates the place."

" I see how it is," said Lucy, smiling towards Anna. " She's left her heart in Ireland."

There was a quite perceptible pause in the general note of mastication, a tiny gap of suspense wherein Joe, Polly, even Frank, shot each a quick look at Anna.

" Maybe," said Anna critically. " Maybe not! "

Then came a silence. Lucy was puzzled; and she did not enjoy this sensation of perplexity. She was about to speak when Frank, who so rarely ventured a remark, suddenly scraped back his chair and declared:

" We're finished now. Let's get into the parlour."

There was a general uprising. Polly rubbed her napkin over her moist red face.

" I'm a one to sweat at my meat," she observed in a loud undertone. " I've got to eat slow or it rises on me." It rose upon her even as she spoke. Gracefully she broke wind, unconscious alike of Lucy's frown and Anna's expressionless stare.

They went into the parlour. Joe unbuttoned his waistcoat, withdrew a cigar, and, carefully retaining the scarlet collar, ignited it with a splutter; Polly, fanning gently, composed herself in layers by the window; Anna sat down upon the sofa; Frank, supporting his favourite corner of the mantelpiece, his gaze adrift in space, made moody investigation with a toothpick.

At the door Lucy paused, her arm round Peter's shoulders.

" You'll excuse me," said she. " I must see the boy to bed."

" No, mother," he wriggled, " it's too early! "

" Let him stay up a while longer," suggested Anna.

" I'm afraid," said Lucy awkwardly, " it's a rule I have. Seven o'clock! "

The boy's underlip hung out.

" Well," he muttered, " Uncle Joe promised to give me a penny. And he hasn't."

" God bless my soul! " cried Joe, " I forgot." With a lordly gesture he disengaged himself from the cigar and, after much straining, produced a warm copper coin.

" Say thank you," said Lucy rather sharply. Her son's action savoured too strongly of usury for her liking; a host to demand money from his guest! She turned abruptly, faintly perplexed and faintly frowning, upset by something she knew not what. Halting upon the landing, she said:

" You shouldn't have done that, son."

" Sorry, mother," he grinned; but he put the penny carefully in his jug for all that.

Upstairs, she reflected that she might have asked Anna to help her to bath the boy: yes, that would have been " nice "; a companionable chat they would have had across the tub! Anna manifestly was too shy to have advanced this suggestion herself. She would have to overcome this reserve of Anna's; make her feel at home.

Reflecting in this fashion, she had almost finished when there came a measured peal upon the front door bell, announcing the arrival of Mr. Lennox. Instinctively she hastened her movements. Though his office was in Glasgow, he, too, lived in Ardfillan, higher up the hill, and it was a notable mark of favour for him to " look in on them "— his own dry definition of these occasional visits. Yet, despite his dryness, she liked Lennox, and she had the soundest reasons for cultivating him. Unaggressive, shrewd, tolerant, he was known as a broad-minded man—or how indeed could he have long ago compounded this partnership with Galton? A Scot and an Irishman in business! Worse than a Gentile and a Jew! But he had done it: Galton had the connection and he the capital. And now, with Galton's death, he was, she knew, cautiously contemplating higher flights: the extension of his interest to the importation from Holland of this new synthetic commodity. It was her opportunity. To-night she did not propose to launch her stratagem; but she would make preparations for its launching.

And now, conscious that hitherto she had handled Lennox with tact—already she saw glimmerings upon the horizon—she kissed Peter good night and hastened to her guests within the parlour.

As she entered, Joe inevitably was in full blast. Throwing out a declamatory hand, he went on, with considerable emotion:

" Let them call us the low-down Irish! We're not much, they keep telling us. Am I contradicting them? Not a word! Just let them watch us. We'll get on for all their talk. Ask anybody in Levenford about Big Joe Moore! They know me there. Right enough they do. I hadn't the chances of the rest of the family, but I've made my way for all that, and made a bit of cash, by the same token. There was me, selling papers when I was a kid, and now—Director of the Green Football Club and Chairman of the local A.O.H. Not much, maybe, but good enough to be goin' on with."

" Leave it to Joe," nodded Polly, with half-shut lids.

Lennox contemplated the glass of whisky before him. He was a middle-sized, grey-bearded man of fifty, comfortable and comfortably assured, dressed in coarse grey tweed of good quality but execrable cut, his eye shrewdly hooded, his mouth small, pursed, his hands bulging his trouser pockets, his plain knitted waistcoat strangely aggressive with a remarkable battery of smoothly sharpened pencils. It was significant of the man that the pencils accompanied him out of office hours. Taciturn by inclination, cautious in disposition, he cultivated shrewdness as another might cultivate wit, existing exclusively, it seemed, for his solid little business. A guarded " long-headedness " epitomised his outlook: he could assume at moments an air of tremendous preoccupation. Without brilliance, without artifice, he was well served by a native penetration. That was Lennox: slow, solid, shrewd, secretive.

" Ay, ay," said he in his odd dry voice, " you're a remarkable man. No doubt about it. Not the slightest." Impossible from his manner to judge if a compliment was implied.

" No! I haven't done so bad," said Joe expansively. " You'll taste as good a drop of John Jameson at the Shamrock Bar as you'll find the length of the Clyde. And for all I've got on I don't forget the poor. Bedam, no. There's a hand in the pocket for St. Vincent de Paul at Christmas. Nor I don't forget the clergy neithers. Every time little Father Cassidy scrapes the kettle there's a sovereign in his hand for luck; not that it's necessary, mind you; I make him take it. Just a triflin' kindness on my own part."

" Blow the trumpet hard, Joe," said Frank, staring at the ceiling, with a faint curl of his lip.

"And why not, boy?" grinned Joe boisterously. "Sure it plays a lovely tune."

"He's a big-hearted man, is Joe Moore," said Polly, blandly easing her corsets.

There was a moment's silence; then Lennox threw a sly side-glance at Lucy.

"And how is the Scottish element?" he enquired; this, with an implication of confederacy, was how he sometimes designated her.

"Well—as usual," she smiled. "Peter's had a slight cold, though. Nothing much."

"A rasher of bacon," interjected Polly somnolently. "Laid on the chest, it puts a coating on the lungs." No one took any notice of the remark; and she relapsed lethargically upon her chair.

"The new idea, Mr. Lennox?" demanded Lucy, quick to seize an opportunity. "That's going ahead?"

"I've just been telling them," he indicated mildly. "I'm real set on it. I was through at Leith yesterday making arrangements at the docks."

"It's going to be a big thing for you to manage alone," said Lucy, leaning forward with immense solicitude.

Lennox caressed his pointed beard, now the most salient feature of his calculating face.

"Maybe," he returned cannily. "Ay, maybe it will be."

A question trembled on her tongue, but before she could speak Joe broke in boisterously.

"By the by, Anna," said he, "what are you doing with your own tin? Your old fella must have left you a bit."

She looked at him with a pleasant, speculative eye.

"Well, Joe," she said softly, "as you've just remarked, there's always charity. And there's always the clergy. But if it came to the bit, I might found a hospital—for Polly, you know." Then, rising suddenly, she looked at Lucy.

"I'm tired, Lucy. Do you mind if I go upstairs? Don't bother to come."

"But I will come," said Lucy warmly, getting to her feet; it pleased her unreasonably that Anna should thus call her by her Christian name. "Everything's ready for you."

They went out of the parlour together.

"My God!" said Polly, sitting up dramatically, undulating with agitation. "Did you hear that about the hospital?"

Joe slid his hand across the roll of fat that bulged over the back of his collar.

"Ah, she's better nor she used to be," said he pacifically. "Her and me have got on fine this last fortnight."

"Too fine!" said Polly, still quivering. "She's a queer one, Joe

Moore, and you're well aware of it."

There was a pause; then Joe raised his head slowly and fixed his brother with a look more direct than usual.

" Does Lucy know—about her ladyship? " he asked pointedly, and he jerked his head in the direction of the vanished Anna.

Frank coloured uncomfortably, thrust his hands in his pockets.

" No, she doesn't," he answered defensively, " and there's no point in telling her this time of day."

" Quite right, boy. Quite right," said Joe smoothly. " No cause to chew that fat over again. No cause at all, at all."

" I must say——" said Lennox, looking cautiously at his pipe. " I must say I've found her very sensible over the settling up of the business affair. Yes, I'll say that for her."

" Ah! you'll never make the leopard change its spots," declared Polly with unusual poetic fancy. " And 'deed you'll never make Anna shift hers."

" Easy on, now," said Joe; " we're only human. No, bedam. We can't be canonised until we're corpsed."

As he spoke the door swung open and Lucy came into the room. And as she entered it seemed to her that a look of understanding passed between the four: a singular flash which irked her, then suddenly was gone.

" What's the matter? " she said, smiling from one to the other. " You look as if you'd all been dreaming. Come along. Draw round your chairs."

" No, Lucy," said Joe regretfully. " It's getting dark. We'll need to be off."

" But surely! " she protested quickly. " It's very early. Can we not have a little music? " Often, indeed, Lennox would demand of her " a tune." Often, too, Polly would insist that she—Polly—must sing; she had a touching ballad interweaving subtly the sentiments of piety and patriotism, which began:

A poor Irish soldier, a Catholic dragoon,
Was—a—writing to his mother by the light of—a—the moon !

Now, however, Joe shook his head.

" I'm bound to be back to count my takin's," he said, as he heaved up his bulk. " Come on, Polly."

Lennox finished his whisky, and looked at his watch.

" I'll be moving too," he said. " Elders' hours for me, you know."

She protested, aware that her party was breaking up too soon, yet somehow unable to prevent its dissolution.

" You'll come in to supper next week, then, Mr. Lennox? " she urged. " For sure now."

" I'll think about it," said Lennox, with his own dry humour.

It was for him tantamount to an emphatic acceptance; yet she had a vague sense of frustration. Reluctantly she accompanied them to the gate, where, taking Frank's arm, she stood whilst Joe heaved Polly into the wagonette, lighted the dips within the lamps, and shook up the shivering nag. When they had driven off valiantly into the night, Lennox took his less dramatic departure. He had promised to come for supper on the following Sunday. With that she contented herself. But because she felt the evening had not been too patently a success, she remarked after a moment:

" It went off all right, don't you think, Frank ? "

" Might have been worse."

" But Anna," she meditated. " I expect it'll take some time to know her. She's a little reserved. Isn't she ? "

" I didn't ask her to come, my dear ! " he said, with unusual feeling.

She made no reply, but looked at him quietly, a little curiously; then slowly she smiled at him, and he smiled at her.

Together they stood at the gate, conscious of the grey quiet which seemed to press downwards with the falling darkness.

" It's pleasant out here together," she said suddenly. Through the stillness the thin thread of a mouth-organ's music came from outside Bowie's yard, where a coterie of youths had their meeting-place; sometimes a low note of laughter broke through the melody as some wench sailed past under a united and gallantly derisive stare; sometimes the muffled greeting of decent bodies—dim shapes passing in the dusk—came to them quietly; and through it all the faint stir of moving water in the estuary beyond drifted inwards with the darkness.

Square patches of yellow light were beginning to spring out along the street, hurrying the pace of the coming night. Doors that had been open to admit the evening's coolness swung shut. Suddenly, from the vague void of the firth, came the beam of the Linton light-house, a flashing meteor across their vision, linking them for an instant to reality, leaving the darkness greater and the stillness deeper than before.

They did not speak: the mysterious invocation of the hour was towards a universal silence. There was no moon, no dust of stars, the darkness richer thus, the silence deeper. A bat's wing brushed invisibly the air that was heavy with the rising fragrance of dewed grass; from a distant field the wafted breath of cut hay came cool and damply moist, drifting around them dreamily. The sweet languor that was in the evening seemed all at once to flood her, and with a rush of tenderness she leaned against him. They had their tiffs, had Frank and she. But still she did—yes, there was no denying of her love. She leaned against him. Possessively she slipped her arm around his shoulders.

" It's late, Frank," she said in a low voice. " Come in to home."

III

Next morning, as Lucy sat at breakfast with her husband and her son—in hospitable regard for that fatigue expressed overnight, she had sent a tray to Anna's room—the telegram from Richard arrived.

A telegram in this household was an event of staggering dimensions, and as Lucy tore nervously at the thin envelope—she it was who dealt with the matter—already she was primed for some calamity. But it was not calamity, merely annoyance, and her gasp had in it a mingling of irritation and relief.

" Bother! " she exclaimed, her eyes bright now with vexation. " Isn't that too bad! " With her slight youthful figure intent, her smooth forehead creased, she exhibited an almost girlish dismay.

" Look, Frank," she repeated. " Isn't that a nuisance? "

Moore read the proffered slip aloud: " ' Dear Lucy please come few days Eva unwell Richard.' " There was a pause whilst he looked at her with raised brows. " Of all the damned cheek! " he declared. " ' Dear Lucy '—that's rich, that is."

" It's most annoying," she agreed in a provoked voice. " Most especially with Anna to be entertained. What on earth she'll think——"

" But—you're not dreaming of going? "

She picked up the telegram again.

" A few days," she read out meditatively. " Till Tuesday, perhaps.' She sighed and said: " Well, I suppose I must! "

" Surely! " he expostulated. " You know they only make use of you. That's the one time you hear from that brother of yours. A couple of years ago, wasn't it, the same thing happened? Then, after they'd used you, they dropped you like a hot potato. A Christmas card in blessed thanksgiving—wasn't that what they sent you? "

She flushed at his tone.

" I've got a sense of duty, Frank," she returned firmly. " It's not what Richard does that concerns me. It's what I do. Eva is ill. Besides, he's my brother."

" My love to the Pope," he exclaimed rudely. " I want you here. You don't have to go."

But quite tranquilly she brushed aside both his rudeness and his objection; she was not one to ignore her obligations; Richard, her brother, had appealed to her in some necessity. Though the inconvenience of this duty was manifest, already her mind was made up.

" It's fortunate in a way that Anna's here," she reflected evenly. " She'll be able to look after you."

" Look after me! I don't want her looking after me." A wealth of protest rang through his tone. But now, as always, that protest merely struck sparks from her resolution.

B—TL

" The ten o'clock is a good train!" she murmured calmly, con-clusively, as though in effect she said: " I've decided, Frank. And when I've done that you know surely——"

No more was said, but as he rose abruptly and struggled into his coat he declared:

" Your own way. Your own way. And nothing but your own way. It's going to land you somewhere one of these days."

" It's not as if I wanted to go, Frank," she murmured reasonably. " And it's only till Tuesday."

He looked at her for a moment, then gradually a smile broke into his glum face; he shook his head.

" It's well seen I'm fond of you," he said, " or I'd never let you tug the reins so hard."

" That's better," she answered, smoothing his collar. Kissing him affectionately, she went to the window and watched his figure dwindling down the road until finally it vanished. Then immediately she went up to Anna's room, her small face suddenly concerned as she tapped upon the door and entered.

" I'm dreadfully sorry, Anna," she exclaimed, and, half frowning, half smiling, sitting on the edge of the other's bed, she explained the awkwardness of her predicament. " It's an atrocious thing to do. But I don't see how I can avoid it. I've got the feeling my brother needs me."

" It's all one to me," said Anna, when she heard; and she began to plait a loose end of hair which hung over her yellow dressing-jacket, observing her fingers as she did so. " I don't mind."

" You're not upset? "

" What for? " She abandoned her plaiting, not tossing back the thick coarse braid, but allowing it to lie quite without coquetry.

" Well——" said Lucy, flushing a little at the expressionless recep-tion of her news. " I'm afraid I'll have to leave on the ten o'clock."

" Suit yourself," said Anna pleasantly, quietly raising her full brown eyes, which were deep against the smooth ivory of her face.

There was a silence between the two women: the one open, eager, and warmly intent; the other indolent, lymphatic, composed.

" You'll look after Frank!" said Lucy at length as she rose. " Don't let him get into the dumps."

" We'll rub along all right," said Anna carelessly. " Frank knows me, and I know him."

Why, thought Lucy as she went downstairs, could not Anna have said spontaneously: " I'm sorry you've got to go. But of course you must. Your sister-in-law is ill. Still, I'll manage beautifully until you come back." But no. Anna had not said that, and in failing to afford this satisfaction had somehow epitomised her character. For a moment Lucy revolved this elusive equation with a certain vexation. She liked so palpably to grasp a thing, it irked her to leave the enigma unsolved. But it must be, she felt, that Anna resented naturally the defection of her hostess—however unavoidable this might be—and as such Lucy accepted the answer, dismissing it finally from her mind.

She shook away her stupid thoughts, turned to the need of breaking her departure to her son.

" Peter! " she called out suddenly.

He emerged from his bedroom, in the process of concluding his dressing: as a greater convenience to his mother and, indeed, to himself, he breakfasted on week-days after his father had gone. She looked at him, hiding the fondness in her eyes.

" Netta is going to give you your lunch to-day," she declared tactfully. " And Anna will be here with you for a bit. I'll—I'll be away.

He stared up at her.

" What on earth for, mother? "

" It would be good fun, wouldn't it? " she evaded, straightening his tie, and adding suggestively: " Will you promise to look after Anna? "

Visibly he toyed with the idea, finding in it something important, unique; yet, with a calculating ingenuousness which she found engaging, which, indeed, she now almost expected, he said:

" If I do, will you give me "—he hesitated—" a—you know "—he spelled out the word—" if I do? For my jug? "

Of course she would—a penny; it was nothing; and he was not the boy to spend it upon cheap and trashy confectionery. No, he saved these pennies with a commendable prudence which could be only reassuring to her maternal heart.

He was given the penny—how indeed could she have refused it?—and a warm and lingering embrace. Netta, too, received her full instructions; then finally Lucy departed.

It was a crisp morning, holding that faint autumnal nip she loved, and she enjoyed her brisk walk to the town. Ardfillan, indeed, had always pleased her. The streets, wide and clean, set out with young lime, ash, and chestnut trees, had the pleasant air of boulevards. The shops, attractive, flaunted their patronage by a patent of nobility blazoned above their doorways. Yes, it was a pleasant town, resembling somewhat in its design an English spa, yet purely residential, priding itself—a wholly justifiable snobbery—upon its culture and exclusiveness, merely tolerating its handful of summer visitors, a town to which the nabobs of the district retired with their money and took in due distinction well-merited delight. There was abroad an atmosphere of order and good taste—" Select " she mentally remarked—which in the first instance had caused her to declare:

" This is where we'll live, Frank. We can't afford the best part, yet. But we shall some day."

It was true that—perhaps because of the faintly inferior situation of her house—she had few friends in Ardfillan. That was understandable. In Perth, her native place, where her father had long held reputable office—he had been a " writer " at the County Court —her social background had been secure. She was known, accepted ; had moved in the professional circle of the city. But since her marriage into this Irish family the background had become less secure, the circle unprofessional. That, she recognised, was inevitable. But she did not care. Well she knew that a woman should lift her husband to her own level. She had proved herself; and she was convinced that one day she would prove herself more fully, that she would establish their position, make their future more secure.

Now, in the comfortable train, her thoughts fell back insensibly to those years of happiness in the town. She could not deny—despite the attitude of her brother, who had foretold calamity in those early days—that she had made of her marriage a most notable success. Frank's family might be a little vulgar. But Frank was not vulgar. Frank was—well, Frank. And it was her nature to make a success of things. Failure ! She did not recognise the word. Perhaps the sound Scottish stock from which she sprang had given her the power to regulate and contrive ; to control so happily the temperamental orbit of her husband's character. But for her, indeed, there would have been no orbit—simply an easy sliding before circumstance. She had taken charge of Frank, shaped his destiny towards a sane and constant horizon. And how easy it had been. Easy, because she loved him. Yes, undoubtedly, her love for Frank was the motive actuating her, actuating her forwards. Frank himself recognised this fact, often with a subtle satire—what was that absurd phrase of his ? : yes, " the carrot before the donkey," he had with irony remarked. In the corner of the compartment she smiled faintly at the ridiculous aspersion. He didn't mean that. Just his way.

She loved Frank. He was so completely hers ; he was her creation ; moulded so consciously by her love that she had almost the possessive instinct of the artist towards the finished handiwork ; become so manifestly a part of herself that she rose with a swift reaction of defence when his weakness was impugned or his failings called in question.

That in a sense was why it gratified her to contemplate her felicity and to exhibit it without self-consciousness : she was glad always to confront Richard with the patent evidence of her happiness, her well-being, her success. Richard was not loath to demonstrate his own success, both familial and professional ; his infrequent letters were full of Eva, " his dear wife," of Vera and Charles, his sweet children, who were perpetually distinguishing themselves in social and educational spheres, and of those cases, invariably important, wherein, against the general opinion, he had triumphed at the Sheriff Court. It was only just, therefore, that she return the shuttlecock. Perhaps Richard was a little self-sufficient; certainly he was uxorious, fond to a degree of Eva. His regard for her had never been so evident. Often with more than the inevitable superiority of an elder and only brother he had tolerantly—that tolerance: an easy vehicle for his derision—dismissed her in a word. Idealist. Well, she had accepted his definition like a challenge. And she had sustained that challenge. What was the object of life, and where indeed was its beauty, were it not based on this formula of honesty and virtue: in her more homely phrase, the satisfaction of " doing the right thing " ? The constancy of love; the loveliness of little children and their laughter; the sweetness of sacrifice; the acceptance of God in all His providence—reject these facts and you were lost in a wilderness of darkness. For her part, she preferred the sunshine; and thus far she had found it warm and comforting.

The train whistled, and she started from her reverie. Gracious! She was in Ralston already. With a brisk movement she got up and descended from the train.

Ralston, a near suburb of Glasgow inhabited by the more successful of the citizens, was, though she refused to recognise its superiority to Ardfillan, an agreeable residential locality, and one well suited to Richard in his profession of the law. Richard's house, too, of red sandstone, surrounded by its well-kept garden, with a small but elaborately ornamental greenhouse at the side, was indicative of Richard's prosperity and of Richard's adequate social standing in this manifestly exacting neighbourhood. It was, like Richard, definitely established, definitely Scottish. But its name was not Scottish. Eva, sustaining her reputation for *chic*, thinking perhaps to stimulate Richard's home-making instinct—already sufficiently engorged—had named it coquettishly *Le Nid*. Touching felicity!

And it was very genteel; yet, despite this scrupulous gentility, it was not a maid, but her brother who himself opened the door to her.

" Lucy," he exclaimed at once. " Ah! Lucy! " His greeting held an unusual cordiality, a note almost of relief. " I knew we could depend on you."

He took her immediately to his study, and there, under the Murray arms that hung above his desk, he faced her—his look less severe, less critical, less superior than its wont. He was a dignified figure, his dark hair and moustache still glossy, his lips still showing that peculiar vivid red against his pale skin. And he had an attitude— left arm bent across his back, chin thrown out, brows heavy, a little aloof, ready to frown, which typified his character.

" It was good of you to come," he began quickly. " I appreciate it. You see clearly that I am upset. Actually I have been unable to get to the office." He paused, aggrieved, frowning impressively. " Eva—Eva has been ill. And that nurse—that wretched abominable woman who came on Saturday—yesterday she engaged with the cook in a drunken brawl. A shocking business! My poor wife! Naturally I flung both of them out of the house. And I am left with Eva in bed, the children on my hands, nobody but a young maid to look after us. It's—it's preposterous! "

His usual manner, precise, dispassionate, judicious, infused with a caustic legal flavour, was gone, and in its place lay exposed the naked pathos of the outraged citizen, the anxious father, the devoted spouse.

" I'm sorry, Richard," she murmured. " What—what is wrong with Eva? "

He flushed darkly, in a virile fashion, his head high.

" A little indisposition," he stammered with an air of mystery which at once revealed the intimate delicacy of Eva's illness. " She'll be over it soon. And on Tuesday we can have her own nurse—she's always seen to Eva and understands her constitution." He looked at her appealingly.

" Of course I'll help you," she declared openly. " That's why I'm here."

" I'm relieved—profoundly relieved." He paused, added self-consciously: " And now I'll take you up to Eva."

As, with a heavy step, he preceded her up the well-carpeted stairs, she prepared herself to meet Eva. The truth was that Lucy had never found herself comfortable with Eva, whom in a peculiar comprehensive adjective she summarised as " small." The ramifications of the word were many, yet Eva was, altogether, a small woman; her waist tight, her limbs slender, her actions quick and exaggerated. She had a pale skin of excellent texture and of which she took excellent care; her hair, shampooed to a high fragrance, and coiled fashionably, was passionately dark; her nose was thin and aquiline, her eyes grey, her teeth good but, to her sorrow, faintly serrated at the edges. She affected elegance, covered a natural stupidity by drooping her eyelids, dressed well and according to the mode; she was, indeed, a student of that fashionable world towards which she ardently aspired. She lisped in her speech, trilled in her laugh, minced in her walk, and was adored by Richard.

That was Eva as Lucy knew her. But now, alas, Eva neither trilled nor minced. Pale, most interestingly pale, she lay upon her pillows, languishing, with every delicate evidence of having suffered in the cause of love.

" Lucy has come, my dear," murmured Richard in a voice appropriately low.

Eva by a faint flutter of her lashes alone betrayed the fact that life was still in her.

" And she'll see you through the next two days," he went on soothingly.

Eva, languishing more entrancingly, opened at last her eyes and turned them—wide and still reproachful—on Richard. Then she sighed, offered a pining hand to Lucy without speech.

" You'll be all right, Eva," said Lucy. " Just don't worry."

Eva smiled wanly—the gentle pathos of that smile! It would have melted marble!

" Well, now," said Richard tactfully; he drew out his watch. " Perhaps—yes—I feel I can get away to the office now. I leave everything in your hands, Lucy. Eva, my poor Eva. I know you'll look after her." He turned to go.

" Kiss me, Richard," lisped Eva, reaching white arms towards him with a sudden burst of passion. " Kiss me before you go."

Lucy turned away. Eva always set her teeth on edge; at the back of her mind she had invariably a lurking suspicion as to her sister-in-law's sincerity. It was not that Eva ran perpetually to pathos and lace pillows. No! Eva could be brisk, entertaining, *chic*—Eva's own word; she ran her house admirably; and she fed Richard succulently and to satiety. But her methods were not Lucy's methods. Not for Lucy this kittenish attainment of a man's subjection. No, no! She attained her objective by something less simpering—a more downright honesty of purpose. And so she kept her gaze averted until the conjugal caress had languished to its end. Then she went downstairs with Richard and saw him to the door.

And now briskly she addressed herself without delay to the work in hand. In the kitchen she discovered Charles and Vera ranged under the eye of the immature maid. The maid, exhibiting a willingness expressive of the force of the tornado which had recently encompassed her, desired passionately to serve. Charles, a boy of nine with a dark and solid taciturnity, betrayed suddenly a most engaging smile; and Vera, who at five could sit upon her flaxen hair with conscious pride, gave encouragement if only through the slow suppression of her tears.

Yet it was not an easy day for Lucy. The house was in some disorder; the servant, despite her willingness, inept; the children, as familiarity developed, a sore affliction; and Eva—Eva was at least a fractious patient. Still there was for Lucy the satisfaction of achievement. Not that she viewed herself with admiration in the rôle of ministering angel—if wings existed in the house, they enfolded Eva's alabaster form—but she had, with a sort of innate obduracy, that sense of fulfilment, the conviction that she discharged a covenant of loyalty.

Richard, returning in the evening with parcels and a troubled air, found his hearth swept, his home lapped in a soothing tranquillity. Bounding—for a heavy man he displayed in this cause remarkable agility—bounding to the bedroom with exotic flowers—white lilies, symbolic of purity—and a bunch of bursting black grapes, provocative of alimentation, he remained some time devotedly with his invalid. Then, descending more slowly, his frown erased, he came into the dining-room and sat down to his evening meal, named by courtesy " dinner "—no such solecism as " high tea " could have endured at *Le Nid*.

" Eva seems pleased," he exclaimed, in a voice more closely resembling his ordinary judicial tone. "And I—naturally I am pleased also!"

" She's eaten well," suggested Lucy, passing him cutlets and peas. " Some jelly I've rather a hand with she's had—chicken broth too—and quite a number of sponge fingers."

" She simply pecks," said Richard, attacking his chop severely. " A bird—no more! I hope you didn't let the children worry her." He paused as if surprised. " These peas—I must say they're very tolerable."

She smiled: she had made up her mind to show Richard what she could do. And apparently he found the remainder of the meal equally tolerable. For he said, finally, caressing his red lips and glossy moustache with his napkin:

" Really, Lucy, I'm obliged to you. That was appetising—almost as good as Eva could have done! "

She said nothing; but she had the feeling that, if Eva did better than this, Richard was a well-fed man.

" You know," he continued, staring at her as with a fresh interest, " if you hadn't been in such a hurry to run off, you might have done much better for yourself."

The remark was vague. But its inference was not vague. And she flushed sharply. To balance Frank against his Eva! Indeed!

" If you're as happy as I am, you'll do," she declared indignantly.

He frowned; yet it was significant of his present mood that he did not pick up her challenge—in the old days they had fought their bitter battles. Now he rose.

" Well," he said composedly, " I think I'll go up and sit with Eva. She likes me to be with her."

She watched his retreating back with a curious indrawing of her lips, then, making a quick gesture, she began to clear the table. Vehemently almost she helped the maid to wash the dishes; and thereafter she went immediately to bed.

With a swift reaction she realised how much she would have preferred to be at home administering her own establishment. Very definitely that night she had this feeling. And during the next two days the feeling intensified. Richard, observed at close quarters after an interval of length, seemed to have become more selfishly absorbed, more uxorious than ever. Eva, improving rapidly, assumed progressively her simper, her trill, her coquettish airs. She used to its fullest extent the prerogative of her condition to have fancies: she had fancies about her diet, her complexion, her flowers. Only the recollection that she had received " house room " from Richard after their father's death—the old man had left little; there had been no alternative!—prevented Lucy from regretting her impulse of sisterly assistance. Yet, even then she had repaid his hospitality by services in kind. Was it conceivable that, as Frank had suggested, Richard was now simply making use of her? Her brows drew down with characteristic suddenness at the mere suggestion!

Moreover, she began at intervals with inevitable solicitude to visualise the state of her own household. Was Peter all right? Had Netta remembered her instructions? Anna! Was Anna being looked after? And Frank—yes, above all, Frank! Was he comfortable? Had he forsaken his moodiness to attend reasonably to the entertainment of his cousin and his guest? With a sudden sentimental emotion she became conclusively aware that home—her own home—was a place of sweetness. Strangely, considering the tranquillity of her departure, she was taken by a quick impatience for her return.

Tuesday she greeted with a breath of full relief. On the previous evening the new cook—subject of glum speculation on the part of Richard—had come; and now the nurse, though it seemed too late, arrived in panoply. It was afternoon when Lucy, attired for travel, came to Eva's bedroom for the last time—she had borne a tray up those stairs many times during her few days at *Le Nid*.

" Well," said she finally, and with a fitting modesty, " if I've been of any use——"

Eva smiled sweetly, sitting upright, smart, but still—at least so Richard asserted—still a little frail.

" Kiss Aunt Lucy, children," she lisped. " And send your love to Peter."

Charles and Vera, who stood grouped woodenly as for a photograph by her bedside, advanced obediently.

" You'll hear from us at Christmas," said Richard significantly— he had returned early from the office. Now he shook her warmly by the hand—a manly grip of gratitude—and came with her as far as the garden gate.

She went down the road with mixed emotions: Richard might at least have accompanied her to the station, Eva have exhibited more gratitude in her farewell. But as the train swept her away from Ralston her dissatisfaction became lost gradually in a warm uprising of anticipation. It was good to be going home!

Making resourceful application of her ticket—on which Richard had not even thought to reimburse her—she included the city of Glasgow in her return trip. The lace d'oyleys were at last acquired —Mr. Gow had " the exact thing "—and with a lively spirit of reactionary generosity—she at least would prove that meanness was not the Murray attribute—she purchased a humming-top for Peter, some tobacco for Frank, and for Anna a charming little flask of Florida water.

She dallied with her shopping, protracting her anticipation, intensifying the pleasurable prospect of her return. And she took tea at Paltock's—a rare treat; still she had the sweet tooth of her childhood, and Paltock's cream cakes were delectable, melting through the power of their own succulence upon her tongue. As for the pastry— well, she knew, privately from Frank, with insight quite professional, that Paltock's used naught but the purest butter in their " stuff."

Seated at the small marble table " upstairs," charmed by the distinctive prospect of the street beneath, her cheeks rather flushed, as they always were after the sipping of hot tea, her lace handkerchief delicately upon one knee, she was pervaded by a sense of completion, of vivid happiness.

She had " done the right thing," satisfied her family loyalty, and now she was going home—to Frank. Well she knew how ridiculous it was that she, married those long years, should so ardently desire this reunion with her husband. But, ridiculous or no, it was so. It was she. Suddenly she remembered another reunion—two years ago, or three, the date was no matter, so vivid was the occasion in her mind: she returning from a few days with Peter at the seaside, Frank awaiting her, Frank who, with amazing, unthought-of premeditation, had placed flowers in her bedroom and a bottle of champagne upon the table. Champagne. And roses. Astounding, incredible tenderness from Frank. But he had done it; and she had loved it. Meditating with remote, shining eyes, she saw herself returning, the evening stillness settling upon the darkening firth as she came along the shore road towards the house, the sudden welcome springing into light of the front room window. Unexampled phenomenon!

With a start she rose and paid her bill; she had to hurry to catch her train at Charing Cross; but she did catch it, and she settled herself in her corner eagerly, a little breathless from her haste.

IV

WHILST Lucy's train came pounding through the twilight along the right bank of the widening river at the frightful velocity demanded by the age, Anna and Frank sat on either side of the fireplace in the dining-room of her home. They had finished tea, which still lay upon the table, and now each seemed to have a meditative eye for the red heart of the fire. Ridiculous thought—a fire in August. But in these latitudes the evenings are chilly, the night winds sharp, and nothing, meteorologically, impossible. Already the lamp was lit, casting a yellow gleam upon the comfortable curtained room and upon the figures of the two occupants: conferring, it seemed, to each face, perhaps through some virtue of the mellow glow, a vague similarity of feature or expression.

They were cousins, of course: Moore's mother and Anna's father had been sister and brother; that no doubt explained this subtle flicker of resemblance. But actually the similitude was deeper, inherent, racial: the manifestation of a common peasant stock sublimated through a generation of prosperity, yet persisting in an altered, weaker form. Despite the difference in their temperaments— Moore's indolent, moody, so easy-going it flowed on like water; Anna's graceless, charming, yet subtly averse—they were under their skins alike: not only of the same kin, but of the same kind.

As they sat without speech, from the kitchen a vague and inter-mittent noise, chiefly in the nature of shrill laughter, indicated that Peter was " having fun " with Netta, when by the laws which governed the universe, he ought to have been in the process of dis-robing for bed. And now, following a prolonged reverberation, Moore said mildly, as he rocked gently in his chair, and exhaled the evit-able smoke:

" High time he was in bed, that youngster! "

Anna removed her gaze from the fire and let it fall on him with a faint smile.

" Let him enjoy himself while he can," she said. " That's always a passable idea, Frank. Besides, he's behaved well. And Netta—it'll keep her right to have a laugh. She's a fine little servant."

" For the Pope's sake! " murmured Moore, with a glance at the door. " Don't let her hear you say servant. She'd leave on the spot. They're highly thought of, her family. Respectable! She's got a connection in the ministry, so Lucy tells me."

There was a short silence; then, induced perhaps by the mention of his wife's name, he looked at the black marble temple on the mantelpiece—the imposing façade was inset with a clock face—and reflectively he remarked:

" She'll be back within the hour—Lucy, I mean."

" I know who you mean," she answered, her curious smile con-tinuing. " No need to come over it. Sure, you've looked at that clock half a dozen times in the last ten minutes."

He lowered his head, made a deprecating movement with the end of his cigarette, which served also to deposit the ash upon the fire.

" You are, though, Frank," she went on lightly, " yes, you are— so don't deny it. A regular old settled-down married man. You've sat there these three nights and done nothing but doze and wear the seat out of your trousers and wonder when she'll be back."

" Well——" he muttered uncomfortably.

" It's written all over you."

" All over me ? " he echoed interrogatively.

" I suppose that was why you'd hardly speak to me when I arrived," she persisted, in her tone of teasing irony. " Didn't want a bad lot like Anna Galton coming into your nice clean little house."

The term, as applied to herself touching some hidden chord of knowledge, seemed to rouse him from his lethargy.

" Half a chance now, Anna," he exclaimed suddenly, sitting upright. " We've got on fine these last few days. We're the best of friends. You know that."

" It's true though, Frank, isn't it ? You didn't want me to come."

" Not at all," he stammered. " There was nobody sorrier than I was when you—when you had that bit of trouble."

" Bit of trouble ! " she repeated, her full, deep eyes faintly mocking him. " That's so like you, Frank ! You don't face up to things. Why can't you be downright and say, ' When you had that baby ' ? "

He recoiled from her phrase, uttered so calmly across his domestic hearth. Though it contained no bitterness, but was uttered with a meditative neutrality, it defined so sharply his vague objection to her visit, recalled so vividly her tragedy—though she refused to regard it as a tragedy, that commonplace misfortune which had disturbed the family circle five years ago in Belfast. Actually, yes, actually the beginning of the trouble, the discovery of her condition —he suspected that, indeed, of having knocked old Galton over— had occurred about the time of his visit. It had not then been an agreeable affair; nor was it agreeable now. But it had happened for all that. It had been such a wretched business for her, cumbered with an illegitimate child, deserted, he felt sure, by the child's father, whose name pertinaciously she refused to disclose. That was like Anna ! You never seemed to get to the bottom of her: under her pleasant surface there ran a deep and turbulent stream. In those days, of course, as in their early days at Levenford, he hadn't thought twice about her; but somehow, though Anna invited no compassion, he had felt for her a vague indeterminate sympathy. She had stood up to things, to her father's raging, to the general commotion—all with a sort of stolid silence which won his grudging, indifferent admiration. Now he looked at her awkwardly.

" Whatever way it's put, Anna," he remarked quietly, " I was sorry about it. And I was sorry for you when I heard the kid had died." He paused. " Why didn't you get married at the start of the trouble and make the best of things? "

" It takes two to do that," said Anna frankly. " Besides, I don't think I'm cut out for the bonds of holy matrimony. I've only got to look at your snugness, Frank, to know that I like something a little less tame. Why, I've had rare good times, off and on, these last years." The lightness of her tone was unforced, her independence quite unaffected, this startling declaration of her philosophy no pose.

" You know, Frank," she went on, still smiling gently, " I'd like to stir you up a bit. You've been here in the house with me for three evenings and you've taken no more heed of me than if I'd been a sack of meal. And I'm far more interesting than porridge! Why don't you wake up? You're asleep, man—you're going through life dreaming."

He gazed at her questioningly.

" I didn't dream my nice villa," he said slowly; this was far from his usual attitude, but somehow he was impelled to defend himself; and he added: " And I didn't dream my comfortable home or the good job I've got."

" Oh, I'm not talking about business," she broke in. " Let business go hang for a bit. I always liked you, Frank, and I don't care to see you settling into the rut. You always were inclined to think small beer of yourself. Why, in the old days at Levenford I believe you would have run around after me but for that."

" No," he returned unthinkingly, " I don't think I would."

She laughed. " Honestly, though, Frank, I feel like shaking you. I believe it's Lucy that's made you like that. You belong to her too much. When she was going away she asked me to look after you as though you were a nice little bit of china she owned and didn't want chipped. Oh, I saw it before that, whenever I came into the house. Sort of riled me, it did."

" I know when I'm well off," he replied defensively.

" It's true though, Frank. A fine-looking chap like yourself ought to be knocking more fun out of life. You'll be an old man before your time if you don't watch out."

He stared at the fire, apathetic towards her words, contemplating his own complex individuality: he was perhaps a queer sort of man—he knew that. He had an idea what she meant: trying to stir him up: but he was not interested. There had been impulses in the past, of course—who hadn't had these?—but they had been for the most part transitory, unsatisfactory in their achievement.

" I'm right as the mail," he said at length, " the way I am! "

" If you'd mix up more," she continued pleasantly, with that delicate air of raillery. " Get some men friends about you. If you'd even buy yourself one of these new bicycles and ride it. Or keep a dog, even—a good snarling hound!"

He looked at her sharply: was she laughing at him? But her face was bland, agreeable. Abruptly he shook his head, threw away his cigarette.

"That's not my style, Anna. I just couldn't be bothered."

Again she laughed—one of her rare laughs—and he, looking up quickly, smiled responsively, sympathetically.

"Well, if you're not going to ride the bicycle, will you be nice to your cousin while she's here?" she exclaimed. "Or are you going to let her mope around and be miserable? Why, even in Levenford, Joe gave me a rare good time—fat and all as he is, he could spare the time. But you, Frank, you entertain a lady by sitting down and thinking about your wife."

He coloured slightly, a little apologetic, a little disturbed: somehow he had not regarded the matter from this angle: and not without compunction he said:

"Perhaps I've been a bit of a stick these days." He hesitated, and with a reactionary influx of enthusiasm added: "But I'll do what I can to liven things up for you."

"That's more like it," she declared, as though between them they had effected a compact. "I'll depend on you."

"Right," he agreed mildly, and, crossing his legs, he entrenched himself once more behind the smoke of a freshly lighted cigarette. A few moments passed, filled only by the gentle ticking of the clock.

As she sat watching him, in her curious way of observing without seeming to observe, with the firelight striking on her rich black hair, on her round cheeks and heavy-lidded eyes, she had a strangely mysterious air. But she was not mysterious, though she had some slight subtlety of address. Her thoughts were plain thoughts, barbed by her scepticism and by a natural satire of mind. But she rarely uttered those thoughts. She had a sort of defensive silence, not malicious, not sullen, but due partly to her history. Betrayed in a moment of weakness by her amorous Irish corpuscles, she had lost her virginity in a damp field whilst returning from a Confraternity Dance. And it was as though she had never forgotten the ironic implication of that dance. Her lover, finding America suddenly more attractive than his responsibility, had left her. She made no complaint, but kept silence, admitting only to herself the burden of her suffering, resolving in future not to cease to enjoy life, but to face it without the compliment of sentimentality.

In some degree she was ahead of her age; she had, too, a remnant of the peasant's coarseness beneath her outward refinement; but she was attractive, vigorous, strongly endowed with sex.

And now, sitting opposite to Moore, she was taken with the idea— not malicious, more provocative, satirical—of shaking him gently from his marital inertia. She had always rather liked Frank—she liked most men—and, on the other side, it was inevitable that her antipathy should be aroused by Lucy, whose idealism and sense of ownership jarred upon her sadly. It would be amusing, most amusing, slyly to spoke that smoothly running wheel.

Suddenly she made a movement more emphatic than usual.

" Fine ! " she said all at once, with a faint derision. " Now we are having a wonderful time."

" Eh, what ? " He looked up, startled by her speech, her sudden amusement.

" You're all tired out cheering me up," she declared. " You deserve a glass of beer for that effort." And she rose and went over to the sideboard. " You'll have one. And I believe I'll have one myself. My kipper was salt at tea, and, as Joe would say, it's thirsty work enjoying ourselves."

" I'm not much caring for beer," said he, watching her as she drew up a bottle from the little cupboard. " I don't usually take it now." He meant actually that Lucy did not care for him to drink at this hour.

In answer, she bent down, looked at him over her shoulder, then pulled the cork, filled two glasses, and offered him one.

" Here, Frank ! It'll do you good. We'll drink to our better understanding."

Rather self-consciously he took a sip and put the tumbler down upon the mantelpiece. As he did so, the door opened and Peter ran into the room.

" Did you hear me, father ? " he enquired breathlessly. " I've been having a fight with Netta. And I won." He had not won; in the culmination of his " cheek " he had been chased ignominiously from the kitchen with the soup-ladle; but it was imperative for his purpose to create an atmosphere of success. So, standing on one leg, he demanded with ingenuous innocence: " And can I stay up a little longer, father ? "

" It's well after seven, my lad," said Moore, and paused; he had no success as the strict parent; the mere idea made him tingle uncomfortably.

" Let me wait up till mother comes home," pleaded Peter. " I'm sure she'll have brought me something. Positive."

" Let him stay, Frank," said Anna. " It'll do him no harm."

" Fine ! " shouted Peter, accepting the affair as settled; and, taking up Hans Andersen, he flung it on the hearthrug and settled himself before it with noisy evidence of content. He was, indeed, a little louder than usual, and in the interval since Lucy's departure his knees and ears had ceased to be immaculate. " I think I'll have the *Tinder Box* this time," he announced audibly, and, finding the place, he planted his elbows widely, cupped his chin in his hands, and began to read.

Again silence fell upon the room, but suddenly into that silence came a brisk sound—a light and lively step upon the path outside. The key turned in the outer lock, the step quickened, almost running, in the hall, then swiftly the door of the dining-room swung open and Lucy burst into the room.

On the threshold she paused, parcels in her arms, her eyes bright, her small face glowing, an almost girlish excitement in her slim figure. There was a freshness about her, an enthusiasm, an eagerness born of the rare delight of reaching home.

" I'm back," she cried. " I'm back, everybody."

Moore started round. " Lucy! Well—that's fine," he said consciously.

Although he had anticipated her return, he betrayed before Anna a characteristic embarrassment as, straightening himself, he sheepishly put down the glass of beer he had been holding.

Still at the door, she stood arrested, it seemed, envisaging the scene: such a picture of domestic felicity as must surely have delighted her! Frank and Anna each occupying an easy chair on either side of the fire, with Peter between them upon the rug. Yet her smile wavered. Why didn't they give some answering sign of joy? And that tumbler——? She was no prude—but beer, so soon after his tea! Anna, she observed, had a corresponding glass conveniently upon the mantelpiece above her. Anna! Drinking beer with her husband! And her eye, roving farther, in a flash detected a dozen details that no other eye could possibly have perceived: a flower half-withered in the vase, a stain on the table-cloth, Peter's knees, a smudge upon her immaculate lamp-shade. Despite herself, she had a faint sinking of her elation, a vague flowing qualm of dismay.

" You don't seem too excited," she declared, maintaining the smile with difficulty. " I thought you might have been along at the station to meet me."

" I never thought," stammered Moore, feeling his own awkwardness.

" What have you brought me, mother? " cried Peter, jumping up boisterously. " Let me see. Quick. Oh, quick."

Standing motionless, her eye shot now by a faint displeasure, she let her son rob her of the packages—did even he think only of the material benefit she could afford him?

" That's right," she said. " Tear off the paper. Make as much mess as you can." Almost with an effort she moved, began to take off her hat and gloves. She mustn't be ridiculous. It was nothing—a glass of ale in the evening. And how could Frank rise to embrace her with Anna in the room?

48

" Anyway," she exclaimed, with factitious lightness, " I'm glad you two have made friends again."

" We were never anything else," answered Anna mildly. And, without the least embarrassment under Lucy's sudden stare, she took a sip at her glass, then crossed her legs before the glinting fire.

" I see," said Lucy slowly. And, for no reason whatsoever, she had a curious clouding of her cheerfulness, the feeling that her entry had fallen strangely flat.

" It's fine to see you home," said Frank, self-consciously, rubbing his chin. " We've missed you."

" Yes, you do seem pleased," she answered, with a little laugh—such a travesty of a laugh! " Come along, Peter! It's high time you were in bed."

It was perfectly absurd; yet her eyes were suddenly blurred and, the thought of that previous reunion passionately in her mind, a deep and poignant longing rising in her bosom, she turned sharply and swept out of the room.

V

BUT on the following morning, which was the day appointed for the visit to Edward, she had quite recovered her spirits. She enjoyed an excursion of this kind: no visitation of necessity, but an opportunity to dress herself tastefully and to exhibit the comeliness, intelligence, and infallible behaviour of her son. The warm sociability of her nature grasped, too, the chance of visiting her husband's relations, the more so as Frank was careless in these matters, and, indeed, openly disdained them.

It was a sweet morning: the sun spangling across the sea, the air still holding the tenderness of summer—a tranquillity in itself a happy portent for the enjoyment of the short voyage across the firth.

As she dressed Peter in his kilt, which was—in honour of her own name—the Murray tartan, she stressed upon him the immense necessity for polite behaviour.

" Remember to say ' please ' and ' thank you ' every time," she pressed, strapping on his sporran firmly. " I'm afraid Anna has been spoiling you. And no personal remarks or I'll be more than cross with you."

Upon a previous visit two years ago he had utterly disgraced her by a naïve reference to the colour of Miss O'Regan's nose.

He promised to be good, to maintain a most polished and refined demeanour, and, excited at the prospect of the trip, he kept jumping up and down, so that she had difficulty in fastening the square metal buttons of his dark green jacket.

" I wonder if Eileen still has the yellow cat? And will Dave or Angus take us over? " he exclaimed at intervals, shifting his weight from one small brogue to the other. " I hope it will be rough, too. I like a toss."

" Oh, you do, do you? " said Lucy, with a little nod—merely the sight of a rough sea made her stomach quail. " And what about your poor mother? Stand still, boy! "

" Take a lemon to suck, mother," he suggested, quite innocently.

She looked at him sideways, thinking that he was his father's son: she had been persuaded to adopt this fruitarian preventive upon her last sea trip, and Frank had not for many weeks let her forget the disastrous consequences.

" There," she said at length, satisfied, holding him away from her; then, making a final inspection of his nails and ears, she turned to her own toilette. Her best, it was, of course, since this was no mission in the cause of suffering—the dark crimson costume of fleecy cloth patterned with white flecks like flakes of snow. Zibelline—a rich resounding name for the material. And the cloth in truth was richly cut: the skirt flared, the jacket short, edged with a basque of wine-red velvet. Her hat, too, a toque of black chenille, drooped its black cock's tail with a coquettish air. Her gloves—black kid—were stitched with white. Her leather purse, " quite the latest thing," swung elegantly by a metal chain.

As a last touch—a rather dashing one, no doubt—she sprinkled a few drops of eau-de-Cologne upon her handkerchief; then with a sigh, she was ready—elegant, glowing, and modestly content. Knocking lightly on the door opposite, she entered Anna's room.

" Nearly ready? " she enquired.

" Do you know," said Anna, who was sitting upon the edge of her bed, " I hardly feel like going. I don't care much about Edward —he's such a high-sounding chap. You and Peter go. I'll stay and see that Frank gets his tea."

Unconsciously, Lucy's look lost its vivacity.

" Netta's perfectly capable of giving Frank his tea," she answered slowly, and paused; " and you've been specially invited."

" I'm not very caring about it," said Anna again.

" But why? It's such a lovely day," insisted Lucy. Obviously she could not comprehend this attitude. " And such a nice outing."

" You like to have your own way, don't you, Lucy? " said Anna, smiling very pleasantly.

" Well "—Lucy coloured—" surely——"

" All right," said Anna suddenly, " I'll come."

There was a moment's silence; then, turning, Lucy went downstairs thoughtfully.

" Will I do, Netta? " she enquired absently, revolving slowly in the centre of the kitchen. They had their confidences, had Lucy and her maid.

" If you don't do, I don't know what will," returned Netta, with hand appraisingly on hip. Left-handed also was the compliment, but a high one none the less from Netta.

" You look lovely, mother," said Peter spontaneously.

There was a pause; they were waiting for Anna.

" Everything go well when I was away? " said Lucy, idly tucking in her watch. She hardly knew why she asked this question—and to Netta, so trustworthy, a " perfect gem " of a girl—but for some reason unrecognised the words left her lips.

" Fine—yes, fine," said Netta definitely.

Here the door swung open and Anna came into the room, slowly, without apology for her delay, wearing her dark dress so negligently that Lucy, quick to react, instantly assumed the zibelline to be flamboyant.

" It's a shame Frank isn't here," said Anna, " then we'd all be going."

" Well," said Lucy, rather dryly, as she moved into the hall " he's at business, you know."

Frank, indeed, had sent to Edward a satiric message of regret which she had promised faithfully not to convey.

They went out, across the road and towards the stone jetty which jutted from Bowie's yard: the two women walking together, Peter trotting, attached safely to his mother's hand.

" It's quicker this way—and nicer," exclaimed Lucy, with all the cicerone's air of responsibility as they walked through the clean pine-shavings to the slip

It was, in truth, much easier for the Moores to favour the small steam launch run by the Bowie brothers than to walk a mile to the pier to take the infrequent steamer. Besides, the Bowies were accommodating: nice young lads were Dave and Angus, the twin brothers who, carrying on their old father's trade, built their dinghies and hired their row-boats and ran the *Eagle*, half ferry, half cockboat, all with a sort of easy, obliging affability.

Yes, either Dave or Angus—so like each other it was all the same —would take a man or a sheep or a barrel of potatoes across the water at a moment's notice without formality of purser's braid.

It was Dave to-day, grinning beneath his peaked cap, who drove the momentous vessel—the *Eagle* was a " one-man " boat. A strapping lad was Dave, wearing his well-oiled dungarees with a careless grace, blushing—now that his grin had passed—for some obscure reason pertaining to the household of the Moores.

" Your dad going on well, Dave? " demanded Lucy cheerfully.

" Fine, fine," answered Dave, the grin starting again. " He'd be all right—so he says—if he had the legs "—this the pithy idiom by which the Ancient Mariner epitomised his debility.

He paused. " Well, if you're ready ? "; and he gallantly assisted them over the low iron bulwarks to the stern, where, in their honour, a long plush cushion had been placed. Then in a moment they were off with threshing screw, curving from the quay, leaving a swift arc of foam which tossed for a moment beneath the following gulls, then rolled towards the shore in a slow succession of undulating waves.

The sea was a flat calm, overhung by a diaphanous haze, through which the sun shone with diffused yet glistening sheen. The air spilled over the ship's sharp bow; the limpid water had a lovely gloss. To Lucy, reassured by the universal steadiness, the departure in this pearly light was beautiful; the slow recession of the land, the widening sweep of the bay, the gradual uprising of the blue hills behind, held her eyes absorbed; mysterious, somehow, it was—the dwarfing of trees and houses, the shrinking of a haystack to a yellow point, the transmutation of a running train to a tiny filament winding beneath a plume of white.

" It's lovely," she said slowly, with a friendly smile to Anna. Anna, her hands inevitably in her lap, her body quite motionless, her gaze remote, inclined her head in acquiescence. The words, unanswered, fell foolishly; and somehow Lucy flushed, as though the warm companionship she offered had been repulsed. Half frowning— her remarks did not usually pass like this—she stared at Anna's profile, faintly provoked by this present apathy; then, with a quick turn of her head, she began to talk to Peter.

Nearing Port Doran, the boy suddenly stood up and pointed excitedly.

" Look," he cried. " There's the *Rathlin*."

" That's right, Peter," said Anna unexpectedly. " I came over in her."

" She rolls all right, too," grinned Dave. " Regular old tub."

Together they watched the Irish mail-boat swing out of the harbour mouth and breast her way down-channel, streaming a pennant of umber smoke. Then they were at the pier themselves, and disembarked.

A bustling town was Port Doran, thriving on strength and sweetness—it had its distillery and cane-sugar refineries—mantling the hill which sloped gradually from the water's edge.

Half-way up this incline was situated the Presbytery of St. Joseph's: a double-gabled grey house, standing in that plot of land which held also the school and the church, the whole guarded discreetly by an iron railing of ornamental and almost ecclesiastical design.

The three entered this enclosure, mounted the stone steps of the house, and, when Lucy had rung the bell, waited. They waited some time; then a servant-girl, with long dark lashes and a downcast smile, opened the door and showed them into a small bare side-room with a table, two chairs, a portrait of Pope Leo XIII on the wall, and a strip of worn waxcloth upon the floor.

"Why didn't Eileen speak to me?" whispered Peter, with an eye on Anna, who had fixed the enthroned figure of Leo with an impenetrable stare.

"Hush," said Lucy. She was sitting upright and had on her company air. "Eileen knows her place. You'll see her afterwards."

She had hardly finished before an older woman came in and droopingly advanced. It was Miss O'Regan, the housekeeper, a tall, thin, pale, pimpled woman with reddish hair, watery-blue eyes, and a cadaverous bosom. She invariably wore black, draping her attenuated figure from the chin downwards in garments which revealed not even her boots; her hands were folded, her voice hushed, her eyes raised only to roll them. A rosary and a bunch of keys—symbols of her piety and her office—swung from her girdle. In her outward order she was scrupulous, but, prohibited by her natural purity from the more intimate ablutions of the bath, there hung about her a sour odour, saintly perhaps, but certainly sudoriferous. Her age was stationary at about forty years, her physical being set constantly to suffering, and when she spoke of her poor health it had been for a long time tacitly inferred that she endured interminably with holy martyrdom the rigours of a virgin climacteric.

Although reputed popularly to be dying on her feet, she existed. But she existed only to serve God and the Revd. Edward Moore. Remove the Deity and she might have lived. But Edward—ah, without Edward surely she must have perished.

"Yourself—Peter too—and isn't he getting to favour the Moores!" she murmured, in a voice still tinged by the accent of Cork. "'Tis the very curl of his father's mouth he has."

She turned to Anna, and insensibly, or so it seemed to Lucy, her manner altered to a faint opprobrium.

"You're over again, Miss Anna. You're stouter—yes, you're stouter."

"I can't say the same for you," said Anna softly.

A tremor that might have been resentment suffused Miss O'Regan's meagre flesh; but, tightening her lips, she turned again to Lucy.

"Yes, indeed, his reverence is expecting you. I'll show you up."

They followed her along the passage and upstairs to a door, where she paused, bowed her head, and tapped reverently with her finger nail.

"Come in," said a mellow voice. And obediently she led them

into a large room, comfortably filled by red plush-covered furniture, a yellow roll-top desk, and a square table—a pleasant chamber, well lit by a wide bow-window affording a sweeping view of the bay.

Miss O'Regan, making a submissive movement—half curtsey, half genuflexion—towards the figure which reclined in an easy-chair by the open window, now said with jealous humility:

" May it please your reverence."

Father Moore looked round and rose at once. He was a tall, round-shouldered man of over thirty, with hair as black as the soutane he wore. His head was oval, like an egg; his face yellowish in colour, with a full straight nose, a long mobile upper lip, and prominent light blue eyes, whose whites were faintly flecked with ochre. Ned Moore, the raw youth of undistinguished parentage, who had entered the seminary of Stairs with gawky timidity, was lost now in the ecclesiastic who had studied further at Valladolid and visited Rome, no less —as though to recompense his swelling virtue the Church had dowered this courtliness upon him.

He elevated his large white hand.

" Ah! Anna!" he exclaimed. " I am happy to see you again. After those years, this is a pleasant meeting. I've often thought of you and wondered how you were getting on."

" That was good of you, Edward," she said, accepting his hand.

He said: " We were sorry to hear of your poor father's death. I hope by now you are recovering from the bereavement." Then he turned. " And Lucy! How well you are looking. And Peter's taller than ever—naturally! Let me see—let me see—yes, two inches at least."

He patted the boy's head gently, and twitched his lip towards them with a prelate's grace, whilst Miss O'Regan in the background, clasping her hands seraphically, set the seal of her fervent eyes upon the ceremony.

When their greetings had been exchanged, Father Moore turned to his handmaiden and included her in the conversation by asking if luncheon was ready.

" Yes, your reverence," answered Miss O'Regan. " I have a beautiful lunch for you. There's a lovely sole that'll eat sweet as a nut. Two birds with sweetbreads and mushrooms to follow. And a sponge trifle that's flavoured fit for the bishop himself."

He listened intelligently, with half-lowered lids. Then his lips pressed themselves together lightly once, and separated with a faintly sounding approval.

" Ah!" he replied. " Well, if it's ready, I presume we're ready for it."

" Yes, your reverence," breathed Miss O'Regan, enraptured by the aphorism; " I'll dish it now."

She smiled at them submissively; glided like a pious shadow from the room.

" A fine woman," he murmured in explanation when she had gone. " A perfect saint, no less—but not strong."

" She does look delicate," assented Lucy; " but she's surely a wonderful cook."

She had been a little overcome by the superlative standard of Miss O'Regan's menu. He nodded his head; then, after a moment, remarked reflectively:

" The spine is weak. She has been to Lourdes twice." He paused solemnly. " No miracle, but—a little benefited, I think."

" You should send her again, Edward," said Anna, looking out of the window, " Third time might be lucky."

" Hardly a question of luck, I imagine," said Edward. " If the cure took place, it would be miraculous."

" That's what I meant," Anna said very naturally.

Edward's brows contracted, but just then the gong rang out, thumped, no doubt, by Eileen, for it was a sonorous note beyond Miss O'Regan's feeble forces.

" Well," he said at once, momentarily relinquishing his reply, " we'll go down."

Gracefully he took Lucy's arm and led the way to the dining-room, where the table, covered by spotless damask, was laid for four. He invoked a blessing on the food. They sat down, and immediately the meal was served.

" A little sherry? " said Edward, coaxing the stopper from the decanter.

Anna advanced her glass negligently, and waited until it brimmed.

" Only half, Edward," protested Lucy; always she felt very youthful and diffident before him; and she had an idea, too, that Miss O'Regan might not approve of any intemperance upon her part. But he insisted generously.

The sherry, of a deep amber colour, glowed upon her tongue as she delicately sipped it. The sole, too, was delicious—that was Edward's word, and it rolled from his tongue unctuously. It was served with a piquant pink sauce.

" Anchovy," he explained, from full cheeks. " And not out of a bottle."

" It's good," said Lucy.

Peter, she noted with satisfaction, was behaving well. He had been given yellow lemonade, gaseous to a degree, and a stiff white napkin lay like a surplice around his neck.

" Really," she thought, " Edward is kindness itself."

He was indeed a perfect host: kind, explanatory, epicurean, moving his hands lightly about the equipage of the table, serving them and, indeed, himself with priestly gestures, rolling the wine upon his tongue, savouring the food elegantly, criticising it blandly, courteous also, and to that end using the heavy lids of his full eyes with suave and subtle eloquence.

And yet, through it all, she saw his glance fall from time to time on Anna and rest there with a curious dubiety.

" I'm thinking, Anna," he said at length, with delicate yet pointed allusion, " of that little remark you made. I hope it was not sceptical. We're all perhaps a trifle wayward in our youth. But I'm sure you meant no irreverence by it."

His air was irreproachable, benevolent, mildly arch.

" You mean," she asked, almost ingenuously, " about Miss O'Regan's spine, Edward? "

" No, Anna. I refer more generally to the question of the miraculous. I'm aware that in these days when they would attempt to explain the universe in terms of science it is sometimes difficult to believe the primary essentials of our faith. Well, we have a stand-by in Lourdes. Those holy waters "—he elevated his hand—" they are pure and healing."

" I know Polly went over once, for her wind," said Anna mildly. " But she wasn't healed. She said it was terrible cold, the water, and dirty. And no wonder either, with all these foreigners taking a dip in it."

" A miracle, Anna," said Edward rather stiffly, " implies something more than the mere cure of wind."

" But if Polly's wind *had* been cured, Edward, surely it would have been a miracle. I mean, you don't ever hear of much in the way of big miracles out there. Now, if a man had his leg off and went into the grotto and came out all of a sudden with a new one, I would call that something substantial." Surely her manner, which seemed faintly apologetic, could hold no hint of mockery, but he coloured, at once aloof. Opportune interruption came, however, through the entry of the " birds," which proved to be two blackcocks, lying crisply upon toast.

" They come best to the table at the beginning of September," he said, with a welcome change of topic, and to these they had Pommard, gently brought to room temperature. Lucy was firm— she felt her cheeks tingling—and would accept only half a glass, but Anna had no reluctance. As he sipped delicately he temporarily abandoned theology and explained the true art of serving wines and the fatal error of sudden alterations in their temperatures. At Valladolid—it pleased him to recall his Spanish days—he had learned something of the nature of vintages and the manner of their preparation; he spoke of the grapes, recounting how he used to rest under a certain vine in the college vineyard where the sweet grapes hung around him; how, by merely stretching out a hand, he could grasp them and taste their warm succulence. Sweet little grapes, like bunches of white currants. De-licious!

Lucy listened with attention; but at the back of her mind was the curious perception of that aloofness in Edward's manner towards his cousin. What lay behind it? Somehow it worried her, spoiled the pleasure of the day.

When they had finished the trifle, that came up rich in cherries and foamed with cream, Miss O'Regan came up herself to receive the verdict upon her efforts. As she stood in her habitual meekness by the door, Edward lay back in his chair, quite his own man again, twirling the stem of his wineglass, a faint smile comfortably twitching his long lip, the light from the window falling gently upon his bump of benevolence.

" Excellent," he said, " quite excellent."

A watery smile ran over her face, but immediately ran off again as he added:

" The only point was—the birds. I think they might have waited a trifle longer. Yes—I like my blackcock well hung."

She blushed a little and looked down.

" Yes, your reverence," she breathed. " I will have to speak to the poulterer again."

There was no timidity in her tone, but merely a profound resignation, as though, deploring extraneous incompetence beyond her earthly powers, she fervently desired the strength to adventure out upon the moors and grass him a brace of blackcock to the appropriate second. Yes, " All for Edward " was the motive of her life; for she loved Edward; physical affection it could not be; but spiritually— spiritually, she was his concubine.

" Mind you, quite excellent otherwise," said Edward smoothly.

" Oh, yes, indeed," added Lucy warmly.

" Delicious," echoed Anna gently, as Edward nodded his head in dismissal.

Miss O'Regan satisfactorily acknowledged, Edward now thanked God for an excellent luncheon, then they went upstairs to the sitting-room to have coffee. There, comfortably ensconced, with Peter departed to enquire for the yellow cat, they should have been at ease. But at first the conversation halted.

" Frank," said Edward, at length, " how is he getting along, the odd fellow? Is he—is he regular with his duties now? " He paused and, watching her urbanely, suggested: " That's where your influence should come in, my dear."

" Frank's not—not too devout," she replied slowly, fixing her eyes upon a speck of grey ash that had fallen upon a button of his soutane. Conscious of her own shortcomings—she had a sentimental attachment to her religion, but she felt now that her belief did not cover the multitude of her deficiencies—she added, " But I know he's all right at heart."

" Of course, of course," he agreed, his gaze resting for a moment impressively on Anna. " He may pretend to scoff, like others; but he has the faith. A little apathy, perhaps, a little indifference, a touch of coldness, but he's sound at bottom. And you, Lucy," he murmured, pressing his pearly finger-tips together and delicately making his point, " you're too fond of Frank to let him be careless."

She smiled at Edward's shrewdness. The excellent luncheon, the sherry, and the burgundy mingling agreeably with the sherry, permitted her to be sentimental.

" Frank and I get on very well together," she said, her smile faintly lingering.

" You're the one to manage him," said Anna pleasantly. " There's no doubt about that."

" For my own part," said Edward quickly, " I think Frank's none the worse of a little managing."

And now, his conscience purged, he turned to matters temporal. " Is business," he said, " going well with him ? "

" Splendidly," she declared. " And there's a good chance—well, I won't say more than this—I'm hoping that there may be something good ahead for Frank."

He nodded his head, pleased at the prospect of his brother's advancement.

" You see," she ran on, enjoying her sanguine expectation of the future, stimulated by the occasion and his interest, " we want to get on in life. Move up, you know. There's the future to think of. The question of Peter's education, too. He's getting a big boy now, and I'm not quite satisfied with the little school he's at." It was evident from the eager resolution in her face that she had her hopes and her determination for their success. So much was certain. She would see that they got on, that something was made of Peter.

In answer to Edward's question, she acknowledged that she had observed in him no signs of a vocation for the priesthood, and admitted that her own inclination lay in the direction of making him a doctor.

" They do good, too," responded Edward amiably. " They are the physicians of the body, but we are the physicians of the soul."

Here Anna, who had followed the conversation in silence, moved a little restlessly. But when Edward looked at her enquiringly she smiled.

" I feel sleepy," she said, " that's all."

He took a final puff at his Turkish cigarette, over which he arched his nostrils delicately, then he said:

" Shall we have a turn round the garden ? That'll freshen you up."

" You two go," said Anna, leaning back and closing her eyes. " I'm snoozy. I'll stay here and have a nap."

" Well! " exclaimed Edward; and again he frowned. Rising with a lofty air, he assisted Lucy to her feet, then took his biretta from the mantelpiece and, from a peg behind the door, a short cloak of thin dark material. It was an old cloak which he had brought from Spain, but, as he now threw it over his shoulders with a magnificent pontifical gesture, never did garment seem more romantically befitted to its wearer. Now indeed could she dimly understand the reason of Miss O'Regan's awe.

Downstairs, they went through the French window of the dining-room and began to stroll slowly round the circular walk of the garden.

Still occupied by his pique, he was for a moment silent, then he exclaimed abruptly:

" What do you think of her—of Anna ? "

" I don't quite know," she smiled. " I like her, I think, but she's rather—rather mysterious, isn't she ? "

" Mysterious! " he shot out. He opened his mouth as though to speak, then suddenly closed it; though she waited for some remark, that remark did not come. There was an appreciable silence, during which Edward re-established his composure; then, having passed the outstretched arms of the coloured statuette exactly twenty times, he paused.

" That's my constitutional," he said. " Twenty times round shakes up the liver "; and he suggested, as he always did, showing her the church. He was proud of his Pugin church, and, when they went in, drew her attention, in a low voice, to the lines of the Gothic arches, the construction of the reredos, and the carving of the wooden angels on the pulpit. Pugin had made that church before God made Edward; yet, observing him, it was impossible to escape the notion that Edward had designed the church, raised it with his own hands, and now possessed it exclusively as his own.

" Yes, it's remarkably fine," he exclaimed finally from between pursed lips, letting his glance dwell upon her serious face. He thought her then a modest and ingenuous creature, not perhaps of the highest intelligence, but honest, deferential to his priestly calling, nicely turned out too—he liked the pleasant elegance of a well-dressed woman.

They knelt down and said each a silent prayer. A little affected by his priestly presence, she did not coherently express herself, demonstrating only by her devotion towards that mysterious altar an inarticulate gratitude for the happiness of her lot in life. Rising, the left they church and, withdrawing Peter from close communion with Eileen in the pantry, they went, following the recognised ritual of these visits, into the school. Edward was proud also of his school! As they passed through the classrooms—and in every classroom the children rose simultaneously upon their entry and exclaimed, with well-trained euphonious exactitude: " Good af-ter-noon, fa-ther "— Edward demonstrated his nephew:

" This big man," he said, handling the youthful head with a proud pomposity. Certainly the kilt looked superior against the background of ragged pinafores and burst boots; nor were the various teachers stinting in their praises of " his reverence's nephew."

When they came away from the school, Lucy, under a pretence of unconcern, concealed an inward glow. For her, by this subtle indication of her son's distinction, the apex of the visit had been achieved. And yet, as she left Edward and the boy and went alone, according to her custom, to pay her visit of courtesy to the housekeeper's room, she had, for all her satisfaction, a vague sensation of perplexity. Something—what she hardly knew—invading the warmth of her contentment. Yes, she could not evade the fact that Anna was puzzling her, a sensation wholly foreign to her downright mind. Anna, to-day, had held herself so pleasantly apart, had, indeed, seemed so subtly out of key with the harmonious concord of the visit. Anna had money, good looks, independence: these entitled her to wear that air of unassertive assurance. But there was more to it than that. At times Anna's careless composure seemed a crust beneath which strange and unexpected forces ran. What, moreover, was the explanation of that aloofness in Edward's manner, of that curious gleam in Miss O'Regan's eye? Her inclination had been to ask Edward frankly; but he had patently sealed his lips upon the subject. Now, however, seated in Miss O'Regan's stuffy little closet —for Teresa O'Regan ventilation was not, except in so far as it pertained to the airing of Edward's flannels—Lucy cast a speculative glance towards the housekeeper.

" His reverence tells me," Miss O'Regan was saying, " that Peter will be over with us for a few days when Anna leaves you."

" Yes," said Lucy. A pause followed, then suddenly, almost involuntarily, she exclaimed:

" Miss O'Regan! Will you tell me something? Why don't you like Anna? "

" Anna! " echoed the other, utterly confused by the unexpectedness of the question.

" Yes! Why do you dislike her? "

There was a pause, during which Miss O'Regan coloured deeply.

" I don't dislike Anna," she said at length, haltingly. " I—I disapprove of her."

" But why? " persisted Lucy.

" Don't you know? " stammered the other. " Your husband—he didn't tell you? "

Lucy shook her head, curious yet confused, a little uneasy at the other's manner.

Miss O'Regan covered her pale lips with her finger-tips, torn manifestly between her desire and her fear.

" I better not tell you," she quavered.

" What! " Impatiently, Lucy waited.

" I don't know——" faltered the housekeeper, then, twisting her thin hands together, she burst out with a sudden spate of words.

Lucy started, profoundly upset. Despite Miss O'Regan's ridiculous embarrassment, there was nothing ludicrous in the unhappy fact which she had just disclosed. Unadorned, shorn of all pious ejaculations, the fact was staggering—Anna, the mother of an illegitimate child!

Shocked, still slightly bewildered, Lucy stared at the other in silence. It was the last thing she had expected. She would never have asked had she even dimly suspected this devastating revelation.

" Five years ago, it was," rushed on Miss O'Regan, with a move-ment of delicate anguish. " And it has died since—the poor child—when it was three years old."

Lucy's eyes clouded. It was a disconcerting situation she had stumbled on: unpleasant, upsetting, so incredible as to be almost novelettish. But it was there, for all that. And with it the warm comfort of the afternoon was suddenly dispelled.

" But why——? " said she at last. " Who was——? "

A flutter invaded Miss O'Regan's eye, which immediately fell down. Her embarrassment now, as before, was painful.

" I don't know," she answered hurriedly. " Nor does anybody know who the father was. Wild horses wouldn't drag his name out of her. Just shut her mouth, she did, and said nothing. His reverence was miserable upset. Oh, she's a queer one, is Anna! "

" But surely," persisted Lucy, " surely——"

She did not finish the words, for at that moment Peter burst into the room, followed by Edward and Anna.

" We'll be late, mother," he cried. " You told Dave four o'clock."

" Yes," she answered automatically, " so I did."

" Hurry, then! Hurry! What with Anna sleeping and you talking, we'll miss the boat."

There was a pause, then a general movement towards the hall.

" I'd come down with you," explained Edward at the door, " but I've a call to pay—a dear old friend—Miss MacTara! "

" Don't miss that on our account," said Anna, smiling. " It's such a lovely name."

He bade them most affectionately good-bye, indicating again

that Peter must return for a few days' stay towards the end of the holidays. Miss O'Regan, too, offered a limp and humble hand. And Eileen, pressing the yellow cat's nose against the side window of the kitchen, presented a fleeting vision which made Peter laugh as they went down the road.

But Lucy did not laugh. She was perplexed, uneasy—touched by a sort of causeless disquiet, as though the housekeeper's unpleasant news had struck somehow at her. No definite distress oppressed her, nor had she a belated sympathy for Anna—impossible to be sorry for Anna: she did not ask for sympathy. Again she looked towards Anna. But Anna apparently had her own thoughts. And then again there arose in her that pricking irritation, unaccountable but actual —a vague presentiment she could not place. " Why," she thought, with a sinking perplexity, " why on earth did Frank never tell me about Anna? " It hurt her, that thought; gave her a sudden heaviness; made her strangely silent. And Miss O'Regan's words came to her again with a curious confusion: " Your husband—he didn't tell you? " The question seemed to burn in her mind: Why had Frank never told her?

VI

THE succeeding Saturday was the occasion of the picnic, an excursion formulated by Peter before Anna's arrival and now insisted on with the relentless enthusiasm of youth. Lucy had little inclination for this picnic: strangely—for a reason she could not have explained— she did not wish to go. But Frank had picked up the idea with unusual jauntiness, discussing various extravagant projects—from the hiring of a lug-sail to take them down the firth to an expedition by wagonette across the Winton Hills. She had replied shortly that if they must go they would row simply to the woods on Ardmore Point. The Point, she briefly indicated, was near, and there she would at least be able to utilise the expedition by picking some raspberries for jam.

She was in a curious attitude of mind as in the kitchen, with sleeves rolled up, she went about her preparations for the picnic: an absurd mood, she was aware, utterly absurd, yet for the past two days it had lain heavily upon her. She had made no mention to Frank of her recent discovery; but she had the feeling that Frank himself should long ago have told her. Why hadn't he told her? She kept nothing from him; she was herself his; and she demanded rightly that he should equally be hers. Moreover, since the visit to Port Doran she had offered him every opportunity to repair his omission;

had given him a lead here, an opening there; had waited, on edge almost, for his belated confidence. But he had said nothing. It chafed her, this palpably deliberate concealment.

Impatiently she raised her head and caught a glimpse through the back window of Anna, Frank, and Peter, their figures bent together, intimately inspecting the turned soil. She heard, too, the thin, excited laugh of her son as he dug deeply for worms beneath the ash-tree. At dinner he had related how he proposed to defeat the cunning of the trout which rumour allocated to the upper pool of Ardmore stream, a fish of legendary size and fabulous antiquity.

She might have smiled at this boast; but she had not smiled. She had been irritable, sharp, thinking of Anna—this so curiously contained woman whom she could not understand—of Anna, now exposed in one aspect, and that an aspect not wholly reassuring. Had she known of the past episode, would she so readily have left Anna in charge of her home, of Peter and—she faced this with an inward wincing—of Frank? Anna and Frank were cousins, of course. But to have left them in a state of palpable indifference, and, returning, to find them pledging their amity in beer—incredible, disgusting bathos! None the less, she did not like it. There must surely be an element of vulgarity under Anna's smoothly indifferent skin.

She paused.

" I must," she thought, her brows creased to a troubled uncertainty, " I must get this thing straight."

To begin: Anna, on this sudden unexpected evidence, was a woman of at least indifferent character. And she, unsuspecting, in perfect sincerity, had left this woman and her husband alone when he, by a single word, could have explained the situation. But he had not uttered that word. Moreover, it was not as if he did not know. Edward knew; so, too, she was sure, did Joe, Polly, even Lennox. Frank must know. Moreover, that very year of Anna's misfortune—five years ago—approximated with his own visit to Belfast. He must have seen the trouble there, must have realised it. And yet he had said nothing.

With a nervous gesture she recollected herself and abruptly lowered her gaze. She had her preparations to complete. She had been brooding too much upon this unpleasant echo of the past. And so, taking a loaf, she cut it into long slices, which she buttered quickly. Upon some of these she spread her home-made apple jelly; on others, rhubarb jam; the remaining slices she used for ham sandwiches, leaving some without mustard to suit Peter's tender palate. Then she buttered a pile of home-made scones and pancakes, fresh from yesterday's baking, cut half a cold dumpling into rich, moist slices, took a promising wedge of fruit cake, and a packet of crisp Abernethy biscuits from the tin which always contained them. Her small, slightly moistened hands, that now had a pinkish tint against the smooth whiteness of her arms, moved competently. Despite her haste, nothing was omitted—not even a tiny twisted paper of salt to savour the hard-boiled eggs—and at length the basket was packed, covered with a white napkin. Then, pulling down her sleeves, she hurried—though there was no occasion for this urgency—to the back door and called out:

" Ready! Ready! " with a rising and falling two-winged cry.

They looked round, Peter, waving with exaggerated intimation of approval, ran up importantly, exhibiting his tin of writhing worms, expectant of her outward blenching. But it was towards her husband that she looked. When he came up, she slipped her arm around his shoulders and again declared:

" I'm ready now, Frank."

" Right," said he, surprised somewhat at her sudden demonstration.

In a few moments they had gathered together their things—Lucy's last injunction for Netta the impressive reminder that she now was in sole charge of the house and its elegant furnishings.

Peter led the way to Bowie's yard, the fishing-rod upon his shoulder, the kettle in his hand; and Moore, carrying the picnic-basket, accompanied him. Lucy, holding a smaller empty basket in which to gather the wild raspberries that grew profusely in the wood, came some distance behind with Anna.

Suddenly, at the edge of the beach, Lucy paused.

" Why," she said in a tone of pleasure, " it's Miss Hocking."

A woman accompanied by a dog was approaching. The dog was a fat fox terrier, panting with its own corpulence, pink and lolling of tongue; the lady—for she was indisputably a lady—was a fine towering creature, massive yet elegant, with the roundly moulded limbs of a Juno and a smooth, statuesque face which suited her age and classic form. Her head was small, her features regular, her nose fine and straight, her brow unruffled, like a white band, her eyes a deep-sea blue, large, limpid under their heavy lids. She wore a well-tailored coat and skirt of grey frieze cloth, which, despite its severity of cut, clung voluptuously to the rich lines of her body. A heavy white silk blouse, with tiny pearl buttons and high collar, elegant buttoned boots and dove-grey kid gloves, a long, tightly-rolled umbrella whose thin handle ended in an ivory tee—this completed her attire. A figure!—yes, a faintly eccentric figure was Miss Hocking; and now, as she drew near, she smiled, looking at Lucy with her large bright eyes, hardly wrinkling her face, that shone smooth and slightly downy beneath the heaped-up lustre of her yellow hair.

" I hope it is not," she exclaimed at once, with a little laugh, " going to rain." She had a cultured voice, deep despite that tinkling laugh, a manner impressive through its very ease. " Your dear little boy! " she went on, envisaging the distant form. " But where is his kilt? Little Highlander. Heather and bracken—so lovely in the autumn—' my foot is on my native heath, my name it is MacGregor '! When are you coming to see me again? " Her remarks were usually a series of parentheses, little squares which fitted one within the other, and in the last of these there might perhaps be found a seed of sentient normality.

" Soon, I hope," said Lucy agreeably; and, turning, she made a murmur of introduction.

" I adore children," said Miss Hocking to Anna. " Particularly boys! " Mysteriously, almost coquettishly, she seemed to imply an interest in male children—not the wistful longing of a lonely and unattached female, but an emotion altogether more intimate and romantic.

" We're going for a picnic," said Lucy a little awkwardly. She knew that Miss Hocking could be supremely reasonable when she chose.

" The omens are favourable," answered Miss Hocking rather dreamily. " Blue sky—blue sea. You haven't been to Capri. Very lovely there. They dive in the grotto. Such handsome figures, the *condottieri*." She paused, lifted her head, and seemed to reflect. " I mustn't keep you. Off! off! Enjoy yourselves. Extraordinary weather for the time of year. But I must go! Something I'm working on. Important."

The recollection of this pressing matter terminated, apparently, the interview, and, like one moved by a sudden compulsion, she bowed, swept Lucy with her animated smile, not a wrinkle marring her smoothly pleasant face, then, turning, she moved gracefully away.

" Good Lord! " said Anna at once. " Who is she? "

At the implication in that tone Lucy's colour rose instantly, the more so as she felt it vaguely justified.

" She's a friend of mine," she answered stiffly, " a great friend. And she's charming! "

The word fell queerly from her lips, yet somehow it seemed queerly adequate.

" She looks an odd lot," said Anna, as they approached the boat which with Dave's assistance Moore had selected and run out for their use. " I don't like the looks of her own omens—with her male children! She'd have made a nice match for Herod."

" She *is* an odd lot," said Frank, picking up the words as he fitted the rowlocks. " Half cracked, she is! And that whelp she's got —Fairy—looks as if she'd used a bicycle pump to it."

" She's awfully big," said Peter, throwing in his word. " Big as "

—he looked round for a simile—" as a boat."

Lucy's lips hardened, and she frowned. She had few friends in Ardfillan, where a refined snobbery was the vogue, and she liked Miss Hocking, whose acquaintance she had quite informally acquired. Their occasional encounters upon the front, where the first fleeting smile directed towards Peter had become in turn a bow to Lucy, a passing word, and a polite exchange of views upon the weather, had resulted in a definite state of friendship between Miss Hocking and herself. They had now a knowledge of each other's circumstances, and Lucy was aware that at one time Miss Hocking, emerging vaguely from England, had " taught "—music was inferred— at the passionately select girls' seminary of Redlands. But now Miss Hocking no longer taught. For some years past, and for a reason not openly avowed, the appointment had been terminated. Yet Miss Hocking had not returned to England. Miss Hocking remained in Ardfillan, living alone, devoted, apparently, to her dog, her music, and the pleasant elegancies of life proper to a lady of taste and independent means.

And now, over the issue of her friendship with this charming if eccentric lady, actually Frank was ranging himself with Anna against her. She was distinctly put out, and in a sudden rush all her previous irritation returned with stinging exasperation. They were in the boat now, and her brow furrowed faintly as she observed her husband tugging at the oars with unusual exuberance. He was showing off, she felt, showing off before Anna. And he had shaved with unusual care, put on his newest suit! Was that for Anna too? Moreover, they were talking again, the two of them, in a strain she hated; having relinquished Miss Hocking, they had fallen to discussing once more the visit to Port Doran, making a mock of Edward between them. Yes, she was beginning to see Anna's character more clearly; and mockery unquestionably lay beneath that outer calm.

" Anchovy," Anna was repeating, with mild, malicious features. " Not out of a bottle."

" It all runs to Ned's stomach," responded Frank, with much less subtlety. " Give him a good feed and a bottle of wine, then he's all set."

" Miss O'Regan's spine," she sighed, trailing her fingers in the water. " Almost a miracle. Delicious! "

" The quarterly collection falls due on the following Sunday. Envelopes may be obtained at the back of the church L. S. D.— I mean L. D. S."

' Interesting occupation though, Frank," went on Anna with her pleasant, expressionless face. " Little secrets in the confessional. Fair penitent. ' And how often, my child, did you——' "

" Sweet perfume in the darkness," he grinned.

" Jockey Club for Father Moore," she returned softly. " Lovely man. Gentle, meek, and mild. Friend of Miss MacTara!" And reclining, with shut eyes she began to hum, " The harp that once through Tara's halls."

Resting on his oars, Frank burst into a roar of laughter, rocking the boat with his merriment.

But Lucy felt the beating of her heart suffuse her throat. She was no zealot, her regard for her religion swayed mainly by sentiment; but this—so utterly flippant—before the boy too! And Edward: let him be pompous; had she not eaten his bread?

" Stop that! " she exclaimed sharply. " I won't have it. Understand that once and for all! "

Anna slowly opened her eyes and smiled across at Lucy.

" Just a bit of fun," she said amiably.

" It's a kind of fun I don't like," said Lucy, a spot of colour high on her cheek.

Moore made a peevish gesture with his shoulders. There was an awkward pause, then he resumed his rowing in silence. She was silent too. It hurt her to see that look in Frank's face; it made her realise how much she loved him. She was glad when they reached the Point and relieved to feel the tension broken as, noisily, they beached the boat upon the shingle. Then, entering the woods, they followed the path which cut across towards the Ardmore burn. Here, after the hot sunshine of the open sea, it was cool and shaded. The oak leaves were already veined with ochre, the olive of the sycamore wrought with scarlet, but still the trees bore full foliage, beneath which tall bracken, still verdant, rose high enough to switch Peter's ears as he pushed through. For him the expedition wore no complexity, but simply the aspect of a high adventure; his eyes shone; the fishing-rod, constructed on principles of a sordid economy and retailed profitably by Mr. Gow at elevenpence three-farthings, was pointed spearlike, with a tilt that made the scrub primeval.

Up the burn they worked. After rain, the stream would rush from the upper moorland in a peat-stained, roaring turbulence, but to-day it trickled crystal clear over its channelled slate-blue bed. Moist mosses clung to the steep banks, and long, pale ribbons of fern hung out, each like a hart's tongue, thirsting towards the singing water. The dank smell of humid growing grasses was seasoned with the sweetish scent of sun-baked clay.

At last they came upon the pool. And, at a distance—his muffled tones frustrating the straining ears of any trout—Peter prepared the hickory rod, threaded the line, which had no reel, covered adequately the shining hook with a long and most reluctant worm drawn from the entanglement in the tin, then, crouching, he made the cast.

Observing her son and his intentness, Lucy's mood altered further; suddenly relaxed. She felt calm, reassured, comforted. All her stupid incoherent reaction was nothing—a silly fancy! Turning deliberately to Anna, she smiled and said:

" Are you fishing or picking? "

" I'll wait," answered Anna, " and see what happens."

" Yes," said Moore, " we'll land a whale for you."

" Stop here till we catch just one, mother," said Peter.

" I think," suggested Lucy, " that it would be nice for you to sur-prise me when I come back. You might have caught two or three by then." She nodded her head persuasively, picked up her basket, and added: " I'll try to find you some ambers." This was the name they gave to the sweet loganberries that grew sparsely amongst the wild raspberries.

" Oh, well," said Peter—he was fond of ambers—" all right."

She moved off, turned and waved, then went on again, making for the upper reaches of the wood.

Beside a low stone wall she struck the raspberry patch. Now she was picking them. Drooping upon their thinly pendent stalks, caught by the invading sunlight, they glowed like clustered garnets, a pattern of crimson points stippled upon a tapestry of green.

Her hands, thrusting amongst the shoots, twisted the silvered leaves. Mostly the velvet pads slipped smoothly from their etiolated cores, but sometimes a riper berry would melt beneath her clasping fingers and spurt its scarlet juice upon them.

Her basket, swinging from her crooked elbow, became more weighty. Around her lay the cloistered silence of the wood. This silence, furtive from its undercurrent of tiny pricking sounds—the movement of a leaf, the crisping of a twig beneath her foot, the murmur of a wood-pigeon from a high beech—sank into her. She became aware gradually of her solitude—a great hand of solitude hovering upon her—and, darting little side-glances, she hastened her picking. She desired suddenly to return to the warm companion-ship of the others, and, with a frowning smile at her own foolishness she turned at last and ran almost from the bushes.

Near to the pool she slackened her pace and called out a greeting.

But no answer came. Emerging suddenly from the bushes, she saw that only Peter was there, and abruptly she stopped, the smile dying upon her face.

" Where are the others? " she exclaimed in a voice whose brusque-ness hid a sudden disquiet. Immersed in his fishing, the boy shook his head without removing his eyes from a thin shadow of brown wavering against the darker shade cast by the overhanging bank.

" Somewhere about, I suppose," he answered vaguely. She stood for a moment motionless, then with an effort she stirred, put down her basket. Her face was entirely without animation as slowly she gathered some dry sticks, lit the fire, and set the kettle to boil.

At the foot of the pool, taking soft wet sand as soap, she began with the same preoccupation to wash her hands. The sand had a fine, clean grittiness, polished by the pouring current. The quick ripple was cold, and frothed round her wrists like milk. Then suddenly, as she stood there, she was startled by a quick shout. They had returned, laughing, breaking out of the bracken together, as unconcerned as if she had not asked them to accompany her—unconcerned indeed as if she had not existed. Her possessive instinct flared. Though she made no sign—her face still as cold as the rippling water—a violent exasperation rose up in her. Out of the blue a vague, intangible emotion struck her: nothing she could formulate, neither jealousy nor suspicion; each was equally absurd. It was not that she suspected Frank's conduct—that clearly was too ridiculous —but somehow it was the hint, the strong suggestion, of understanding between these two which at once outraged and baffled her.

And now, for the first time, she dissembled. Straightening, she forced a smile·and said with factitious tranquillity:

" Where on earth have you been ? "

" I wanted to show Anna the view," he retorted easily, " from the other side."

She stared at them. The view—it had the sound of the traditional excuse.

" We could have seen it afterwards," she declared almost vehemently.

He raised his eyebrows.

" But surely, Lucy——" he began.

She cut him short, her slight figure vibrant, her eyes suddenly intense.

" Leaving me to gather the sticks and light the fire after I'd picked the rasps. Not very thoughtful of you." She paused, swallowing hard upon her resentment, whilst he looked at her sheepishly.

" Anyway, I'm all ready for you now," she concluded making herself smile once more. " Come along."

They sat down.

The sandwiches had a moist succulence; the egg yolk crumbled seductively; the tea was hot, with a rich tang from the stream water. Bluish-white flakes lifted lightly from the charred wood; a curling wisp of smoke nipped their nostrils with a piquant relish. But for her there was no savour in the food; she was not enjoying herself; all the time she was telling herself that to-night she would have a word with Frank—just a quiet word. Meanwhile, in a sudden reaction of her mood she kept pressing him to eat, helping him to the choicest pieces.

" You're not eating anything," she said suddenly, looking towards him in some concern. " What's happened to your appetite ? "

He moved rather restively.

" It's all right," said he. " Give Anna some of that cake. I've finished."

" But you usually eat so well," she expostulated, " when we come over here."

In answer, he drank the last of his tea, got upon his feet, and went over to the rod. They had caught nothing, and now, pulling in the line, he examined the inanimate worm on the hook.

" Dead! And never called me mother! " he muttered glumly.

Anna, who also had risen, laughed shortly at the atrocious flippancy—one of her rare laughs—which rasped instantly on Lucy's nerves.

" I'm sorry I took the trouble to pack the basket," she declared crossly. " Nobody seems to want anything I've brought."

" You've eaten the least yourself," said Moore dryly, without turning round.

" That's true, mother," laughed Peter, wiping his fingers on the grass with an air of complete conviction. " I ate most, father second, Anna third, and you last."

" Use your handkerchief, boy," she said, looking at him rather sharply. " And remember your manners."

With curious abruptness this terminated the meal; the dishes, washed by Lucy in the running water, and dried, apologetically, by Frank, were packed in the basket; they set out down the stream to follow its short course towards the sea.

The afternoon was now steeped in a warm languor; the scent of the gathered raspberries, crushed by their own weight, ascended like a rare ether; and as she walked amidst the hum of insects she felt sweep over her that old nostalgia, that almost painful longing which so often took her, a yearning for something which she must seize and grasp with all her strength.

Fording the stream by the flat stepping-stones, she turned and took Frank's arm. Let Anna sneer at this display of proprietary right —she did not care. She had her devotion, and would not conceal it. Thus they crossed a narrow field where the buttercups pollened their boots to bronze; then a briny tang stung the softness of the air, the stream grew wider, shallower, split by sandbanks. From the stones of its bed waving fronds of amber seaweed lifted, twining, floating idly, languidly; from the slope of its banks coarse grass and salted rushes stiffly rose amongst the beaded heads of bright sea-pinks. At last, with a twist of the ending course, they emerged upon the shore.

Lucy drew a long breath of the saline air and let her gaze leap out upon the blue water of the estuary where, through the shimmer, the white sail of a ketch veered like a swinging gull. She felt freer now; yet still her mind was not at ease, that strange emotion latent within her, dormant and unappeased.

On the return trip, lulled by the indolent impulse of the boat, she closed her eyes in a pretence of sleep; she had indeed a curious fatigue, a lassitude ensuing from some unconscious spending of her spirit. The three others were singing: singing in perfect amity, it seemed; and upon the still water the sound fell hushed and soft, blending with the quiet rhythm of the oars. But she had no heart to join with them. Such sentimental songs they were, too, raising an unaccountable turmoil in her breast—the last, at Peter's earnest request, the childish, stupid little lullaby she had so often crooned to him:

> " *My Bonnie is over the ocean,*
> *My Bonnie is over the sea,*
> *My Bonnie is over the ocean,*
> *O bring back my Bonnie to me.*
> *Bring back—*
> *Bring back——*"

That haunting implication of desire breaking through the hot, hushed afternoon awoke in her a yearning, a sense of reaching out, which was poignant as any pain. Only the firm pressure of her closed lids prevented a stinging, ridiculous tear from starting from her eyes.

When they reached the jetty and Dave, running out from the sheds, helped them to disembark, she had almost a sensation of relief.

" You had a grand day for it," said Dave, smiling down at her, as he gripped her arm firmly whilst she leaped upon the slip.

" Yes, it was grand," she agreed, with a faint answering smile; she liked Dave.

But why she knew not, it had not been very grand for her. Yet it was good to be back, good even to see Dave's lively face again, reassuring and substantial. It seemed suddenly an age of time since she had left the slip. She was glad to enter the clean coolness of her own home.

She bathed Peter and put him to bed, then changed her dress, came downstairs. Busy with her ribbon embroidery, she evinced tranquillity; yet, as she made the stitches, inwardly she chafed impatiently for Anna to retire to her room. But to-night Anna lingered. Ten o'clock had struck before she yawned and turned an eye towards the clock. At last, however, she rose and said good night.

Lucy was alone with her husband.

It was the awaited opportunity, and with a quick gathering of determination she laid down her sewing, came over, and sat down beside him on the sofa where he was reading the evening paper.

"Frank," said she in a resolute voice, "I want to speak to you about Anna."

"Speak away, my dear," he murmured, without moving his head. "I'm listening."

She took a long breath. Before she broached the subject of Anna's past she would afford him one last opportunity to do so. And she said slowly:

"You knew Anna well before we met. Didn't you, Frank?"

"What a question," he said lightly. "We lived in Levenford, in the same town, for years. Played kiss in the ring when we were kids." Unconsciously her lips drew in.

"And you saw a deal of her, I suppose, when you were in Belfast."

"Yes," he admitted off-handedly. "I suppose I did."

"Then why," she said, even more slowly, "why did you not tell me about her?"

He did not look up, but she saw his eye fix suddenly upon the sheet, the fingers drumming upon his knee become arrested.

"What do you mean?" he answered, after a perceptible pause.

"What I say!"

Slowly he raised his head, turned towards her; but he did not speak. And, perceiving in his silence an avoidance of the issue, she cried out suddenly, with a voice which trembled:

"Why didn't you tell me she'd had a baby?"

Actually it rang out like an accusation. His jaw dropped in a fashion almost ludicrous; for a full half-minute he stared at her.

"What?" he stammered. "How do you know about that?"

"Not through you, anyway," she returned with nervous vehemence, releasing in one painful rush all her repressions of the last two days, all her sentimental tension of that afternoon. "You should have told me. You know you should. Letting me invite Anna here without a word, when you knew about this all the time. And more than that. Letting me leave her here in charge of my house when I went to Ralston. It's not right. I don't understand it. And I don't like it. Why, Frank, in heaven's name didn't you tell me?"

"Half a chance," he protested, flushing. "Don't swamp me."

He was dismayed to be confronted by this evidence of her knowledge of Anna's history, if only for the plain reason that he had meant to tell her. Yes, he had intended to do so, but somehow—that innate apathy of his—he hadn't bothered. It was not that he was moved by any noble or bombastic instinct—the exalted fatuity of "sealing his lips on Anna's shame." It was simply that he had let the matter drift. Once or twice he had begun to think of it, hesitated, then let it slip. And now, conscious suddenly of all this, he flushed more deeply, exclaimed with weak pugnacity:

" I didn't tell you for the simple reason that it's no business of yours. That's why—if you want to know. It never did concern you. And it doesn't concern you now."

" Indeed," she declared, with quickened breathing. " So it doesn't concern me what kind of woman comes into my house. Because you choose to be dumb, because you feel you've got to hide something from your wife, we're to have someone in our home whose reputation, to say the least of it, is utterly discreditable."

" Go easy now," he cried in a louder voice. " Anna's my cousin. She's all right. And you know it."

" Now we're coming to something," she returned with suppressed intensity, her eyes brightening angrily. " And it's something we're going to disagree about. So let me tell you it straight. I don't like Anna. Now that I know too, and know of her, I do not like her. You understand. In the boat to-day, just to give you a single example, it was perfectly abominable the way she went on about Edward. She's my guest. She can finish her visit. But I'm not going to stand any nonsense. No, not one inch of it."

" Nonsense ? " he echoed incredulously, and the colour heightened on his cheek. What the devil are you talking about ? "

Her own small face was flushed and her lips resolute as she gave him a direct look.

" As if I didn't understand at Ardmore," she said with a biting Acorn. " To look at the view indeed ! The view ! " And she gave a hard little laugh.

" We did go to look at the view," he almost shouted, " and nothing else. What in God's name do you think we went for ? "

" Don't bawl at me," she said in a low, vibrant voice. " And don't let Anna hear how you behave towards your wife." She paused, quivering, and, because she loved him, sought for the phrase with which to cut him deepest. " You—running after her all day, then raging at me like this at night—making this scene—— You should be ashamed of yourself."

" Haven't I said that I wasn't running after her ? What earthly harm is there if I try to entertain my cousin ? Didn't I promise to do it ? "

" I know you, Frank," she said slowly, from between her set lips, " and I know you're not the entertaining kind. Don't think that deceives me for one moment. More than that—I love you. I've stood by you those nine years through thick and thin. I've kept nothing from you. I've given you everything. I've been loyal to you—and I'm not going to have you make a fool of yourself at this stage of the proceedings. So you'll kindly let Anna take care of herself in future."

" So that's it," he sneered defiantly. " I'm to have my orders. Well, let me say it again. Anna hasn't been running after me—as you call it—and I haven't been running after Anna. You know that I wasn't anxious for her to come. It was you who invited her. Yes, you! Have her you would! And, now that you have got her, you calmly turn round and tell me to snap her nose off. I think you're crazy! But, since you have brought this up, let me inform you that I'm not going to be dragooned by you. I'll be as nice to Anna as I like. And much nicer now that you've tried this on me. Perhaps Anna's a better sort than you think." And with a jerk he straightened out his paper, raising it like a screen between them.

For a moment she considered the stiff sheet which she knew he could not be reading, her face pale now, her warm eyes dismayed, hurt, and angry. This, then, was the upshot of her quiet word with him, this defiance, this utterly unreasonable resistance to her over-ture, her advice, her caution. She knew that she had acted rightly, that her action was just; and he had met this justice with a cascade of reproaches. No explanation of his conduct, no elucidation of his concealment! The last thought pricked her like a lance.

Abruptly she rose, standing rigidly above him. " I warn you, Frank," she said in a firm, controlled voice. " For some reason you've hidden this from me. And you don't know how it's hurt me. But I'm much too fond of you to let you hurt yourself. Remember that! It's the explanation of anything I do." And with her head held stiffly in the air, her eyes blurred by a sudden rush of tears, she turned and walked swiftly from the room.

VII

THAT night she slept badly, a troubled, restless sleep that left her unrefreshed. And she awoke—her mind still clouded by fancies which had flitted like phantoms across her slumber—to a consciousness of her quarrel with Frank. This, of course, was over, but the burden of it remained, the sad sense of a barrier still between them that would be removed only by their passionate reconciliation. Warm with sleep, her thin nightdress disarranged by the unconscious movements of her limbs, a thick braid of hair darkly upon her shoulder, she con-templated him covertly, taken suddenly by a desire for this recon-ciliation. Really, she was most awfully fond of him! And, aware now of his nearness, she had a quick impulse to slip her arm around his neck and tell him so. She liked so well the set of his head, the straight line of his nose, that stamp of refinement which seemed—though Edward possessed it in lesser degree—to distinguish him from the rest of his family. Not only from his family, she thought, but from everybody. The very familiarity of his countenance made it unique:

he was Frank; he was hers. Now, as he turned and faced her, she smiled constrainedly, watching intently for his answering smile.

" Another lovely morning," she murmured tentatively.

" Fair enough," he answered.

Her face altered, not at the words, but at his manner, which indicated, by a subtle indifference to the weather and to herself, the stiff persistence of his resentment. But she gave no sign of being hurt. Last night it had not been pleasant for her to define so firmly the position. But she had been justified in doing so. And now she would not reopen the matter. Enough that she had spoken. Let there be formality between them; that formality would dissolve, and dissolve more quickly for what she would this day do for him.

For a few moments she waited, wondering if he would offer to fetch her a cup of tea: on certain Sundays he did himself bring up her morning tea—Netta's strict upbringing precluding her entry to the conjugal bedroom: but he gave no sign of this good intention. And so, with a sudden movement, she put her smooth-skinned legs over the edge of the bed. Then he spoke.

" You don't want to get up yet," he protested fractiously. " The day's young."

" It really is time, Frank," she she, with equal formality, " I've a lot to do. Remember, Mr. Lennox is coming to-night."

He yawned, followed the movements of her dressing moodily, saying at length:

" When I've made my pile I'll never get up before ten."

" You've not done that yet," she answered, with her back to him, coiling her hair swiftly: she was not too sympathetic towards his indolent inclination.

" I'll do it all right. One of these days," he replied glumly, " if you don't finish me off first."

" Don't speak like that, Frank," she answered, in a voice unexpectedly hurt; his flippancy gave her this morning a queer heartache; but she concealed this pang and said evenly:

" Wait and see what I've got to say to Mr. Lennox to-night. In the meantime——" She paused as she went out of the room, and her look signified: " Get up and come out to Mass with Peter and me."

His face turned petulant again: manifestly it was not conviction which drew him regularly to church, but an influence which now apparently he recognised anew. Am I never to have peace ? he thought lazily; and it seemed not; for as he lay back, relaxed, brooding, the door opened and Peter came in. Sounding his father's mood with a guileless eye, he assumed instantly the privileges of Sunday morning by launching himself on to the large bed.

" Now fun, father," he commanded, without delay. " I want fun ! "

Moore looked at his son querulously.

" A story? " he said slowly—this the least enervating form of entertainment.

" No, fun! King of the Castle! "

Moore groaned; he liked the boy, of course; loved him indeed; yes, he supposed he did. But the playful parent! Him? And this morning particularly: after that wretched business with Lucy last night, that stupid scene all about nothing. And what was this fuss about Lennox coming?

Lucy was all right; he recognised her worth; loved her, in fact, infinitely more than the boy. But sometimes she had a way with her, the bit clenched between her small white teeth, which upset him entirely. Made him look such a fool.

He wouldn't put up with it, not this time—no, he wouldn't. He would make a stand once and for all: assert his position as head of the household.

" Come on, father," cried Peter again. " King of the Castle."

" All right, all right," said Moore impatiently, stung by the ironic implication in the words. " Don't you start next."

The historic game began: angled elevation of the paternal knees accompanied by liturgical chanting and sudden terrific subsidences; shrieks of laughter, flapping up of a short blue and red striped night-shirt, and a lethargic pretence of castigation. For Peter the humour of this last antic was convulsive even to tears. But Moore, as always, seemed not to capture the full rapture of the moment. He tired of it quickly, and, in his own words, " called a halt."

Meanwhile a rich smell of crisping bacon had mounted the morning air, and now a thin note from the breakfast gong rang out at Netta's persistent touch.

" Off now, boy," said Moore, " and get your clothes on." Then, with a final yawn, he himself got up, dressed—an easy process—and in a few moments followed his son downstairs.

Peter and Lucy were already at table as he sat in; Anna had not appeared: straining her prerogative as guest, she would " have her tray " in bed and " hear," if indeed she " heard " at all, a later Mass.

And so the three members of the family breakfasted together. The pleasant light of the morning streamed through the window, and fell upon the candid face of Lucy, revealing some force behind her eyes, some power outflowing with the quiet movements of her hands, a power with which she strove, it seemed, to draw the three together and hold them closely thus in a warm mystical unity. Always it gratified her, this sense of unity, strengthened the mood of confident tranquillity with which she faced the universe. Later, on the way to church, with Peter marching between, linking them by his outstretched hands, she had again a warm gush of feeling, a sense of almost painful vindication tightening her throat. Was it not better, she thought, to rise decently, to dress decently, to advance decently to church as a united family, rather than lie slovenly abed and cast a mocking disparagement upon religion? Let that be Anna's inclination. It was not hers. Nor so long as she drew breath would she permit it to be Frank's.

After Mass she turned to him as they reached the sea front, halted, and said:

" You and Peter have a walk before dinner. I'm going to be busy —getting ready for to-night."

" I'm not very caring about a walk," he muttered. " I'll come back with you."

" No, Frank," she insisted. " I want you both to get the air. It'll do you good."

" Come on, father," cried Peter, tugging violently, " we'll go and gather chestnuts in the Gilston wood."

Moore made no reply, and, having straightened Peter's tie, she stood for a moment with a faint smile watching them go along the promenade together. It was a proprietary smile, of course, but now, somehow, it had a quality almost wistful: the recognition of how much they meant to her, those two—Frank and Frank's son. Turning, she went slowly home.

Still, her remark that she intended to exert herself was just; and these exertions centred upon the preparation in advance of the supper for this evening. Dinner to-day would be, in her own words, something of a put-off; but for the defections of the midday meal the evening repast would more than compensate. Not that stark gluttony was the object of her cuisine. No! Ignoring the disturbing influence of Anna's presence in the house, she had decisively resolved to take to-night that step which had long been maturing in her mind. To this end she had invited Mr. Lennox, and to this end would she feed him richly. Then, at the ripe moment, she would approach him; and he, unguarded, indulgent, gently stimulated, must surely be amenable to that approach.

Surely! Yes, as she moved about the kitchen she felt that her plan must succeed. She had long been aware that Lennox was well disposed towards her: he accepted her invitations always with a gratifying regularity. Moreover, he was not a young man; recently he had lost his partner; and he was now proposing to extend his business by the importation and distribution of this new commodity. Assuredly a propitious combination of circumstances. It was more. It was a golden opportunity.

Besides, from the other side, she was conscious that Frank's advancement was overdue. For long enough now had he been working for a wage—a comfortable wage, no doubt, but none the less a wage

—and it was time, high time he took an upward step. Her ambition for his future demanded this step; and her resolution, she felt, would compass it. She proposed, indeed, to ask Lennox to admit Frank to a partial interest in his business. And why not? Nothing could be more natural. For ten years Frank had worked as the travelling agent for the firm. And he would, of course, be prepared to purchase his share. True, their present capital was limited—she blushed almost at its inadequacy—but the balance of payment could be settled in instalments. Or Richard might come forward—where, indeed, was the risk—with an advance. The main point was to interest Lennox; and she had a premonition that by the exercise of all her tact this might be achieved to-night.

Lennox, Galton & Moore—perhaps simply Lennox & Moore. How well it sounded! Richard would be staggered when she told him; Anna would stare; and Frank—he would more fully realise her love, her loyalty, her worth. She smiled at her own conceit; but there was a purpose even behind that smile.

And all at once her mood altered; her spirits rose with a forward gallop of her thoughts.

At dinner—which, by the exercise of her undoubted talents, was not so much of a " put-off " as she had predicted—she was in a strange yet happy humour: a little unlike herself; riding the crest of her enthusiasm; exerting herself to please. She made unexpected little sallies; her repartee was amusing. To Anna she was " nice," rather openly nice perhaps, and, facing her guest across the table, her sparkling eyes seemed to say: " Be as entertaining as that if you can! " Relinquishing, momentarily, her ban on caricature, she gave a short account of Eva upon her pillows which drew a smile even from Moore.

" What's turned you this way all of a sudden? " said he with a conscious look.

" Just wait," she answered, " and you'll see."

It was a favourite phrase, suggestive of her capacity to arrange, to administer, to astound. Her nature was not reticent, yet now most certainly she did not propose to exhibit in advance, for their disparagement and discussion no doubt, her cherished purpose.

" You can be awfully funny when you like, mother," grinned Peter.

" I think she's come into money," remarked Anna to Frank. " Or maybe something important is on the way."

" You'd be surprised," said Lucy conclusively, almost like a challenge.

After dinner she rose and expressed her intention of resting— a departure far from her normal habit. But this evening she was determined to be at her best; and so she went up to her bedroom.

From the window she observed her son running over to the boatyard where Dave was busy on the *Eagle*—the ferry, if need be, would make one Sunday-breaking trip to the opposite shore. Unconsciously her brow creased. Peter's absence inferred that Frank and Anna were downstairs together. No matter! Her mind, excited, engaged by her project, rejected for the time all interference with that project. She slipped off her frock, lay down upon the bed, and closed her eyes.

Fatigued by her restless night, it was late afternoon when she awoke: already the sun slanted a low beam upon the beribboned forget-me-nots of the bedroom wall. Nevertheless, a glance at the clock reassured her that there was ample time. For a moment she lay passive, possessed by a sense of unreality—awakening in this light, at this hour, and alone. But she shook it off, rose. She dressed carefully, slowly; did her hair becomingly. Freshened, fortified, fit to do her utmost for Frank, she went downstairs and made with Netta a final survey of the table—" set to the last spoon," as Netta confidently declared.

At six the door-bell rang. She had been waiting, reassuring her faint nervousness by a last investigation of the meticulous perfection of her dining-room, and now, in honour of the occasion, she herself ran to the door.

" Come away in, Mr. Lennox," she cried warmly. " I knew it was you. Let me help you off with your coat. Are you well? "

He parted his beard in an agreeable smile, exposing his yellowish false teeth.

" Ay, ay, I'm not so bad," he affirmed with caution—meaning that he was in magnificent health. " And I believe I'm the better for seeing you."

She smiled back at him. It was an excellent start.

" We've always got on well, you and I," she said, with a modest intimacy: there was a definite atmosphere of intimacy in the narrow little hall, made narrower by the hanging of his bulky coat.

" We have. Ay, ay, we have that," he affirmed, rubbing his hands together briskly. True enough. He liked Lucy Moore, in his own way. " She's fresh as a daisy," he often thought, " and a regular smarter." He pressed her arm as she showed him into the parlour, where the others were assembled.

" Peter! " she exclaimed swiftly. " Get up, boy, and give Mr. Lennox that chair."

" Thank you. Thank you. I don't care to be too near the fire. This'll do me fine."

She saw him comfortably established, then diplomatically led the talk into easy channels of ordinary affairs—not for her a blind, immediate rush towards the obstacle. No, no, that was not her nature! At half-past six, everything moving smoothly: Peter behaving well, Frank conversing amiably, Anna sitting in silence: she rose.

"Now," she declared, and not without effusion, "I'm going to make the coffee myself. I know exactly how you like it, Mr. Lennox." The blandishment was unblushing; and she knew it to be unblushing. But the cause was good.

Nevertheless, in the kitchen she did take especial pains with the coffee: a full ten minutes were occupied in its preparation: and finally, her cheeks faintly flushed from the fire, she went into the hall and sounded the gong; then slipped into the dining-room. She was waiting, hospitably, to meet them as they came in.

Supper—that banquet on which she eagerly based her hopes— began auspiciously, on a note of cordiality. It was so excellent a supper! There was tongue, an excellent cold tongue, and a plump-breasted chicken, boiled and cold. There was salad, a delicious salad, a tart juicy with those Ardmore raspberries, and cheese—a prime Dunlop. At the pleasant sight Lennox's eye mellowed further; he widened his knees, tucked his napkin above the second button of his waistcoat.

"My word," said he, with an admiring glance towards Lucy. He said no more. But it was enough.

"Some chicken, Anna?" said Moore, hacking at the bird. He gave her a thick white wedge of breast. "Blunt as usual, this knife is," he added, under his breath. Carving always found him at his worst.

"Give Mr. Lennox some chicken too, Frank," suggested Lucy; "the other breast."

"I'm partial to the tongue," said Lennox, delicately apportioning the mustard with his knife. "Try some yourself, Mrs. Moore."

"I'm all right," she answered quickly: to-night her interest was centred upon his plate. "You think about yourself."

"It's little wonder I like to drop in here occasionally," said he meaningly, audibly savouring his coffee; then, wiping his beard, he turned conversationally to Anna.

"Have you made up your mind when you go back?"

Anna smiled. Had she picked up that subtle challenge of Lucy's at lunch? Having guessed "what was on the way," did she mean in her contained ironic style to have a little quiet amusement from the evening? Certainly her manner towards Lennox was unusually pleasant, her general air more provocative than before.

"I'm enjoying the change right well," she said, lifting her eyes towards him.

"She's got no need to hurry," broke in Moore. "She can stay as long as she chooses."

Lucy put down her cup; looked at him fixedly across the table.

"We mustn't interfere with Anna's arrangements, Frank," she

said evenly. " Perhaps she's got her own plans."

" Oh, I've no arrangements at all," said Anna pleasantly, and as she lowered her head the light glistened across her black hair, so smooth with its natural oil. " And I never make plans. I just do what suits me best."

" You're a very up-to-date young woman," said Lennox amiably.

" Is that a compliment? " she murmured intimately.

" I wouldn't say ' no,' " he answered, with a sly side-glance over his napkin. " But it's well seen you believe in taking life easy."

" That's where Anna and I differ," said Lucy, with an assumption of lightness, rasped a little by this *camaraderie* between Lennox and Anna. " I've got to have some object in view. I like to work, to get on. I'm afraid I couldn't drift along with the stream so easily as that."

" It's pleasant, though," returned Anna, with her vague unwavering smile, her own particular quietude, " to take things as they come. If you put your head down and rush at them, you're liable sooner or later to run into a wall. What do you say, Frank? Do you like struggling for things? " And she looked at Moore, who had kept his eyes upon his plate.

" I don't know," he answered uncomfortably. " I suppose I'm like most folk. I don't see any more fun in work than the rest. You work because you have to; not because you like it."

At the head of the table, Lucy stiffened. Was he mad, to talk like that before Lennox, and to-night of all nights!

" What nonsense, Frank," she exclaimed, marking her annoyance with an utterly factitious raillery. " You're most interested in your work. Nobody knows that better than I do. Why, only the other day you were telling me how much you liked the business; what a splendid opportunity it might give you."

" You ought to go in for it yourself, Lucy," said Anna gently, " seeing you think so much of it."

Lennox gave a sudden laugh as he passed up his empty cup.

" She's right," he said abruptly—to Lucy. " You've got the spunk for it. Yes, I honestly believe you'd shape better at your husband's job than he does himself." And he capped his remark by adding facetiously, " If ever you want the post—just let me know."

She coloured violently, realising that for some reason, precipitated by Anna's inopportune remark, the whole strategic position was turning against her. At this moment, when she desired urgently to convince Lennox of her husband's undoubted qualities, here he was, decrying Frank's worth and stupidly affirming hers. It was intolerable. Suddenly she felt the situation slipping from her, felt vehemently that it would not avail to let the matter slide, felt the uselessness of relinquishing the issue in order to broach it weakly, later.

No! it had arisen, and she must seize it now, grasp it definitely before it escaped her.

She took a long breath, gathered her courage determinedly, unconscious of that subtle gleam of mockery in Anna's observant eye.

" I wanted to speak to you, Mr. Lennox," she exclaimed, with a little rush, " about this very thing—about Frank's work."

" His work," he echoed, looking at her sideways, enquiringly. " Well? "

" I know you're extending your business." She hesitated, but went on resolutely, " I know that you're going to develop it. And I've been thinking that you'll probably require someone to help you to manage the extra amount of work involved."

There was a long silence; she felt them looking at her. Then suddenly Anna broke in with a quick movement of her hands.

" Your coffee's out, Mr. Lennox," she declared solicitously. " Let me pass it up for some more."

" Ay, ay," said Lennox doubtfully. " Much obliged."

Lucy accepted the cup with a restive air.

" Have you thought of that yourself, Mr. Lennox? " she persisted firmly. " Considered what this development may entail? "

" Well," said Lennox, prodding a slice of ham with a sudden caution, " I'm not sure about the extra work. You see, I'm thinking of letting the Irish trade go easy for a bit." He paused; laid down his fork. " Besides, I'm not so young as I used to be."

She leaned towards him, fixing him with her earnest appealing glance, her very breath quick with her eagerness.

" That's why I felt you might want to "—she faltered a little, but went on bravely—" might want to give Frank a move up—to let him have a small interest in the business."

It was out. And now, indeed, he stared at her with complete and undivided attention.

" Well—well," he ejaculated at last. " You're not blate, woman."

At the foot of the table, Moore moved restlessly, his face flushed, his attitude expressive of acute embarrassment.

" We don't want to bother about that just now," he said suddenly. " Let's eat our supper."

" Will you give him the chance, Mr. Lennox? " entreated Lucy, undeterred, her lips suddenly dry. " I know you'll never regret it. I promise you that. Oh, I do promise."

He looked away under the force of her eyes: the blue was so deep, compelling; and his gaze fell on Anna, who sat wearing her curious smile.

" What do you make of that? " he asked her a little sheepishly. " Putting a question like that to a man at his supper."

Anna looked up at him with her large full eyes. She was not tense

—rather condolent, perhaps, of his present embarrassment.

" I'm sure you don't want to talk business now, Mr. Lennox," said she gently, " not at supper, and least of all on Sunday."

Lucy started with an irresistible impulse of anger, then swiftly checked herself. Her glance flashed towards the other woman, but, drawing herself together, she ignored the remark and said determinedly to Lennox:

" It would be an advantage for you to have a partner. And I'm convinced my brother would make any advance that might be necessary."

" But, Frank," said Anna, widening her eyes at Moore, in an assumption of surprise. " Didn't you say? I mean—you wouldn't— surely you wouldn't like——? "

Moore winced, his colour still high. What man likes his wife to improve his position? And before Anna too! It made him feel lazy, impotent, inept. And only that morning he had—to himself—pro-claimed his intention of asserting his position in the house. Darting a resentful glance at Lucy, he muttered weakly:

" The whole thing's news to me. I'm not responsible for bringing it up."

" We'll leave it, then, in the meantime," said Lennox with a short, conscious laugh. " Ay, ay, we'll leave it, and maybe we'll think about it! "

Lucy's face paled and her bosom filled convulsively. She felt instinctively that Anna was thwarting her, and the thought impelled her forward fiercely.

" Why not settle it now? " she insisted in a strained voice. " The fact that it's supper-time on Sunday doesn't prevent you from saying ' yes ' or ' no.' "

" Well," he said, darting a quick glance at her, " maybe that was why you asked me to-night."

She recoiled from the baldness of his statement, knowing that in essence it was true, but knowing also that it would never have been uttered but for Anna's interference. Yet she ignored the issue.

" You've known us a long time now, Mr. Lennox," she persisted, keeping her tone level and forcing a smile; " and Frank's been with you ten years. Surely it's worth considering. Please do think of it."

Again he laid down his fork and pulled at his crinkly beard, manifestly disturbed.

" It's hardly a question of ' yes ' or ' no,' " he said awkwardly. " There's more to it than that. I'm not one to favour quick chopping and changing."

And again Anna broke in with her reasonable voice.

" And if you were changing," she inserted gently, " wouldn't it be a fair idea to give Frank the Belfast agency? He did well that time

83

he was over. And the man you've got now isn't much good."

Lucy's head drew back sharply: really it was too much! Anna, interfering, distorting the vital issue in question, advising Lennox to give Frank this paltry advancement—this agency only slightly superior to his present post. It was maddening.

Again that impulse swept over her, the impulse towards some outrageous speech, towards violent outrageous action. What business was it of Anna's—this unpardonable, maddening interference? She could contain herself no longer. Turning from Lennox, she looked fixedly at the other woman, and in a quivering voice declared:

" This seems hardly your affair, Anna! I have no particular desire to go to Ireland."

" It's not a bad place, mind you," said Anna agreeably. " It rains a lot, but that keeps things green. My word, you should see the shamrocks." Her ingenuousness was diabolic.

" It wouldn't suit us," returned Lucy, breathing quickly, pressed by an urgency to strike back furiously. " Though it may suit you. No doubt you've found it very entertaining there? No doubt you have your reasons for liking it? "

" Well, maybe I have," said Anna meditatively.

" Some reason of your own perhaps? "

" You never can tell," answered Anna, without the movement of an eyelid.

A strained moment followed, during which Lennox cocked his eye at the ceiling and Moore looked glumly at the fire. The harmony of the evening seemed suddenly disrupted.

" You see," broke in Lennox—he had now had time to collect his obduracy—" I've got my own ways of working. If you study everybody, you study nobody. Wholesale confusion."

There was a long silence during which she felt the painful throbbing of her heart.

Wholesale confusion! And he had been on the verge of yielding. She knew it. And now, through Anna's insufferable interference, he had all at once turned unsympathetic; and he might remain unsympathetic, intolerant, unamenable to suggestion for months to come. It was unfuriating. Her enterprise, defeated, shattered, smashed to atoms. And by Anna.

" Give me some more coffee," said Moore moodily. " I'm parched."

Lucy hesitated, then stiffly she stretched out her hand for his cup; the curtness, the latent resentment in his words pierced her. As though, indeed, it were she who was to blame! There was a stiff silence, and her face too was rigid, suffused by the colour of her wounded love.

" Dave took me out in the *Eagle* this afternoon," ventured Peter at length; he had but a vague idea of the tension which encompassed him; but no one gave heed to the remark.

" Why has Netta put so much sugar in this tart? " broke out Moore. " It's poisoned with it."

" I made the tart myself," said Lucy coldly; but her voice quivered.

" It's right enough for me," said Lennox quickly. " Just lovely."

Moore moved uneasily; he had not thought; usually it was Netta who made the tart. Anna said nothing, but bit into a biscuit as though something amused her intensely. There was a long pause.

Loudly Lennox cleared his throat.

" Anyway, I'm for some more," said he pacifically, passing up his plate. " The pastry is fine."

" It's nice to see you sharp set," said Anna politely, as Polly might have done.

He had his second helping, and was the last to finish: his air that of a man who had enjoyed the meal in the face of circumstance. And, as Lucy observed him, sensed his partiality for her, she thought bitterly on what she might now have done but for Anna's insufferable meddling. It goaded her, the thought; agitatedly her fingers crumbled the wheaten cake that lay untasted on her plate. They sat in silence for a long time; then at last Lennox made a move.

" Time I was off," he said, brushing his waistcoat. " I came early because I knew I must get away early."

She did not protest, yet as they rose she was conscious of the falsity of his excuse.

" I'll come along with you," Moore declared, " as far as your gate."

" I could do with some air myself," said Anna speculatively. " It's a fine night."

Again Lucy felt the blood rush into her face, felt Lennox looking at her, felt an overwhelming surge of rage come over her. She could not offer to go: it was Netta's evening out; she must put Peter to bed. In a red haze of confusion, she accompanied them to the hall.

" Good night, and thank you," Lennox was saying, with the usual warm pressure of his hand.

She stood at the front door—the air striking upon her heated face —watching them go down the path. Then, with a sigh which broke involuntarily from her lips, which seemed to come from a rending in her breast, she turned, went back into the house.

This, then, was the climax of her achievement. Nothing! And Frank—she winced, feeling bitterly the injustice of his attitude. She—more anxious for his advancement than anyone, with that advancement already consummated in her mind—to be spoken to as he had spoken to her. And Anna—always Anna—interfering in so dubious, so detestable a fashion. There was in Anna's interference so manifest a pretext that she immediately suspected it. Anna, indeed! Wearily in the empty room she leaned her brow against the cool marble of the mantelpiece, contemplating the figure of the other woman. How she detested her! Her indifference, her composure, her enigmatic eye drawing towards Frank. The softness of her speech, even her movements, which had at first seemed quiet and natural, were become odious and insincere. Now, to look at Anna, even to think of Anna, evoked instantly a shiver of aversion.

Controlling herself, she saw Peter upstairs, cleared the table, and returned to the dining-room. She knew she must not think; and that was why she thought. Her excited mind, seething with a leaven of anger and suspicion, turned fiercely upon her humiliation—for it was surely a humiliation. The precipitation of this anticlimax, the sudden frustration of her brilliant scheme, awoke in her a galling sense of deprivation, brought back with redoubled violence all those previous nebulous misgivings.

Why had Anna dared to interfere with Frank in this insidious, insufferable fashion? Anna had no right to shape his future! Surely something lay at the bottom of it all, something which she must seek and apprehend. Vehemently almost she desired to grasp some tangible solution of this elusive, exasperating perplexity.

And she began to go back, piecing together what might be evidence —the evident solution of Anna's attitude: a look here, a word there: adding up the total of her doubts, trying vainly to crystallise the substance of her fears. Because she knew her position to be unimpeachable, it was inevitable that she assumed Anna's to be amiss. Because she felt her conduct to be blameless, it was natural that she saw Anna's motives as the converse of her own. Besides, had she not that wretched echo of the past rising up and resounding perpetually in her ears? And involuntarily she commenced to think of that unhappy episode, to formulate its circumstances, to visualise even the image of that child—nameless and now dead—of which she knew Anna to be the mother. Unaccountably she began to feel that the mystery of this hidden child was linked in some vague and devious manner to her own perplexity. Or at least, by an unconscious association of ideas, by some common bond of obscurity, she herself linked them in her mind, bound the two subconsciously into a unity as yet unrealised. If only she knew more about that episode in Anna's life, would she not then have a clue to Anna's conduct, a clue to Anna herself? And, understanding Anna, would she not then comprehend her attitude to Frank? Anna and Frank—always now she reduced her reasoning to this inevitable impasse: those two names, coupled together, provoking her by the very inconclusiveness of their association.

All at once she started, hearing the opening of the outer door, the sound of their voices in the hall. Her face took on a set, determined

86

look as Frank entered the room. He was alone.

" Well," he said immediately, in a low voice, " you made a pretty fool of me to-night. And all for nothing! "

Her lips compressed themselves. The fact that he, who with Anna had compassed his own defeat, should now accuse her, was too painfully absurd to allow her even to defend her action.

" It was you made a fool of yourself," she cried out. " I know Lennox would have given it you. I could have managed it." She dropped her arm with a hopeless gesture. " And it would have suited us so well."

" And are you to be the judge of that? Don't think you can boss him into it. And don't think you can boss me all my life! "

" That's not true, Frank," she cried passionately. " You know it isn't. I want everything to be for you—your good."

" My good," he sneered. " Everybody sees you've got a chain on me. Even Anna."

" Anna! " She threw an indescribable intensity into the word.

" Yes, Anna. And, whilst we're on that point, I may ask you to be a bit more civil. You've been damned rude to her lately. Remember she's my cousin! "

" Your cousin! " she repeated in a quivering voice. " I like that! Is she more important than your wife? "

He took a cigarette and lit it, watching her all the time; then, jerking the spent match into the fire, he exclaimed curtly:

" I think what I said was to ask you to be civil to her."

Ignoring this issue, she faced him with burning eyes.

" I'm going to ask you a simple question! Why are you so taken up with Anna? "

He made a fractious movement of his head.

" What the devil's wrong with you these days? Do you own me or what, that you cross-examine me like this? "

" Cross-examine you! " she exclaimed vehemently. " You know I'm not doing that. It is a straightforward question! "

" Straightforward question be damned! " he broke in angrily. " Keep your straightforward questions and don't hang over me— don't smother me. You've been doing it for years. Is that not plain enough? "

At the childish irrationality of his words her eyes flashed with vexation. Something goaded her to say, in a low suppressed voice:

" I think I've always done the right thing by you, Frank. I think you know if you've been happy."

" That's right," he said sulkily. " You're perfect. When you walk I can hear them flap."

She made no reply, but with a face still flushed, she fixed him with a look of passionate reproach. For a moment she stood there, then

87

abruptly went over to the sofa where, in a pretence of occupation, she took up her needlework and began to sew with trembling fingers; and he, too, sealed up to a gloomy taciturnity. Thus they sat in silence; then at last he rose. Despite herself, she made a quick movement; her eyes clouded suddenly with tears.

" Is it anything "—she was filled by a flowing desire for reconciliation—" anything I can get you? "

" I'm going to bed," he answered, " bed! "

She stared at him, aghast.

" But, Frank, it's not nine o'clock yet." She stretched out her hand. " Let's make it up. After all—we love each other."

" Let me be," he said; " you've done enough for me to-night." And he went out of the room before she could utter another word.

She sat quite still for a long time, hearing his slow movements upstairs, hearing finally the cessation of these movements as he got into bed. Her eyes remained fixed, transcending the limits of the room; her resentment gone, erased by a curious regret; her mind filled with an unconscious dismay.

At last she moved her head impatiently, rose, and wound up the clock on the mantelpiece: all such duties, which by right and precedent devolved upon the master of the house, belonged entirely to her: then she went upstairs.

She undressed in the darkness and got into bed beside him. He was not sleeping, but he was pretending to be asleep. His deep breathing did not deceive her, and she gauged the certainty of this pretence from the almost imperceptible rigidity of his body as it lay touching hers. She wished him to speak to her; yet she felt that he would not; nor would she herself risk another rebuff. She had her pride. And so she lay beside him without moving, without giving any sign, closing her eyes to shut out the moonlight that streamed palely into the room, thinking—thinking with a faintly furrowed brow, straining for something which still eluded her.

VIII

SHE had firmly determined to have the matter out with Anna—so much was definite; and in her mind she had fixed the afternoon, when Peter would be safely out of the way, as the time of her attack. She would be calm; she would remember that Anna was her guest, yet she would demand at length an explanation of Anna's conduct. But next morning, quite unexpectedly, Anna went to Glasgow, upon a shopping expedition—although nothing that Anna undertook could justly be defined by so exact and premeditated a phrase. She had said off-handedly after breakfast:

" I'm going to get myself some clothes," and, rising at once, had caught the ten o'clock train without enthusiasm. No preparation, no excitement, no mention of Lucy accompanying her.

Not that Lucy would have dreamed of accompanying her. Indeed, despite the frustration of her purpose, she viewed the departure of the other woman with a sense of incredible relief. Her head this morning felt heavy, confused, her mind obscured by this strange obsessing doubt. Perhaps it was as well that Anna had gone. She wanted to be alone to think, to reason clearly with herself. Again and again she had that conscious sensation of something within her straining to be delivered, something which was of her own substance and must painfully be born before she could find assuagement.

As she went about the house, almost automatically preparing Peter's things for his visit to Port Doran at the end of the week, she felt herself remote from her surroundings. Moving restlessly, she attempted with racking intensity to define her suspicion, to conjure up this phantom which now intolerably possessed her.

From the beginning she had tried to make friends with Anna— so much she immediately admitted. She had welcomed her, had made every effort to like her. But, looking backwards, she now saw that from the moment when Joe had brought Anna into her house she had been conscious of a subtle antagonism flowing between this other woman and herself. The initial conviction that she liked Anna had been a delusion, mere imagining, a pretence born of her own hospitality; she had never liked Anna: they were at opposite poles: she distrusted Anna. And the first realisation, the first suspicion of this distrust, had come at that moment of her return from Ralston, when she had found Anna sitting so intimately with Frank. Then gradually, one stone upon another, had arisen this incredible structure, an unformed structure perhaps, an unshaped mass of doubts and suspicions and mistrust, but all—yes, all emerging and arising from the character of Anna Galton and the bearing of that character on Frank. In consequence, Anna's visit, looked forward to so lightly, so eagerly, had become, not a happiness, but a menace; something painful, almost sinister. It was evident to her as she stood there that she was not to blame for this condition of affairs. How, indeed, could she be to blame? Frank was her husband, living with her in contentment and perfect happiness. Anna had come, and thereafter contentment had gone. It was unanswerable. Anna must be responsible. But how? She bit her lip, and with furrowed brow retraced once more the tenuous line of her suspicion. Had she not detected a curious undercurrent in Joe's remarks, perceived a peculiar significance in Edward's conduct? That singular atmosphere at the Presbytery, too, the almost painful embarrassment of Miss O'Regan's manner—had this its origin simply in outraged modesty? And then—Anna's attitude to Frank. Frank's own attitude—his obstinate silence. If he had been obliged to be silent, if there was something which he had been forced to conceal, then she would at once have understood. But he had nothing to conceal. Nothing! And yet he had concealed it. He who had been there, actually in Ireland in that same year, had not said a word about the matter. Oh! it was a goading, insistent thought.

Frowning, she drew in her breath sharply. She had raised a strange edifice in her mind, and lacked only the keystone with which to crown it to completion.

Perhaps there was no keystone. Perhaps it was jealousy alone that moved her. Though she winced at the thought, she confronted it. And she repudiated it calmly. No, no! Jealousy. That was a motive of unutterable selfishness. And her love was not selfish. Everything that was she strained towards the ultimate object of his good. She knew him so well, understood him so thoroughly, loved him so consummately, that she would brook no interference with his happiness nor see the contented passage of his life disturbed. That was not jealousy. It was loyalty, devotion, sanity—yes, the sublimated essence of her love. So she thought. So, indeed, she knew.

Anna, of course, was different. She had no ideals, no ambition, no objective, no code. The unhappy episode of the child seemed to typify exactly her attitude towards life. Why otherwise had she not married the father of this child and settled down determinedly to a new and regular existence? But that was not Anna. No doubt she had sneered her way through the whole trouble with a sort of detached perversity, to emerge harder and more indifferent in the end. The man, of course, must necessarily have been weak—someone unstable, foolish, injudicious—who had desired with all the obstinacy of weakness to escape his obligation in the end. And Anna had let him escape. Even now she could hear Anna saying with cold indifference: " Then go to the devil. I don't care what you do." Yes, that was how it must have been.

But it was all so wrong, so misguided, so contrary to her own open line of conduct. Suppose, for example, she had adopted those careless standards with Frank, who could himself, she was well aware, be unstable, foolish, even injudicious: to what end indeed would she then have shaped his future and her own? Only towards disaster.

She sighed, and with a pressure of her knee closed the drawer wherein she had been arranging Peter's clothes. Then abruptly she straightened herself and went into Anna's bedroom to make it tidy. But at the door she paused and for a few seconds surveyed the room with a gathering frown. Really it was so disordered, disgustingly disordered, she thought: the bed unmade—she at least as a guest would have made that bed—the dressing-table littered, a stocking exposing its shiny sole outside a half-shut drawer, a chemise lying nakedly upon the floor. It was too bad. And Anna's underwear, thus displayed—of a most seductive pattern it was, and a material strangely different from her own white lawn—even that evoked in her a causeless, uneasy irritation. Involuntarily the wish rose passionately in her mind: " I hope she'll go soon." No, it could not be long now before Anna must surely terminate her stay. She must go. And she, Lucy, would not be sorry. She admitted, at last, the full force of that antagonism which had sprung into existence between Anna and herself.

Her frown still lingered as she began to clear up the room—Netta had her own work in the kitchen, but, quite apart from Netta's obligations, Lucy had the singular urge to do this tidying herself. Unconsciously she felt the action to be symbolic: let Anna cast her life about; she would arrange hers, and arrange it decently.

She restored the room to order, then gathered some trinkets—a brooch and an opal ring scattered carelessly; the rest of the jewellery at present adorned Anna's person—to place them in Anna's trinket-box that stood beside the mirror. And she opened this small green box. Then suddenly—the movement of her hand arrested—she stood motionless. A curious intentness came into her eyes, her face, her whole figure. She was staring at something in the box. Immobile, she stood staring—staring rigidly. And, fixed by that stare, her face blanched coldly.

Then slowly she moved her hand, picked out something from the case. It was a photograph; not a locket—nothing so sentimental could have been Anna's—but a small, cracked photograph which might perhaps have rested unheeded in that box for years from very insignificance. And it was the likeness of a child—a paltry image, faded, long laid away, but still exact, distinct, and curiously arresting. So arresting, it absorbed her fascinated eye. She knew at once: it was Anna's child, mysterious, hidden, that child long since dead —that was the likeness which now so suddenly confronted her. And suddenly, too, arising from the image of this child, came another image to confront her—the face of her own son. Peter's face, shorn of the years, ranged beside this other face with staggering resemblance—the nose, the set of the eyes, the very curl of the lip almost identical—swimming together before her blurring vision into one single face. No, not a face, but a suspicion, a horrible, atrocious suspicion.

Was she dreaming, possessed suddenly by some disordered fancy, some false sentiment of melodrama, something wholly foreign to her sane and normal nature? But no, it was not fancy. This likeness, striking so acutely into the suspense of her excited mind, was to her not merely a shock, but a revelation. That Anna's son and her own son should be as one admitted of but a single explanation—a single terrifying solution which was indeed the solution of everything which she had feared.

She trembled. And within her also something trembled unliberated, straining to escape. Everything that had hitherto evaded her, the unrealised presentiment of these last few days, the whole undercurrent of her mind seethed upwards to consciousness and overwhelmingly engulfed her.

"Oh, God," she thought blindly, "now I understand everything." Now it was complete—the edifice. Five years ago Frank had lived for months in Anna's home. Then Anna's child—their child had come. It was true, then. Frank was the father of Anna's child. She knew it to be so.

With a movement of frightful agitation she thrust back the photograph, snapped down the lid, sank down upon the edge of the bed. Stunned, her eyes wide, darkened by fear, she sat stricken. Her heart stopped beating. She was dazed, beaten, confounded; virtue had gone out of her and out of life. The echo of a thousand voices resounded in her ears, a low muttering, insistent voices all whispering— whispering of Frank, her husband whom she loved unfaithful to her.

With a little cry she recoiled. Violently she straightened her sagging figure. She did not believe it. Quivering, she drew in a long, determined breath, swept by a quick revulsion of feeling. She would not believe it. It was impossible. This stunning likeness between Anna's child and her own child was a circumstance of chance, the outcropping of some family resemblance. It was not the keystone of her edifice. There was no edifice. All—all meant nothing beside her love for Frank. She had her love, her loyalty. I'm mad, she thought with fierce compunction, to suspect Frank! It seemed suddenly monstrous that on the evidence of a word, a look, a chance resemblance in a photograph, she should accuse him of an action inevitably destructive of their happiness. Clearly she was not a woman to be meanly jealous or suspicious; she was above that. It was the sheer intensity of her love for him which had driven her to this pass, had made her feel the wound within her breast before the arrow had been loosed. And there was no arrow. Frank had no connection with this wretched business. She would not believe it of Frank—this atrocious suspicion—Frank who through these years had been her husband, who had caressed her, loved her without once alluding to this nightmare fact which now so painfully oppressed her.

But why—she paused, her eyes again clouded—yes, why had he made no mention of the matter? It would have been so easy, so natural to drop a word, a hint, before Anna's arrival. And why had he opposed her coming when now his every action gave evidence of his regard? With a gesture of despair she flung her arm upon the bed-rail and leaned her brow upon it.

She had no proof. She was mistaken. She was making a fool of herself. It was a pure coincidence, Frank's visit and the birth of this child happening within the compass of a year.

But what—what a hateful coincidence! And was it mere coincidence? Merely at the thought she shivered. Besides, to have hidden it from her—therein lay the fiercest anguish of it all. A flood of bitter recollection swept over her: looks she felt to have been interchanged between Anna and Frank, words passed slyly. She started fiercely. Had they even a sign of secret understanding?

She bit her lip, clenched her hands tightly in the effort to command her reason. Her pulses pounded in her ears, and in her throat was a dry constriction like the clutching of a painful grief.

Suddenly she raised her head, her chin curved to a resolute set, her body arched to a fine-drawn tension, her will fighting something unseen. Violently her instinct of possession flamed. Frank was hers. Let the past contain what it might; she was concerned now with the present and the future. Abruptly she started to her feet and with a firm compression of her lips went down the stairs. Accepting the fact as certainty, she forced herself fiercely to confront it. She would confront it.

But she could not continue with her work. She went into the parlour, sat down upon the sofa. And then, sitting stiffly upon that sofa, gradually the lines of her figure drooped, her lips softened, her eyes became again remote. Her shoulders drooped listlessly. She began to go over it again.

Her face torn by the conflict of emotions, her form outlined against the clear light of the window, she made a figure strangely youthful and pathetic. An air like that of tragedy enveloped her. But was that tragedy her discovery? Or was it deeper, coming solely from within?

She was still sitting there when Netta came in to announce that lunch was ready And with the same intense preoccupation she rose, went into the dining-room. Peter was there, seated at table, his napkin already around his neck; and at the sight of him warm tears of sentiment ran into her eyes. He at least is mine, she thought, and always will be mine. With a sudden restrained movement she slipped her arm over his thin shoulders and swiftly kissed him.

" Where's Anna, mother? " he cried, attacking his broth with vigour.

" In Glasgow," she answered in a low voice.

" I missed her this morning," he said cheerfully, " I like Anna. She's a good sort."

She made no reply. That her son should have become attached to Anna struck her as incredible—a repellent thought.

"She said something about a yacht the other day," he went on; "with real sails, you know."

She tightened her lips suddenly lest she betray something of the turmoil within her. In this moment of desperate disquietude she saw even in Anna's attitude towards Peter something unnatural, excessive, suspicious: Anna being good to the boy because he was Frank's son, because he reminded her of her own son of whom Frank also was the father.

Abruptly she got up from the table, anguished, her hand pressed against her cheek.

"Mother," cried Peter, "where are you going?"

"I've finished," she answered with difficulty. "I've got some sewing to do." And hurriedly she went out of the room.

The afternoon dragged on; steeped in the pale autumnal sunshine, marked by the slowly ticking seconds, evoking sadness, touching her with the poignant recollection of other afternoons, quiet and sleepy and intimate, when Frank and she had proved their love.

She had no sewing to do. There was nothing that she could do. She must wait—wait feverishly for his return. And when, at last, it drew towards the time of his train, her quivering impatience drove her to action. She would go to meet him. She rose, put on her hat and coat, then set out for the station. She went by the front road— this was the usual route of his return—and, keyed to meet him, she suppressed the impulse to take Peter with her. It was Frank alone whom at this moment she desired. Oh! how poignantly she longed to be alone with him, to plumb this wretched business to its uttermost depth, to be convinced, to tell him that she loved him, to be assured conclusively of his love for her.

As she drew near to the town, her gaze sought vividly amongst the passers-by upon the promenade, ready to light at the approach of that familiar figure. But he was not in sight. Surely he had not taken the other road when this invariably was the way he favoured? Gradually her pace slackened; at the middle of the esplanade she halted indecisively, her face pale and troubled, her eyes anxious, perplexed.

Then suddenly a voice at her ear made her start and turn with swift expectancy. But instantly her look fell; she swallowed hard upon her disappointment: it was not Frank who stood there, but Miss Hocking, gravely appended to her dog, beaming towards her with generous serenity.

"I," said Miss Hocking reasonably, "shall stroll back with you."

Lucy was in no mood for this meeting—it was the last thing she desired; she wanted Frank: her very heart, it seemed, swelled urgently towards him.

" I'm meeting my husband," she answered stiffly.

" At least let me walk with you," suggested the other, with greater logic than before.

" All right," said Lucy miserably. " I'll go back now."

They began to walk together.

" If you could come to tea with me," advanced Miss Hocking mildly, " there will be crumpets—and a cream cake."

Lucy gazed up at the other with swimming eyes, then smiled lest she might do worse. But it was a wan, strained smile.

" Not to-day," she answered wretchedly.

" And after—I should play to you on my 'cello. Classical, perhaps; but not tiresome. Very low and sweet."

Lucy shook her head.

" I can't come," she said in a low voice.

" A thought," murmured Miss Hocking without regret. " Simply a thought. No harm has been done."

They went on for a while in silence.

" You haven't," said Lucy with difficulty, almost in spite of herself, " you haven't passed Frank—my husband? I came to meet him."

Miss Hocking's face drew to a profound consideration, then ultimately she said:

" No! "

They walked for a further spell in silence; then with calm directness Miss Hocking declared, as only she could declare:

" You are looking for him. But it is he surely who should be looking for you! "

Lucy coloured violently: the words, ingenuously amicable, held no implication, but they struck at her with painful force.

" A woman," went on Miss Hocking, with unexpected eccentric philosophy, " should be pursued. I do not pursue, but I know instinctively that I am pursued."

Lucy bit her lips at the fantastic words; it was all such nonsense, yet through the nonsense gleamed a thin shaft of truth. Her hands moved nervously; there was a break in her voice as she said:

" I'm referring to my husband. I hope you understand."

" Ah! " said Miss Hocking mildly.

Nothing more was said. They parted at that point beyond the pier which marked the divergence of their ways—Miss Hocking ascending to her flat in the select quarter upon the hill, Lucy continuing along the front towards her home.

Unreasonably, she felt distressed, disturbed by the recent circumstance, by Miss Hocking's grotesque but none the less exasperating suggestion that she had been running after Frank. Who indeed had better right to seek for him than she? She had gone simply to meet him. She did not demand that he run after her; that, in Miss Hocking's ridiculous phrase, he must pursue her. But was the phrase so ridiculous? She frowned. Her mind, again insinuated into the channel of suspicion, chilled at an odious thought; her body, conscious of the bleak autumnal mist marking the approaching twilight, turned colder.

What a frightful thought it was, piercing her, that Frank had once pursued Anna, had loved Anna, had lain with her, filled her with his child; that he, himself, everything she had felt to be hers, had been Anna's also. And all—all happening without her knowledge. Yes, it was back once more, torturing her.

And again, with amazing association, she recollected her brother's frigid opposition to her marriage, his constant aspersions against the Moores, even his warning of catastrophe. Surely this was inexplicable on the mere grounds that by her marriage she demeaned herself. Had Frank and Anna—was it possible they had been lovers even in their early days at Levenford? Did Richard know something of which she had then been ignorant? From that indeed, though in her heart she felt it might be true, her pride recoiled violently.

Then into this recoil came a moment of calmer reason, a shaft of light striking through the haggard obscurity of her mind. Why, if Frank and Anna were lovers—she was hounding her surmise to its bitter end—why had they not married in the beginning? Frank's weakness, Anna's perversity towards a settled life—neither of these facts explained conclusively their failure to take a step so logical and sane She started, and for a moment felt light, relieved, almost happy. For this reason alone that suspicion was unfounded. She was wrong!

Then suddenly from some secret cell within her brain rose a prompting which chilled her happiness and tore away this new-found hope. Frank and Anna were cousins, a relationship which made their marriage forbidden by the Church. Her tormented mind, aghast yet avid, seized upon this unessential fact with an almost sinking dread. She felt cold again, conscious of a raw dampness sweeping inwards from the firth which seemed to freeze her very soul.

Now it was almost dark, and tiny points of light were pricking out around the sweep of the bay. She had been out longer than she had anticipated; already Frank might have arrived; but she made no movement to hasten her pace. How curious it was that she, so open and loving, taking such pride—a conscious pride—in her house, should be apparently reluctant to enter that house—afraid, as it were, to enter her own home. Even now at the gate she hesitated, as though, hidden by the vast outer blackness, she were safe; as if, indeed, it were she who harboured some secret which she must conceal.

Then again came the passionate uprising of her love. She must see Frank, her Frank, immediately. Her heart yearned suddenly towards him with all the intensity of her present suffering. Let them be alone together; let him explain; then all would come right. She was no tyrant; she would listen to him, and would understand. With a movement almost vehement she twisted the handle of the door and, her eyes glistening, her lips resolute, she entered the house.

She wanted Frank. And Frank was there, occupying an easy chair before the glinting fire in the parlour, with Peter on one side of him. But upon the other was Anna. Anna! She paled, winced as from a blow at the sight of the other woman. Her figure drew together, taut in the half-light of the doorway. Frank and Anna had returned together.

It came like oil on the fire of her suspense, like gall thrust into the raw wound of her jealousy—a sudden confirmation of her fear. All the open tenderness went out of her in one sudden inexplicable rush, and in the instant her softness turned to bitterness, her face hardened, her lips sealed into a narrow line. Blinking defensively against the brightness of the lamplight, she felt like some stranger intruding unexpectedly upon a group that already was complete. She, the mistress of her home, to feel like this. For a moment she stood, watching, then all at once she cut in, her words vibrating harshly in her ears:

" So you ran into each other."

Peter gave a lively, excited laugh.

" Ran into," he echoed. " That's a funny way of putting it. They came home in the same train, mother."

" So I see," she answered, in a choking voice.

" And look, mother," he cried, and in his tone the rapture still persisted. " Look at what Anna has brought me." Entranced, he held out a model yacht, a lovely, slender, white-sailed craft, a most enchanting and expensive gift.

" It's a treat of a boat," said Frank enthusiastically. " It must have cost Anna a mint of money. I'll sail it myself on Sunday."

She stared at him fixedly.

" Speak, mother, speak," cried Peter, tugging at her dress. " Say that it's wonderful."

" You all seem to find it wonderful," said Lucy with painful bitterness, and in the hot room she had a sudden flushing of her wind-stung cheeks.

There was an awkward, unexpected silence; then Anna, who had been watching her, her lower lip protruding, that look upon her face as though she smiled yet did not smile, exclaimed:

" We thought you were lost! "

" No," said Lucy, with cold deliberation, " I'm anything but lost."

D—TL

" My boat," said Peter, aggrieved, smoothing the shining hull.
" My lovely boat. You might have said you liked it."

" Be quiet," cried Lucy fiercely. " I've more to think of than
your toys."

She could not help herself: she, torn by her anguish, faced by the
crisis of her life, to be harassed by this triviality—this gift of Anna
to her son.

The gong rang for tea.

" Well," said Moore at length, rising, " even if we can't be pleasant
we must eat."

Her flush deepened, but without a word Lucy turned and went
into the dining-room.

" Where did you get to? " said Moore again, when they were
seated. His humour was good; he seemed anxious to please, even to
placate her. " You don't often go out at this time."

" I have my own affairs to attend to," she answered in a hard
voice; she saw his desire to placate, and bitterly she suspected it.
" I suppose you realise that."

" Yes," he agreed mildly, " that's right, my dear."

A pause followed, a stiff, unnatural pause. Then Anna spoke.

" It was funny, Lucy," said she with unusual graciousness, " Frank
and I came down on the same train, and we didn't even know it till
we got to Ardfillan."

" Indeed," said Lucy with a curl of her lip, " That's almost unbelievable."

Yet the effort to produce that inflection of disdain made her heart
break. She knew, of course, that Anna was deceiving her—how else
to explain her mood of unusual complaisance. Poor Lucy! Had
Anna's mood been sullen, she, in her present anguish, would surely
have construed it to this same suspicion.

But it was for her an intolerable meal. Scarcely could she swallow;
each mouthful seemed to choke her. She had a sudden impulse to
rush out into a freer air, a desire to escape from the insufferable
burden of her thoughts. But she could not move; she could not
escape. She was compelled to sit, to listen; and all the time to
watch—yes, compelled by some growing force to watch painfully
for some look or word passing between these two which would confirm this dread which tortured and infuriated her.

But at last it was over. Anna went back at once to the parlour;
Peter ran upstairs hugging tenderly the disparaged yacht; Netta
cleared the table and retired to the kitchen. They were alone—a
moment which Frank too had apparently awaited. For he said at
once, quite openly:

" Lucy, what's wrong, my dear? I thought we'd got over all that
difference."

She rose, closed the door which Netta had left ajar, then with set lips she sat down and faced him. Her mood of tenderness, frustrated, was gone: she was resolved now, passionately resolved: and without hesitation she said firmly:

" I want to speak to you, Frank."

" Well," he answered, with a peaceable smile, " that's no reason to wear a face like a funeral."

" We'll leave my looks out of this," she answered, with hard deliberation, " seeing that you don't approve of them."

" Now don't take me up wrong, Lucy," he said hurriedly, mildly. " You know that was simply a joke."

" I'm in no mood for jokes," she replied bitingly. " I've never been more serious in all my life."

" But, Lucy," he almost pleaded, " what's the matter with you ? "

" I'm in deadly earnest, Frank," she declared, with a slow intensity, and there was no mistaking the significance of her tone. " I suspect you of something. It's a horrible thing. But that doesn't alter the fact. And more than that. There's only one way out of it. You've got to speak the truth. Tell me "—her voice rose suddenly and quivered accusingly—" tell me if you were Anna's lover."

" What ! " he gasped.

" Not only that," she cried passionately. " Tell me if you were the father of her child."

He stared at her stupefied, whilst a high colour mounted his brow. So that was it—the explanation of everything: she had jumped to a horrible conclusion. And she was wrong—horribly wrong.

" So that's what you think," he stammered, at last. " That's what you think of me."

" Tell me," she cried again in a high voice. " Can't you see I'm waiting ? "

" But, Lucy ! " he stammered, completely abashed, his embarrassment making him the picture of guilt; " don't be absurd. The—the thing's ridiculous."

" Not so absurd," she burst out, her breast filling convulsively, as she perceived his palpable distress, " not so ridiculous but what it upsets you."

Her senses strained to the utmost, she searched unconsciously his face, observed each shade of meaning, each inflection of his voice. And, aware suddenly of this scrutiny, he flared up.

" Who are you looking at ? I don't like it."

" Then you have something to be afraid of ? " Her face was pale, her tone suppressed, as, stung by the defensive note in his voice, she added bitterly: " Why, there's guilt looking out of your eye. You can't deceive me, Frank. I know you. Oh ! why can't you be a man and face up to this honestly ? "

Her words came with swift vehemence, treading one upon the other; and under that vehemence he moved restlessly, flushed more darkly, because he knew that he was weak, felt himself confirming her suspicion.

" This is madness," he shot out. " I'd nothing to do with that affair. Nothing! You know surely that it's you I love. I've never in my life had a thing to do with Anna. If you don't believe me, ask her."

" Anna! " she cried fiercely. " Do you expect me to humiliate myself by asking Anna? Me, your wife, to abase myself before her! Besides "—she sneered—" what could I expect from Anna? Certainly not the truth! I've no doubt there's some horrible understanding between you."

" Good God! " he exclaimed, his temper rising at his own inability to master the situation. " What are you getting at? You've got it all wrong, I tell you. It's damnably wrong."

" It is wrong," she flung back passionately, " and it's you who have made it so."

" Have it that way then," he shouted. " If it suits you to hang something on me I never did, then do it and be damned to you! "

They confronted each other, strung to a vital tension. Then suddenly the hardness of her face relaxed. Swept by an uncontrollable impulse of tenderness towards him, the bitterness faded from her eyes, which shone now with a glistening appeal.

" Can't you understand, Frank," she cried, " how this is torturing me? Let's have it out. Then we can start afresh."

But now, at last, he was thoroughly enraged, and with all the obstinacy of injured weakness he refused to listen. Instead, he jumped to his feet.

" I've had about enough. I can't stand any more of this."

Quickly she, too, started up and took his arm.

" Frank," she entreated passionately, " you know I love you. Surely you know that by this time. You must know I'd do anything for you. Anything on this earth. Can't you even ask me to forgive you? "

He made for the door without looking at her. " What should I want your blasted forgiveness for? " he cried. " Keep that till it's asked for."

" Don't go, Frank," she pleaded desperately. " That only convinces me you're to blame."

With an exclamation he shook off her arm.

" For God's sake let me alone! " And he swung round and went out of the room.

He was gone. She sat rigidly, her eyes, filled with tears, fixed upon that closed door. He had denied her accusation. Yes, inevitably he had denied it. But the manner of his denial had served merely to confirm her insufferable belief. If only he had been honest. Oh, how gladly would she have forgiven him if only he admitted it. But instead he had blustered his way out of the room. That was not Frank, not the man she loved; it was a shell, a mask to cover what lay beneath. She knew his weakness, his moodiness, his queerness; that indeed was why she wished to lend him her strength. She did not love him for any qualities he might possess, but for that indefinable something that was he. And, loving him, she had tried to help him. For eight years they had been happy: it was impossible for him not to recognise her devotion to him: and now she was faced by this incredible, this dreadful turn of circumstance. It was possible, from his manner, that something had happened even now between Anna and him.

And again she shivered, her eyes still fixed upon that door, which seemed suddenly symbolic—something shut against her, giving access to a state she might never regain. Suddenly from the parlour, whither he had gone, came the chorus of " The Minstrel Boy," thumped out by Anna upon the piano. She started. Her head ached; she felt upon her an unutterable despondency. Alone in the room, the moment and the place were propitious for a bitter outburst of her grief. But she did not weep. Her lips came together firmly; into her small, resolute face there flowed a fresh determination. No matter that her suspicion was confirmed. She loved him. And she would save him from Anna, save him from himself. Her anger was spent; she would make no scene; but she would watch, she would wait, she would be ready to act when the need for that action arose. Deliberately she got up and went quietly into the parlour.

IX

Now, when she awoke, always that heavy load lay upon her like a weight pressing on her heart. For a few seconds she would have the drowsy happiness of awakening, that subconscious pleasure in the new day, then all at once would come swift realisation, which destroyed instantly the brightness of the morning. It was intolerable, this painful oppression, extinguishing all the lovely eagerness of life. With wounded eyes and set lips she would remain quiet, facing the opposite wall of the bedroom. There, in frightful mockery, hung a pleasant picture she had always liked: " The Reconciliation "—two lovers, romantically attired, clasped in a chaste embrace on marble steps beside a fountain, whilst in the foreground a faultless deerhound pointed and in the background an old servant, manifestly affected, supported a salver with wine. A sweet tableau. But Lucy saw nothing of its sweetness. She was thinking wretchedly behind her clouded brow: " I cannot endure this. The strain of it is killing me!"

But she must endure it. She would endure it. She—to give in, capitulate, admit defeat? Why, it was unthinkable! Quickly would come the answering resolve: " I'll see this thing through—yes, to the bitter end."

Then, her determination more finely tempered, she would arise, dress silently, and descend to see about his breakfast. For she did not cease in her attentions. No, no! These, on the contrary, she intensified, without appearing to intensify them, holding herself coldly apart whilst she proved her worth. His breakfasts had never been better, nor had they ever been better served. She warmed his fresh underclothes with a sedulous neutrality, heated his gloves before the fire, came even to the door to help him silently into his new overcoat.

But, oh, how feverishly, beneath this calm worked the leaven of her excitation.

It was the following Saturday, and she was no wiser, no easier in her mind. Actually four days had passed—how had she endured them?—every morning of which had greeted her in unfelt splendour. Clear and sunny, yet freshened by the roving airs of autumn, these last days had dragged strangely past her. She could not get satisfaction—that was the phrase she knew to be expressive exactly of her situation, and it was a phrase which fretted her to distraction. If Frank had only taken her in his arms and made with serious intensity a simple denial of the single fact she dreaded, then would she immediately have been happy, appeased. But following that scene when she had first confronted him he did not do this. He did not defend himself. He was by turns ironic, facetious, flippant, deliberately going out of his way to aggravate her anxiety by a new and quite open attention to Anna. It was as if, indeed, under her eye, betraying a strange similarity of humour, they discovered themselves flung together into an alliance of necessity. Unfaithful once with Anna, why not unfaithful now, again? Her face piteous, she winced. She knew Frank, and knew him well. In the past they had had their disagreements—who had not?—but he had always " come round." Now, however, he was a long time " coming round." Did he think actually that she had accepted the situation, that she was beaten? Her head reared like an angry horse at the iniquitous suggestion.

Standing there in Peter's small bedroom, watching him at what he gravely termed " his packing," a heavy wave of injustice rolled painfully over her being. Even in this contemplation of her son she had the feeling of having been abused. Yes, even here she had been trapped, betrayed into a false position. Peter was going for a few days to Port Doran, but, though she herself had suggested that going, she did not in the least desire that he should go.

The boy had been her outlet during those last days. She had talked much to him, had made much of him, finding in him a fountain of relief. More especially had she paraded her son and her affection for her son before Anna, all with a sort of bitter ostentation. Precluded by her pride from a direct attack, she was determined, passionately determined, to use every weapon she possessed to wound Anna and to induce her to terminate her stay. With this latter purpose firmly in view, she had said on Thursday, holding the boy closely and fixing a direct look upon the other woman:

" You'll go to Port Doran on Saturday, Peter. Uncle Edward wants you over when Anna has gone."

But Anna had taken no hint from this plain precipitation of the situation. Anna was still here. And her son, rising joyously to the prospect of the change, was leaving her—was nearing even now the moment of his departure. Even upon this trivial issue she had the feeling of frustration; it was as if, almost, she had been defeated by her own hand.

" I think I've got everything in, mother," he declared seriously, suddenly looking up from the small Gladstone bag that stood open on the carpet. Viewing his kneeling form sadly, with a sort of melancholy pride, she recognised him as an amazing child, saw his propensity for order, for neatness, to be astounding. He knew exactly what he had and where he had it. His clothes—she of course might look after these, but towards the rest of his possessions, from his toys, yes, even to his ties, he exhibited a careful ownership— derived, surely, from herself—which was incredible in one so young.

" Are you not sorry, son, to be going away from me ? " she said, yearning for a crumb of comfort, her eyes a little humid towards him.

He closed the bag and jumped up gaily.

" I'll soon be home, mother," he declared, with proper optimism. " I'm sorry, though, about Anna. She may be away when I come back." Then his face brightened hopefully, and he added : " Perhaps not, though. You never can tell."

As he spoke, a loud knocking sounded on the back door.

" There's Dave," he cried ecstatically, making for the stairs. " Time I was off." He paused suddenly, arrested by a thought. " I must say good-bye to Anna, though."

" Go, then," she said coldly. " I can promise you'll not see her again."

As he went to Anna's room : the hour was early—nine o'clock had just struck—and Anna was not yet up : she descended slowly to the kitchen.

" That's young Bowie—come for Peter," said Netta, brushing at a boot. It was Angus who had come, not Dave, and Netta worked off her disappointment in a furious attack upon the leather.

" You'll see him over safe, Angus? " said Lucy going to the open door. She had again that strange qualm at this parting from her son.

" I'll do that," he declared seriously. Though he was like Dave, he had not Dave's laughing humour; he was reserved guarded, more sure of himself; and he added, echoing her words: " I'll see him safe over for you."

" Thank you," she said quietly; and she turned as Peter burst into the kitchen bearing his bag in one hand and a new shilling in the other.

" Here I am " he cried boisterously, " and Anna has given me a whole shilling. Isn't it great? Come along, Angus. I'm ready."

" You'll not spend that money on trashy sweets," she said severely, feeling herself forestalled; she had meant to give him a shilling herself " for his sporran." " I don't want your stomach upset."

" No, no, mother," he affirmed at once. " I'll buy nothing coloured."

She gazed at his laughing, eager face with an indescribable emotion. This separation for a few days was nothing, a triviality, yet, coming upon the frightful tension of her spirit, it struck her with almost overwhelming significance. She had the strange sense of something impending, something irrevocable occasioned by, and arising from, this obscure parting; and she had, too, a vague, intangible immanence—a presentiment—concerning his return. Suddenly she stirred.

" Good-bye, then, dearest," she said, holding out her arms. It was almost unique, her use of this superlative of affection, but somehow the circumstance compelled it from her lips.

As he went down the path with Angus, she followed him with her gaze, feeling still with an exquisite lingering emotion the pressure of his warm lips on hers. Stupid, stinging tears were in her eyes. Then she turned swiftly: it would not do to make a fool of herself in front of Netta.

She went into the parlour and, standing in the front room, she gazed fixedly through the window, brooding upon the view before her. She was conscious of a sense of deprivation; conscious, too, that the departure of her son must bring the crisis to its head. He had been, she recognised, a sort of buffer State, deadening the sharp clash of conflict between Anna and herself.

And now she asked herself again why she had not determined the situation once for all by asking Anna to leave her house. Though she may have felt it to be so, no mere tenet of hospitality had restrained her. No; the reason was deeper, subtler than that. To resolve the matter in this fashion would be a tacit admission of her weakness, her fear, her surrender. It was not she, but Anna who herself must sound the retreat. Besides, though she knew it not, her suspicion was like a canker which demanded the sinapism of surveillance. She was sure, yet she was not sure. And violently she wished to clench the truth, to nail it down finally and for ever. How often, with searing, introspective vision, had she contemplated the facts of the position, shredding the evidence, weighing this against that, probing deep down into the raw wound of her suspicion. She was convinced that Frank was the father of Anna's child, convinced that he had again been unfaithful with her. And yet—still she did not *know*.

She did not know—and therein lay the crux, the goading nucleus of all her misery. All her intuition recognised the case as proved, but the final evidence was lacking. That was the position and the very thought of this suspense gave her a sense of straining impotence.

And she could not ask. She had questioned Frank, and he had evaded her question. Now, if the universe hummed with this awak-ened secret, she would not stoop to ask again. Her pride forbade it. Besides, there was no universal hum: the secret was dormant, sealed, sought after only by her: and one person alone must positively hold this knowledge she desired. One person. Anna! If only she could for a second see within the mind of Anna.

She stirred restlessly. Again the imperative need came upon her to know—to know conclusively, to grasp this elusive, torturing bubble of uncertainty, and finally to burst it. How maddening was her position.

Once more the bare realism of fact, endured interminably, struck her with unexhausted violence; and she shivered at the picture in her mind: Frank and Anna, together, in the consummation of their love. She bit her lip fiercely.

How could she say calmly: This is past—a long time past, when the woman herself was in her house, eating, sleeping, living under her roof, confronting her with that perpetual enigmatical antagon-ism. It was too unbearable, too unjust, that this should descend upon her from the blue; and too impossible that she should receive it in quiescence. She who made her love for Frank the loyalty of her life —the mere thought of all these happy years of her married life brought tears to her eyes—she could not accept it placidly.

She would not tolerate it. It had gone on long enough—too long; it must be that her sense of decency, of hospitality, had overborne her judgment. Yes, she felt now with a hot tide of conviction that she could no longer suffer merely to wait and watch. That she should have sent away her son in this vain reminder whipped her with a sense of ineffectuality. She—ineffectual! If Anna were too thick-skinned to accept that hint, then some stronger interference was necessary. The need for action pressed upon her feverishly. It was no surrender to confront Anna. And it was not as if she was afraid of Anna. Her lip curled at the thought, and all at once something rose up in her. This was no ordinary situation; it could be dealt with by no ordinary methods. Her hands clenched firmly. The sound of Netta's singing striking on her ears served merely to lash more fiercely her determination; but for Anna, she, too, might have been happy and singing at her work. She thought passionately, " I won't endure it! I won't! I'll go up to her now." Yes, she would do it— and that instantly! Impulsively she turned, went into the hall, began to ascend the stairs.

For all her agitation, for all the slightness of her figure, she had an air almost formidable. With a tightening of her throat and a quickening of her heart she entered Anna's room.

Anna was in bed—now she never rose for breakfast—lying with her hair strewn darkly upon the pillow, the marks of sleep unerased about her eyes, her nightdress open, edged at the neck with a frill of lace. Her breasts showed round, her under lip that interminable fullness, her face no shadow of surprise at this unusual and wholly unexpected entry.

Silently Lucy sat down upon a chair: so close she could see the points of yellow flecking the brown of Anna's eyes; and in silence the two looked at each other steadily.

" You're not up yet? " said Lucy at length, calling on all her strength to keep the quiver from her voice, to make the words deliberate, cold.

" So it would seem," answered Anna easily.

" You take things very easily." It came more quickly, louder than she intended.

" Isn't it the best way? "

Lucy drew herself together; moistened her lips, which felt dry and stiff.

" I cannot understand you, Anna," said she with a suppressed intensity.

" What is there to understand? "

" You have no occupation, no standards, no religion—nothing. You exist solely for your own pleasure."

" What's life for? " said Anna carelessly. " Get what you can out of it. It's a race for what you want. And the devil take the hindmost."

" So that's what you believe," said Lucy sharply. " That explains your attitude."

In answer, Anna smiled—was it a smile, that expression mingling indifference, amusement, contempt, which emanated entirely from her unresentful eyes? At that look, so exasperating in its negligence, Lucy turned pale.

" So that's your idea of life," she persisted in a hard voice. " You haven't a single loyalty."

" And have you ? "

" I have my husband," stammered Lucy, with a sudden vivid flush. " And my son. And—and my religion."

" The Father, the Son, and the Holy Ghost. Amen," said Anna with a sort of meditative mockery.

There was a sharp pause, during which Lucy felt a sudden uprising of all the restrained and accumulated emotion of the past week.

" That's horrible! " she cried out. " Simply horrible! How can you talk like that? It's sordid—it's blasphemous. You make a fool of everything in life that's good and noble." Swept away by her own emotion, she used the final word without self-consciousness.

Anna raised herself upon her elbow, her manner suddenly scornful, her voice harsher than before.

" Don't make me sick," she exclaimed with unexpected vehemence. " All that sentimental mush. You're like the rest of them— standing on the wrong foot. The sanctity of marriage! The beauty of motherhood! What is it when all's said and done? You marry for something you're afraid to get other ways. Then, because of that something, you have a kid. That's how life begins. The voice that breathed o'er Eden." She paused, and threw an ineffable derision into her stare. " Isn't it sweet? And as for the other, you may kill yourself looking after your nice little son and in the end he'll turn and spit in your eye. And that last piece of clap-trap. The immortality of the soul! Wait till you die—then you'll find out you've been chasing balloons."

" How dare you talk like that? " gasped Lucy, quivering with anger. " How dare you? I'll not have it."

" Not have it! That's just your trouble. You squeeze the balloon that hard you're going to burst it one of these days—then you'll find your fancy notions up in the air, like smoke."

" I'll see them go before I believe you," threw back Lucy in a voice strained by her exasperation. " I'd rather die than have your idea of life—your—your explanation! " Abruptly she paused, strung to an irresistible impulse. " But when you're about it—can you explain this? " she exclaimed; and, suddenly stretching out her hand, she opened the green box upon the dressing-table.

But the dramatic gesture was entirely ineffectual—the case was empty. And all at once Anna laughed outright, her unusual, harsh, scornful laugh; her whole manner was unusual: her habitual mildness gone, her full eyes alight, she seemed equally ready to give and to receive.

" That was real funny," she said. " No, I chucked the photo in the fire the very day after you spied it out."

A small spot of colour now burned high on Lucy's cheek, and her eyes burned too, with a steady anger.

"I'm glad you find it amusing," she cried. "Perhaps you'll tell me the joke."

"It's gone stale now. Not worth the telling."

"You never did say much about it, I understand."

"No, sure enough I didn't."

"You don't need to," cried Lucy, strung to an intolerable pitch. "I know all about you—and the child you had."

"Well, it was me that had it," said Anna mockingly. "You don't have to worry."

There was a pause while Lucy, outraged, choking back her indignation, clenched her hands and fixed the other with a determined eye.

"You're going to tell me," she declared in a desperate voice, "something that I want to know."

"Yes?"

"Yes! Why did you come here at all?"

"You asked me, didn't you!"

"I didn't know you then."

"And do you know me now?" The words, provocative, levelled with a deadly irony, made Lucy flinch, and again that frightful aggravation welled up violently in her. She cried out fiercely:

"What does Frank mean to you?"

"Well—I've always liked Frank," answered Anna, in a reasonable, taunting voice. "When I came here I'd almost forgotten. But you—you've sort of made me realise it again. If it hadn't been for you, I don't believe I'd have taken a bit of notice. No, 'deed and I wouldn't."

"He's my husband, you understand," said Lucy in a low, vibrating tone.

"Does that mean that you own him—body and soul and divinity? You won't let him out to graze occasionally?"

"It means that I love him. Sneer as much as you like. I don't care." A note of defiance crept into her tone. "I don't care what you think. I'm not ashamed of it. Even if he was mixed up with you in the past, it makes no difference."

"Then why worry?"

A look that was dangerous flared into Lucy's eyes. Her lips quivered; it seemed as though she might fly at Anna.

"This," she cried out. "This is how you return the hospitality I offered you. You've come here, you've traded on something that's past and forgotten, you've estranged my husband from me—yes, you've done your very utmost to take Frank away from me."

For a moment Anna calmly returned that stare, then slowly the old look drifted into her face.

"You're all wrong," she said evenly. "I've done nothing. You've done it all yourself." She paused, turned her head, and gazed out of the window. " I admit I did try to shake Frank up a bit. He looked that much as if he belonged to you I thought he needed it. But I've done no more."

" I don't believe you," panted Lucy. " You're lying. There was something between you. For the last time I ask you to tell me."

" What good would it be ? " said Anna negligently. " You've just said it. You wouldn't believe me in any case."

" If you don't," threw back Lucy in a suffocating voice, " you'll —you'll leave my house to-day! "

" Well," said Anna reflectively, " I knew we were coming to that. It's easy enough done."

Speechless, Lucy faced the other, fighting to control that sudden inward rush of intolerable resentment. It was the last straw! No longer could the same house contain this woman and herself. Abruptly she rose.

" You'll go then," she said in a low voice, " and at once. That's the best way. There's a train at twelve."

" I hadn't meant to stay more than a week when I came," said Anna slowly. " Just think that over."

Without a word Lucy spun round ; the door closed behind her with a snap. Her face was pale, almost drawn, as she went downstairs. She had done it—Anna was going—but strangely, she had no sense of victory. Instead, she had a curiously dull feeling of distress.

" She's inhuman," she thought bitterly, " quite inhuman! " To accuse her of creating this frightful situation, she who loved Frank, who had sought merely to defend the integrity of her home. Yet a dry sob rose in her throat. She had to pause in the hall, her hand pressed to her side, before she entered the kitchen.

" Netta," she said quickly, her head averted, " run along to Frew's and ask them to send a cab."

Netta's red hands moved slowly to her apron-strings.

" She's not—is she going ? " And her tone epitomised her surprise.

" Go and get the cab," answered Lucy, in a strange subdued voice.

Netta went out ; returned ; and thereafter the cab arrived and stood for a long time significantly at the door: the cabman upon the box crouched beneath his hat, the horse stretching its neck towards the vision of a nosebag, striking an impatient shoe upon the metalled road.

At last Anna came down, calm, negligent, indifferently averse ; and smiling—was it a smile?—that enigmatic mingling of amuse- ment and contempt. Now, as at the moment of her entry, she con· veyed that same strange sense of stillness.

" Here I am, you see," she declared lightly. " Doing what you want. Now you've got it all your own way."

In the half-light of the hall Lucy's face looked small, white, with eyes strained to a dark intensity. It struck at the rooted instincts of her being to do this thing; but it was, she knew, the right, the only thing to do.

" Good-bye," said she, feeling the violent beating of her heart. And she put out her hand. But Anna did not take it.

The jarvey, activated at last, staggered out with the trunk upon his back.

" Good-bye, then," said Anna. She halted a moment on the step. then over her shoulder she remarked: " You'll think it strange. But I can't help feeling sorry for you. Don't forget what I said about that balloon." Then, with a crunching of the wheels, she was gone.

Lucy turned with a painful constriction of her throat and closed the door. A faint elusive perfume, all that remained of Anna's presence, drifted to her nostrils with a sickening sweetness, and almost hurriedly she moved, went unknowingly into the front room. She felt weak suddenly, and there was a vague trembling in her limbs, but, relieved of that oppressive presence, she felt calmer, lighter somehow in her spirit. Yes, she was relieved, immeasurably assuaged. With lips still quivering she stood, one arm leaning upon the mantelpiece, gazing into the fire. The flames leaped upwards— alive they seemed and eager, soaring towards some ultimate desire. For a moment, born of her agitation, the old intangible longing gripped her, that curiously poignant yearning that often took her, welling upwards, as it were, from something long, long past. What was that desire? Bent forward, the light dancing warmly within her dark eyes, swept by that flowing qualm, she was a figure ageless and universal. What was her desire? It was, it must be, her love for Frank, her wish to see him happy, secure from the danger which had threatened him.

And she had made him secure. Out of that emotion came con- viction. Yes, she had done well. She knew it. And through all her agitation she felt suddenly appeased.

X

THAT evening before Frank returned from business she made an especial effort with her preparations for his reception. In the after- noon, impelled by some urgent need, she had cleaned her house until it shone: Anna's room particularly she had scoured and polished, changing the bed-linen, flinging wide the windows, letting the breeze lift the curtains and pour in freshly from the sea, removing every trace of that hateful and contaminating presence.

Something symbolic was in that action: a purification of the temple of her home. And now, with this same straining eagerness, she cooked his favourite dish, tilted his slippers to warm against the fender, assumed carefully her grey voile, did her hair with unusual care. She took infinite pains with her appearance—unique solicitude in one who dressed usually with brisk severity!—and in the end she was not satisfied. She felt that she was " at her worst," that Frank might think her lips pale, her face pinched, at this crisis when she desired most ardently to attract him. Turning from her mirror with a faint sigh, she descended and went into the front room, where she began nervously, needlessly, to arrange the Goss china on the corner bracket.

How unendurable these last few days had been, how frightful this situation she had been forced to meet. But she had met it, had faced the worst, and it was not insupportable. She had confronted the situation and she had mastered it. Anna was gone. And Frank was here, her own, ready with her to forget the past, and to recapture the rapture of their happiness. Ah! She was thinking of Frank, and of the fact that he and she would be together, alone in the house: a feeling at once so poignant and so rare it moved her with a tremulous appeal.

Gone now was the immediate effect of the recent departure, with its momentary assuagement of her nervous tension. Gone was that subsequent quiescence, and in its place had come an eager tenderness, an emotional impulse to forgive, to love and to be loved. Perhaps she had been severe during the past week: a little sharp to Frank; and rude, especially rude to Anna; torn by the pangs of her suspicion that had been supremely natural. But by accepting the actuality she had shown her fortitude, and now by her own act she had achieved, if not a victory, at least salvation—the salvation of her happiness, of Frank's happiness, of her home. Had she not heard somewhere of women in history—or was it legend?—women who fought to protect their homes, who cut away their breasts so they might draw the bow. A long time past. Yet she could understand. That was she. She had defended her home, and now, with inevitable reaction, she celebrated by a sweet surrender, not to circumstance, but to her love.

Nervously, keyed to a high expectancy, she waited. He was late. On most Saturdays he had an afternoon of leisure, but to-day he had been required by Lennox to journey to Leith Docks in connection with arrangements for the delivery of consignments from Holland. And, though her gaze turned often towards the clock, it was close on five when, listening intently, she heard the familiar click of the front gate. At once she jumped to her feet, a faint flush rising then fading

quickly from her cheek. Although she did not go into the hall—
that would have been too full a revelation of her altered disposition—
she stood, her eyes alight, her lips parted, awaiting the moment of
his entry.

It was, as usual, an unobtrusive entry: his head was down, his
shoulders forward, his air the slight sardonic mildness that was he.

" Tea ready? " he enquired, rubbing his hands with a quiet
rustling sound. " Turned colder outside, it has. And a mist coming
off the water fit to choke you."

" It is colder," she answered quickly, eagerly—yet it took a
powerful effort to control the tremor in her voice. " But I've got a
fine hot shepherd's pie for you."

He looked at her sharply, surprised, but, withdrawing his eyes, he
advanced to the fire and began to warm himself without speech.

" Have you had a hard day? " she asked warmly.

" Not too bad," he answered non-committally. " It was a longish
trip. Just like L., asking me to do it Saturday." He paused, seeing
more fully the favourable import of her manner.

" Get the boy away all right? "

" Yes," she said, pulling the bell. " He got off nicely."

Tea and toast and pie were brought by Netta, hot and crisp and
savoury. Then in silence Netta withdrew.

" Sit in," said Lucy from the head of the table.

He raised his head sharply, as though questioning his first perception of her mood.

" But Anna? " he exclaimed. " You don't want to begin without
her."

" She won't be in for tea," she answered, her eyes averted, her
hand which poised the sugar-tongs taken by a faint tremor. " She
went out some time ago."

" Went out? "

" Yes." With an effort she achieved a casual air. She would exhibit
her action in her own time, and not a second before. And, manifestly
surprised, he sat in, accepted his cup and stirred it thoughtfully.

" Has anything gone wrong? " he said at length.

The last few days had turned him more moodily mistrustful of
the universe.

" Nothing at all, Frank," she answered, flushing. " It's the other
way round. I hope we're going to get things right now."

Slowly he picked up his knife and fork.

" I hope so," he said significantly.

The meal progressed, and with its progression the colour upon her
cheeks intensified. Handing his second helping of pie, she remarked
suddenly:

" It's nice to be by ourselves again, don't you think? "

With one eye on the paper that lay beside his plate, he nodded, as though merely half hearing her question.

" It's the first time for days," she went on hurriedly, " that we've had a meal alone. We're more like ourselves to-night."

" You mean you are more like yourself," he said moodily.

She flushed and drew back, watching his bent head with a troubled eye; but she made no reply.

At last he had finished, and, picking up his paper, he went over to the sofa.

" I wonder where Anna is," he exclaimed, his gaze still upon the sheet. " Where can she have got to? "

She was silent; then, feeling she could wait no longer, with a quick movement she rose, advanced to the sofa, and sat down beside him. It was a moment reminiscent of the occasion when first she had confronted him with her suspicion. But since that moment the flux within her soul had fused to another purpose. Now, though more painfully agitated, she collected herself for no attack. That issue was sealed. Now she asked only that they bury the past and face the future together. And, making an effort to speak lightly, she exclaimed:

" Frank! It's just like old times, having the house to ourselves like this. Don't you remember? "

The paper crinkled as he turned to another page.

" Of course I remember," he said. " Surely you don't expect me to forget."

" But, Frank, don't you remember? " she repeated nervously, taking his hand and pressing it between her warm fingers. " I've been thinking all afternoon about things—that mean so much to us. That day we had—that day in Craigmore Wood—we don't seem to have thought much of that—lately." Stirred by her own words, again that nostalgia rushed over her and she moved restlessly, feeling once more the hot sun on the pine-needles, the warm scent of the humming bracken; below them the bay, she glowing, passive in his arms, a wild beating within and against her breast.

" What's the matter with you? " he demanded, turning slowly, and perceiving the shamed colour in her face he added, " What have you done now? "

Coming nearer to him upon the sofa, she lifted his hand and placed it close against her eager cheek.

" All that I've ever done has been to love you, Frank."

He looked at her uncomfortably, drawn to her, yet conscious of the strangeness of her mood.

" You've had a peculiar way of showing it this last fortnight," he said slowly.

" I want us to start over again," she murmured agitatedly. " Dear Frank. We'll forget everything that's happened. If only we love each other, nothing matters."

" But, Lucy," he said uneasily; then suddenly, struck by a violent thought, he pulled himself up, stared at her. " You haven't—no, surely—where did you say Anna was? "

Her eyes averted, she pulled nervously at a thread in his cuff answering painfully:

" You know I didn't want to do it, Frank. You know it wasn't easy for me."

" In the name of God! " he broke out, and as abruptly paused. There was a strained silence. " You don't mean to say," he resumed slowly, almost dazedly, "you don't mean to say you asked her to go? "

" And why not? " The mildness of her tone masking the turbulence of her heart was infinite.

" You made her go? " he stammered. " Made her get out? " Apparently he could not credit her admission.

" Yes." The word was more emphatic, the turbulence breaking through the mask.

Violently he wrenched his hand away.

" You've chucked her out of my house! " he cried out. " It's—it's unbelievable. Anna—my own cousin! "

" I've had quite enough of this cousin business," she answered in a suppressed voice. " I asked her to go for your good."

" My good! " he cried. " The way you've treated her this last week! And now—now you put the lid on it with this! "

Her bosom filled convulsively; anger brightened her eyes.

" You didn't wish her to come," she said, striving vainly to maintain her calm. " Why be sorry that she's away? "

" She was going next week," he cried, and in the acute exasperation of the moment his words rose almost to a shout. " Even if you didn't like her, why couldn't you put up with it for a few days longer? "

" Because I love you, Frank." It was the culmination of her argument, the explanation of her conduct, the epitome of everything, the sublime second of her oblation.

They faced each other, strained unbearably by the tension of the moment. Pale, her eyes hot and dry, she was breathing quickly, conscious of a quick throbbing in her side, filled by an agonised yearning for him to take her in his arms. Then all at once he moved restlessly, the corners of his lips turned downwards.

" Do you think you own me? " he said gloomily. " Do you think you're my keeper? If you loved God Almighty you'd want to put a chain on Him! "

" Frank! " she cried out appealingly. " Did you expect me to blind myself—to let things slide? "

" Slide! What was there to slide? You think you know everything.

But you don't. Not by a devil of a way. Anna was no more to me than anybody else. Yet you've shoved her in my teeth ever since she came. Go on like that and you'll destroy everything—destroy yourself too!"

Bitter words of denial rose to her lips, but she stifled them. This was what he said; this was how he answered this present offering of herself; this how he named her honesty, her sincerity, the intensity of her love for him; and after all that had taken place between them, those intimacies so enduring they could never be forgotten or effaced! Abruptly she turned away, angry at heart, feeling a humiliation turbulently mixed with longing. She knew she had been right, and she would persist in her intention. She knew he must be conquered; it was the only way; left to himself, he would slide weakly to disaster. His attitude served only to confirm her conviction that she had acted for his good.

" I'll leave you now," she said in a voice that was tremulous under her control. " I know you'll come round when you've thought about it." And all at once she rose, turned on her heel. As she went out of the room, she visualised poignantly the time when he would thank her for what she had done, admit that she had suffered equally with him.

She went into the parlour, where she sat at the window, foreseeing with a humid eye and heavy lip that hour when she would be justified; her thoughts ran faster and farther, too, and with a strangely childish turn of her dejection she saw herself working at some humiliating toil, scrubbing even on her knees, immolating herself for him, making some exalted sacrifice that should be for his good, and he who had ignored her demanding pardon, perhaps, when it should be too late.

For a long time she remained passive at the darkened window; then all at once into this mood of singular inversion came the sudden slam of the door. She started; turning, she hurried to the hall. He had gone out of the house! The unexpectedness of it dismayed her, shocked her like a blow. He never went out at nights, preferring always to lounge by his own fireside, and this swift departure from his inevitable habit moved her with a sense of keen dismay. With eyes puckered, she entered the dining-room, sat down in the chair which he had that moment vacated.

It seemed to strike her now with utter certainty, the conviction that her suspicion was justified: his reception of Anna's departure the final link in her chain of evidence. A heavy sigh broke from the very depths of her bosom. The blow was shattering. Yet she would accept it because she loved him.

But with what providential fortune had she recognised the situation, with what incisive foresight had she acted upon it. Was she the woman to sit passively in her own home and endure the recrudescence of this old, dishonourable infatuation? Was she the woman to wait weakly until this same senseless prepossession had run its gamut and then to say, " Come back, Frank. It's just the same as ever." No! A thousand times no. That was not marriage. She had asserted her rights, and she was glad. Possession! It was not possession, but love, her love—a welling tenderness towards him that rose into her eyes now as she sat waiting—waiting for his return.

XI

WHEN he had slammed the door—that sound which vibrated unexpectedly upon her nerves—Moore came down the steps and swung along the road moodily, his indignation still colouring his face, that line of bitterness still twisted upon his lips.

Pulling down his hat, he turned sharply towards the front, quite deserted at this hour, and with hands in his pockets and shoulders raised set out along the promenade. The mist had thinned, weaving like a living fleece above his head; the night seemed warmer, close, and quite oppressive. Where was he going? Exasperated to the point of oblivion, he did not know, nor did he care. He knew, however, that he had no wish to be here, at this time of night, when he might have been in comfort at his own fireside. It was she who had driven him out with the very earnestness of her desire to keep him in. The insane paradox moved him with a sense of moody futility.

To think that to-day she had actually ordered Anna to leave his house—it was monstrous. Anna, his cousin, who five years ago had come through her trouble; who ought now in all justice to have lived down that trouble. He didn't know anything about it: where or how it had happened; who the man had been. Nor did he care. It was nobody's business. He had never thought twice of Anna in those days, but now he had a rising sympathy for her, initiated by Lucy's action—a feeling of companionable compassion. Not that Anna needed his compassion: a reckless devil she was—he had all the weak man's admiration for Anna's particular hardihood; and there was something more than hardihood in Anna. She was—yes, he supposed she was rather a wild lot; taking life as it came and her amusement where she could find it. Yet, though this had been his reason for objecting to her coming, now, strangely, he had no quarrel with her on that score.

But to think that Lucy had conceived the ludicrous idea that Anna and he had once been intimate; that he, actually he, had been the father of Anna's brat. It would have been funny had it not been so intolerable: gloomily he admitted the humour of the situation to have worn thin. He had laughed it off, sneered it off, yes, blustered it off—all to no purpose. Was the fault his? It was so typical of his ineffectuality, this failure to convince. Why had he not the capacity to meet the situation with a cold and powerful assurance? To have mastered the ridiculous thing, smashed it with a firm and decisive contempt.

But no, he was not like that—never had been. No guts, he thought, miserably. Unstable as water, thou shalt not excel. In the Bible, was that? The word of God, or was it Shakespeare?

All at once the old complex of inferiority cast him down and he had a hot rush of self-contempt: curious devil, he was, curious unlucky devil; he couldn't get away from it. Something would happen to him one of these days. For sure.

He frowned into the mist. It was not as if he had bothered much about women; no, not even in his palmy days, and now, of course, still less. Stray fancies perhaps: those photographs a customer had shown him, artistic, Parisian, state age when applying; but always a barrier lay between himself and freedom. That barrier was himself: laughter and easy companionship cut off by the curious inhibition of his temperament. Besides, when all was said and done, he had his wife. With stinging exasperation came the realisation of his fondness for Lucy. He did love her; but how obstinate she could be when she chose; so—he sought for a phrase—so wrong-headedly in the right. It was not that she was jealous in the ordinary sense: take, for example, those few days she had left Anna and him together—here came vaguely a sensation of missed opportunity—it was that she seemed to appropriate him pertinaciously, exclusively, as her own.

Content to move through life with easy indolence, he had never troubled about this proprietorship, but now it rankled with all the bitter violence of an indignity suddenly discovered.

By this time he was opposite the main street of the town, and with a sudden impulse he crossed the road, put his shoulder to the light swing door of the Shandon Bar.

He had a drink, which had a bitterness that matched his mood.

" Another, miss! "

He brooded over the second glass, which, as usual, was never as good as the first. He wouldn't have a third. Couldn't be bothered. Didn't really care for the taste; he would never make a drunkard, never make anything.

Wiping the brown froth from his lips, he looked around, then instinctively pulled out his watch. Nearly time to get home; she would be wondering where on earth he'd got to. Lucy! She was a good wife, her motives high, her qualities self-evident. Wherein, then, lay the essence of his discontent?

A fresh surge of irritation took him as he flung out of the bar. Why was he thinking like this? Why was he here at all, troubled by this ferment of his mind? For a moment he stood indecisively, looking up and down the street, where the lamps glowed with a soft-ringed radiance; then, as he made to turn for home, a voice accosted him with easy familiarity.

" Hello, Frank. How's yourself? "

He spun round, staring, and instantly his face lighted to a warm amazement.

" Anna! I thought you were away! "

Standing there wrapped warmly in coat and fur, the curious gleam of her skin enhanced by the lamplight, her lip moistened by the damp air, her eyes deep, expressionless, she made a charming figure, vaguely mysterious, vaguely enticing.

" I thought," he stammered, " I thought you had left us."

" I changed my mind at the station. I was going, and then I didn't. Took the notion. I'm at the Craig Hotel for the night. To-morrow I'll get over to Port Doran for the boat."

" I didn't want——" he stammered again. " I knew nothing about——"

" Miss all that, Frank," she cut in. " I'm as well at the Craig as anywhere. And it's time I went home. The boat leaves for Belfast to-morrow night."

" But, Anna——"

" Come on for a walk," said she, " and forget to apologise."

He looked at her. For the first time he had the strange consciousness of promiscuous encounter. Had he met her in the ordinary way he would have smiled and taken her at her word; but now, this meeting, so unexpected, so contrary to Lucy's inclination, almost forbidden, it seemed, stirred him with a curious reaction. Anna·had been flung at his head. And now Anna was here, beside him!

But the reaction was momentary, a fleeting sense of intimacy which touched him lightly and left him self-conscious as before.

" Do you want to go up the town," he asked nervously, " or along the front? "

" The front is as good as any place," she answered carelessly. " We can talk there."

And so they turned and set out towards the deserted promenade. When at night he had taken this stroll with Lucy, she would slip her hand in his warmly, companionably, in a particular fashion: their " way of walking," she termed it; but now, having passed the darkened pier in silence, he it was who clumsily took Anna's arm. Why he hardly knew—perhaps a vague impulse towards self-assertion.

" It's clearer now," said he, with an effort to appear at ease.

" Why drag in the weather, Frank? " she answered pleasantly.

" You know you don't mean it."

He made no reply; and in a moment she added in a tone of con-
dolence:

" Poor Frank! so you're in trouble for something you never did."

Startled, he could find nothing to say, as with her low laugh she
exclaimed:

"It's funny, Frank. You've had all the blame, and none of the fun."

" So long as it amuses you," he muttered, his face troubled, ill
at ease.

" That's the spirit," she answered lightly. " If you can't get the
good of it, have a laugh anyhow."

They walked on together, enclosed by the darkness, hardly an
echo to their footsteps in the shrouded air. What was he doing here
with Anna, at this hour? How exactly had it come about?

" Honestly, though, Frank," she said suddenly, in a more reasonable voice, " I'm dead sorry if I've made any bother for you. Lucy's
one of the best, but she's so gone on you she kind of put my back
up. It's the last thing I'd have wanted to do—to upset you. I always
liked you too well to do that."

" You know it's nothing to do with you," he answered moodily.

" The fact is," she rejoined, in a sly tone of logic, " yes, the fact
is that you're married, and you've just naturally got to put up
with it."

" Don't! " he said in that same troubled voice. " Don't rub it in."
If he had his worries, he didn't want to discuss them with Anna.

" I never could see you as a family man," she meditated. " But
there—you went and did it. Now you've got to walk in step till you
finally step off. You've got to keep the collar on for life."

" Well, it's my collar," he muttered resentfully, feeling her curious
smile upon him in the darkness. And she had been smiling, for now
she laughed outright.

" Good enough, Frank," she declared in an altered manner.
" I've got hopes for you when you answer up like that. I thought
you'd want to pour it all out and weep. I was afraid all the spunk
had gone out of you. That's why I first made up my mind to shake
you up a bit. But, glory be! I'd no idea Lucy would start this cock
and bull affair. It regularly riled me. Mind you, I'm not caring for
myself. I don't need to bother. Now I've got the old man's tin I just
enjoy myself and bless the Pope for what comes along! "

" You have a good time," he said, " and you know it."

" Tell me though, Frank," she asked suddenly, reverting to that
first ironic key, " did you never feel a bit reckless about me? Am I
such a regular old hag as all that? "

He looked at her quickly, trying to pierce not so much the enigma
of her words as of her unseen face. Uncertain, intimidated, conscious

all at once of the pressure of her side against his, he swallowed uncomfortably, in the darkness.

"No," he answered carefully, "I can't say I did."

She laughed again—her humour was unusually gay—and gave his arm a reproving pinch.

"I believe you're made of sawdust," she said cheerfully.

They had now reached the farthest end of the promenade, and before them stretched a white sweep of beach, edged by grey vapours, lapped by the faint sucking of the receding tide.

"The night's young yet," she said, looking towards him. "But it's time you were back."

He knew that it was time he was back, and, in a fashion, he desired to be back, yet something in her manner provoked him.

"It'll be time for me when I say so," he asserted.

"We'll go along the shore then," she said. "It's sort of nice down there."

"All right," he muttered.

Without another word, they turned and set off along the beach; but they had not gone far before she halted.

"This sand!" she said, lifting one foot whilst she supported herself against his shoulder. "I can't walk on this stuff. It gets in my shoes."

Hesitating, he faced her, wondering whether he should suggest their return. But in a moment she said:

"Let's sit down a while. It's quite warm. Have a cigarette, and we'll sit on my coat." And she unbuttoned her coat and spread one half upon the sand for him to sit beside her. The sand was soft, her warm form close, the night full of hushed sounds—a muffled quietude. He lighted a cigarette awkwardly, because somehow her nearness limited his movements. For a moment there was silence, then she said close to his ear in a familiar whisper:

"Give us a puff!"

He started at the unexpectedness of the request.

"Do you mean it?" he said. He spoke more for the sake of proving his composure—to occupy the coat he was obliged to come very close to her.

"Of course," she murmured. "I'd try anything."

For a second he hesitated, then he turned and held the cigarette towards her lips, vaguely seen in the mysterious white oval of her face. He was awkward, fumbling, and as she bent towards him he felt the moist warmth of those lips upon his fingers. She choked a little as she let out the smoke.

"It's not so good as it looks," she coughed.

Her coughing sent her against him in little spasms, and in an absent fashion he slipped his arm around her waist to support her.

"That's better," she said, with a tiny final choking, and she let

120

her hand fall idly on his knee.

A thought rushed through his mind: how incredible that he should be here with Anna, his arm round her waist—so incredible it seemed to pass, shadowy as a dream.

" Try another puff? " he asked suddenly.

She shook her head, then leaned against his shoulder, looking up with her large luminous eyes, as though she waited. With an involuntary movement he leaned over and kissed her.

" You shouldn't have done that, Frank," she murmured, when it was over, and she pressed his hand gently. He still had that same absent feeling. Was it he, here with Anna, feeling the warm softness of her lips, the warmth of her body soft under her outdoor clothing? He kissed her again, and she answered that kiss.

" You know, Frank," she whispered, as in a reverie, " we're not really responsible for this. We've been so much blamed, we've just been flung into it. You know that as well as I do."

Agitated by a sudden uncontrollable impulse, provoked by the gentle logic of her manner, he stared at her. It was just what she said. He had done nothing, absolutely nothing; and yet from that moment she had entered the house they had been flung together with almost preordained inevitability. And it was Lucy's doing—all her doing.

" You don't," he stammered again, " you don't seem very excited about it."

Still vague, his mind misted as by the vapours of the night, he scarcely knew what he was saying.

" You'd wonder," she whispered, turning to him slowly, " you'd wonder when it came to the bit." And her moist lip was near to his; in her eyes, dark-pupilled, points of curious unrest.

Some things you could not escape. And this he had no desire to escape. A flowing urgency ran through his veins, and with a sudden movement he leaned towards her, against her. At once her head fell back and, her hands holding him, she gave way towards the soft yielding sand.

" Why didn't you think of this before? " she whispered, with a sudden intake of her breath, and, unresistant, she closed her eyes, now so near to his.

The tide lapped quietly, unseen, and by then unheard; then the night seemed colder, the mist more damp, and raw. At last she disengaged herself silently with a little shiver; and he, too, sat up, staring with a melancholy self-consciousness towards the sea. So it had actually happened, after everything—how he hardly understood; and now he felt so foolish and ill at ease. For some moments nothing was said.

" Well," she murmured eventually, " we better be getting back."

She squeezed his arm as they rose, and added:

" You're not a bad old sort, Frank."

He made no reply as, stumbling through the sand, they regained the promenade. This time it was she who took his arm.

" You're not going to let it worry you," she said in her tone of sympathetic irony. " Nobody'll be a bit the wiser. And I—I'm not the kind to hang around your neck. I'm off to-morrow."

Her words gave him a sort of melancholic gratitude, and he was glad, relieved that she was going.

" When—how do you go? " he stammered in a low voice.

" I'll get that *Eagle* over. The *Rathlin* leaves at four o'clock."

All at once he felt abashed and mortified, more ineffectual than ever: in his own thought, sick of himself.

" It seems hardly fair," he mumbled in a troubled tone. " I'll see you over if you like."

" Well, that's good of you, Frank," she answered in a pleased voice. " See me to the other side. Then like enough you'll see no more of me."

Half-way along the promenade she stopped abruptly.

" Don't come any farther," she said—how exactly she understood his mood. " But call for me to the Craig to-morrow." Then, with a quick gesture, she brushed his cold cheek with her lips, swung round, and was gone.

He stood motionless, a figure strangely solitary in the mist, then he, too, turned and moved off. Again he asked himself wretchedly how this thing had happened. He had neither premeditated nor desired it. If Lucy had not suspected him, had not treated him as she had done, had not ordered Anna to leave the house, had not caused him to rush out at this hour, then assuredly this encounter would not, could not have occurred.

As he slouched along, his mood holding a reactionary disgust, he wondered how, returning at this hour, he would confront his wife. Only one course, clearly, was open to him. He must assume the continuance of his ill-humour, feign a sullen anger which now he little felt, and go immediately to the spare room where he sometimes slept. To-morrow he would see Anna across to the steamer. Then, the whole wretched affair wiped from his mind, he would return to begin afresh. Yes, he would do that. But a look of sardonic misery came upon his face as he was taken by a swift recollection of himself saying fretfully: " I don't want Anna in my house." And now this. Unbelievable how it had all come about.

As he turned off the promenade, his footsteps sounding softly in the empty street, suddenly from out of the grey haze that hung upon the water there came the low yet piercing note of the siren of a passing ship.

XII

LUCY awoke upon the following day at a later hour than usual.
Again she had slept badly: that broken sleep through which dis
torted fancies of disaster had floated in slow, uneasy stream, drifting
coldly as the thin mist which swathed the passive trees outside.
Then towards morning, pressed by the heaviness of an unseen hand,
she slipped back into a torpid slumber from which, now awakening
with singing ears, she recollected painfully the circumstance of his
return on the previous night. Morosely he had flung up to the spare
room, without a word, without a look; then she had heard the key
turn in the lock with a sullen snap. She winced at the remembrance.
That he should return thus when she waited with her heart, her
whole soul open to receive him, struck her as the most cruel cut of all.

But her intention was clear. She loved him—how intensely she
loved him only she realised—and now, as always, she would protect
him, protect him from himself. How often had she known this contrary moodiness of his nature, that stubborn weakness which only
she could combat. " Poor Frank," she thought, as she had often
thought before, whilst now a tear clouded her eye. " He's his own
worst enemy." Yes, a hundred times in the past had she called
upon her love, her resolution, her fortitude, to save him from that
easy-going wilfulness at once the bane and charm of his character.
And at no time with more purpose than this past fortnight. Even
through the drawn-out wretchedness of those last days that purpose
had not wavered.

What calamity, indeed, might not have befallen had she not
acted as decisively and determinedly as she had done? No matter
that in the beginning her suspicion had been interwoven with a
baffling uncertainty, had she not her instinct, her loyalty, her innate
prudence to guide her? And her love for him—that indeed had been
the touchstone of her judgment, the force which warmed her, drove
her straight to the heart of the entanglement. And above all did she
not desire his good, their united good, and their united happiness in
the integrity of their home? She had no wish to dominate, nor
would she admit her idealism to be perverse. Yet she must guide
him. Loving him with all his imperfections, recognising in his nature
the complement of her own, she could not permit their felicity to be
dispelled. It would have been madness to stand aside and placidly
observe their happiness disintegrate.

Now, with an unconscious sigh, she approved again the wisdom
of her recent course. Once and for all she had settled the matter.
Frank was upset—how well she knew that almost petulant protrusion
of his lip, that swift turn to resentment of a nature which could swing
with equal facility through excitement, credulity, scepticism, and

elation—but he would not long be upset; and she was ready—ready when he should be ready, waiting for that moment when he would turn to her. Even now, expectantly, she visualised that reunion— not the first occasion of her vindication—when he would " come round," confirm the wisdom of her conduct by the very penitence of his approach. That was the sweet moment she desired.

With a glance at the clock upon the mantelpiece she sighed again, threw back the counterpane, and rose. She dressed slowly, a meditative slowness, then, going out of her room, she hesitated, knocked lightly at his door.

" Frank," she exclaimed in a mild voice. " Are you coming out with me at ten ? "

There was no reply.

Although she waited, listening anxiously for a full minute, acutely conscious of his presence behind that door, she did not repeat her query. The last thing she desired was a further quarrel; she was prepared to let him sulk, to let his mood travel to its fullest limit. Sufficient that she be there to catch the pendulum upon its backward swing. Then—ah, then would she have her recompense.

And so, straightening her head, she went downstairs, where, with a curious sense of solitude, she breakfasted. He would not accompany her this morning : so much was evident : and, instructing Netta to prepare his tray, she herself took this up and left it outside his door. Then she went out alone.

The day was grey, the trees dripping, the mist still hovering, the opposite shore a vague smudge drawn at random through the haze. Underfoot the leaves, no longer crisp and rustling, had at last a lifeless look—mere sodden plaques flattened into the earth, from which they had emerged and which now assumed them back into its own substance. A dank depression hung upon the shrouded air, a feeling of decay, the sense of something ended. At intervals a fitful sun broke through and smeared a pallid light across the glassy water of the estuary, whither out of the brackish hanging haze the slow challenge of unseen ships drifted and passed—drifted inshore to the clanging bell of the Ardmore Buoy, clanging, clanging in monotone and desolation.

Despite herself, the cold dampness fell drearily upon her; with a shiver she hastened her steps towards the church. There, because devotion was not her mood, everything seemed slower, the sermon longer, more tedious than she could remember. Her face intent, her eyes upon her little prayer-book—it was *The Key of Heaven*—she kept thinking of Frank, desiring urgently to return to him. At last it was over; she came out with the consciousness of a duty accomplished, and quickly, with contained eagerness, she set out for home.

In the hall, when she had taken off her hat and coat, her first impulse, despite her assumption of serenity, was towards his room. But with an effort she restrained that impulse and went instead to the kitchen, where at once she saw his tray. She paused: he had eaten his breakfast, then, a good meal: and, turning to Netta with factitious calm she said:

" Mr. Moore, has he come down? "

Without turning her head from the sink, where she was peeling potatoes, Netta replied casually:

" He's gone out. He said something about going to see Mr. Lennox."

" Oh, yes," answered Lucy slowly. " I remember." She composed her features and repeated: " Yes, I remember now."

She did not, of course, remember; but it was well to support the fallacious explanation of his conduct. He was not at Lennox's, but had gone, she was convinced, for one of those solitary walks which marked always the culmination of his moods. Her lips drooped faintly: again their reconciliation was delayed. Still, he would return from that walk. And he would return to her.

Turning, she went into the front room, sat down by the window, and picked up a book. But she found it impossible to see the lines: from time to time she discovered herself, with eyes arrested, staring in curious abstraction through the window. Once she heard a step outside, and, drawing herself quickly together, she prepared with a beating heart to receive him. But it was not he. And the sight of her own face reflected in the overmantel gave her a sudden, a strange uneasiness. Had he gone to Lennox's? Or was he walking somewhere in this grey haze without?

One o'clock came and he had not returned. She began now to feel a definite uneasiness, through which worked a curious vexation—really, it was too bad of him to behave like this; and, with Netta appearing at half-past one, anxious to get the dinner over and escape for her free afternoon, she declared in that same tone of factitious composure:

" Very well! I'll have mine now. Mr. Moore may be detained."

Yet—perhaps he was detained? It was improbable, but it was not impossible that he had after all gone up to Lennox's house, been pressed to remain for a cut of the Sunday joint. A faint gleam came into her clouded eye as with a start she considered the possibility of his having gone to Lennox to reopen himself the question of the partnership. That indeed would be a supreme gesture of atonement! But was it likely? Her eye dulled again. Was it conceivable? Harassed by her thoughts, she made a poor meal, a mere pretence of eating to satisfy the inquisitive eye of the maid and ease that curious discomposure of her own mind.

" Keep something hot in the oven, Netta—in case," she said as, finally, she rose from the table. It was her sole indication that her pretence of normality might be assumed.

She was back again in the parlour, seated, not at the fire, but at the window—waiting. Useless now, the pretence of reading; she was simply waiting. And, as she waited, the strange disquiet of her mind deepened.

How would he return? He would be wet, soaked by the drizzle. Yet, following his quiet entry, he would be loath to meet her. For a long time he would be in the hall, hanging up his hat and coat, moving about without apparent purpose. Then, suddenly, he would come into the room. Affecting not to look at her, intensifying his conscious embarrassed air, he would slouch to the fire, sink into his chair. There would be silence. Then swiftly she would rise, yearning for reconciliation, drop on her knees beside his chair, and cling to him. Ah! that moment! She started at her own thoughts, caught her breath. He was not back.

Half-past two; Netta gone out; herself alone in the house; and he had not come back. It was—it was preposterous. Despite herself, she could not prevent a quick thrill of apprehension. Surely he had gone up to Mr. Lennox's? This clearly was the only possible solution —he must have gone to Lennox's; he could not have been walking interminably through the wet mist. That was incredible.

Abruptly she rose, her eyes deeply troubled, her hand pressed with a curious characteristic gesture against her cheek. Then, with typical resolve, her eyes strengthened and she moved suddenly towards the door. She would go herself and make sure; that was the only thing to do: perhaps, too, she might meet him on her way.

Outside it was lightly raining, a fine impalpable drizzle that came sweeping up from the grey firth like clouds rising from the surface of a misted mirror. And again, as she ascended the hill towards Lennox's house, s he shivered. She found herself hurrying—hurrying she knew not why .On the way she tried to quell her ridiculous alarm, to reason with herself: to devise some excuse for this extraordinary call which she was about to make.

But she was spared the necessity for such excuse: in the upper reaches of the town, at the corner of Garsden Street, she ran into Lennox, returning, she instantly perceived, from his usual Sunday afternoon promenade. And, taken aback, she stopped at once, her heart sinking, realising that Frank was not here.

"Well, well," said Lennox, halting and genially including her beneath his dripping umbrella. "You're in a great hurry for the Sabbath."

"Yes," she stammered unhappily. "Yes, I am."

"You're on the wrong road to meet them, though," he went on, smiling down at her.

Breathing quickly from her ascent of the hill, her slight figure close to his, her hair and cheeks glistening from the rain, she echoed quickly, yet without full comprehension:

" To meet them ? "

" I passed them on the front "—he indicated with an easy movement of his head. " Your husband and Anna. Going back the way."

Transfixed by his words, she paled, and her eyes widened towards him in a sudden anguish. It was as if a chasm yawned suddenly beneath her feet. She made to speak and could not.

" They'll be home now," he continued, unobservant of her distress. " Come in and have a cup of tea before you turn."

Her tongue seemed fixed, wooden; she was choking. So Anna had not gone away! She had waited, waited with inconceivable duplicity, and Frank had met her. And what—oh, what would be the upshot of this meeting?

" Come away in," said Lennox again.

She struggled with her speech.

" No," she stammered at last, " I must—I must get back."

" A cup of tea'll take the fog out of your throat."

" No, no," she said hoarsely. " I'll not—I can't wait." And, before he could reply, she turned, blinded by her emotion, moving away from him with rapid stumbling steps.

So she had been right. Tears of anger and misery ran out of her eyes and mingled with the raindrops on her cheeks. She had known it; but at last the certainty was absolute. And they had renewed their previous intimacy; fostered it despite her every care. Having done everything to prevent it, by some incredible circumstance she had failed to keep them apart. It was anguish, a maddening thought.

Violently she bit her lip, clenched her hands in the pockets of her coat. Her slight figure hastening along the wet, deserted street so thickly plastered by these sodden fallen leaves became dynamic with the painful force of her resentment. Recovered from the first stunning impact of the blow, the thought of her deception infuriated her. It was not as if Frank had not loved her. She knew that he loved her; and she knew too that she loved him. He had been compelled to this against his will.

Why had it happened ? Panting with her haste, she struggled to find the answer, to lay her finger on the fault. Oh, why had it happened ? She had tried so hard; it was unendurable she should have failed. Desperately she tried to calm herself. She had not failed. Nothing had happened that was beyond repair. Her conviction had become irrevocable. But pressing closely upon that certainty came another. She would immediately control the situation, smash up this menace to her home, restore Frank to sanity and to herself. She was neither a weakling nor a fool. Outraged though she was, her love was greater than the outrage. She had no mawkish modesty; she knew her power over Frank; and use that power she would! She would go home, await his return; and she would save him, save him from himself.

With an effort she forced herself to slacken her pace, feeling through all her anguish that she must be calm, conscious that she must not make herself conspicuous in the open street. She was now nearing her house, and approaching in the opposite direction she observed the figure of Dave Bowie. Firmly she composed her features; she at least would make no exhibition of her distress, nor expose her humiliation to the public gaze. They met opposite her gate, and with a set face she inclined her head, made to enter. But he stopped.

" You're not away over with them ? " he exclaimed pleasantly.

She spun round, staring at his red face cased by the shining south-wester tied beneath his chin. Little crystals of water beaded the oilskin's yellow rim.

" What do you mean ? " she said, with curious slowness.

" I'm sorry about it. A regular nuisance, this weather," he apologised mildly. " But I had the *Eagle* up at Linton this afternoon. If I had known that your husband wanted her I could easy have been back earlier."

Her eyes remained fixed, still bewildered, but filling gradually with a strange dismay. A strained sensation came upon her that he was not real, that she lived this in a dream.

" What are you trying to say, Dave ? " she demanded in a low, intent voice.

" Did you not know ? " he answered awkwardly. " I'm just this minute back. And they wouldn't wait; they were in such a hurry— my father told me. Angus had to get out the dinghy to pull them over."

" Over where ? " Her tone was feverish now, but her eyes did not leave his face.

" Across for the mail boat," he stammered. " That lady you had staying with you. And your husband."

" The mail boat," she cried out, with sudden uncontrollable emotion. Then all at once struck by a horrible fear, stunned by the unthought-of, the unthinkable acme of her dread, she paused. A great throb of anguish broke within her, like a cord strung taut and then intolerably snapped. Frank was gone—with Anna. That was the reason of everything, the consummation of all her foreboding. He had left her and returned to Anna.

Unconscious of Dave's presence, a low cry escaped from her lips as, standing at that gate where so often she had awaited him in love, she realised with crushing violence that he was gone. He had deserted her. Her face, wreathed by her wet hair, seemed shrunken, and her lips pale, as though drained suddenly of blood.

For a moment she stood motionless, pervaded by a sinking hope-lessness of loss, an insufferable feeling of defeat. Then with a violent movement she raised her hand to her brow. Was he mad? He must surely be mad, infatuated, or both, to compass this incredible, this final folly. To desert her, disintegrate his home, and ally himself with that loathsome creature.

Anna! Her lips drew in over her set teeth. How could he expect to be happy with her? And as by a tide she was swept by the recollec-tion of Anna and her laziness, her vulgarity, her utter shamelessness.

She couldn't let Frank do this thing. So weak, so easily influenced, he had been dragged into it against his will—yes, drawn into it despite her efforts to safeguard him.

As with a sudden inspiration of courage her eyes flashed, the colour ran back into her face and she flushed with the intensity of her feeling.

Defeated! She was not defeated! Was she the woman to stand in wretched apathy or sink down in helpless tears whilst this creature ran off with Frank? Through her tense figure there flowed a vital resolution. She had said that she would save him.

Abruptly she turned and, seizing Dave by the arm, she declared passionately:

" You're got to take me across—now—at once."

" What's wrong? " he stammered. " I don't understand."

She made no answer; but, still holding him by the arm, began to hurry him across the road towards the yard. The gate swung shut with a violent slam.

" How long is it since they left? " she demanded in a hard voice as they went along.

" I don't know," he muttered, much put out at the strangeness of her manner; " maybe quarter of an hour; maybe less. I wasn't expected back so soon. But what's—what's the matter with you? "

" Quarter of an hour," she repeated intently, as though to herself. " We'll be over in time."

They were in the yard now, advancing towards the stone jetty which ran out and seemed to lose itself in the vague white haze beyond. Then all at once Dave hesitated and drew up.

" I'll not go out," he exclaimed uncomfortably. " It's too late. And there's a fog coming up."

Giving no sign of having heard, she continued on her course, mounting the narrow slip, quickening her step upon its moistened flags. And, in constrained fashion, he finally came after her.

" I'm saying that we can't go over," he repeated in a louder tone. " I don't like the weather. It's thickening. You can't see a hundred yards ahead."

Turning opposite the *Eagle's* moorings, she faced him with eyes that blazed.

"You're going, Dave," she said in a choking voice. "And I'm going with you."

"I have no steam," he answered surlily, gazing out at the shifting vapours that moved uncertainly above the glassy sea.

She looked at him fiercely.

"You've just come in," she cried. "And now you're going out again."

"I don't like it," he muttered, his eye still evasive of her burning stare. Thus they stood for a moment facing each other, whilst the tide made a quiet sea sound beneath their feet. There was a second of suspense: this second, sublimated, reduced, seemed to poise the balance of Frank's future and her own. Then suddenly Dave's head dropped; he moved to the rope around the tiny bollard. It was over! She had done it. Without a word she swung round and clambered over the low iron bulwarks of the *Eagle*.

"I'm telling you," he said hesitantly, but, compelled by that unusual force which drew him against his will, he bent over the bollard, cast off the hawser, and came aboard the tiny launch beside her.

"I'm not wanting to go," he muttered again as with one hand on the wheel he threw in the gear. "Remember that."

She made no reply as, with a sound that was strangely muffled, they slid away from the jetty, losing the shore instantly, moving into the dumb softness of that fleecy sea. Outwards they slid, outwards and away.

"Be quick, Dave!" she whispered suddenly in a low voice. "Quick as you can!"

Consumed by an intolerable emotion, she stood rigidly beside him, looking ahead with eyes which were like wounds in the blurred pallor of her face. If she should fail? Yet she knew she would not fail. She had the conviction that she must succeed. Frank could not yet be across; he was not far ahead; the very swiftness of her resolution would be his salvation. If only she could see, pierce through these loose folds of mist that fell about her like a fleecy garment. But it was thick, the mist, and it seemed, out upon this still sea, to turn thicker: a pale, amorphous vapour, intangible yet actual, brackish as a polluted breath, choking her with its vapid density. Clasping the collar of her coat around her neck, she bent forward, stifled by its oppression and by the oppression of her choking breast. Then suddenly, softly, half-way over, the fog deepened, descending upon them like a shroud, blotting out everything but their own figures. They became in an instant two shadowy forms isolated in a wilderness of fog.

Immediately Dave cut down the boat's speed.

"What did I tell you?" he cried. "We'll need to turn back." His voice came, dulled, as from afar.

She made no movement.

" Go on," she insisted, her eyes fixedly before her.

" We might be into something—any minute."

" Go on," she cried out in a louder voice. " We can't turn back now."

He made a hopeless gesture with his arm, then tugged violently at the siren cord, loosing a thin, shrill whistle into those opaque billows of white.

" Look out, then," he shouted. " In the bows."

Without another word she crept forward. Crouched in the bows, burning with fierce impatience, feeling nothing of the wetness or the cold, she was like a figure-head driving forward, herself the motive, the very impulse of the boat. Her will it was alone which drove them forward. Swathes of fog rolled past her like coils of smoke working within a vast and desolate cavern. She could see nothing, nothing but this impenetrable whiteness which numbed her eyes, choked her, condensed upon her hair, and coursed like tears upon her cheek.

Desolation pressed itself around her, raw as the rimed air of winter, clammy with a wet sea breath. And faintly in warning came the thin, bleak clanging of the Ardmore Buoy, clanging far off, clanging, clanging in monotone and desolation. She shivered and set her teeth. It was as though some phantom hovering unseen had laid cold fingers upon her brow. Trembling, isolated, she could see nothing. No matter; she was going forward. Forward to save Frank.

" What was that? " shouted Dave suddenly. " Did you hear oars? " And he loosed a violent blast from out the whistle.

Listening with straining ears, she heard no sound; nothing but the siren's echoes, the plashing of unseen water, the faint clanging of the Ardmore Buoy, clanging its dirge in monotone, sad monotone and desolation.

" Did you hear it? " he cried again.

But she had heard nothing.

Then all at once, from ahead and beneath, there came a loud cry swelling upwards through the fog, so close it seemed to draw them towards it.

" Ahoy! " shouted Dave, wrenching upon the rudder.

Rigid in the bows she heard that cry repeated, louder, nearer, and with a sudden vital urgency. It pierced her, the urgency of the call. Then in the same swift second she felt the shuddering of an impact which ran through her with awful paralysing numbness: no violent crash, but a soft concussion as though the fog or some soft shape had cushioned the violence of the blow: a tearing, crushing impact which drove the blood out of her beating heart.

Instantly a shriek soared up from beneath her, a confusion of cries, a grinding noise, then everything fell away astern to silence. Grey silence and shrouded desolation.

" God Almighty! " shouted Dave in panic, " we've hit something."
Already he had jerked the engine to reverse, and with a violent
threshing they went astern, the launch, torn by two impulses,
quivering along her keel. And her body quivered too, rent by a
frightful thought. Yet, held as by a vice, she stood motionless while
they slowed, drifted, stopped. The fog clung thicker, darkened by
the coming night.

" Ahoy! " bellowed Dave wildly through his cupped hands.

" Ahoy! " came the answer, vague, yet near, like a lost cry from
some vast wilderness.

" My God! " he cried again despairingly. " It's Angus and the
dinghy! "

Trembling, she rushed towards his side as, leaning over the stern,
he searched the obscurity with his call.

" Frank! " she shouted desperately. " Frank! "

The fog was like a wall from which her voice rebounded in a vain
elusive echo: an echo which mocked her, chasing through the caverns
of despair. Then suddenly there came an answer, close at hand.

" Fling a line! "

Instantly the coil in Dave's hand curled out towards the muffled
cry, fell slack, then tautened incredibly.

" They've got it," she sobbed. " They've got it "; and, straining,
she helped him as he hauled arm over arm upon the dripping rope.

Out of the fog as by a miracle a wet hand appeared, clutching upon
the gunwale, then a dark head glistening like a seal's. It was Angus,
holding in his arm the figure of Anna.

" Take her," he gasped; " there's another."

As Dave dragged Anna aboard, he grasped the rope once more,
slid back into the water, and disappeared.

Her teeth sank into her lip with the frustration of her hope.

" Frank! " she shouted passionately. " Frank! "

With hands clenched upon the bulwark, she gave no heed to
Anna, who sat down weakly against the engine casing; but, straining
towards that opaque screen, she waited in an agony of suspense.
The slow seconds passed like hours. Frantic, in a cold sweat of fear,
she willed him to be saved. Her heart was fluttering like a trembling
flame. Then all at once a cry of inexpressible joy broke from her lips.

" Here! " she panted. " Here! " Leaning far over the stern, with
all her force she pulled in the rope, bearing upon it with desperate
strength. A choking cry broke from her lips as she helped Angus to
scramble aboard, to lift the figure of her husband across the gunwale.

" Frank," she sobbed, her arms around him, " I thought—
I thought you were gone! "

He made no answer, but collapsed and lay limply upon the deck.

Then all at once his eyes opened towards her with a dull and painful recognition.

" The boat——" he said, with difficulty. " You hit me here." And slowly, in a frightened sort of way, he let his hand fall weakly upon his chest, which seemed strangely sunken and deformed.

She caught her breath.

" Frank," she cried, falling upon her knees beside him. " You're all right."

" The bow——" whispered Angus, shivering with cold, whilst water ran from his streaming clothes. " The bow struck him in the breast—took him under the keel——" He shuddered. " A fearful blow."

" Frank," she sobbed, stricken by a new and feverish fear. " You're not—you're not hurt, my dear ? "

" I don't——" he answered in a slow, slurred voice, " I don't feel well. Something—something warm coming into my mouth," he said with greater difficulty. She shivered. In his voice there was an inarticulate choking which terrified her. Instantly she flung herself towards him, but not before he coughed : a dreadful bubbling cough. The choking, retching issue of that cough—it spread over her bosom in a warm, living stream. Nothing seemed to arrest the gushing, insatiable tide of unseen blood that ran from him and flowed thickly between her breasts. The horror of it paralysed her. Desperately she tried to move, to help him. But in his panic he clung to her, would not let her go.

" Frank! Frank! " she shivered. " Let me—let me help you." She was terrified, locked to him in the white darkness, moved by the spasm which shook him, convulsed as by the consummation of some deathly orgasm. Suddenly she felt that she would faint. Then all at once the rigid intensity of his grip relaxed, his limp hands fell away from her, and with a final expiration, a gasping sigh, his spent body fell languidly upon the deck.

Trembling, she lifted his head, lifted it upon her lap.

" Oh, God!" muttered Angus in panic, with chattering teeth. " He's bad "; and again he whispered, " 'Twas the bows hit him. Right—right in the breast." He had lighted the lantern, and now, with a wavering hand, he held it near : a weak yellow flame which threw a sickly smear upon her pale face vested by her hanging hair, and upon the sodden garments that clung and dripped about her.

The light fell also upon Moore's figure, motionless, inert ; and on his pallid face—an empty face, as though some frightful force had sucked out the vital essence of the body, draining it of life.

The shock of that look upon his face, so swiftly changed, made her shiver ; the clammy garment, no longer warm, clung to her ; her knees shook—shook weakly as she crouched beside him.

" Look at me, Frank," she cried. " I love you." And she held him closely like a child upon her lap whilst the boat swung gently on the unseen water, and always that bell clanged slowly from afar, tolling a passing soul.

He did not move, but lay motionless, his face sunken, already ghostly. His hand, clasped in hers, was cold and pliant, and had a fleshless feel, yielding and without substance, chilling her. For a second of agony she hesitated. Then a desperate strength flowed into her. It was impossible. She loved him. She was here to save him. Frantically she looked up, met Dave's eyes.

He had left Anna—who lay dazedly against the casing—and now, bent down, a dreadful anxiety in his gaze, he said:

" He's bad. He looks awful bad."

" Get some water! " she cried out, in a voice of anguish, and she clenched her free hand so tightly that the knuckles showed white beneath the reddish streaks that stained them. " Bring it quick! "

With the water that he brought she washed his face, laving his lips and brow tenderly with trembling fingers.

Then suddenly, incredibly, he opened his eyes, which filled with a last faint flickering recognition.

" Lucy," he gasped, making a feeble effort to cling to her, " don't leave me."

A quick, stifled sigh broke from her constricted lips, hung suspended.

" No, Frank," she sobbed, " I couldn't let you go. We'll be together, always."

" But why——" he gasped once more; and stopped. Then, slurring weakly the words, he whispered: " It was nothing with Anna—only seeing Anna—seeing her to the boat."

Her heart stood still. At first she did not understand. Then all at once, as with a lightning stroke, something struck her—a paralysing shaft of horror which sank quivering in her breast.

" I'm thirsty," he whispered, and with a frightful travesty of his old-time irony he panted weakly, " But—but I can't swallow."

She could not speak for the rending in her bosom. The universe, with all its constellations, had ceased to move. She was void suddenly, wishing for death. What—oh, what had she done!

" It's dark surely," he gasped feebly. " Is it here; or—or—there ? "

" Oh, God! " she sobbed out suddenly, her posture suppliant with her desire, tears gushing from her livid eyes. " Save him for me! Frank, beloved, come back—back to me! I'll—I'll get you better. I love you! "

But his jaw went slack; those heavy eyelids dropped, shuttered the dulling eyes. His head rolled over, the lips fell leeringly apart, leaving a final emptiness which mocked her.

BOOK II

I

" CHECK ! " said Uncle Edward, blowing his nose delicately. " Mate ! "

Peter frowned. He knew the moves of all the pieces: a pleasant thrill to jump the knight about ! Yet, somehow, it always happened —this—without the slightest warning.

" Funny," he said. " I thought——"

A half-smile lay on the priest's face; his long white fingers caressed the glass of port, which shone like a warm ruby beside the dish of walnuts on the polished mahogany table. The red velvet curtains of the room, tight against the wet wind blowing gustily from the firth, shut out the encroaching darkness and enriched the mellow gaslight, which fell comfortably upon the two players. Uncle Edward raised his port, savoured it with slightly pursed lips, when suddenly a loud batter of wind and rain rattling the window made him look up, and, after a moment, complacently remark:

" More pleasant inside to-night—don't you think so, my good sir ? "

Peter let himself slide down so that his head rested on the back of his chair.

" Wet often comes after fog," said he oracularly; he had heard old Bowie make that remark, and now he repeated it with a strong air of originality.

" And what comes after I've taken your queen ? " said Uncle Edward slyly.

They both laughed, and into the middle of their laughter came a knocking upon the door—an unexpected knocking, for they had hoped to have the evening to themselves.

" Come in ! " called out Edward; and Miss O'Regan glided into the room.

" Your reverence," she began hesitatingly, faltered, and began again: " Your reverence——"

Then all at once her downcast eyes lifted to heaven with a wild rolling gesture, so that the whites were exposed in an orgy of resigned misgiving: distracted, almost, she seemed for some obscure reason, and her upturned face had the look of the martyred saint that hung upon the wall behind her.

" This—it came," she ejaculated from her pale lips, and, withdrawing an orange envelope from behind her back, she proffered it tremulously.

He opened the telegram mechanically, whilst his ivory skin whitened and his mouth drew in. Then all at once he made a curious sound in his throat.

" Dear me ! " he said in a vague, frightened voice. " Dear me ! "

Then all the blood rushed into his face again, making it look full, and he rose up agitatedly, scattering the litter of walnut-shells that lay upon his lap.

" I've got to go into the church," he stammered, without looking at Peter, but addressing the little statue of the Madonna by the door. " Yes, I've—I've got to go into the church. I must go to the church."

He took his biretta from the mantelpiece and stepped forward, his large buckled shoes crunching the shells upon the hearthrug. Holding the open telegram in his hand, he went out of the room and Miss O'Regan followed him, shivering like an agitated shadow. As she passed through the door, she dipped her fingers in the little holy water font and signed herself with a fearful spiritual abandon.

The boy's face clouded at the sudden change in the happy warm room, and he sat up in his chair, his thin body stiff and apprehensive.

The waves of wind which billowed against the windows became sea waves which flowed coldly around him as he traversed in fancy the nine miles of rough water which separated him from his home across the estuary. With the remote yet positive intuition of his age, he had incredibly a glimmering of understanding, and vaguely the tall figure of his father rose up before him. Clad ridiculously in a long white nightdress was this figure—grotesque, disturbing.

What a nuisance to have the pleasant evening broken into like this, especially when Uncle Edward had promised him a threepenny piece if he won a game. Actually it was there—the pledged reward— shining beside the board. Petulantly he picked up a walnut, made to crack it, laid it down again. Then he picked up the threepenny piece. He would have won it—really he would; yes, now he was positive he would have won it; and so, with an abstracted air, he slipped the coin into his pocket. Then he rose up quickly, and began to put away the chessmen.

When he had put the box and the board into the proper drawer of the roll-top desk, he thought again for a moment, with his head lowered. Then he went out of the room.

Seeking companionship of some sort, he descended the stairs and walked along the cold, waxcloth-covered passage. Miss O'Regan and Eileen were in the kitchen: Miss O'Regan weeping and walking up and down, saying her beads with her long heavy rosary in her thin hands, Eileen standing by the fire watching the housekeeper with concerned eyes. When he came in Miss O'Regan paused in the middle of a " Hail Mary " and shot out under her breath to Eileen:

" He hasn't been told "; then she resumed: " Pray for us sinners now and at the hour of our death, Amen." And her tears fell afresh from her red-lidded eyes.

He knew that Miss O'Regan was not crying because of what was in the telegram, but simply because his uncle was upset. Yet, for the sake of saying something, he exclaimed:

" Why are you crying, Miss O'Regan ? "

" I've a headache," the housekeeper returned through her sobs, pressing her hand to her brow.

It was a reasonable excuse: Miss O'Regan's headaches ranked equally in incidence with her ecstasies. Still, the room felt uncomfortable; the fire had gone out; and the blister on his finger, where he had burnt it the other day whilst roasting chestnuts, began to throb again painfully.

" My finger's hurting, too," he remarked idly, regarding it sympathetically. But he was not to have much attention to-night.

Eileen, as often as not, would look at his thin shanks, and laugh: " Hasn't he the leg for the kilt. the boy ? " or make a joke about his sporran—why was that sporran a source of secret joy for Eileen ? But now she said, with a glance at the clock, merely:

" It's near nine, Master Peter. I'll give you a glass of milk and a biscuit. Then I'll take you to your bed."

Miss O'Regan stopped praying whilst he sadly sipped his milk and nibbled his ginger snap; delicately she wiped her nose several times with her small lace-edged handkerchief. She and Eileen watched him whilst pretending not to, and through their eyes he felt the finger of calamity pointing at him. But the finger was too unreal for him to be impressed. When, in spite of prolonging his meal, he had finished, Eileen looked at the housekeeper for authority, and said:

" I'll take him up now, will I, miss, or not ? "

Miss O'Regan nodded her inclined head once slowly, and in this acquiescence he felt the unusual significance of the evening. At the beginning of his stay, when Eileen had offered to undress him, Miss O'Regan had shrivelled the awful suggestion with a burning word which had shamed the young maiden to a blush.

" If you can't," the elder virgin had remarked, " get modesty in the priest's house, Eileen, where in God's name will you get it ? "

To-night, however, was clearly different, and upstairs Eileen tucked him in warmly. First, of course, he had to look at the Linton Lighthouse, which threw its flat revolving beam across the wet blackness of the firth. Three sweeping beams, then a long pause; three lovely beams again—it was an ecstatic sight.

Then a quick rattle of prayers—' Glorbefar-sun-olygost-men——";
it was fun to see how soon you could finish them—and a jump into

bed. Eileen smiled gently—that missing tooth in front gave her such a lovely piquant air—and she kissed him with a sudden surreptitious solicitude, so that one of her curls fell into his eye. Then he was alone.

The tiny peep of gas flickered behind its pink-rimmed frosted globe—for the window was open a little at the top—and outlandish shadows chased across the wall towards which he had turned. Although he was nearly nine, these monstrous racing figures still retained the power to make his room a strange chamber of fear. Sometimes he would fall into a sweat to think that long, gripping hands cast these shadows, and it would be minutes before he could clench his teeth hard enough to twist round and confront the emptiness which was always there, and yet might not be there.

But to-night the waving forms were not the forms of his swift imagination. Another figure—grotesque, white-robed—floated back once more into the sensitive screen of his sight, aweing him somewhat but causing him neither grief nor fear. He had, besides, a comfortable feeling at the back of his mind. Fumbling drowsily, he all at once remembered. The threepenny bit! Yes, that was it. Then he slept.

Next morning began with a warm sun that sent wheels of yellow light over the waters of the firth, with a high blue sky that held a quivering expectancy for the day. And yet the same disastrous sense of the unusual clung like a stale odour to the fabric of the household. He did not see his uncle at breakfast; Miss O'Regan's head, which he knew to be the barometer of her feelings, was still set to a melancholy inclination; even Eileen, who silently brought him his porridge and boiled egg, seemed a different and more complex being from the soft and intimate creature who had clasped him in her warm embrace on the night before.

Altogether, he began to feel a slow depression settling upon him like a lethargy. He went out after breakfast, and, after weighing the matter, bought himself some sweets—peardrops: a new confection he had recently discovered in a shop where the lady, a parishioner of Uncle Edward, might be trusted to give him generous measure: but he did not succeed in lifting his discomfort. For a moment he stood observing some troops filing up the gangway into a long yellow ship at the pier; then he turned, looked at some shop windows without interest; listened to a man who was singing " Beautiful Flossie "; went finally and disconsolately to the Presbytery.

In the hall he found Miss O'Regan awaiting him.

" Peter! " she exclaimed as soon as he came through the door. " I've looked for you everywhere. Where have you been, child? "

" Oh, out," he returned listlessly.

" I know, but——" she paused.

The duty she must perform at once distressed and flattered her. His reverence had said that morning:

" You had better tell the boy, Miss O'Regan. He'll take it better from *you*." And at these words her lowered eyelids had flickered with a profound though humble satisfaction. She felt, indeed, that such a task favoured her with a high esteem, elevated her to a confidential position far above that of mere housekeeper. Yet she shrank a little from projecting this thunderbolt through her palely pious lips.

" Peter," she began at length, " come upstairs." She took his warm palm between her thin, cold fingers, and as she led him up the figured Axminster he felt those fingers like the thin legs of a frog he had once touched in the garden—cold yet living—productive of a feeling of great discomfort.

They went into the sitting-room, which was empty; sat down on the plush sofa by the window; faced one another. For an awkward moment silence hung self-consciously between them; then the housekeeper's lips trembled, her eyes rolled twice in their orbits and widened with a faintly curious expectancy.

" Peter, my boy," she whispered, " you'll have to be brave." She put her arm round his shoulders, still gazing at him sideways. " Yes, a big brave boy," she continued. " I've got sad news for you, Peter."

He felt her watching him, and her look troubled him; he began to wish ardently that she would tell him quickly.

" You know, Peter," she resumed, with a little sniff, " your— your father's ill—very ill indeed."

His discomfort grew, yet he saw that Miss O'Regan was doing her best for him, and he nodded his head jerkily in acquiescence, as though, in effect, he encouraged her.

" But, Peter," whispered Miss O'Regan at last, " your father— your father's not really ill any more. He's in heaven with the blessed angels—he's dead, Peter."

He had prepared himself, and immediately he burst into tears. By some strange presentiment, from the moment she had appeared with the telegram, he had suspected; yes, despite the specious pretence of concealment, he had known; but now her manner, the sudden expression of his knowledge in words, the very anticipation with which she awaited some demonstration of his grief, all conspired to make him weep. He sobbed loudly; then, drawing him to her, she mingled her tears with his, wallowing in her grief. Thus, close-pressed, they wept together.

He stopped crying to blow his nose and, turning his head without moving his body, gazed mournfully out of the window. Below him the movement of the streets continued; the thin stream of soldiers— more like ants than men—poured still into the troop-ship; on the window a sluggish wasp crawled to the top of the pane, buzzed loudly, then fell down again; a bone from Miss O'Regan's corsets was sticking into his side and hurting him.

At last reluctantly she relinquished him.

" When you go back with his reverence you must tell your mother I've looked after you well," she exclaimed, wiping a tear-drop from the end of her nose. " A thing like that would please his reverence proudly."

" Yes, Miss O'Regan," he assented willingly. " Of course I will."

He hardly thought of what he said, for at the sudden thought of his mother an immense joy possessed him that he was to see her again. A sudden thought struck him:

" Shall we have lunch on the boat, Miss O'Regan?" he asked timidly. Returning with Uncle Edward meant an exciting voyage on the steamer *Lucy Lamond*. Shocked, she looked at him, was about to reply, when suddenly the door opened and Edward came into the room. Immediately she rose to her feet, clasped her hands in front of her, and lowered her head.

" Yes, your reverence," she murmured in reply to a muffled question, " he took it well, very well, considering. I did my best."

She seemed thus to claim modestly some success for the warm tact of her womanhood.

They both turned, gazed at Peter, and under that united look he blushed, looked down, as though conscious that he had not wept enough. Then Miss O'Regan beckoned spectrally; and, following her, he went out of the room.

Yet he did not go home on that day; nor yet on the next. It was incredible, he could not understand it, but actually an entire fortnight elapsed before a general stirring awoke in the household, and he knew this as the day of his departure. When Miss O'Regan had washed his face and hands, and brushed his hair smooth, he hurried down to the foot of the garden to take a last look at the frog which lived in the dampness of the grotto. But, although he looked everywhere and dirtied his hands again by turning up the leaves of the ivy that overgrew the rockery, he could not find it. He spat gently upon his hands and wiped them upon the back of his kilt, so that Miss O'Regan should not be annoyed with him; then he went to inspect his own initials which he had cut as straight and deeply as he could in the lime-tree by the back gate. The sight of those yellowish letters, the consideration of their permanence—a monument to his name—afforded him a swelling gratification, made him even smile. Reluctantly he left them to return to the house.

They had a light luncheon, followed by a heavy leave-taking, which left him gasping; before his trotting body had recovered breath he was on board the steamer with his uncle.

The crossing passed in a curious suspense, half excitement, half fear—a stomach hollow that deepened the nearer the boat drew to Ardfillan. At first he wandered about the deck, but soon, very soon, he came back towards Uncle Edward and Uncle Edward's hand. They disembarked in silence.

On the way along the front, his steps flagged, he felt a lump in his throat; yet shortly he was at the end of the promenade, had passed at the corner the long smooth iron drinking-trough—the one into which he had once loosed some minnows; then the familiar white stone house confronted him with incredible reality.

As he watched his uncle quietly pull the bell, a fearful desire came upon him to run, to run anywhere so long as he could escape from this unknown terror. Then the door opened, and he saw his mother's face, a face which seemed strangely small and young, with large eyes washed strangely bright. Instantly his legs ceased to strain to run, and began instead to tremble. The hard lump rose from his stomach into his throat, and melted in a sob. Tears of real happiness and real sadness welled out of his eyes. Without knowing, he raised up his arms, and instantly the half-forgotten sweetness of his mother's kiss flowed through him.

II

In her frightful desolation he was beside her at last, her son, pressed against her. She felt tears of love and tenderness driving out the tears of misery from her eyes.

" You're not to cry though, Peter," she exclaimed, trying to smile at him, " or I'll cry too."

But her smile and the strange blackness of her dress racked him into fresh sobs, through which he stammered:

" I'll stop, then, mother; I'll stop. Oh, yes, I'll stop."

She took his hand tightly and turned to Edward.

" Come in, Edward," she said in a low voice. " It was good of you to bring him. Joe is here, too."

The door closed behind them, and, passing through the hall, they entered the parlour.

" Come along, Ned," said Joe at once, in a sad, hushed voice, speaking from the armchair in which he sat. " I was just wondering when you would be over, and Peter, too. It's time we had a fambly talk. Well, well! You're a fine big boy now, Peter. Don't cry, Peter boy. Take a look at that brave little woman that's your mother, and don't cry another drop out of your eye."

Obediently, Peter looked up at his mother, and, tightening his choking throat, nodded. " Yes, Uncle Joe."

" Good boy, good boy," replied the other approvingly, his short stumps of fingers playing with the seals on the heavy gold chain that glistened across his stomach. His eye, glistening too with a sad benevolence, swept the three in turn, and finally settled upon Edward, now seating himself with a melancholy solemnity.

Lucy, her arm around her son, drew him close suddenly to her knee; the small parlour seemed over-full and heavy with an apprehensive silence. A slant of sunlight broke through the window and gashed into the shaded room like a yellow blade. No one seemed to know what to say.

" Well," said Joe at last, looking slowly around again, " I've said it before and I'll say it again. It's a fair knockout." He sighed. " But there's no way out of it. He's gone now, poor fellow, and God rest his soul." He cocked his eye at Edward. " Can we look to the cloth to speak? "

Edward stirred uncomfortably. Should he put up a prayer? Hardly, he thought, with just the family here; besides, he had himself officiated at the funeral.

" Well," repeated Joe, " what have you to say about it? "

" Have you—have you gone into things? " hesitatingly enquired Edward of Lucy. " For example, the bill for the funeral? "

He was, despite Joe's patent affability, keyed to a less magniloquent note in his elder brother's presence. And now, indeed, Joe lifted a hairy, arresting hand.

" No! " he exclaimed dramatically. " I didn't mean you to start on that line. That's my affair, if you please." He faced them in generous aggression. " God pity my soul! " he cried indignantly. " What do you think I am? Didn't I tell you I'm going to pay for the whole shoot? Am I a low-down begrudger? As if I couldn't do that for my poor dead brother! "

His blunt nostrils heaved; his round paunch quivered spasmodically; a tear hung upon his eyelid. He was genuinely moved, and he continued impressively:

" Yes, and I did give him a lovely funeral, didn't I? Lovely! " And his words passed over his lips with a slow deliberation as though he relished them. " Begod and I did! The best brass-plated coffin that money could buy! And lashin's of flowers. And everything handsome and proper. And every farden of it I'll pay myself! Money's no object to me. And him dyin' sudden on us like he done. God pity my soul! If I couldn't have buried my own brother right, what kind of an object would I be? "

He drew the back of his hand across his eyes, and gazed towards Lucy for approval.

Pale and very silent, worn out by the anguish of the last two weeks, she bent her head whilst her eyes traced the pattern of the carpet. Would Joe never cease his effusive recollection of the funeral? He had insisted that Frank be buried in the family grave at Levenford—a proceeding involving a long journey by carriage; had declared vociferously that he would pay for all. And, prostrate, she had been unable to combat the vulgar ostentation of his grief.

Holding her son closer to her knee, she shivered again at the recollection of that day. It had been wet. Strange how frequently the last dismal function of interment invokes the drabbest and most dismal complexion of the sky. But so it was. That day was very wet, and the rain poured ceaselessly with a hurrying patter, mocking Joe's arrangements; pouring on the professional mourners, lugubrious and stiff, on the sumptuous hearse, black yet glittering with glass, on the sickly banks of white flowers, on all the show and futility of a pretentious funeral. The last thing Frank would have desired; the last thing that she desired.

But Joe was in his element: his top-hat set to a rakish slant, his thumbs straying seldom from his arm-holes, grief glistening in his excited eye.

Rain. Rain. Rain.

It poured mercilessly upon the elaborate *cortège* during the long journey to Levenford—a drive beginning with a slow solemnity through the town but whipping quite gaily into a quick trot at the end of Garsden Street. The carriages bumped and splashed along the empty country roads. Dully, she thought of the limbs of the dead man shaken and flung into strange and listless attitudes inside that wide and costly coffin. Why was he there? It made her shudder, that piercing thought.

At a bend of the road she saw perched on the hearse a cowering mute sucking his fuming clay, and within her something recoiled at the wretched incongruity of it all. It was well that she had opposed Peter's coming: Joe had desired that he attend " to take a cord " at the graveside: for now she recognised this travesty of mourning was no fit exhibition for her son.

At the graveside the rain turned the soil to cloying mud, bruised the petals of the wreaths into a limp misery. Edward, in black stole, looked pale and fearful of the damp; Joe's blubbering—for blubber he did at the last moment—froze her own grief; she stood stiffly whilst they pulled on the black cords and lowered the coffin into the raw gashed earth.

Afterwards they went to Joe's house above the Shamrock Tavern —a fitting climax to the tragic day. The house itself repelled her— dirty, disordered, littered with clothes and food, Joe's whippet leaping the air wildly, Polly's fur coat on the dresser beside the raw pork steaks—the whole redolent of its own composite odour, the lingering smell of every rich meal that had been prepared within these greasy walls.

The room was full of smoke; the conversation rang in her ears:

" True enough—that was the year Branagan came over."

" Even money it should have been "—this from Joe as he sucked his cigar.

" 'Twas pulled if you ask me."

" The blazes it was! " They were gathered in a genial coterie, all Joe's friends, none of whom she knew.

Apart, with curious reserve, stood the others, her own friends: her brother Richard; Lennox watching her with a curious sympathetic eye.

She had seen them, seen it all dimly through the numb curtain of her wretchedness, the frightful misery of her spirit.

But it was over! Now abruptly she raised her head, straining to banish the recollection from her mind, striving, for her son's sake, to face the future.

Joe was still speaking.

" I tell you," he declared at large, with that intimate manner, lately increased, " I'm going to see that Lucy and the boy come out of this right. What kind of things are we if we can't stand by our own? "

" Well," murmured Edward diffidently, " if you mean it, Joe."

He knew his brother to be comfortably off; he, naturally, was at a disadvantage: by virtue of his calling, he had no means, merely his paltry yearly competence.

" Of course I mean it! What do you think I opened my mouth for? " returned Joe, widening his eye aggressively. " So you can take that as gospel."

There was a pause. Then Edward spoke again, now quite hurt at Joe's monopolising an attitude which should, by virtue of dignity, devolve on him; and he said, rather loftily:

" What exactly are your plans, Lucy? "

" Yes," broke in Joe, hanging forward in his chair. " What are you thinking of doing? How much did Frank leave? "

Edward drew in his breath. Had Joe no decency, no respect for the precedence of the cloth, grossly to distort his questions like that?

Lucy blushed painfully, wincing from the words. Yet she knew that she must face this interrogation with courage; Joe did not mean his manner to be offensive.

" I don't know," she said in a low voice. " There's various things to pay." She had herself proposed to indemnify the Bowies against the dinghy's loss. " But when everything's settled there should be— should be more than a hundred pounds left."

At her words Joe's mouth hung down slackly; then he let out a long whistle and lay back in his chair, fixing his gaze pointedly at the ceiling. Edward, too, looked somewhat startled.

"Frank was just beginning to get on," she said in that low, strained voice.

She faltered slightly, looking from one to the other, her colour still high upon her pale cheeks.

"Was he not insured?" shot out Joe.

She shook her head; as if Frank would have troubled about insurance!

"Well, it isn't a great deal," said Edward slowly, in a logical sort of voice. "No, it isn't a great deal."

"Pah!" cried Joe contemptuously, jingling the loose change in his trouser pocket. "It's nothing, nothing at all. It's less than nothing. What in God's name Frank was thinking of I don't know, but it's pure suicide leaving a wife and child with only a hundred pound. I'd have put him in the way of making a bit myself if he had only asked me, but he was one of them kind that wouldn't look near you, wouldn't ask a favour off the Pope himself."

"I tell you, Frank was getting on well," said Lucy with a full throat.

"I know, I know. I'm not saying a word against my poor dead brother." He lowered his eye towards her. "But that doesn't alter the case—not at all, not at all."

A sudden thought struck him, and he jerked out:

"Is that brother of yours going to help you?"

Lucy's eyes, still moist, clouded over at his tone.

"I don't intend to ask him for help—or anybody else, for that matter," she said slowly. A vision of Richard's cold, detached look at the funeral suddenly confronted her. Even now she could hear his guarded condolences.

"I'm grieved, you know—grieved about the whole affair. Eva—Eva has been deeply upset."

Though Richard had talked to her agreeably, his enquiries into her position had been cautious. He had given her clearly to understand that it was only just that Frank's family should safeguard her interests in the future. As to himself, he stressed the liabilities that lay heavily upon his own shoulders. It was no surprise, this attitude.

"I've got a certain amount of independence, Richard," she had then replied, "and I think I'll keep it. I'll be under obligation to nobody."

He had nodded his head without speaking, concurring with this sentiment. expressing thus his approval of this manifestation of the Murray pride. Now, looking at Joe, she added quietly:

"My brother has his own family and his own responsibilities. He's got enough to do without me troubling him."

Edward moved restlessly. He had been meditating, and now he felt that it was time for a little discourse.

"There's sure to be some way out," said he. "There's no need for anxiety. God is very good. Something is sure to turn up for you, Lucy."

He knew that it would be in the worst possible taste to suggest that she should marry again, but this was indeed at the back of his mind, and he inferred it blandly.

"Tell us what you mean to do, then," said Joe slyly, who, from behind the shadow of his hand, had been all the time observing her.

"I can work, surely," she returned.

"Work?" His tone was incredulous.

"And why not?" she asked defensively. "I can't sit down and look at my fingers."

The two brothers gazed at each other with an equal astonishment. It was not the age when women went freely into the world to work, except in the most subordinate positions. And she had no qualifications. A shop assistant? Something in the line of domestic duties? Unthinkable, reflected Edward; and with this in mind he queried dubiously:

"Have you anything particular in view?"

"Yes, I have," she replied, striving to make her quivering voice composed. "I have the chance to carry on Frank's work. I've asked Mr. Lennox. And he's promised to let me have the chance."

It was a fact. Faced by the urgent necessity of combating her grief, of facing the future, of safeguarding her son, she had approached Lennox. And he, at length, had consented to give her a trial.

"He'd never let you do it," broke in Joe incredulously. "No, bedam, and he wouldn't."

"But it's conceivable," said Edward, pursing his lips, placing his finger-tips together. "And not uncongenial work, either. Quite lady-like—yes."

Joe said nothing, and for a moment there was silence.

"You'd never do it," said Joe again. For some reason he seemed aggrieved at her intention.

But she did not reply, and again he was silent.

"What about Peter, though?" exclaimed Edward suddenly. "You'll be away all day, and late sometimes."

At the words Joe's manner relaxed; he slapped the arm of his chair.

"Yes, you'll need to put the boy to school," said he, "and I'll give you a hand over him. We'll send him to the Brothers' College at Laughtown. That's where my own boy was—a fine place; there's Spaniards and everybody there. I know Brother John Jacob meself —had him down at the Green's sports last year; he can lift a football with his one hand, can John Jacob; big lump of a man, J.J.! Big as a house! Of course I'll help you with Peter."

Dully, she looked at Joe; vaguely she had hoped that he would take an interest in the boy's future; she was not satisfied with the school Peter was attending; and yet—was she to lose her son too?

" Quite a good school," assented Edward judiciously. " They are not ordained, of course, the Brothers—still, quite passably good."

" Ah! It's a fine place, I tell you," broke in Joe shortly. " Set up my Barney, it did. And you can leave the paying to me."

Edward raised one eyebrow, but made no further comment. He felt indeed that some definite decision had been reached, that the awkward obstacle of the future had been surmounted. He detested trouble; although he was just, although his conscience never failed to function adequately, he nevertheless abhorred any contingency which might threaten to disturb his own peace of mind. He looked towards Lucy tolerantly, implying the truth of his assertion that the Almighty would disclose the proper pathway for the future.

With her arms still around her son, speaking to him through the tenderness of her touch, Lucy returned that gaze in silence.

" Well," said Joe at length, " we've settled something. Peter's for Laughtown and I'm payin' the whole shoot." Again he looked at her slyly. " And you—you'll see how you like the travelling, maybe. You'll get tired of it soon enough." He paused importantly. " And now I'll take a squint at the time," said he, pulling out his large gold watch and puckering a beady eye towards it. " Bedam, I'll need to get along or I'll miss my train." He stood up, took her hand in his, patted her shoulder effusively. He did not speak of his return, but his manner inferred intimately that he would return, and, after an affectionate leave-taking, he shook his head, tiptoed with obvious grief from the house.

Nor did Edward remain long after his brother had gone. The conversation had found him less assured than usual, left his manner a little over-stretched, as though his own mellow tones, after Joe's downright brag, echoed somewhat weakly in the room and filled him with a sense of bathos. As he rose he shot a cautious look at the boy.

" Anna," he said guardedly ; " have you heard from her since she got back ? "

She shook her head, her eyes suddenly cast down.

" No," she answered, in a quivering voice, " I don't—I never want to hear from her again."

He made no answer, but took his departure in subdued yet digni-fied manner, promising to come over shortly to satisfy himself as to her comfort and well-being. The door closed behind him gently, suavely.

They were alone, then, Lucy and her son, a constraint upon them through their very love and the awful strangeness of their situation.

Tenderly she looked at him. His return, the sight of him standing n gawky timidity upon the doorstep, had come as a consolation almost divine. The frightful tragedy of Frank's death had torn her like the sudden evulsion of a limb. Prostrate, she had abandoned herself to an intense grief which clouded her vision to everything but her loss, and the irrevocable finality of that loss. But she had, after all, something to live for. She had her son; an inspiration towards fresh hope. His face was the face which she saw through the encircling haze of her sorrow, and she turned towards it passionately. A realisation of the future, the future before them both, dawned upon her and filled her with the growing knowledge that her life was not over; a new epoch it was which had begun, in which she would bind herself more closely to him.

Moved as by a sudden weakness, she did not know how she could part with him to send him to school. She wanted him beside her always. As she gave him his tea—and from time to time they looked at each other across the table almost diffidently—she felt this passionately. They did not speak much, though occasionally she made a little conversation, trying to put him at his ease. No mention was made of the awful forbidden subject; nothing, not by a word or even by a look between them.

Yet, from time to time, as with a fresh pang, her body seemed to shrink a little, her eye, still bright, became haunted, and her face took on a strange look of listening.

It was after tea that the doorbell rang—a sudden peal, vibrating upon her tautly drawn nerves. Startled unreasonably, she went to the door. But it was only Miss Hocking, standing, incredibly, with a mould of jelly neatly wrapped within her large gloved hands.

" I'm sorry," said Miss Hocking, rather foolishly. " I know you are upset, but I thought you might care to have this. You looked so ill. It would do you good."

There was a moment's silence, during which Lucy looked doubtfully at Miss Hocking's smooth, too-reasonable face: her giving was like a child offering a toy; an action light and unconsidered, empty of anything but a sort of laughing simplicity.

" It was kind of you," she said, as reluctantly she took the mould.

" I've enjoyed making it," answered Miss Hocking apologetically. " It's the mixing—and the colour! " Her smile faded—when she was not smiling her face was quite expressionless—then she added: " You must come up and see me often now."

No depth of motive lay beneath her tone, merely a benevolent friendliness.

" Yes."

" I've been sad to-day," said the other again, dreamily; " some-thing of your sadness has come up to me—like a dark flower ! "

Lucy made no reply, but drew back slightly from the doorstep.

" I mustn't keep you," exclaimed the other quickly. " But any-thing I can do I will do. Yes, I will, for I understand." And she turned with a slow sweep of her skirts, and went slowly away.

Lucy closed the door. She was used now to these capricious mani-festations of Miss Hocking's favour, but to-night her mood was filled solely by the urgency of tenderness and grief. The approach of night chilled her, gave her again that frozen sensation of her sorrow.

She entered the parlour and sat down beside Peter, who was on his elbows on the floor, playing a game of soldiers upon the carpet, watching the smiles strain through his intent and serious face.

After they had played together they went early to bed, lying together in the small bed in the spare room, where they talked in low voices, saying to each other those things which could be said only in the darkness. They had suddenly an intimacy, a warmth, a comradeship; his breath was upon her cheek; under the flashing promises he made—of the furs and motor-cars which he would buy her, of the greatness he would achieve for her sake—the future opened before them both.

At last his voice grew jerky, then drowsily his breathing deepened. She raised herself up, and, quietly bending over him, watched in the dim light his sleeping face. As she gazed, she heard the vague sound of music coming from without, afar, swelling into a slow strain of sadness, falling thinly into the silence of the night. She lay down, swallowed with difficulty, curved her body against her son, then she closed her eyes, and, worn by the long passage of broken nights, her breathing eased into sleep.

III

NEXT morning she took a firm grip upon herself and set her face doggedly towards the future. Despite her assumption of confidence before Joe and Edward, the fact was that she had with difficulty persuaded Lennox to allow her to continue her husband's work.

" I could only give you a trial," he had said dissuasively. " If you didn't do, then we couldn't keep you."

He had hesitated, uncertain, swayed a little by his regard, yet half persuading himself that the move might be a shrewd one. Although he had entertained for Moore a certain regard, although he liked Lucy, sympathy and affection did not lie entirely at the back of his acquiescence. He saw that she was young, presentable; likely, more-over, to receive a sympathetic reception from his customers because of her recent sensational bereavement; he committed himself to nothing; her remuneration would be adjudged chiefly upon a commission basis; and the work itself was simple, of a nature involving merely a knowledge of prices and quality which she could easily acquire. Yes, he was careful—very careful: he explained that such a departure would be a novelty totally lacking in precedent, a novelty which could hardly be successful, but he inferred at least that she should have her opportunity.

" It's a risk I'm taking, mind ye; it's a risk," he had declared in conclusion. " Me that's as long in the head as the Tron steeple. But I'll give you the chance."

She saw clearly, therefore, that she must fight for success, that to ensure this success she must first make provision for Peter.

How she would part with him she did not know—but it was apparently inevitable. At her work she would be away all day; often, on her wider visitations, until late at night; already she had decided on the grounds of economy that she must part with Netta, and in consequence there would be no one to look after him or to prepare his meals. Besides, never could she be happy to be away from home, constantly in fear that some unforeseen mishap might befall the boy. Again, his present school was inferior, and attended chiefly by a poorer class of children; she had for him a great ambition; he was now virtually nine years of age; finally, there was Joe's generous, even handsome offer to send him to an admittedly excellent board-ing-school. It was unthinkable that she could place her own feelings in the way of the boy's best interests and refuse this excellent opportunity. Yes, she faced the melancholy, indisputable fact: she must part for the time being with Peter. It was a sacrifice, a great sacrifice, yet she must make it.

Lest her resolution should falter, she sat down quickly and wrote to the Brother Superior at Laughtown.

And quickly, too, in return came a courteous personal letter from that Superior thanking her profusely for her enquiry, pointing out that the new term began in ten days' time, indicating the extremely reasonable range of fees, and enclosing a green and gold illustrated prospectus which explained in eloquent terms the manifold attrac-tions of the school. Earnestly she read through this neat little book, beginning: " Designed to afford an eminently sound and practical education for the sons of Catholic gentlemen, the college is delight-fully situated within the salubrious country town of Laughtown, so justly dubbed by the poet Brown ' The Pearl of the Eastern Low-lands.' Soundly built, standing in its own tasteful grounds, and so agreeably fanned by the balmy yet bracing breezes of the eastern seaboard, it commands——" and ending: " The food in particular is wholesome, nourishing, and plentiful. Delicate and backward boys are especially cared for. No extras. The Brothers mingle with the boys and engage freely in their sports and recreations. Fees in all cases and without exception are payable in advance."

It was an elegant and moderate essay. She was impressed—indubitably impressed. She sighed and turned again to the photographs; the School Band; the School Orchestra (almost the same photograph); the School Choir; the School Dramatic Society—in the costume of that classic piece *Nero ! or the Christian Slave*; the groups of the various forms—every boy in the college had his face in the book, and Lucy looked at them all.

She read glowing extracts reprinted from the *Laughtown Courier*: " A distinguished gathering . . . the Lord Bishop of Nofar presiding . . . amongst the laity were . . ." She read the long lists of prizes which could be won. Then she laid the book upon her knee and gazed across at Peter.

Strangely, he was fired by a desire to leave her. Inconceivable it was, but indisputable. This timid, sensitive, childish boy, who had wept in her arms less than a week ago, now desired urgently to forsake these arms. He had read the usual fictitious literature of school life; he had read, too, this prospectus; and now he saw himself leading the orchestra, beating the big drum in the band, holding a vast audience rapt by his impersonation of the Christian slave; he craved nothing more of life at this moment than to see his photograph staring proudly from that green and yellow book. Even through her relief, the fact that he made no demur saddened her. Irrationally, she wanted him to consent, yet she wished him to protest lovingly: " I don't want to go. I couldn't leave you." But he made neither of these protestations. Instead, he leapt visibly at the idea.

The buying of his outfit—according to the prescribed list—was for him an expedition as joyous as it was tragic for Lucy.

They went, naturally, to Gow's. Mr. Gow himself—dreadfully overcome to hear of Frank's death—was kind, almost paternal, and generous to the tune of three shillings discount. Yes, it was a sad business for Lucy, this setting out of her son upon the business of life. But Peter was ravished by his new and manly garments.

He came home elated, tried on his new pyjamas, and at the same time his bowler hat, which had been chosen, on Mr. Gow's advice, on the large size, to allow for the natural growth of the head, and which reposed backwards on his ears with a faintly Semitic archness. He postured before the mirror with supreme gratification, and demanded with an unblushing vanity that Miss Hocking be brought along to view him. She did come, and delightedly viewed the outfit, praising particularly the colour of his new braces, which superseded his old and worthless ones. She passed no comment upon the school; her father, to whom she remotely alluded, had been educated, it appeared, at an exclusive English Public School; she herself had been to Leipzig; but she did like those braces, and she laughed unrestrainedly as he jumped about in his pyjamas, exposing his small person shamelessly at every excited leap. Every leap sent Pinkie into a fresh peal. That strange interest flashed happily in her blue excited eye. But Lucy's answering smile was wan.

That the term should begin so soon—it was an unexpected pang, and it seemed to her that the days rushed past. They swept along, indeed, in a stream so swift that the last inevitable day had reached her before she realised it. Yet it was here.

They set off for the station in a cab; the new shiny black trunk, with his initials inscribed upon it in white paint—ineffable refinement of modern civilisation—lay tenderly bestowed above them; Miss Hocking, who had come down to see him off, ordered the cabman about to distraction, and waved them good-bye with a pink sash from the doorway. To Lucy the occasion was one not only of sorrow but of solemnity; and the high solemnity of the occasion warred with and almost overcame her sadness. To her this setting out was momentous. She saw in it the first step into life of this young and captivating creature that was hers, the opening out of a highway which he should walk with an illustrious tread. In the train she was silent, now gazing out at the moving landscape, now suddenly returning her look to the excited figure of her son.

Her determination firmed within her. She had pride and she had an immense love, both moving her to a resolution. It was like an aspiration: a swift pang of yearning tempered by her own courage.

The past was the past: she must not, she could not, brood upon it—therein lay only wretchedness and defeat. She determined that she would succeed; as for Peter, his success would be hers; together they would achieve it, and she would see that it was incomparable.

The journey was long, and involved a change with a considerable wait, but they reached Laughtown in the early afternoon. As the train drew in, she carefully wiped the smuts from Peter's cheek with her moistened handkerchief, and they got out upon the bustling windswept platform. She had expected that someone might meet the train, but in the press of people—it was market day, and the station was full of farmers and their stock—she could discern no face which looked expectantly towards her and the boy, standing in his stiff new hat so obviously beside the shiny trunk.

The porter whom she approached betrayed only an unsympathetic knowledge of the school and its whereabouts; she was jostled by some passing yokels; the cows mooed and lifted their tails incontinently; the sheep bleated mournfully; and the pigs mingled their grunts discordantly from the adjoining pens. She became aware that this arrival at " The Pearl of the Eastern Lowlands " was hardly the picture that her fancy had drawn, and as she stood holding Peter's hand her brows drew together with a slow perplexity. In the end, however, they found a cab and drove with a continuous chatter of iron-girt wheels over the roundly cobbled streets. Clop-clop, went the sluggish hoofs of the jogging nag, and somehow the town seemed sluggish, too. It had a blousy and bucolic air: shops full of the instru-ments of agriculture, barrels of potatoes stacked upon the pave-ments, in the market-place a crowd of rustics who merely stood in apathy or moved their heavy boots towards the nearest tavern: yes, a disappointing town, threaded but unredeemed by a greyish river which wandered aimlessly beneath some low-arched bridges.

At last, with a jerk, they drew up at the school, and here at least there was no disappointment for Lucy. The college buildings of white sandstone had a neat and compact air. The laurel-edged drive was precise and scrupulously raked. The whole establishment exhi-bited a genuine solidity, which reassured at once her anxious mind.

At her ring a manservant in a green baize apron opened the door, and at the sight of them an agreeable smile parted his dark, shaven face.

" Will you please to step this way, ma'am? " said he, and showed them along a polished corridor to a small hushed chamber. Lucy and her son sat down formally on the edges of two straight-backed chairs, gazed at each other as from a distance, forbidden almost, by the strangeness of their situation, to speak, then looked round the room. An aspidistra in a china pot stood in the centre of a brown drugget tablecloth; a marble temple of a clock upon the mantelpiece loudly marked the seconds; and rows of darkly bound books against the wall conveyed a serious sense of erudition.

In a few moments an old man came slowly into the room.

" I'm Brother William," he said, advancing a tremulous hand, explaining further with a naïve satisfaction: " Superior of the College."

He wore a small black skull-cap, a habit shiny from use and pollened upon the chest with snuff; askew, a short black shoulder-cape drooped from him. He was bowed, shuffled somewhat as he walked, and his redly veined, clean-shaven face was pendulous with age: his brows hung down, his neck fell into folds, even his cheeks sagged in limp dewlaps over his chin like those of an aged bulldog.

But, for all this patent evidence of senility, he looked a wise and kind old man, now turned a little simple in his sagacity, perhaps, yet with a mild astuteness, the more subtle because it sat on him so openly.

" Yes, I'm Brother William," he repeated, as he sat down, with a faint nodding smile; and when Lucy saw that smile she forgot Brother William's age and knew only that she liked him.

" You'd like to take a little walk and see some of the other boys ? " he said to Peter, after they had spoken for a moment. He struck a small bell upon the table, and almost at once a young Brother entered: dark, he was, alert and trim about his person.

" Brother Aloysius," continued the Superior, " take this young man and show him round. Don't be afraid," he went on, looking at Peter; " your mother's not going yet."

But Peter was not afraid; his excitement still swept him buoyantly along. He went out of the room almost at a trot, clasping the hand of Brother Aloysius.

" A fine boy," remarked the Superior, with just the right amount of weighty deliberation, as he turned slowly to Lucy; " an exceedingly sensitive boy."

He said this to every maternal parent. To the fathers he used the words: " Manly little fellow." Oh, he was a very nice old man. And so, too, thought Lucy, as, knowing nothing of ten thousand similar interviews which stood in heaven to Brother William's credit, she accepted the implied compliment, and faintly blushed in gratification.

" A little cake and wine after your journey, I think? Yes, I think so! " murmured the other, and, making a ruminating movement with his jaws, he went to the sideboard, where a decanter of sherry stood beside a cut seedcake. In a moment he returned, offering Lucy a glass of wine and a portion of the cake. Then he sat down opposite her, without himself partaking of the refreshment, and went on mildly: " He'll be very happy with us once he gets used to us."

Lucy nodded her head, and, lifting her black veil, removed one neat kid glove and made a pretence of nibbling the cake upon her plate. The imminence of the parting with her son had gripped her. Speech became increasingly difficult.

" He's very young, you know," she declared dryly through the cake, " and I'm anxious about his health."

" We've many here younger than he," he reassured her reflectively. " Yes, and from a long way; but they come to us. I mother them. Myself! "

There was a short pause; then Lucy said, with diffidence, hesitating over the words:

" I hope you'll take care of him. I've only got him, you know."

He came a little nearer, patted her arm protectively, and murmured an affirmative. Then he looked at her black dress, said in a tone persuasive of her confidence:

" You've had a sad bereavement recently, I understand ? "

" Yes," she admitted.

" And it has upset you," he suggested gently. " I see that."

A quick warm tear rushed to her eye as she again nodded her head.

" Poor thing, poor thing," he murmured soothingly.

It gave him a strange benignant pleasure, fleeting and atrophic, to see this warm, vivid young creature grievous and opening to his sympathy. He liked this gentle, sensuous stimulation—a rare delight; often in default he would draw the younger boys to confide in him tearfully in this fashion.

" Was it a long illness ? " he murmured.

But a warm drop fell from Lucy's lashes, and splashed into the wineglass. The still, strange room, the cloistered quiet, the sun striking a mote-filled beam upon the old books, this aged Brother offering his benignant sympathy, and, above everything, the separation from her son—all these moved her suddenly. Inward it was, except for that single tear, but to her it seemed a shameful grief.

He held her arm tightly in his veined hand, and murmured his condolences gently. He had no Orders empowering him to the confessional, but this—this sensuous impression, powerful yet mellow—stole into him gracefully, like the bouquet of an old wine or the whisper of an old romantic melody.

When she had composed herself and controlled her voice to speech, despising, indeed, her own weakness, he talked to her about the school, how they hoped soon for a newer building, how he had been here for forty years. Attentively she listened. She had no idea of inspecting dormitories in the traditional manner, nor did he offer to conduct her thither; no matron appeared for her to interview— Brother Adolphus, the Infirmarian, held the matron's post; he it was who sewed the boys' trousers' buttons when they so required him. Woman, inevi ably, did not exist within that building.

" The first term's fees," she said; " I would like to pay these now "; and she drew out of her purse eleven pounds, which was the necessary amount. Joe had not yet been to see her, but she preferred to discharge the obligation now, knowing that he could reimburse her at a later date.

Brother William waved away the matter and the money—yet somehow the deprecating hand received her sovereigns, and in a moment his stamped receipt was in her purse. She rose.

" The boy! " he exclaimed, and rang the bell again. Then he turned and gazed tactfully from the window. She stood quite still in the middle of the room, clasping her bag tightly in both hands, looking towards the door. It opened, and Peter came in, still animated by the excitement of the occasion. He had apparently encountered other boys, whom he had been very sorry to leave, whom he desired speedily to rejoin.

For her own sake, she refrained from embracing him, but kissed him lightly through her veil.

" You'll be all right? " she enquired stiffly.

" Oh, yes, of course," he assured her eagerly. " Certainly, mother."

She said good-bye to Brother William, who, turning at the right moment, laid his hand on Peter's shoulder before she swung round and with lowered head went out of the room.

The journey home was a succession of images: his childish face, moving in every expression against the background of the fleeting, darkening landscape. The separation, accomplished without bitter tears or protestations, had been so swift it left her with a sense of blankness, almost of unfulfilment, of a climax yet to come.

The house was cold and empty when she got home. The sad business of Netta's dismissal had been achieved—regretfully but without recrimination: Netta had accepted the matter as inevitable—and now no fires, no meal, awaited her. But she had neither desire for food nor energy to cook it. She made herself a cup of tea and drank it. " Tea again," she thought dismally. She was taking too much tea these days. Still, a measure of comfort flowed through her with the warm drink, and, reassuring herself with the consideration of her son's well-being, she turned her mind to the momentous question of her future work. She was to begin her duties on Monday morning. Sometimes the very idea of her attempting to enter, single-handed, without experience or talent, this world of business, startled her by its incredibility; sometimes its incongruity flashed upon her as ridiculous. She of all people to be attempting this! was the exclamation so continually before her mind, but to-night, although she felt herself inept, a tremendous desire swayed her and flowed into a determination to succeed. She went to bed in the lonely house hopefully, and not without the beginnings of a certain valiant cheerfulness.

IV

" Do you know what you are to do now? " said the man Andrews, gazing at her distrustfully.

" I'm certain," she answered, as confidently as she could.

He looked at her doubtfully. He was an under-sized, middle-aged man, with a bushy but melancholy drooping moustache, and a mild cast in his left eye which intensified his air of pathos.

" You've got the names of the customers? "

" Yes."

" And the price list? "

" Off by heart."

" You'll mind all I've told you ? "

She nodded, essaying to give herself courage by the thought:
" If this under-sized creature can do his work, then I assuredly am
capable of doing mine." But she was not so confident as she looked.

It was the fateful Monday morning, and she stood in the office
dressed in a neat dark grey costume—reluctantly she had discarded
the black as sentimental and inappropriate—awaiting the arrival of
Lennox. She had been early, very early; he was late; and in the
meantime Andrews had been grounding her in the simple essentials
of her duties.

His interest was purely and exclusively selfish. He had no regard
for Lucy, nor any altruistic desire for her success; but he had a
strong regard for himself, and a pressing urge to retain his own position. At one time he had known the vicissitudes of " travelling," and
Lennox had hinted that in the event of Lucy's failure Moore's round
might be his. It was an uncomfortable thought for Andrews, who,
in his own idiom, was sick of the road.

For many reasons, indeed, he cherished his present post, not the
least being that his house lay in the Gallowgate, near to the office,
and he liked, above everything, to get home regularly for his meals.
But he had small hopes of her success. What good was a woman outside of her own kitchen ? And his opinion was clearly shared by
young Frame—the office-boy—who, busy with his morning task of
filing the previous day's letters, fixed her from time to time with
an almost patronising stare.

A curious and inappropriate figure, she seemed, standing in that
office. There was a neatness about her dress and a lustre upon her
hair; her face was calm, but it was a calmness that was slightly
strained, and in her tightly clenched fingers she felt the rapid
running of her beating pulse. So much depended upon her now—
actually upon herself, for no one else could help her. That was a
curious thought, and it filled her with a sense, not, strangely, of
impotence, but of strength: some force unlocked within her, liberated,
and rushing through her veins.

" Anyway," said Andrews, turning away with gloomy finality,
" I can do no more."

She made no reply, but, detaching her eyes from his retreating
figure, she let her gaze travel round the office. In a sense even this
office disconcerted her. Always she had imagined " Frank's office "
to be something elaborate, refined, dignified; but this—this she felt
to be sadly lacking in distinction. There were two rooms: the office
and an inner room marked " Private," but stuffed chiefly with cases
that had spilled their straw randomly: and the rooms were old,
untidy. She stared at the fixed windows, the cracked cornices, the

drab green walls, at that vacant desk which must in truth have been Frank's and to which now, with a sudden pang, she apportioned his lanky, stooping form. Even the approach to the office had dismayed her: the entrance from the Saddleriggs guarded by the sign *Lennox & Galton* on a rounded rib of brass—not polished, alas, but yellowed, greened in parts with verdigris almost to illegibility—had been dingy, dark, leading to a circular stone stair round which she had guided herself by a rope banister. And the door itself, with one cracked panel, had been in keeping with the rest—holding almost the shambling decrepitude of senility. Clearly Lennox wasted little on the upkeep of his premises.

With a start she collected her forces, conscious of the office-boy's stare: Frame, she knew his name, Dougal Frame—an under-sized boy of about fourteen, untidy of hair and collar, suspiciously sombre about his neck, his ears added like an afterthought, the one balancing a pen, the other a nipped stub of cigarette, his eyes holding a hostility which defeated the density of his large steel spectacles. At least vaguely she suspected that hostility, and in an effort to master her nervousness she turned to the boy.

" Is this place never cleaned ? " she enquired mildly.

He stared at her broodingly for a long time, answered cryptically: " Whiles." Then with laconic urgency he resumed his filing.

" You should clean it oftener," she persisted. " It's so dusty."

" I'm not paid to clean it," he retorted coldly, without looking up.

For a moment there was silence. Then into that silence came the sound of a step upon the stairs.

" Here's Lennox himself," said the boy, still distantly, but with less asperity, as though perhaps already he repented the full blast of his frigidity.

Her heart leaped, and abruptly she turned as the door swung open and Lennox entered. His face, set already to an unusual severity —it was not the expression with which he entered her house—soured further at the sight of her; pushing back his hat from his brow, he immediately exclaimed:

" You've turned up! "

The rebuff stung her—why did he speak like that, when the matter had been arranged, confirmed even by his own word, only a week ago? But she forced herself to smile—the smile of a woman too anxious, too eager to please.

" Mr. Andrews has told me everything," she replied with a specious briskness. " I'm ready to begin right away."

" I'm a fool," he returned in a crabbed voice. " You'll never do it."

" Don't say that, Mr. Lennox," she answered quickly, still with that forced air of brightness.

" Mind you, off in a week if you don't get results ! "

What kind of a sentimental fool had he been to take on a woman like this, or a woman at all, in fact? To think that once over her tea-cups he had said with incorrigible rashness: " If you want the post, let me know ! "—to think that now actually she was here, in his office, about to take up that post—the monstrous turn of circumstances pricked him sharply. Yes, in the cold light of this Monday morning he was questioning the wisdom of his compact. And so he declared:

" And if you lose me a customer, don't show your face here again ! "

" That's the last thing I'll do," she answered, at once, decisively.

" Humph ! " he said impatiently, and turned to Andrews. " Where does she start ? "

" Linton," said Andrews, " and I've put her up to it all I can."

With his feet planted wide, Lennox gazed in moody abstraction out of the window. Then suddenly he turned upon Lucy, who was watching him anxiously.

" Well, what are you standing there for ? " he shot out testily. " You're not paid to do that ! Get away and get on with it ! "

" I was waiting on you," she returned, upset more than ever at his manner. " I thought——"

" Don't think. Do ! "

He grinned sourly at his aphorism, and, taking a pencil from his waistcoat pocket, he stuck it beneath his hat, where it projected aggressively, like a cannon.

She looked at him indignantly, but no word left her lips. Yes, she controlled her rising temper, collected her new book and papers from the desk, then, with cheeks burning, went slowly from the room.

Humiliating, it was, to be constrained to submit to such an indignity. She had half a mind to return and throw his wretched post back into his grinning teeth. Half way down she heard a clattering of footsteps, and, turning abruptly, received the full impact of Dougal's flying figure.

" You forgot your pencil," he said clumsily, recovering himself.

She took it, looking up at him in silence. He glanced at her self-consciously.

" I've sharpened it for ye," he declared, colouring to the ears. Then, before she could speak, he jerked his thumb, and added: " Never mind Lennox. He's aye in a bad temper on Monday mornings. You'll get on fine ! " Then swiftly he turned, and, three steps at each stride, was gone.

She stood for a moment, then slowly her lips twitched; her brow cleared, she smiled faintly as she went out into the street.

It was a fine fresh morning, whetted by a crisping of early frost; the breeze, bustling through the Saddleriggs, bowled her along towards the station. At the swift change from the dingy office into the brightness of the day a sudden emotion, mingled of courage and resolution, came to her with intensity. Around her streamed the quick flow of the city, the incessant impulse of the restless streets: a string of stallions straining at their drays; the lumbering swing of brightly coloured clanging trams; the quick rattle of a hansom cab: in everything some vital quality which she unconsciously absorbed. And, propagated by this flowing stream, the low insistent note of the city's noise—clipped by the toot of a tug from the near-by river, the whistle of an engine, the shout of a huckster at his barrow—came to her vividly through the resonant air.

She crossed the road and cut into Young Street; the pavements here more crowded, the road more cluttered by its traffic. She went on into Queen Street Station, traversed the cloudy, sub-aqueous light of the glass-roofed high-level station, descended through the sulphurous smoke which choked the dripping, vaulted arches of the low-level platform.

Here she took train for Linton, and again during the rattling journey she had a quick impulse of resolution, a thrusting forward of her endeavour. Again she thought:

" I must forget the past. I've got Peter—and the future."

At her destination she drew a deep breath, set a determined face towards the town. And it was a busy town. The air rang with the chink of a thousand hammers: the endless rat-a-tat-tat of the riveters' beat and the ring of the platelayers' sledge; against the skyline a fretted framework of half-formed ships carried the swarming figures of men like ants; giant cranes swung out prodigious arms from which hung huge linked chains, the thickness of a man's thigh. Across the road from the shipyard gates a squat engine puffed, leaving behind a ragged pennant of steam. The earth reverberated to its passage. Crude and vital it was, raw as the turned-up clay where they were building a row of houses. But it thrilled her. The batter of steel upon iron; the roar of steam; the creak of a windlass; the rattle of a winch; she felt it all, and the power of it. The air rang with a high purpose, and she had a purpose, too, in life: not the mere barter of this wretched margarine—something behind that, vital, intense.

At the corner of the High Street and a narrow lane running to the shipyard she came upon her first place of call—a baker's shop, with a small fly-blown window holding a row of loaves and two circular glass cake-stands. One cake-stand was empty; the other bore some oleaginous pastries: strange bloom upon a stunted tree; and above the window was the sign: *Danl. Harbottle & Nephew.* She would never forget that name or this moment. The name of Harbottle, transcending all other names, became to her of paramount significance as through those glaucous panes she observed the figure of a man standing behind the counter. He stood meditatively upon one foot, rubbing a floury leg with the opposite boot. His bare arms, daubed with dry dough, pressed upon the counter, threw back his aproned body and elongated his thin neck. He had an almost stork-like abstraction. The nephew or Danl. himself? It was of little consequence. She perceived in him her immediate victim, and she marched into the shop determinedly.

" Good morning, Mr. Harbottle," she exclaimed. " I'm from Lennox's."

Her manner was firm, outright, even uncompromising. " Have you an order for me to-day? " she demanded brazenly.

Shades of the unobtrusive Andrews! Where, oh, where, was the evidence of his advice, that she edge effacingly into the shop and initiate insidious converse upon the weather?

" An order? " he repeated. Immured in his underground bakehouse since four that morning, and now dozing in the shop while his daughter breakfasted upstairs, he confronted her mazedly, as though doubting the evidence of ears and eyes.

She opened her notebook.

" I'll be calling on you in future," she declared with factitious confidence. " I've taken my husband's place, you see."

He continued to gaze at her. Then at last the light of understanding broke over his floury features.

" I see! I see! " he exclaimed. " Yon fella! So that's it, and you've got his job. Well, well! Funny days we're living in to see a woman come into my shop and speir like that for orders! "

She took up her pencil and looked towards him.

" I'm needing something, mind you," he responded guardedly; " I've no prejudice. I could do with something from Lennox."

Her pencil poised eagerly above the paper.

" Ay, ay, you might send me a tub of the usual."

Swiftly she wrote—she knew from Andrews what was his " usual"; there was a silence.

" Some oleo? " she suggested. " We can do it at fourteen/three."

A master stroke, that quotation, she afterwards reflected, and one indicative of her profound knowledge of the intricacies of the business.

" Well, when ye're about it," he averred slowly, " you can send me a half-tub of the marge an' all."

Her fingers trembled slightly as she made the final entry. When she had finished, then only did she smile and thank him briskly.

He stared after her almost sheepishly as she went out of the door. " Well! " he thought to himself. " Did ye ever? "

Outside, she paused. Yes, she had demanded that order and she had obtained it. Her heart thumped excitedly under her outward composure. It was a beginning—it was success! She knew that she could do it. Her triumph with this small, insignificant baker convinced her of the tremendous excitement of life. She was elated, but she calmed herself. Deliberately she forced herself to be tranquil as she moved off towards her next call.

She went through the town assiduously. Not always did she find a receptive ear attendant in an empty shop for her enquiries. She had to wait; she had to cool her heels whilst master bakers—sometimes impatient, sometimes inquisitive—emerged from subterranean depths. In the larger shops she had malapert young ladies to confront. Not always were her enquiries so downright. She had her rebuffs; but that beginning had been auspicious—almost an omen. She gained confidence, if this was necessary, and slowly she accumulated a list of commissions. In a sense it was inevitable; she was no fool, and Lennox's was a good firm, a firm with a reputation. Their stuff, as Frank had once phrased it, sold itself.

She emerged from the last interview and pulled out her watch from her patent-leather waistband. " Gracious," she thought, " it's three o'clock! " So tremendous had been her immersion that the relatively unimportant question of food had entirely escaped her. Now, however, thrilled by her victory, she felt hungry, voracious almost. Looking around, she discovered and entered a small eating-house opposite the yard gates. It was a modest place, and empty at this hour; though, from the wet rings and crumbs upon the tables, it had not recently been so; and here she sat down, ordered a ham sandwich and a glass of milk. How good they tasted! Relaxed, she spun out the last drain of milk deliciously.

Into the stillness of the room came the quick clamour of those beating hammers—rat-a-tat-tat and chink-chink-chink they went, mingling interminably. Some flies snoozed upon the greyish ceiling, comatose, untroubled by the noise. Nor did it trouble Lucy. She accepted it, dwelt upon it almost lingeringly as the stirring symbol of her new life.

Later her mood was different—calm, almost frigid—as she bore down upon the Saddleriggs and mounted briskly the stairs of the office.

A silence fell as, with an almost spectacular precision, she entered. She did not speak—no, she had been humiliated that morning. Tacitly, filled, now, with the recognition of her worth, she demanded an apology.

" Well," said Lennox at last, looking at her queerly, " how did it go? "

In silence she handed him her book, and with an equal silence he took it. It was a dramatic moment, with Andrews and Frame an audience entranced, as Lennox swiftly ran his eye over her commissions. At length he put the book down.

" Not bad," he murmured, and his voice had changed. Then he rubbed his hands together, cocked his beard at her, and showed his yellowish teeth in a sly smile. " Not so bad for a start."

For a start, indeed! She knew that she had done well, and she knew that he knew it too.

He picked up the book again. " Is it the first quality they want at the stores? " he demanded.

" It is the first quality, at eighteen shillings the tub," she returned, with a perfectly professional air.

He smiled again, admitting her more intimately to his regard. Of course, he had always known! A most tidy little woman: and his judgment always was marvellous. Of course! Of course!

" Yes. You've done fair," he murmured, and, turning, he went into the inner room, whistling softly.

She looked at the others, and with a definite gesture of invitation Dougal smiled at her.

" You can make out your invoices here," he declared, indicating his own desk.

He accepted her definitely as a member of the firm.

V

SHE reached home after six, viewing her own front door with an unconscious air of achievement. She was, in a sense, profoundly relieved by her success, realising suddenly the limitations of the field open to her, stricken by a fear as to what she would have done had not this opportunity of employment so fortunately appeared. And as she passed through the doorway she observed a letter lying upon the hall floor awaiting her. From Peter, she thought instinctively, and instinctively a smile trembled upon her lips as she bent to pick it up.

It was from Peter, but it was not a letter. It was a plain postcard—wilted, creased, dog-eared at its corners, wearing every evidence of hasty writing and surreptitious posting—a postcard which said, with incredible brevity: " Take me away at once." No signature, no superscription, merely a blot, a smear that might have been a tear, and these five atrocious words: " Take me away at once! "

Stupefied, she repeated them aloud. She stood stock still, petrified; then, walking into her sitting-room, she sank into a chair. What did it mean? A dozen different explanations raced through her mind.

With a vague alarm she saw her son in some dire and desperate predicament. Was he merely unhappy in the novelty of his surroundings, or was he being ill-used, bullied? Were they beating him? Actually this limp card, clasped now in her limp hand, had descended upon her with the unexpectedness and devastating violence of a bombshell.

And yet—that reassuring kindliness in Brother William's venerable voice; those dark, commiserating eyes of Brother Aloysius; the modest dignity of that green and gold prospectus—she could not in reason doubt such evidences of integrity.

For all that, she passed a night of misery, chafed by the very uncertainty of her fears. She was exasperated by the unexpectedness of this development, coming at a moment when she imagined she had triumphantly arranged the future, even to the payment of that first quarter's fees; and it was a matter which demanded her attention. Her instinct, indeed, was to rush to Laughtown upon the following day; yet this she would not permit herself to do. The impossibility of leaving her work at this juncture, and the manifest weakness of such a step—these factors made her temporise; and it was not easy for her to temporise. Yet, after a night of broken and restless sleep, she rose early, and wrote a short letter to her son, indicating that she would return to see him upon the following Saturday, which was her half-holiday.

For the remainder of the week she fought her uneasiness, setting her will firmly against that insidious inclination to rush off to see him; but on Saturday, the moment she could leave the office, she hurried to the Central Station, and caught the 1.15 for Laughtown.

What a journey it was—the same dull country and the same duller town! It seemed to her the apotheosis of imbecility that she should be taking it. The expense, too, though she curtailed this by refraining from taking a cab, was a considerable item to set against her weekly earnings. She realised that in this direction she must now be careful. And what would they say to her? What would Brother William say to her as, presenting herself within the compass of one short week, she demanded again to see her son?

But she did not encounter Brother William, and here, perhaps, he achieved the crowning glory of his wisdom. Though she was shown by the same servant to the same room, Brother William did not appear, nor did she receive those hospitable libations of wine and cake. Instead, after a few moments, Peter arrived with a countenance pale and miserable as a sickly moon, and the instant he saw her he burst into tears. Atrocious tears they were, mingled with a recurrent whine, whereby he implored her to remove him from the school.

She looked at him with bright eyes, strangely unable to indulge his grief.

" What's the matter? " she demanded quickly.

" I'm homesick, I'm homesick," he repeated over and over again.

This had, indeed, become the catchword of his position, for upon the day following her departure his confident elation had collapsed and left him stricken, devastated by his abandoned state. Since then he had wept consistently.

By a pressure of her hand she made him look at her.

" Do they treat you properly? " she enquired sharply.

" Yes. Oh, yes," he sobbed. " They treat me all right. They're kind, very kind. Brother Aloysius kisses me every night. Oh yes, all right, all right."

Again he had that almost hysterical repetition of his words.

A great struggle went on within her. She saw clearly the triviality of his emotion, divined the petty cause which had drawn her back so ridiculously. It was too bad; really, it was too bad of him. Yet she was profoundly touched by his dependence on her.

Suddenly she desired passionately to abandon her pretence of severity, to feel the warm intimacy of his wet, tear-stained face on hers, to strain his sobbing figure against her bosom; but she would not. Instead, she conquered herself, and rose.

" Come along," she said pleasantly, stretching out her gloved hand.

Instantly he took it, yet if he had harboured any sudden illusion of immediate departure this was quickly dispelled as she added kindly: " We'll go out and take a walk."

He accompanied her meekly along the corridor, where, though a murmur of voices exuded from the various classrooms, they encoun-tered no one. She wished to ask if he might have leave to go, but as no one appeared she opened the front door herself, and they went out and along the drive at a fairly rapid pace. Insensibly, at the swift movement of his limbs his grief abated.

She wished to give his woe time to expend itself, and, when they had fully traversed a back road which wound along the outskirts of the town, she looked at him covertly. Yes, he had stopped weeping.

" A big boy like you! " she said at length, now looking straight in front of her. " I'm surprised at you! " Deliberately she re-opened the subject.

" I was lonely, mother," he explained. " I began to cry, and I didn't know why, and I couldn't stop. Then the boys told me I was homesick. You'll take me away, sure, won't you? "

Apparently he saw not the slightest difficulty to prevent her removing him and plunging back into the impasse from which she had so recently withdrawn.

" Do you like the other boys? " she demanded abruptly.

" Yes—they're all right," he admitted. " One of them has fits.

He falls down and froths. Then the Spaniards have a funny smell, and some have got yellow boots with pointed toes. They play handball."

" Do you play too? "

" I've played at marbles. I didn't want to, but Brother John Jacob asked me to."

" Brother John Jacob! " she echoed; Joe's friend—and the phrase rose before her mind: " The Brothers mingle with the boys and engage freely in their sports and recreations." They had tried even to coax him from his grief by that childish game.

She glanced at him sharply.

" But the other boys? " she persisted. " Have you made no nice friends? "

" Yes." He considered gloomily. " There's a big boy called Ramford. He's fine. He can mimic. He can do anything. He wants me to be his pet."

" His pet? " she exclaimed. " What do you mean? "

" It's nothing, really," he explained. " You just say you're his pet, and that's all. All the big boys have pets. It's a custom. If you're a boy's pet he might give you some of his cake for tea."

" Does Brother William know about that? "

" Of course—he knows everything."

She gazed at him in silence.

"Think of it, too," he protested further; " we've got to go to church every morning. Isn't it sickening? And the lessons we get! They teach you here, all right."

Her brow cleared slowly. She comprehended something of the novelty of her son's situation.

" Well! " she exclaimed, drawing a long breath. " We'll have a real good talk about it all."

" That's right, mother," he agreed mournfully; " then you must take me away."

She looked round determinedly. She wanted now to sit down and thrash out the matter thoroughly. Upon her left she discerned the pleasant enclosure of the town cemetery, conveniently dotted with seats, and, diverting her course, she led him through the wrought-iron gateway. The ironic humour of the situation was apparent to neither, as, enwrapped by their own thoughts, they sat down beside a yew-tree that shaded a large tombstone.

" It's like this, Peter," she began; " you see——"

But it was difficult to make him see; her position was to him altogether remote; and already he had accepted her as his deliverer. How could he realise that in the space of one more week the symptoms of his nostalgia would vanish? Yes, it was difficult, difficult to impose her will upon this sensitive and diffident creature who was hers. But she forced herself to do it; she talked to him seductively, then firmly. His tears flowed again and his sobs rent the grisly air in that so suitable graveyard. The tombstones breathed a sympathetic melancholy; the yew swung overhead softly, with a dark approval. Her own eye was humid, yet, in spite of that weakness, an undercurrent of impatience flowed through her. It was too ridiculous, such a fuss he was making; a terrific disturbance out of nothing, ignoring her immense devotion to him—and he had lost his handkerchief!

" It's no use, dear," she said, with finality, as she offered her own handkerchief. " You must make up your mind to it."

He dried his eyes, and stared for a long time in front of him.

" Well—if you say it, I suppose I must."

" That's right," she declared triumphantly. " You're a brave boy."

He composed himself further; he seemed to be thinking of something.

" Some of the boys have tuck-boxes—bottles of sauce and things," he remarked at length; " and I haven't."

" Would you like one? " she queried quickly, seizing the change of topic willingly.

With an under-lip still drooping, he nodded his head once.

" Come along, then! " she exclaimed with gaiety. " We'll go down to the shops."

He rose and followed her out of the cemetery. Another victory lay to her credit, and not, mark you, at the cost of spoiling him!

They reached the town, and a watery cheerfulness infused him as she purchased for him a jar of pickles, a bottle of tomato ketchup —the boys spread this on their bread at teatime, he informed her— some potted shrimp paste, a tin of biscuits, and a pound of aniseed balls. He became cheerful.

They walked hand in hand by the river, and afterwards had tea in a small tea-shop where she let him sate himself with pastries. At intervals of his gluttony he would stop and stare at her uncertainly.

" Now, Peter! " she would break in warningly. " Remember! "

As she delivered him at the gates of the college, which from motives of delicacy she did not again enter, she repeated that injunction firmly.

" You're to work hard and get on," she adjured him finally, " then you'll be a famous man with lots of money."

He nodded his head submissively, and, standing at the gate—a small, indescribably pathetic figure—he waved his hand to her dutifully as she withdrew.

It was over. She went to the station with a baffling feeling of weakness, but she had won; yes, she had won.

VI

FOR three months she had been working, and the result was a comfortable feeling that she had established herself. Upon some weeks, to be sure, her commission was lamentably small, but on others she would earn as much as three pounds; in addition, by economy and ingenuity, she contrived to save always a certain small sum from the expenses allowed her by the firm. Admitting always a certain amount of good fortune, there were moments when she felt her success to be amazing; and Peter was now progressing well at school, that initial misery long forgotten, his official weekly letters monuments of composition in elaborate violet-inked penmanship. He had advanced to the middle of his class—this, indeed, she had expected—but there was talk actually of his admission to the band. How her heart leapt to these ingenuous bulletins.

In her physical being she felt strong, pervaded by a sense of energy and health, intensified by the quick-changing movements of her days. She had little leisure for brooding, but, even so, she admitted to herself that the pain of her husband's death was slowly easing, although at times a wretched feeling of her solitary position in the house would invade her, and she would be swept by the sudden desire for his companionship. At the tragic moment of his death she had felt that her life was finished, terminated by this loss; and now he had already begun to assume the condition of a memory, idealised —his faults forgotten, his virtues magnified—and dimly seen through this very afterglow which now surrounded him. With inflexible resolution she refused to permit herself to brood upon the manner of his death. That at first had driven her frantic, the dim consciousness of how the awful thing had worked to its tragic end. But she would not think of it. Nor would she think of Anna. Anna she obliterated from her mind, finally, irrevocably. Yet sometimes she would sit quite still, trying to remember intimately Frank's face— shutting her eyes and striving to see it as though it were now before her—yet, with a melancholy realisation, she discovered that this was now beyond her power. She saw his face, but not as a real and actual face; it was far away, luminous, intangible. Only one detail stood out with vivid intensity: his hands, limp and waxen, as they had been folded across his breast within the coffin. She saw these hands many times, until they became to her almost symbolic of his memory.

Altogether she was not unhappy, and her confidence was amazing. Miss Hocking, moreover, in her own peculiar fashion, had become increasingly attentive, and often Lucy would go up the hill and sit with her in the evenings, listen to her playing, even play a little herself upon the richly sounding German piano, whose deep tone so out-matched the tinkle of her own cottage instrument.

One thought only sobered the warmth of her satisfaction. She had not yet received the promised visit from Joe, and this fact caused her a certain indefinable suspense. The account for the funeral had been posted—quite naturally, she realised—to her, and it was for the large sum of forty pounds; further, she had the florist's bill, which was not large, but which Joe had insisted that he himself would pay. From a sense of order, apart from honesty—she had always paid " ready money "—the presence of these accounts hanging over her head irked Lucy. And there was, moreover, with the new term approaching rapidly, the matter of Peter's fees. Everything was all right, of course! Although she felt him dilatory, she had no lack of trust in Joe. Had she doubted him, her confidence must assuredly have been restored by the arrival of a present—curious, perhaps, but none the less a rich and generous gift.

One evening, at the mysterious hour of dusk, three wooden boxes of varying shapes had arrived upon a lorry. To the carrier she immediately disclaimed all knowledge of his freight, but with a jerk of his head he had indicated that they came from Levenford; he had brought them over at the request of Joe Moore—Big Joe of the Shamrock Tavern and the Green Football Club. Why, everybody knew Big Joe—he himself often carried from the station to the Tavern crates which Mr. Moore ordered from the wholesale markets in Glasgow.

When the man had gone, she gazed with startled eyes at the rough cases which defiled the orderly symmetry of her tiny hall. Then, using the poker, which bent under her vigorous but unskilful blows, she at length succeeded in opening them. Straw and papers littered the spotless linoleum; then she saw what the boxes contained. The first held a Belfast ham, large and brown as the haunch of a horse; the second contained one dozen dark bottles labelled Royal Ruby Port Wine; the third was filled to bursting with bananas—not merely a bunch, but a tree; a miniature colony of Canary bananas, yellow and aromatic with their escaping ripeness. What on earth could she do with all these bananas? Some had looked quite rotten at their ends.

The sight of this strange assortment of food and drink plucked her bewildered eyes, made her gasp stupidly; then the good intention, the liberality which must lie behind the gift, slowly dawned upon her.

Certainly the bananas became a difficulty. Immediately she sent off some of the sound fruit to Peter, but as the days went on her efforts to cope with the rapid progress of the rotting fruit became frantic. It was like a desperate race: the quicker she ate, the quicker the fruit decayed; the more she ate, the more bananas sprouted from that central unconquerable stem. Lucy's economical heart was chilled, but the struggle was hopeless. Eventually she was affected by a most inconvenient disorder, and the climax was achieved when Miss Hocking mildly but firmly declined a third bunch of the inexhaustible fruit.

The ham, too, became a source of positive exasperation. She began by having it frequently: for breakfast; often for tea: but soon the repetition of the dish blunted her fondness for it. She sickened of it, like a sailor fed with briny pork upon a scrofulous ship. The smell of frying ham was never out of the house; it began to hang about the curtains like a pollution; it haunted her; she was obliged to get up in the night to drink water from the saltness that lay continually in her mouth. That ham became a skeleton in the cupboard of her kitchen.

As for the port, it remained untouched, standing in one long row —useless, intimidating, rather sinister!

She admitted to herself that the present was not an unqualified success. Nevertheless, there was no doubting of the liberality of Joe's bounty.

Thus, she waited hopefully, and towards the end of November she received a postcard—his inevitable medium of communication—saying that he was coming, that he would arrive for tea upon the following day. Gratified, she made her plans. She had an idea of the realism of Joe's appetite and of what might be his conception of the meal he termed " tea." She had, moreover, a strong incentive towards exerting herself to please him. And so she hurried home early, and hastened pleasurably with her arrangements, covering the table with her best stiffly laundered cloth, setting it elegantly, and cooking an appetising meal, savouring the novelty and zest of her own labours.

At last, everything was ready. She trimmed the fire in the sitting-room, and sat down to wait. The heart of the fire was clear and white and strong, and the light of the flames shone warmly upon her face. Outside was the darkness and a rising wind amongst the trees.

Suddenly, into her reverie came a long and confident peal upon the bell. At once she rose, went into the hall, opened the door.

" Well! Well! Well! " cried Joe from the doorstep. " Here we are as large as life! "

He had on a thick reefer coat; his hat sat well back upon his head; his whole presence exuded a full and genial affability.

" I wondered if you'd get me card in time. I just took the notion to look over all of a sudden. Came over me, like! "

He shook hands, engulfing her fingers in his large doughy fist. Then, struggling a little with the effort, he let himself be shelled out of his coat; hung up his hat on the peg, with a clop; rubbed his hands; then advanced towards the open door of the sitting-room.

"Come away in, Lucy!" he exclaimed, almost hospitably. "Come away in!"

She followed him in.

"Aha!" he cried out at once. "Aha! That's a fine smell you've got here. 'Tis enough to draw water out of a dead man's teeth on a cold night like this." And he sat down before the fire, and grinned at her.

"Well," she answered, with a twist of her lips, "it's your tea. I've just been cooking."

"You don't say!" he cried, widening his eyes and sniffing appreciatively, with expanded nostrils. "Sure, if I'd known this was waiting on me I'd ha' been over to see you long ago."

Then all at once the creases died out of his face, which instantly became heavy, serious. He shook his cropped head, and said gravely: "No, no, my dear. I was only wanting to give you time to settle down a bit, and get over things. True it's taken me hard enough to get over the loss of me poor dead brother meself."

He shook his head, pulled quickly at his broad nostrils, then flicked the back of his hand across the end of his nose. It was a characteristic gesture with which he often terminated a sentence, as though its performance erased an emotion from his mind, released him from that feeling of joy or sorrow into which his own words had momentarily plunged him.

He smiled again. "You're getting over it, though, aren't you, Lucy?"

"Yes, I suppose I am."

"That's right. Ah! But don't I know it's hard? Haven't I been in the same boat meself? Don't I know what it is to lose the partner? Ah! when my Katie was tooken I was all smashed to pieces. Aha, we're only human, aren't we now? Is the tea ready, did you say?"

"Yes," she replied, "and I can give you a choice. I didn't quite know your taste, but I've got bacon and egg, or would you care for fried chops?—whichever you like. They're ready and in the oven."

"Bacon and egg, or chops," he repeated reflectively, thrusting out his thick jowl and rubbing his palm over it with a crisp bristling sound; he swivelled his round head towards the table. "Bacon and egg, and chops. They sound good, and, bedam! they smell good!" He smacked his lips like the crack of a whip, and concluded slowly: "How about the whole caboozle, then, seeing we can't make up our minds—you and me?"

"Why, certainly," she agreed. In her desire to please him she felt delighted with his generous choice, and went off immediately to serve the meal.

When she returned, with an ashet of bacon, chops, and eggs, still spluttering, he was standing with his back to the fire, his tails elevated, warming himself intimately.

" Come along, now! " she said, putting the ashet upon the table. " Sit in while it's hot."

" Be the Holy, Lucy! " he replied, coming over at once. " That looks good to me. There's a shine on that fat would raise a hunger on a corpse, bedam! I'll sit in right enough. Just let me get at it. I'll skin the plate."

He lowered himself into his chair, helped himself liberally by tilting the ashet towards his plate, buttered some toast, and began to eat. After a few mouthfuls, he moved restlessly, pulled back his sleeves, dug at his armpits, then glanced up.

" Do you know now," he exclaimed, " I'm a plain sort of a man— so damned used to eating my grub without a coat that I an't be easy with one. Would I be annoying you if I sat down comfortable, like I do at me own place? "

" No—oh, no," she returned, making an effort to conceal the shade of hesitation in her tone. " I don't mind." But the unusual request had almost startled her. He nodded gratefully; rose; got out of his jacket; sat down again in his shirt-sleeves; and re-applied himself to the food with undiluted gusto. Lucy, at the other end of the table, watched him silently. It gave her a fantastic feeling to see this fat man in his shirt-sleeves eating at her table, after her weeks of solitude; never had she observed such zest, such abandon, such obvious enjoyment of each mouthful! When he pulled a wedge of meat off a fork, or sucked a slab of egg from the flat of his knife, or chewed with all the muscles of his face working, he did so with such manifest relish that he invested the process of eating with a sublime importance. As he ate, the goodness of the food seemed to permeate his system, and glisten out of his face with a rich and mellow glow. Nor did he talk much, but between bites would stand his knife and fork upon the table, looking straight in front of him, masticating the fullest savour from the food.

At last, however, he was finished. He rattled his knife and fork carelessly on to the plate, swallowed the final drops of his fourth cup of tea, wiped the last of the gravy off the ashet with a soft piece of white bread, thrust this gently into his mouth, sucked his fingers, lay back, sighed, and said simply: " That's the finest tightener I've had in a month of Sundays, Lucy. You could cook me sister Polly into an old cocked hat. We ought to have you over at the Tavern."

His mellow eye bathed her with a glow of invitation, but she murmured definitely: " We've been over all that before, Joe."

" To be sure, to be sure. It's the independence you're after," he agreed amiably, picking his teeth with his thumb-nail; he withdrew his thumb, sucked crisply with his tongue, rose up, and went over to the armchair by the fire. " You can have a shot at it, to be sure."

He wore the broad look of the man of the world, who, indulging her in this whim against his better judgment, would ultimately see his judgment vindicated.

As he sank back he pulled out his pipe, and changed the subject affably: " Well, a smoke and a little drop of the crater would just about put me right for Dublin."

Her face fell. Despite her careful preparations, she had forgotten something.

" I don't believe I've a drop of whisky in the house," she said confusedly. Then her look cleared. " What am I thinking about? I'm forgetting your port."

But he stopped her movement towards the cupboard with a look. " No," he protested, " not for me. That's a lady's drink, that is." He shook his head profoundly. " The hard stuff is the only thing that suits me stomach."

She paused, feeling from his manner that she was deficient in hospitality. Then at last, somewhat awkwardly, she declared: " There's some brandy in the house that was left—that I got for Frank at one time. Would you like some of that? "

" Indeed, an' I would," he averred, with a wave of his pipe.

She went to the medicine cupboard in her bedroom, and came back immediately with a long green bottle which had a blue label and was half full of spirit. As he took it from her his upper lip crinkled compassionately.

" Poor fella! So this is his brandy," said he sadly. " And Three Stars, bedam! It's the best." He paused, flicked his nose. " Well, there's no use to waste it. Frank'll never drink it now, poor fella. Have you a tumbler? As big as you like."

When he was established with his glass of brandy and water, he indicated the chair beside his and said out of that corner of his mouth not occupied by his pipe: " Now, my dear, how is the world rollin' for you? "

" Well, I've made a start," she answered at once, as she sat down.

" A start, indeed! " he replied, eyeing her humorously. " And how long will the start continue? "

" As long as I want it to, I hope."

He broke into a rolling laugh, and slapped his leg. " You'll give me a stitch, Lucy. The idea of a little thing like you going about at that kind of work! 'Tis enough to make a cat laugh."

She did not know how to take his genial ridicule, and, to cover the indignation which she felt must show in her face, she bent forward to her wickerwork basket and picked up the grey scarf she was knitting for Peter. As she threaded the wool between her smooth fingers and began slowly to knit, she said: " It seems rather a joke to you."

" Ah! You should put the thought of that business outa your head," he returned indulgently. " Can you not let Big Joe look after you? "

As he spoke, she was confronted by the vision of the unpaid bills lying in the pigeon-hole of her desk, and she wished ardently that his lavish expressions of generosity would assume a more concrete form.

" Peter's getting on excellently," she ventured, with a suggestive change of subject.

" Good! " said he. " Good for the young fella."

She felt that now surely he would broach the topic of the liability he had undertaken, but, after he had poured himself out another glass of brandy, he cocked an eye towards her wool and remarked slyly, quite irrelevantly: " Will you do me a pair of them some day? "

His archness fell awkwardly across her mood, but she made herself smile over her flashing needles.

" Of course I will. I'll knit you half a dozen pairs."

" Will you now? That's great." He was pleased.

" I'm not much of a walker, to be sure, so I don't wear 'em out that way, but it's the sweat off me feet that rots holes in 'em."

She coloured at the odious vulgarity of his tone; his manner—so different from the reserve of her husband or from Edward's actual diffidence—gave her a curious constraint. Yet she tried to excuse his bluntness upon the grounds of downright honesty.

" This is a scarf I'm knitting for Peter," she said.

But the brandy was percolating his system agreeably; he gave no heed to her remark.

" I'm a man that's got on, you know, Lucy," he declared, with a fat laugh. " I'm a plain man, but I've done pretty well for meself. No, I'll not deny that I've made money, and I've got the position. When I walk down the street the folks all say, ' There goes Big Joe Moore.' Big Joe, begod! that's what they call me! "

He puffed out his chest, and let his paunch fall down between his legs; he had now finished the brandy.

" Do you not find the room too warm? " she exclaimed uneasily, moving her chair back from the fire.

" But I tell you I'm a lonely man," he went on; " yes, it's the lonely, lonely man I am, and I'm not above telling you it comes hard on a big lump of a man like me."

His upper lip worked into a grimace of self-pity. He shook his bullet head on the thick socket of his neck, and scraped his big boots restlessly along the fender in his urge to express himself.

" Sure, you're a fine little woman, Lucy," he went on, giving her a slow covert stare. " My poor brother had an eye in his head when he picked you. I wish I'd been as lucky as Frank, but my Katie, rest her soul, fell away to a bag o' bones before she went to God. Well, Frank's gone and my Katie's gone, so here we are! You and me, the two of us."

She threw him a strained look. Again the sight of him sitting in his shirt-sleeves in the chair which had been her husband's, sitting so intimately with her, gave her suddenly a strange bewildered feeling, which passed like a shiver along her spine and plucked at the roots of her hair. A curious oppression from his presence touched her like a wet finger drawn across her brow. Under his eye she dropped two stitches, fumbled clumsily in picking them up. She saw that her reflections were forcing her into a ridiculous position with a man who was by marriage her brother. And he, indeed, must have perceived her confusion, for he went on with a gross complacency, his upper lip spreading out slowly in a smile.

" I'm not an eddicated man, mind you. I'm plain Joe Moore the publican. Maybe I've a clumsy tongue in me head, but there's no humbug about me, and I'm downright fond on ye, Lucy; so help me God I am. I took a notion on ye the first time I seen you and I'm going to keep me eye on you."

" Well," she began hurriedly, " I'm grateful to you, I'm sure."

" Ah! Time enough for that," he exclaimed broadly. " Don't you never feel the need of a man about the house now? I could come over here often to see you."

The drift of his remarks still eluded her; she felt an acute discomfort under his leer, but its full significance was too incredible to be realised immediately. She maintained a stiff silence, which, in the grip of his mood, he took to be propitious. Although he had intended to be cautious, he was now full of meat and drink, and swayed by obtuse desire. He felt her dependence upon him; the sight of her trim adjacent figure, tinted warmly by the firelight and by his own desirous eye, urged him on. She was breathing a little quickly; her breasts rose and fell with a soft insistence. His mouth felt dry as he leaned forward and laid his hand upon her knee.

" We're only human, aren't we now, Lucy? " he said thickly. " You and me could be good to each other."

The movement of his hand more than his words struck her with a sudden horror. Her skin drew together, and she felt an answering constriction of her throat. The knitting fell to the floor.

" What do you mean? " she cried. She thrust her hand against his, but as she did so he seized it. Wrenching her wrist free, she stood up, her lips pallid as her face. Her own breathing seemed to smother her.

" What are you running away for? " he coaxed her, getting to his feet unsteadily.

" Don't! " she jerked out fiercely.

His eyes peered at her from beneath his thick overhanging eyebrows like the eyes of a warm, living animal. She was aware dimly, as he came towards her, that they were alone in the house, and, as in a nightmare, of what he desired of her.

" Don't get excited," said he thickly, trying to make his features smile ingratiatingly; but the smile became fixed—a grimace—as he came towards her.

" I'd look after ye, me dear."

She backed until she struck against the table, and her hand, thrust out to save herself, knocked over his empty tumbler. In a cold fury she seized it, confronting him in silence.

" What's your worry? " he said again.

He was close to her now. She perceived a twitching in his cheek, faint beads of perspiration on his brow. Her legs felt weak under her, and the room moved round. She was not afraid, but sick with anger and distrust.

" What do you mean? " she cried again, from between her teeth.

He paused. " Ah! Be easy," he muttered. " I've always been fond on ye. You and me could hit it off fine and not a soul a bit the wiser——" and he hesitated.

She looked at him frigidly; then a sudden overpowering rage swept her. It was not enough for her that he hesitated. With all her force she swung her arm and splintered the tumbler against his grinning teeth. A fierce and joyous thrill ran up her arm at the impact of the blow.

Stupefied and sobered, he raised a clumsy hand to his gashed mouth. The tinkling echoes of the shattered glass filled the room. Her own hand began to bleed, though she felt no pain. Then animation returned to her rigid body, and, with a start, she turned swiftly, walked determinedly out of the room, and in a moment had thrust open the front door. She stood upon the threshold of the lighted hall, trembling in the cool air, her eyes glistening, filled by a bitter blazing rage. She waited for what seemed to her a long time while the gas-jet flickered above her bared head; then she heard his slow step in the hall, heard him put on his coat and hat; and he came out, still moving slowly. He looked at her. A handkerchief held to his mouth almost concealed his features, but an uncouth, miserable mortification welled out of his small eyes.

" What did ye want to do that for? " he mumbled thickly, from behind the folds of the handkerchief. " Ye could ha' said what was to be said without doing that."

Now she was conscious of no alarm, but suddenly she hated his stupid loutish face.

" Have you finished? " she demanded, with bitter coldness.

" I never meant nothing," he muttered. He was almost blubbering.

She was silent, staring at him. Then she said, with icy distinctness: " Because I've finished with you."

For a moment he looked at her; then his eyes filled; and, without a word, he turned and went heavily down the path.

When he had passed, she stepped into the hall, slammed the door shut, bolted it, and for a moment leaned weakly against it. Now she felt utterly weak. No relief filled her, but instead a dreadful nausea; she felt physically sick. The unexpectedness, the shock, the outrage of it, all filled her with a sickening resentment. She was incapable even of tears. In the smoke-filled room she threw up the window dully, and let the night air rush in around her motionless figure. Her large dark eyes looked towards the darkness of the night; then she turned, and those eyes—sombre, darker now from the absorption of that outer darkness—fell upon the table, still covered by the remains of her pitiful preparations for him. The very sight of them shamed her. She had set herself out so eagerly to please him. Her lip curled as she remembered how he had gorged himself. Frank's brother! Frank had been right! Life seemed to her suddenly bereft of virtue.

Shrinking back into herself, for a long time she stared at the dying fire, then she shivered, closed the window, and went to bed. But it was not to sleep.

As she at last dozed off, all at once she came to herself, and sat up, startled. Suddenly she had realised the almost vital consequences of this irreparable breach with Joe.

VII

Upon the next day she paid every bill she owed—those bills which Joe had accepted as his liability; which, in fact, he had so largely incurred. Morally she had not felt herself responsible for these accounts or they would have long ago been settled, but now, despising her original acquiescence, she seized these obligations proudly, and with a bitter alacrity discharged them utterly. As a result, she was left with a capital of under forty pounds, but she was in no mood to dwell upon either the smallness or the magnitude of this sum. The sordid considerations of money were as nothing in the balance of her outraged pride.

In some measure, the very payment of the bills relieved her wounded feelings; she felt vindicated; but still a frightful rankling remained. She would pause sometimes in the midst of her work, suddenly stricken by the remembrance of that scene. Often at nights she turned restlessly in bed, swept by a feverish recollection. After such a night, she made up her mind to inform Edward of the circumstances of Joe's conduct. Sitting down with compressed lips and a tumultuous indignation, she wrote swiftly a letter of the bitterest resentment. But she tore up that letter—slowly—and threw the fragments into the flames. No, she would not so demean herself. Silence she adjudged the most cutting weapon!

Nevertheless, despite her bold front, she had her moments when she felt sick at heart. Life dragged during the ensuing week, and upon the following Saturday, returning home upon the 12.30 train, she felt tired and depressed. Then, as she stepped on to the platform at Ardfillan, she found Miss Hocking, standing statuesque in her tailor-made, quite unruffled by the bustle of the station. The sudden unexpected sight of someone awaiting her made Lucy's face light up in swift animation, and with open pleasure she exclaimed: " Surely you didn't come to meet me? "

Miss Hocking nodded her head gravely, and in a tone equally impressive replied: " Come! "; then, heightening her air of mystery, she added: " With me."

Lucy laughed outright—the first time she had laughed for days.

" Are you going to do away with me? " she enquired, implying that Miss Hocking's motive was that of abduction under violence.

" Perhaps! " answered the other seriously. She could be very serious in the presence of merriment; her own laughter came unexpectedly and often when the situation demanded the utmost gravity.

" What, though? " persisted Lucy pleasantly.

How nice, she thought, to be met in such a fashion by this well-turned-out and friendly woman!

" Allen's! " declared the other, with a laconic sententiousness.

They went, therefore—and Miss Hocking led the way with conscious dignity—to Allen's, which was a restaurant; but no ordinary restaurant. Allen's was fashionable, even famous. Differing greatly from the modest tea-room where Lucy often took her luncheon in Ardfillan, Allen's represented the pinnacle of contemporary elegance in pastrycooks. Allens had palms, seductive carpets, waitresses with streamers, distinguished patronage, and charges which were not moderate. The age of orchestras had not yet arrived, or Allen's would undoubtedly have exploited Mendelssohn!

Miss Hocking knew her way about in such establishments, and, compelled almost by the suction of her majestic weight, Lucy was drawn to a charming table for two, near the window and beneath the stellate fronds of a stupendous palm.

Seated, Miss Hocking drew off her gloves and looked round regally. Instantly a waitress appeared—to Lucy's attentive eye how suavely the streamers floated—and, without once appearing to observe the waitress, Pinkie declared they would have this and they would have that. Her little finger, curving elegantly, charted a charming course through the mysterious latitudes of the French menu. Yes, it was nice, again thought Lucy, to be treated like this—most awfully nice for a little woman who had been lately so rudely used by fate. She had, indeed, unexpectedly a little rushing mood of intimate self-sympathy. Not often, recently, had she yielded like this; but still she could yield. Take her the right way and she was soft, charming; the wrong way and she was hard and uncompromising as a shut oyster.

Now, after a few spoonfuls of a creamy soup, reminiscent of chicken but surely more ambrosial, she looked up and murmured: " This is very pleasant." She smiled appreciatively—her breakfast had been hasty that morning. " But I don't understand why."

" A little treat for us both," answered the other offhandedly enough to expose her satisfaction. " I often go out like this. Dick takes charge of Fairy and out I go."

Lucy crumbled her roll. Dick—curious abbreviation—was Mrs. Dickens, Miss Hocking's daily woman; Fairy, of course, the fat fox-terrier!

" Well, it's kind of you to invite me," said she slowly.

" Nonsense! Beautiful nonsense, my dear! "

After the soup came asparagus. Mingling their flavour with the melted butter, the limp green buds dissolved upon the tongue, surrendering the succulence of spring.

" This toast is not crisp, waitress! " said Miss Hocking haughtily. " It bends weakly."

Lucy started. A tiny spot of butter rolled down her chin. She had been enjoying herself excellently, and now she wondered if a sudden wrangling might spoil the harmony of the moment. Frank had wrangled with waitresses in his day in lesser establishments than this. But this waitress was obsequious, utterly obsequious.

" I'll get some fresh at once, madam." And in a moment fresh toast was apologetically brought.

" One must keep them up to it," said Miss Hocking with a little laugh, when the girl had gone. " They like you if you scold them. *The Taming of the Shrew* ! Wasn't it amusing? "

" I wouldn't have dared," thought Lucy, but she answered: " This asparagus is delicious." Very correctly was she eating it—with her fingers, delicately.

" It's a little thin," said the other, in a manner of benevolent patronage. " At home we grew it much thicker. Oh, yes, I assure you! The vegetable marrows were enormous! " No boast this—merely a casual comment.

Their plates were removed deftly, and an ethereal meringue—supreme novelty—was served.

"Take more," urged Miss Hocking dreamily; "you like sweet things. Sweet as honeysuckle. I am the bee."

Yes, Lucy admitted her affection for sweet things, and this—this surpassed all expectation. Dreamy, it was, like Miss Hocking's change of mood, and evanescent, fleeting as froth—new milk chilled, sweetened by the subtle breath of cowslips, whisked incredibly into solid form. Miraculous! Or, as Edward might have said: "Delicious!" Its last spoonful evoked faintly a sigh of rapture that could not be repeated.

"Good gracious!" exclaimed Miss Hocking in a too-casual tone, looking at her fine scrolled watch. " We'll be late if you don't hurry. ' Oh, dear! oh, dear!' said the White Rabbit, ' late again!'"

"Late!" echoed Lucy, her eyes widening a little as she put down her empty coffee-cup; but her companion was paying the bill and leaving, very generously, a shilling for the streamers.

Out in the street, a fine drizzle had begun to fall from an overcast sky.

"What a pity!" said Lucy. " We might have taken a walk."

To go home seemed rather a drab finish to such a banquet; but the shadow of a smile flitted across Miss Hocking's mobile features.

"Just the right kind of day for a concert," she asserted, with an air of having arranged the weather and the universe, "and it so happens there is the recital at the Victoria Hall. Lehmann!" The last word was vibrant!

Lucy said nothing. She understood the inference, but she had exhausted her superlatives. She knew all about this concert, which was in a sense the pick of the season's subscription concerts at the Victoria Hall—an afternoon recital by Lehmann. She had seen the posters, had felt the instinctive desire to go to that concert. Only a sense of her position and of her bereavement had debarred that desire from her conscious mind; and now Miss Hocking had arranged everything and sanctioned everything by taking her! They were, in fact, by virtue of the two stiff yellow tickets in Miss Hocking' gloved hand, being escorted to the best seats in the front row of the auditorium. From around them rose the subdued rustle of the polite and well-informed audience, a sound which fell gratefully upon the ears of a woman who had lunched at Allen's and who had her natural aspiration towards refined society.

"His last performance, I understand!" proclaimed Miss Hocking most audibly, by way of intensifying the enjoyment. Lehmann, at this epoch, had already inaugurated those farewell recitals which he was to pursue dramatically during the next thirty years.

"Indeed," murmured Lucy, much impressed. Then she joined in the polite applause as the pianist came on to the platform and bowed stiffly over a short white hand, which clasped the lower buttons of his imperial frock coat. He was a big, thick-set man, with a flat, pale face, darkly haloed by the lank locks of his hair; and the movements of his body were abrupt, almost staccato. He parted his tails with a jerk, and with military precision lowered himself upon the piano stool. Then, amidst a further subdued murmur of applause, he gazed slowly around; suddenly threw back his head; conjured his inspiration from the hanging chandelier; and began to play.

It was Chopin, and, as his powerful fingers rippled with incredible delicacy through the Polonaise in A Minor, Lucy drew in her breath. Around her the air quivered with the throbbing ecstasy of invisible strings. She sat entranced through the first part of the programme.

" A *tour de force*," said Miss Hocking calmly, at the interval, standing up and looking about her; " quite a *tour de force*."

Lucy sighed, withdrawing herself, returning to reality; a tiny shiver traversed her; her eyes were still fervent.

" It was wonderful," she said. " I don't understand it as you do, but it's—it's overwhelming."

" Technique—technique," murmured the other, ogling the bowing figure on the platform with her lorgnette. " They say he practises six hours a day. Touch—touch! " She patted her fingers together, joining her approbation to that of the audience, who, relaxed from poses of stern virtuosity, eyes removed from straining towards the infinite, heads no longer sunk between palms in abysmal contemplation, applauded resolutely.

" Bravo! Bravissimo! " cried a few bolder devotees.

Lehmann had shown the audience; and now, delicately, the audience returned the shuttlecock, exhibiting their taste, their nous, their discrimination of his genius. A cultured town was Ardfillan. Cosmopolitan, almost, in its affection for the arts!

But Lucy's feeling was instinctive, artless, and sincere. When the second part of the performance began, she closed her eyes, occluding everything but the swelling waves of sound which now encompassed her. She became detached, alone. She was in a cave, a vaulted cavern, which sang with the melodious insistency of a vast sea-shell, still humming with the spent echoes of rushing wind and rolling water. Through these echoes came a note more vital, striving to penetrate the cavern from without, retreating at times but returning more loudly, clamouring with a quickening urgency. And then she saw more clearly; she was on a rock lapped in dim light and ringed by water of a green translucency. Her figure was permanent, ageless; within her something reached yearningly towards that outer force that came towards her appealingly in a swell of sound. It grew louder, then louder, at last broke through the narrow rift, and came towards her visibly—like crested water. It rushed upon her in three distinct waves. She saw the first advance and gird the rocks with slavering tongues; the second, louder, larger, broke in foam across her feet; the third, last wave came eagerly, combing the grotto with a surge of surf, and when at last it ebbed, the rock was barren of her figure. The green water quietened, and beneath its opalescent shimmer the swift darting of phosphorescent fishes quivered like flashing lights. Then these died slowly, quenched by a universal silence.

She opened her eyes with a start, almost of alarm. The recital was over.

" I thought you were sleeping," said Miss Hocking with a little giggle. " I believe I heard you snore."

" Oh, no! " protested Lucy, with a liquid eye. " I loved it, really I loved it. It was like—I don't know—something I wanted to grasp, but couldn't."

" He's such a fine upstanding man," returned the other, as they came out of the hall. " But I couldn't "—she giggled again and moistened her lips—" I couldn't think to kiss him."

They went up the road in silence. It was dry now. Already some early stars pricked points of light within the remote and ragged gaps of sky.

" I don't know how to thank you," said Lucy at length, rather awkwardly. " This afternoon has meant so much to me."

" Good gracious, that's nothing! " returned Miss Hocking and she took Lucy's arm and pressed it playfully. " I'm hoping we shall see a great deal of each other now. In fact," she paused dramatically —" I met you to-day especially, because, you see—well, I wanted to speak to you."

" Yes? "

" You see," resumed Miss Hocking again, " we're just two nuts rattling about in different shells."

Puzzled by the picturesque but rather pointless metaphor, Lucy looked up at her companion perplexedly.

" Oh, you poor thing! Don't look like that! " returned Pinkie immediately. " You look as though you were thinking preposterously sad things—the child lost in the forest—Doré's picture. I shall weep, also! "

Lucy smiled, and said: " I was just wondering what you meant."

" I mean this, my dear—really, I've thought of it before. We're both alone. Only some laths and plaster between us, and there shouldn't be. I am very attached to you. Why don't you come up? Share my flat with me? "

Lucy looked down quickly; there was a pause.

" Oh, I don't know," she answered slowly. " I couldn't think to give up my home."

" But, my dear," returned Miss Hocking, with a protective air,

" you don't need it. You're out all day; your little Highlander is at school. He'll come to us at the holidays. Yes, we'll give him a lovely time. Besides, forgive me, but surely "—with extreme tact she added, " less expense might——"

" It's kind—very kind of you to offer, but really—I couldn't think of it."

" Nonsense! I'd love to have you."

When a desire obtruded itself upon Miss Hocking's mind, she pursued it gaily, with the impetuous eagerness of a child chasing a butterfly.

' Come along now, do—say you will! Yes, do say you will! "

" Well, I'll—I'll think about it," said Lucy evasively.

It was unlike her to be evasive, but she was fond of Miss Hocking, and now particularly she could not think to wound her by a direct refusal.

" Besides," gushed on Miss Hocking, " Fairy wants you, too."

She advanced this quite seriously as an argument.

" He only takes to people who are really nice, I assure you, the darlingest thing! "

Again Lucy smiled at the other's enthusiasm. She had, in fact, in the light of her recent experience, dwelt lately upon her solitary position: those moments of darkness when at nights the house seemed unendurably lonely; and her responsibilities were a heavy burden for her shoulders to support.

Vaguely, she toyed with the suggestion. The motive of economy was a compelling one—but, no, she had no wish to relinquish her home; her own home, secure, filled with her own furniture, was like a rock to which she clung. And, yet again, there was the stronger motive—the craving for companionship. She liked Miss Hocking, saw her to be a lady, had experienced already the ramifications of her extreme kindness. She admitted the other's eccentricity— that peculiar dreamy, effusive, romantic coquettishness, a combination of dignity and playfulness, a manner at once open and impenetrable, which seemed both to offer and to conceal. A most curious idiosyncrasy! What lay behind it she did not know. It so essentially was Miss Hocking that she did not even question it. Yes, Lucy admitted this eccentricity; admitted it freely; but she was not repelled by it.

" We've had a most delightful time," Miss Hocking was saying. They were nearly at the point of parting, ascending the hill together. " Such a shame to separate. Only some laths—and plaster! "

" Well, I promise you I'll think about it," said Lucy definitely, with a smile. " And thank you again for your kindness."

They parted affectionately, set out to enter their respective shells.

And Lucy did think about it, though, of course, she did not decide at once. She turned the matter over in her mind with her native caution, weighing everything for and against the proposed change. Then, ten days after that initial offer—it had been frequently repeated—an incident occurred which, striking upon her mood, influenced her strongly towards a decision.

It was a visit from Polly. Yes, Polly arrived one evening—perspiring, panting slightly from the stairs, hanging with good clothes: the fur cloak, the hat with the feathers, the heavy jet beads, the half-buttoned bursting boots: yet, despite it all, slatternly as a fishwife, and nervous, too, under her enormous affability. Lucy received her frigidly. Polly had done nothing; she was not Joe; but she was, nevertheless, from the enemy's camp, and she had so patently come at Joe's suggestion " to see how the land lay " that her attempt at subtlety hung upon her ludicrously as her lamentable garments.

" The boss was wonderin' how you was gettin' on," said Polly, after much preliminary chatter. Often in the higher flights of her ponderous wit she alluded to Joe as " the boss."

" Oh," said Lucy uncompromisingly.

" Have you seen Neddy lately? " Neddy was the Reverend Edward Moore.

" No! " said Lucy, more uncompromisingly.

Polly looked relieved. How much she suspected Lucy never knew, but she suspected something; and she was so obviously an emissary bent upon conciliation, upon the salving of Joe's damaged reputation.

It was so like Joe to have sent her; impossible for him to be consistent—even in this! No! He must blubber a little, no doubt, and propitiate his conscience by sending out Polly as a peacemaker. Lucy's lips drew in. As if she could even tolerate to look at him after what had happened!

" Why don't you let the boss do a bit for you ? " Polly was saying. " He's a good sort. Look what he done for me."

She ruffled her feathers, and smoothed her fur suggestively.

" Not a penny less than twenty pound, this cost, and it's all bought and paid for by me brother."

" Yes ? " said Lucy.

" Ah! You've only got to stick in with the man to get the right side o' him. It don't do no good rubbin' him the wrong way. He's free with the money when he's in the mood. Sure, there's too much o' the poker up your back, Lucy."

" That's where I've been to blame," agreed Lucy, with a biting irony.

Polly stared at her suspiciously. " Well, I've an invite for you to come over to the Tavern, a personal invite from Joe himself, and if you're not too high and mighty you'll take it. In fact, it's my own opinion that Joe means to put his hand in his pocket for you, so it's a fool y'are if you don't come."

Lucy's lip curled.

" I prefer to be a fool," she shot out with a curling lip.

Again Polly stared at her, gathering together her coat, which had fallen widely into folds slack as her own adiposity.

" Sure, you're a fool," she said slowly, getting up. " You're that perfect you can't see what side your bread's buttered on. If you'd only watch yourself, you mighta come over and stayed with us."

" I'm sorry," bit out Lucy, on the spur of the moment. " I've other plans. I've been asked by a lady—a lady, I said—to share her house with her."

" You have, have you? " A half-malignant astonishment tempered the words.

" So you may tell your brother I don't require his generous assistance. No! " Lucy gave a short, contemptuous laugh. " I shan't require to join you above the Tavern after all! "

The irony was lost on Polly, but her red face flooded with a higher colour at that laugh.

" It's a wonder ye ever married on to our family at all," she declared, with a toss of her blousy head. " You'd think we was dirt beneath your feet! "

" I married Frank Moore," returned Lucy sharply. " He was a gentleman."

" Oh! He wasn't that different from Joe! " threw back Polly maliciously. " He was fond enough of the girls himself when he was younger. I could tell you a thing or two if you'd care to hear it."

Lucy's small nostrils dilated; her eyes sparkled with a frosty glitter.

" Get out of my house! " she said with cold distinctness. Inflamed by her rage, she was a little theatrical; but she was not conscious of being theatrical. She wanted this contemptible, vulgar-tongued woman out of her house; and so, without scruple, she instructed her to go. And, indeed, Polly went, muttering above her palpitating chins, compelled by that hard stare in Lucy's eye.

It seemed, therefore, as though fate had prearranged that she accept Miss Hocking's offer. But it was not fate which had designed it; fate had not even swung the balance in favour of acceptance; it was she, and that which was within her, which so shaped the course of her destiny. She had told Polly that she was going, and go she would; nor, on second thoughts, did she wish to draw back. Upon the day following Polly's visit she told Miss Hocking that she had agreed to fall in with her suggestion, and Miss Hocking was delighted. How delighted she was! The wave of optimism whose crest she perpetually rode swelled even higher than before. She was enthusiastic about the happiness each would derive from the change, urging Lucy to express her lightest whim upon matters of comfort or cuisine, making Fairy sit up on his fat haunches by way of demonstrating his approval. It was all very pleasant and amusing!

At first Lucy had the idea of retaining her house and of letting it furnished: it would have been a welcome additional source of income; but the agent who controlled the affairs and amenities of the villa was adamant. Both saturnine and adamant! No such thing had ever been done, or ever could be permitted to be done, in so select a locality as Ardmore Road. He indicated, however, that it would be a matter of ridiculous ease to relieve her of the remainder of her lease and find a new tenant for the empty house.

She was faced, therefore, with the necessity of selling her furniture. Storage was, from its high rental, out of the question, and Miss Hocking's single flat could not accommodate the furnishings of two. Lucy almost hesitated. It was a drastic step, and she was aware of its irrevocability. Nevertheless, the needs of the immediate future were more pressing than the remote, and Peter would be at school for another five years. Besides, she had weighed up everything before; she had decided; and she would not draw back.

Her furniture went down to a local sale-room, and was disposed of, without auction, through the agency of a dealer. She was wrung by the parting. It cost her a bitter pang to relinquish the familiar objects which time and usage had made so absolutely her own. When she had bought them so eagerly with Frank—she remembered her sanguine expectation on that day, the profound and intimate arguments with Mr. Gow upon the virtues of oak and mahogany, her own earnestness, her smiling side-glances to Frank—yes, when she had polished them through the years with the warm pride of possession, had she ever considered that she would dispose of them like this? And she received so little—a miserable sum of little more than thirty pounds!

Certain things she retained—her own wardrobe, a picture that had been her mother's, the rocking-chair from her bedroom, on the round knob of which, still faintly dented, Peter, clutching at her skirts, had cut his teeth.

Then, one night towards the beginning of February, she came home from business, and went along the front towards her house for the last time. There was no need for this journey—the house had that day been emptied—but the peculiar sentiment which sometimes swayed her was the impulse of the pilgrimage.

She let herself into the naked little hall. The house, stripped of everything, wearing an aspect void and unfamiliar, holding nothing substantial, yet peopled, it seemed to her, by images, teeming with actions past, hung with a tapestry woven from the intimacies of her life, held a strange yet hollow dignity.

Tears rushed into her eyes. Here Frank had loved her; here

Peter had been born; from here, violently, madly, had she rushed into that fog to defeat herself, to destroy her love—and Frank.

And suddenly she sobbed uncontainedly. How had it all come about? Turning, she went out into the garden: the crusted soil, sealed now against the winter, held but a few stalks, sapless stems, and the callow apple-tree all shorn, immobile, its two arms outstretched, a thin and gawky scarecrow of a tree. The pebbles upon the path, washed by the rains, polished by the frost, glistened whitely —those pebbles which Frank and she had gathered to strew upon the walk.

With a final wrench she tore herself away, locked the house, came sadly along the front, her eyes red-dimmed with weeping.

The key she left at the agent's office, and, overcome by a strange lassitude, she came up the hill, ascended the stairs to Miss Hocking's flat in Victoria Crescent, and paused before Miss Hocking's door. Then, slowly, she entered that door.

VIII

MISS HOCKING's flat was artistic. No bunched roses or beribboned forget-me-nots adorned the walls, which were, instead, papered to a reseda green, admirably adapted to display the Burne-Jones mezzotints and the Rossetti women who, with up-tilted chins and sensuously curving lips, gazed palely from their rough oak frames. In general, the furniture was good—furniture, doubtless, that had descended in the family—and it wore the stamp of genuine antiquity; Miss Hocking's bed, indeed, was a large four-poster that carried its canopy with historic dignity. But there were newer pieces—a whatnot, a canterbury, some playful little knick-knacks—which betokened a feeling for the modern decorative art.

In the drawing-room, the piano, bearing no photographs, was swathed by a fringed satin scarf, and the 'cello, leaning by the canterbury like a *roué* at a buffet, justified that scarf with an air of romantic negligence. Yet there was nothing raffish in the air, nothing Bohemian! Holman Hunt—also upon the walls—forbade that strictly, inducing something of a devotional austerity.

And there were books—quantities of inherited books, and some uninherited and uncut—lying upon the table, denoting a *penchant* for the dilettantism of the day.

Moreover, an easel stood unashamedly in its corner, and a bowl of pot-pourri upon the hearth. No bourgeois aspidistra could be seen, but instead, tendrils of wandering sailor, trailing from a bamboo stand, tastefully supplied that touch of greenery demanded by the age. Green, indeed, even to the lampshades, was the tone of the flat, and Miss Hocking herself—when she discarded her tailor-mades—affected this colour: trailing green square-yoked dresses with full sleeves, fashioned of a shot-silk fabric that rustled with seductive majesty.

Certainly the house had quality, a charming quality shared equally with its owner, a quality which Lucy found impressive but which, in some strange fashion, eluded her. She liked the house, she liked her new companion—to do otherwise was impossible—yet she could not " place " Miss Hocking, who, admitting herself to be a wanderer —outcast was the word she laughingly employed—remained in Ardfillan for some reason unexplained. She had few friends—a little changing coterie, perhaps—and no relations but a brother, seldom mentioned, who lived still in her native town in the south of England. Yes, there was something which escaped Lucy, some underlying quantity which puzzled her.

This was what she felt as she sat at the window of the drawing-room upon a Sunday some weeks after her arrival. They had just had luncheon, an excellent cold luncheon left ready by Mrs. Dickens—Lucy refused to recognise the sobriquet—and now she was in a mood of quiet introspection. Glancing out of the window, she observed the pleasant waving screen of foliaged trees, now masking, now revealing, the discreet view of the private gardens opposite; she saw a carriage roll slowly away from one of the mansions underneath; the faint throbbing note of a piano came to her through the quiet of the afternoon; the sun shone upon her and cast her shadow behind into the room. Through the uncertain state of her mind she felt the charm, the orderly peace, of those surroundings, drawing from her being a sensuous response which wavered tenuously between happiness and regret. Suddenly Miss Hocking came into the room.

" Time for our constitutional! " she exclaimed positively. " Walk and the world walks with you. Sit and you sit alone."

Lucy, whose morning had been occupied by church, and who had meant now to take her ease, looked up.

" I rather wanted to have a rest," she said mildly. " I'm tramping all week, you know."

" Time for your walk! " insisted the other, in her usual high humour. " A glorious day! Fairy is simply bursting to get out! A wind on the heath. Walt Whitman's weather. He can't miss his exercise, neither can you."

Fairy, sunk in the torpor of digestion, endeavouring to secrete himself beneath the sofa, now exposed one protesting eye.

" Well," began Lucy—she hardly cared to offend the other, whose effusive good-nature alone excused the insistence of her manner—

" I don't feel like walking much."

" Tut-tut! Not tired of living yet! " broke in Miss Hocking, with her customary raillery. " You don't know how pretty you are to-day! Mustn't die until you've worn out that new dress. It's too becoming. Upset all the lady angels! "

Lucy smiled. " All right—if you'd like me to come "; and she rose to get her hat and gloves.

" Excellent! " exclaimed Miss Hocking. " Come, Fairy! Fairy! Mustn't be a lazy dog."

She made an excited note of invitation with her tongue, and cried: " Bunnies! Bunnies! Bunnies! Come and get bunnies! " To which the animal, emerging upon its stomach, essaying twitchingly to find its legs, at length responded with a feeble growl.

They went out, Miss Hocking still talking, Fairy wandering despondently at heel.

The walk was to be short—so much had been agreed—but Pinkie marched exuberantly; before long they found themselves away from the usual Sunday promenaders, amongst the high woodland which screened the foothills above the point of Rhu.

" Might as well get down to Rhu! Come back by the sea road! " said Miss Hocking gaily. " We love a long tramp, and it's a bewitching day."

" It's rather a far way round, though."

Lucy's new shoes were stiff, the right one already hurting her heel.

" Oh, no, no! Do come along! Wonderful here "; and she marched off again, taking a path which swung into the adjacent woods.

Reluctantly, Lucy followed; she disliked being dragged about like this; yet the wood was lovely, shady and calm. The lime and beech leaves, limp from their own freshness, hung suspended in a green spray; the chestnuts, burdened already by a bristle of white spears, drooped languidly; profuse wild flowers enamelled a blue and yellow pattern upon the turf.

" We'll have a rest, you know," called out Miss Hocking encouragingly. She was still ahead, like the forager of an expedition. " Of course we shall! A lovely spot near here! "

She went on talking over her shoulder, discussing the weather, the trees, the flowers. She made little poetical declamations; she whistled back the bird-calls with a merry air; desperately she enticed Fairy to the chase of unseen rabbits; she betrayed a giddy, intoxicated love of life.

Then, half way through the wood, she paused beside a flowering wild-cherry tree.

" This is the place! " she exclaimed. " This is where we have our siesta. Lie down! Lie down and be at ease! "

Triumphantly she flung herself upon the grass, straightening her long limbs luxuriantly. Lucy sat down beside her; she took off her hat and lay against the bole of the tree, letting her palms rest on the cool foam of fallen blossoms by her side.

" I'm hot," she said reproachfully. " You walk like a regiment."

A few white petals fluttered lightly downwards from the branches through a web of sunlight, and settled on her hair. Half closing her eyes, she added: " And I feel sleepy."

" Sleep, then," suggested Pinkie; she was making a daisy-chain for Fairy. " I'd like you to sleep. If I'd my 'cello, I'd play you to sleep. You would sleep beside me!"

But Lucy did not sleep; instead, from beneath her half-lowered lids she gazed at the other curiously. It gave her a strange sense of intimacy to be here alone in the heart of the wood with this extraordinary and beautiful woman, whom she seemed hardly to know. The thought now struck her forcibly as she observed the other's massive yet elegantly moulded form, stretched in some abandon upon the grass. Almost an embarrassment the thought became, the longer she dwelt upon it.

" My legs?" said Miss Hocking, looking up suddenly. " You're admiring them!"

Lucy coloured, and withdrew her eyes sharply. She had in a sense been thinking——

" They're rather good, I think," continued the other, smoothing her calves appraisingly. " A Grecian curve, you know. Oh, yes! You should see me when I'm undressed, or even in my bloomers. Quite charming!"

Lucy looked pointedly away, and drew the hem of her own skirt tightly around her ankles. She detested that sort of talk. Her modesty, like her pride, was excessive. She was not the sort of woman who studied intimately her own form, let alone the form of another in the act of disrobing. But Miss Hocking displayed an eager pertinacity, an almost avid enjoyment of the topic.

" Our duty to our bodies—keep them beautiful. Mustn't be ashamed of them! Don't you think it's good to be like that? The nakedness of woman is the work of God. Tell me," she went on unexpectedly, " were you happy when you were married?"

" Yes," said Lucy shortly. She neither approved the conversation nor understood its purport.

" Did you have great happiness?" persisted Miss Hocking. " Won't you tell me?" The subject, or the situation, seemed to rouse in her a strange excitement.

But Lucy was silent, coldly silent.

" Really, I have a reason," continued the other, with wide, ingenuous eyes. " I should love you to tell me."

" I'd rather not," said Lucy decisively, suddenly frigid.

" Marriage—a sweet abandon," rhapsodised Miss Hocking, hanging the completed daisy-chain around Fairy's plethoric neck. " Of course, not everybody can—can they, my Fairy, darling? But I—well—I——" Miss Hocking broke off, and laughed with a self-conscious skittishness which set Lucy's teeth on edge. Never had she seen the other so ridiculous as at this moment; it grated upon her, this persistent hovering upon the outskirts of sex. Suddenly she had the recollection of that occasion: of Miss Hocking leaning forward entranced by the sight of Peter dancing half-naked in his pyjamas; yes, it was the same excited curiosity which lurked now in those dreamy eyes. She was distinctly put out.

" Let's get on," she said restlessly; and abruptly she got to her feet.

Miss Hocking, reclining with her hands behind her head, looked up languorously.

" Such a nice talk—so intimate—we're having! I'd like to go on and on and on. Just like Tennyson's brook! "

In answer, Lucy began to walk down the path. A faint glimmering of understanding, a dim, uneasy intuition, had begun to trouble her.

In a few moments, however, Miss Hocking made up on her. She was gay once more, and once more full of chatter. But Lucy was not gay; thoughtful she was, and silent, as they emerged from the woods and took their way along the shore road to Ardfillan.

" I said I didn't want a long walk," she said, rather crossly. " We've come miles."

Indeed, the road seemed interminable; her heel, she was sure, had blistered; Fairy, the daisy-chain askew upon his left ear, wore a tortured look as he panted along beside them, pausing repeatedly to lap disreputable water from the adjacent ditches. Even Miss Hocking began to show signs of dishevelment from wind and sun, but she was not dismayed. She took a cake of chocolate from her pocket, and, offering a piece to Lucy, who refused it, she began to munch it contentedly.

" I always carry a bar about with me," she said cheerfully. " About a bar! A bar about! " And she bit into it. A brown smudge smeared itself on her cheek. Lucy said nothing. She was limping now.

They reached Ardfillan, footsore, tired, and hungry, about six o'clock, just as the bells began to peal. As they began the ascent of Garsden Street, Lucy made an effort, and, conquering her ill-humour, she turned to her companion.

" We'll have a bath when we get back," she said; " and I'm dying for a cup of tea."

These were the first words she had spoken in the last mile. But Miss Hocking's perspiring features assumed a slow and dreamy smile.

" You go ahead and have your bath," she returned agreeably, " and your cup of tea."

" What? " exclaimed Lucy in astonishment. " Aren't you coming too? "

" No, my dear." All the facile chatter of the last hour was gone; she was constrained, bashful. " I'm going in there "—and she pointed to where, half-way up the road, the Episcopal Church stood with open doors, already receiving a string of worshippers for the evening service.

Lucy gazed at the other in amazement—at the mud on her shoes, the tilt of her hat, the wisp of hair plastered against her smudged cheek, and finally at the almost incredible expression now stamped upon her face.

" Surely you won't trouble! " she expostulated. " You were out this morning. And I'm certainly not going to Benediction to-night. You must be dying to sit down. Come home and have tea."

Miss Hocking shook her head. " No! " she answered coyly. " No, no! "

" But you're so untidy! "

" I must go. Yes, I must," she murmured. " He's preaching to-night. He would miss me if I wasn't in my seat."

" He! " ejaculated Lucy. " You don't mean——"

" Yes, the Reverend Mr. Adam—Malcolm, I should say." She blushed with an awful coquetry. " Heartbroken he would be—if I wasn't there."

" Heartbroken? " echoed Lucy, completely taken aback. " Why? "

She did not know, but she knew of, the Reverend Malcolm Adam: by reputation a quiet, methodical man, a man of abrupt and taciturn habit. She stared at Miss Hocking. She was convinced, positively convinced, that Miss Hocking was romancing.

" You—you're not serious? " she exclaimed.

" Completely serious! " answered Miss Hocking, with a grotesque primness. " You ought to know—there's an understanding between Mr. Adam and myself, a perfect understanding. We may be married any day now."

Lucy's jaw dropped. She could not believe her ears. Literally she was staggered by the announcement.

" Are you in earnest? Has he proposed to you, then? " she gasped.

Miss Hocking halted. They were now just outside the church, and, with a frightful simper, she said: " Oh, no! He's said nothing, not a word. He's too shy to speak. It's the way he looks at me, just that look. Oh, the way he looks at me! " She sighed. " That's how I know it! He adores me. I know it; yes, I know it. And I keep it all for him! " Then she smiled, and swept up the steps into the church.

Lucy stood quite still. She was dazed. She remained motionless while that large, majestic figure vanished under the Gothic arch; then slowly she turned and set off for home.

It was out, out at last, the secret of that girlish playfulness behind the full, excited majesty of manner. Yes, the murder was out—out irrevocably. It was as though the afternoon had been a gradual progression towards the bathos of this frightful, ridiculous *dénouement*! Miss Hocking's eccentricity might have been—well, anything! But it was this! She was profoundly dismayed, confounded by her conflicting thoughts. But there was no shadow of doubt; she saw clearly, and, indeed, she wondered why it had not dawned upon her before. She had cast in her lot with a woman virtually deranged, a woman affected by a grotesque and unbelievable obsession. Yes, it was incredible. Had she been told of this obscure yet violent passion, cherished secretly in the traditional manner, for a clergyman, she would not have believed it. Absurd, she would have said, unconvincing, the inevitable, prescribed, and immemorial commonplace. Yet here it was, an actuality, thrust suddenly before her, thrust into the middle of her life.

She let herself into the flat with a serious face. Immediately she turned on the bath, and, discarding her limp and dusty garments, she slipped into the warm comfort of the hot water. She lay back, her face flushed by the steam, still frowning faintly. She went over the whole thing in her mind—the scene in the wood, the scene at the church. It was clear to her, absolutely clear. She did not blame herself. Drawing upon her pride, sustaining herself by the thought that she could see this thing through, gradually she became less disturbed. When she got out of her bath, she had prepared herself for some sudden dramatic event, some event which would immediately precipitate the situation, and she waited calmly in her dressing-gown for the return of her companion.

But nothing dramatic happened. Miss Hocking returned quietly— a little dreamy perhaps, but again ingenuously cheerful. She began, indeed, to make a salad for Lucy. A most delicious salad it was, cool, refreshing, with French dressing—Miss Hocking had a masterly touch with such dishes—and she discussed the ingredients with an amiable enthusiasm.

So Lucy ate the salad, and said nothing.

IX

SHE had prepared herself for a sudden rupture, an immediate cleavage of their companionship. But no rupture came. She went on living with Miss Hocking and she went on working. As time went on—and how swiftly it passed!—the weeks drawing into months, yes, the months drawing into years—she became gradually aware of the full extent of Pinkie's aberration. She became aware of all these hidden and adoring attentions, these gifts which the recipient never acknowledged. Adam was, of course, utterly oblivious of this secret and languishing affection directed towards him; yet, out of this very ignorance, Pinkie withdrew subtly the implication of a secret understanding. A stray glance falling upon her in church, an involuntary turn of his head as he passed her window, an inflection of his voice as he addressed her with some casual and unconsidered remark about the weather—all would strike her with a ravishing thrill, strengthen her delusion to a delicious and positive belief. She sent him presents anonymously—gloves, ties, scarves, even sets of the finest woollen underwear. For an entire year she worked upon a large illuminated address of her own design and composition—an exquisitely painted scroll eulogising his virtues. On certain mornings she got up early, and sat patiently at her window for the pleasure of observing him pass.

Upon every other point of reason she was normal—a little frivolous, gay, perhaps a little affected, yet near enough to normal; and she was sufficiently normal to conceal on most occasions the more glaring evidence of her partiality.

The essence of it all was this: Pinkie out-reaching powerfully to find the outlet for her repression. No matter that this outlet was fatuous. Instinct was satisfied.

And now Lucy accepted this state of affairs calmly, as a thing unavoidable and constant. It would go on, she felt, in this indefinite state, interminably. When mention of it arose in the conversation, she discouraged it by a stiff and uncompromising silence.

Yet sometimes Miss Hocking became an anxiety, even an irritation. From that first week-end when she had been burdened by the very insistence of the other's kindness, Lucy had suffered repeatedly under an amiability—a succession of attentions, arising, no doubt, from a genuine warmth of heart, but transmuted into something so exaggerated as to become almost aggravating! These constitutionals, the enforced *tête-à-têtes*, the gushing conversations, the little rippling laughs, the exclamations: " Oh, you must, my dear! " and " But I insist, my pet! "—all became tedious through repetition and their very emptiness. Often she would come home at nights tired from a long day's work, desiring quietness and the solace of a restful evening, to find Miss Hocking excited, lit with laughter, in this mood of tiresome exuberance. Then they would quarrel, Lucy retire sharply to bed, Pinkie to the drawing-room, where she made slow, sad music in reparation. It was a spectacle—Pinkie clasping the body of the 'cello between her legs, tenderly, as though she embraced the form of the Reverend Malcolm Adam.

At times the thought came over Lucy: " Why am I living here? Am I living with this woman for what I get out of her? " But she repudiated the thought; it was not so. Often, indeed, she stood between Miss Hocking—whose notion of money was of the slightest —and a lavish prodigality. And she was no parasite. She paid her share of the flat's expenses determinedly. It was, of course, for her, an unparalleled chance. She lived with economy, yet in surroundings of taste and even luxury. And she was able to educate her son! Yes, that argument weighed with her most heavily; to every doubt she had the answer that she was doing it for her son.

Nevertheless, she had moments when she made up her mind to leave the flat for good, and establish herself alone on a less pretentious scale. Several times she had been upon the verge of this step, but always the recognition of some essential obligation towards Miss Hocking had acted at the last moment as a deterrent. Miss Hocking had, after all, been good to her in her own way; her intentions, never malicious, arose from a well-disposed nature, and defeated themselves only through their own foolishness. Further, she had been good to Peter, which was now, with Lucy, the final and universal argument. There had been, for example, that holiday at Fort William, a joyous interlude for the three of them, suggested and—apart from Lucy's modest contribution—financed by the older woman. Lucy often went over it in her mind—the short train winding along the toyish single line, through the blue and purple mountains of the Western Highlands; the sudden silver vision of a loch lying beneath them, fringed by ragged pines, still with its own depth, placid with an ageless antiquity; the heather rolling endlessly, the briny tang of peat and bracken; a stag startled, racing with lowered antlers from the engine; the isolated stations, pebbled with their names, banked against the winter snowdrifts, but gaudy then with trailing nasturtiums and the fiery spurts of fuchsia. A wave of nostalgia came over her when she thought of it—it was her own country, and she loved it. Although during this holiday Miss Hocking had surpassed herself in giddy exuberance—flaunting a tartan skirt, a shawl upon her shoulder, a plumed hat, and a cairngorm as large as any buckler, and posing picturesquely, with arms akimbo, by every mountain tarn, after the manner of Flora Macdonald, whom she now decided she resembled—although she had been foolish, still she had been good to Peter. Previously, she had raked from the lumber cupboard a fishing-rod that had been her father's—no bamboo this, but a real whippy green-heart—and a pigskin fly-book containing multitudes of plumaged hooks, some rusty, with crumbling feathers, but most holding still their gaudy brilliance. Peter had fished in the Spean, had returned one afternoon pale with his intensity, his hand still tremulous, bearing a sea trout of at least two pounds. The memory of that look upon her boy's face, triumphant almost to ecstasy, had weighed in the balance many times against the decision that she must leave the flat and abandon the other to her own resources.

Peter—yes, she admitted him to be the keystone of her life.

All through this period the school prize-givings afforded her the greatest happiness, and it was incredible how quickly they came upon her; incredible, too, the changes which they brought upon her boy. She remembered the first still, vividly, and with that initial rush of pride which she had then experienced—to see him advancing with a modest yet distinguished bearing—he had distinctly an air, she admitted to herself—to receive from the ringed hand of the Lord High Bishop of Nofar himself the silver watch and chain for Christian doctrine and the pile of books—prizes in geography, orthography, and mental arithmetic.

" He's the lucky boy," she had heard the obese parent of a less successful scholar mutter, while Peter crushed his way through a labyrinth of outstretched legs back to her side in the steaming hall.

" Lucky, indeed! " thought Lucy indignantly, as she slipped her hand furtively under her son's arm, and clasped it tightly. Her face was flushed as his from her excitement; she frowned faintly in the direction of the heavily plumed hat from beneath which the remark had emanated. No, it was not luck. True, every boy in the school received a prize—it was said that Brother William had an astute contract with a bookseller in London. " Bill wasn't born yesterday," Ramford had been heard to exclaim in this connection. True also that every boy's name appeared in the elegantly printed prize list of the prospectus, even if it were only against the symbol: " Fourth Pianoforte Playing," or " Fifth Good Conduct." But what of that! And, whatever the inference of Ramford's graceless remark, assuredly it was not luck which had culled for Peter these firstfruits from the tree of learning; nor was it good fortune alone which had earned him the privilege of reciting " The Burial of Sir John Moore "—with appropriate gestures—before the same well-dressed gathering. Of *that* the *Laughtown Courier* said a week later: " The charming little man showed unquestionable histrionic talent, and, on taking his bow, was cheered to the resounding echo." And Lucy treasured this cutting, yellowing through the years, to her heart.

He had played, too, in the school band. Overture by Weber had been the piece, and, although he had not achieved his ambition of the big drum, which was, in truth, belaboured by a stout Spaniard with spectacles, he had been given—much more appropriately, she thought—the piccolo. Her eyes had devoured the graceful dexterity of his fingers, moving one bar behind the others; and to her the whole thin volume of the band's harmony had seemed to emanate from his ripe, distended cheeks.

Afterwards, Brother William had placed his hand benevolently upon Peter's head, and said on his passage to another parent: " We're proud of this boy." Brother Aloysius, too, in the background, had fixed on her his dark sloe eyes, and murmured: " It's a pleasure to teach *your* boy, Mrs. Moore," making the note more intimate, the triumph more personal.

Her head had been high, the night air cool upon her cheeks, her heart singing exultantly as, after the ceremony, she had taken her way back to Lang's Private Hotel: strongly recommended by the Brothers—" An estimable woman, widow Lang! " Why, she had four sons day-boarders at the college.

Lucy slept little that night, and next morning, taking Peter home for the holidays, she had looked at him proudly across the carriage, and let her mind drift dreamily towards his triumphs of the future, which should be her triumphs also.

Yes, that had been the beginning, a beginning which had been magnificently sustained. He was going to be clever. Her initial exultation became moulded into a constant purpose. She became reserved about his successes, for, although she was a fond mother, she was no fool. She perceived that the college was a most excellent institution, the best, indeed, available to her; and the round annual expenditure of forty pounds was within the limits of her narrow purse. She saw, also, that the régime and regular life suited Peter, who was developing to an adequate strength and stature. The fear of his health—she had always thought his chest " not strong "—lay at the back of her mind like a spectre, and, although she refused to acknowledge this dread, it gave her, notwithstanding, an indescribable satisfaction to see her son growing with every evidence of normal health. The slow changes which turned him gradually from an ingenuous child with a pocketful of marbles to a heavier boy, still incomparably charming, but now a lunging boy, destructive of his clothing, requiring size five in boots, who sang loudly and with an air of finality at every holiday the traditional rhyme:

> *No more Latin,*
> *No more French,*
> *No more sitting*
> *On the hard old bench,*

and from that to a lanky youth, diffident of his breaking voice, yet remarking casually upon the advisability of his assuming long trousers—these changes slipped over her with the slow precision of the inevitable.

She saw that all this must happen, and, because it happened gradually and in a direction which was good, she was not disturbed. Her attachment to him grew in a mingling of love and devotion. He had become tall, reserved now in his manner, even more tidy in his habits, and with an occasional tendency towards studying himself profoundly in a looking-glass. She became aware of a quality in him somewhat different from the ordinary—not merely his unquestionable distinction and charm, not merely his lack of boisterous clumsiness, but something indefinable which stamped him as her son amongst the millions of other sons belonging to a million other mothers. She began to see in him a growing resemblance to his father—the moulding of his lips, his smile, the strong white teeth, shining and perfect—to discover little mannerisms which made her start by a sudden plucking at the chords of memory. She thought him, privately, a handsome young fellow, lived with him in her mind, drew an intense satisfaction equally from his enthusiasms and his successes.

She supposed that certain changes must be manifest in herself, but she did not often consider this. She traversed that phase which runs flatly and uneventfully in every life without the consciousness of alteration in herself. Her figure had become a little more solid, her waist less flexible, her smile shadowed by a greater reserve. But she rarely considered these changes in herself. Nor did she consider extensively the possibilities of romantic adventure. Joe had, in that direction, given her at the outset a rude shock, Miss Hocking's absurd passion disgusted her, and above all she had her son—so, though she knew it not, the circumstances of her life induced a curious repression, diverted her love entirely towards Peter. Her clients, whatever their attitude, were to her mere floury figures, emerging and disappearing with equal suddenness, entirely without significance in her life. Lennox was fond of her; so much she knew. But he had his business, to him all-engrossing, almost an obsession. Once, however, in the office, he had sheepishly advanced an arm around her waist. Quite calmly she had instructed him to remove it. And he had at once complied, confused, apologetic, infinitely more disturbed than she. On the whole, she deliberately discouraged in herself all tendency towards introspective reverie, which inclined to make her sad, to induce, she felt, a morbid self-pity. And it was seldom she had leisure to lay her hands upon her lap and relinquish herself to those moments of abstraction.

She had her work. She became accustomed to a hasty breakfast and the morning rush for her train; she waited on railway platforms in wind and rain and sunshine; she went round the district on her weekly pilgrimage, and stood for hours without impatience in damp shops and underground bakehouses. She cultivated optimism and, in the way of business, the art of cheerful salutation. When the rush of orders, evoked by sympathy, had subsided, she settled down to the routine of the work. Her income became smaller but more regular, and in this she was at least content. Often she would pause and consider the absurdity that she, of all people, should be doing this work, spending her life in selling an undignified commodity. Undignified or no, this margarine had come to stay, and Lennox was pressing it—yes, even to the detriment of his butter business. It was almost ludicrous, yet she went on selling it. She was not unhappy, and, indeed, actually she had no choice. In her present mode of living her income enabled her to exist comfortably, to dress neatly, even smartly—at her son's request—on her visits to the school, to enjoy the moderate refinements of life, and, above all, to pay for her son's education. Naturally she had no balance in the bank. Her capital consisted of her fortitude and her love for Peter.

But she was aware that she had reason, as Edward put it, to be grateful for God's mercies; but at times it struck her as inconceivable that her relations should evince such little interest in her position. It made her perhaps a trifle bitter. Edward was undoubtedly the most punctilious; he wrote to her at intervals, saw her occasionally, had Peter over for the holidays, spoke in lavish terms of the boy's scholarship, and was, according to his limited means, spasmodically generous. He made no allusion whatever to Joe, but she had the uncomfortable conviction that he surmised the reason of the other's persistent silence, and forbore—from modesty, no doubt—to mention it. Yes, insensibly her attitude towards Edward had altered: in her own phrase, she " did not think quite so much of Edward " as before. As for Richard, her own brother, he maintained his usual reticence. He presumed, she imagined, that she was " doing well," and deduced therefrom a further tribute to the Murray brain and character. At Christmas she received once a penwiper sewed by Vera and again a pink satin tea-cosy worked by Eva, sent with the love of the entire family, as tokens of their esteem for her.

Yet somehow these pleasant attentions made her draw more within herself. She began to lose a little her social instincts. She abandoned nothing of her generosity: on the occasion of Netta's marriage with Dave Bowie—a momentous matter, indicative of the triumph of true love and the passage of the years—she bestowed on her former maid a handsome gift of linen out of all proportion to her income. Yet insensibly her interests narrowed. She took, for example, small cognisance of the business of the nation. The re-conquest of the

Sudan, the formation of Australia's commonwealth, left her unmoved. She never knew that Marconi used the wireless telegraph, nor that Langley caused his tiny air machine to fly. The name of Kruger was not to her a fearful and obscene obloquy. She suffered the death of Queen Victoria without a pang.

Still, for all her lack of interest in the world's affairs, she was happy; she had her own affairs, her purpose, and she was content.

X

On the 3rd September, 1904, she entered the office in an excellent humour, and went straight to her desk to make up her book. Nothing unusual had occurred to influence her mood except, perhaps, the scent of autumn in the air. She had always loved this season, and to-day at Darroch the crisp wind sweeping up from the loch shore had brought a fume of fallen leaves—a delicious fragrance of the earth which made her pause suddenly and draw a long, deep breath.

Calling out an off-handed remark to Andrews, she took up the invoice book and began to duplicate her orders. How many times had she done this? She did not consider, nor, as she had once done, did she now pause to tap her teeth and ponder anxiously some point, in fear of making a mistake. No, she had an air of confident proficiency as her copying-ink pencil raced freely over the paper.

" What's the worry to-night? " she threw out to Andrews, without lifting her head.

He had made no reply to her previous greeting. And again he made no reply.

" Is it the indigestion? " she persisted amicably, still writing at her dashing pace. Lately this devotee of his wife's cooking had begun to suffer stern internal pangs, and, by a constant tribute of pills, to make belated reparation to his liver.

But again he was silent, sitting moodily upon his stool, caressing his drooping moustache with a languid touch, casting on her a lacklustre, squinting eye. She laughed, and turned the page crisply.

" Every picture tells a story! " she quoted. Could this be she who had once trembled in this very office, and said: " I'll do my best to remember what you tell me, Mr. Andrews "?

" You're laughing," he responded slowly. " Well, laugh away. Ye may as well get all the jokiness out of your system when ye're about it."

His inveterate pessimism moved her to another smile.

" Where's Dougal? " she remarked.

Dougal, in the years, had belied his dour and unpropitious promise. He was now " a pleasant chap " and a great friend of Lucy's.

Andrews moved his bald head slowly towards the inner room. " With the boss." He paused gloomily. " I've been in myself—and when he comes out you'll go in *yourself*."

This time she did look up, and, holding her pencil against her cheek, she inspected him more carefully. Yes, his dejection seemed pitched in a lower key than ordinary.

" What's wrong? " she demanded.

" You'll find out, sure enough," he answered slowly; " and you'll not be laughing then, I'll warrant."

" Tell me," she persisted, curiously. He did, indeed, look extremely upset. " Tell me what's wrong."

" Everything! " he declared, with unusual vehemence.

Just then the inner door opened, and Dougal came out into the office, followed immediately by Lennox himself.

" You're back, are you? " Lennox exclaimed, on seeing Lucy. " Come in here a minute, will you? "

She got off her stool slowly; the sight of Dougal's face and this summons, following upon Andrews's prediction, gave her a peculiar disquietude; but she knew she was all right; she had made no errors, her work was up to standard; there was nothing to be afraid of.

" Sit down, Mrs. Moore," he invited her, and, again, equally in this invitation and in the use of her name—a title which, in fact, he never gave her—she perceived the unusual drift of the event.

" I've just been seeing the others," he declared, fingering his pencils almost nervously.

" Yes? " she advanced expectantly.

She discerned now in his manner a restlessness, a suppressed elation, seething beneath an unusual compunction. There was a silence.

" It's a hard thing for me to have to do," he said suddenly, playing now with a ruler, " but it's got to be done, for all that."

He threw down the ruler decisively. " I'll have to give you your notice."

She went quite pale, with the total unexpectedness of the remark. For a moment she stared at him in silence; then she gasped: " But my work's all right, perfectly all right! You know that as well as I do! "

" I know, I know," he declared with open regret. " I'm downright sorry."

" Then what——" she faltered, and broke down.

" I've sold out—yes, sold out, lock, stock, and barrel, to Van Hagelmann's! "

He lay back in his chair. Despite his compunction, the elation was getting the upper hand; his high voice became frankly triumphant.

" You know I've been a thorn in their flesh—for all the size of their concern—ay, I've pricked them long and weary. They tried to down me, but they couldn't. I've sold Dutch margarine in spite of them—I sold it under their very noses—and now they're sick of it. They want no competition; they're wanting to get the monopoly, indeed. I knew it; oh, yes, I knew it. I saw it coming a long way ahead. That's why I pressed on with the margarine and sacrificed the other. That's where the foresight came in. And now it's done, and the bargain sealed. I'm out and they're in! "

At his words a high colour had flooded her face. So that was what he had been working for?

" But—they'll keep us on here? " she exclaimed anxiously.

He shook his head slowly. " That's the pity," he returned, with a sudden change of manner. " They've got their own place, their own staff, their own travellers. I think they'll take on Dougal, mind you. He's a young lad they might use. But Andrews and yourself—well——" He paused significantly, and added: " I'm downright sorry about it."

Though he tried to draw his features into a frown of commiseration, he was not acutely sorry. He was delighted to have pulled off the deal, exuberant at his good fortune in disposing of his small business to a large, progressive firm, which had purchased it more on a principle of policy than to obtain the monopoly.

She saw this clearly, and a sudden sense of injustice oppressed her fiercely.

" And I'm to be turned off after all those years! That's what I get for all my hard work! "

" You were paid for it," he murmured mildly.

" It's not fair! It's unjust! " she burst out unreasonably. " You might have let us know this was coming! "

" I didn't know myself for certain." He hesitated, added more mildly, " No use to lose tempers over it."

Perhaps the sudden memory of that distant warm afternoon when he had weakly slipped his arm around her waist restrained him from a more definite rebuke. Perhaps he realised even now something of his lingering regard for her.

" I've been meaning to retire for a long time," he went on. " You'll get something else to do. A tidy little woman like you."

A quick reply formed upon her lips, but she tightened them upon it. She rose up abruptly, facing him with sparkling, resentful eyes.

" When do I finish? " she shot out, from the door.

" In a month," he declared, pacifically almost.

She went into the outer room. A rankling indignation burned within her. She saw herself humiliated on that first day when she had entered this wretched office; yes, humiliated, she had been; and now, again, she had been bitterly humiliated by this sudden enforcement of departure. And in between, how she had worked, slaving in all weathers, to secure for this wretched Lennox a fat retiring competency!

" I told ye, didn't I? " Andrews remarked. " I knew you would get the sack."

" Leave me alone! " she snapped.

Dougal was silent. He was not sacked, and he had, in consequence, the painful air of one who has betrayed his associates.

With compressed lips, she picked up her book, finished it, and at five o'clock left the office.

She came out of the narrow archway, and walked half-way down the wet street before she noticed that it was raining. Her hair was already misted with raindrops before she raised her umbrella automatically. The yellow blurs of shop windows wavered past her; a newsboy at the street corner was calling hoarsely the winner of the last race; dark forms marched with her towards the station.

She got into the train. In the corner, a man leaned over to his companion and spoke of the trade depression over his lowered newspaper.

" They're sacking them off like flies in the shipyards," he concluded importantly.

She looked over at the man calmly. That, she considered, was exactly her position. She had been sacked. Those years of steady, uneventful life had terminated with a casual, almost grotesque, suddenness. A comical phrase, " to be sacked," yet to her it was a catastrophe unexpected, even uncontemplated. No, in her confidence she had never, never foreseen this. With a returning gush of resentment, her lips drew together again as she sat realising more fully the significance of her dismissal.

At Ardfillan it was still raining, in heavy slanting sheets, and when she let herself into the flat the hem of her wet skirt clung limply to her ankles.

" Brrrh! " cried Miss Hocking, coming into the hall with a rush. " You're as wet as a herring, my child! "

" Yes, I'm wet," she forced herself to reply. " I'd no coat with me."

" Come along quickly, then, and change," gushed the other. She wore the inevitable green shot-silk, and high lights sparkled in her eyes.

Lucy shook the raindrops from her head.

" I'm not coming," she said definitely. " I'm tired." They had been invited out to supper; but now she had no desire to accept that invitation.

" But you must—oh, of course, you must! " protested Pinkie effusively. " It'll cheer you up. We'll have music. A little singing before supper. Very restful for you. Come, come."

" I told you I'm not! " returned Lucy brusquely. " I don't feel like it."

" You must be made to feel like it, my dear. I'll help you dress."

" Let me be! " returned Lucy, and, pushing away the other's encircling arm, she blurted out: " I've lost my job! "

" Your job! " came the incredulous, rather fastidious echo.

" Yes, my job—my work—my position. I'm sacked, if you know what that means."

" Dear me! " said Miss Hocking pleasantly, and then, with a blandly reassuring smile, she added: " You'll find something else. In the morning. Surely! Do come! Yes, come, come."

Lucy made no answer, but brushed roughly past into her own bedroom, where she began to take off her wet clothes. It was an added aggravation to come home to this inane reception.

" What a fool the woman is! " she thought, in the bitterness of her mood. " And what a fool I've been to put up with her! "

She dried her legs with the energy of her vexation, put on new stockings and her house shoes; then chose her grey velvet dress from the wardrobe. A fingered tattoo upon the door made her pause. Then Pinkie's voice came through, lilting the words archly: " Are you coming now, my dear? I'm all ready."

With an effort Lucy controlled her reply.

" You go along yourself," she called out. " I can't possibly come."

" You must! You must! " cried Pinkie excitedly, and she rattled the door-handle like a thwarted child, but Lucy, wise in her experience of the other's persistence, had locked the door. The silence which followed was heavy with pique; then the slam of the outer door relaxed Lucy's constrained attitude, and freed the hidden tension of the air. She finished her dressing; then she went into the kitchen and made herself some tea and hot buttered toast.

Sitting down to the meal meditatively, she placed Peter's last letter in front of her, and read it again slowly. The neatly written lines comforted her, yet they crystallised the position more definitely than many hours of meditation. He was in his second last term at school, and when he returned at the end of the year she would be confronted by the immediate necessity of dealing with his future. The vision of the last prize-giving again rose up before her. Brother William—more pendulous than ever, tottering a little, but still, in his own phrase, " going strong "—with hand, not now upon the head, but upon the shoulder, of the prize-winner—saying to her: " There's a career in front of this boy." If it had been difficult before, how much more difficult was her position now! Yet, though the future was not definite, her ambition for him lay clearly defined in her mind.

After all her efforts to educate him satisfactorily, the idea of allowing him to take up some trifling and nugatory occupation was not only absurd, but a waste of all her effort, a clear admission of her failure. An office-boy? A clerk? An apprentice to some trade? All equally unthinkable!

No, her present hurt and rankling mood served only to intensify her determination. She had her objective—that the path to this objective was obscure did not dismay her—she could not see clearly, but she had faith in herself. She would get another situation immediately; she would do anything, everything. Grimly she folded the letter, and let her thoughts run forward.

She went to bed early, but she could not sleep. Again and again the recurrent thought of her dismissal flicked her on the raw. Restlessly, she drank some water from the carafe at her bedside, but the moment she lay down to compose herself that over-active brain seized once more upon the thought: this happening to her—dismissed by that shoddy little man, after she had worked and slaved for him:

She was not asleep when Miss Hocking came in. Lying in the darkness, she heard the flat door open, opened in a fumbling, uncertain manner; then suddenly slam shut. She heard the other step along the lobby—not that usual bouncing step, but a slack, curious tread, which instantly engaged her notice. Listening, she forgot momentarily the trouble in her mind, as those dragging sounds went into Miss Hocking's bedroom, and draggingly continued.

Most unusual, she thought, and she roused herself upon her elbow and looked towards the door, where a thin crack of light indicated that the gas had not been extinguished in the hall. Yes, it was all exceedingly unusual. She had expected that habitual exuberant entry, the subsequent bustlings about the flat, the little hummed snatches of song, perhaps an attempt to enter and declaim, with frequent ecstatic interjections, upon the delightful attractiveness of the party. Then, still resting upon her elbow, she heard another sound which came through the darkness with a startling clarity; neither tears nor laughter, but a combination of both—the sound of hysterical sobbing. At once she jumped up, drew on her felt slippers, and threw on her dressing-gown. She opened the door, and, thrusting her head into the lighted hall, called out: "What's wrong?"

No answer came, only an exacerbation of that awful exaggerated grief.

Lucy frowned, and, drawing her dressing-gown tightly around her, she went down the lobby. She knocked at Miss Hocking's door, paused for an answer which did not come, then turned the handle sharply and went into the room.

Again she paused, in astonishment and dismay. Reclining in her long chair, as though she had flung herself there in the midst of her undressing, her face and figure tinted oddly by the gas in its greenish coloured globe, was Miss Hocking. In extreme disorder she lay, her dress and petticoat cast upon the floor, her laces ruffled, her shoulders bare, her thick yellow hair half hanging down her back—a magnificent creature, lying half-naked in a queer voluptuous abandon. One pink-tipped breast lay exposed above her corsage and above her long black stockings her white skin shone with the lustre of satin. Thus she lay, and she was sobbing, wailing aloud in utter misery.

" What's the matter? " cried Lucy; and there was a sharpness in her tone.

For her, the sight of the other woman relaxed in this loose position of abandon was altogether too exotic, too indelicate, to provoke her sympathy; nor did that loud-voiced grief affect her. Not moving, it was to her, but absurd. She drew her dressing-gown more tightly around her trimly moulded figure.

" I'm asking you what's wrong? " she exclaimed, in a louder tone.

" He's thrown me over—over—over! " burst out Miss Hocking. " I heard it at the party." And her big eyes gushed fresh tears.

" What do you mean? " demanded Lucy acidly. She was outraged by the other's behaviour. She recognised the grotesque obsession, but it was different somehow, and she was constrained to ask again: " Tell me what you mean! "

" Over, over, over! " He's thrown me over. He's got engaged to another woman—it was announced to-day," wailed the other. " He's thrown me over after all those years, after all I've done for him, after the way I've loved him, after the way he looked at me." And she had a fresh spasm, kicking her heels into the carpet distractedly.

It was inconceivable! It was too wildly impossible! But it was so. The unfortunate woman flagellated herself with a frantic grief for the loss of something which had never been hers.

" Be quiet! " said Lucy, in an altered voice, " and let me help you into bed."

" How can I be quiet? " shrieked the other. " I loved him; yes, I loved him, and he loved me. I know it. I'm positive of it. We trusted each other. Waiting for him. I was—I was! "

The enormous fabric of her self-deception, that one monstrous illusion, had been crumbled by a single unexpected shock. The mainstay of her life was shattered, and it looked now as if she were shattered with it.

She moaned again, and her eye had a wild gleam.

" I loved him! I loved him! " she cried again. " We were married in the sight of God."

Lucy was alarmed. " Stop crying now," she coaxed, patting the other's shoulder, and at the same time attempting to cover that vast expanse of nudity.

" You believe me, don't you? " sobbed Miss Hocking, clutching that outstretched hand and rubbing it wildly against her tear-ravaged cheek. " Kind Lucy, kind Lucy."

" Yes—yes," said Lucy hastily. " Come now, we must get you to bed."

Actually she induced the other to rise, began with persuasive fingers to undo her corsets and undress her.

At this touch Pinkie stopped weeping, and stood passive, a tragic dishevelled spectacle in her long lacy drawers; a ravishing figure she was, but her face, fixed and now dry of tears, was blank—void of all but a grotesque bewilderment.

" What's to become of me? " she declared suddenly. " Now! "

" Hush," said Lucy determinedly.

At last she got rid of the corset, which had pressed the white skin into pinkish creases, and she slipped a nightdress over the other's shoulders and helped her to climb into the huge four-poster.

" Would you like a cup of tea? " she demanded. She had a profound belief in the efficacy of this beverage as a restorative.

Miss Hocking nodded her head with that same absent look. Lucy went out and made some tea, bringing in a full cup—the large breakfast-cup which Miss Hocking always used.

" Here! " she said directly. " Take this."

Pinkie stretched out an obedient hand, that large, beautifully manicured hand, and took the cup; but no sooner had she clasped it than it slipped apathetically from her grasp and fell to the floor. The cup did not break, but the tea spilled instantly, and flooded the carpet with a steaming puddle.

" Now look what you've done! " cried Lucy.

At the senseless action her temper flared. As she bent down to pick up the cup and saucer, she declared: " You can do without it now."

" I beg your pardon," said Miss Hocking abjectly, " I was thinking about something. My love for Malcolm. Is it not sublime? "

Straightening herself, with a flushed face Lucy stared at the pitiable creature on the bed. She had no sympathy for her, simply a pricking annoyance. With an intense exasperation, in her phrase " she wished she could knock some sense into her." Passionately she despised herself for having so long tolerated this foolishness. And she had her own worries; at the back of her mind she balanced the triviality of this idiotic woe, this utterly fatuous emotion, against the serious anxiety of her own position, into which she had been so suddenly thrust to-day.

Yet she was moved to say: " Would you like some of your bromide? "

" I would like some bromide," echoed the other, like a child; and when Lucy gave her the dose she took it in the same helpless, unresistant fashion, covering Lucy's hand with her own as the former raised the spoon firmly to her lips.

She was no longer devastated by her grief; she had become remote.

Lucy continued to look at her with a frown.

" Good night," she said at length.

" Good night," said Miss Hocking placidly.

Lucy turned out the gas, and went quietly out of the room. She had been at first profoundly disturbed, but now she was almost reassured. As she went along the corridor, a neat and modest figure, the stereotyped phrase kept running through her head: " It never rains but it pours." She thought of herself, and again the thought recurred. Her life had gone on quietly for years. She had tolerated Miss Hocking; she had felt herself reasonably secure; and now, in the course of a single day, this double catastrophe!

Yet she was not profoundly disturbed about her companion.

" She'll be better in the morning," ran her thoughts, rather severely, as she got into bed.

XI

BUT in the morning Pinkie was not better. After breakfast, fully dressed preparatory to her departure, Lucy went into the other's bedroom—Miss Hocking never rose before nine—for her usual good-bye.

" Are you all right? " she enquired.

" I'm all right," echoed Miss Hocking languidly. " You see, I—I've been thinking."

They made a strange contrast, the two women: the one standing erect, neat, assured, tapping her tightly rolled umbrella against her shining shoe; the other lying indolently in *négligé*, her hair blousily across the lace pillow, her large, beautiful eyes blurred into a tragic dullness.

" Yes," she continued, with the same stuporous air of reason; " I think it must be because I don't play the church organ that—you know. If I could play that organ, he would take me back." She paused. " I must learn to-day."

Lucy frowned uneasily beneath her taut veil. How different was this from the other's usual gushing good-bye: " Bye, bye, my dear Lucy. Home soon! "

" Did you not sleep well? " she enquired.

" I slept," declared Miss Hocking, " and to-day I shall learn to play. I'll go down to the church this morning." She sighed. " All— I'll do it for him. Malcolm! My husband in God's sight."

" Stop that, now," said Lucy brusquely, as though by her very will she could infuse a modicum of reason into that fatuous head. " You know I can't be bothered with that talk."

" I know you can't be bothered, Lucy," repeated the other dully. " But you don't understand. I have to be bothered. I've got to think about him. I can't help it."

Lucy bit her lip, and looked at her watch. She must go for her train; she had her own affairs to attend to; she would not spend her entire day looking after this silly creature; and so she turned on her heel.

" I'm going then," she said abruptly, and went out of the room, leaving Miss Hocking still staring in front of her with that air of dreamy lethargy.

Yet in the hall she paused; she would have liked to give a few words of instruction to the daily woman, but that laggard—her very unpunctuality a direct tribute to Miss Hocking's easy-going nature—had characteristically not yet arrived; and so, still unsettled in her mind, Lucy was compelled to leave the house.

Throughout the day she put the matter determinedly away from her. She impressed upon herself the urgency of her own affairs: that she had a month in which to discover a new occupation; that she had her son to consider; that this consideration and the consideration of his future took precedence before all others. Yes, even upon this first day she started—started by asking her customers lightly, and with a specious infusion of jocularity, to suggest an opening commensurate with her talents. Most expressed concern that she should be constrained to relinquish her work—" Good sakes, you don't mean to say! " " Well, to my mind it's a downright shame, and it beats me how a woman of your ability——" But in these exclamations she perceived rather bitterly that same superficial solicitude which had been evoked by Frank's death. Did they mean, after all, what they said? Not all, however, were serious. Some, with an answering jocularity, propounded in the abstract the attractive possibilities of matrimony; some even were more jocular and less abstract; but all promised faithfully to bear her in mind; yes, should they hear of anything which might be suitable, " they would mind her, for certain." That at least was something. She had set the wheels moving.

She came home with a feeling of accomplishment. So constant had been her purpose that only when she turned along Victoria Crescent did her mind revert to the subject of Pinkie.

"She's sure to be out of it now," she thought optimistically. "Silly creature!"

But Pinkie, apparently, was not yet out of it, and there was, moreover, the unusual sight of the daily woman in hat and coat waiting in the hall, her departure delayed until the arrival of Lucy.

"I had to stop on, ma'am," began the woman immediately, in a low voice. "She's been that queer. Thinks I, ' Extra money or no extra money, I'd better wait on till you come back.'"

"What's been the matter?" demanded Lucy quickly.

"She's that different, ma'am. You know how she is, ordinary, singing and laughing half the time, and playing that big fiddle of hers, with a ' Will you have this, Dick?' or ' Could you do with that, Dick?' but to-day—well——" She paused.

"I see," said Lucy shortly.

She gave the woman a shilling, and let her go. Then, composing herself with a factitious expression of cheerfulness she entered the sitting-room.

"I've decided against the organ," said Miss Hocking immediately —she was dressed with some untidiness in her grey costume, and sitting upright on a hard chair in the middle of the room. "It wasn't the slightest use."

"What do you mean?" said Lucy, in spite of herself.

"I got the organist—nice man—oh, yes, he knows me well—up in the organ loft to show me, but no use—I saw it at once—that piece of wood. Between the knees it sticks—how could I do it— play, you see, manipulate that, with my skirt?" She paused idly, as it were, to reflect in a manner supremely reasonable. "Unless— there's that tunic I used to drill in. I could wear that under my skirt, you see. Take the skirt off when I got to church. Still—I think——"

"Oh, don't Pinkie!" said Lucy. Her severity was gone; she was stricken by sudden alarm, by such alarm that she uttered the words entreatingly. "Please don't talk like that."

"No, I think not," returned Miss Hocking, in the same reasonable manner. "I think I shall learn Hebrew. Yes, I'll get the book and learn Hebrew to-morrow. Then we'll talk together, he and I, wander-ing nigh. He'll love me for it"; and she turned her large bewildered eyes on Lucy.

"Don't talk like that, Pinkie!" cried Lucy again. "You know it's so silly. You'll upset yourself—and me, too."

"I'll get a Hebrew Testament first thing in the morning," logically averred the other. "Wandering nigh—Malcolm and I—reading the Hebrew together!"

It was ludicrous, but it was also profoundly distressing. Lucy was no longer angry; she was moved, and disturbed also beyond everything; and she was, for a moment, at a loss for what she should do. She was mystified, and yet——

She spent the evening trying to coax the other out of her frightful strangeness. She was sorry now for her original curtness, and she openly apologised by her attitude.

Next morning, too, which was Saturday, she waited and arranged that Mrs. Dickens—who arrived, from curiosity rather than from virtue, with unexpected earliness—should remain until lunch-time, when she could return. She arranged also that Miss Hocking should rest in bed. Then she set out for the office.

Again, but with a greater effort, she turned her mind upon her own predicament. " I've got to do it," she told herself. Hurrying through her work—she had small compunction now about shortening her calls—she finished early, and returned to Glasgow about eleven o'clock. Then, following her premeditated plan, she went immediately to the new office of Hagelmann's in Alston Street and demanded to see the manager. Yes, she demanded! But Hagelmann's was not Lennox's, nor was the elegant tiled entrance as penetrable as those small grimy back stairs in the Saddleriggs. She was barred by an Enquiry Chamber. She was asked first to give her name, then to state her business; and she did not see the manager. Suavely but firmly she was informed that she could expect neither an interview nor any prospect of employment with this firm.

Out into the street she went, her head high in the air. They did not know what they were missing, these people, to disdain her, an experienced business woman, a traveller with a clientèle, without an interview, without even a single expression of regret! But they would regret it! Yes, she would see that they regretted it. Some competitive firm would have the benefit of her connection. In the rebound of her indignation, and as it was not yet quarter past eleven—to think that she had allowed a full hour for that interview and composed carefully such persuasive arguments!—she decided to pursue the matter further, immediately.

Three other firms she knew to whom she might reasonably apply, firms carrying on the business of produce import. The largest of these was quite near—in Carswell Street, to be exact—and without delay she took her determined way thither. Here, at least, it was not difficult to obtain admittance: she smiled almost to herself at the complete contrast of her reception. She ought, she reflected, to have come here in the first instance. But when she stated her case, and she saw to it that she made her statement plain, a different complexion fell upon the matter. Trade, the manager averred, was bad, worse than ever it had been; that foreign competition was doing it.

Besides, already they had an adequate staff of travellers, and in these hard times it would be unjust to deprive a man of his livelihood for the purpose of engaging a woman. Why not try Margotson's, was the suggestion. They might be able to do with her.

She did try Margotson's, which was, indeed, the second firm which she had in mind. Then she tried the third firm. Finally, she tramped back to the office, her head in the air, a spot of colour still upon her cheeks, feeling somehow disquieted, an unusual despondency within her. A faint thread of doubt ran through her confidence.

Hadn't she been fortunate in arriving so easily in her present position? She perceived now that circumstances which she had then failed to appreciate had, perhaps, enabled her to fall somewhat easily into this work. But she made an effort, and pulled herself together. It was ridiculous—she was a woman who had proved her worth. Later, at the station, she bought two papers, the *News* and the *Citizen*; and, sitting back in her compartment, she went through the advertisement columns carefully, marking with her stylo every vacant situation for which she judged she might reasonably apply. Reasonably! Yes, she made that term elastic, but the situations were, alas, unreasonably few. She saw with a sudden insight that she was not adapted for office work. She could not type; she knew no shorthand. Why, she asked herself almost fiercely, had she never set herself to learn? Nor was she in the strictest sense young: " Young lady required." No, she was not that. She perceived that, with good fortune, she might serve behind a counter for seven and six a week, or cook the dinners of some undistinguished family for the princely sum of twenty pounds a year—both courses equally unthinkable.

And then there was Miss Hocking. Now she could not keep that thought completely from her mind. She admitted that she was acutely anxious; but she had the whole week-end before her. Surely she could do something, make some effort to withdraw the other from that frightful strangeness which had taken her!

She got out at Ardfillan, and began the ascent of the hill, slowly, because she felt tired. The day unexpectedly had turned warm. A gentle day it was, filled by the subtle languor of an Indian summer, filled by the quiet rustle of the fallen leaves, each leaf protesting softly—a melancholy sound, distant somehow, receding like a fading memory.

Half-way up Garsden Street a boy was selling the local weekly paper, and, partly because he vaguely reminded her of Peter—absurd idea, but it was her mood—partly because the thought of obtaining that post lay continually before her, she purchased an *Advertiser*, and as she went on she glanced idly at the sheet. Suddenly she paused—an involuntary pause—her eye taken by a small paragraph, a short paragraph which announced the official engagement of the Reverend Malcolm Adam. So it was authentic, after all—this normal, supremely normal, incident of life which had pricked the glittering bubble of Miss Hocking's illusion. She folded her papers together, and went into the flat.

" Well? " she enquired immediately of Mrs. Dickens.

" She would get up," said Mrs. Dickens in a tone of self-defence, " in spite of what you said. But she's been sat in the drawing-room all the time with her books."

" I see," said Lucy. Her curt manner had a repressive effect upon the other, who displayed an obvious desire to discuss the matter intimately.

Having removed her things, Lucy went into the drawing-room. At her entry Miss Hocking looked up impatiently. She was seated at the bureau, which was littered with books; upon the floor around her were strewn more books.

" Can't you see I'm busy? " she exclaimed immediately; she had a studious air, abstracted yet fervent, and as she spoke she ruffled her hair impatiently.

Lucy glanced at the books—mercifully not the Hebrew she had feared, but some works on botany taken from those upper shelves so rarely touched.

" Why do you disturb me? " said Pinkie again. " Can't you see I'm trying to find out about myself? "

" I thought you promised to stay in bed," said Lucy mildly, and she came a little farther into the room.

" Don't come near me! " cried Pinkie instantly. " A lady always keeps a certain distance. And I don't know what I am yet. There may be a reason for all that's been going on. I'm looking for it here."

Lucy hesitated, her eyes fixed upon that smooth and feverishly absent face before her.

" Don't you want any lunch? " she demanded slowly.

" No, I don't," declared the other, with unusual conviction. " I've more important things to think of. If I don't find out in time for church to-morrow, I shall have to compromise. Non-committally! A kilt I'd have to wear. Yes, I'm determined. At least, that comes in between the two."

" I see," said Lucy.

She turned, and went slowly out of the room, shutting the door firmly behind her. At last the fact struck in on her with a crushing certainty. She knew she was dealing with a woman utterly insane. She was profoundly disturbed. What was she to do? As she took her lunch, not tasting the food, she considered broodingly what step she must take. It was painful, both unbelievable and painful, to think that Pinkie, who had for years cherished her silly delusion, like a child its plaything, should now, in losing it, lose also all that had been reasonable in her life.

Paradoxically, that delusion had kept her on the borderland of sanity; but, now that the delusion was assailed, she supported it with other delusions which removed her utterly beyond the pale of reason. Now indeed she was blundering about the labyrinth of sex like a huge, lost animal.

When she had finished, Lucy pushed back her chair and rose abruptly from the table. The more she thought of it the more the thought galled her. She gazed out of the window. Again her mood swung round, and she thought, almost passionately: " She must— oh! she must come out of it. It's a phase, a passing instability. I'll get her out of it in time." And she reassured herself by her own desire. Moreover, to invoke outside assistance seemed an exposure of her companion's weakness amounting almost to betrayal. With a sudden resolution she decided again to wait. Yes, she would wait for at least to-day; this afternoon she would leave Pinkie alone; solitude and quietude might resolve the enigma to its original simplicity.

When the table was cleared, she took her papers and her stylo, and composed herself to answer the advertisements which she had marked when returning in the train. Always slow in her composition, she was to-day slower, weighing her words carefully, choosing those phrases which most adequately expressed her fitness for each position. Into each letter she put a laboured intensity, yet between times her concentration dissolved, and, with head raised and pen suspended, she listened for some signs of activity within the drawing-room. Once she heard the door open and shut; but beyond that there was nothing.

Her letters finished, sealed, and stamped, she straightened her bent back and regarded them. Neatly stacked, they made an imposing little pile, out of which she drew some comfort: by Tuesday at the latest, she told herself, she would have the replies.

" You'll post these when you go, Mrs. Dickens? " she remarked, as the daily woman entered the room.

" Yes, ma'am," said Mrs. Dickens; she had all the afternoon been in and out of the sitting-room, hovering about the table, darting surreptitious glances at Lucy's bowed figure; now, seizing her opportunity, she definitely demanded: " And if it's not asking too much, what are you going to do—about Miss Hocking? "

Lucy looked up at her. " We'll wait for a bit," she replied, with an assumption of confidence. " I expect this—this little attack will pass off."

" Do you not think her friends should be let know?" persisted the other. " She's got a brother somewhere—cleaning up I've seen

the letters he writes, off and on—laying on the bureau odd times——"
She excused herself—" You couldn't help notice them."

Lucy's expression became rather colder; clearly Dick had exceeded, and was now again exceeding, the responsibilities of her position.

" I think you must leave it to me," she affirmed, with an air of closing the matter. " I shall do what's best."

" But don't you think——" insisted Mrs. Dickens. She broke off self-consciously, paused, and added lamely: " I'd be frightened to stop on all night alone with her—like and all as she is. It would make me grue. Truth to tell, I wouldn't do it for a ransom."

" I'm not frightened, Mrs. Dickens," said Lucy briskly. " Rest assured of that."

She picked up the letters, said suggestively: " You can post these on your way home."

" Yes, ma'am," murmured Dick, and, wiping her large red hand upon her apron, an action of courtesy rather than of necessity, she accepted the letters deferentially. " Good night, then, ma'am." She paused. " The tea's set on the tray."

" Good night."

Mrs. Dickens went out, and in a few moments the outer door closed behind her. At the sound Lucy got up. She was pleased, almost reassured by the ease of her moral victory over the daily woman. In her heart she had never actively approved of Mrs. Dickens.

And now, going briskly into the kitchen, she infused the tea. It seemed to her that actually she had not tried sufficiently to remove Miss Hocking from her present wretched state, and in a sense she reproached herself for that indifference. " I'll get her out of it," she said to herself—not for the first time—" yes, if I've to shake her for it."

In this mood she carried the tea-tray to the drawing-room. After all, Pinkie had been kind to her!

" Time for tea," she remarked determinedly from the doorway, " and you're going to have some, whether you like it or not."

" But I do like it. Who said I didn't like tea? " exclaimed Miss Hocking at once. " Tea from spicy breezes blow! " She had abandoned her books, and was now sprawling in an easy chair, opening and shutting her umbrella, which she had fetched from the hall, with an air of impulsive playfulness.

" Come along, then," said Lucy, putting down the tray and beginning to pour out; she ignored the umbrella as long as she could, but at last, holding out the cup, she was constrained to say: " Put that down for a moment, won't you? "

" I like doing it," returned the other immediately. " That's why I've left the books. I can't make it out yet. This is better. It eases me! "

She went on with her opening and shutting, but at length, catching sight of the cup, which Lucy still steadily proffered, she suddenly flung the expanded umbrella from her and as impulsively took the steaming tea and gulped it.

" This is fine! " she exclaimed, after a moment. " But I want to secure love, that's what I want."

" Some cake, now? " said Lucy firmly.

" Cake! I can't be sure about cake. It may be too sweet. It comes under the category."

" This is really quite nice," went on Lucy determinedly. " It came in fresh to-day from Allen's." Allen's! Suddenly she was confronted by the memory of her first luncheon with Miss Hocking, so distant now in time, so different from this present travesty of a meal. Her eye glistened, and she exclaimed affectionately, spontaneously : " Come, now, try a piece." She held out the plate. The slice of cake became suddenly a symbol—its acceptance victory; its refusal defeat. " Come! " she coaxed, as to a child. " Take a piece to please me, Pinkie. You know how fond of you I am."

But Miss Hocking waved the plate away.

" Do I attract women as well as men, then? " she exclaimed, crossing her powerful legs. " That seems to be the question! "

Lucy put the plate down sharply, indignantly.

" Let me have your nightdress to sleep in," remarked the other largely. " Then I shall know for certain."

" For the last time," said Lucy, " I ask you to stop talking like that."

But Miss Hocking met her imploring eye with an empty stare.

" I know it is dubious, but if God performs a miracle I shall be all right. There is one question which I must know. So tell me truly. If I went upon the streets, how much would I be paid? "

Lucy gave a short, despairing exclamation that was half a sob. It was utterly hopeless. She must have assistance.

" Don't laugh! " cried Miss Hocking, with an instant change of manner. " Don't laugh, I tell you! " Her tone was sullen; suddenly leaning forward, she struck Lucy a light blow upon the cheek.

For a moment the two women stared at each other; then Miss Hocking broke into a high, derisive laugh.

" You little fool! " she exclaimed contemptuously. " Don't you know I'm your superior in everything? "

The colour in Lucy's face deepened; she got up without a word and, taking up the tea-tray, went out of the room. Indignation rather than defeat throbbed within her. Stiffly she stood in the kitchen, seeing nothing; that this woman—this senseless creature for whom she had been doing her utmost—should have struck her! That was the final straw. Now, indeed, she must do something. For another moment she stood with a colour still heightened, thinking; then, taking her decision, she went into her bedroom and rapidly put on her hat and coat.

" Where are you? " shouted Miss Hocking from the other room. " What are you doing? "

Lucy made no reply.

" Come here! " bawled the other once more. She seemed excited, restless, lunging powerfully about the room. " I want you here immediately."

In answer, Lucy tightened her lips; she went quickly into the hall, and reached the front door.

" I want you! I want you! " came that excited voice again, and in a moment Miss Hocking herself appeared at the other end of the hall, filling the doorway of the dining-room with her bulk. " How dare you refuse to come when I call you! "

" I'm going out," said Lucy shortly. " I'll be back soon." And, before the other could reply, she slipped the key from the lock, opened the door, and went out of the house. She shut the door behind her with a nervous violence; stood for an instant considering; then walked off swiftly.

Outside, the darkness was already falling, and a high wind swayed the opposite trees into fantastic shapes. With head bent down against the breeze, Lucy hastened along the road, heedless of the moaning trees, the wind's resistance merely sharpening her purpose.

In five minutes she had reached the gate of Dr. Hudson's house: he was the nearest to the Crescent. As she hastened up the short gravelled drive and pulled at the bell, she had a sudden distressing thought of what Miss Hocking might be doing in her absence: a sudden premonition of disaster.

Suddenly she had become impatient; the thought of her original delay angered her; and from the maid who opened the door she demanded immediately to see the doctor. He was in, though engaged upon a consultation, yet, at her request, conveyed urgently by the maid, he interrupted this, and came at once into the waiting-room.

She knew Hudson—upon one occasion she had called him in to Peter—a slight, middle-aged man, his manner restrained, polished to a high degree. And in his person he was polished too: his small pointed iron-grey beard pomaded, his neat feet encased in varnished boots, his hair worn rather long, groomed to a glossy curl, his linen glistening, immaculate. About him was an evasive delicacy, and, gliding in, he advanced towards her. She wasted no words: looking at him directly, she said: " Miss Hocking—the lady I live with—I want you to come and see her at once. She seems strange."

" Strange! " he repeated, and looked at her queerly. " I know her —has she not always been strange? You ought to know. Haven't you lived some years together? "

Her wind-stung cheeks flushed easily; she saw in that one glance a questioning, an odd suspicion, cast upon her for her association with Miss Hocking—cast indirectly and unjustly upon these last five years of her life.

" There was nothing but a little peculiarity," she declared, accepting his challenge. " But now—it's different."

" How different? "

She told him, giving the salient points of the last few days. Whilst she spoke, his eyes roamed the room. She did not fully comprehend the reason of his manner, but she saw clearly that it was inimical to her.

" You never know where you are with these people," he said at length, " and from what you tell me it looks as though this so-called peculiarity has become something remarkably like——" He paused significantly.

" What? " she exclaimed, watching him intently.

" Mania," he replied coolly, as though he uttered a term of reproach against her; " acute mania."

Although in effect she had been aware of what the condition must be, she was shocked by his words and the coldness of his manner. For years she had been living with a woman on the brink of insanity. And it was as though he suspected her of something, she knew not what.

" You'll come, then? " she demanded, anxiously.

" I'll come," he said briefly. " Wait here till I've finished next door—then we'll go up together."

" Oh, no, no! " she exclaimed, pressing her hands together. " I'm afraid for her. I couldn't leave her alone any longer."

" I advise you to wait," he returned guardedly. " You never can tell."

But already she had the vision of some disaster occurring in her absence—some disaster for which she would hold herself responsible. She shook her head, moved to the door, anxious, ill at ease.

" I'll go up now," she declared hurriedly. " Come as soon as you can."

His expression did not change. " As you wish," he remarked evenly.

She went out of the house and into the cold, windy dusk with a little rush, and at the same pace she hastily took her way down the hill. If she had entertained a doubt before, the encounter with Hudson had completely dispelled it. As if she could have dreamed of waiting, now that she fully understood the gravity of the situation! All the kindness which she had received from the other woman rose up before her, and she was swept by a gush of feeling which wiped out instantly the rankling memory of that recent blow, and filled her with a quick compassion.

She ran up the stairs, and—out of breath from her running—unlocked the door and entered the house. Immediately she paused, still panting. The hall was now quite dark. She could see nothing; but across the blackness came a strange tearing sound which fell coldly upon her ear.

" Where are you? " she called out, the blood pounding in her ears.

There was no answer but that slow rending noise which came insistently from the sitting-room. And in a panic Lucy rushed into that room. Then she saw Miss Hocking, and abruptly paused. Pinkie was there, standing by the table, the outlines of her huge figure shadowy, magnified by that fast-fading light. Stooping she was, her shoulders bulky, her head drooping, her hands moving unceasingly with a slow vindictive malice, tearing into tiny shreds the papers which Lucy had left upon the table.

" Pinkie! " gasped Lucy. " What are you doing? "

The other woman looked back at her.

" Where have you been? " she demanded, and her voice—no longer composed—was harsh, heavy with a sullen animosity.

" I only went out for a moment," said Lucy, her breath still coming quickly.

" You said that before," burst out Miss Hocking, and her lip hung down in a malignant sneer; " but I know where you've been. Going—going—going behind my back in everything." She paused heavily, and, indicating the torn strips between her fingers, she called out in a loud voice: " Is this your paper? "

" Yes," gasped Lucy, " it is mine—but don't go on like that. You frighten me. Let me—let me light the gas."

Suddenly she was appalled by that wild stare with which the other transfixed her; in the gathering darkness that immense amorphous form loomed with an indescribable menace.

" I haven't done anything—really I haven't, Pinkie," she faltered.

" You have! " shouted Miss Hocking, madly, accusingly. " You've admitted it. I saw that notice about him in your paper. I saw it when you were out. I read it, I tell you; I read it myself." Yes, she had read that fatal announcement; by a wild deduction of her insane logic, fastened the entire blame on Lucy. " You're against me," she shouted again, in that loud, malignant voice; " you've done it all. Everything! You hate me, and I hate you."

Still keeping up that lowering, malicious stare, she began slowly to move round the edge of the table. She advanced on Lucy.

" Don't, Pinkie! Don't look like that! " cried out Lucy, shrinking back against the wall.

" I will! I will! " shouted Miss Hocking; at last she had found an outlet for all that pent-up passion, an object on which to spend the bewildered forces of her immense vitality. Madly she began to tear off her clothes, whirling them behind her with wild movements of her arms. Her face, vaguely pallid in the darkness, shrouded by the wild tangle of her hair, transcended by an insane fury, was a sight indescribably terrifying.

" For God's sake, Pinkie! " panted Lucy. " I've done nothing! Don't do that! "

But the other gave no heed. She ripped the last of her garments from her, and her huge white body swam terrifying as a ghost towards Lucy.

She was close to her now, her nakedness complete, obscene, and as in a frenzy she clasped her firm breasts.

" You did it," she shrieked. " You have ruined my life."

" Leave me alone," cried Lucy, and she tried to slip sideways towards the door.

" I've got you," shouted the other madly, " I've got you here."

Then all at once she lunged forward.

Lucy screamed, but, even as she screamed, out of that darkness two powerful hands seized her suddenly by the neck. The hands had thumbs like steel, which dug into the softness of her neck and compressed themselves upon her gullet like a vice. She struggled; she struggled desperately, trying to tear herself free. Again she shrieked —or made to shriek. She did not know. Those two hands were choking the life out of her. Desperately she flung herself against that naked body which so closely oppressed her and so gladly received her struggles. She kicked; she twisted her head, and sank her sharp teeth firmly into those devilish compressing hands. But those hands only held more closely. That soft, warm body closed over hers more ardently. She tried—she tried—again she tried to scream—to utter some feeble cry. She was in agony; dumbly her body writhed; then slowly began to yield. Her head slipped, then sagged slowly backwards; her eyeballs were bursting; the darkness vanished, supplanted by a red and swimming haze through which there floated elusive lights. Dazedly, terrified, she thought of Peter. She was dying—what would he do without her? Her blue lips fell apart; feebly she tried to whisper; then suddenly a roaring—a battering— burst upon her ears; limply she sank back, and utter blackness rose up to envelop her.

She knew nothing of that blackness, but vaguely throughout its span there came to her a flickering of lights, shouting, a sense of crowding, rushing forms; then silence.

When she woke up again, she was on the sofa. A powerful smell of ammonia was in her nostrils; the place seemed full of light and stamping people; Hudson was there, bending over her, and, ridiculously, a man in uniform—a policeman. From the adjoining room—or a mile away, perhaps—came a high, insistent shrieking, like the frantic madness of a wounded animal. It was Pinkie's voice.

" That's better," she heard Hudson say. " But didn't I tell you not to come? "

Why was that policeman looking at her so anxiously? What was he doing here? She tried to smile at him, to nod her head, and again that stab of agony ran into her throat. And so, once more, she fainted.

XII

FOUR days elapsed before she could struggle out of bed. Hudson had said a week; but she had her own ideas about things; and so, upon the afternoon of that fourth day, when she had dismissed the attendant Mrs. Dickens, she raised herself and made determinedly the effort. But as her foot touched the ground she winced from the jarring shock, and with difficulty restrained an exclamation of pain. Her neck, upon the slightest movement, sent a twinge along her spine which was excruciating. She was obliged to step cautiously, to hold her head quite motionless, to keep even her features expressionless and rigid in order to avoid that shooting pang. Still she went on.

Supporting herself by the furniture, she made the passage of the room, and looked at herself in the mirror. She was pale, and upon the pallid skin of her throat two great purple weals lay spread like the wings of an enormous butterfly. Curiously she gazed at these for a moment, then, with a faint shiver, she turned away. In the same stiff fashion she pulled on her dressing-gown, and shuffled slowly into the hall. She felt extremely weak, but she had an almost impatient desire to get away from the restraining influence of her bed.

Instinctively—this time the pang was that of recollection!—she avoided the sitting-room; and, entering the kitchen, she sat herself cautiously by the window. Before her lay that same shining scene of sea and sky which she had so often viewed from her own house. For three days after those first hours of semi-consciousness she had stared stiffly at the opposite wallpaper—a patch of unchanging green—and now, in the present weakness of her body, this lovely familiar sight gripped her with a voluptuous sadness. Everything was quiet. Around her, empty of all sound, was the flat; and it was empty of Miss Hocking's presence. They had taken her to the asylum. How strange it was to think of that—driven her off in a closed cab to Blandford Asylum, upon the outskirts of Glasgow. She had often seen it from the train—a noble building of grey stone, turreted like a castle, set upon a hill in charming grounds. Yet she had never dreamed that Pinkie—— In retrospect, she viewed the whole calamity dispassionately, like a woman gazing with studious detachment at a picture. It had moved so swiftly: that frightful screaming of Miss Hocking under restraint, which she had heard dimly through her dream, then her awakening; later, Hudson's enquiries; his wire to Miss Hocking's brother—a tall, dark, angular man. with a keen and worried face above his high white collar. Somehow that collar stuck in Lucy's mind, which had been feverish when he arrived—a stiffly rigid collar, unpeaked, shaped like a clergyman's. But though, somehow, that collar typified him, he was not a clergyman. He was a barrister, with a reputation—a coming man, Hudson had inferred to her—which he guarded jealously.

" We've always been afraid of this," she heard him say again, in his clear English voice. " We've dreaded it." He dreaded, too, the repercussions upon his practice. " It mustn't be known," he had repeated, not once, but twenty times, with an anxious insistence " It would be fatal—in my profession." A wise consideration, in a way, she thought; no one would want to trust a lawyer with a mad sister.

And so that sister had been certified—what had they called it? Acute mania! Yes, that was the phrase; and the outlook, Hudson had told her, was beyond doubt, hopeless. For more than five years she had lived with a foolish woman who was now a certified, incurable lunatic! The thought appalled her; it made those ordinary years of life so startling, so unique. Strangely, she remembered nothing of Miss Hocking's peculiarity, harboured no grudge for that awful and unprovoked assault; she thought only of the kindness she had received from her. " Yes, she was kind," she thought, with a slightly humid eye.

And now she had to get out of this flat within the month. The furniture would be removed then—stored or sold—which she did not know; it had been all arranged by that barrister brother. How kind he had been; but with that curious look like Hudson's in his eyes. And she did know that alone she could not support the expenses of the flat.

Abruptly, her thoughts swung round to her own predicament; her eye, no longer humid, lost its spell and hardened into reality. Her position was really serious. She had a handful of possessions— a wardrobe, a rocking-chair, a picture. She had some good clothes— how she grudged now what she had spent upon them at Pinkie's rash enticement—and she had twenty pounds in money. Finally, she had her son: her dear son, whose face had risen before her at that agonising moment which she had thought to be her last. Him she counted no liability, but her chief asset upon the balance-sheet of life. She had also—an afterthought instantly dismissed—her relations. No, she would never, after these years, swallow the bitter lees of humiliation by approaching them. The gentle suppliant was not her rôle. She had changed, lost that mildness which had once been hers. And yet, by the end of this month, unless she bestirred herself, she would have neither occupation nor home.

She moved restlessly, and was twinged by her pain. Exasperated by her own weakness, she twisted her head deliberately into that pain, encountering it fiercely, till it waned into numbness. Yes, that was her attitude towards life.

Still, she chafed at her enforced inaction, deploring the loss of these last few days, realising that she could make no move till Monday. Her present absence from the office did not trouble her; she would be paid, and that sufficed her; already in her mind she had finished with Lennox's. But she must quickly get herself right— that was imperative.

At this she rose. It was four o'clock, but she did not want tea— she always knew herself to be ill when she took a distaste for tea— and, pouring some milk into a saucepan, she heated it on the gas-ring. She drank the milk slowly, then, feeling a little faint, she returned to bed. There she lay plotting out the future—thinking, till at last the darkness fell upon the quiet house, and sleep descended with it.

It was Monday before she was able to go out, and even then she was shaky and giddy in the street, as she struggled up to business. At the office, she was utterly reticent about her accident—that was what they termed it—and she herself offered no contradiction. Nor did she yield herself to their sympathy; even when Dougal had remarked: " You're not looking well, Mrs. Moore," she had simply nodded; and Dougal was a favourite of hers now. Though her head throbbed, she went out upon her round in the usual fashion. It was not, of course, the demands of her present post which drew her, but her purpose to achieve another. She was in earnest now, she told herself, and, indeed, in grim earnest she began.

Even yet she did not realise the full difficulty of her task, or she did not, at least, admit this difficulty. The district at this period lay stagnant, sunk in that bog of trade depression which long followed the Boer War. Everywhere a policy of cautious pessimism prevailed. Most of the shipyards were already on half time, the largest steel-works in Winton had closed down two blast furnaces, and, in sympathy, many of the pits were idle, or working only a single shift. These were actions upon the grand scale; but they had inevitably their reactions upon the lesser. Small tradesmen lengthened their faces and shortened their credit. Even upon her final rounds for Lennox's, she found a dwindling of orders; a general glum anticipation of bad times ahead; in the colliery villages, miners, squatting upon their haunches, supported thus the walls of their dwellings, eyeing her despondently as she passed; in the Clydeside towns crowds of unemployed gathered in apathy outside the public-houses; the beat of the hammers—pulse of the district's industry—no longer vigorous and vital, now throbbed with a feeble and intermittent note. Instinctively she felt these omens of misfortune. Those who had promised glibly to inform her " should they hear of something," inferred, when she ventured to refresh their recollections, that it was a bad time to be looking for work.

Moreover, it was not even yet the age when women were admitted freely to equality in business, nor had she qualifications fitted for this still unequal struggle. Those letters which she had so confidently despatched brought her not a single reply. She had moments, indeed, when she contemplated with a sort of dull amazement the lack of response to her applications. Did those people not comprehend what they were missing? She, Lucy Moore, so brisk, so competent, so eager to serve, to be overlooked in this atrocious fashion. She could not understand it.

Still, she knew her worth and she persisted. She would achieve a magnificent post, somehow, in spite of them, in spite of everything. Every day she bought her two newspapers—that almost fatal newspaper!—approaching them each morning with fresh hope, studying one by one those advertisements, marking with her pen each slender chance.

She wrote her applications with a sort of dogged pertinacity, forcing herself to a note of optimism. She bought better notepaper; she spent shillings upon postage-stamps; she began even to apply for the impossible: the matronship of an orphanage—a secretary's post in London—actually the post of manageress in a laundry. Finally, in desperation, she inserted an advertisement offering her services in any capacity which might yield a modest wage.

And nothing happened but a passage of the days. She had not fully recovered from her shock; Hudson had spoken vaguely of a holiday, but that she' dismissed instantly as impossible; still, her assumption of vivacity began to wear thin. She had moments when she discovered herself staring at nothing, with doubtful eyes. Sometimes at night she would wake up, wondering what would become of her. And Peter! He, of course, was her main concern. Still unconscious of her altered circumstances, he continued his blandly optimistic letters, demanding in one a better fountain-pen, alluding in another to the prospects of his career. Each letter was to her a sublime incentive, a happy spur, urging her forward to succeed.

She must and she would succeed for him. And yet she could not.

With a feeling of galling desolation she came into the office in the Saddleriggs on the Saturday which was her last day. Despondently she went to her desk, and began those entries which were the last she would ever make in that drab and grimy den. Yet, painfully almost, she embraced its drabness and regretted her departure from its grime. She knew it now so well. Frank had worked here; her livelihood had sprung from here; she had filled it with something of her life.

At length she looked up, to find Lennox regarding her. He cleared his throat awkwardly, at once removed his eyes. But in a moment he was over at her desk. They were alone in the office.

" Have ye got anything to do? " he enquired, with the same awkwardness; and she saw in his face that curious concern which had been growing for those last few days. For a moment there was silence, then she faced him directly, confidently.

" Yes," she lied, stung by the compassion in his eyes. " I got fixed up nicely yesterday."

His face cleared slightly. " Did you, though? That's fine, now, that is." His eyes lightened and he gave his conscious little laugh. " I was beginning to worry about you. You've been looking real poorly these last days. It's an extraordinary thing, but it's fair upset me."

" I'm perfectly well," she answered calmly. " Perfectly strong and healthy."

" I know," he said hurriedly. " You're fit as a smart-stepping pony. I've always known that. But it's just that you've looked down in the mouth lately. I wouldn't for anything think that I was maybe responsible."

He broke off, caressing his neat beard sheepishly, as though scarcely comprehending why he spoke. Strange man that he was, he had cherished for her unawares a curious regard, which, overlaid by the passion of his business, squeezed away by his natural shrewdness, had been compressed through the years into small compass: present yet unrecognised. And now, by his own act, he had wrenched himself from business. He was a little lost; he had not yet found his feet in this new and unsubstantial world. But now, as he encompassed her trim small figure, he had a sweeping recollection of that quiet after-noon when involuntarily he had slipped his arm around her waist. How neat it had felt, neat yet soft! Unconsciously his sallow, perky features coloured. He had been a bachelor by inclination—of course, he knew that—but he was only fifty-seven, and, in his own words, spry as a sparrow.

" I was so taken up with the signing of the settlement that other things went out of my head," he said at last, rather vaguely and with unusual diffidence.

" Quite so," she said, with an assumption of briskness. She did not understand his attitude. The first shock of her dismissal over, her resentment had thinned. She had even seen something of his point of view.

" I'm glad, though," he persisted, cocking his beard. " I'm real glad you've got settled." He looked at her sideways, and added : " What is it ? "

" It's teaching work," she replied at random—a little wildly. " An excellent job."

" I see," he replied somewhat vaguely. " I see," he said again ; he stared hesitatingly at her a moment, then moved off to the window, turning a pencil in his fingers, turning a strange intangible consideration within his mind.

She looked at his square back covered by the inevitable grey homespun. Why had she lied to him ? It was so unlike her. She did not know, yet she did know with clear-cut, painful apprehension that she must at all costs escape a final expression of his condolences : for him to say, " I'm sorry—real sorry you've nothing to do ! " That, at least, her swelling heart could not endure. She could suffer anything but an exhibition of her own misery.

Yet, as she bent low over her book, she was aware of his turning from the window as though again he meant to speak. But at that moment the outer door swung sharply open and Andrews entered the office with Dougal. At once Lennox halted, thrust his hands into his pockets, began his conscious undertone of a whistle. Instinctively she felt the eyes of Dougal and Andrews upon her. They were safely settled ; Dougal secure with Hagelmann's ; Andrews tidily looking forward to a pleasant existence in a small newspaper and confectionery shop in the Gorbals which he had purchased with " a bit of the wife's money." Yes, they were all right, but she—she was not all right : she was all wrong : a liar, a humbug, a fool ! Well, let it be so ; she did not care. She would keep her head up and make herself to smile.

She finished her book, shut it, put down her pencil, and looked at the clock. As she did so, it struck one—a slow, portentous stroke.

" Well," she cried cheerfully—or so it seemed—" that's the end of Lennox's ! " They greeted her remark with fitting solemnity. It was quite an occasion. They all shook hands with each other. Lennox gave them their pay envelopes.

" I hope we'll meet again, Mrs. Moore," said Dougal, quite earnestly. Now he was a head taller than she, well dressed, clean, and businesslike—even his ears seemed less obtrusive. Incredible what the passage of the years had done for him. But what had they done for her ?

"We'll run up against each other, Dougal," she answered briskly. "That's certain."

"I hope so, indeed," he said seriously.

"And don't forget to look me up," cried Andrews, shorn from his melancholy by the moment. "Look in if you're passing"; and, combining sentiment with business, he added, "We sell all the papers."

"Glad to hear you've gotten fixed," said Lennox, in a confidential undertone, still rather sheepish, still hesitating, holding her hand a little longer than he ought. "I'll be coming to take a cup of tea with you one of these days." Tea! Was it likely that he would ever take tea with her?

She put on her hat and coat, took a last look round, then at the door she gave that neat little nod, smiled towards them collectively.

"Good-bye, then," she exclaimed briskly, "and good luck."

Still smiling, she turned and went down the stairs. But, outside, that smile went wrong. Her lips quivered as she made her way to the station and entered her train. Seated in the empty compartment, she gazed at the opposite cushions with a set face; then all at once she dropped her head into her hands, broke down into a flood of silent tears.

XIII

THOSE tears, though unaccountable, were assuredly not the symbol of her defeat. Inevitably she felt better when she had shed them; she became aware, with swift reaction, almost with a smile, that neither this termination of her present employment nor her enforced departure from the flat was synonymous with the deluge. Hope was inextinguishable within her.

She would find another post. Unencumbered by any obligation, she would find it. Herself! Naturally, too, she must find some temporary lodging; a room—an inexpensive room; and she decided at once that she would not rent this apartment in Ardfillan. Though she was little known in the town, she shrank somehow from exposing to the public eye the sudden change in her fortune and position, from any revelation of her altered circumstances. She wanted to get away completely; to make a fresh start; and it was essential for her to be at the heart of things, ready to seize upon the slenderest opportunity; in the city, moreover, she knew she could obtain easily a cheap lodging such as she desired.

And so already, in advance, the next step was decided. Her mind, again alert, speculated actively; yet never—no, not once—did she entertain the thought of demanding assistance from her relations. That was the last unthinkable resource. She would cringe before nobody. Joe, of course, had placed himself utterly beyond the pale; Edward's past spasmodic interest had merely irritated her: and, as for Richard, her own brother, she would, in her own phrase, have died sooner than ask him for a penny.

Her stock of money was ridiculously low—a few pounds. But, against that, once again her spirit was high, her determination firm, her fortitude unquenchable. She began her intensive campaign. She bought no more papers, but the reading-room of the public library became her resort. Once more she scoured the advertisement columns with an almost painful intensity. On Monday she wrote twenty letters of application. On Tuesday she went to Glasgow and again made a scrupulous canvass of every firm even remotely associated with her previous line of business. On Wednesday she discovered an advertisement demanding a personal application for a travelling agency in connection with one of the smaller spinning-mills at Raisley. Immediately she set out. The town lay outside the zone covered by her season ticket, and, to avoid expense, she travelled by workman's train, sitting with repugnance amongst a row of corduroyed labourers who smoked and spat inordinately. But the situation had been filled an hour before her arrival. Had she no luck, she thought bitterly? Would her affairs never turn? She came home in cold exasperation.

Thursday she spent writing letters at the flat. Some men came to arrange for the removal of Miss Hocking's furniture on the following Monday. She took out and packed some of her own clothing.

Despite herself, she felt again that her situation was growing desperate. Four long days of effort and nothing to show for it. Nothing.

Restlessly she wandered about the flat, sat down, touched the piano, then got up again. A strange agitation lay upon her, due, she thought, to the imminence of her departure. She took up a book, but, her ears attuned for the postman's knock, she could not settle herself. Would nothing ever turn up for her? When with a sinking heart she heard the postman go past her door, she laid down her book listlessly and went at once to bed.

On Friday she said to herself frankly: " If nothing happens to-day, I must go to-morrow to see about my room." And on Friday nothing happened.

Accordingly, on the following day she set out for the city to find this apartment of necessity. It was a repugnant step, which she had put off until the final moment—anything in the nature of a temporary measure filled her with a sense of insufficiency—but now she could procrastinate no longer. Facing the bitter necessity, she took an early train for Glasgow, and on her arrival, her face strangely sober and contained, she came out of Queen Street Station and turned along towards Unity Street.

Then suddenly someone collided with her. Turning, she raised her head sharply and found herself looking up at young Frame's smiling face. It was an encounter strangely reminiscent of that moment when, on her first day at Lennox's, running after her with his usual velocity, he had bumped into her on the stairs.

But so little had she expected this present meeting that she exclaimed involuntarily: " It's you."

" I told you we'd run into each other," he said, smiling more broadly. " But it's sooner than I thought."

" Yes," she said, a trifle coldly. " But I didn't expect you to run me down."

" I'm sorry," he exclaimed hurriedly, his smile fading. " I was in too big a hurry, I suppose." He paused, disconcerted by her singular lack of effusion, whilst on either side a stream of people slipped past them along the pavement.

" I've been up seeing my aunt," he said, explaining himself with growing embarrassment. " She's cashier at Henderson & Shaw's— the house factors, you know."

She gave him a wintry smile, wondering how she could be rid of him, inferring by her manner that now, of all times, she was in no humour for his ingenuous conversation.

" A regular bother she was in," he persevered, flushing, however, at her silence. " One of her collectors has left without giving notice, and she's at her wits' end to find somebody reliable straight away. Wanted me to take on the job. But no fear. I'm starting with Hagelmann's on Monday."

Abruptly she raised her head, stared at him: not that frosty smile, but an eagerness leaping suddenly like a light into her dark-blue eyes.

" It's a position," she exclaimed in a different key. " Did you say it was a position she offered you ? "

" Only twenty-five shillings a week. Walking about all day collecting rents. No, thank you," he answered contemptuously. " And such work! I wouldn't look at it."

" Do you——" she asked slowly. " Do you know if they've got anybody else ? "

He shook his head. " They'll have to advertise, I expect."

" Dougal," she exclaimed, with sudden outright vehemence, " do you think—would they give it to me ? "

He looked at her, his lips adrift, his eyes widening in surprise.

" But you're fixed up," he stammered. " You told us at the office. Besides, you wouldn't like it."

" Like it ! " she breathed; this was no time for a specious picture of her achievements. Speaking rapidly, she said:

" Look here, Dougal, I want to get something to do. Never mind why. I just must get settled into something. If you think they'd take me at that place, I'd jump at it—yes, I'd jump at it if I had the chance."

Still astounded, he replied slowly:

" You'd have the chance all right. She's been cashier there for years—my aunt. Practically manages the place. She'd give you the job, I haven't the slightest doubt."

All unconscious of the sublime irony of the situation—this one-time office-boy, whom she had viewed with so dubious an eye, offering to assist her towards fresh employment—her gaze shone towards him. He was perhaps her deliverer. Yes, at last it was a chance—a chance of that very work which had for weeks eluded her, an opportunity which changed instantly the whole complexion of her life.

" Tell me about it," she cried quickly. " I'll go straight along now."

" Mind you, it's not much," he answered hurriedly. " Only twenty-five shillings a week. I don't think you'd consider it. And the work's not exactly pleasant."

He paused, envisaging her eagerness. " But it might—you might take it—for the time being."

" It'll suit me all right if I get it." She laughed delightedly, a little breathless with her own excitement. And to think that a moment ago she had almost snubbed him. More intimately she added: " Quick, now, tell me where I am to go."

" Well," he said at length, smiling in sympathy, " the office is at the end of Davis Street. Henderson & Shaw. House factors. You can't miss it. Ask for Miss Tinto and mention my name. I'm sorry I can't come along with you. Not that you'll have the slightest difficulty. It's just that I don't think that you'd care about the kind of work."

" Never mind the kind," she answered, flashing a warm look at him. " It's work I want."

" I see," he said doubtfully. But it was evident that he did not see. There was still a questioning smile on his face as she took his hand and shook it quickly, gratefully.

" Good-bye," she said warmly, " and a thousand thanks."

" That's all right," he answered awkwardly. " Nothing at all. We'll—we'll run into each other again one of these days."

She nodded with a final quick glance, turned, and set off along the pavement. At last a stroke of luck had come to her; she must at all costs turn that luck to account. With a swift memory of that situation at Raisley which had been filled before she arrived, she swung into Davis Street, hurrying from her eagerness. She did not pause to take a tramcar—that in her mood she felt to be too slow—and in a few moments she had traversed the length of the street. Then, all at once, she drew up, her vivid eyes upon the sign before her: Henderson & Shaw—House Factors.

It was, she saw immediately, a dignified office, shop-fronted, the window screened by wire mesh, the door of mahogany, the fittings of solid shining brass, a very different office from those back rooms above the Saddleriggs. But she was not intimidated. With a determined thrust of her chin she advanced, turned the handle, and pushed through the door.

She found herself in a wide and rather lofty room, facing a long and shining counter railed with brass. Behind the counter stood a large, stout desk, and behind the desk a large, stout woman. Other articles of office furniture: two tables, some chairs, an enormous greenish safe inset against the wall: were also behind that counter, but the desk and the woman were significant, outstanding, starkly arresting to the eye.

For a long time Lucy stood upon the tessellated floor gazing in silence over the brass-railed counter—there seemed a superfluity of brass about the establishment—at the woman who, betraying no consciousness of her existence, moved carefully a pen over an enormous ledger.

To engage that rapt attention she coughed; but her cough was without avail. The pen scratched faintly; the woman stopped writing, inspected the nib reproachfully, cleansed it fastidiously of an invisible hair; then she began slowly to write again.

" I beg your pardon," said Lucy suddenly.

Slowly the woman turned round, exposing an expanse of shining red face focused by a pair of gold-rimmed spectacles. She was in black, rather stiff black, high-necked, and wore no ornament but a fine gold chain. And now in silence she slid off her stool and swept to the counter. Seen at close quarters, she was more massive than ever, and her high bosom was terrific.

Gazing down at Lucy over that expanse of bosom, in a voice unexpectedly mild she said: " Well? "

Dwarfed by that impressive presence, Lucy felt suddenly a strange sense of insignificance come upon her, but with that resolute tilt of her chin she enquired: " Miss Tinto? "

The other inclined her head, tapping her pen gently upon the counter.

" My name is Moore," said Lucy quickly. " I've come to see about the vacancy you have." And, before Miss Tinto could reply, she rushed swiftly into a full account of the circumstances of her coming.

It was a long account, and, when she concluded, abruptly, again she felt herself tremulous with the eagerness of her intention.

" Just so," said Miss Tinto at length, following a prolonged survey through her gold-rimmed glasses; then, with unexpected confidence, she added: " He's a nice young fellow, my nephew."

" He is indeed," agreed Lucy with fervour.

" He was left badly off," said Miss Tinto reminiscently, " but I must say he has done remarkably well for himself."

Lucy concurred eagerly with this concise eulogy of young Frame's progress.

" It's a pity though," said Miss Tinto guardedly; " it's a man that I require."

Not that Miss Tinto attached a literal significance to her phrase! Miss Tinto at fifty-five knew all that was to be known of man, and of man's duplicity. Miss Tinto was a business woman, pioneer of her age, calm, capable, respectable, and virgin, with a bridle capable of reducing any male to abject impotence. Yet through all her dryness Miss Tinto had amiability—when she felt that amiability to be deserved. And now, with another survey of Lucy's intent figure, she added: " We've got to collect our rents in some curious places."

" That wouldn't worry me," said Lucy swiftly. " I've been doing a man's work for six years now."

" You mightn't stand up to it," said Miss Tinto thoughtfully. " There's not much of you."

" But what there is of me is good," answered Lucy. " Just give me a trial and you'll see."

Incredibly a slow smile spread over Miss Tinto's shining features. " You've a good conceit of yourself," she said with caustic pleasantry. She patted her mouse-coloured hair with the pen, then smoothed her cheeks back to their normal impassivity.

" The very highest references would be essential," she added after a moment. " Our collectors have the handling of money, you understand."

" I can give you references," broke in Lucy eagerly. And at once, without compunction, she advanced Lennox's, Edward's, and Richard's names.

The effect was astonishing.

" Your brother! " gasped Miss Tinto, immediately engaged. She stared at Lucy with new eyes. " So you are Mr. Murray's sister." She paused. " He's a most respected man. I know. I live in Ralston myself."

There was an impressive silence. Then slowly Miss Tinto moved and lifted the flap of the counter.

" Come in and sit down," she said, and there was even a tinge of cordiality in her manner. " I'll speak to Mr. Rattray about you."

With cheeks faintly flushed, Lucy obeyed, taking one of the smaller chairs whilst Miss Tinto mounted a short flight of stairs to a glass-panelled door upon the first landing, knocked and went in. It was for Lucy a moment of crisis, this momentous balancing of her fate. Surely here she would be successful. Surely she was right in thinking that Miss Tinto seemed well disposed towards her. Had she not observed a sympathetic flash of understanding in the other woman's eye? Sitting there, gazing unseeingly at that enormous safe, her eyes remote, her small hands clasped upon her knee, her hair—struck as it were by a new lustre—coiled delicately upon her white neck, she had an air both vivid and intense.

The issue was not magnificent, but, oh, how vital it was to her! Let this wage she sought be paltry, it was at least sufficient for her present purpose. Let her be successful and she would abandon all thought of that repugnant single room. Plotting ahead, she saw herself taking a small, unobtrusive place. Her few things she could have removed to the city at small expense. She would have at least a roof above her head for Peter when he returned. And in Glasgow. She had that deeper motive, that more powerful thrust of her endeavour in the thought of establishing herself here. Violently she willed that she might maintain her independence, that she might get this post. She would get it; she must get it; it was vital, urgent, imperative for her good and for Peter's good.

Suddenly, with a leaping of her heart, she looked up to find Miss Tinto descending the stairs. With a trembling of her limbs she rose and faced the other woman, whose face betrayed nothing of that immense decision which she must now convey.

"Well," said Miss Tinto slowly, "I have seen Mr. Rattray."

"Yes?" said Lucy in a low voice, and to herself she thought, "If I fail here, what in God's name is to become of me?" Never in all her efforts had she advanced so far towards the threshold of success.

"He's the head of the firm," went on Miss Tinto; she seemed in no hurry to disclose the palpitating issue of her interview; and now she explained: "Henderson & Shaw is simply the name. Really it is Mr. Rattray's business."

"Yes?" whispered Lucy again. And again she felt the trembling of her limbs.

"Of course, he really leaves the managing of things to me," said Miss Tinto, bridling a little. "I've been here for thirty years. He's got every confidence in me."

"Yes?" Once more Lucy gasped out the word. Was she never to know?

There was a short silence.

"And so I've decided to take up your references," said Miss

Tinto finally, smiling almost benignantly over her glasses. " If they're satisfactory, you can start next week."

Something swept over Lucy. She wanted to weep, to laugh, to cry aloud. They had taken her. Again she had her start; again the future lay ready—ready to be moulded by her own capable hands. With one flashing stroke, the recollection of the past month's misfortune vanished like a spectre dispelled. Gazing up at Miss Tinto's ample form, she had a wild, hysterical, almost irresistible impulse to fall on that maternal bosom. But she restrained herself.

" Thank you," she stammered in a low voice. " I'm—I'm glad——"
Then she could say no more.

XIV

A MONTH later she sat breakfasting in her new house—eating a slice of bread and butter to her cup of tea—by the light of a tongue of gas which whistled upwards noisily from its burner. Not yet eight o'clock, a blanket of fog lay over the city, excluding the faint light of the breaking dawn and pressing darkly against the window of the room wherein she sat.

It was not a prepossessing room, nor from her present look did she so regard it, yet it had at least some features of utility. In front of her, beneath the window, was a chipped sink fed by a tap which, though it dripped incessantly, was none the less a most convenient source of water; to the right was the kitchen range, bearing on its blackleaded surface a small gas-ring linked by a swooping pipe to the bracket above the mantelpiece; on her left, fixed against the wall, stood a battered wooden box, half bunker, half settle, combining the storage of fuel with the advantage of an occasional seat. These were the simple fixtures of the room, and the furniture—the small square table at which she sat, two cane-bottomed chairs, her own fluted rocker, and a small iron bed standing behind her in an alcove—was equally severe. Through the open door of this kitchen-bedroom the remainder of the house was visible—a dark and well-like hall joining on to another bedroom, empty except for a wardrobe and another iron bedstead—and a small cubicle of a bathroom containing a bath encased in its mouldering wooden frame and coated with cracked and blistered yellowish enamel. The walls of these rooms, like the walls of the kitchen, were papered throughout by a brownish varnished paper of undecipherable pattern; and in the foggy light they had an aspect almost melancholy.

This, then, was her new house—that " quiet place " which she had so eagerly anticipated. Yet she had done her best. For two days she had searched—" searched high and low," as she put it to Miss Tinto—and, even with the discerning assistance of Henderson & Shaw, this " one room and kitchen " house, with its so-called bathroom, situated on the top storey in a large block given over to such dwellings, had been the only habitation to fulfil the requirements of her respectability and her purse. And how narrowly it missed evading both! The rent was seven shillings a week, which was as much as she could afford, and the house—indeed, the entire block of houses, which ran the length of the street, euphoniously and inappropriately named Flowers Street—breathed of a drab and seedy indigence.

The building, with its narrow " close " entrances and dark, ill-lit stone stairways, was not quite a tenement. The street itself was not quite out at elbows, but its elbows had worn suspiciously thin. Something—perhaps a clinging vestige of a more glorious past— saved the building and the street, preserved them from an utter meanness. Here, then, to 53 Flowers Street had she come, here of necessity had she settled for the present.

Her immediate desire had been to brighten up the rooms and to furnish them with some degree of comfort. Reluctantly, however, she had been constrained once more to defer inclination to necessity, for, with Peter's last term's fees to be paid from her small reserve of money, she had been able to afford only the barest necessities: these two beds, some second-hand chairs, and the cheapest cooking utensils. How bitterly, now, did she regret her parting with her own original furniture so lightly, and for so paltry a sum. But that was done, and done irrevocably.

No, this new house was not quite what she had anticipated; it was not yet a home, though shortly she would make it so—or, if she improved her position and her fortune turned for the better, shortly abandon it for a more suitable abode.

By this time she had finished her breakfast and, with a glance at the cheap nickel alarm clock—this another of her purchases—on the mantelpiece, she rose. Turning out the gas, she entered the hall. Here, in the well-like obscurity, she removed her hat and coat from unseen pegs, slipped into them, and, as her key lay already in her pocket, opened the door and went out.

The fog, lying in wraiths upon the street, enveloped her hurrying figure as she emerged from the close mouth. Hereabouts—perhaps from the nearness of the river—these fogs lay with a thicker and more persistent intensity, yet now the brumous haze was lifting, pierced by a red orb of sun which disclosed more clearly the features of the district which, stretching back through Kelvinbank to the

Docks, ran a hard-pressed race against the approach of those adjacent dockland slums.

Even now, as she hurriedly traversed it, she felt unconsciously the meanness of its air. The streets were narrow, cobbled, profusely littered in some mysterious fashion by torn, dirty papers, defiled always by orange-peel, a stray tin can, and the scattered yet persistent evidence of dray-horses passing to the docks. The shops were undistinguished. The fronts of those shops, even the pavements chalk-marked by playing children, had an untidy look. Then, at the corner, where Flowers Street reached its tortuous end, stood a large hall, with a board which said, in rich gilt letters: " Garner's Assembly Rooms. Balls Wed. & Sat. Gents 1s. Ladies 6d." And beneath, in smaller type: " Gloves optional. Slippers essential."

That hall, with its blatant board, typified for Lucy the essence of this locality. It was common; it was ordinary; it offended against good taste in general and her own sense of refinement in particular. As she boarded the red tramcar which took her to her work she could not forbear to think on the rude turn in her affairs which had thrust her so unexpectedly into this indifferent background.

And her work. How she regretted the comparative sinecure of her last employment, with its easy train journeys and a remuneration which in retrospect appeared munificent.

Henderson & Shaw factored slum property. That summarised everything, epitomised the hardships of her present occupation. She saw now that young Frame had been right when he submitted that " the post was not much "; she admitted frankly that she detested it. Still, she accepted her position in the same spirit as she accepted 53 Flowers Street, saying outwardly, as it were, with an ironic smile: " You've come down a step, my woman! " yet thinking inwardly, without irony, with indeed a resolute intensity, that it would not be long before she stepped up again.

At the corner of Davis Street she got off her tramcar and with a brisk step made her way to the office. Glad to be out of the raw air, she entered quickly.

Already the large and lofty room had ceased to be impressive; with quite familiar ease she slipped past the counter, answered Miss Tinto's agreeable nod, and went at once to her own small table. At the opposite table sat a man with his hat and overcoat on, and at her entry, without looking up, he rasped out the single word: " Morning."

" Good morning," answered Lucy, smiling slightly. Dandie's continual aggression towards the universe had not yet ceased to amuse her. He was the other rent-collector—Adam Dandie—a stocky, burly, thick-set man with long arms and a weathered, craggy look. His bearing, too, was bluff and downright. Even his dress—the seedy square hat clapped firmly above his bluish bitten ears, the shiny pilot-coat taut to his sturdy figure—betrayed the same uncompromising bluntness. His face had a hard ruddy colour—a fine network of reddish vessels in which his eyes, beneath the greyish tufts of his brows, were small and scrutinising. Stout he was in figure, short in wind, and shorter still in temper: when irritated, he had a testy belligerence, delivering his words with an impact which struck like the kick of a mule. Such was Adam Dandie in all but one essential—his legs. The dreadful fact remains that Dandie was bandy, incomparably bandy: his lower extremities when he stood still described a perfect letter O, and the transverse diameter of that O was wide. This explained his grudge against a universe containing fleas, fog, women, insufficient whisky, and tardy tramcars. This much could be said for Dandie: his grudge was not malicious, and he himself enjoyed it thoroughly.

" Damn these pencils," he now said, looking at the one he was sharpening and had again broken. " They can't make them nowadays. Can't make anything."

" I'll sharpen it for you," said Lucy helpfully.

" Humph," he growled. " Think you can do it better than me, do you? I don't think. Probably cut yourself and sue me for damages."

" So long as it's not for breach of promise, Dandie," shot out Miss Tinto from her high desk. She did not speak much, but when she did, it was pertinent.

" Capable of that, too," said Dandie, grinding away at the lead. " I know women."

Bandy-legged or no, he implied an intimate acquaintance with the tender sex which had left him scornful yet scatheless, and, as though to make sure, he added, " Don't I just? "

Miss Tinto lifted her eyelids towards Lucy in companionable understanding: despite her superior position, she had now definitely accepted Lucy—for all her formidable figure and slightly bearded face Miss Tinto had a generous heart—and a growing friendship was the result.

" For some men," said she grimly, addressing the air, " hanging is too good."

The conversation was not continued, for at that moment Rattray entered the office, or, more correctly, walked through it to his room. He was an unobtrusive man, tall, angular, rarely seen; now he nodded generally in his passage and was gone.

" Well," said Lucy, rising, " fog or no fog, I'd better get begun. White Street for me to-day. Worse luck! "

" Don't get lost, now," said Dandie, with a sort of saturnine solicitude.

Lucy smiled and shook her head. Then she took her book and her bag, those insignia of her position—the black leather book and the well-polished leather bag—and went out of the office.

For the moment the sun had gone out, and the fog again worked down in yellow twisting coils. It caught her throat with a stinging rawness and made her cough. Her coat, she decided, was not heavy enough for this weather. Around her, swirling like the fog, was the life of the city; but no longer did she feel that quick answering thrill which once had stirred her. She was used to it now, and she was older (yes, she reflected, she was getting older); she didn't care about her work, and she didn't like the fog: she coughed again from its fume as she entered White Street. No, she didn't like the fog; nor, most emphatically, did she like White Street.

White Street was narrow—a narrow canyon enclosed between two rows of tall tenements, dark and dismal, untroubled by sun on the sunniest days of summer, and now merely a narrow gutter, a chasm, a sewer choked by fog.

It was half-past ten in the morning as she entered the first close to begin her work. The close held a glutinous blackness beside which that outer darkness was as snow to pitch, and it held, also, that odour, indescribable, polluted—the smell of the slums which she already knew, and which already she detested.

Arrived at the first door, she knocked sharply upon the thin panel, using the butt of her pencil—a professional touch acquired through bitter experience after that first week, when she had worn the skin off her knuckles by much misguided rapping.

After she knocked, she waited. In the beginning she had been inclined to scorn the length of time allocated to her for each tenement —with some she was allowed an entire day to complete the collection of the weekly rents—but now she did not scorn that length of time. She knew instead that it was too short. There were, for example, in this one entry, four landings—each corresponding to a storey of the building—and upon each landing were eight one-apartment houses, making a total of thirty-two " houses," accessible through this one narrow close. Twenty such closes in the tenement gave in all the incredible yet actual figure of six hundred and forty dwellings in one small building. Six hundred and forty homes—packed and teeming with a wretched humanity, crammed up together on an acre of mud. And in the short length of White Street there were three such tenements. In this narrow span of street there dwelt, under the civilised conditions of the twentieth century, a total of four thousand human beings. " Ticketed houses," these were, each bearing upon the door a ticket by right of which a night inspector of the Corporation might enter to ensure that no " overcrowding " should occur.

Salutary precaution of a benign authority. Yet, despite that precaution, twelve persons—and three generations—had been known to sleep in harmony and comfort in one of those rooms ten feet wide by fifteen long. At least the harmony and comfort may be assumed; for the landlord heard no complaints.

Abruptly Lucy knocked again. The door opened to the width of an inch and a voice said, " Who's there? "

" Henderson & Shaw," said Lucy briskly; upon her visitations she assumed now this dual personality: Henderson always the aggressor, Shaw the sympathiser. Besides, the term was more impressive than a mere demand for rent.

" Oh! " returned the voice, not enquiring, now merely resigned. There was a pause, more expressive than the exclamation; then the door swung back slowly and a woman appeared within the dimly lighted frame. Dark and tangle-haired, her face darkly sallow from its dirt, she turned one gleaming eye towards Lucy. The other eye would never gleam again, for it was gone, and in its place the socket pouted with a blank and rather sinister evasion.

But the woman was not sinister. " Come in," said she, in a tone mild with habitual acceptance of the inevitable.

Lucy went in. The room was bare—destitute of furniture save for two wooden boxes and a straw mattress lying on the floor along one side of the room. Upon one of the boxes sat a labouring man; before him upon the other was his breakfast of sausage and bread and tea.

Eating noisily, gulping his saucered tea, he gave no attention to Lucy's entry, but continued his hearty breakfast. Nor did the baby, lying upon the mattress, apparently give heed to her, but, flat upon its back, with lack-lustre eyes carrying some wistful vision of the limbo whence it had recently emerged, it mumbled comfortably its rubber teat whilst a stream of lice strolled sluggishly across its puny face. Two rickety children, their twisted legs curled under them upon the floor, did, however, look at her, ceasing their playing with a battered mug to stare at her with interest. Beside the mug, stretched like a streak of God-forsaken lightning, was a yellow whippet bitch, answering to the name of " Nellie." Indeed, as Lucy had already learned, in the slums nine female dogs out of every ten responded to the call of " Nellie."

Meanwhile, the woman, hurrying to the mantelpiece, had swept her hand along its dusty surface, retrieving an object which lay thereon. And now, with a covert twisting of her head, she slipped her fingers across the socket. Then, lo! there was no longer a socket, but a beautiful glass eye, shining, out-glistening its neighbour.

" You'll excuse me," said she; " I wasn't expecting you so early."

Honour satisfied, she produced her rent-book and, after much fumbling at her person, the sum of two and six.

" Here you are," she said, proffering the money and the book; then, as Lucy took the one and marked the other, she added almost jealously: " It's still clear, you see."

" Yes," said Lucy. " You're up to date." She looked round the indescribable apartment, and, moved, perhaps, by Mr. Shaw and the thought of her own position, she added: " You've got a struggle, I suppose—I see you haven't much——"

" No," agreed the woman, with a nod towards the burly deglutinating navvy. " No. Him—he'll never let me buy furniture. We aye get behind with the rent—sooner or later, you see—then the landlord steps in and takes all we've got. ' What's the use of it? ' says he. ' When there's nothing to take we just move on and that's the end of it.' "

" But surely your husband likes more comfort than this? " suggested Lucy.

" True enough," agreed the other pleasantly. " He was fond of his own good comfort, was my man, but he's been away for two year now. Five year he got altogether. This gentleman "—another nod— " is just staying with me."

" I see," said Lucy, and her gaze ranged from the pallid children to the six months' infant whose paternity was thus, alas, so rudely called in question. But the infant didn't mind, nor did the children; nor, least of all, did the gentleman.

" Give the lady a song, Alfie," said he suddenly, turning to the eldest upon the floor. He wiped his mouth and glanced at Lucy. " He's great, that one, at a tune."

Lucy looked at Alfie. She was in a hurry; she had her work; but again Mr. Shaw prevailed.

" Go on," she said suddenly. " Sing and I'll give you a penny."

Alfie—he was about five—smiled unblushingly, moistened his lips, and said: " I'll give you ' Maggie Murphy '—I like it best."

Then he raised his precocious pipe in this short ballad:

> " On Sunday night 'tis my delight
> And pleasure, don't you see,
> Meeting all the boys and girls
> Who work down town with me.
> There's an organ in the parlour
> Just to give the house a tone,
> And you're welcome any ev-en-ing
> At Maggie Murphy's home."

It was a strange, disturbing scene in that bare room: the thin voice of the rickety, hopelessly deformed child arising to the fog; the cheerful, grinning " gentleman "; the glass eye glowing with maternal pride; the infant dribbling on the straw; the whippet fallen back upon its own resources; and through it all the unconcerned movement of the lice wandering about in ceaseless, unmolested ease.

" That's all," chirped Alfie, when he had finished. " Good, wasn't it? " And, reaching out his claw, he received the coin.

Something rose up in Lucy's throat. She wasn't fitted for this work, really she wasn't: it was too bad, this indescribable, overwhelming misery. With an effort she collected herself, moved to the door. There was an exchange of compliments, then Lucy said: " This time next week." She nodded, and went out of the room.

She had to go on. There was no help for it: it was her livelihood.

Resolutely she tapped upon the adjacent door, which with surprising alacrity swung open to disclose a room different indeed from that which she had quitted. It was cosy, cosy as the fire that leaped within the grate, cheerful as those flames sparkling across the china dogs upon the yellow chest of drawers. And, despite its poverty, comfortable—comfortable as the ample little woman who stood with her tattooed arms akimbo at the door.

She had a battered, ruddy face, and roguish, contumacious eyes, like beads of jet; upon her hair a black hat sat, and round her neck was clipped a straggling string of mangy fur. Lucy had never seen, and never was to see, this honest soul without her hat and mangled necklet. She wore them out of doors and in; almost indeed, it seemed, as though she slept in them; the reason being that in White Street the touchstone of quality was a hat so worn—not a shawl flung cowl-like upon the head—and a fur so clipped. The fur, indeed—it touched the very acme of the mode—was not discarded even when the wearer went about her charring.

" The rent again, is it, miss? " said Mrs. Collins. " Truth, 'tis never paid but it's round again."

" Every Tuesday," said Lucy, gazing at Mrs. Collins and at Mrs. Collins's son—a lumpish young fellow who, couched beneath the blankets in the alcove bed, threw a captivating eye across his mother's back.

" Ah! 'tis the oftenest day of the week," said Mrs. Collins. Following Lucy's eye, she swung her head round and exclaimed: " Ben, there, he's on the night shift now. That's why he's laid down like that. Think of it, too, only fifteen shillin' a week he brings in. And eats double."

She turned testily to obtain her rent-book, which, despite the protest, lay ready with the money on the table. Lucy marked the book, accepted the money.

" You'll not forget that bit of charring you pledged me? " pursued the other, after she had reclaimed and inspected her book. " I'm cheap for stairs and suchlike."

" I'll remember you," returned Lucy. " I expect I'll want you when my son comes home."

She came out of the house; then she knocked at the next. Tap, tap, tap went her pencil on the door.

She tapped, indeed, at every door in that foul and gloomy entry; she marked the soiled books, collected the greasy money, wheedled and demanded, heard excuses and complaints; her bag grew heavier and her head—because she was not yet habituated to the work—grew lighter. Each visit occupied, upon the average, three minutes of her time: more than an hour and a half was spent within the dwellings opening from that first close, and it was after noon when she emerged into the narrow street. Yet her work was not finished. It had merely begun; and without hesitation she entered the next close, knocked immediately at the nearest door, waited, uttered her formula: " Henderson & Shaw! " And so it went on. What work for her to be doing, she somewhat bitterly reflected—she, a woman who had once had her own little villa, her maid, her garden with its apple-tree, its pansies and petunias! She sighed, shifted her heavy coin-filled bag, and beat another insistent tattoo. " From Henderson & Shaw! " It was like a password, admitting her to a dark and weary citadel. The almost unbelievable dirt, the vile odours, the squalid congregation of all the miseries of humanity, relieved but rarely by a cheerful face, became to her at times a nightmare.

It was after three when she had gone through the tenement completely. She should, of course, have taken her hour for lunch, but somehow her inclination lay towards finishing the work without a break. Miss Tinto had agreed, too, that this was the wiser tack, and sanctioned it with her benign authority. Now, however, as she came out of White Street and left its nauseating smells behind she felt unaccountably hungry. At the corner she boarded a slow-moving tram, which swam out of the fog with its lights ablaze. With her bag upon her knees, she sat upon the smooth wooden seat, resolving the possibilities of the cuisine. Her appetite was healthy, and for five hours she had been working hard. Various dishes passed seductively before her mind; then finally she decided. At Kelvinbank she got off the tram, and, entering a small butcher's shop which she had already patronised, she demanded a mutton chop. The butcher—Tutt he was by name—was fat and hearty: he seemed, moreover, to know her now as " regular." Perhaps he felt her eye upon him as he sliced and swung his chopper. At any rate, the chop was prime, well over weight; and his manner was agreeably polite.

From the greengrocer next door she obtained two pennyworth of potatoes—she was just " out " of potatoes; at the baker's she purchased a loaf.

It was awkward carrying the parcels with the bag; and the loaf was clumsily wrapped in newspaper, which flapped open as she walked. Still, she had her lunch, and the sight of a woman so burdened was neither here nor there in Flowers Street.

Her house, gaining by contrast with those she had just quitted, had at this hour a quiet and restful solitude. She let her eyes wander. It was, after all, " not too bad for the time being."

Her first movement was towards the bath, where, standing in all her clothing, she thoroughly shook her garments. These fleas were a nuisance—but you couldn't avoid them in White Street; even now three leaped the air agitatedly from the bath. Still, with care she kept free from the slower and more loathsome vermin.

She stepped out of the bath, turned on the tap, washed her face and hands. Then, removing her hat and coat, she lit the gas-ring and began to cook the chop. It was a bother having to set about these preparations, yet there was no alternative. For the time being she must forget the refinement of a well-cooked, appetising meal awaiting her arrival. Still, whilst she waited, the odour of the grilling meat sharpened her appetite further, and when at last it was ready— browned exactly to her liking—she sat down and began to eat with all the relish of a hungry woman. How good it tasted! Subconsciously she approved her choice of Mr. Tutt.

The warm food filled her with a new comfort. It was amazing how this simple meal restored and fortified her. Insensibly her outlook altered. With the bulk of the day's work behind her, she had a satisfactory sense of accomplishment. Instinctively her thoughts turned to her son; always an indication of her cheerful mood.

When she had finished, she sat for a moment, still meditating. It would have been pleasant, she thought, not to go out again into that fog; but, with a glance towards the clock, she rose rather reluctantly. This time she left the dishes; she would be back again at six.

She went out, clasping again that inevitable bag. She hated it, but she could not escape it.

At half-past four she entered the office.

" What a fog! " said Miss Tinto. " We've never had the lights off all day here."

" It's not so bad indoors," returned Lucy mildly, " but it's really dreadful out. I was glad to get through."

Miss Tinto nodded her head, almost with satisfaction; reaching out her hand for the bag, she declared:

" I'm glad you're getting into the work. It comes hard at first."

For a moment Lucy was silent: she had a sudden vision of that tenement wrapped in squalor and misery; then, with a sudden tinge of bitterness, she exclaimed: " Who owns that property—the one I did to-day? "

" That property? " repeated Miss Tinto in some surprise. " It belongs to a man—Tully. He has that shop in Alston Street. As a matter of fact, he lives in Ralston—out my way. Yes, Tully's his name." She paused. " What makes you ask? "

" I was just thinking," returned Lucy. She remembered that shop —a jeweller's shop—its great windows grilled and crammed with silver plate, but, around the corner, above the narrow side-entrance, the ominous sign—three brass balls! " If ever I meet Mr. Tully," she declared slowly, bitterly, " I'll let him know what I think of him! "

XV

SLOWLY she walked towards the end of the platform, waiting with an outward calm which cloaked the intensity of her eagerness. The warm June sunset glowing through the city's haze poured into Central Station with an amber light, gilding familiar objects, making of them a mirage both luminous and remote. Facing her, arched by the vaulted roof, a segment of open sky shone with a secret glory. Like a spell, it was, the strange unreality of that light, blinding her, drawing her by its swimming radiance.

She was waiting for Peter. Miss Tinto, with that brusqueness which masked her sudden generosities, had virtually commanded her to leave the office at half-past four, thus enabling her to rush home, to smarten herself up, and to be here in time to meet the three o'clock from Laughtown. She had been, indeed, too early, running rather breathlessly to be confronted by an indicator which informed her that the express would be five minutes late; but now, turning to retrace her measured, impatient pacing, a whistle shrilled, and into that mellow glow the long darkness of the train wound with a tired clanking, slowed with a last expulsive hiss. She paused, her figure taut, her eyes seeking, vivid with her emotion. Then she saw him swinging out of his compartment, advancing in the crowd to- wards her: not now the little boy who had taken her hand and trotted beside her upon this very platform, but, by some miracle of time and fortune, a neat, upstanding youth, who walked with a confidence beyond her guiding. She did not move, but stood watching him, a smile trembling upon her lips, waiting until he should see her. Then, indeed, that smile leaped into her pale face, and instantly transfigured it.

" Hello, mother! " he cried at once. " Sorry we're so late." And the grace with which he raised his hat to her, his mother, enraptured her. She felt weak, suddenly, as she kissed him.

" You're back then, Peter."

" Back for good now," he agreed cheerfully. She looked at him, seriously now and absorbedly, whilst he grinned down at her with that same ingenuous candour of his childhood.

" What about my luggage? " he demanded, at length.

" Yes—your luggage," she echoed, and stirred slowly. He took her arm spontaneously as they walked up towards the guard's van and again she felt that thrill of physical happiness traverse her like a sweet languor: the joy of having him back for good, as he had said —it was unbelievable!

" There it is! " he exclaimed.

The familiar trunk, no longer shining—the leather cracked, the initials yellowed but still bravely decipherable—lay upon the platform before them. How small it seemed! Once, when it stood upon its end, it had dwarfed him into insignificance. He exclaimed, indicating a porter. " Will he put it on a cab for us? "

She hesitated; it cost her an effort; still, she said: " I think—yes, I think we'll have it delivered by the van."

He raised his eyebrows. " But it might as well come with us, mother."

" We'll take the tram," she returned, with a reasonable air. " It's really handier for us that way."

With a reassuring nod, she went over and quietly made arrangements with the porter for the delivery of the trunk; then she closed her purse with an imperious snap, turned, and remarked briskly: " That's settled! "

As they moved off towards the station exit she continued, in the same manner: " I'm sorry I didn't get down for the breaking up. I hope you didn't mind? "

" No. Oh, no."

" I'm pleased you did so well again."

" We ought to be used to that now," he returned, rather abstractedly.

Indeed, a silence fell between them whilst they came down the incline into Young Street, and paused at the tramway stop, a silence which persisted as they boarded a red car and sat down upon the narrow wooden seat upstairs. Only when the conductor had punched the two tickets, and she had surrendered the penny piece in payment, did he remark slowly: " You haven't said much in your letters about —about the change, mother. You told me about Miss Hocking and about the new work, but what exactly does it all mean? "

" Nothing much, really," she declared, with a careless air; she knew that he must be told, but she would spare him the damaging details at all costs. " We haven't quite so much to live on, dear, but we'll manage—we'll manage perfectly."

" It's not going to interfere with my—with——"

" Oh, no," she cut in confidently. " That's going to be done at all costs. You mayn't find things so—so nice "—it was a convenient word—" as at Ardfillan, but we can put up with them for a bit. We'll be together, and we'll soon be out of the wood."

" I see," he said. His look cleared, and he gazed over the edge of the tram as it bumped its way westwards.

Nearing the corner of Kelvinbank Street, she rose. " Here we are, then," she exclaimed briskly, and, pointing from the top of the swaying tram like one who demonstrates unquestionably the momentous, she added, " Near enough to *that* for you, anyway."

They both looked towards the building which she indicated, a long grey building, with a central tower that stood upon the summit of a hill, above the Park of Kelvingrove. Touched upon its high hill by a level slant of sunlight, the cold, dark grimness of the stone dissolved, and the tracery of the tower, enriched, became delicate, tenuous as a web of gossamer. It was at that moment a lovely sight, and for Lucy it was more: a passionate incentive, a hope, an inspiration which was reflected in her eyes and on her shining face.

" Doesn't it stir you? " she exclaimed suddenly, with bright eyes.

" That's the place right enough," he agreed slowly; but the look upon his face was different: more meditative and detached it was, with an inward calculation which made his gaze a scrutiny, unemotional, almost acquisitive. " When I'm finished with that place, I'll be ready to make my way right enough."

She gave him another quick smile, and, turning, began to descend the steps. They got off the car.

And now, with a sudden inward qualm, she led the way towards Flowers Street. Never, she thought with a swift unhappiness, had the street appeared so crowded or so objectionable, and somehow she felt a sudden responsibility for all its imperfections. She had wanted Peter to see it in quietness—at its best—but now the warm night had drawn the inhabitants to the outer air, like rabbits from a warren. Children played and capered upon the pavements, some smaller infants sprawling with such exuberance as to expose their persons and their sorry soiled underclothing; they laughed and shrieked and fought, raising shamelessly their happy din. Women stood at the close mouths, with folded arms and flapping tongues, pausing to stare curiously at passers-by or to shout a caution to their writhing progeny. At open windows men in shirt-sleeves sucked pipes and read their papers, lifting now and then contentedly a brimming beer-can or spitting with casual complacency into the convenient street. At the corner, too, the dance-hall was in full and noisy session. Through the doors, swung wide for the heat, the thumping of feet and the jingling of a piano came mingling with a clapping of hands from the Master of Ceremonies, and the occasional cheerful—or was it odious—shout: " Swap judies and burl! " Moreover, outside the hall a gang of youths stood knowingly, with shoulders slouched and caps pushed down upon their eyes, the very droop of their cigarettes epitomising the wisdom of the ages. They stared as Lucy and her son went past, and then they laughed with all the derision of a rich experience.

" This is terrible, mother," said Peter, in a voice suddenly constrained. " I had no idea! Really, I had no idea it was like this."

" It's not always so—so busy as this," she replied in a low voice.

" Busy! It's not the busyness. The whole place—it's terrible. Terrible! "

She made no reply, but continued to look straight in front of her until they reached the entrance to No. 53. They went up the stairs in silence; then she took her key and threw open the door of the house.

" Here we are, then! " she exclaimed, with a cheerfulness belied by the quick anxiety of her gaze. " It isn't much to speak of, but it's our own place—and that's the main thing." She paused, closed the door, and followed him in. " This is your room," she explained, " and this "—she indicated the kitchen—" this is a sort of sitting-room where I sleep."

It took him a moment to penetrate the full significance of the establishment; then his eye fell upon her in acute dismay.

" Is this where we live now? " he demanded incredulously.

She nodded her head. Somehow she had got used to the place; she had not expected him to take the change so badly. And she had done her best to brighten up things for him, putting new curtains on the windows, polishing the waxcloth till it shone. She had even whitewashed the ceilings during the last week-end.

" But the furniture! It's all so bare," he almost gasped. " A bed and a wardrobe in my room—and next to nothing in the other! There's an echo like you get in an empty house! "

Her face grew troubled and slowly coloured.

" We'll not be here always," she declared, " and I'll get more furniture as time goes on."

" It's terrible, mother—really it is. To think of living here—this wretched place—a down-at-heel locality! "

" It's the best I could do," she answered pointedly. " We must put up with it for the time being. It's not as if we had nothing to look forward to. We've got such a lot that we've got to make the best of things till we can get away from here."

He sat down and looked at her. " Well," he said, at length, " if it must be—then I suppose we'll have to put up with it."

Her brow cleared instantly. " That's the spirit! " she exclaimed.

" I knew you'd be sensible; and you'll feel better when you've had your tea."

He turned his head towards the table, which was already laid, then he smiled back at her doubtfully. " The sight of that crowd out there was enough to take a man's appetite away."

But his appetite was not gone, and later, when they sat at table, he ate with a hearty relish; yet from time to time he glanced at her and at his surroundings with a dubious eye.

" You can cook, anyway, mother," he asserted at length; " that's one thing I will say."

" Wait and see what I'll give you when you're studying," she replied warmly. It roused in her a strong protective instinct, this thought of all the nourishing and tasteful dishes she would make for him. " You'll be glad you're home then."

He lay back in his chair. " Yes, that's all very nice," he said slowly, " but let's get this thing straight. You seem confident, but —do you know how you're going to manage? "

" I'll manage," she declared at once, with that very confidence of which he had accused her; then she broke off, and in a different voice suddenly enquired: " But you—you're not thinking you won't get the——"

He waved aside her words before she uttered them. " I haven't the least doubt about that! I can put myself through flying. I've got the whole thing worked out to the last penny." He paused, and continued with a brevity and methodical assurance which thrilled her: " I got the University calendar from Brother William. Fees on an average thirty pounds a year; books and sundries—say a total of five pounds. Against that there's the Carnegie Fund, and of course the scholarship—there's twenty open to me, and any one of them I can take standing on my head. Well, that's worth twenty-five pounds, for every one of the five years." He advanced an explanatory hand. " My income, sixty pounds; my expenditure, say, forty at the outside. Result: I'm twenty pounds to the good to keep me in clothes and pin-money."

" It's splendid, Peter," she breathed, " simply splendid."

She was thrilled by his competent knowledge and his position; thrilled, too, by this intimacy between them which bound them to the same cause.

" Yes, it's all right," he answered, with a short laugh. " But there's the other side to the question."

Her eyes puckered. " I've said I'll manage," she repeated.

" It's no good just saying it, mother," he returned restlessly. " That's stupid. It's like a mole burrowing along in the darkness."

" The mole gets up to the light in the long run," she replied slowly; now she felt his exactitude a chill upon her ardour.

" Yes, but how? That's the point. We've got to live for five years, you know, and that's your part of the business." He summarised the deficiencies of the room and the meagreness of the table appointments with a pointed glance. He paused. " Now tell me outright how much you're earning."

She hesitated, her eyes still troubled.

" Tell me," he insisted. " How much have you got when the rent of this salubrious palace is paid? "

She raised her eyes, and looked at him. " Eighteen shillings a week," she answered steadily.

His face fell instantly; he stared back at her stupidly.

" Eighteen shillings a week! " he gasped. " Less than fifty pounds a year to keep the two of us on—and buy your clothes! " He gave a short, sardonic laugh. " And pay for your box at the opera—it's utter madness, mother."

" I tell you I can do it," she declared firmly.

He shook his head slowly from side to side. " It's utter madness," he repeated. " It's an utter impossibility—and I know what I'm talking about. I understand how to put two and two together. You can't just rush at this with your head down. You haven't thought enough, mother—all along, I mean. Look at the way you sold your furniture, for example. If I'd been sixteen then, and not simply a kid, I'd never have let you do it. Then that little affair with Miss Hocking—surely you could have foreseen——" He broke off significantly, and added: " But you can't do this thing by being headstrong."

A lump of indignation rose in her throat. She felt the bitter injustice of his remarks, of this almost judicial attitude; and after the way she had worked to keep him at the college, after she had planned everything for the best! Yes, and struggled so successfully to maintain their independence! No one but he could have spoken to her like this and escaped the cutting, devastating anger of her reply. But she loved him, and so she said simply: " You must let me do as I think fit."

" What good is it for me to have everything arranged, and you to spoil it all by being so obstinate? " he declared petulantly. " And what good is it having relations who are decently off if you don't ask them to stand behind us? "

" I'll do my share," she answered resolutely, " and without their help."

He looked at her with a sudden plaintiveness, moved by a sense of her inflexibility.

" Don't you see that everything centres on me, now? I'm the one that'll get us both out of this rotten hole," he said miserably. " It would upset a saint." And then, indeed, he was upset, choked all at once by a ridiculous rush of grief.

"Don't, Peter dear!" she cried instantly, melted by his unexpected tears. Despite his size, for all his brilliance, he was still her little boy, the child who had come running to her skirts, eager for her compassion. The sweetness of that thought, following the long separation, made her wish suddenly, inexplicably, to yield to him.

"We'll think about it," she soothed him, taking his hand in hers. "Perhaps I'll take a run over to Richard or to Edward to see what they say."

"You'll need to do it," he said, with a final sniff. "I'm telling you it's the only way."

"Yes, yes," she answered. "You leave it to me, dear."

His piteous face, this grief, so strangely reminiscent of Frank's weakness; this attitude, so close and so dependent; that sweet relationship which she wished always to continue, moved her with a powerful impulse of protection. She comforted him, she felt him close to her; and violently within her there rose the unconquerable impulse of her love.

"Funny thing for me to do a thing like that!" he exclaimed at length, turning towards her a slightly shamed face, and he made a feeble attempt at jocularity, adding: "It'll not occur again."

She pressed his hand, arose. "You're tired, my son," she said calmly. "I'll go and turn down your bed."

She went into the half-empty room—into that travesty of a bedroom—and in a moment he followed her, going to the window, where he stood, idly looking out into the gathering darkness.

"Look, mother," he said, after a moment, "you see it well from here."

She came beside him and slipped her arm round his shoulder, whilst she followed the direction of his gaze. There upon the hill, vague now and indistinct, yet lit by the last pale lance from the retreating day, stood that edifice, the focus of their ambition and their hope. Sombre now, and to them imposing, even magnificent, it seemed to bestride the mean and shabby district which surrounded them. A few lights pricked bright points from the professors' houses beside the umbered trees; then, as they gazed, a deep bell from the tower rang out the hour with heavy clanging strokes. A small and undistinguished university, set on the summit of a gloomy provincial city; two ordinary creatures gazing towards it from a dingy room. It was nothing—a commonplace—a matter of no possible importance; and yet, strangely, there *was* something. It was a poignant moment. In Lucy's heart there rose that swelling pang of aspiration; her eyes, seeking beyond, fixed themselves upon a faint star, which swung remotely, brightening against the darkening sky.

XVI

SHE had turned the matter in her mind until her head ached—until she felt the justice of the accusation that she was stupid. She had thrashed it out whilst tramping round her district; had entertained the thought of asking Miss Tinto's advice, then dismissed it on the grounds that Miss Tinto lived in Ralston and knew, or at least knew of, her brother Richard. For she had, at least, decided that if she took this drastic step she must approach Richard. Edward had no solid means to support his indeterminate goodwill, and he was indeed a quantity to her now strangely unreliable and elusive.

But, viewed from every standpoint, it was a frightful ordeal. To ask for herself was unthinkable; yet to ask for Peter—that was a humiliation which she might perhaps endure.

And here, on this Saturday afternoon in June, she was reluctantly upon the roadway leading from Ralston station to Richard's house. Now, indeed, she was at the green iron wrought gate, had opened it and entered the garden. As she went up the neat walk, she saw that since her last visit the garden had been altered: the lawn now laid out as a tennis court, a row of young lime-trees planted to shade the path; even the small greenhouse wore a coat of fresh white paint. She took heart from these evidences of Richard's prosperity, and rang the bell firmly.

A maid showed her into the drawing-room, where she sat down by the open window and waited. She waited for five minutes, letting her eyes travel slowly over the figured velvet furniture, the ebony piano, the tall pot of spirea, and the row of photographs upon the mantelpiece. A photograph of herself with Peter stood too prominently in the centre of the row, and she had the instant suspicion that Eva had placed it there for the occasion. She did not like Eva— a fact she admitted frankly—and this was a polite insincerity of which Eva might well be guilty. She had begun to feel herself forgotten when Eva entered the room with outstretched hand and an apologetic patter of her small feet.

" I'm so sorry to keep you waiting, Lucy," she now lisped. " I was resting after lunch—I always have my little siesta, you know. Really, I find it so restoring, and I'm afraid——" she broke off. She had a convenient habit of deserting a phrase in a difficulty and diverting her conversation engagingly to another point—the line of Eva's conversation left an erratic trail. " And the children have gone off to play golf," she ran on. " They'll be sorry to miss you."

" I'm sorry too," said Lucy. " I haven't seen them for a long time." Had they, she thought, been sent safely out of the way of the poor relations?

" It's ages since we've seen you. Quite wicked of you to stay away so long," said Eva reprovingly. " I'll ring for tea immediately."

She rang, with a pretty gesture of her small, well-manicured hands. Tea came upon a tray: a silver service, Wedgwood cups, and a many-tiered cake-stand; there were at least no flaws in Eva's equipment. With a curious pang Lucy had a quick vision of her own delf cups and earthenware teapot—products of the Caledonian Bazaar; and her lips drew together tightly.

" You've got Peter back now? " said Eva, offering the cake-stand.

" Yes, he's back."

" Such a nice little boy, I remember. You see, we've got his photograph." She indicated the mantelpiece pleasantly with a crooked little finger. " I had some taken myself at Annan's the other day."

" Did you? "

" Richard wished it, you see," explained Eva coquettishly.

" Did he? " returned Lucy. The other's effusiveness constrained her strangely, made her replies brusque, laconic echoes. But Eva was not constrained; and never disagreeable. She skated along brightly, veering continually, keeping far from the edge of ice which might be dangerous.

After a few moments, the door opened and Richard came in. Perhaps by contrast it gave Lucy a sudden warmth to see Richard again; she knew that his regard for her had never been intense; their natures were set at opposite poles, and they had drifted widely apart in these latter years: but he was her brother, and the relationship, for her at least, still held an indefinable quality of association.

" Late for tea again," twittered Eva. She turned to Lucy in fond explanation: " He's been working in his study—these cases—oh, dear me—what a struggle it is to make ends meet these days."

" You're looking well," said Richard, taking his cup of tea and stirring it gradually.

" She's looking marvellously well," chimed in Eva brightly.

" I have been rather poorly myself lately," said Richard, taking a slow sip of tea over his high-peaked collar. " The doctor insists it's arthritis, but I doubt it." Drinking, he sucked in his cheeks: " Yes, I very much doubt it."

" It's overwork, my love," said Eva. She betrayed unashamedly in her attitude all the touching solicitude of an excellent spouse, and, again turning to Lucy, she remarked, in a confidential aside: " Did you know—he's in the running for the vacancy—fiscal, you know—and no one deserves it more."

" That's good, surely," ventured Lucy. She saw that Richard had become more formal, more magisterial than ever; indeed, he filled his chair as ponderously as though already the mantle of the public prosecutor lay upon him.

" You mustn't believe all Eva says about me," he said with rare indulgence.

" But you do deserve it, my love. Such an honour."

" Well, well! We shall see. I may refuse it. Snap my fingers at the honour. There's not enough money in it these hard times."

A short silence followed, then Eva, assuming an air of extreme tact, rose up and with a sweet smile said:

" I'll leave you two together now. You must have lots to say to each other." She left the room with almost a prearranged celerity.

" Well, Lucy, we haven't seen much of you lately," said Richard directly, when his wife had gone. " How are things with you? "

Lucy was relieved; she had dreaded the prospect of herself broaching the subject; and now she said gratefully: " That's what I've come out to see you about."

He constricted his dark brows in agreement. " I was sorry to hear you had lost your connection with Lennox. On the other hand, you've done well to get this—this other post. Plucky of you—very plucky! " He paused, and remarked judicially: " But why have you never married again? It would have simplified everything."

" I don't know," she answered confusedly.

" Tut-tut! You're quite a presentable woman yet."

" I suppose I've never had the chance."

" It's the natural law," he returned, moistening his vivid lips. " Eva and I are very happy. Yes—I assure you."

" I'm quite happy with Peter," she replied, " only—I must see him getting on in life."

" Quite natural," he asseverated, after a pause.

His unusual acquiescence gave her encouragement; she gathered herself determinedly, and said—but not without a tremor—" We haven't seen each other for a long time, Richard. Perhaps it's been my fault. But now that Peter's left school I want your advice and your help. Will you help me with the boy? "

" I will," he said at once.

" You'll help me with Peter? "

" Yes—I'll do what I can," he returned precisely.

She breathed again. " Thank you, Richard," she said, with unconcealed emotion. " It's good of you. You don't know what it's cost me to come out here. I'm not built for asking, but I must have a little help if I'm to put him through the University."

" The University! " Blasted from his habitual composure, he jerked violently in his chair. " Good heavens, woman, what are you talking about? "

" Yes—that's what I mean," she faltered. " I want him to go through as a doctor."

" Put him to the University—and for medicine——" He had lost

his imposing manner; he looked at her with startled eyes. " You must be crazy."

" He's clever, Richard," she said desperately. " He could win a scholarship. And I've always wanted him to go in for a profession. I want him to go in for medicine."

" You're not serious," he reiterated slowly, his heavy brows still elevated.

" I am serious! " she insisted urgently. " I must give him his chance."

Her words had given him time to recover; his eyebrows fell; he was himself again.

" My dear Lucy," he said, severely magisterial, " you really cannot understand what you are talking about. Fortunately, I do. You could never put your boy through such an expensive training even with the help I could give you. I am not a wealthy man. I have got my own family to think of." He narrowed his eyes and leaned forwards, whilst she watched him with a strained face. " Charles, as you know, is articled to Kidston's. That cost money, I may inform you. Then there are his fees to be considered. Moreover, I've got to think of Vera's art. She has a wonderful talent. She is attending classes now—her mother even wants her to go to Paris if I can afford it. You see, I am not made of money, Lucy. Don't let our house or our way of living deceive you. We have got to keep that up, whether we like it or not. My position demands it." He threw out a protesting hand. " I'm not proud. Often I feel that I'd like to live more humbly."

" You said you would help me," she burst out, the moment he had finished.

" Yes! Yes! " he expostulated. " In a fitting manner. I have certain influence. I might get your son in somewhere as a clerk."

" A clerk! " she echoed harshly.

" And why not, pray? " he countered frigidly. " You've given him a good schooling. It's high time that young man did something for you. Besides, if there's any good in him, he'll soon rise above the office stool. Let him fight his way up."

" You can keep your office stool," she exclaimed bitterly. " I don't want that kind of help. My boy can do better than that! "

He contemplated her for a moment, then said emphatically: " You have not changed."

" I haven't changed enough to thrust my only son into an office," she returned fiercely, " while your children have the best of everything."

" Let the Moores do something for him," he returned dryly. " That publican fellow has lots of money."

" I don't want his help," she exclaimed in a hard tone; " nor his money. And more than that—let me tell you straight—I don't want yours either."

" No? "

" No! " She fired it at him like a bullet. He looked at her coolly, twisting his watch-chain, then without apparent significance, remarked:

" I warned you from the first against marrying into that family. I said you'd regret it."

Her eye glistened; her nostrils quivered.

" What did I care for your warning then? " she retorted fiercely. " As much as I do now. And I regret nothing."

" Well, you can't say that I haven't given you my advice again," he replied evenly. " It's folly to entertain this university idea. You haven't been fortunate, and you must cut your cloth accordingly."

" We'll see about that." She began to draw on her gloves.

" Be logical," he persisted, in a more conciliatory tone. " Why must you always swim against the stream? You'll get into deep water and drown yourself. I'll give you reasonable help. I'll get the boy some respectable work. His wages will be a great help to you. Don't go on with your eternal striving after the unobtainable. Be content with what you've got."

She fastened the last button of her glove and stood up suddenly; her face was pale and set rigidly.

" You'll see what I can do! " she said in a vibrating voice.

He got awkwardly to his feet, exclaiming:

" Now don't be ridiculous, Lucy." Her emotion did indeed seem ridiculous; the intensity of her feeling out of all proportion to the situation. " Listen to reason. Leave the impossible alone."

" Good-bye, Richard," she said, her hand shaking slightly from her agitation.

He gazed at her for a moment, then shrugged his shoulders coldly. " Of course, if you insist on being melodramatic," he exclaimed, " the whole thing's hopeless."

Here the door swung suddenly open and Eva entered, fluttering into the tense air with an entrancing smile.

" You're not really thinking of going, Lucy? " she lisped. " You haven't stayed nearly long enough."

" Too long, I'm afraid," returned Lucy stiffly; but the irony had a pathetic ring.

" So sorry you can't stay to dinner. And I meant to cut you some flowers from the garden," protested Eva sweetly, as she moved towards the door.

Flowers, thought Lucy; she had asked for bread and they offered her flowers. One day she would " give " Eva flowers! She controlled herself sufficiently to bid them goodbye, but as she passed down the neat garden path her cheeks flamed with indignation; the bitterness of her humiliation stifled her. Yes, she had abased herself; and to what purpose? Richard, who could enter his son for the law and send his daughter to Paris, had offered her son a clerkship, had likened her love for Peter to a ridiculous pose. Even now he would be relating the incident, discussing her critically with Eva. Her lips trembled and drew together; she walked on unseeingly. Eva, of course, might be at the bottom of the entire affair; Eva's detestably winsome manner had its influence—its insidious, sickly influence—on Richard. In her imagination she heard Eva's light laugh dismissing the affair; she shivered sensitively in shame.

On the journey home, her pride clenched itself to a fierce intention. She walked into the house in Flowers Street with a quivering determination. Her son was awaiting her: not, she reflected, flaunting himself lightly in pleasure upon a golf-course, but reading seriously in the kitchen: and, keeping her voice as normal as her agitation would permit, she said:

" Do you think you can win one of those scholarships you were speaking of? "

He looked up, his face somewhat startled at her strange intensity. " Yes, mother," he said. " But did Uncle Richard not——"

" Be quiet," she flung out fiercely; then, with an effort, she took hold of herself. She looked at him tenderly. " I want you to enter your name to-morrow," she said calmly, in an altered voice. " You're going to win a scholarship, my son—and I'll do the rest for you."

Melodramatic, indeed. She would show Richard, with his two undistinguished children; and above all she would show Eva. Yes, when next Eva laughed, she would be in a position to answer her with a calm and contemptuous smile. Her eye, seeking the distance, drank in a vision of the future, and she clenched her teeth with the grim intensity of her purpose.

XVII

HER key made no sound as she inserted it carefully and turned the lock; her entry was as noiseless as she could make it. In the small hall, darkly lit by the fanlight above the door, she laid down her leather satchel: not the famous collecting-bag, this, but a reticule for parcels newly bought in the Caledonian Bažaar; then she took off her coat and hat, hung these on their pegs, turned, and went quietly into the back room.

He was studying: elbows upon the table, head supported by both palms, hair ruffled by his unconscious fingers: bent over the strewn litter of books and papers which so engrossed him that he did not look up to acknowledge her presence. She made no sign, but began quietly to make her preparations for tea: putting the kettle to boil, lighting the gas-ring silently, letting her glance fall from time to time upon his bent form. For almost three weeks this intensive study had continued, and the sight of his bowed, absorbed figure moved her indescribably. When at last her preparations were complete, she paused and said mildly:

" May I have the table now, Peter? "

" Hello, mother," he returned, looking up as though only now aware of her presence. He lay back in his chair. " Disturbing me again."

" I can give you another five minutes, if you like," she murmured.

" Oh, that's all right," he returned agreeably. " I've had a pretty hard afternoon altogether."

She thought he looked pale as, taking great care not to lose his place, she began to lift his books on to the scrubbed wooden box— now called by courtesy the dresser. He lay back for a moment watching her intent actions with a half-smile on his face, then he got out of his chair and, with his hands in his pockets, began to move about the house. As she covered the table with a cloth and quickly set it, she heard him pacing up and down in the next room, muttering aloud snatches of erudition far beyond her comprehension.

" Ready," she called out cheerfully when the sounds ceased. " Tea's ready." She had, she reflected, no need of a gong in this house.

" Charming quarter this is, really," he asserted as he came in; his first dismay overcome, he had lately turned his wit upon the district. " I've just been watching some kids outside—playing football with a tin can—along the gutter." He sat down and helped himself to toast. " We can't be out of it too soon for my taste."

" Well," she agreed, handing him a well-browned fillet of fish, " we'll do that between us some day."

" You leave it to me," he asserted confidently. He meditatively stirred his tea, then picked up his knife and fork. " Fish again," he commented, not unpleasantly.

" I thought you'd like it," she put forward quickly. " It's quite fresh. I went down to the market for it—I don't mind the walk—it's such good value there. It's light for you, too, when you're studying. They say it's a brain food."

" Brain food be blowed," he said indulgently—and in his voice she heard Frank's gentle scoffing. " But it is good," he went on, taking a large mouthful. " Fine flavour." He had almost finished before he looked up and said suddenly: " Where's yours? You haven't had any."

"You know I don't care for fish," she laughed. "Besides, I've just had coffee and a cake—Miss Tinto and I went into Chisholm's on our way into the office. It put me quite off my tea."

He looked at her dubiously as he put the last of the fish in his mouth; he had the suspicion that her sprightliness was mendacious.

"Well," said he, "if that's the way of it. Spoiling your stomach like that." This aspersion so often cast upon him in his childhood flew back like a shuttlecock; she smiled, watching him as he picked up the *Evening News* and opened its pink sheets at the sports page. At first he read in silence, then, finding his cup by sense of touch, he took a long drink of tea, and said critically: "The West ought to have a good season this year. They've a rather decent team."

"Yes?" she answered, with a show of interest.

"Splendid," he returned; "you mark my words."

She would not have known a football player from a weight-lifter: her interest sprang from the animation which coloured his pale face; it thrilled her to hear him speak so intimately, exposing his tastes, his interests, so unreservedly to her. Whilst he read, she sipped her tea, observing him with a faint smile, throwing out appropriate comments, when he would explode suddenly:

"Now listen to this of all things, mother."

Yes, she, his mother, was at least content.

At last he let the paper slide to the floor, yawned, and stretched himself.

"This won't get me to the top of the list. Still, I've stuck at it all day."

She had a rule never to press him as to his progress, but now she permitted herself to say humorously:

"You've got on well by the look of you. You seem pleased with yourself."

"Wait and see how pleased I'll look when the results come out," he returned sapiently. "I'll top that list—or nothing!"

"Yes, you've always done well," she said reminiscently, "the whole way along, from your very first term at school."

"Well, do you want me to stop now?"

"So long as you get one of the scholarships," she suggested; "it doesn't matter whether it's the first or the last."

He watched her meditatively as she got up and began to clear the table.

"I'll dry for you to-night," he said at length, when she had set herself to wash the dishes.

She held up a moist, steaming hand.

"Sit where you are, boy."

But he got up, took the dish-towel from its hook, and began to dry the dripping dishes as she placed them on the cheap japanned tray. It gave her a curious feeling to have him beside her, almost touching her—and standing now half a head taller than she—helping her with this menial occupation at the kitchen sink. She reflected that some day she would say to him across the perfectly appointed table of their dining-room, one day when, perhaps, he had returned from a brilliant operation—yes, then she would say to him amusedly: " Do you remember those days when we did the dishes together at Flowers Street? " It would be an almost ludicrous memory! Meanwhile, however, she cherished his assistance as a token of their comradeship.

" Thank *you*," she said, when they had finished; she wrung out her dishcloth. " Now you go out and take a walk before you settle down for the evening."

" Do you think I should? " he queried undecidedly: Frank's voice speaking to her again—not quite sure, depending upon her opinion.

" Of course," she replied firmly. " It'll do you good."

He took his cap and went out with that fleeting, almost hesitant smile which he sometimes gave her, which warmed her with a glowing appreciation of his affection.

Whilst he was away, she arranged the dishes, tidied the room, placed his books back upon the table—adjusting them with careful touches—then changed quickly into her grey house-dress. All the time her ears were set for his quick step upon the stairs, for the sharp, prearranged whistle by which he now announced his coming.

When she did hear this shrill sign, she ran to the door, opened it, and, leaving it ajar, was back sitting in her chair, calmly knitting, when he arrived—the obvious inference being that the door had somehow sprung ajar; that she, of course, was neither so fond nor so foolish as to have opened it for him.

He had been round the Park, had watched the tennis, sat for a moment at the public bowling green, dived finally into the Grove Café (Antonio Demario, proprietor) for an ice on the way up: " Just to cool off that fish, you know, mother." Though she frowned a little at his entering the café, she withheld the correction on her tongue.

Again he was busy with his books. Seated at the other end of the table, knitting his socks, pretending to read the novel that lay in front of her, she wondered, with an amazement, how she had ever endured to send this boy to school; only because it had been for his own good, because of inevitable circumstances; yet now she knew that through some change in him or in herself she could never separate herself from him again. Secretly she studied him, followed his efforts intently, supported them even by the unconscious exercise of her own will.

From the mantelpiece the clock ticked down a quiet rain of seconds upon them; the soup that was for his supper simmered gently upon the stove; from the house beneath a muffled sound—a step—a snatch of words—arose at intervals; outside, the faint evening hum of the city ascended around the tenement and fell, like the note of a subdued and distant organ, softly upon the windows of the room. Devotion was in that room, coupled with a high endeavour, and a strange softness—a softness in her love such as for many months she had not known.

As the days rushed on—for, as the examination drew near, time spilled a swifter sand—it seemed to her that he was working too hard. So many scholarships of equal value were open to him that she felt this striving to top the list unnecessary and prejudicial to his health. So long as he was amongst the first twenty candidates he would receive a bursary; but nothing less would satisfy him than to carry out his assertion to achieve the first place in open competition. Violently she willed that he might succeed, and with unusual devotion she prayed for this intention. As she tramped round the slums she had the habit of slipping into the church situated in her district—a poor church, it was, but one convenient to her purpose—and there, for a few earnest moments, to petition his success. Often her votive candles burned before the plaster statue of St. Anthony and her copper coins rattled as frequently into the black tin box between his sandalled feet. The widow's mite, she sometimes thought, with a wry twisting of her lips, and St. Anthony—patron saint of youth—could not refuse these supplications for her son.

As the time drew in she became, actually, moved by an increasing solicitude; when, that morning of the examination, she kissed him—for her the rarest demonstration—and saw him depart composedly upon the great adventure, a tear hung upon her lashes as she ran into the front room to watch him down the street. Pride and tenderness swelled within her as he turned and waved affectionately, even confidently. His confidence thrilled her. Ordinarily, toughened by experience, her hardihood was boundless, but to-day she felt nerveless, limp from her anticipation.

She did her work, talked rationally, made adequate answers when addressed, yet she had no real consciousness, and, later, no memory of how she accomplished these acts. She did not return home at middle day—Peter's luncheon was to be taken at the University—but went by herself to Miss Chisholm's tea-room, where she sat abstracted, eating a twopenny pie—an excellent pie, with plentiful gravy—without tasting it. Actually she was seated in the examination hall watching the flying pen of her son; her fork, indeed, might have been a pen, and the pie's rich gravy ink, for all the savour which she drew therefrom.

When at last the interminable day dragged towards its close, she left the office at five sharp and took the red tram for home.

Mounting the stairs, her breath came quickly; though she realised that it was too early for him to have returned, she felt already the presage of his news. Her mood was not propitious to accidental conversation, yet as she unlocked her own door and made to enter, the door of the adjoining flat swung open and a young woman holding some parcels smilingly accosted her.

" These messages came when you were out," said she, tendering the packages to Lucy. Fair-haired, her upper lip touched also by a faint golden down, her face round, smiling, red, her body inclined already to plumpness, she had a look at once innocent and voluptuous; and now almost diffidently she added: " I took them in for you, to spare the boy coming back."

" That was good of you," said Lucy, taking the parcels and turning to go.

" I'm Mrs. Finch," ventured the other, lingering on the doorstep. " Yes—Bessie Finch is my name."

" Indeed," returned Lucy, without encouragement. She had marked the recent arrival next door unenthusiastically; she had, moreover, endured one experience of neighbourly solicitude which it was not her intention to repeat; yet some artless quality in the other's open face restrained her from closing the door.

" You're new here, I'm told," advanced Bessie again. " Just like ourselves." It was clear that in her own vernacular, which Lucy was to learn later, " her tongue was just hanging out for a talk."

" Yes," admitted Lucy, in spite of herself, " we're new here."

" I'm downright glad to make your acquaintance," returned Bessie frankly. " You know, folks are not very sociable like on this stair. At least, that's what I find. And I'm a sociable kind of a girl myself. Over at Whiteinch—where my mother keeps a fruit shop—there was always plenty of company about—we're a well-known family, you see, having the business. It's that old established, we're well known over there! But here it's different. And Mr. Finch—that's my husband "—here Bessie blushed—" well, Mr. Finch and myself are not long married. Mr. Finch is away at his work all day, and sometimes he's that tired when he comes in he can't be bothered with much entertainment. I find it kind of dull sometimes."

" I'm out all day, too," returned Lucy discouragingly.

" That's your boy that I see about, isn't it? " persisted Bessie. " He's such a nice young fellow. He lifted his hat to me on the stairs the other day—oh, the perfect gentleman, believe me. Mr. Finch and myself were wondering what trade you were putting him to."

At these words, which found the weakest point in the armour of her pride, Lucy's hand paused in its decisive shutting of the door.

" My boy is going to the University," she asserted coldly. " I'm putting him in for medicine."

Bessie Finch was visibly confounded; her eyebrows lifted from her simple brown eyes; she was silent for a moment, then she gave a little embarrassed laugh.

" Mr. Finch works for Lush & Co.," she advanced, " the whisky firm, you know—a splendid position he has, mind you, and excellent money forbye."

Lucy's smile was constrained. She had no interest in the ubiquitous Mr. Finch, whom she had observed distantly as a fat little man who left behind him on the stairs a strangely spirituous odour; nor would she now willingly surrender to that instinct of friendliness which once—when she herself was a young and lonely wife—had strongly moved her.

" Thank you for keeping my parcels," she said conclusively, pulling the door towards her.

" It's a pleasure," said Bessie, smiling once more. " Yes, I'm delighted." Yet something faintly agitated lay behind that smile, as though some inner nervousness still strove to unburden itself in speech. But Lucy gave no further opportunity for speech; inclining her head, she quietly closed the door.

She went into the back room and laid down her parcels, the trifling interlude of the encounter immediately forgotten.

She waited, and as she waited the muscles of her face drew rigidly downwards under the press of her anxiety. Her pride refused to admit that anxiety, yet immediately she heard his knock—he had not whistled, which she took instantly to be an unfavourable omen— she was startled by the sudden loud quickening of her heart. Stiffly, she went to let him in.

He looked pale and tired; a smear of ink marked his left cheek; and he said nothing as he entered. They went into the kitchen.

" I've got something hot for you," she said precisely. " It's ready now if you'd like it."

He flung himself down on the bed within the recess—there was, of course, no sofa in the room—and stared at the ceiling.

" Good! " he said at length.

That single word, and the manner of its utterance, vibrated through her like a warm delight. Beneath the mask of her composure her heart kindled as she began to dish up the savoury stew she had prepared for him.

" Well, you don't take much interest," he said suddenly, after a moment, still contemplating that particular cornice with a factitious tranquillity. " Why don't you ask me how I got on? "

She paused, his hot plate, held by a cloth, arrested in mid-air. " You did do well then? " she enquired, raising her brows calmly. It was an arrant pretence of indifference; she felt her knees tremble weakly as she spoke.

"Got on like a house on fire," he answered quickly. "It's early yet to speak, of course. But I found the papers easy—dead easy. I sailed through the maths. and did the English standing on my head." His enthusiasm grew with his own words. "Amazingly well I did, and when I came out and spoke to some fellows they told me they'd done vile papers."

She did not stir, but suddenly her eyes shone towards him; she had a flash of transient sympathy towards the sad mothers of those "fellows who had done vile papers"; then all her relief and pride welled into her swelling throat. For a moment she could not speak, but stood quite still, envisaging his lanky, recumbent figure with her transfigured gaze. In her tenderness his form became invested with a kind of pathos. She saw his bony wrists protruding from his insufficient sleeves, the shiny elbows of his suit, his pale face, and—lasting evidence of his endeavours, evoking a culmination of her emotion—ink upon his fingers and his cheek.

But now that he had achieved his effect a profuse account of the day broke from him in a spate of words; he described, with a reactionary detail, what he had done and the manner of its doing. She hung upon his quick speech, reflecting upon the virtue of her sacrifice in sending him to school at Laughtown, demanding of herself how she could reward him for having so long and so diligently applied himself. Yes, she thought, he's stuck in nobly; as Brother Aloysius had said: "The willing horse never needs the spur." The spur, indeed, for a boy like Peter. As she served him with his meal and urged him eat his fill, this thought of recompense lay at the back of her mind. She wanted him to have some treat, some just reward for this victory which she knew that he had won.

XVIII

DURING the next few days, bereft of the stimulus of the great event, Peter was caught in a backwash of apathy. It would be actually a full month before the results were known, and meanwhile he had nothing to do. His humour changed; he hung about the house, commented moodily upon the hotness of the weather and the dustiness of the city streets. He lamented his lack of friends, his lack even of a bicycle which might have taken him into the coolness of the countryside. It was of course unthinkable that he should consort with the youth of the district, and she could not—"in the meantime," she phrased it—afford a bicycle for him. Once, too, as she returned in the evening, she had observed him coming out of

Demario's saloon, where he had justifiably gone to quench his thirst with an iced drink. She became concerned; she dreaded that slack droop which showed sometimes in his shoulders. Anxiously she felt that his health might be affected for lack of a change of air.

Then suddenly, out of the blue, arrived a letter. It bowled her over, she who had always denied her luck and asserted that fortune came to her only through her own endeavour. For it was a letter from Edward—expressive, though she knew it not, of a twinging sacerdotal conscience—a letter wherein he indicated that he had hoped to take Peter for a few days' holiday, but now regretted his inability to do so. He had been recommended a voyage to Madeira on account of his liver, and in tangible evidence of his regret he enclosed a present of five pounds. It was like Edward, who detested being asked for money and preferred to give spontaneously and in his own fashion. But a five-pound note. She was staggered; the crisp feel of it between her fingers was like an ecstasy, so long was it since she, who dealt now in greasy copper and well-worn silver, had handled such concentrated wealth. She had an immediate instinct to conserve it, or to buy sensibly some much-needed article of furniture. Peter required at least a carpet in his room; her own bed, bought second-hand, already had sundered one defective spring. But passionately she put these thoughts away from her. A sudden recklessness took her—a madness. Though she felt her yielding to be weak, insanely weak, the circumstances which induced it were unique. Peter's period of study, his present jaded looks, the enervating air of the city striking them both, the pricking conviction that in justice some relaxation was due to them, the fact that as an employee of H. & S.—despite her very recent assumption of that dignity—she would receive ten days' holiday in July: all these factors swayed her. She saw in her mind's eye, as she tramped languidly along the hot and squalid pavements of her district, a vision of the blue and dancing sea; she saw Peter and herself beside that sea; in her own words: "something came over her." They could not achieve Madeira; but they could have a holiday none the less. They had earned it, had Peter and she, and go they would, if it took every penny of that five-pound note!

When she announced the news to her son, his eye brightened and his shoulders raised; he ceased instantly to execrate the weather, which became instead ideal for the coast. They talked in marine terms for the rest of the week, took a trip round the stations to study the various chromatic posters, and, after some enjoyable research amongst the railway folders upon the subject of excursion fares, decided, ultimately, upon Miss Tinto's advice, to visit Doune. Miss Tinto knew a lady in that resort who " kept " rooms—a Miss Tweedy —whose character and cleanliness she vouched for with a dogmatic bridle and a more than usually emphatic tightening of her lips.

Hurriedly Miss Tweedy was written to, and in due course Miss Tweedy replied, explaining her failure to find an objection against receiving Mrs. Moore and son for the trifling consideration of thirty-five shillings a week—exclusive of baths, lights in bedrooms, blacking, high teas, and use of the kitchen stove. And so it was decided. The scorching heat of the city, heat that came up from the pavements through her shoe soles, which heightened the vile odours of the slums wherein she spent her day, became as nothing in the rapture of her anticipation. Methodically, too, she made her preparations. On the eve of their departure she packed their things in Peter's trunk, and, countering his irony—he mentioned the word " honeymoon "—she displayed an unexpected joyous repartee. She arranged, moreover, with a brigadier's foresight, that Mrs. Collins's husband, again out of work at the docks and glad to earn a sixpence anyhow, should take their box to the station whilst they followed on by tram —an auspicious beginning, which would mean the saving of a clear two shillings.

Upon the morning—the momentous morning—it was fine. Mrs. Finch, appearing unexpectedly upon the landing, had promised blushingly and quite gratuitously to keep an eye upon the house. Kind of her, thought Lucy, in the indulgence of the moment. Down the street they went. At the corner they boarded that tram of so familiar a colour—but with how unfamiliar an emotion. She could not admit this to be the same vehicle which bumped her down to White Street. No; to-day its dull sides took on a cheerful and vermilion glow; even the conductor's buttons scintillated with prismatic brilliance.

At the station Collins was waiting with the box, relieving those faint qualms which she had entertained upon his sobriety, and shortly they were seated in the train. They were off. The day was warm and sunny, the railway cuttings vivid with the golden yellow of dandelions; the swirling steam white against the blue, actinic sky. As Lucy lay back and placed her cheek against the rough, warm cushion of the seat she had a sensation of release, an incredible lightness, a happy emancipation in this quick passage from the town. It was as if she had forgotten, and now recognised with new delight the sweet greenery of the fields. Unbelievable almost that her eye, striking a patch of dandelion weeds upon a grass embankment, should leap to this sudden ecstasy. But it was so. After the sultry squalor of the city this journey was like a swift intoxication, a new realisation of the beauty of life, the awakening of an almost painful longing for its joys. She was silent, rather, when they arrived at Doune.

Miss Tweedy's house, which they found with difficulty, far from the madding seductions of golf-courses and hotels, was situated at

the sober end of the town; and Miss Tweedy herself was a sober little
wisp of a woman, with a small head, a long limp white neck, large
pessimistic eyes, and a drooping inflection to her thin voice. She
welcomed them gently.

" You found the house, I see," she declared dejectedly.

" Yes—oh, yes," agreed Lucy pleasantly.

" Everybody knows me," said Miss Tweedy with a melancholy
pride. " I'm a well-respected woman in the town. Not faddy on your
food—I hope you're not." She swept them with a lack-lustre eye.
" Plain cooking is what I give. Plainest of the plain. But everything
of the best."

" Yes! I'm sure," assented Lucy.

" But the price of things," resumed the other, throwing her eyes
upwards with startling effect. " It's shameful. Everything a ransom
now. Butter up twopence, sugar a penny, flour a halfpenny. How
well-doing people are to live beats me." Under her challenging
glance Lucy became faintly uncomfortable.

" If you would like me to pay a trifle more than what we agreed,
Miss Tweedy," she said, " I'm perfectly willing to meet you."

Miss Tweedy held up a limp, protesting hand.

" Not a penny, Mrs. Moore, and not if you went down on your
bended knee," she said dramatically. " My terms are reasonable, and
reasonable they will remain. There's landladies—I could name them
in this very street—that would jump at your offer. But me? No,
Mrs. Moore! Let them float about in their ostrich feathers if it gives
them any satisfaction—I'll keep my reputation spotless if it chokes
me "—she paused for breath—" but if you think you have been well
done by when you're leaving there's nothing to prevent you giving
sixpence for the lepers. For years I've helped to save the lepers—
poor stricken mortals that they be." Again the little landlady drew
breath, then, fixing a languid eye upon Peter, she remarked slowly:
" Your son? " Having received the inevitable information, she lifted
a limp strand of hair from her pale cheek, placed it carefully behind
her left ear. " I'm not saying but what it isn't handy to have a doctor
in the family. I've nothing against doctors. Oh, dear no! They do
their best, I've no doubt. Sometimes they can and sometimes they
cannot." She lowered her voice, added in a tremulous undertone:
"They could do nothing for my nephew's wife."

" I'm sorry," said Lucy. " Is she ill? "

" Was, Mrs. Moore. Was," returned Miss Tweedy, solemnly and
with a hollow emphasis. " We buried her last winter, and I laid her
out with my own hands. She made "—her lower lip quivered and
she raised her eyes pathetically—" she made the most beautiful
corpse I have ever done, Mrs. Moore. Like an angel. I put a arum
lily in her little hand. Everybody said it was the last word. I have

the touch, you see. I could have grat when they screwed her down—she was such a picture of loveliness." A light which was almost animated flowed into Miss Tweedy's wan features as she spoke. She said: " Some day I'll show you the locket the husband gave me for a token. He was most grateful—and a well-doing young fellow he is. Though he does mean to take another come Lady Day."

There was a pause. Then with a sigh Miss Tweedy became more practical. She indicated the times of meals and the neighbouring places of worship, predicted a breakdown in the weather, warned them against dangerous bathing and late hours, then faded, with a drooping satisfaction, from the room.

An expressive silence followed her departure.

" Beautifully clean, anyway," said Lucy, looking round cheerfully.

" Anyway? " queried Peter.

" Well—she seems a little lowering herself, doesn't she? "

" ' A arum lily,' " he quoted pointedly.

They looked at each other, then gradually between them came a smile which widened, deepened into a burst of laughter. It mastered them, that merriment; they laughed and laughed.

" A arum——" he stuttered weakly, rolling helplessly against the mantelpiece. Lucy wiped the tears from her eyes.

" Stop," she gasped at last, " she'll hear you "; but her lips still twitched as she took up the tea-pot.

Yet Miss Tweedy improved upon acquaintance: some quality in her melancholy which purged it of depression: and her cooking and baking could not be surpassed. " Miss Tweedy's buns " became a byword ranking in incidence with " the lily "; and she " drew to Lucy," as she herself expressed it, " put herself about " for them, unburdened, too, her withered bosom of a family history of ponderous weight and lugubrious intimacy; a family history distinguished not so much by the remarkable achievements of its members as by the morbid significance of the lingering and painful maladies which had beset them and borne them finally to a happier land.

Nor did the weather yield to that first dire prediction, but maintained instead a succession of halcyon days which passed with dreamy softness. Lucy did little; idleness was her chief joy. She liked above all to sit on the warm rocks and look out to the sea—not the blue ocean which her fancy had painted, but a grey, shimmering expanse of sea surging with a restless, endless insistency: waves licking the boulders at her feet—long dripping tongues of waves. The motive of the moving water, persistent, was like the motive of life; it became an inspiration to her, an inspiration not realised, but drawn in unconsciously by her acquiescent body, as she sat, passive and relaxed. A spring-board jutted from these rocks above a deep green pool, and here Peter bathed every morning. When he dived, the sight of his body arching the thin air gave her a strange romantic pleasure. His mocking phrase came back to her and made her smile. A honeymoon with her son—what an absurd idea! And yet?

When he was dressed he came up to her, his hair still damp, his towel draped manfully around his neck, and, after he had demanded her verdict upon the merits of his performance, they took a sharp walk along to the harbour for the benefit of his circulation. They were continually together. Occasionally he seemed to desire a wider field of amusement, and directed an envious eye towards some passing golfer carrying a bag of clubs upon his shoulder; at odd moments he had a momentary petulance against their limited exchequer, but she gave him for his pocket as much as she could afford; and, indeed, for the most part he was charming to her.

He began to assume an air of genial indulgence, and when, during their walks, an appraising masculine eye was turned upon her, he would remark:

" You're quite a good-looking woman yet, you know, mother ";
and nod encouragingly. He invented and invested her with a most tender passion for the leader of the pierrot troupe, twitted her for languishing under a secret and unrequited attachment.

In the evenings, after tea, they strolled along the grassy front arm in arm, and went, as an event, to these pierrots. Fourpence permitted them to enter the reserved enclosure and sit comfortably in chairs, but this luxury was, they decided, an economy; to stand outside was to be haunted by the little red velvet bag, and Lucy had, in her present mood, no heart to withhold her contributions. The entertainment, moreover, was excellent—Val Pinkerton's Troupe had a reputation second to none upon that sea-beach, and Val himself, by day a quantity unknown but by night a hero distinguished from the commonalty of the troupe by a broad red ribbon which split diagonally the white front of his evening dress with an almost Continental distinction—yes, Val Pinkerton had a presence that was aristocratic—even haughty—and a baritone voice of surpassing soulfulness. To Lucy and Peter it seemed that he achieved the pinnacle of his art when he sang, with one hand romantically outstretched and the other eloquently upon his ribbon-covered heart:

> " Daisy, Daisy, give me your answer, do,
> I'm half crazy just for the love of you.
> It won't be a stylish marriage ;
> We can't afford a carriage ;
> But you'd look sweet
> Upon the seat
> Of a bicycle built for two."

" We'll be able to afford the carriage all right, mother," Peter remarked with sly complacency. " Don't you worry about that."

Again that eager assurance towards their future which thrilled her. And always he linked her with him in the upward scintillation of his flight. Often they sent up a request for the " Daisy " number, and when the admirable Val himself announced that he would " oblige with the old favourite," they had the feeling that he sang it exclusively for them. On the way home, moving intimately together in the warm darkness, they hummed the catchy tune, and into the refrain came a low bourdon note—the sea sound that rose and fell upon the unseen beach. As they walked, the air came damply upon their cheeks, mingled with a saline freshness; the distant harbour lights threw pointed yellow pencils across the black water; the turf beneath their feet was plastic with the lightly fallen dew. Outside the Marine Hotel—whose large illuminated windows proclaimed its unabashed magnificence—Lucy often pressed her son's arm, and they would stop, secure in the darkness and the distance, to watch the glittering progress of life within. A row of rose-shaded tables, the swift passage of waiters, the curve of a woman's shoulder rising from her evening gown, the whole moving picture of an easy and refined existence was revealed before them. Filled by the hidden watcher's intentness, each had a secret ardour towards this scene, his eager, hers passive; yet for each an inspiration which rose into the throat and became intensified, moulded to a firm reality. She saw herself, at the end of the long struggle which lay before her, moving in that atmosphere of leisured ease; and he, with parted lips, placed his future against a background of equal elegance and wealth.

When they moved off, filled with their own thoughts, they did not speak much; yet she was aware of a closer union between them, of a common aim which bound them.

Throughout this happy period, filled with such delightful intimacy, she ceased almost to regard him as her son. His companionship occupied her day; she hung upon his word, waited for his smile, anticipated, as best she could, his every want. The dishes which she requested the landlady to prepare were those which he desired or demanded. To gratify his whim became her joy, yet mostly she gratified it under a guise of brusqueness. Never did she permit her intention to be weakened by her fondness. She did not spoil him. That thought was clearly preposterous. Her giving was not an indulgence, but the token of an affection which demanded an equal affection in return.

That was their relationship during this period at Doune, and when, at last, after the fashion of all holidays, this holiday did indeed draw to its end, the relationship seemed solidly and permanently established between them. Lucy returned to Flowers Street with a feeling of assurance, girded for battle and the future.

They had spoken little of the result of the examination at Doune, avoiding the subject through a tacit understanding of its certainty. Her own feeling tended inevitably to support his belief: what had he not done in the past? Nevertheless, as the day upon which the results were to be made public drew near, her excitement ran again a little feverishly within her. And when actually the morning of this day arrived, the stiffness of her hands betrayed her as she dressed.

It was a Saturday, and he proposed, he said, to attend at the University at eleven o'clock, by which hour the results would assuredly be posted upon the general notice-board; he would be in a position to let her know the best or the worst when she returned at lunch-time.

" Oh, it must be the best," she said hurriedly, as she stood dressed for the street, yet lingering unconsciously at the door.

" I think so," he admitted. This suppression of their feelings made them constrained with each other. It was with an effort that she said:

" I'd better get along now or I'll be late "; and she tore herself away from him.

As she went down the street, which held still the freshness of the early air, she felt restless, strung to a high impatience. Although she had already waited an entire month in stoic equanimity, now she was fidgety, and the few hours until lunch seemed to stretch out interminably before her. At the corner of the road the old man who kept the small paper-shop was busy affixing the morning placards outside his window, and, as she passed, by an association of ideas a sudden thought struck her. She stopped abruptly, returned, entered the shop, and bought the *Glasgow Herald*.

On her way to the tram station she held the folded paper in her hand, half regretting her impulse, realising now that it was impossible for the results to be published in the morning paper.

And yet, seated in the red tram, her hands were tremulous as they opened the white sheets. Her eyes, travelling heedlessly over the trivialities of news: the earthquake in Japan, a tidal wave in Borneo, a murder in Leeds: sought anxiously for intelligence of greater moment. But she became aware gradually that there was no mention of the supreme tidings. Had Peter's name been in that paper, it would have arisen instantly out of the jumbled medley of dead words and useless letters. She half lowered the paper to her knee, then, all at once: " University News "—she saw the heading, perceived also a list of names. Her eyes devoured the short list—only twenty-five names—and all names of no importance, names blank with a horrid futility.

It was not the proper list. Her startled gaze jumped to the head of the paragraph. Then instantly her mind doubled upon itself, veered towards another issue. It was the list; but some mistake had been made. A misprint! Her son's name had been omitted from this paltry register. She swallowed dryly and read the whole again. Twenty-five successful candidates out of nearly two hundred competing for the open scholarships. Every detail of these pedants was given: their schools; the bursary allocated to each; even their stupid, pretentious, bombastic middle names. Her brows drew together bitterly.

At last it was evident: she was confronted, not by his defeat, but by her own. A long sigh went out of her stiff body like the expiration of all hope. She let the paper slip under her feet. She sat staring in front of her, filled by a galling despair. The intensity of her disappointment made her physically sick. Dully, at her station, she arose and got off the car. She wanted, not to walk through these busy streets, but to lie down limply and weep.

At the office she said nothing, yet, as she went about her work, she could not wholly comprehend the reason of it all; at the back of her mind hope still lingered. His career at school had been satisfactory; he had worked hard; he had expressed gratification at his own performance upon the day of the examination; and she, for her part, had prayed; yes, she had prayed. The whole thing struck her with a sudden bewilderment.

In this same confusion of mind she hastened home shortly after one o'clock. Saturday was her half-holiday, and on this day she reached home earlier than usual. One swift glance at his face sufficed, confirming her rising fears, shattering her last faint hope. He was lying back in his chair, his head sunk into his shoulders, his hands thrust deeply into his trousers pockets: in the same attitude of apathetic misery that he had manifested in his bouts of childish pique or sickness at Ardfillan. She had always known this dejected attitude to represent the lowest level of the barometer of his feelings. And now she saw that he had touched the pit of his wretchedness.

" Never mind, son," she cried out at once, forgetting instantly her own grief at the sight of his distress. " You did your best."

" It's a swindle," he said miserably, keeping his pale face averted from her. " The whole thing's a fraud."

" What do you mean? " she faltered, her own vague suspicions confirmed by his manner.

" They don't half read the papers," he shot at her glumly. " Fling them up to the ceiling and see the one that sticks there longest. That gets the first prize." He paused, then broke out again, " I tell you I did great papers—splendid papers, every one of them."

" Perhaps the others were good too," she murmured haltingly.

" Perhaps——" She was thinking paradoxically of those youths who had confessed to having done vilely at the examination.

" It's all favouritism, I tell you—the school you come from," he muttered almost sullenly. " They haven't given me a dog's chance."

" But surely——"

" That's right," he cried, " blame me. Go on and take sides against me. After me nearly killing myself."

Her lips trembled; she placed her arm lightly, caressingly on his shoulders. But he shook it off and said, with a hint of weak tears in his voice:

" Let me be, mother. Can't you let me be? You know as well as I do I should have got a place. It's not fair, I tell you."

She said nothing, and her hand dropped back to her side; she had no thought but for him and the bitterness of his disappointment. His resentment, though perhaps misjudged, seemed to her supremely natural. She stood for a long time in silence; then with a heavy heart she started to move about the room, making a pretext of tidying things up.

At length she was about to venture a remark when suddenly the flap of the letter-box clicked open and shut. She heard a letter flutter on to the floor of the hall. She gazed towards his stiff profile doubtfully, concluding from his apathy that this was the confirmation of the wretched news: the official notice of his failure.

" Go on," he muttered sulkily, without lifting his head, " go out and get it. But don't show it to me. I'm sick of the whole thing."

He had the same premonition as she; nevertheless she went slowly into the hall and picked up the letter. When she returned, she gave him another compassionate glance, and, with a melancholy foreboding, tore open the envelope.

For a moment she stood perfectly still, then her hand fell upon her bosom and a short, inarticulate cry came from her lips. Her dull face quickened; her eyes, still unbelieving, still fixed upon the letter, widened and filled with a shining light.

" Peter! " she gasped. " Oh, Peter! "

" What is it? " And at her tone he started up and snatched the letter from her hand.

" Don't you see? " she said weakly. She could say no more; her eyes brimmed; she gave a short, hysterical sob and sat down in a chair. His face was a study, traversed by the conflicting emotions of surprise, amazement, and finally by a leaping ecstasy of joy.

" The Reekie Trust! " he said eagerly, " I never heard of it."

" But I did," she cried. " Miss Tinto told me about it. I entered your name just—oh, just in case. Oh, isn't it splendid? "

He looked at the letter again. It said concisely that he had been elected to the Reekie Trust—a bursary of twenty-five pounds per annum, tenable for five years—created by the late Kezia Reekie for the assistance of the sons of widows in specifically indigent circumstances. With almost brutal brevity it informed him that, although he had been placed ninety-seventh in the list of open competitors, he was the first to fulfil the conditions of eligibility. Would he therefore communicate with the writer—of Fullerton & Co.—at the given address at his earliest convenience.

" I didn't know anything about this. Did you enter my name? "

" I heard about it in the office," she admitted eagerly. " I didn't think there was any need, but one afternoon I was passing Fullerton's, and somehow—I went in and gave them all the particulars about—about myself—and what—what I was earning."

He stared at her.

" Well, I've got something, anyway," he returned slowly, looking up at her.

" And we can do it after all," she said exultantly. Her face had become flushed; words rushed from her lips. " I couldn't think what we were going to do. I was at my wits' end. I thought it was finished. Oh! isn't it wonderful! "

Her gaiety infected him; yet for a moment his eye clouded.

" I like their cheek, making me out ninety-seventh." He favoured the examiner's ruling with a final and facetious contempt.

" It's wonderful, though," she persisted. " We've got all we wanted—and remember—you came out above more than a hundred of the others who tried."

This aspect of the case which he had not considered now struck him happily.

" You're right," he cried. His elation rose; he flung himself back in his chair, with his eyes upon the ceiling, exclaiming: " I've done it, and in spite of them."

Than this nothing more could be said. All had been lost and all was now regained. That span of anguish which they had endured left in its miraculous banishment an ecstatic sensation of relief. A sanguine conviction of the future stole into her, and her eye glistened with a trembling happiness.

XIX

LIFE, which now seemed wonderful, swept on gaily for them both. They had intimate talks in which they discussed his future at the University. He mentioned the word Union with the conscious air of one who might shortly claim membership of that distinguished body; he took, moreover, long striding walks, chiefly in the evenings, when the swing of his stick and the forward thrust of his head betokened the consciousness that he was, or might shortly be, a figure; a young man poised on the threshold of the darker sciences.

Returning later than usual from one of those excursions, he was surprised to find his mother seated in the rocker with an open letter in her hand. Quite a spate of letters, this had been: three in one month—which was three more than they ordinarily received. His lips shaped to a query, but before he could speak Lucy called out:

" You'll never guess who from, Peter." She paused, felt slippers neatly crossed, still rocking gently to and from. " Mr. Lennox! "

But he was not impressed. His memory of Lennox was vague, a letter from Lennox to him a relatively petty incident in the joyous sweep of life.

" It leaves me rather cold," he retorted, the faintly ironic twist of his lips befitting his future profession.

" No, really though, Peter," she replied, looking up quickly. She lowered the letter and tapped her knee meditatively, glanced again at him a trifle self-consciously. " And now he wants to come up and see us—on Saturday."

" You don't say." He let out a whistle; then, with a speculative raillery, he added: " Let him come, and we'll have a jolly party in the palace."

She looked round slowly at the palace—this now his satiric designation of their home—and said:

" How could I ask anybody here? It's too bad—after the way he used to see us in Ardfillan."

The recollection of the fastidious elegance of her villa, an illusion gilded by time, made her forehead pucker; then all at once her face cleared.

" I could get him to meet me, though, and have tea at Miss Chisholm's," she exclaimed decidedly. " Yes, that's just what I will do."

He burst into a roar of laughter, which doubled him up convulsively.

" You and old Lennox, mother," he gasped, " strolling like this. It's good—it's good—oh, it's good! "

Straightening himself, he crooked his arm and, affecting a frightful simper, gave a ludicrous impersonation of their united passage along some fashionable thoroughfare.

She observed him, half frowning, half smiling.

" Laughing like that! " she protested, and paused. " I will meet him, though. He's not a bad sort—whatever I may have thought of him."

She had, indeed, a vague, incomprehensible desire to see Lennox again now that she had definitely set her son upon his career; and this idea of taking tea with him—her own suggestion, but one, she knew, with which he would instantly concur—appealed to her. After a moment's further thought, she took pen and wrote her reply.

During the next few days she did not quite forget about the matter. It lay pleasantly at the back of her mind, touching some instinct long neglected and overlaid; indeed, she was at moments surprised by her own anticipation, yet explained it by the recollection of part indebtedness to Lennox and the paucity of her present pleasures.

Upon the Friday night she considered the condition of her wardrobe—an inspection performed slowly and rather sadly. The " grey " had now become her stand-by, and she was tired of it; it showed, moreover, on closer inspection, a faint suspicious shininess of hem and cuff.

" Dowdy," she thought, holding it from her critically. Still, she was resourceful. She had a lace collar—real Cluny it was, a gift of Frank's, long treasured—and this, after some searching, she retrieved from the bottom of her solitary drawer. Washed, ironed, and neatly stitched over the lapels of the costume, it made a pleasant change, freshening up the sober habit with a touch suitable to the occasion and the season.

When, on the Saturday afternoon, she stood dressed before the mirror, she noted the set of the collar approvingly, felt instinctively that it suited her. Yes; done up like this, the old grey was not too bad, after all.

Peter, who had viewed her preparations with an eye wherein irony was swamped by a greater curiosity, had arranged to attend a football match. Catching a glimpse of some unspoken question in that eye, she said good-bye to him rather consciously, promising to be back in ample time to cook his evening meal.

The halfpenny tram was again the vehicle of her election; this time a yellow one, and swift—which made her fear she would be early at George Square: the meeting-place she had arranged. She had resolved on this occasion, in contrast to the first historic day in the Saddleriggs, that he it was who should be early, she who should be late.

It was a pleasant day, the sun warm, the sky a dreamy blue, the streets quiet and freshly watered against the dust. And her humour was pleasant, too. Her lips bore that pleased, faintly reminiscent smile which indicated always a relaxation of her mood; a rising to the surface, as it were of all the mildness which was in her.

And she was not too early. Lennox was already there, looking, indeed, as she had hoped, from the impatience of his expression, as if he had been for some time awaiting her.

He saw her when she was still a long way off, and, raising his hat jerkily, he started to smile—that rather conscious smile which, in his effort to maintain it, grew fixed and somewhat strained by the time she came up to him.

" Are you early—or am I late? " she demanded briskly, and there was nothing strained about the look she flashed on him.

" I'm early, I expect—yes, yes, I'm early," he said sheepishly; and the Tron Clock chiming the quarter gave him back immediately the lie.

She laughed; feeling it rather pleasant to have reversed their customary relationship so neatly.

" Well," she declared, at length, " how does it feel to be a man of leisure."

He caressed his beard cannily. " Not so very good, you know," he said. " And not so very grand, either."

A short silence fell between them, and for a moment they stood awkwardly upon the pavement; then, throwing out his chest, he exclaimed: " You'll have a cup of tea with me? You said in your letter——"

" I'd like that," she declared warmly. " I'm dying for tea."

" That's right—that's right."

Her assurance seemed to give him a sense of inward satisfaction; he squeezed her arm in quite his old manner, and together they went towards the nearest branch of Chisholm's in Alston Street. It surprised her somewhat, this plain evidence of the recrudescence of his regard, but she made no sign, and as they entered the tea-room she paused, looked at him pleasantly, and demanded:

" Where shall we sit? "

Though the place was fairly full, he did not hesitate. It was an age when Miss Chisholm, in the heyday of her fame, drew to her tea-shops a polite and discriminating patronage—" tea at Miss Chisholm's," was, indeed, the refined accepted usage of the day. But Lennox had no qualms; observing a vacant table by the window, he indicated it positively with a cock of his beard.

They went over and sat down; but no sooner were they seated than a waitress appeared—hurrying.

" This table is engaged," she declared.

Lennox looked up. " It doesn't say so," he returned, quite undisturbed. " And there's no other vacant."

" I tell you it's engaged," returned the waitress emphatically; she looked harassed and bad-tempered from the heat.

But Lennox's hand had strayed suggestively to his pocket, and now strayed more suggestively towards her.

" Well, sir," said the waitress in a different key, " I'll see—yes, I'll see what can be done." She wavered, smiled, and went away.

Lennox's eye drooped towards Lucy with a naïve satisfaction.

" That's the value of money," he said, studying her face. " I'm beginning to alter my notions, you see. I used to think that money was just for keeping—but there's pleasure to be had in the using of it too."

Lucy made no reply; but she agreed with his remark: it was pleasant to have the tiny wheels of life oiled like this. Tea was brought, and poured in silence.

" You're not annoyed," he ventured at length, " at my having written to you? "

" Certainly not," she answered with an open smile. She paused: " I've got over it now I'm settled. But perhaps I was a little unreasonable when you sacked me."

She used the phrase deliberately, with a sort of provocative raillery. But he drew back from it.

" No," he said seriously, " I'm not wanting to talk about giving you the sack. It's just the other way round. You see—you see, it's been an awful wrench, this giving up of my business. I wouldn't have believed it, but to me it's just been like a man losing his wife. Yes, I felt fair lost at first." He paused, felt absently for a pencil which was not there, then suddenly went on. " But gradually I've come round a bit. I've begun to see that there's more things in life than driving a bargain."

Amidst the noise and chatter of the room, she regarded him in silence, toying absently with her teaspoon, feeling actually that here, beneath this crust of self-assertion, was a strange pathos: a lonely, unattractive little man, who had built up his life on one loyalty— and what a loyalty! so different from that which she pursued—and now discovered it crumbling beneath his feet. Misguided—ah, yes, misguided! Hers, of course, could not so crumble.

" So there was something I wanted to say to you," he persisted, with a curious note in his voice. " Something important."

" Yes? " she answered in a detached manner.

She waited. His face, for all its native shrewdness, wore a most unguarded look.

" You are not very comfortable where you are? " he said at length, observing her closely.

" Quite comfortable," she answered tranquilly.

" But you can't work like you're doing," he asserted. " It's only a stop-gap. It's not the thing for you, at all."

" You can make yourself do anything, if you try. Besides, I'm doing it for my boy."

" Give it up," he said slowly, importantly.

" I'll give it up when Peter's through! That'll be soon enough." She smiled confidently. " Unless you've something better to suggest? "

" Give it up," he repeated, more slowly, more importantly.

She stopped playing with the teaspoon, raised her head, and looked at him with a sudden intentness. She was startled, not so much by his words as by his face, self-important yet sheepish, holding something which astounded her. She drew in her breath sharply.

" I'm not a young man," he said. " But then, again, I'm not an old man. Yes, I'm healthy. Spry as a sparrow. And I've got the siller. I'm wanting someone to help me to enjoy it. Besides, I'm lonely—dashed lonely now I've parted with my business."

He paused, seeing that she read his mind.

She gasped, her attention riveted. It was incredible, but it was so. Lennox, who had for years been—well, " Lennox "—in the background of her life! Here in this crowded teashop—the last place suited to a romantic declaration—he was proposing to her. She had a sudden ridiculous impulse towards laughter, an impulse restrained only by the sight of his important yet curiously pathetic face.

" I believe I've been fond of you all along," she heard him say, as though it cost him an effort to utter it. The straining of a sentiment, repressed through the years, vibrated, not without absurdity, through those words; yet there was something tragic in the cry— something repressed until it was too late.

" But it's impossible," she declared slowly; " you know that "— advancing the obvious pretext, the incompatibility of their creeds.

" I'm a broad-minded man," he answered largely. " That's not the slightest objection to me at this time of day."

She looked at him seriously, thinking of those days when he had sat at her table at Ardfillan, affected strangely by his declaration. But she had travelled a long way since those days when she smiled at him from the garden of her house. Slowly she shook her head.

" It's no use. I've got my boy, you see," she said, looking downwards. " No, it wouldn't be any use."

He started, stopped smiling. " What! " he exclaimed incredulously. " You won't—you wouldn't——"

" It's just that I couldn't," she answered.

" You're not serious? " he stammered, all his little crust of self-importance caving in. " I'm a tidy man—you don't know what I'm worth. I could buy you all manner of things."

For a single second she hesitated. She knew that he was rich; that he was a decent man; that he represented comfort and security. Had he spoken that last day in the office, when she lay plunged in the well of her desolation, no doubt she would have accepted him. But now he was too late. Now—ah; now she was in different case: her son set upon the pathway of success, her loyalty pledged unalterably, her face set to the wind, not begging, but demanding, not

278

lying down weakly to let the turmoil of life sweep over her, but fighting—fighting for her ultimate triumph.

" Think about it, then," he said suddenly, almost entreatingly.

" It wouldn't be any use," she repeated compassionately, and as she spoke the sudden tension between them fell away limply.

Once more she heard the voices and the laughter, the chink of china and the tinkle of teacups. He did not persist; he was so staggered. But, essaying to cover his discomfiture with that familiar conscious little laugh, he said: " I think you're making a big mistake. But there was no harm in asking, anyway."

" No," she answered seriously, drawing on her gloves. " I'm sorry —that's all."

" If you would let me say one last thing," he declared more sharply, his sallow face still coloured: " I wouldn't sacrifice myself too much, if I were you, for that boy of yours, you know."

She smiled at him gently; construing his remark in terms of a justifiable pique, she chose altogether to ignore it. She was herself, and Peter was Peter; these unique and unassailable facts removed her case far above the lot of universal experience.

" And if you don't keep up with your friends—or keep your interests wide," he went on wryly, " you get set too much on the one thing. I've found that to my cost."

" But you and I will always be good friends," she asserted confidently.

He looked at her curiously, without replying; then he pushed back his chair and awkwardly arose. They went out of the tea-room in silence.

Outside, as they neared the Square, he broke a long pause.

" I'll get away for my train," he said at length. " I've nothing else to do."

The thought of his departure touched her with a strange compunction; now, perversely, she did not wish him to go. But how, and on what pretext, could she detain him?

" I'll be seeing you again soon? " she said, pausing, facing him at the entrance to Queen Street Station.

" That's right—that's right," he answered; but she did not in the least understand the oddly penetrating look which accompanied his words.

Instinctively she stretched out her hand. His was warm, and the veins stood out soft and compressible upon the back.

" Good-bye, then."

" Good-bye."

She stood watching his retreating figure just as, years past, she had watched it vanish down the roadway from her gate; and now there was again that indescribable nostalgia. She conquered instantly a foolish impulse to run after him; then she turned, and walked slowly away.

Rather sadly, she reflected: " I'll see him again soon—very soon. He's not a bad sort. He's too good a friend to lose right off." Yes, she did want to see him again, and at that thought she remembered suddenly that final remark which he had made. Suddenly, too, she seemed to perceive its meaning, and to feel within it a hidden reproof. She frowned, but the thought persisted: it lingered and rankled in her mind the whole way home: this thought that she had lost the gift of friendship. And that look which he had given her! Did he think actually that because she had refused him she would cease to think of him, cease to regard him as a friend? Those others, too. Was it her fault that Joe had vanished completely from her life, that Richard had used her so shamefully, that Edward manifested merely the most spasmodic interest in her affairs? She drew in her breath sharply. A thousand times no! Then, suddenly, she thought of Miss Hocking, with whom she had spent actually five years of her life. Six months had elapsed since the wretched woman had been removed to the asylum, and she had not once visited or enquired for her. Here, indeed, she felt herself at fault. She let herself into the flat with an uneasy sense of self-reproach. She was not selfish—she repudiated the thought—but, somehow, that frown between her brows deepened and remained.

When Peter came in his meal was ready, but she was still abstracted, disinclined to tolerate the somewhat boisterous inclination of his humour.

" Did old Lennox make love to you? " he enquired largely, striking the truth through the very wildness of his surmise.

" Be quiet! " she snapped. " And don't let me hear you talk about a decent man like that! "

He raised his eyebrows; but he was quiet. He had the faculty of realising when she was in earnest.

All that night she was restless; she did not sleep well. Something, she knew not what, was plucking at her. And her restlessness continued. She determined—and it seemed almost like a salve to her conscience—to visit Miss Hocking at Blandford. It was little enough to do; yet, somehow, she felt that she must justify herself in some fashion against the rankling of that reproach.

Consequently, upon the following Saturday—which she had ascertained to be a visiting day—she went out to the asylum.

Again the day was fine—another lovely day of that most lovely, lingering summer—and as she walked up the main avenue, through the pleasant grounds, she was conscious of a feeling of surprise. Nothing unusual was here—it was like the park of some well-ordered estate. Three tennis-courts lay on her right, and to the left an orchard hung with ripening fruit. She passed two gardeners, brushing in a slow, methodic manner the early fallen leaves. In the distance she observed a little knot of people walking sedately in all apparent normality. Farther up the drive, where it suddenly diverged, she came upon another gardener sweeping steadily with his broom and, uncertain of the path which she must take, she paused.

" Can you direct me to the West House? " she enquired agreeably.

He raised his head and stared at her. But he did not answer. Instead, he closed his eyes, and thrust out his tongue with a frightful childish grimace of distaste; then, quite quietly, he opened his eyes, restored his lolling tongue, and, bending his head, began once more that steady, unconcerned sweeping of the leaves. She flushed, and turned away quickly. She was wrong: strange currents ran beneath the seeming quiet of this tranquil spot.

She found the West House without difficulty: here also it was quiet—cool and charming as any country house: nor was there any difficulty raised when she asked if she might see Miss Hocking. She followed the nurse—a stout, elderly woman with a key chained to her girdle and a bonnet primly perched upon her head. Along corridors she followed her, and through many devious doors, not one of which but must be first unlocked before they could pass through. The key became, indeed, a talisman, the very emblem of the place, and, as it turned noisily in the ultimate door, the nurse paused, exclaiming succinctly: " This is the room."

Lucy went in. It was a curious room, and immediately she entered a curious thrill of fear went through her. It was so strange. The walls and floor were grey—a dullish putty grey—and soft, they were, like putty, cushioned to the touch. No ordinary window admitted the pleasant sun, but instead a small square aperture, a grille set high upon the wall, permitting grudgingly the entry of a few stray shafts of light. Nor was there any furniture. No, nothing was in that room but the figure of a woman crouching in the corner. Cowering there, she gave no attention to the opening of the door, but rested silent, absorbed, immersed in a ceaseless task. She was tearing paper, and at this task her fingers worked interminably. A newspaper lay in her lap, and this she tore into tiny shreds—fragments so indescribably minute that each was smaller than a small pin's head. Around her lay the product of her labour, a fine dust of white, heaped up in places like a bank of snow, and every now and then the woman ran her fingers through this dust with a slow caressing touch. Suddenly she looked up. It was Miss Hocking! A spasm passed over Lucy's face; she started forward.

" Pinkie! Don't you know me? " she cried.

But Pinkie made no answer; nor did the faintest shadow of recognition lie in her dull and wide blue eyes, eyes no longer dreamy but flat, somehow hopeless, and opaque.

" Pinkie! Surely you remember me? " She was touched, frightened, immeasurably distressed.

" It's no good your talking to her," said the nurse plainly. " When she's like this you won't get a word out of her for weeks at a time."

" But surely——" gasped Lucy.

" And don't go too near her, please," exclaimed the other, quite pleasantly. " She's liable to turn on you."

Lucy stood quite still, watching this woman who had been her friend and who now crouched in the corner of the dreadful room like some strange, bewildered animal. She had by contrast a quick vision of that first luncheon at Allen's, of Pinkie in all her kindness and childish vivacity. And now this—this creature! And those fingers, too, at their endless tearing, tearing, with a crazy, concentrated venom destroying the evidence of those printed sheets. A labour of futility!

With an involuntary shiver, Lucy turned. She could stand it no longer.

" We give her these newspapers to keep her quiet," said the nurse, as they unlocked their way back through the chain of doors. " It's the only thing that——"

" Yes, yes," said Lucy hurriedly. She saw vaguely the mad motive behind the insensate task.

" I'm up to all their little ways," remarked the other complacently. " I've been here thirty years by now."

Lucy looked at her sideways—at the fat, prosaic face, the rather importantly pursed lips, the waddling, consequential walk—and the key, emblem of her kingdom. Thirty years in this place—thirty years of unlocking doors! What a pattern of a life!

She took leave of the nurse, who smiled at her companionably—all in the day's work, it was, for her—and went hurriedly down the drive.

She was profoundly disturbed by her visitation of Miss Hocking. Involuntarily her hands clenched. It seemed to her suddenly monstrous, a travesty of the divine justice, that such frightful inequality should be permitted. All the human creatures within these walls emptied of reason, cast down lower than beasts! And for what cause? That squatting figure in the cell, tearing, tearing its way through futility—it haunted her; and for years to come that figure might still be there, inane, useless, imprisoned by its own nothingness.

She came through the fine scrolled gates, and away from the asylum, troubled and depressed.

For days this baffling, distressing feeling persisted with Lucy; but gradually it faded. She had her own purpose. The opening of the University was at hand, and the thought of her son's immediate entry absorbed her. She had her own brave ambition. No tearing of paper for her! Her purpose was momentous, and one, she knew, far from the realm of futility.

XX

She had twenty-five shillings a week. Out of this sum, seven shillings went on rent—deducted, indeed, from her wage by Henderson & Shaw before she received it; gas for cooking and lighting, coals at eightpence a bag, a charwoman, for the washing of the stairs, at sixpence—though sometimes, on the bad weeks, it was Lucy and not Mrs. Collins who " did " the stairs—consumed together, upon an average, three further weekly shillings. She had, in effect, fifteen shillings a week to provide two people with the bare necessities, and even certain of the minor luxuries, of life.

Fifteen shillings a week—it was not much. She did not disguise the fact from herself that it was a struggle—it was indeed, for her, a bitter battle—but the battle was not eternal. Herein lay her comfort. She was no martyr, and she rejoiced in the fact that the period of her privation was limited; that day by day it steadily grew less.

She was, despite his simile of the mole, an admirable manager. She knew the shops which offered the best value—she would walk two miles to secure a bargain. And she had a way with shopkeepers: pleasant yet firm; she was, in her own words, not to be imposed upon. Was it likely that she would allow herself to be so deluded when the career of her son turned literally upon the value of every penny which passed through her reluctant fingers? She had the " knack " of exacting the best both as to matter and measure in all those dealings. She so established herself with Mr. Tutt—the stout butcher with the pock-marked neck and the cartilaginous nose—that she obtained her inconsiderable quantities of steak—usually a quarter of a pound —" cut thick," an impossible achievement contrary to all the laws of orthodox butchery. Still, so it was. Though Mr. Tutt's heart must have bled to do it, he regularly defiled the symmetry of his rump under her anxious yet compelling eye. Again, accepting for the ultimate good those ingenuous advances of Bessie Finch, she often obtained, as a result, bargains of fruit from the maternal establishment: fruit, for example, which was good on Saturday but would not be good on Monday. Three miles, that journey to Whiteinch and back: but in the cool of the evening she walked it gladly: Peter was very fond of fruit. Indeed, to suit his tastes she stretched her purse-strings to the breaking-point. She was, for example, on many a Saturday, the blessed festival of pay day, betrayed to rashness by her innate boldness and the suggestive clink of silver in her purse; thus it fell out occasionally, towards the end of next week, that not a single coin remained in this same black purse. Then she devised little economies. During a whole week, for example, disdaining the tramway, she would journey in to the office on foot, and at the end of that week, utilising her petty savings, present him with some trifling delicacy: a cake from Cooper's or a carton of those ginger chocolates which he liked so well. Not that she fed him on such fripperies. She had indeed a genius for simple cooking. Knowing nothing of calories, she had, nevertheless, an instinct for those dishes providing the maximum of nutriment. From the beginning she had made up her mind that Peter, as a student, a growing youth with a delicate tendency, must above everything be fed. She knew the value of a well-grilled piece of meat. But, unfortunately, she knew its savour. Fifteen shillings bought English steak for one, but not, alas, for two. It was at these moments, when cooking his dinner, that she weakened and almost knew defeat. Rushing back from her district to prepare his meal, bending over that small gas stove, her healthy appetite would assail and almost betray her. She became conscious of wild and primitive instincts surging within her; the delicate odours arising from the grilling steak would fall upon her nostrils temptingly, causing her an acute anxiety, and water would run freely into her mouth. The very colour of the browning meat, the very richness of the gravy, made her lips twitch like the lips of a hungry dog. But she conquered. She would not submit. As she followed covertly the brisk movements of his knife and fork, it was a delight to mark the excellence of his appetite; it removed in no small measure her qualms as to his health. Yes, she knew the rapture of that steak vicariously.

But the food question was not her only difficulty; unexpected problems kept appearing from the most ridiculous and vexatious quarters. Take, now, the matter of her shoes. Clothes were, so to speak, easy, in that she knew beforehand that she must make her present wardrobe suffice. Her underwear and stockings could be repaired and darned as need be. No one now required her to wear dainty lingerie. But with footwear it was different. Her work involved a vast amount of walking—and she walked more than need be in order to economise in tram fares—travelling freely over pavements which were hard and unsympathetic to shoe-leather. As a result, the manner in which she wore out her shoes was deplorable, and, though she had always prided herself upon her neat-shod foot—it was a small foot—she came gradually to the conviction, after several successive days when she returned home with soaked, chilled feet, that this was false pride. Thereafter she wore shoes with the thickes soles she could obtain; heavy they were, and somewhat clumsy She got them in a small cobbler's shop not far from White Street, and, by an unstinted use of iron protectors, induced them to last until the uppers cracked.

With Peter it was different. He was light upon his shoes and careful of his clothes. Further, if only for reasons of conformity, it was necessary for him to be well dressed when he attended his classes; and it was possible for him to achieve this with that small yet adequate surplus of his scholarship remaining after his fees had been paid. His managing also—in a different sense—was quite astounding. But he knew always to the ultimate penny how and where he stood. The history of his childish " jug " again repeated itself; he kept a little memo book, discovered soon the wise economy of buying his books second-hand at Stenhouse's; he was exact, punctilious, and never once the prodigal. Nor from the beginning did he countenance her efforts to assist his calculation. It was, he pointed out, his own money; and he knew exactly what to do with it.

Thus it was with his clothes: though Lucy did her share by discovering, after repeated and careful enquiry—Miss Tinto was the ultimate fount of knowledge—a tailor named Ward who promised to shape his cloth and prices to Peter's slender figure and still more attenuated purse. The first visit to Ward was memorable—almost reminiscent of the choosing of the school outfit—for, in this instance also, Lucy led her son into the tailor's shop. Posed stiffly like a lay figure before the long pier-glass, he exposed his worn braces and suffered the indignity of the yard-stick with a faintly conscious blush. But Ward was no boor, no mere snipper, lassoed by a tape measure and stuck with his own pins; he was a dapper young man, recently started in business, short in figure but vast in tact and understanding; in his own dress, too, he revealed himself a model of waisted and bespatted elegance. He addressed Lucy respectfully as madam; enquired, indeed—though unsuccessfully—if he might not have the pleasure of cutting a costume for her; and, with a speculative eye upon the future, he maintained towards Peter an affable and knowledgeable friendliness.

The suit was a speckled grey homespun, chosen by Lucy after much careful fingering, more for its warmth and wearing qualities than for any startling effects of colour. Peter's taste lay towards a lighter and more lavish check; but Ward, whilst sympathising with the son, agreed wholly with the mother; it was unwise, he said, for a gentleman to become known by his suit; the grey might be quiet, but would " make up " well, and it was unimpeachably *distingué*; it was, he continued, " the cut " which mattered—cut was every-thing, and he (looking knowingly at Peter) guaranteed himself as gifted in this mysterious, elusive, but all-essential art.

The suit certainly was a triumph—the jacket curving downwards gracefully from the judiciously padded shoulders, the waist neat, the lapels small and square, the trousers two parallel lines of extreme precision—the whole a triumph of elegance and the sartorial genius. Moreover, in the making and completion of the suit Peter and the tailor grew friendly: after each fitting they " adjourned "—it was Ward's word and invitation—and over a coffee discussed the future which opened so brightly before them in their respective spheres. It was entrancing for him, sitting at the window-seat, whilst the trams swam up and down the street and all the stirring movement of the city flowed in a fascinating stream before him, to feel this delicious opening out of life.

Over these coffees he tasted in advance the savour of existence: to be so surely aware of his University career; and above all, like a *motif* running through the piece, to have the consciousness of the ultimate certainty of his success. It was delightful.

He was good to that first tailor-made suit, changing it for the older garments of his youth whenever he returned from classes, hanging the jacket meticulously upon a chair-back, reposing faithfully each night upon the trousers, flatly pressed beneath his mattress. And, by the inevitable justice of time and circumstance, he was rewarded. When the next instalment of his bursary came round and his fees, which were light that term, had been duly paid, it was natural that the surplus should be applied to supplement this first component of his wardrobe. Another suit—it was the check—and a neat spring overcoat came in cardboard boxes and tissue paper to 53 Flowers Street. Peter became a well-dressed young man, the admiration of his mother, of Bessie Finch, of Mrs. Collins, and— proof positive of his pre-eminence—the object of an occasional derisive catcall from the corner boys outside Demario's Venetian Café. Mrs. Collins, indeed, relinquishing her pipeclay to throw a half-blinded eye after the effulgence vanishing down the stairs, remarked to Lucy on one occasion:

" 'Tis the air of a duke he has." She tugged at the straggle of fur that choked her neck. " 'Tis a crime to think he'll come to smoke and go wid the girls like the rest."

Lucy accepted the just compliment, ignored the ridiculous aspersion in complacent silence. She had no qualms; she knew her son: his constancy, his purity of heart, his loyalty to her. Other sons, perhaps, might falter and fall by the wayside, but Peter—well, he was hers, and that unanswerable fact alone sufficed.

He had not yet become the president of the Union, but his progress, like his conduct, was good, and she marked it with a passionate interest; it became, in fact, the source from which she drew a steady and increasing comfort, the deep and secret well of all her happiness. During their long evenings together he would favour her, on precious occasions, with a full and expansive confidence. Thus, spellbound, she followed his zoological adventures with the dead dogfish and the sluggish amœba, joined in his profound chemical research with silver nitrate and the chlorides, heard mazedly of the botanical wonders of the cambium, and—in physics—of the hitherto un-dreamed-of principle of gravity. Her glowing eyes, fixed upon his moving lips, transcended the laws of optics he indulgently defined as actually she perceived his progress through these shining scenes. She saw him at his microscope, with slides and stains at hand, with scalpel poised delicately over a dead lumbricus (had he once called this disdainfully a worm and used it casually for bait?); she felt the swiftly rising heat of blue-flamed bunsens; the aromatic scent of benzine mingling with Canada balsam rose to her nostrils in a stimulating fragrance; she heard the voice of the professor, the movements of his fellow-students, the slow pacing of feet echoing through the cloisters beyond. She lived her life in his, not only when he spoke, at nights, of the great doings of the day, but during her own day also; when, at odd moments, as she stepped with relief out of some condemned dwelling, or saw perhaps the sudden beauty of a slant of sunlight striking through the squalor of a back court, her mind would lift with a sudden overwhelming buoyancy to the thought of him, working within that classic pile upon the hill. The very chime of the University clock as it rose over the city and fell faintly upon her ears drew her to him, linked them together in love and unity of purpose.

In the evenings, at his request, especially before examinations, she would hearken him his work, struggling with the pronunciation of a dead language or the formulæ of chemical equations. His tolerant amusement of her efforts to follow his enumeration of such pro-fundities as the nomenclature of schizomycetes made her smile in sympathy; and in dealing with the invertebrates her solecisms created a neology which moved them both to spasms of hilarity. Soon, however, he passed to studies beside which these early researches were but children's playthings. Here, of course, she could not follow him, nor was her proffer of assistance of the slightest service. He shook his head mysteriously, even warningly, so that she felt she had intruded upon the realms of the taboo; nevertheless, in expansive moments he chilled her blood with an occasional morbid detail of the anatomy room, or terrified her with an anecdote per-taining to the antics of a decerebrated ape. Temporarily, coincident with his descent to the caverns of the dissecting-room, he went off his food, and evinced a disinclination for the wares of Mr. Tutt, especially when presented in an underdone condition. But this phase soon passed, and he was able to refer hardily, with a manly smile, to the stiff subjects of his glistening knife. Admitting his student robustiousness, she could never quite condone this attitude towards those unfortunates who finished in this fashion upon a marble slab. For her, this end, tragic in its failure, epitomised the most piteous calamity of life; and once she had a terrifying nightmare filled with the horrors of the mortuary chamber. To die defeated and unknown; to be stretched upon this ghastly bier; she shuddered.

But she reflected that he could never perform such work without assuming a veneer of indifference. Moreover, his success in the recurrent professional examinations justified the means towards the great and glorious end.

Yes; he was getting on. Her heart swelled at the thought. The episode of the bursary competition had given her a transient apprehension, but this was now forgotten, buried in the limbo of unworthy thoughts. He worked nobly, and passed his examinations honestly, not with the flashy achievements of honours or the specious distinction of prizes, but with a comfortable solidity, sure sign of a stable and well-balanced mind, more to her than all the questionable pyrotechnics of genius.

Only yesterday, it seemed, gazing from the window, had she seen him walk—with steps restrained through the correctness of his new garments—to his first lecture at the University; and now he was through his second professional examination, sated with the profundities of anatomy and physiology.

" That's the *pons asinorum* I'm over," he asserted, with a satisfied sigh. " Easy going now."

She knew enough of the learned tongue to understand his remark.

" That bridge was never built for you, Peter," she returned calmly.

" Apparently not," he agreed meditatively; then he laughed.

" There's two or three old fellows still trying to get over it, though, mother. Been stuck for years. Bit of a joke—what? One man's married—with two children."

She shook her head, said almost judicially, " Everyone can't be born with brains——"

When she saw his name definitely in black and white among the list of passes in the second professional, a positive conviction of her own judgment, a sweet vindication in the course she was taking, passed through her in a quivering elation. " That will show them," she thought exultantly, including in this category all who had impugned the wisdom of her conduct. She was proud, and her justifiable pride was shared, apparently, by Edward. The reverend gentleman had seen the results in the *Herald* and, gratified by this new lustre on the name of Moore, feeling perhaps that it redounded to his own growing ecclesiastical importance and popularity in the

diocese, he had mused pleasantly over the paragraph and his morning chocolate: asking of his handmaiden, " Would the Bishop see
that, now, do you think? " And Miss O'Regan, answering faithfully:
" He's bound to know it's your nephew, your reverence," had firmed
a conviction tending already towards the affirmative. Considerately,
Edward had written an encomium to the student coupled with an
invitation to share his coming holiday, not this time to Madeira but
to St. Andrews, where the ecclesiastic, still under medical instructions, proposed to stimulate his liver with a niblick.

Lucy was pleased at the compliment. Apart from the material
benefit—somehow Peter's health and the question of his holiday lay
always rather harassingly at the back of her mind—she drew no
small measure of personal satisfaction from this indirect admission
of Edward's approval. She had no regrets that she had not been
invited to accompany them; it was unsuitable in every way: she had
no clothes, the " two men " wanted to be together, she would be a
perfect nuisance to them; and, though she had seen little of Edward
lately, she accepted inevitably the present divergence of their lives.
But it was with a pleasurable sense of justification she saw Peter
off to join his uncle at St. Andrews. The experience of life in a good
hotel would improve his manner, remove the last lingering diffidence
of his boyhood; she knew too that he was, beyond words, safe in
Edward's unimpeachable company, and this, though she knew it
not, drew all sting from the separation. She herself had not had a
holiday since the expedition to Miss Tweedy's, but this, she affirmed,
was of little consequence to a woman strong, literally, as any horse.
She took the change of air with him in spirit.

A chromatic postcard of a palatial hotel—his bedroom indicated
by a star—came to the flat in Flowers Street at the lunch-hour one
hot August day. She smiled at the conceit of the symbol, which lay
like a climbing spider upon the middle of that imposing façade. It
seemed a most attractive hotel. She had no aversion to hotels; suit-
ably clad, and with money in her purse, she felt, indeed, on this
languid afternoon, that the porch of a seaside hotel—she discovered
the palms and cane chairs in the postcard—would present a cool
seductiveness. There she would wear blue shantung, with, she
thought, a hat wide and somewhat shady, and, of course, a parasol.

It would be a relief to get out of her shabby costume—with all its
acceptable durability, it had barely sufficient mode for the Grand
Hotel. Yes, she favoured the blue. Closing her eyes, she saw herself
sitting under a palm, with Peter ordering her an ice. It was a pink
ice, with the sweet wafers she liked so well; and the waiter who
brought it was obsequious to a degree. She had always been rather
in awe of waiters—even in those early days of her courtship when
Frank, moved for once from his inertia, had taken her about—

but now, supported by Peter's immaculate and devoted presence, she was rather contemptuous of that waiter. She could not see his face, only the bald spot on the top of his bowed head, but she was sure he thought her charming and a lady. She gave him sixpence; then she opened her eyes, which fell upon the remains of a knuckle of veal which had confronted her without comfort upon three successive days. She had not much incentive to cook with Peter away; she preferred instead to make the most of the rest—often it was quite a rush for her to come from her district to prepare her meals in the limited time available—but now she regarded the unappetising dish without rancour. Her eyes looked towards a future not far distant; her vision transmuted the ragged bone to a jellied capon with, perhaps, asparagus. The savour of life was still in her, and (with a warm satisfaction) she felt her period of parsimonious endurance drawing swiftly towards its end.

In a cheerful humour she placed the postcard on the mantelpiece —visible object of inspiration—washed her teacup and saucer, and tidied up the room. It was the same room, holding the same bare oddments in lieu of furniture. But how could it be otherwise? How could she furnish the house when sometimes a single shilling was all that lay between her and absolute necessity? Still, the shilling was there. And for the rest, she could wait. She was still cheerful as she took up her bag and went back to her work. Back to the slums she went; back to her peremptory knocking on those inevitable doors; back to the inevitable declaration, " Henderson & Shaw "; on and on, up the dark stairways, handling the dirty money, carrying that same ridiculous bag, stung by the squalid sights, nauseated by the foul smells, the vermin, the filth, keeping her head up to it, clinging to her loyalty.

He returned from that seaside holiday brown and with an almost nautical jauntiness. " Spiffing," was the word he used to describe the excellence of his enjoyment; and his views upon Uncle Edward had—like his own constitution—undergone a sea change; Uncle Edward was now classed as " Not a bad old bird."

After he had dazzled her with the splendour of the vacation, she surprised him by asking absently if a bald-headed waiter had served him in the hotel. He looked at her askance, then laughed. " Waitresses, mother, all waitresses! Not a waiter in the place."

" Well—there will be," she returned dreamily, " and a strawberry ice cream."

His laugh became uproarious.

" You're a cure, Lucy," he gasped: he had lately fallen into the indulgence of denoting her by her Christian name. Though she felt the affection of the term, she did not quite like it.

" Mother," she corrected sharply.

" But, all the same," he persisted with streaming eyes, " that about the waiter——" And he tapped his head significantly.

She paused, a little cross at his unwonted liberty. But it was the liberty of a strong affection; of this she was sure; her resentment melted under his smile.

That autumn he began to walk the wards. He began actually to shave—not spasmodically, but in regular, deadly earnest. Uncle Edward, an esoteric in the business of the toilette—he used even a face cream after his sensitive ablutions—had given him one of his razors, a noble blade which, though not exactly of Toledo, had at least shorn the prelate's bristles during that memorable sojourn in Spain.

The idea of his shaving affected her curiously. Every morning she heated him specially some water in the kettle before he arose. Her devotion increased. She would look at him occasionally with a sort of brooding happiness: again she had a man within the house.

And autumn was in the air. A holiday was not for her, but this change of season was as freshening as a change of scene—that frosty nip she loved so well, the leaves sailing softly downwards in the park, a zest filling the crispy air. She drew fresh courage from the vigour of it all—courage that vitalised her purpose.

XXI

" You know, mother," he said, and when he made this casual presumption of her precognition she was aware, from long experience, that she did *not* know, " there's a dance coming off to-morrow."

" Oh! " she answered, without much interest; then, after a moment, she added: " Do you want the table cleared now? "

" If you like."

" It's not six yet," she remarked, getting up from her chair, " but I'll light the gas, anyway." The premature dusk of the late autumn evening had already shadowed the quiet room to crepuscular twilight.

" That dance——" he persisted.

The gas exploded into illumination with a sharp plop; she was usually a careful lighter of the gas, and it was the quick report no doubt which made her slightly start.

" What dance? " she asked sharply.

" I wouldn't mind going, you know."

She looked at him in astonishment; for one wild moment she thought he meant one of those dances held in the Grove Assembly Rooms—loud and odious gatherings advertised as " Select balls—

gloves optional, slippers essential." What other dance, indeed, lay within the compass of her house? But, before she could speak, he said:

"It's at the Union—the Beta Club. I'm told it's an excellent buffet." This last esoteric word seemed to remove his remark into the realms of the fantastic. Buffet, indeed! And they had just supped so meagrely—he upon a scrambled egg, she on a disconsolate heel of cheese. She had felt unwell during the day—a hard day it had been—Friday, too, the day when her exchequer always worried her—and her throat, never strong since that laryngitis at Ardfillan, ached suspiciously; now, with a stocking around her neck and her feet at last warm in felt slippers, she was prepared for comfort. And he spoke about a dance!

"Wait till we're more settled before you talk about dancing," she said more brusquely than she meant. "Where on earth would you get the dress suit—and the money for the ticket? Expensive enough, I've no doubt, with their buffet!" She returned him his word crossly.

"Don't get excited now, Madam Lucy," said he pacifically. "I got the ticket from a man on the committee—free gratis, you know —trust me for that. They're short of men—see!"

She watched him whilst he inspected his fingernails.

"But the dress suit?" she said at length, in a more subdued manner.

"That could be done, perhaps. Oh, yes, possibly—possibly."

"You wouldn't hire one," she exclaimed quickly, struck by a degrading recollection of the various "Dress Agencies" that lay upon the disreputable fringes of her district. "I wouldn't let you do that."

"Great Scot, no," he cried in a shocked voice. "A man couldn't do a thing like that." Then his manner reverted to its former knowing complacency. "I couldn't wear a rag off a peg like that. No! I know a better way than that."

"What, then?" she demanded tartly; he was provoking her with his tedious procrastination, and on such a preposterous, vexatious subject.

"Well, I was in at Ward's the other day," he returned quickly. "You know we're the best of friends. The question of dress clothes came up."

Dress clothes, indeed, she thought. Why not dress suit?

"I told him I couldn't possibly afford them for a couple of years yet. He wanted to give me credit, but I wasn't having that." He paused significantly while his eye, now ingenuous, invited her approval; but, as she did not speak, he continued: "Well—you know, Ward's one of the best of fellows. He has an evening dress in the shop belonging to a man that's gone out on a voyage to China —left to be refaced. I—I tried it on—it fits me like a glove." He tapped his teeth dispassionately. " Beautiful cut it has, too."

The dress suit of a man in China! He was now, at least, utterly fantastic.

" Mr. Ward couldn't lend you it," she said slowly.

" Oh, but he will," he returned at once. " He's promised definitely. I can have it to-morrow morning. Nobody'll be a bit the wiser."

" But—can you dance? " she persisted, with unconscious misgiving.

" Oh, I can get round," he grinned. He was astounding her. She saw that he had thought it all out; it was, in fact, arranged; she was startled at his resourcefulness. She did not wish him to go; she was, indeed, bitterly opposed to his going; but he was waiting— waiting on her word.

" If you've got the suit and the ticket you may as well go," she said at last, in a reluctant voice, which came, it seemed, from a long way off.

" Good enough, Lucy," he returned with a teasing satisfaction. " That's settled. Now we'll have the table cleared and get on with the work."

She cleared the table; yet, during the evening, her eye fell upon him with an odd hesitation. The sudden broaching of this topic—it was like a trap sprung without warning in her face; and she was, though she admitted it to be ridiculous, distinctly startled. She knew the adage, " All work and no play "; she was aware of Peter's incorruptible rectitude; it was, she told herself, because of her incipient chill that she felt as she did; yet the idea of a dance—a form of pleasure so different from that holiday with his Uncle Edward— filled her with a vague uneasiness which persisted during the evening and recurred at intervals during the following day.

Next evening, too, she felt her throat more inflamed, though she made no reference of this to Peter. He took his tea quickly and without appearing to notice what he ate; then, with a humorous sideglance towards her, he went into the front room with the cardboard box which he had brought home that afternoon. She put his hot water into the bathroom without comment; it seemed to her, as she listened to his movements, that he was a long time shaving—he was usually so quick. She thought also upon all the accoutrements necessitated by the " dress clothes "—how had he achieved these? It struck her suddenly as utterly incongruous that he should be dressing up in such a fashion in this mean, impoverished house; had he no sense of the fitness of things? Her mood returned more strongly, more indignantly than before.

Yet, when at length she heard his step outside the door, she looked round from the sink expectantly. He entered calmly, walking neatly upon his borrowed patent leather shoes.

" Well," he remarked tranquilly, " how does it go? "

Speechless, she could only stand, her hands still dripping with the dish-water, her lips apart, gasping, like a fish. This was not her son! —this debonair and godlike creature whose face shone with a pink translucency above his immaculate high collar and expanse of shirt, whose back revealed a lithe and tender elegance beneath the sensuous lines of the fine black cloth. He surpassed everything! Val Pinkerton, despite the decoration of the slashing red, was a mere simpering nonentity to this. She was moved, so profoundly moved that her eyes brimmed with tears.

" Oh, Peter! " she murmured, " really—really you look awfully well."

The sight of her son standing against the cheap background of the kitchen, filling these borrowed dress clothes like a young Apollo, touched her as poignantly as a grief. At that instant she had an emotion towards him which she had never before experienced— a rushing tenderness—admiration mingling with love. Frank had never had a dress suit! Frank! No, not even Frank had ever looked like this. She had never loved Frank as she loved her son at this moment.

" I can't get over it," she whispered again; it was one of the rare occasions when she involuntarily exposed herself to him. " I hardly seem to know you. You're—you're——"

" Clothes make the man, you know," he said. At that look in her eyes he had the grace to feel uncomfortable. " You must admit they're pretty tony, though. You're not going to sit up for me," he continued, adjusting his tie before the four square inches of unframed mirror on the wall.

" Oh, yes, I will," she inserted quickly. " I couldn't think not to."

He shot his cuffs for practice, then said:

" Almost time to move." He looked up suddenly and saw her intent face. " Why, I believe you'd like to come too, Lucy," he teased her. " And you wouldn't be a wallflower so long as I was there."

She made no answer, but she winced; then her face hardened. There was a moment's silence.

" You'll not be late," she said stiffly.

" No fear! Business to-morrow as usual! Give me a brush, though, mother, would you? "

She brushed him, then, finally, the richness of the suit shrouded by his coat, the effulgence of the shirt shaded by a claret silk muffler which she discovered in her drawer, he waved her good-bye and ran gaily down the stairs.

She went back to finish the dishes in chilled abstraction; she hardly saw what she was doing; the house seemed suddenly silent and empty, bereft of a presence almost luminous.

It was her night to wash down the stairs, but—although now, as always, she felt this a weakness on her part—her cold had so upset her that she had asked the charwoman to come. Mercifully, too, she reflected with an ironic twist to her lips. She would have looked well, cleaning the stairs, stepping aside from the wash-pail to let her son go sailing past.

Despite the rapture of the recent vision, her spirit commenced unusually and unaccountably to drop; she began even, as a means of distraction, to anticipate the arrival of Mrs. Collins, who on most evenings had a philosophic humour epitomised in her phrase: " I've a joke in me for all that."

But to-night, when she came, Martha was, in another of her phrases, " black miserable "; and, obtaining her utensils without much parley, began her work outside, slopping her cloth about to the mournful strains of her favourite song: it went like this—slightly falsetto, the words slurred together with an almost gloating relish:

> " I wish I was a maid again,
> But a maid again I shall never be
> Till an apple grows
> On an orange tree.

> " I wish my baby it was born,
> And crowing on some nurse's knee ;
> And I was dead,
> And in my grave,
> With the green grass over me."

Through the thin door the lugubrious ditty came to Lucy with irritating insistency. Yes, to-night she had little humour for the ballad, but at the end of Martha's labours, as she handed over the customary sixpence, she demanded:

" What's wrong with you to-night, Martha? Is the husband out of work again? "

Martha Collins straightened her hat—constant token of her respectability—and said at once, without an eye-blink:

" It's my youngest son, lady. He's a devil when the bead's in him. And now I've got to marry him or see him damned."

" Some trouble is it? " ventured Lucy.

" Oh, I know it's nothin' unusual; 'tis nothin' to fuss over at all at all. Yes, 'tis the will of God, I suppose, but when it's the youngest it comes hard on a woman." Her eye fired. " 'Tis a trollop that's trapped him no less and named him for the father of her misbegot."

" I see," said Lucy slowly. That young fellow—she remembered his ingenuous grin, like Peter's it was! It gave her, by some queer analogy, a vague feeling of misgiving.

" And him bringin' fifteen shillin' a week regular into the house," lamented Mrs. Collins. " Much good may it do her—the bag and baggage that she be's."

Lucy stood at the door while the outraged mother, invoking the curse of Cromwell upon the enchantress who had seduced her Benjamin, went slowly down the stairs.

And it had an obscurely depressing effect upon her, this incident. She went in, hung about the house, put away her son's discarded clothing, tidied up his shaving things in the bathroom, returned to the back room and sat down. She looked at the clock three times in half an hour; then, restlessly, she got up and put on some soup to simmer on the fire: he might like some when he came in; and a cup of it might do her throat good.

Again she seated herself; she had no energy for her knitting; the clock indicated that it was past his usual bedtime, yet she felt it strange not to see him there seated opposite her. She wondered if he were enjoying himself. Staring in front of her, her hands idle in her lap, she had upon her face a somewhat cold severity.

Then suddenly she was surprised to hear a light knocking at her door. For a moment she thought it was her son, and at once she started from her chair. But it was not he; it was, strangely, Mrs. Finch from next door, standing nervously upon the doorstep.

" I saw you weren't in bed by the light," Bessie began, with a flickering shadow of her usual smile. " I wondered if—if I could come in and sit with you."

" Sit with me," echoed Lucy. For a reason clearly understood, she admitted no one to her house; and it was, she felt, at this hour an extraordinary request.

" Yes," faltered Bessie. " A sort of frightened feeling came over me. It's—it's one of Mr. Finch's late nights. Sometimes he's not in till twelve." Her full face had a pallor in the dim light of the landing.

" Come in then," said Lucy, after a moment's hesitation. She had now an obligation to Bessie and to Bessie's mother which her sense of justice forbade her to repudiate. But her tone was cold. They went into the kitchen, where, despite her trepidation, Bessie had a quick curious glance for the furnishings of the room; they sat down opposite each other.

" It's downright good of you," breathed the visitor, with a short gulp, " to have me."

" Not at all."

" I don't know what came over me! You know—all day by yourself—sitting for hours——" She paused, almost in irritation; but Lucy, though observing the other's agitation, made no overture of curiosity; there was an awkward silence.

"Peter's out at a dance," she said at last, making an effort to ease the strained stillness.

"A dance!" echoed Mrs. Finch; her eye lit up with a pale gleam. "I used to love the dancing myself—I was that fond of a cheery tune."

"Yes?" said Lucy politely.

"Oh, yes, indeed," returned Bessie, her eye suddenly moist, the golden down upon her upper lip invested with a tremulous quiver. "It was at a ball I—I met Mr. Finch. I wore a white dress and a yellow ribbon in my hair, and a lovely yellow sash. He said I was——" Her soft plump face drew into ludicrous creases, and she burst outright into tears. She laid her head sideways on the table and wept unrestrainedly; between her sobs she gasped out, in broken lamentations. "I'm sorry—I'm sorry," she wailed, "coming in and greeting on you like this. But I can't help it. I can't help it, I tell you. It's John—my own Johnnie. I love him that much——" She broke off, choked by her sobs, and Lucy had a swift, startled vision of Johnnie, the mild little man next door, fat, bald of head, and middle-aged. Johnnie was no Romeo, but he was none the less the bridegroom, the paragon, the fount and origin of Bessie's bliss.

"What's wrong then?" she cried.

"The drink—the drink," wailed Bessie. "I've kept it till myself for months, and now it's choking me. It's soak, soak, soak all the time for him, I tell you. I never knew when I took him—I thought he liked a glass and that was all to it. Oh! it's killing me—me, mind you, yes, me that was brought up respectable. There's not a night in the week but he comes home drenched with it. And my mother—she warned me too—but oh, I'm fond, fond of him. That's the pity of it."

A frightful suspicion ran into Lucy's mind.

"Does he—does he beat you?"

"No, not him," the other woman moaned. "I wish he would. I would like it even if he leathered me. Yes, leathered me stark naked," she moaned again hysterically. "I want him, I tell you—and all he wants is the drink. He falls into the bed and snores like a pig— that's all I get out of him now—snores!" she laughed wildly. "Then next morning he eats ham and eggs and swears he'll go off it. Then in he comes at night as bad as ever he was. Blind, rotten drunk!" And she went on rocking herself hysterically, bumping her head fiercely against the hard table as if rejoicing in the pain of each concussion. Lucy did not know what to do. She was not demonstrative; she could make no facile show of sympathy; but she was concerned. She sat stiffly, gazing compassionately at the bowed figure, waiting in a wise silence for the other's outburst to cease. At length Bessie raised her head, wiped her eyes with the back of her hand like a tearful child.

"I've made a fool of myself," she sniffed. "A downright fool. Haven't I just?"

"No, no," said Lucy soothingly, "and I'm—I'm sorry."

"It's done me good, anyway," returned the other, "and I'm sure I'm much obliged to you." She paused, then added with a gentle defiance: "You know all about me now. But I don't care. I'm a healthy girl, and I can't help myself." As she spoke, she inclined her ear to a listening attitude, then said limply, "I think I hear him now. I'll better go and see."

They went to the door, and there viewed in silence the slow ascending figure of John Finch. He came carefully, with a meticulous step, his wary hand firm upon the balustrade: he was calm—too calm—and his breath inflamed the air. Preceded by the powerful odour of cloves, he advanced, amiable, dignified; his eyes, surveying the world, admitted, nay proclaimed, the brotherhood of man.

"Ah!" he said tranquilly, noting them profoundly, but without surprise as he achieved the head of the stairs. "Mish Moore and my Bessie. Good!" His morning taciturnity was gone; he had now the careful, slightly-slurred speech of the habitual toper. He closed one eye and added conversationally: "Nish nigh touside."

"Come away in, John," said Bessie hopelessly.

"Mush speak Mish Moore," said John pleasantly.

"Oh, come in, John."

"Mush speak, Bessie—mush speak."

She took his arm and tried to lead him into the house; but he straddled his short fat legs and exclaimed with a rush:

"Mish Moore, I know your bro'-in-law Joe. Big cushtomer mine 'n Levenford. Fine big Joe——"

But Lucy, with a last pitying glance towards Bessie's tortured face, had closed the door; she stood for a moment, rigid, listening; then at last she heard them go in, the drunken speech finally resolve itself to silence.

She went back into the kitchen. What an evening! She was dismayed by its strange irregularity. The departure from her fixed routine, the startling sight of her son emerging in one swift breath as a man of fashion, his absence at the dance, and then—as if these had not already been enough—the sudden unexpected intrusion of these two tragedies—ordinary, undignified, even disgusting, yet out of which two separate fears emerged and crystallised slowly within her mind. And these fears began to torment her. What if his fate should be that of the unfortunate Mrs. Collins's son? Or even that of the wretched Finch? He had said, too, something about a buffet. Her mind's eye conjured up a circular bar, glittering with lights, where gilded youths in evening dress lolled in debauchery, tempting her son to braid vineleaves on his brow. She had been mad to let him go. Her face hardened incredibly. She scowled at her own weakness in permitting him to go; yet inwardly she trembled—shaken by a painful presentiment of disaster.

Thus she sat waiting. And then, out of the strangeness and incredible torment of the night, a step sounded on the stairs—light, assured, and rapid. She did not move; but her eye lightened. It was her son! And immediately he appeared, pink, cheerful, unconcerned, and slightly damp around the region of his collar.

" What, still up, old girl? " he exclaimed as he came into the room. " You should have been asleep hours ago! "

Asleep! She almost laughed! Her relief, indeed, at the sight of him moved her suddenly with a swift elation. He was back: normal, unassuming, perfect, his breath untainted by the reek of liquor, his cheek unsoiled by the wretched caresses of a harlot. Never would she suspect him again. Never!

" Did you have a nice time? " she asked kindly.

" Oh, fair enough," he returned, after appearing to consider the point. " Poor lot of females there "; and he shrugged his shoulders with a disparaging air.

Her heart leaped within her.

" I'm sure you danced with somebody nice," she persisted, torturing herself to make sure.

" Not a one! " Then he gave a short laugh. " One good lady told me I walked all over her feet." Although she did not realise it, the evening had not been for him a brilliant success: he had been told occasionally that to get round the room was not the act of dancing. He yawned prodigiously.

The sight of that yawn, so natural, so spontaneous, so infinitely reassuring, restored her confidence in him completely. She gave him a cup of hot soup and watched him drink it. Then, at half-past one, she went to bed happily, smiling at her own absurdity. She fell asleep instantly.

XXII

" It's a confounded nuisance making us come up like this," Peter said, as they left the offices of Fullerton & Co. " You would think it was charity they were giving us."

He had been to receive the quarterly instalment of his bursary, and Lucy, fulfilling the stipulation of the philanthropic but mistrustful benefactress, had been constrained to accompany him.

"You never know," she returned mildly; conceiving the outrageous but not impossible case of a student who might hasten with his bursary to the nearest tavern, she added: " Some might abuse it. It's not everybody can be trusted." She did not add, " like yourself," but that was what she meant. His conduct in regard to the money had all along been irreproachable; not a penny wasted, everything spent in the right direction and upon himself.

"Crusty old fool she must have been," he muttered under his breath, and his tone deposed Kezia Reekie and her trust finally and for ever beyond the pale of decency.

"What was that?" said Lucy. Sometimes she thought she was getting a little deaf.

"I was blessing Kezia," he declared ambiguously, "relict of the grocer."

They walked down to the tram in the bright afternoon spring sunshine. She had asked permission to leave her work early, and now it gave her an unusually companionable feeling to be with her son here at this hour. It was seldom they had the opportunity of going out together: the relaxation of "a match" naturally claimed him on Saturday afternoons, and on Sundays she had formed now the habit of going to an early Mass while he went out at eleven—in order to devote the forenoon to cooking him a hot dinner.

Since her absurd fancies on the night of the dance—she still had remorse when she recollected this—she had clung to him perhaps a little more eagerly. Now she could afford to smile at these delusions, yet for some time after that event she had been nervous, and easily disturbed. Coming upon the dress suit hanging in inoffensive limpness within the wardrobe, she had said irritably:

"When is that thing going out the house? It doesn't belong to you, does it?"

He had smiled at her, and replied:

"No hurry, mother. It won't bite you. Time enough when Ward asks for it."

His very mildness had been like a reproach. Now, as they turned into a busier street, the recollection of these ridiculous suspicions was far from her mind. She was content to enjoy the sunshine, his society, and her emancipation from the slums, where, by reason of a scarlatina epidemic, her work was at present unusually trying. She enjoyed, also, an occasional glance at the shop windows as she passed along this, the most fashionable thoroughfare in the city. Strangely, when alone she shunned this street, with its large, expensive stores and throngs of modish women; or at least she hurried swiftly through; it gave her, by contrast with the pavements she usually trod, and by reason of her undistinguished dress, a feeling of inferiority and discontent. Now, however, with Peter by her side, she absorbed a pleasant sense of his elegant escort; and she maintained a leisured way, drawing in with satisfaction the occasional glances directed towards them by the passers-by.

Jabots were being worn, she noted, and pale pink—which she had always suited—seemed to be the prevailing shade. Although she had not bought a dress in the last four years, it was almost a pleasure to discover that her interest in the fashions had not abated; she reflected that she was really fond of clothes—she had always liked to be well dressed—and when Peter was through she would, she told herself, have her fling. The sight of the windows intensified her good humour.

" It's a lovely day really," she said, withdrawing her gaze from the windows and smiling up at him. " Don't you smell the spring in the air ? "

" Plenty of scent about here, anyway," he returned rather constrainedly. He had been taciturn during the expedition, and now held his head aloofly from the crowds and from her.

" Lavender water used to be *my* favourite," she replied. " You'll need to give me an enormous bottle some day."

She had hardly uttered the words before her open expression suddenly narrowed; she paled to the lips and let her gaze run in front of her towards infinity. Coming out of Ray's—the most exclusive costumier in the street—she had observed the smartly turned out figure of a woman. It was her sister-in-law, Eva—Richard's wife.

It was not the first time she had seen Eva, who was an indefatigable shopper in this district and in the city generally; yes, she had often seen Eva, but the truth was that Eva had never seen her. Perhaps on Lucy's part consciousness of inferiority in dress and occupation, perhaps her recollection of their last encounter at Ralston, favoured this mutual slipping past of glances; but she had nevertheless the bitter conviction that Eva, from motives of unconcealed snobbery, avoided the recognition.

With this in mind, she had begun unconsciously to hasten her step when all at once she heard Eva's refined and rather affected voice addressing her. She started; rescued her glance from oblivion.

" It isn't you, Lucy, surely," Eva was saying with her familiar lisp. " Imagine meeting you here ! "

" Yes," returned Lucy with conscious irony, " it's strange." The blood had rushed back to her face, and she felt, angrily, that she was blushing. She was not afraid of Eva, nor was she afraid to show that she detested her. But Eva smiled : she was cool and pleasant and socially at ease. With a slight tightening of her lips Lucy observed the smartness of the other's tailor-made grey costume, her pink hat, her lace jabot—they *were* being worn—the long umbrella slanting coquettishly along her crooked arm; no item of the costly outfit was missed.

"I'm often in town, but I'm so shortsighted I hardly recognise people in the streets these days," continued Eva—and in this artless excuse Lucy read a confirmation of her suspicion.

"My work takes me to another part of the town," she returned meaningly, and with unmistakable curtness.

Eva emitted a sympathetic sound—which came easily on her lisp—then her smile swept on to Peter, encompassing his well-groomed appearance appreciatively.

"This isn't your boy, surely?" she exclaimed. "Why—he's positively a man now!"

"Oh, not quite," said Lucy definitely; but she thought: So that's why you stopped—because you wanted to find out about my son; and she added: "We're just hurrying to get our tram."

But Eva made no motion to go; she remarked instead to Peter:

"I'd hardly have known you—and you my nephew. Isn't it ridiculous? Why haven't we seen something of you all this time?"

"I don't know, Aunt Eva," Peter replied; his aloofness was gone, wafted from him by her air of modish friendliness; he was smiling, rather effusive. "We don't go out much really."

With a mild resignation he made his seclusion an anchorite's.

"That wicked mother of yours—keeping you to her apron-strings," chided Aunt Eva, turning to Lucy and wagging a smooth-gloved digit reprovingly. "Why—we want to see you out at *Le Nid*."

"Peter's got his work to do," exclaimed Lucy sharply, "and I've got mine."

"Oh, mother——" said Peter indignantly.

Eva gave her little laugh—like a bird—in contribution to the conversation: with her sharply angled nose thrown back, she gaily pecked the air.

"We haven't much time for running about," threw out Lucy. She knew she was being outrageous, but something antagonistic rising under the other's suave and well-dressed elegance forced her to add: "*We've* got to work hard."

"Really, mother," said Peter again. He seemed frankly ashamed of her lack of courtesy, and looked across at his aunt apologetically.

"I only wanted you to come out on some Saturday," said Eva brightly. "It's absurd, our hardly knowing each other."

Absurd! Yes, thought Lucy grimly, but the absurdity was not of my seeking.

"I'd love to come out," Peter was saying. "It's very pleasant out Ralston way."

"We have tennis-parties occasionally," said Eva. "Quite informal."

Informal! Whoever heard of a formal tennis-party, thought Lucy bitterly.

"Tennis!" he echoed. "Lovely!"

"You do play, don't you?" she cajoled.

"Well"—he hesitated—"I suppose I could. I've often wanted to." Certainly the vision of his adolescent fancy had often arrayed him in spotless flannels of an immaculate cut and thrust the accessory of a racquet into his receptive hand.

"Well, I insist that you come," lisped Eva. "And bring your mother too—of course. I'll write you for certain."

"I'm afraid Peter has no racquet," said Lucy in a strained voice. "He won't be able to go." She was, she realised, placing herself in a false position. She loved Peter, yet she was deliberately alienating him; she was aware that she wished him to play tennis to his heart's contentment; nevertheless, something rose up tightly in her throat and constrained her to oppose his acceptance of this invitation. She did not like Eva; she felt jealously that the other woman had no shadow of right to interfere with Peter; neither Richard nor she, the wife of Richard, had acted fairly by her or by her son. Eva's well-dressed air of superiority stung her; Eva's presence poisoned indeed the balmy air, darkened for her the brilliance of the day.

"No!" she repeated. "He won't be able to go!"

"Well," said Eva, smiling, after a moment, "I must run along"; but her air said confidentially to Peter: "I'm much too much of a lady to press the matter, but we shall see if this nice young man will *not* come to *Le Nid*." She shook hands—at a high altitude—with them both and minced herself away.

Lucy and her son boarded their tram in silence. Her lips were compressed, her head stiffly erect. And he—he was in a huff: his aloofness settled once more upon him with a loftier and more domelike dignity. Nevertheless, after a long pause, it was he who spoke first.

"Why, may I ask, were you so rude to her?" and in his tone lay a forced judicial calmness.

"Oh, I don't know, Peter," she sighed, and looked up at him apologetically. "I suppose it was stupid of me. I just don't like her. I don't think she's sincere." This, indeed, epitomised, with telling frankness, her accurate opinion of Eva's character.

"Well, I think she's charming," he rejoined quickly; "and it was good of her to ask me out."

"How can you possibly go?" she retorted sharply. "You know your final is coming on. You've neither the time nor the clothes for that sort of thing. Do you want to get your flannels from China next? " She twisted her lip sardonically, yet she regretted this allusion to the borrowed dress suit the moment she had uttered it.

" Aunt Eva seems both delightful and kind," he threw back haughtily.

" Kind!" she echoed, not without bitterness. What did he know about Eva—whether it was milk or vinegar that circled under her smoothly cold-creamed skin.

He observed her pause and, eyeing her intently, exclaimed loftily:

" I hope you're not jealous of her because she happens to be well dressed and better off than you are? " His aspersion was so near the mark, divided from truth by so thin a pellicle, that she blushed with an indignant colour which flooded even her neck.

" Don't say that to me," she snapped.

" No? " he interrogated tauntingly.

" And remember that I'm your mother," she shot out fiercely. " Richard and all his have done nothing for us."

" Oh, well——" Under her tone he wilted; but even as he subsided he added sulkily: " You would think people ought to run after us and spoon feed us. You can't be unreasonable these days. Everybody's got their own affairs to worry about. And if you do want friends you've got to go out for them, and not hide yourself away in a back street." As his remarks tailed off, her lips compressed themselves tightly over her indignant answer, and she gazed fixedly in front of her. She saw the futility of furthering the quarrel. Living together as intimately as they did, the quarrels which they had were, she realised, inevitable, but they left her always with such a physical sense of disturbance and desolation that she made every effort to avoid them. Nevertheless, he was still nursing his displeasure as they got off the tram; he did not speak much, and when they reached the flat their estranged relationship continued. She set about making the tea while he began to steam his face with hot cloths. Lately he had been affected, to his concern, by an outcrop of comedones—he had corrected her use of the term blackhead—and now, placed before the mirror, he appeared to do penance by exorcising these painfully from his steaming skin.

Dispassionately considered, the affair became less ominous, and she admitted that she saw his point of view. He was young; upon the threshold of his life; until such time as they could remove to a congenial background his natural instincts towards enjoyment—and indeed her own—were being thwarted; the philosophic detachment with which she steeled herself to wait could never be achieved by his impetuous youth; she became in the end compassionate towards his petulant impatience.

Out of this train of thought the idea grew that his relaxation was too sadly restricted; she had the persistent desire to sponsor some suitable enjoyment which would encompass them both. For several days she considered the question unsuccessfully, feeling that to keep him closely to her she must lend herself more sympathetically to his pleasures; then, unexpectedly, fortune played into her hands. Miss Tinto offered her two tickets for the Empire.

Inconceivable that the stately and even puritanical bosom of Miss Tinto could harbour an inclination to frequent this edifice of pleasure. But such was indeed the case; Miss Tinto's bosom was virginal, but it was not pinched; nor was the bosom of Miss Tinto's elder and more majestic sister. Miss Tinto and her sister often " took a jaunt " to the Empire, booking their seats long beforehand—for noteworthy coming events—in the best position of the house with a meticulous exactitude and foresight. And now Miss Tinto's sister was ill; the sisters were attached—they came, as Lucy had often heard with a sad reminder of her own different lot, of a " very united family "; there was no possible question of Miss Tinto adventuring selfishly and alone to the gilded portals of the Empire while her sister lay racked with lumbago upon a bed of suffering. The tickets were offered graciously and surrendered without a murmur to Lucy, who accepted them gratefully, yet with proper protestations of regret.

She was, in fact, deeply gratified. These tickets had cost three shillings each—a sum she could not possibly afford—and they were just where she desired. That night, as she went home, her step held a brisk alacrity, and when Peter came in she exclaimed, quite excitedly:

" What do you think? I've got two tickets for the Empire to-morrow."

He lifted his eyebrows, and, after an expressive pause, declared:

" Not paper money, I hope, mother! "; then, observing her blank look, he added knowingly: " Free list—tickets for nothing—rotten show."

" Oh, no, Peter," she protested. " Miss Tinto would never do a thing like that! "

" What's on, then? "

" Well—I'm sure—I hardly know." Under his eye her crest drooped slightly.

" Let me see——" Stroking his chin, he affected to consider, as one more versed in such matters than she. " Let me see—yes—it is— I believe it's Marie Lloyd that's top of the bill."

" Marie Lloyd! " she exclaimed, perking up again. " Oh, she's splendid, isn't she? I'd love to see her. Quite a London favourite! I knew Miss Tinto couldn't possibly——" Under his quizzical stare she broke off smiling. drawing gratefully from Miss Lloyd's fortunate appearance a vindication of Miss Tinto's honesty and an asseveration of her own good taste.

"She's getting long enough in the tooth now, I imagine," he remarked. " Still, it might be amusing."

" Of course it will," she assented warmly. " We'll have a splendid time."

Certainly, upon the following evening, she felt as though she must enjoy herself. She smiled to herself as she thought of Marie. Yes, she had inspected the poster outside the Empire, and she expected to get a good laugh—just what she was needing—from Miss Lloyd. What was that song of hers they were all humming? " I'm the ruin that Cromwell knocked about a bit." Yes, that was it: too funny for words! She began to hum it herself.

Peter was not in: detained at a late clinic, he had arranged to meet her at Charing Cross: and so, with a final reassurance that she had the tickets safely—what a calamity to forget them!—she locked the house and went out.

Outside, the air was cool and vibrant, even in the centre of that dull grey city, with the promise of spring; a carthorse passing wore a bright ribbon twisted coquettishly through its mane; some sparrows, fluttering in the dust, made pretence at an evening bath. She was reminded vividly of those days, so pleasant and seemingly so near, when, arm in arm with Peter, she had walked along the front at Doune, drawn by Val Pinkerton and his attendant galaxy.

At Charing Cross she was early. She strolled up and down at Paltock's Corner, enjoying the evening air and her own anticipation of the evening's pleasure. People were waiting—it was a favourite meeting-place; the scene had a pleasant vivacity. Then all at once she was startled by a tap upon her elbow—a peremptory and pleasantly possessive tap.

" Move on, please," said a voice close in her ear. She jumped and turned swiftly. It was Peter, smiling, raising his hat and replacing it at that astute angle befitting an evening of sophisticated entertainment.

" What a turn you gave me," she said slowly; but her eyes were bright with the sudden sight of him.

" Shakes up the liver," he answered her, with a grave imitation of Uncle Edward's manner, as, taking her arm, he began to escort her along the darkening street.

She concealed her smile, which became a secret smile, evoked not so much by his ridiculous words as by the swift realisation of a sudden happiness.

" Have we the tickets, madam? " he enquired with extravagant raillery as they reached the gilded portals of the Empire. " Or have we left them on the bunker of the palace? "

They were in her hand even as he spoke, and, with a nod indicative of her own competence, she passed them over to him.

They sailed past an admiral of a commissionaire and entered the theatre at the exact moment when the orchestra, risen from its secret catacomb, burst triumphantly into Blake's " Grand March," Her cheeks flushed a little at the prominence of their entry; but his aplomb was magnificent: surrendering the penny for the programme with an air, finding their seats with ease, he surveyed the audience with nonchalance before flinging himself down beside her.

" Plenty of swing, hasn't it? " she declared at the end of the overture. " Lovely seats we've got too." Looking around, she felt that she did not disgrace him; she had removed her hat and jacket and was agreeably conscious of her freshly ironed blouse and neatly arranged hair. She was conscious also of the delightful knowledge that she was going to enjoy herself. Actually it was five years since she had been inside a theatre.

" Athleto and Angelo," she murmured, reading from her programme, " weight lifters." And as she spoke the curtain parted upon a scene of sylvan loveliness, where against a background adorned with arborescent forms which wound like limbs of octopi, bowing, stood Athleto and Angelo. Stout, massive of foot, and impassive of mien they were, with long, well-waxed moustaches and whitish tights clasped firmly to them by shining plaques of steel.

" The Babes in the Wood," he insinuated gently into her ear. She laughed; so escaped as to find in his atrocious pleasantry the scintillant shafts of wit.

" The little one is like Mr. Andrews," she whispered reminiscently; " it's the moustache, I think." They watched in silence whilst Athleto and Angelo raised with bursting eyeballs dumb-bells of prodigious and progressive weight. " Quite good," she averred critically as the curtain fell to a thin rattle of applause strengthened by an orchestral blare.

" That's only the first turn," he returned indulgently. " Never worth much."

But even as he spoke the curtain rose on the second turn, and hurriedly Lucy slanted her programme towards the lighted stage.

" P. Elmer Harrison," she announced to Peter, " coloured vocalist." Then eagerly she looked up.

Elmer was coloured: he was black. But, no matter the quality of his hide, he had a voice of resounding richness. And he had a lovely smile: a ravishing, red-lipped smile wherein blubber and ivory mingled entrancingly between his enormous ears. He sang the Toreador number from *Carmen*, and " When the Ebbtide Flows."

With the ebbtide he was masterly, descending gradually to unknown caverns of the chromatic scale, his last notes so hollow and abysmal he was loudly encored from the gallery. Rebounding instantly from the depths to a pinnacle of sublimity, Elmer replied with " Home, Sweet Home." It was very slow, very sweet, very sad; and it was fervent: there could be no possible question of the enduring affection of P. Elmer Harrison for his first aboriginal abode.

They agreed that Elmer was good—" passable " was Peter's word —but there was more than passable to follow. It was a " splendid programme," as might have been inferred from Miss Tinto's perspicacity, and Lucy felt the full enjoyment of it course through her being like wine.

The Cascarellas came after Mr. Harrison, in a triple bar turn. And, when they had revolved giddily at unbelievable heights, Otto and Olga walked sedately on to soothe the excited nerves with song, rendering: " Now I have to call him father " and " Have you got another girl at home like Mary? " with delightful and ubiquitous harmony. Then came Primavesi—" a dexterous juggler," as was said of him in the *Evening News*, " of no mean order "; Ebenezer Edwards, immaculate in pink, " the ventriloquial huntsman "; Elle Tortamada, the boneless wonder, a contortionist of almost repellent subtlety.

But, of course, the breathless anticipation of the evening was centred on Marie, who came—whetting the appetite—late after the interval. And Marie was sublime. Actually there was no adjective sufficiently superlative for Marie: Marie was in tights and terrific form. She sang first, with her own provocative archness, " I'm afraid to go home in the dark." And oh, how every male in that audience yearned to make Marie less afraid. Then she sang a song about a French lady affected in some mysterious manner by that insidious blight, *embonpoint*. " Um—bon—pom," sang Marie, and every time she sang it, which was often, she winked an eye, wagged her tights, and added the knowing affirmative, " Wee-wee." " Um—bon—pom "—pom-pom—" wee-wee."

It was devastating. Marie rolled about the stage. She strutted, she postured. With expert hands she made undulating movements suggestive of adiposity around her calves, around her bosom, around regions more intimate than her bosom. And always with a roll of drums would come that shattering, side-splitting, sempiternal cry, " Um—bon—pom " and its echo, with cymbals, " Wee-wee."

The house rocked. Outside, in the city, trams clanged wearily along, policemen stood moodily at street corners, husbands were beating their wives, children—yes, even children were being born. But within—ah, within, Marie was the centre of the universe; the beloved of every male within the audience; the sister—under the skin—of Lucy.

The tears rolled down Lucy's cheeks; ecstatically she clasped Peter's hand.

" Oh, Peter," she gasped, " she's—she's marvellous."

Limp with laughter, he muttered weakly: " Wee-wee."

Helpless, she made signs that she was expiring.

" I'm—I'm——" she panted. " I'm——" But she could not say it.

" Um—bon—pom," sang Marie for the last and hundredth time. And the whole house hurled the glorious reply: " Wee-wee."

But that was not the climax, for, having reduced her audience to impotence, Marie proceeded metaphorically to stamp upon them with her genius. Bursting back upon them as one dishevelled by a drunken frenzy, she sang finally, " I'm the ruin that Cromwell knocked about a bit." The ruin—Marie, dainty Marie, the ruin ; and Cromwell, you know, Oliver Cromwell—oh, it was too much !

It was more than flesh and blood could stand. Strong men wept with mirth, Peter had the hiccough, and Lucy—Lucy lay back in her seat and let the tears of helpless joy run down her cheeks.

So, overcome, she saw Marie's ultimate exit through a glorious ecstatic haze. So overwhelmed were they both they hardly saw the concluding item of the bioscope entitled : " The Cabin-boy's Sister." They could scarcely stand erect for " God Save the King." Oh, rare, delicious, and enchanting treat ! How she had loved it. Life with Peter by her side was glorious after all.

They came out of the steaming theatre into the cool street, where already a queue had formed for the second house.

" To think they've got to go through it all again," she said more soberly, with a sympathetic memory of Athleto and Angelo. " But oh, Peter, it was marvellous ! "

" They're paid to do it. Money. That's what makes the wheels go round."

He stopped to buy a paper from a yelling newsboy, then at the corner held up his hand imperiously to a yellow tram. The tram obeyed with a protesting screech.

" Up top ? " he enquired, looking over his shoulder as they boarded it.

She nodded her head. On the way home he read his paper indus-triously. She sat very close to him, glancing occasionally at him from under her hat, thinking how charming he had been to her ; even to this last request as to which seat she preferred upon the tramcar. How she had enjoyed herself ! She was happy, as happy as ever she had been with Frank. A feeling of extraordinary felicity stole over her ; half closing her eyes, feeling his shoulder against her, she willed the tram to go swinging on and on like this. Always—always—always !

Then all at once he exclaimed :

" I say—here's news for you." She opened her eyes and looked at him. " Listen to this—they've made Uncle Edward a Canon." In an excited voice he read out a short paragraph relating the elevation of the Rev. Edward Moore to the dignity of Canon by virtue of his seniority and long service in the diocese. " That's splendid for the old boy, isn't it ? " he declared.

" Splendid," she agreed ; she was not enraptured by the news, but in her present mood she felt it mildly agreeable.

" I must write and congratulate him," he said meditatively, after a moment.

" That's right," she assented.

He looked at her curiously, and later, as they went slowly along Flowers Street, he remarked suddenly:

" Why aren't you always like this, mother ? "

" What do you mean ? " she asked quickly.

" Oh, you know what I mean." He was perfectly serious. " Natural —not so touchy and stiff."

She made no answer.

When they got home, a letter lay on the floor of the hall.

" From Uncle Edward," he exclaimed. " But it's fiddler's news now." But the letter, which bore a large gilt monogram upon the envelope, was not from the new Canon. It was from Eva, asking him to play tennis on the following Saturday, and with a postscript which said: " Bring your mother with you if she cares to come." He gazed at her as though to say, " Now you know what I mean. What have you to say about this ? "

But, though she had a sudden sense of discomposure, she said nothing. She reflected: " He knows I don't want him to go. And he won't go." But she determined that she would not express this reflection in words. In silence, therefore, she watched him throw Eva's letter in the fire and sit down to begin a glowing letter of eulogy to his Uncle Edward.

XXIII

But he did go to the tennis-party, and she did not go with him. There was no scene. Everything fell out with perfect simplicity. All that week the subject had been taboo between them. She had thought vehemently, " I know he will not go." But he had been making up his mind to go. On Saturday forenoon he dressed himself with extreme care in his lightest suit: it was a matter of acute vexation that he had no flannels, but on this occasion there was no redress from China, and as for his lack of a tennis racquet, he decided to protect himself by saying he had sprained his wrist; and he wrote out a note for Lucy explaining his absence. It was a rude turn of the wheel—for this system of notes had been initiated by herself. When the time of his classes interfered with his lunch-hour and she was obliged to depart before his return, she would leave a pencilled message—this for example: " Dinner hot in oven: will be back early. Love "; and now how bitterly was the guillotine to recoil upon her own head!

He said, cloaking his defiance with an idiotic facetiousness: " Off for an afternoon at little Eva's.—Signed, Uncle Tom."

Then, quite ready, he stood for a moment before the wardrobe mirror inspecting himself; gradually a smile of satisfaction came over his features. He bowed to his image and went through the motions of shaking hands, raised his other arm, and, despite his injured wrist, swung a vigorous racquet; then he laughed at his own conceit, adjusted his tie, took a last look at himself, and went out.

It was a delicious summer day—one of those days when the very air holds a glitter from the sun's brilliance—and as he walked down the road he straightened his shoulders gallantly. He swaggered slightly as he passed Alice Maitland coming up the road from her music lesson, acknowledging her diffident flushing glance with a rather distant upraising of his hat. She was not much, of course, was Alice—that he knew—and his head was screwed too tightly upon his shoulders for him to commit the mildest indiscretion in that direction; but it was pleasant, none the less, to accept the warm tribute of her eyes. That faint answering smile of his might make her happy for the rest of the day. Who could tell?

At the station his mood continued, and with a sudden unaccountable rush of extravagance he demanded a first-class return for Ralston. It was unnecessary, a prodigal excess in one who counted his coins to such purpose; but as he flung himself back in the solitude of his compartment and put his neat shoes upon the elegant upholstery he admitted the experience to be worth the extra sevenpence.

The journey passed quickly: it was not yet three o'clock when the train drew into Ralston. Naturally he was aware of the deplorable solecism of punctuality, yet, although he walked at a most leisured pace, it was still early, much too early, when he reached *Le Nid*. Outside the gate he paused indecisively. Before him lay the lawn, spanned by a net, marked to the wavering form of a tennis-court, flanked by a row of attendant chairs. But the lawn was empty; so, too, were the chairs. Suddenly something of his assurance deserted him. He couldn't play tennis; he shouldn't have come; he had a sudden fear of appearing ridiculous. Quite disconcerted, with a quick movement he turned and moved hurriedly up the road, keeping his head lowered to avoid detection from the windows. Gradually his steps slackened, and for a quarter of an hour he wandered about, annoyed.

Yet, despite his mood, he found himself admiring the pleasant villas of this most pleasant suburb. One especially took his fancy—" The Towers " was the name upon the wide white gate, and the house strove nobly to sustain this title by a lavish display of baroque half-timbering and little stucco turrets visible through the rhododendron clumps of the winding drive. An imposing place, he thought, and somehow the name remained in his mind.

His assurance at last recovered, with a final look at his watch, he made his way back to Aunt Eva's house.

Now he was late, and the row of chairs occupied by quite a crowd of people who, with backs towards him, laughed and talked with every appearance of intimacy. Moreover, a car stood at Aunt Eva's gate, a large red car, with beautiful high seats of red morocco leather and a natty little brass radiator with a blue lion embossed upon the front. An Argyll, he saw at once, with an inward tremor; actually an Argyll at Aunt Eva's gate; and as he opened that gate he hesitated, once more disconcerted, not knowing whether to approach the group or to advance towards the front door.

The latter course seemed safer, and, ascending the three steps, he gave the bell a gentle pull, announced himself with a nervous gravity to the maid who answered the door.

He was shown into the drawing-room, already in readiness for afternoon tea, with a profusion of sandwiches, cakes, lace d'oyleys, and polished silver. Very stiffly he waited upon the edge of his chair, his eyes upon the elaborate preparations, his ears attuned to the conversation which came like a chattering of starlings through the half-open window. Actually it was his first real social adventure; and he was nervous. His early anticipations that he would cut a figure at the University had hardly been realised: at that dance, for example, he had gracefully supported a doorway for the greater portion of the evening. And now he started almost as Aunt Eva came pattering in, followed more slowly by Charlie. Both were smiling, welcoming him.

" But your bag? " cried Aunt Eva girlishly after a moment's talk. She wore white piqué and an orange bandeau twisted gipsy fashion round her dark hair. " Don't say you're not going to play."

He blushed and stammered.

" It's my wrist—sprained, you see."

Aunt Eva looked at the wrist, then twisted her head sideways and wagged a coquettish finger.

" You must play," she declared chaffingly. " We're depending on you. Run up with Charlie. He'll lend you some of his things."

" Really, though—the sprain—it's quite stiff, you see," he protested, with a still heightened colour.

But Aunt Eva, urging them upstairs with a commanding lisp,

would have none of that sprain. Before he could discover a more
convincing symptom, he was in Charlie's bedroom, a cheerfully untidy
room lined with books and coloured prints, watching his cousin toss
out an assortment of flannels from a well-filled bottom drawer.

" These should fit," said Charlie, straightening himself. He was
about Peter's height and age, dark, serious, a little consequential
like his father, but friendly; now he surveyed the other and, apparently satisfied, smiled his wide and rather charming smile. " Have
a cigarette while you change," said he, offering his case. " I've got
a racquet stowed away somewhere you can have."

" Very decent of you," mumbled Peter, unhitching his braces.
" I felt so laid out, I'd no idea of bringing my own togs."

Charlie leaned against the mantelpiece and let out a long, non-
chalant stream of smoke.

" Rotten court we've got," he affirmed casually. " Balls keep
getting into the shrubbery. Silly game too. I do it to keep my
weight down."

" Haven't played for long enough myself," said Peter in the same
manner—his cigarette, which was giving him confidence, dangling
from the corner of his lips. " More of a game for girls, I think." And
he pulled off his shirt, unashamedly exposing areas of skin with a
companionable hardihood.

" Two nice girls here to-day—Kitty and Rose."

" Yes ? "

" I'm interested in Miss Darting myself—that's Kitty."

" Oh! " replied Peter. He wanted to say something appropriate,
something rather clever, but for the moment he couldn't think of it.
So he let some smoke down his nostrils sophisticatedly, and finished
lacing his borrowed shoes in silence. When he was ready, they went
downstairs and out on to the lawn. Again he felt awkward and ill
at ease as they approached the group upon the chairs. Smart people,
he thought, nervously preparing his smile. His borrowed flannels
made him feel a clown; Charlie's tennis racquet was like a banjo in
his hand; but he got through the rush of introductions successfully
with much hand-shaking, exclamations of " Pleased to meet you,"
and an almost continuous ripple of laughter. Really they were nice
people, like all Aunt Eva's friends, and quite young—she liked young
people about her. There was Mrs. Ivy MacBride—bosom friend of
Eva—blonde, smart, gesticulatory, the youngish dashing widow of
a deceased gentleman who had made his money in the corset business.
And Kitty Darting, an alert, vivacious little brunette with a roguish
eye for Charles and a papa who recently had multiplied and dignified
some thousands made in butchery by an excursion into the frozen
meat trade. Vera, too, was there, anæmic, spectacled, drooping,
neatly gowned but not very interesting, beside her a tubby youth

named Jim, red-faced, beefy, somewhat hearty, and his sister—Rose!

He was sitting in the chair next to Rose now, was Peter, looking fixedly at a broken string in his banjo (or was it his racquet?), but seeing her round the corner of his too obvious absorption. About him flowed the talk which his arrival had interrupted: the smart gossip of the set—who was giving the next whist drive, weren't they getting on with the new picture house in Maidenhall Street, yes, weren't they just, and wasn't it shameful that Mrs. Moody (of all people) had been asked to open the jumble sale next Thursday. At last he looked up at his companion abruptly. She was tall, brown-eyed, and somehow remote, with a soft milky skin faintly dusted by freckles and a coppery tint to her hair, emphasised by the green ribbon which bound it. Her seeming aloofness rather intimidated him, yet he blurted out: " Do you play much—tennis, I mean? "

She smiled, altering immediately the immobility of her features to an engaging softness.

" Yes," she said candidly. And he had thought her distant! " Do you? "

Surer of himself, he made a non-committal gesture with his eyebrows.

" Cricket's my game," he answered meditatively. Had he not once, planted before the chalked stumps in the " little rec.," made seventeen against Brother John Jacob's bowling? He added, quite convinced through repetition of his infirmity, " And I've crocked up my wrist."

She was impressed by the one statement, sympathetic about the other.

" You live in town, I suppose," she remarked shyly: her dignity was but the mask of her softness; yes, for such a divine creature she had, he now saw, a most submissive shyness. " I haven't seen you this way before."

" Yes," he admitted slowly, with an eye on Aunt Eva, who, out of earshot at the end of the row, paused in her prattle to give him a vivacious nod of encouragement.

" Actually our place was in the country," he added. " But we've taken a flat in town whilst I'm at the 'Varsity."

" So you're at the University? " Her eyes glowed towards his interestedly.

He nodded; added laconically: " Medicine! "

She clasped her hands. " Oh, how splendid! Father wanted Jim to go in for that. Such a noble profession. But he would go into the business. I think to be a surgeon—wonderful! "

There was a pause, during which he looked notably quizzical. " You live here? " he demanded at length.

" Yes. It's not so very far from here, our house. The Towers. Dreadful name—but father would have it."

The Towers! He pricked up his ears and gazed at Rose with a new interest strangely mingled with respect. She seemed a fascinating creature, her eyes warm, her neck very white, her hands soft, placid, her dress attractive, of a thick and most elaborate silk belted with a bright green leather strap.

" How did you come? " he said suddenly, half teasingly. " I didn't pass you on the road."

She looked at him with a smiling surprise. " We came in the car. Jim's mad about it."

The Towers! And that stunning big Argyll! Really, it was exciting beyond his dreams. This was the society he preferred; for which, indeed, he was justly fitted.

" Court's waiting," cried Aunt Eva playfully. " Rosie and Peter against Ivy and Jim."

He rose obediently, with hardly a qualm.

" You'll need to help me," he murmured significantly to Rosie as they walked on to the court. " It's so long since I've played."

She smiled at him almost intimately in reply.

Fortunately the game was not cyclonic. It was mild, easy, and not unlike the ping-pong he had once or twice played in the Guild Hall at Port Doran. Jim's style was rash—rather fierce shots into the net; and the plump widow, too stiffly girded by corsets of an intimate marque, might giggle freely but she moved in a restricted orbit: her plump breasts outbounced the ball at her attempts to run. And Rose was steady, helpful with her advice. Through that advice he did nothing stupid, but, by holding his racquet up the handle and keeping the ball well in the air, acquitted himself, he thought, not unfavourably. They won, did Rose and he, and came off the court to quite a rattle of applause.

" Good set," lisped Aunt Eva. " Now it's our turn! You take Kitty, Charles, I'll take Vera "; and she led them on to the vacant court with a lively toss of her head.

" You did splendidly," murmured Rosie, sipping the lemonade which he had gallantly brought her from the small side-table. " With your bad wrist too."

He took a long pull at his own glass, his eyes upon the game in progress. This was the life. Indeed it was! He stretched out his white legs—really, he looked remarkably well in flannels—smoothed his well-brushed hair, then threw up a glance at Rose.

" I had a jolly decent partner, you see," he remarked daringly.

She smiled, watching the tennis in silence. Several sets were played —Aunt Eva was enthusiastic, with a boundless social energy for forming fresh permutations amongst her guests.

" Ivy, you take Peter this time, and Kitty, you——"

So it went on. Watching her, he thought his aunt charming, the epitome of kindness, and he expanded under that kindness. His confidence grew; he was enjoying himself. Once more he played with Rose, and they encountered each other like old friends. Again they won. Then, shepherded gaily by Aunt Eva, they went in to tea. This was a delightful function, impressive through its very informality, his first experience, indeed, of " tea in the drawing-room " since Uncle Edward had taken him as a little boy to the formal halls of Miss MacTara. Without the memory of his recent triumphs upon the court to sustain him he might have blenched at the swift passage of cups and the feats of balancing demanded of him. But now it was impossible for him to feel self-conscious. He lounged back in his chair beside Rose, his air engaging, slightly superior, finding her a charming companion—quiet and almost gentle.

" Try some of this cake, won't you ? "

" I dote on Abernethys."

" More tea, won't you ? "

" Let me take your cup, then."

Yes, she was extraordinarily easy to talk to, and restful, giving him her whole attention. Not like Miss Darting, whose glances darted archly about the room, or Vera, who had a languid indifference to all but the buttered buns. He was pleased with himself, with Rose—yes, with everybody. When the stage of cigarettes was reached, Charles handed over his case.

" Have one of these, old man."

Old man, indeed! It was an enchanting acceptance of equality, the definite seal set upon his social success. A little rush of warmth filled him. These people were friendly, kind, charming. It was too idiotic of his mother not to want to have anything to do with them ! He turned casually to Rose:

" I hope we shall run up against each other again," he hazarded. " One meets so few really nice people these days."

She smiled unaffectedly and looked down at her soft, large palm.

" That's true," she agreed reflectively.

There was a pause. At the sight of her downcast eyelashes, which seemed now to shade her rounded cheeks, he was moved suddenly by a desire to say something flattering, intensely complimentary. He racked his brains, trying to think of some remark not too forward, and at length his gaze fell upon the brooch that pinned her dress, which, in the new fashion, was open at the neck.

" How well that brooch suits you," he murmured awkwardly.

She fingered it idly.

" I don't care much for these things," she remarked, " but it's a good stone."

He drew in his breath abruptly, quite confused. He had imagined the ornament to be of crystal, and it was actually a diamond—such a large watering stone that with this new knowledge it made his eyes water in sympathy.

" You must come and have tea with me in town some day," he heard himself say, with unthought-of hardihood.

Their glances met.

" I'd love to," she smiled.

But now Aunt Eva rose, declaring that if they had finished they must get out into the simply gorgeous sunshine.

" You seem to be enjoying yourself," she whispered to Peter in passing. He grinned at her, holding the door open gallantly.

There was more tennis, more laughing, more talking. Between sets he helped Rose to look for a lost ball in the shrubbery. Their heads, bent under a laurel-bush, came so close together that he could see the tiny droplets of perspiration upon her upper lip. Enchanting sight!

Towards six o'clock Uncle Richard strolled out, after his fashion— with nose well up, but with a certain jocularity tinging his severity— to see how things were getting along.

He seemed pleased to see Peter, and after a few moments sat down beside him—somewhat apart.

" I'm sorry your mother couldn't come," he exclaimed guardedly, crossing his legs. " How is she ? "

" First rate, thanks."

Richard nodded his head.

" I'm glad. I'm very glad." He paused, his eye upon the toe of his boot. " Sometimes I have the feeling that your good mother is not just to us. We are not answerable for her, of course. But we wish you well, nevertheless."

" Of course," answered Peter hurriedly. " I can see that." There was a pause.

" Perhaps life has dealt hardly with Lucy," suggested Richard. " It's understandable. But I bear her not the slightest ill-will. I would like you to know that, my boy. And you're always welcome here. Your Aunt Eva——" His glance strayed fondly to the distant figure of his wife. " Yes, your Aunt Eva is very fond of young people about her. Come out any time you wish."

Peter was grateful, profoundly grateful.

" And I am delighted at your success," went on Uncle Richard. " At one time I admit I was dubious. But now I see you I'm not surprised. Stick to it, my boy, and you'll come through with flying colours."

" Thanks, uncle," stammered Peter. What exactly he was thankful for he did not then consider; but he was thankful none the less.

" Remember me to your mother, then," said Richard, pulling out his gold watch with a resumption of his normal brusqueness. " Now I must go."

Why, thought Peter when his uncle had gone, did the recollection of his mother suddenly make him uncomfortable; fill him with a curious sense of shabbiness ? It was as though some tie, some restraint, were upon him which he could not explain; and he wished to break that tie, throw off that restraint. However, in a moment this went out of his head; he began again to enjoy himself.

But at last the sun slid off the lawn and a faint breeze sprang up which made the thin-blooded Vera shiver. At this there was a general movement towards the house, and, unwilling to spoil this glorious day by outstaying his welcome, he at once went upstairs to change. First he had a cold spray in the large porcelain bath—so unlike the cracked and blistered tub at home—then he dressed with extreme care, brushed his hair with cousin Charlie's brilliantine till it shone, and went down.

Rosie and Jim were on the point of going—somehow he had the impression that she had delayed her departure until he came back—and now Rose turned to him and in her soft voice remarked:

" Can we give you a lift to the station ? "

" Let's all go," exclaimed Kitty gaily, in her usual slapdash fashion.

He took his leave of Eva and Richard with a profuse and eloquent gratitude: how could he thank them sufficiently, he said; then he followed the others to the big red car. Incredible that he who, a few short hours ago, had stood diffidently at this very gate was now gliding away from it by motor—a member of this jolly party.

He was squeezed very close to Rose by the pack in the back seat, and with each movement of the car he felt the sliding movement of silk against that smooth skin. Was she blushing ? He did not know; but he did know that he was happy, elated.

They tumbled out on to the platform, where—Ralston was a terminus—the train awaited him. And how he blessed his first-class ticket! He entered the compartment with a lordly air of indifference, and leaned out of the window, facing the little group beneath him. There was more elegant raillery, more laughter. Jim, blooming suddenly as a humorist, produced a handful of coins and rifled the automatic machine. They all ate chocolate round his window, then the engine whistled, the coaches jerked once, twice, and he was off.

Gallantly he lifted his hat and held it in his hand, keeping his eyes fixed upon the dwindling group. Was it his fancy, or had Rose answered that pressure of his hand ? She now gave him a last little wave as he swung out of sight around the bend.

Exultantly he raised the window and threw himself back upon

318

the cushion. He wanted to shout, to sing. It was fine; it was great; it was wonderful! He had enjoyed himself! He was a handsome fellow, and how admirably he had acquitted himself—an extraordinary success he had had! And what charming people! Rosie, especially, with her background of those turrets and the big Argyll, with that diamond sparkling so unconcernedly upon her rounded bosom. Suddenly he laughed outright. Life was opening out marvellously for him. Then he closed his eyes, and lay back with a faint smile still lingering upon his lips.

XXIV

AND she—she was late in returning from her work: when, at quarter to two, she entered the house, he simply was not there. With a strained look she picked up the foolish note: " Off for an afternoon at little Eva's.—Uncle Tom." Nothing about being back early; no thought of her; no message of endearment. Her face coloured violently when she read it, then she tore off her hat and flung it fiercely on to the dresser. She felt stifling. He had gone, then, in spite of her. She sat down, let her thoughts rush out of the close room. But in a moment she drew herself up sharply. Why was she thinking like this; so jealous, so intense, whipping herself into this bitterness of mood? What had come over her? Years ago she would have delighted in an expedition of this nature—a sudden vision of that excursion with Peter to Port Doran rose up before her; but since then she had altered in some strange, insidious manner. She had, of course, no suitable clothes; she disliked Eva; she had a legitimate grievance against Richard; she was, moreover, tired after a hard week's work; but some reason beyond all these had made her decline that invitation. Had the cumulation of her years of work and struggle and anxiety, and the realisation of the wretched locality wherein she lived, suspended her desire for social intercourse? No, that was not the reason. Eva, of course, would know that her son had disobeyed her. Even now the memory of that recent encounter rose up and stung her. Yes, the victory was Eva's. Eva had connived the whole thing. It would, she knew, be a delicious, piquant triumph for that lisping little snippet of insincerity to have so smartly turned this finesse against her. She began to entertain an almost diabolic bitterness against Eva. She wanted to be left alone with her son. That was it. They must keep their hands off Peter. He was hers. She wanted him all to herself; and when he was away from her she was miserable. Yes, she admitted it.

Automatically she rose up and put on the kettle to boil for her now unfailing solace—a cup of tea. Controlling herself, she marshalled all her forces. There was no universal conspiracy to take her son away from her. And he was devoted to her. She soothed herself with the memory of that delicious evening at the Empire.

She drank her tea, took up a book, and tried to read. Downstairs, Alice Maitland began upon the piano those interminable scales which so invariably annoyed her. But she neither heard the halting notes nor saw the printed words before her.

She was waiting, consolidating her resolve not to antagonise him by her anger. Yet, when he came back from Ralston, she saw with a curious sinking of her heart that he was elated; nevertheless, she said in a forced yet kindly voice:

" Did you enjoy yourself? "

Manifestly relieved at her reception, he unburdened himself of his experiences at *Le Nid*.

" They all sent their regards to you," he concluded meaningly, out of breath with the rush of his enthusiasm.

" That's right! " It cost her a frightful effort to maintain her determination to be calm. Their regards, indeed! Would their regards have put him through the University?

" I can see nothing wrong with them," he resumed unguardedly.

" No? "

" You've got to swim with the stream these days—not against it."

" What's Vera like now? " she demanded abruptly.

" Oh, I hardly spoke to her." He paused, and gave her a charming smile. " But there was a crowd of jolly people there. One lot came along in one of these new Argyll cars. Lovely thing it was. Must have cost tons of money. I'll never be content till I've got a car like that —and the money to run it." He laughed. " You can do anything nowadays if you've got money." Then his laugh died out and he looked disgustedly round the room. " It's awful to come back to a hole like this after a decent house. You should see their bath! How could we ever invite anyone here? "

" Well," she rejoined almost wearily, " we haven't long now."

" Thank God for that! "

His tone was to her almost insupportable; she was on the verge of a frightful outburst; but no words left her tongue. She watched him in silence as he went out of the room to change his suit. Then he returned, flung his books on to the table, and began to work.

" That's over, anyway," she thought after some moments, con-gratulating herself on her restraint. " He's been to their wretched party. Now he'll think no more about it."

Apparently he thought no more about it; for he never spoke of it to her again. Yet strangely she was not comfortable in her mind.

Was it her imagination—that very peculiarity of which he had accused her—or did he seem altered in some manner indefinable? She was uneasy; but she was not sure. Had some mysterious seed of unrest been sown in him by that one ill-advised excursion? It was absurd, a ridiculous thought, and yet somehow it clung to her. Often in the evenings she would look up from her knitting and find him staring away from his books in quite a vacuous manner; she observed that he became even more meticulous in his dress; he complained more bitterly about the shortness of money; he brought a face-lotion back from the dispensary. Once when she returned unexpectedly, having forgotten something, she found him writing furiously at the table. All this indefinable evidence pointed nowhere. She saw that she was making a fool of herself for nothing. Besides, had she not firmly resolved that never would she allow suspicion to transfix the sweetness of her love? Not again would she defeat herself by that misguided step. Her frightful mistake with Frank was enough. No, no, she suspected Peter of nothing.

And then one afternoon late in May, when she entered the office after her day's work, she was greeted by a loud burst of laughter, which made her pause. Nobody observed her, the merriment was so intense, and Adam Dandie, holding the centre of the floor, was at once its focus and its source. Standing in the doorway, she smiled in spite of herself. Dandie, a natural mimic given to derisive acts of caricature in which he used his physical oddity to its most clownish limit, was now engaged in such an act, to the unrestrained amusement of Miss Tinto and, inevitably, of himself. With head upturned engagingly, arm crooked tenderly, small bandy legs curved amorously as a cupid's bow, he escorted an invisible companion—manifestly feminine—around the room. " As sure as I'm here—that's how I saw him," he exclaimed, with a gesture of broad pantomime. It was very funny; and laughter convulsed him. " Down Maidenhall Street! ' Allow me, my dear,' said he. ' My arm, if you please.' "

Miss Tinto was about to relax her high front once more when suddenly she lifted her eyes and saw Lucy. Instantly her double chin dropped, her face coloured in confusion; she turned abruptly and gave her attention to her ledger.

" What's the matter? " said Lucy, as she shut the door and came into the room. She had an uncomfortable intuition towards that pantomime which once—a long time ago—had been enacted satirically for her benefit by Peter.

Miss Tinto made an inarticulate, non-committal noise in her throat; but the inimitable Dandie, his hardihood surviving his discovery, fronted the situation with bravado.

" Tell me," insisted Lucy.

" It was nothing," said Dandie.

Lucy stared at him, her mind filled by an unpleasant suspicion.

" Was it anything about me? " she asked severely.

" Not a thing! " he repeated. " It was just a bit of fun! "

" It was about me," she persisted sharply. " Come on—out with it."

A sourness came over his features.

" I tell you it wasn't," he exclaimed. " I happened to see that boy of yours this afternoon—arm in arm with some piece of goods. That's all it was! " And he swung to his desk, slapped down his book with an aggrieved air, and began his addition audibly.

She felt herself flush vividly; an indignant repudiation of his assertion trembled on her lips. But she hesitated. Supposing— supposing he was right? He knew Peter, who on an occasion had called for her at the office; and he had sharp sight; yes—wretched prying eyes.

" I wouldn't worry my head about it," said Miss Tinto suddenly, addressing her ledger. " Any young man will make a fool of himself once in a while."

Lucy made no answer. Her son a fool! She bit her lips as she felt the other woman glancing at her stealthily. She walked over to her table, slammed down her bag, and made up her book furiously. At five o'clock she left the room without saying good night to either of them. Almost racing, she could not get home quick enough. He was back, awaiting her, when she arrived at Flowers Street.

" Come along, Lucy," he exclaimed amiably. " I'm starving for tea."

She drew a deep breath and faced him.

" Where were you this afternoon? " she shot out.

" Why—what's the matter? " His face had altered at her tone.

" Where were you? " she repeated more violently.

" At dispensary—out-patients—where I always am."

" Where did you go after that? " The words came furiously.

He looked at her strangely.

" Oh, come now, mother. What are you getting at? "

" Answer me! "

" Who do you think you're talking to? " he exclaimed with a sudden heat. " You would think I was a schoolboy, the way you go on."

" Answer me! " she persisted in a high voice.

" Oh, be quiet, for heaven's sake! "

" Answer me! " she shouted, for the third time.

" Don't be mad! " he shot out; but he looked now a little afraid of her. They gazed at each other in a tense silence; her lips were pale; she could feel her heart struggling like a bird within a net.

" You were seen in Maidenhall Street this afternoon with a girl— walking arm in arm." The last words came pantingly, ridiculously, in a rush—the culmination of her impeachment.

His face fell.

" What if I was? " he said, sullenly. " It's no business of yours."

He did not deny it! The feeling within her became intolerable.

" No business! " she returned furiously. " What in the name of God are you talking about? You that's got your work to do—wasting your time on that sort of nonsense. And with hardly a penny in your pocket! "

" Well, whose fault is that? "

" To think of it," she exploded. " To be seen like that in broad daylight. You—you would lose your bursary if it was known. It's humiliating! It's disgraceful! "

" Here, what are you talking about? " he exclaimed heatedly. " Don't start running people down. Where's the harm in what I did? "

" Harm! "

" Yes—harm? "

Her lips quivered as she stared at him.

" Are you mad? " she cried fiercely. " Are you forgetting our position here—stuck up in this tenement? Here you go gallivanting about with some empty-headed creature from Maidenhall Street "—her fear drove her to a preconceived opinion on the form of his debauchery—" and me slaving myself to put you through. Have you nothing else to do that you must make such a weak fool of yourself? "

" Put me through? " he returned loftily, picking up this issue. " I understood I had a bursary."

" And am I not," she panted, " taking the very bite out of my mouth for you? "

" Don't be vulgarly disgusting," said he with a chilling disdain.

" What ? " His manner, cutting into her apprehension, drove her beyond control. She swung back her arm and struck him a frightful box on the ears. The sound of the heavy blow resounded through the room like an explosion.

He staggered back from the very unexpectedness of the attack, and, clutching at the table-cloth, dragged the tea-things to the floor, where they broke with a resounding crash. His face, ridiculous and crestfallen, was pale; his cheek began slowly to assume the reddish print of her fingers.

" So that's it, is it? " he stammered. " Well—now we know how we stand." He scrambled up from his absurd position, and, with a high attempt at dignity, walked into the front room, shutting the door behind him with a violent bang.

She followed him with her eyes, which were now glistening with tears; she breathed painfully, as if she had been running. Then suddenly she heard a noise in the hall; in the agitation of her entry she had left the front door open, and now Mrs. Finch came rushing into the house.

"I thought—I thought I heard something," cried Bessie with large round eyes, which, since the exposure of her own misfortune, seemed on the outlook for kindred calamity. "Did you fall?"

"Yes—I stumbled," said Lucy, staring at the other like a woman in a trance; then, making the explanation clearer, more obviously false, "against the table."

"Are you ill?" stammered Bessie. "Can I get you anything?"

"I'm all right now." She uttered the words with difficulty, supporting herself against the table by one stiff arm. Mrs. Finch bent down and picked up the fallen tea-things—a cup and one plate had been broken; then, raising her flushed face, she suggested diffidently: "I could give you a drop of spirits."

"No!" Lucy waved the assistance away. "Just leave me. I want to be alone."

"But——" persisted Bessie; then something in the other's attitude compelled her. She went out of the room with a bewildered look on her round red face, closed the front door almost apologetically behind her.

When Mrs. Finch had gone, Lucy sat down. She felt ridiculously weak, and the hand resting upon her knee showed a fine, faint tremor. For five minutes she remained seated, then she rose and took a drink of cold water. Slowly the colour came back into her face. She set about making the tea, adjusted the table, dropped the broken crockery into the bunker, and finally composed herself completely with an effort which was almost painful. Then she went to the door of his room and knocked firmly.

"Peter," she exclaimed in a low, controlled voice, "your tea!"

She did not await his answer, but returned immediately to the kitchen, whither, after a moment of acute suspense, he followed her. He came in slowly, with his hands in his pockets, his lip heavy and, for all his years and size, his face expressive of an almost dismal discomfiture. Sitting down at the table, he began his tea in silence. Her hand, as she passed his cup, was deliberate and steady.

"Some toast," she said distinctly, pushing forward the plate.

A long silence.

"Thanks, mother," he said, with an effort masticating the hot buttered toast as though it were wood.

A deep and powerful emotion swept over her, mingled by an immense relief—a torrential rush of feeling under her outward calm. Her eyes fell upon his lowered head compassionately. She had lost her temper. She had not meant to subdue him like this; her victory was like a pain to her. But it had been for his good. Only for his good, and perhaps for hers. Yes—for their ultimate united good.

XXV

SHE felt that she had re-established their relationship, and, attempting, as it were, to vindicate her attitude, she increased her efforts to prove her worth to him. He was now working for his final professional examination, and she set herself in her own fashion to a final passionate endeavour. It was difficult. During that summer, whilst he was studying, her economic position grew steadily worse. Lately, prices of foodstuffs had risen; but her wages had not risen. The advance in values was not much; merely, as Miss Tweedy had once indicated, a halfpenny here and a halfpenny there; yet for Lucy those paltry halfpence were the jealous tokens of existence which must be fought for, guarded with a painful intensity. She ought by this time to have bettered her position. It was with this optimism that she had entered the office of Henderson & Shaw; but for a long time now she had accepted her own limitations. She was not clever— indeed, the adjective " stupid " had more than once been levelled against her—and she perceived that never, now least of all, could she ameliorate her present humiliating occupation. It must serve its purpose; then she would cast it from her. And, if she was not brilliant, she was dogged, with a proved unyielding doggedness: a spirit which, increasing with increased adversity, grew within her grimly.

To see her coming along Flowers Street of an evening—a sultry summer evening when the air hung listlessly between the tired buildings—was to observe a spirit transcending the confines of its jaded flesh. Slowly she would come, her costume—worn to utter dinginess—clinging to her from the heat, her hat—battered now and of a greenish tint—evenly upon her brow, her figure erect, but with one shoulder drooping, weighted by the satchel holding her day's purchases of food. Her lips were pale, her eyes remote and large, her face colourless, with a fine-drawn gauntness which made her cheekbones high and almost harsh. And about her hung that singular quality of isolation.

She gave no heed to her surroundings, avoiding the playing children quietly, careless of the staring women who stopped their close-mouth gossip to follow her with their eyes. They had their own name for her now, these women; but she was oblivious of that name, totally indifferent to their opinion of her conduct.

Though she was conscious of no martyrdom, she was, indeed, like a woman persecuted—persecuted by herself, marching to some tortured purpose of love and sacrifice. Yet whilst obsessed by this purpose, she was not insensible of the suffering it caused her. She did suffer; and she realised, too, despite her assumption of invincibility, that she was fast reaching the end of her endurance. Often, in the middle of the night, she would wake up in the closeness of her room dripping with the cold sweat of a frightful nightmare. Peter had failed in his examination; he had broken down in health; or, with unspeakable anguish and a hand clenched on nothing, she had lost her purse. Supreme bathos. Yet she was haunted by this last fear—the dread of her defeat through some monetary disaster. No matter that her budget was balanced in pence, her sleeping brain would laboriously reckon, reckon over and over again painfully, explore a better way of expending her paltry wage. She awoke sometimes exhausted, as if her body had been beaten by a pitiless hail of coins.

The essence of her life was this: she denied herself everything for the purpose of her ultimate supreme gratification. No sacrifice was too great in this, the culmination of her endeavour. Dress, holidays, she forgot about them all—she tried, too, to forget about her food. Her diet became fixed, unalterable as her own will. It was a meagre diet; not her favourite chicken and asparagus, but it was enough to live on—she had the evidence of White Street—and this momentarily was all that she demanded. Nor did she suffer great physical disability, beyond certain transient attacks of giddiness, from this too farinaceous diet. But it had begun, though she failed to recognise the cause, seriously to affect the condition of her teeth. Once her teeth had been firm and even, white—as Frank had often declared— as new milk. At first in Flowers Street she had continued to take great care of those teeth, brushing them night and morning with camphorated chalk; but toothbrushes—especially the cheaper ones— became so quickly denuded of their bristles that in time she had stopped buying them; begun, instead, to use a scrap of folded linen. Then, with her eye fixed always on economy—Peter always purchased his own tooth-paste—she had abandoned the camphorated chalk in favour of salt—that coarse salt she knew to be an excellent cleanser.

Now, as a result of these limitations, her teeth were decaying rapidly. Lately, indeed, she had suffered excruciating attacks of toothache, arising from two hollow molars—now mere shells of teeth—on either side of her lower jaw. She did not know what to do about these teeth. Determinedly, she made up her mind not to trouble Peter with the mention of the matter; deep in his final preparations for the examination, he had his own worries.

Nevertheless, this ceaseless nagging exasperated her, the more because she was absorbed, and desired to be absorbed, by the final stages of his study. It irked her, that pain, when, with her whole soul, she wished to fling herself into this last effort. She was trying to do everything. By day she raced through her own work, hurrying home to suit his convenience; his meals appeared upon the table as if by magic; for fear of disturbing him, she sat for hours perfectly motionless, in her favourite rocker; she took her knitting to the next room, lest the click of the needles should distract him; adventuring downstairs with rare fortitude, she prevailed upon Mrs. Maitland to determine for the present her daughter's Lydian measures. She thought of everything, and omitted nothing; she rose, indeed, despite her difficulties, to heights which surely were sublime.

But this toothache, yes, this ridiculous intervention in the face of the sublime—what was she to do about it? Just when she wanted to be at her best, to make the last spurt during his examination, it paralysed her with its pain.

On the eve of the examination, hurrying on her weekly round of White Street, as she stood for a moment with Mrs. Collins, she was taken in the middle of a sentence by a dreadful twinge. Immediately her hand flew to her cheek, her face stiffened.

" The face-ache, is it? " ventured Martha sympathetically. She was nursing, affectionately, the offspring of her erring son—temporarily surrendered to her care by " the baggage," who, immured for the moment in Rotten Row, was engrossed by a further demonstration of her fecundity.

" Yes, it's toothache," said Lucy slowly, when the edge of the pang was blunted.

" Why don't you pluck up your heart and have it out? " returned Mrs. Collins, clapping the infant's bare bottom soothingly, and dangling seductively a china dog before its dubious eye. " My Benny had one out at the Dental Hospital last year, and never knew a thing about it. After spending good money on a gill of whisky to kill the pain, he went up and had it out for nothing."

" Did he? " returned Lucy slowly, struck by an idea. The Dental Hospital—she could attend this free!

It was, in effect, not the pain, but the price of the extraction, which she dreaded. Yet somehow her pride recoiled from the thought of degrading herself by attending at a free institution; she—Lucy Moore—to do that. It was unthinkable.

But the toothache got no better, and, after five o'clock upon the same day, as she went along Young Street, she paused at the shop surgery of an American dentist—a cheap establishment which in passing she had often observed. She hesitated, then abruptly she went in. Her intention was merely that of enquiry, but the dentist —title of courtesy, for he was quite unqualified—had a bustling way with him. A big square-shouldered man he was, with a blue serge suit and a brilliantly gilded smile, and he had her in the red plush chair before she could protest.

" Wouldn't be a bad idea to clear the mouth and have artificial," he suggested cheerfully, playing with the forceps.

" No—no. I only want rid of my toothache," she returned.

"We'll take four out, then, to start with"; and he lifted his syringe. "You'll never feel them, with alvatunder. It's easy as shelling peas."

She put her hand on his sleeve.

"But the price?" she protested. "That's what I want to know."

"Five shillings the lot."

Her look became troubled.

"I couldn't——" she began.

"Say four shillings, then."

She shook her head, and made as though to rise from the chair.

"Say three and six then," he exclaimed, restraining her. "That's rock-bottom—hardly pays me for the anæsthetic."

Three shillings and sixpence! It was still an impossible sum. She thought for a moment, then, looking at him, she said slowly:

"How much without—without anything?"

He stared back at her, sensing at last something of utter indigence.

"Oh, that," he returned. "I'll take them out for a couple of shillings."

Again she became thoughtful.

"Very well," she said at length.

She lay back in the chair, gripped its arm tightly, closed her eyes, and opened her mouth.

The torture was exquisite, like tongues of fire lancinating her jaw, searing into her very brain. She had never dreamed that anything could be so agonising—the crunching of the forceps on the last tooth ran through the marrow of her bones. But she made no sound.

At last it was done. She sat up, washed the blood from her mouth with the water he gave her, then, with a pallid face, she rose and, opening her worn purse, handed him the two shillings. It was a small price to pay for the conservation of her pride.

On the way home she felt weak, overcome by a vague nervelessness.

"Good Lord, mother," said Peter, looking up as she came in, "what on earth's the matter?"

"Nothing," she answered. "It may be the heat. But you—how have you been getting on?" And she began as usual to make his tea.

Next day the examination began: the final test.

Her mouth was slow of healing, but, free from the persistent pain, she was a woman refreshed. During the succeeding days she gave no sign of strain. She was calm, reassuring him with her unspoken confidence. For the space of a week she saw him come and go: speeding him with fortitude, meeting him with an unshaken composure. Then it was over. Then, also, a quick reaction took her. She felt limp, languid as from a lavish spending of her forces, liable to strange fits of agitation.

When the day drew near for the announcement of the results, this agitation, long concealed, broke through, and almost betrayed her. Success meant everything to her. She felt, with a sort of fatality, that if he failed now she could never repeat this supreme effort. In it, she knew, she had touched the pinnacle of her powers.

Another week passed slowly, but this thought did not pass: it was, indeed, still in her mind as she went into the office on the morning of the appointed day.

XXVI

" YOU'RE a mass of nerves, my woman," said Miss Tinto, treating her with a magisterial dignity which held a hint of reproof. " As if your worrying would make the slightest difference."

" Is this how you feel? " broke in Adam Dandie from the far corner of the room, and, affecting to tremble violently, he shook his crescentic limbs in palsied agitation.

" Not exactly," said Lucy, with forced smile.

" Ah! " said Dandie, ceasing to shiver and returning to his normal acidity. " What's the good of upsetting yourself? He'll get through all right. They let anybody through nowadays. It's too easy for words."

" Easy! It's desperately difficult," she answered sharply, and paused. " Not that Peter won't manage it."

" Why worry then? " said Dandie cunningly. He had the stupendous faculty of diverting the issue to get the better of an argument.

" Oh, I'm not *worrying*," said Lucy, with a jerk of her head.

" That's right," said Dandie, grinning maliciously.

Miss Tinto vented a refined snort.

" You'll know all in good time," said she with a conclusive air of wisdom, " and the world won't stop going round if——"

Suddenly the phone rang. She paused, lifted the receiver, and listened. Then, with a curious expression, she turned to Lucy.

" You," she said. " You're wanted."

They both looked at her as she went over to the desk.

It was Peter's voice which came over the wire as clearly as though he stood beside her.

" Is that you, mother? "

" Yes."

" Well—— " he paused. " I thought I'd ring you up, you know ——"

" What is it? " she exclaimed urgently. " It's not—nothing's——"

" Oh, no. Nothing's wrong."

" What, then? " A sudden weakness took her. It was unprecedented for him to ring her up, and now his hesitation convinced her of some impending disaster.

" Well—it occurred to me you might like to know——"

" Yes," she broke in quickly.

His laugh came teasingly over the wire.

" Don't get excited, Madam Lucy."

She said nothing; she was trembling; sick with her suspense.

" Anyway," his voice continued jocularly, " I thought you might care to know that it's Dr. Moore that's speaking to you."

For a second she did not understand; then she gasped:

" Peter—it's not true! "

" Yes, it's a fact," he assured her lightly. " I've just been up and seen the lists. It's positive."

She could not articulate; her eyes blinded suddenly with tears; a tremendous ecstatic sweep of joy surged over her.

" You knew all along I'd pull it off, didn't you? "

" Yes, yes," she stammered; her tongue felt stiff; her emotion was choking her.

There was a silence; he seemed to be waiting for her to congratulate him; but she was still too overcome to speak. Then again his voice came back.

" I'll not be in for lunch to-day—I'll be with some of the others here—a little celebration."

" Of course," she agreed quickly.

" That's right then, mother."

" Peter——" She found at last some expression of her happiness. But he had gone. She stood facing the telephone, dazzled by an inward light; then she hung up the receiver slowly. A supreme, a sublime beatitude possessed her; her face was strangely illuminated. She had struggled, but the struggle was over. She had fought, but the fight was ended. And she had won; yes, victory was hers. She had vindicated herself! Between them they had won that frightful unequal conflict. From nothing, and with nothing, she had elevated her son to a noble and exalted profession. He might have been a pettifogging clerk, a shop assistant, an artisan, a common worker in a shipyard. But no—she had said otherwise; she had stood alone to say it; and with what determination had she consummated her decree. Suddenly her heart soared. She wanted to call out in the ecstasy of her happiness. She looked round the room exultantly. Victory! Victory! It was hers!

" He's through! " she cried, with an excusable emotion. " My boy's through! "

They gazed at her for a moment in silence.

" What did I tell you? " exclaimed Dandie. " Didn't I say it was easy? "

" Good! " said Miss Tinto, with a mild approving nod. " Good! Did he get honours—or anything? "

" I don't know—I don't care," returned Lucy excitedly. Their lack of enthusiasm astounded her. This new wonder of the universe caused them neither to marvel nor to admire. Politely they made a lukewarm murmur of congratulation. They were pleased; but they were not enraptured.

" You're the proud mother now," said Dandie, not without a shade of sarcasm.

" You're out of pain, anyway," said Miss Tinto succinctly, " and that's a mercy."

" She'll be too big for her boots now," said Dandie sagely, addressing the ceiling. " She'll be leaving us for her estate."

" I should think so," returned Lucy gaily. " I've had about enough of this work." And she smiled at them.

She went out of the office in this same warm glow of happiness. In the streets the life of the city seemed suddenly transfigured: the colours of the trams seemed cut from rainbows; men rushing past her to their work had a gay impetuosity; shop windows seduced her; the sun had a high brilliance; even the air was rare, and had the sparkle of a bubbling wine.

All day as she did her work, in which there was, strangely, no labour, the thought of her triumph—for her son's triumph had become hers—was constantly before her mind. At intervals she made little exclamations to herself of wonder and delight. Her face, relieved for once of its habitual fixity, was animated as a young girl's; her lips, no longer drooping, had that upward contented curl of her youth. Her foot regained its spring, her back its suppleness.

Ten words upon the telephone and ten years slipped miraculously from her shoulders. She did not view the matter as she might have done. A woman of no consequence, a woman employed in a low and almost menial capacity, a woman who spent her entire days working amongst the squalid sights and odours of the slums—this woman had pinched and scraped and starved herself to allow her undistinguished son to complete the curriculum of a provincial college and to emerge, finally, in company with one hundred others equally ill-fledged and inexperienced, who, mouthing with false measure the dog Latin of the Hippocratic oath, would shortly be loosed upon an unsuspecting universe. No wonder, then, that Dandie had with difficulty suppressed his yawn, that Miss Tinto's tone had sounded tamely tepid. But for Lucy it was not like this. No! A million times no! To her the battle had been homeric; the prize supreme; and now the victory—so hardly won—was ecstasy inexpressible.

That night, when she returned to Flowers Street and, ascending the chipped and damaged staircase, entered her house, he had returned before her. She paused, her eyes moist with sudden tears. Then she dropped everything she was carrying.

" Peter," she cried, stretching out her arms. " Peter."

XXVII

It was here, the great triumphant day!

She was dressing for the ceremony of the graduation, her cheeks somewhat flushed, her movements, from her excitement, a little flustered. Peter, immaculate as a groom, had already departed—drawn by the exigency of hiring a gown—and now, with an eye upon the clock, she began hastily to put on her new dress. Yet, as she pulled the garment over her head, her haste was tempered by a subtle apprehension. She had made that dress herself, out of an odd piece of brown voile—a special bargain at the remnant shop down the street from Tutt's—cutting it from a pattern in the *Weldon's Home Dressmaker* and stitching it quickly as best she could without the accessory of a " machine " during the evenings of the past week. She was, in consequence, rather dubious of those stitches, and now, gazing at herself in the mirror, she became, not for the first time, rather dubious of the dress. It was neither worn nor shiny like " the relic," and it covered her. But this, in effect, epitomised its virtues. It was not the dress she wished—something soft and filmy, relieving the outlines of her thickening figure, that would have been—but it was, reluctantly, the best that she could do.

But what matter the dress? It was the graduation that mattered, and the fierce delight of seeing him—her son—capped in open assembly.

For years she had anticipated that scene, and now, triumphantly, it was here. Her triumph it was, equally with his, and, watching, she would share it secretly, in the deep recesses of her heart.

With a final inspection in the mirror she hastened to get her shoes.

She picked up her shoes from the rack above the range, looked at them; then suddenly her face fell, fell miserably.

She had entertained a doubt, a strong suspicion, about those shoes. They were old; they were worn; when damp, they had been dried and dried again at nights on this same rack to facilitate their being comfortable in the morning. And now this last rash drying had consummated their defeat and hers. A frightful disaster! The sole of the right shoe had cracked completely through. It was not so much a crack as a hole—a ragged angular hole in the shoddy sole, through which she might have inserted her little finger. Around that hole the weakened leather—if, indeed, it were leather—peeled and curled, making her eyes widen wretchedly.

She had wanted to buy herself a new pair of shoes, but she simply hadn't been able to afford them. The extraction of her teeth, the hat, the remnant for her dress—these recent indulgences had ruined her; and now both the time—it lacked but a quarter to eleven, the hour of the ceremony's commencement—and the day—it was Friday, the barren morning of her pay-day—definitely precluded her obtaining new shoes. She had a sudden wild idea of demanding the loan of a pair from Bessie Finch, but, though Bessie would have been " only too glad to oblige," Bessie's enormous shoes would be like boats upon her own small feet. And there was no alternative; she would have to make the best of it.

Slowly she went to the bunker—refuge of every oddment—and took out a piece of stiff brown paper. This she folded and refolded, then inserted it—an accessory sole—inside the damaged shoe. She even rubbed a little blacking on the outside, to conceal and perhaps consolidate the junction of the paper with the wreckage. Then she put the shoe on. Tight, it was, much tighter than the other, but it had at least a sense, and a deceptive sense, of tense solidity. Still, what did she care about the shoes? No more than the dress. It was the day that counted—the glorious day!

Outside, as she emerged on to the landing, she found the Finches' door open, and Mrs. Finch herself hovering in the hall beyond.

" I thought you might like this," said the sentimental Bessie. " I got it at my mother's for you—special like—knowing where you were going "; and with a quite romantic air she presented Lucy with a pink rose trimmed with maidenhair. " Here's a pin, too," she pressed, and, before Lucy could protest, she pinned the rose upon the baggy bosom of the ill-made dress.

" That's lovely," she concluded, throwing back her head admiringly. " Just sets you off."

" Thank you," said Lucy awkwardly. She doubted the wisdom of the adornment, but she nevertheless submitted to it. At one time she had questioned Bessie's kindness. Did not that soft eye, falling upon Peter, gleam unconsciously with a frustrated ardour? But now, of course, that thought perished. They would so soon be away! With amazing fortune Peter had fallen into a hospital appointment —a " stop-gap " for six months at the Royal Eastern. In the interval she would make her plans. Then they would move.

Then, after a further word, she descended the chipped staircase and, with her head in the air, the rose on her bosom, and the burst shoes on her feet, she set out for the University.

Strange that never before she should have entered this building—
that for five years it should have over-topped her life without her
once approaching it. To-day it seemed—like her—in festival: cabs
and motor-cars converging towards its entrance-gate, a crowd upon
the terraces, a flag floating languidly upon its high white staff.

Suddenly she had the feeling that she was late, and she quickened
her step upon the gravelled drive. It was a rash impetuosity. The
rough surface of the drive rent her paper sole unmercifully; like teeth
the flints were, chewing her flimsy subterfuge to ribbons. She had
not advanced a hundred paces before she walked upon her stockinged
sole, nor yet another hundred before that stocking parted, and she
felt the cold gravel upon her skin. It was a calamity. But she would
not stop. Excitedly, with a mantling colour, she topped the summit
of the hill. The clock struck eleven meditative strokes as she entered
the quiet of the cloisters.

Following the last stragglers upon the circling stairs, she entered
the Bute Hall with a still heightened colour—and by good fortune
found a single seat against the wall, high up in the crowded gallery.
Here she drew a deep breath, feeling herself secure and unobserved.

She looked around, but she could not see Peter. The place was
filled by a stylish gathering. Unconsciously she hid her damaged
shoe, kept herself erect proudly in her seat.

Suddenly an organ pealed—a high, triumphant note, which
drowned the hum of conversation, and, rising, swept the hall in a
rushing ecstasy. She was lifted up by that soaring sound. It became
the symbol of her victory, a wind on which her spirit suddenly took
wings.

The music ceased, and, with a start, she came back to the hall.
Dreamily, almost, she observed the entry of the professors, passing
pair by pair, following the mace-bearer along the aisle, sedate and
learned in their gowns and curious caps. Their hoods made vivid
slits of colour—scarlet and blue and yellow—as they ranged themselves in their dark stalls. The Principal, a short-necked figure
with a peering eye and a pointed beard, mounted the daïs. There
was a Latin prayer; singing.

Then the capping ceremony began.

She leaned forward eagerly in her back seat, watching one after
another the gowned figures advance to the daïs, where, kneeling
in a suppliant attitude, each was touched by the Principal and
solemnly presented with his parchment. Impressive sight!

Suddenly her body grew tense—rigid with expectancy. At last—
Peter's name had been called. A high colour leaped into her cheeks
as she saw her son emerge from beneath the gallery and advance
to the daïs, his figure erect, his gown sustained behind him smoothly.
He was pale, she saw, but collected; and he performed with perfect

poise the ritual required of him; kneeling, bowing, rising—he did it all so well! Her heart thrilled within her—no mere beats but a flutter, like the flutter of wings. Quite a burst of clapping greeted him as he arose; a loud applause which almost startled her, coming from somewhere in the body of the hall. For herself, she did not move her hands, which lay stiffly upon her lap. She was too proud, too conscious of the moment, and too overwhelmed by it. She would tell him afterwards what she had felt. It was an emotion too deep, too secret, to be openly expressed.

Well, it was done! The final seal was set upon him. For her, the proceedings terminated in a daze of sound and movement. Once again that organ pealed—now it was a pæan of thanksgiving—then with the others she rose and began to make her way out of the hall.

It was a slow progress. People stood and talked and laughed; they were in no hurry; they made little groups, little parties barring her way. Some looked at her curiously, she thought—an up and down survey, then a quick removal of the eyes. She did not like to press past them, and yet she wanted to get out. She had promised to meet Peter outside—in the cloisters.

At length she reached the cloisters, which were not now quiet, but crowded by part of the same well-dressed throng. She saw that she was out of place, utterly incongruous, her travesty of a dress as unbecoming as a piece of sacking tied about her. What did she care? Soon those things would be of the past: satin, not sacking, for her then! She was waiting for her son. They would go away together.

She waited with her back against one of the arches, surveying the animated scene with an impassive face. Then, all at once, the crowd parted, and she saw him. Immediately her eyes began to smile; then, suddenly she started and drew herself up. Her hands clenched, her brows came together in a sudden dark perplexity which merged slowly into a fixed and brooding stare. Her son was there, bare-headed, his gown floating easily about him; he was talking, laughing, the centre of a group. As her astounded eyes envisaged that group, her lips tightened with a sort of grim repulsion. She passed her hand slowly, dazedly, over her eyes. Yes, it was incredible; she had not dreamed it possible—but it was so. They were all there—all her relations were there, all those who had conspired to defeat her—Richard, with Vera and Charles and, inevitably, Eva; Edward, too; and, lastly, Joe, accompanied by his sister Polly. It was Joe, indeed, who saw her first, and waved his large hand with a sheepish gesture of invitation. Every eye turned towards her. Immovable, she stood for a long moment; then slowly, like a woman in a dream, she advanced towards them.

" Allow me to congratulate you also, Lucy," said Richard immediately, with what she felt to be an odious pretence of candour.

" A remarkably fine achievement on the part of your boy."

She took his hand stiffly, mechanically, still dazed by the shock of seeing them.

" And a very fitting time for a family reunion," said Edward, with suave urbanity. He indicated Joe and Polly. " When Peter wrote me, I decided we should all meet here. We're all proud of him."

" Sure—we was only too glad to come along," blurted out Joe, in an excess of affability. " And I'm goin' to stand a feed at the Grosvenor for the whole shoot."

" If we couldn't come along to give you a clap," remarked Eva agreeably, pinching Peter's arm, " simply too unkind, it would have been." She smiled at Lucy from under her elegant floppy hat, and, with a wave of her gloves towards some young people behind her— merely a blur they were to Lucy—she added sweetly: " We brought some of Peter's tennis friends to swell the cheering."

She murmured, in introduction, some names which Lucy, still confronting the group stiffly, did not hear. Nor did she wish to hear. A slow anger burned within her, an animosity which again sent the colour surging into her pale cheeks. What right had these people to come here, under the specious pretence of friendship, to interfere with her son? What had they to do with him—or, indeed, with her? By what authority did they presume, now, at this juncture, to participate in her desperately-won victory? It was she who had led the van in battle, and now they came, these others, to share unjustly in her triumph. They had ignored her; they had despised her; they had left her to fight alone. A memory of her struggle—in all its bitterness, its anguish, and its grinding poverty—rose swiftly before her. She clenched her teeth to keep back a rush of stinging tears. A reunion, indeed. Good God! It was unbearable!

" It seems rather late in the day for your reunion," she heard herself say to Edward, in a voice of ice.

" It's never too late to mend," said Eva, with a little titter; and at the vacuous absurdity the tension was broken by a general laugh.

" Come, mother," whispered Peter anxiously in her ear, " don't be queer—especially to-day. They all mean well by us."

She threw him a burning glance.

" And what about that feed, now? " broke in Joe hastily, with a pacific jocularity. " I'm starving meself. We'll have a proud spread at the Grosvenor. McKillop's a good friend of my own; he'll give us a private room. And as for the drinks, there's goin' to be champagne —lashin's of it."

He turned sheepishly to Lucy, and added: " We're all friends, now, aren't we? And it's a poor heart that never rejoices."

There was a general laughing murmur of approval, and a general movement towards the quadrangle—a movement which swept

Lucy onwards with the group. Her eyes were hard; something within her breast was rending her.

" We were delighted to hear of your promotion," said Eva, with an ogling, appreciative eye upturned towards the princely purple of the Canon's stock. " When we want a new Archbishop in the diocese ——" She paused significantly.

He waved a pearly, deprecating hand.

" The Grosvenor's the place, sure enough."

" Peter, who was the youth who tripped over his gown? "

" I'm very partial to Veuve Cliquot—if it's dry enough."

" Luck, your getting into the Eastern! "

They were all talking at once; she could not get a chance to speak.

" We'll pack into the car," said a voice from behind her. " It'll be a lovely jam, but Peter can sit on your knee, Rosie."

A shiver ran through Lucy; she wanted to turn round, but could not. She was walking with Polly—yes, Polly, fatter than ever, wheezing under her panoply of vulgar, expensive clothes. And Polly, looking at her solicitously, was enquiring: " What's wrong with your foot? You're lame, as though you'd got varicose."

She made no answer to the abominable words; she wanted to get to Peter, to take him away from here, to be alone with him— the two of them—by themselves. But she was swept along, through the archway, to the drive, where, amongst a row of cars and cabs, a big red motor stood, its brass-bound radiator glittering in the sun.

" All aboard, now! " exclaimed that same voice. " We'll pack up the old waggon."

It was a young man who spoke, and now, with an encouraging smile, he threw open both doors of the car, and jumped into the driving-seat. " Come along, Rosie—you can stand a crush—you're the first sardine."

" Won't you go in, Mrs. Moore? " said someone close to Lucy. She turned swiftly. A tall, well-rounded girl, with the same hair and eyes as the other, was smiling at her pleasantly, a little nervously. But Lucy did not smile back. She was chilled, outraged, infuriated; the whole thing seemed a shameful conspiring to defeat her.

" I can't come," she answered shortly, torn by her feeling.

A general outcry of protest arose.

" You must come, though, mother," urged Peter gallantly; he had disposed of his gown, and now bent towards her solicitously. But angrily she felt his very solicitude an affectation.

" You know I can't come," she threw back, giving him a cold look which lacerated her own heart.

" Come along, Lucy," inserted Edward blandly.

" No, I can't come," she answered painfully.

" But why not? " expostulated Joe, his thumb stuck in his armhole—how she hated that posture! " And all of us not been together for years! "

They looked towards her. " I have my work to do," she lied, facing them stiffly.

There was an awkward silence; Eva gave a little titter—but it had a nervous inflection—and she abandoned the pavement for the car. Peter's face coloured deeply, whilst Rosie looked at him uncomprehendingly.

" Let those who can get in, then! " said Richard suddenly, frigidly. " We can't stand here all day, and Lucy knows what she wants to do best." As he bent his head beneath the hood he added something under his breath to Eva.

At the words they got into the big car—all but Lucy. The engine raced under the red bonnet; smoke puffed from the exhaust; she felt her son's eyes upon her in a troubled, magnetised stare. Before the car could leave, she stirred, and, forcing her features to a formal expression of politeness, she said good-bye quickly, turned, and moved off down the road.

She heard the roar and departure of the motor without turning her head; nor when, from the silence, she knew it finally to have disappeared, did she turn from her path. It was the wrong road she was taking, the long way round to Flowers Street, a further distance of at least a mile, through a maze of the mean streets of Partick. Simply by turning round and retracing her steps she could have avoided this. But no; she would not. With her head in the air, she kept on—going her own way!

Yet, when she reached her house, there was an agonising lassitude upon her, and at once, without removing hat or gloves, she flung herself on to her bed in the kitchen. There she lay, motionless, staring fixedly at the cracked and yellowing ceiling.

She had, of course, lied about her work. The whole day lay before her, a generous donation from Miss Tinto; she was free until—naturally, and from necessity—she should present herself at the office at five o'clock to collect her wages. Why then was she here, numb, miserable, straining towards some unknown bourne, when she might have been at that luncheon-party with Peter, drinking champagne?

She moved restlessly, stung by a jealous pang. It was so unjust, so iniquitous—the whole affair! Peter was hers—by stronger ties than the mere accident of birth. Since that day when, a little boy of eight he had flung himself into her arms on his return from Port Doran, she had bound him to her by a chain forged by her own hands.

She closed her eyes; the tender perfume of the rose upon her heart rose gently to her nostrils—so exquisite it was, like a pang, like the pain of an insatiable longing.

At one o'clock she rose, made herself some strong tea, drank the dark and bitter brew. She felt better, calmer. Meditatively she removed the damaged shoe and torn stocking, observing that her foot was cut and had apparently been bleeding. It was nothing—a mere trifle; she had not even felt it; but she washed the cut, darned her stocking, rehabilitated the shoe (on the former principle), and resumed it. She saw now that she had been unduly upset. This party, this sudden congregation of these unwanted relatives was merely an incident, an event which would soon be finished, and would never again occur.

Her calmness strengthened. In this mood she pottered about the house, tidying things up, placing the rose in a tea-cup of water, and finally, at four, she went out, took tram for the office. There she was reticent and composed. Everything, she declared under Miss Tinto's scrutinising eye, had passed off admirably. But when she had received her wages she took the first opportunity to leave the office. The reason she advanced was the necessity for immediate shopping, and here, at least, her excuse was just. She made, indeed, the round of her favourite shops, making a surprising variety of purchases. Nor was it her usual penurious bargaining that she now indulged in, but a different, altogether a more reckless, marketing. Her mood, mellowing still further, caught something of a spirit of abandon. Clearly, she had been surprised into losing her temper this morning—the shock, the unexpectedness of it all, had betrayed her into quick resentment. " That temper of mine! " she thought wryly. Then, her spirits quite recovered, she smiled, for the first time since the morning. And really it was exciting to spend money recklessly like this! She even bought a bunch of wallflowers from the old woman at the corner of James Square. Flowers! Wild extravagance, induced by this new humour and, perhaps, by the memory of Bessie Finch's rose. Could anything be more preposterous?

She jumped off the tram at Kelvinbank, and, laden with her parcels, passed quickly along the street—a manner different from her usual meditative progress. He had not yet returned, a fact which strangely rejoiced her, and, with all possible dispatch, she removed her hat, changed into her felt slippers, and began her preparations for the dinner.

Yes; it was to be no wretched high tea, but actually a dinner. He had lunched at the Grosvenor, apparently. Well, he should judge now between the merits of that expensive cuisine and hers. This dinner would be at once a celebration, a vindication, and an atone-ment.

It was the rare luxury of a chicken which she had bought, and, when the promising pullet was stuffed and sizzling in the oven—it was small, and sizzled quickly—she set about preparing the accessories of the feast. Her menu was ambitious: cream of tomato soup, roast chicken with potatoes in their jackets—none, he had often averred, could render a tuber so indubitably flowery as she—a Swiss tart fresh from the Colville Bakery, and, finally, coffee, rich, black, aromatic. It was a menu. Could Miss O'Regan have done better?

With sleeves rolled up and face engrossed, she had an almost youthful eagerness.

Whilst the dinner cooked, she laid the table, choosing the least chipped of the assorted crockery, covering the patch in the middle of the cloth with the blue vase of wallflowers. Then, at last, she was prepared to receive him. She sat down, pleasantly fatigued, pleasantly expectant her eye upon the clock, which lacked but one minute to seven. He would soon be in; he was punctual, and he had that morning, in answer to her query—she had even then entertained vaguely the purpose of the celebration—mentioned the hour of seven as the time of his return.

There she sat, waiting, listening for his step upon the stairs.

But she heard nothing: no step, no whistle of greeting. At half-past seven she rose, went into the front room, and looked out of the window, down the street; but he was not in sight.

She came back into the kitchen, and looked at the clock. Quarter to eight! She was disturbed, but, her eye straying towards the table, was soothed from momentary disquiet. Everything was perfect; the dinner was waiting in the oven. She straightened a spray of wallflower, and sat down.

But she could not sit still. She got up, paced up and down the room, hesitated, went once more to the window, contemplated with anxiety the prospect of the empty street, then came slowly back.

Again she was seated, her eye once more upon the clock, waiting with a growing dismay.

Gradually the bright edge of her anticipation became dulled; a furrow creased the centre of her forehead; the eagerness died out of her face. What had happened to him? It was now after eight o'clock. A rush of uneasiness flooded her. She strove to calm herself, but tranquillity would not come to her. She was up again upon her feet, moving about restlessly, looking at the clock, standing with straining eyes at the window, hovering about the door; yes, even opening it, as though to anticipate the quick sound of his step upon the stairs: waiting, waiting, waiting, her ears straining for his step.

Nine o'clock came without his arrival. She forced herself to sit down. Half-past nine, and still he had not come. The dinner was ruined—the fowl done to a stick, the potatoes leathery, the coffee a puddle of muddy grounds in the bottom of the pot.

Chilled by the empty greyness of the falling darkness, the joy of the day finally extinguished, she rose at last, cleared the table, threw out the coffee, poured the soup into an earthenware jar, placed the chicken in the cupboard—effaced every evidence of her presumptive banquet. Her lips drooped with an inexpressible pathos; but her eye, full and humid though it was, would shed no tears.

When he came in at last—just on the stroke of ten—she was seated knitting; her brow firm, her face inscrutable.

" I couldn't get away from those people," he exclaimed immediately; he was breathless but smiling, in a brilliant good humour. " Did you think I was never coming? Were you worrying? "

Never pausing in her knitting, she looked at him fixedly. " No—I knew you would come," she answered; then she added slowly, each word concentrated and intense: " And why should I worry? There's all the future to look forward to! "

XXVIII

FIVE months later, with the end of his hospital appointment in sight, she had quite made up her mind as to what they should do. To his not infrequent hints that someone should finance him in a practice she had returned a tolerant smile. He was only twenty-two; and where, pray, was the money to come from? No; only one course was feasible, and a pleasant course, though involving perhaps the prospect of hard work. But work was essential if a young man were to get on, and, as for its hardness, surely both she and he were used to that?

He would take an outdoor assistantship in England—somewhere in the provinces—and there she would keep house for him. England appealed to her for two reasons: salaries paid there were higher than in the north, and she desired above everything to sever completely her connection with her present locality. She had drudged too long in Glasgow to cherish it, and she was, moreover, so known a figure in certain districts that always the chance existed that the stigma of her occupation might fall upon her son and blight his growing practice. So they would get away to England. She visioned a small neat house in a comfortable market town—nothing pretentious it could be to start with, but neat and decent, yes, with a square brass plate upon the door. And how she would have that brass to shine! She had actually in her mind at the moment a truly brilliant idea. Studying the *Lancet*—she investigated this periodical regularly in the Mitchell Library—she had last week come upon an advertisement which made her eyes sparkle suddenly. Two assistants were required by the North Stafford Medical Aid Society, two active young men—actually Glasgow graduates were preferred—and, in return for his whole-time services, each would receive a free house, coal and lighting, together with a salary of £350 a year. An assured income; all this without having to advance a penny piece of capital. It made her gasp. And two posts vacant. Surely Peter could obtain one of them.

Immediately she had rung him up at the Royal Eastern, filled with her project—hers because she identified herself inevitably with him. He too had seen the advertisement; but, strangely, he demurred. Contract practice did not appeal to him; the B.M.A. did not approve of it; it was killing, that club work, and work, moreover, which stamped a man and lowered his professional standing. On the whole, he had expressed himself, rather judiciously, as being against applying for the post.

But she felt very differently; yesterday she had telephoned him, and now on this Saturday afternoon, she was resolved that they would thresh out the matter when he came up to see her. It was his habit to come at this hour and on this day, but lately, owing to the exigencies of his duties in the wards—" sweated labour " he proclaimed it—he had been somewhat irregular in his visits. Lately, also, a vague uneasiness had ebbed and flowed within her, but from what cause she could not discover. She seemed hardly to know how she stood with him; he had become elusive, a quantity which she strove fiercely to grasp and could not.

She had missed him these five months infinitely more than she admitted. In her loneliness, seeing him so infrequently, she took comfort even from the fact that the Royal Eastern was so near to her; and often at nights she drew sentimental solace from this nearness, sitting in the darkness of the front room watching the lights of the hospital break out beneath the University against the opposite hill.

Now, as she sat, her elbow resting on the arm of her chair, her cheek cupped in the hollow of her palm, she had still that strange, unsatisfied feeling; and that frown of perplexity—almost constant now—lingered curiously upon her brow. Her face was plumper, as though recently her meals had been more regular. And she wore a neat serge dress—the home-made gown had long ago been dowered upon a grateful Mrs. Collins—but still she did not look at ease. Her eyes were restless. Perhaps she needed a holiday! She had indeed arranged to take her fortnight's leave early in the following month. Thereafter she would be definitely abandoning her work, and, on Miss Tinto's subtle implication, had agreed to the wisdom " of taking the holiday out of H. & S." before she left. For her own part, she would hardly have troubled—her mind was set so fixedly upon her future with her son.

Suddenly, as she sat, there came a pull at the bell. She rose slowly, conscious that it was not Peter, who had still his own formula of announcement, and, going into the hall, she closed the front-room door, which stood ajar. Lately she had become more sensitive of the emptiness of her house, and this void apartment—easily visible from without—demanded the continual necessity of concealment. Then she answered the bell.

It was an elderly, red-faced man who stood upon the doorstep, his features fixed in an enquiring smile which displayed a golden tooth, and crinkled the shiny skin of his bulbous nose to a fine-scored network of wrinkles. He was short, his overcoat of smooth black cloth with satin-faced lapels, his collar low, lapped by the creases of his ruddy neck, his wide cravat bearing a glowing garnet pin. His fingers, decked by three rings, deeply embedded in the flesh, carried upright by its middle a heavy silver-topped Malacca cane, and on his head, set roundly above his ears, was a cap of astrakhan fur shaped almost like a turban—a curious cap, which made the little man at once a figure.

" Mrs. Moore? " said the stranger, still keeping up his smile, identifying her with a shrewd gleam of his puckered eyes.

" Yes! " she answered rather brusquely, not too well taken by the oddity of his air.

He nodded his head at his own cleverness, and said, after a short pause: " I've a notion to speak to you."

She stared back at him, then exclaimed:

" What do you want? I don't know you."

He shook suddenly with a sort of internal merriment, as though the idea of their not knowing each other afforded him intense amusement; then remarked:

" We'll soon know each other—surely—surely! "

" What do you want? " she threw out again.

He half closed his eyes, slyly.

" It's about your son I wanted to see you."

She arrested the movement of the door, which she had been about to close in his face.

" That's better now! Don't," he exclaimed, wrinkling again his shiny nose—it was his smile—" don't be so stiff with me. I'll come in and have a word with you."

She hesitated, then, almost in spite of herself, she stepped back. The talisman of her son's name had afforded him an entry.

" What is it? " she said again abruptly, facing him inside the house with a beating heart. This was a rude interruption to her mood of quiet meditation. Was he some moneylender, some disreputable individual into whose hands Peter had fallen?

He sat down, widened his knees, placed both hands upon the knob of his stick.

" I had a job to find you," he remarked agreeably, leaning forward. " He's as close as can be, is that boy of yours—about some things, anyway. Other times butter wouldn't melt in his mouth. Fine young fellow though." He beamed on her. " Stylish as they make them! "

She was utterly confounded.

" What do you want? " she pressed, in a hard disagreeable voice.

" Come, come, now, ma'am," he expostulated. " Don't be so stand-offish—you and me are going to be friends." He chuckled with a knowing air, tapped the knob of his stick lightly against the golden tooth, then suddenly exclaimed: " Tully's the name." He watched the effect of the word, then added: " You know the name —Tully the jeweller—in Alston Street. That's me."

Dazedly she stared at him. Her glance swept over him, taking in his tiepin, his rings, his cane, envisaging even the ridiculous hat that lay upon the table beside him. So this was Tully; this smug, grotesque little man bedizened by unredeemed pledges. Somehow, despite her amazement as to his presence in her house, her lip curled, and she exclaimed:

" Yes, I know who you are; you're not a jeweller. You're a pawn-broker—and a slum-landlord."

He broke into a roar of laughter, and tapped his stick upon the floor. " Good, good, good," he cried, quite unperturbed. " That's right. I like it straight—like my John Jameson." He paused, and wiped his eyes with a canary yellow handkerchief. " Yes—they told me you were a tartar, and, by Gord, so you are."

" Who told you? " she shot out fiercely.

He winked at her amiably.

" Some friends of yours in Ralston, my dear. But mum's the word. That's where I live, you see. I've a fine house out there, and a couple of acres of ground laid out in beautiful gardens—you'll need to come and see it—and it's all done out of pawnbroking and property. Ha! Ha! Ha! " He shook again at his little joke.

With an effort she controlled herself. She sat down at the table directly opposite to him.

" Will you be so good as to tell me what you require? " she said in a hard voice. " I suppose my boy has got into your wretched moneylending clutches. How much does he owe you? "

At her words, more especially at her tone, his manner altered at once; he blinked at her, then exclaimed:

" Good Gord, no, woman. I'm not a moneylender." He paused. " Your boy's running around after my daughter Rosie—that's all." And he lay back in his chair with an offended air, as though awaiting her apology. But she made no apology; she was stunned; her lips drew together as she faced him speechlessly. It was he, indeed, who first broke the silence.

" Yes, he's come around after my girl. And a beautiful thing she is too, by Gord. The image of her dead mother that's with the angels. She's the very core of my heart, is that girl of mine." He sent a look at her pale, set face, and resumed indulgently: " Mind you, I've nothing against your boy. He hasn't got a brass—but that don't matter. I've got plenty. Plenty, plenty. My Rosie will have a pretty penny to her name. And he's got the position. Yes, he's worked himself into a fine profession. I like him properly, for all his blarney." She flinched; but unobservantly he went on: " It says a lot for him to have done it, but he has his head screwed on right; he knows that two and two make four. _That's_ in his favour." Still she sat numb— bewildered; but through the haze of her conflicting thoughts she had a dim recollection, then all at once she remembered. Rosie! The tennis-parties! Eva's friends at Ralston. And that tall, reddish girl at the graduation, looking down at her a little nervously beside the car: " Won't you go in first, Mrs. Moore? " And again the brother's laughing voice, " Peter'll sit on your knee, Rosie."

A frightful spasm transfixed her. Rosie Tully—the daughter of this wretched pawnbroking slum-landlord for whom she had slaved and slaved, extorting iniquitous rents from pauper wretches to pay for his villa and his gardens, to put money in his purse and fine clothes on his detestable daughter's back! She shivered, then her teeth came together.

" Has my son anything else to recommend him? " she said in a restrained tone of bitterness.

" Yes, yes, yes," he agreed largely. " He's got the right faith. That's another thing in his favour. I'm having no mixed marriage for my Rosie. When she does go to the altar, it's got to be the right one."

His gross complacency drove her frantic; a swelling fury rose up through the frightful shock of his disclosure.

" And now that you are satisfied," she said in a hard, lucid voice, " what about me? "

" Eh, what? "

" Does my son know you have come here? "

" No, indeed and he doesn't. That was Tully's idea—meaning my own."

That he could be facetious broke the last straw of her endurance.

" And so it's all settled? " she sneered.

" Good Gord, no, ma'am. There's lots of things to be gone into."

" Indeed! " Her sarcasm was devilish.

He gazed at her. " I know what you feel about it. But you wouldn't come out the loser by it. I'd see to that." He looked significantly around the sparse furnishings of the room. " I'd send you up some sticks for your house and some carpets and what not. See, now! I'll send you up——"

" Be quiet! " she cried out fiercely. " Do you think I want your wretched charity—I or my boy? "

His jaw dropped. " Charity? Ah, you don't know me yet," he jerked out, " and you don't know my Rosie! "

" And I'll never know her," she retorted bitterly.

" What—what——? " Touched upon his most tender point, his red face became a vivid beetroot. " By Gord, ma'am," he retorted heatedly, " he'll be a lucky man that gets my Rose."

She stared him out of countenance.

" My son will not be that man," she returned in a low. concentrated voice. Then she rose and looked at him fixedly.

" Good Gord, you *are* mad! " he gasped; the assurance of his manner was gone. " It's the chance of a lifetime for him. And me doing what I've offered to do for him." He threw out his hand protestingly. " Let's get the business straight, ma'am. I love my daughter and I want her to be happy. That's what brings me here. Now, will you meet me half-way? "

" No! " she said violently.

" Why not? " he expostulated.

" I refuse—that's all you need to know." Would she bandy words with this wretched usurer?

He stared amazedly; at last got up to his feet.

" You're not reasonable. No, no, you're not reasonable. But they told me—yes, they told me."

More calumnies behind her back!

" If that's what I am," she bit out, " you need have nothing to do with me."

He looked at her again, blowing out his red cheeks. " By Gord, you're a queer one," he said finally. " And I promise you I *will* have nothing to do with you "; then slowly he pulled on his ridiculous hat, shook his head, and went out.

Immediately her stiff attitude relaxed; she sat down weakly. Her eyes filled once again with that first look—that pitiful bewilderment occasioned by the shock. Yes; the shock was frightful, the coincidence so savagely unjust! The daughter of this Tully, of all people! Eva, it was, who had occasioned that friendship—her lips came together at the thought—Eva, with her tennis-parties, her social affectations, and her languishing pretence of friendship. That indeed was a further hurt—salt rubbed into a wound already rankling.

And Peter—why had he not told her? Now her lips quivered. A pang of jealousy shot through her—a lancinating pang. But quickly came the answer: He was young, popular, infatuated, susceptible. Everything else was impossible. No; his intentions could not be serious—again jealously she repudiated the thought. But she must

346

act at once—she must speak to him this very afternoon. She must do it! Not for her to sit in silence whilst her son was entrapped into some foolish entanglement which might mar the wonder of the future. With an intent expression she glanced towards the clock. Quarter past three! It was beyond his usual time; perhaps to-day he was again too occupied to come. Yet if he did not come to her she was resolved that she would go to him. She moved into the front room and let her look strain toward the hospital.

XXIX

By a conscious effort of her will she forced herself to wait for half an hour, standing immobile at that window, with eyes fixed under her contracted brows. Then, with that forward thrust of her chin, decisively she moved. She put on her hat, took up her gloves, and went abruptly out of the house.

The day was quick with an impatient wind; but her mind was more impetuous than that wind. Yet, as she walked swiftly down the road, she resolved above everything to be calm. That, she knew, was the only way. Calmness for this unexpected crisis! This time no wild and desperate rush: calmness.

As she crossed the dusty park and drew near to the hospital her eyes attached themselves fixedly upon its wide grey sweep. To enter without permit or knowledge these unknown and mysterious walls was, in itself, a strange adventure. But she would do it. She could not delay. Determinedly she crossed the broad paved courtyard, between the outflung balconies of the wards, where patients in scarlet jackets were reclining in the sunshine.

At the main entrance she approached the porter within his sentry-box.

" Dr. Moore," she threw out briefly.

The porter laid down his paper and looked up; he was an old man, and now he regarded her over his glasses with all the pessimism of a wide experience.

" Dr. Moore will be out," he said, with a doubtful shake of his bald head.

" I don't think so," she countered, and went on shortly to explain herself.

" Of course," said the old man finally, " if it's important and you like to try—it's the first floor right." His gesture indicated to her without optimism the stairs which she might ascend.

Following his directions, she went up a flight of stone steps and along a white-tiled passage; the pungent odours of chloroform and carbolic came strangely to her; through a glass swing door she had a quick vision of a row of beds.

At the end of the corridor indicated by the porter she paused, confronted by three doors, then suddenly she heard a burst of laughter, the middle door swung open, and a sister appeared abruptly before her. The sister was a tall, middle-aged woman with a flowing headdress; her cuffs and wide starched belt shone with a high glitter. The smile which still lingered on her face faded as she looked at Lucy.

" Yes? " she enquired briskly.

" I wish to see Dr. Moore," said Lucy with equal curtness.

" About a patient? "

" No! "

" An admission? "

" No! "

They faced each other. The sister paused, recognising a spirit that matched her own.

" I'm afraid you can't see him," she returned, and her manner held an important impatience. " The doctor's off duty, and in any case he's engaged at present."

" He'll see me—he's my son."

" Your son? "

The sister's face altered slowly through astonishment to a re-strained amiability. " Well," said she at length, " in that case you'd better come in. I'm Sister Cooper—the sister of the floor." She paused. " He's giving a little tea-party—or, rather, I'm giving it for him." Her features relaxed further, and her professional air slipped from her. " Just to keep things fit and proper—you know."

Lucy said nothing. She had no idea what this stiffly laundered sister meant; nor was she in the mood to seek that meaning. But when she followed her into the house surgeon's sitting-room she saw instantly the full implication of the words. Her face, which had softened to meet her son, paled suddenly, and hardened into a bitter mould. A small table covered with a white cloth was set for tea. Peter was there, a cup balanced in his hand; yes, he was there, seated upon the sofa; and beside him, seated upon the same sofa, balancing another cup, was Rose Tully.

A perfectly polite and banal situation—a nice young man, nicely contented with the universe, entertaining to tea a seemly young woman apparently equally content, under the matronly eye of the sister of his wards.

But to Lucy it was not ordinary. It was dreadful, desperate, utterly shattering. Another shock, ghastly in its unexpectedness. She was staggered by the intimacy of those two upon the sofa.

There was a rushing in her ears, a sudden pain in her side. Her eyes, still startled, could not withdraw themselves from the generous, youthful figure of the red-haired girl sitting so near her son. Beautiful she now saw her to be—again that same heavy ache of jealousy!—fair-skinned, with a dust of freckles, brown-eyed, with fine white hands and a soft and faintly pouting lip. How could the inexpressible Tully have produced so sweet a slip as this! How could this pink and whiteness have risen from beneath the glitter of the three brass balls! Her own lips paled and drew down; her own hands, worn in the service of her son, clenched themselves tightly.

" Here's your mother come to see you, doctor," said the sister, with a sort of bustling heartiness, through which her sharp eye gleamed observantly. Peter's cup jerked. He looked round, and instantly his face changed, dropped into a startled embarrassment.

" Oh, yes," he exclaimed foolishly. There was a strained pause—a dreadful pause—during which Miss Tully coloured slowly, painfully.

" Take this chair, Mrs. Moore," broke in the sister, with greater heartiness. " I promised to pour out the tea. Let me give you a cup too."

Lucy sat down stiffly, her back a ramrod, her eyes never leaving the figure of the girl upon the sofa. It was, alas! no longer a contented ether in which the sofa's universe revolved.

" One lump? " The tongs were poised lightly, enquiringly. " That's right." Lucy had said nothing. " And cream, too, I suppose." The sister, sniffing the tenseness of the chilly air, like a charger the distant battle, prepared to enjoy with greater gusto this new and unexpected turn of the party. " I do hope that's to your taste," she said with great solicitude as she passed over the cup. Again there was a pause: Rosie still red as any rose; the Cooper " full of spirits " and capably intent; Peter desperately reaching for his composure.

" This—this is an unexpected honour, mother," he stammered at length. Weak and ineffectual attempt at jocularity!

" Yes. You could have knocked me over with a feather," advanced Cooper. " I would never have taken you for the doctor's mother. Never! " She paused, leaving the inference open, then, smiling round at the others, she returned her gaze to Lucy. " But you couldn't have come at a nicer time, could you? "

" Apparently not," said Lucy, with an effort; she felt the hand which held her cup tremble: not with agitation, but with anger. Calmness, though, she thought. Calmness. Once, in a crisis such as this, into what awful consequences had her precipitation led her.

Sister Cooper laughed appreciatively: she was not ill-natured—but what a situation! What a story she would have to tell in the common-room to-night!

"You live in the country, don't you ? " she enquired progressively. " Ardfillan, I think your son said."

" I live quite near," said Lucy flatly.

" Indeed! " answered Cooper, surprised. " I understood it was the country."

" Quite near, I said." The words were uttered with a dangerous brevity.

" Another piece of cake, mother," blurted out Peter with frightful embarrassment.

" Why, she hasn't touched her first piece yet," said the sister airily.

There was a silence. And that silence continued till Rose, at length plucking up her courage, turned to Lucy.

" It's a beautiful day, isn't it? " said she with little originality but great good feeling; her blush had faded, leaving only her lips red in the appealing softness of her face. Peter looked quickly at his mother; so, too, did Sister Cooper; hanging upon the response to this mild invitation to amity. But Lucy, studying the carpet with a set face, made no reply. She had the measure of that soft creature upon the sofa. The intensity of the bitterness which filled her swept over her like a sudden hatred. Her jealousy—a queer unnatural jealousy—was like a burning in her breast.

" It's nice," said the sister, with a little vivacious sigh, " outside." She smiled pleasantly, and added: " Another cup of tea, Miss Tully? "

" No, I couldn't really." She looked, indeed, at this moment as if another mouthful must choke her.

" You then, doctor? "—this a little playfully.

" No—no." He pulled his collar away from his neck. " No more, thanks." He looked sulky and uncomfortable; his inability to cope with the situation gave him a sense of humiliation which expressed itself in a swelling resentment against his mother. Why couldn't she leave him alone? Why did she sit there with a face like ice—saying nothing, fixed obstinately on making trouble? He looked gloomily at Sister Cooper, now complacently pouring out her second cup of tea.

" I'm afraid I'm a great tea-drinker," she now explained at large. Only her presence maintained the dismal situation at the bare level of artificial civility, and in this knowledge she became more than ever conscious of her office. " Yes, I find it suits me. You see, I've a responsible position. Two wards, with fifteen beds in each. A staff nurse and three probationers to look after—and, of course "—here she smiled with a starched waggishness—" there's always an eye to be kept on the young doctor I get here."

Lucy looked at her with a grim and silent coldness.

" Yes, indeed. You'd be surprised if you'd seen what I have in my time. The things they can be up to. Climbing in and out of windows—at night—painting each other with methylene blue, drinking the brandy out of the stimulants cupboard. Not that there's anything like that about Dr. Moore—oh, no! He's the quietest resident I've had for months. Of course, I think a serious attachment steadies a young man so much. Don't you? " And she threw her archly interrogative glance upon Lucy.

But Lucy was not listening. Her attention, fixed upon that sofa, was riveted by a rustling movement. Suddenly she started. Rosie, unable, it seemed, to sustain the situation—or the stare—stirred, got upon her feet.

" I'll go now, I think," she said in an undertone to Peter.

He too mumbled under his breath, and, rising, he went to the door.

Rose turned. " Thank you for having me up," said she to Sister Cooper. Then, fronting Lucy without rancour, with, indeed, a quite modest confusion, she said diffidently:

" Good afternoon, Mrs. Moore."

" Good-bye," said Lucy, with a terse and freezing finality. With that first and last word she dismissed Rose Tully from her life. As she uttered it, and observed Rose leave the scene of her discomfiture, she had a rushing sense of triumph. Yes, she had been calm: no rashness: a cold, considered finality. Rose, beautiful though she might be, was like chaff before the fierce blast of her purpose. How easily she had routed her! But, then, she had determination, experience, courage—yes, and right upon her side. Abruptly she turned to Sister Cooper.

" I would like to speak to my son," she declared directly. " Would you mind? "

Cooper gazed back at her with elevated eyebrows which deplored the other's manner.

" I was going," she answered huffily. " I've got my work to do, you know."

She rose; behind her the door closed with a scornful snap.

Lucy turned to her son. At last they were alone. For a moment she looked at him in silence, then slowly her face softened—softened at last to the ineffable tenderness of her love for him.

" I wanted to get rid of those people," she said slowly. He stared back at her sulkily, made an impatient movement with his head, answered angrily:

" And a fine job you've made of it. It's an unheard-of thing—behaviour like that. It'll be all over the hospital before the evening's out. Trust that fool Cooper to spread the story."

" But I had to come, Peter. Can't you understand? "

" No, I don't understand."

His tone disturbed her; but she would make him see the logic of her position.

"I waited on you for an hour," she explained, with a forced evenness of tone. "I didn't know if you would be home. I had to speak to you."

He gave a short, sulky laugh.

"You would think I was a child at your apron-strings to hear you. Can't I look after myself now? Why do you have to run after me, bursting in on me at every turn—making me look foolish before —before everybody?"

She gazed at him, that betraying flush mounting high upon her cheek.

"It is because I don't want you to be foolish that I am here," she returned firmly.

"What have I done?" he burst out. "Tell me that. Do I drink, do I gamble, am I a thief?" He swelled with a virtuous indignation. "What did Sister Cooper say about me? The quietest resident she's had for months. And yet you talk as if I——"

"I am thinking of your future," she broke in, with a rising inflation to her voice.

"Well, if you are, don't you want me to be happy?" he returned immediately; and, after a triumphant pause, he improved his point. "It's only natural that I should take an interest in—in Miss Tully. I don't deny it, and I'm not ashamed of it. She's a splendid girl."

Immediately her face changed—changed to a greyish tinge. His words lacerated her; she gripped the arm of her chair tightly and leaned forward.

"Don't talk like that," she said harshly. "Am I going to sit still and see you get mixed up with a soft little nobody?"

He looked at her with a sullen resentment.

"Nobody," he repeated. "Let me inform you that Miss Tully is a very wealthy girl."

Could he think of nothing but money—and such tainted money as it was?

"And don't start calling names," he persisted. "You were rude enough when Rose was here. Can't you be civil?"

"What!" she exclaimed in a feverish voice. Who had once asked her to be civil to another woman? She did not pause to think! "So that's what you call her? Rose?"

"And why not?" he retorted, kicking at a footstool which lay upon the floor. "It's a name that suits her."

Again that agony of jealousy. Her limbs trembled as she sat, and, despite her control, she burst out:

"What has she done for you to deserve that?"

He faced her: the reaction from his recent humiliation goaded him to face her.

" She's done nothing," he cried. " I don't want her to do anything. I happen to love her—and she happens to love me—that's all."

" Love! " she exclaimed violently. " What does she know about love—that soft, pink and white creature? Would she work her fingers to the bone for you? Would she fight for you and slave for you and starve for you? "

" I don't want her to do any of those things," he said, flushing. " There are other things in life besides that."

" How long have you known her? " she persisted, in that fiercely concentrated tone. " A few months—and because she's got a doll's face, because you think she's pretty, you forget about me." Her breath came hoarsely, as though she choked. " It's shameful of you to behave like this. Have you no gratitude, no sense of decency in you? "

" What do you expect me to be? " he retorted angrily. " Do you expect me never to get married, never to get on in life? Do you think you can always tie me to your apron-strings? "

" You, not twenty-three yet," she cried, outraged, " to talk like that. How dare you? To think that you speak so glibly of marriage —at that first sight of some silly smirking face! "

" Don't go on like that," he answered sullenly. " I don't like it."

" I will go on," she panted, her hand to her throat. " And I'll settle this once and for all. You're all that I've got—and to see you behave like this—at your age—it's maddening! " With a painful effort she controlled herself; a cold perspiration was upon her skin. Her face was stern as she said distinctly: " What exactly do you propose to do about this Rose Tully? " She bit out the name with a grim determination.

Her words startled him; his composure began to give way; he glanced at her uneasily, and muttered:

" What are you going on about—upsetting yourself—making a fuss about nothing? It's foolish."

" You won't make a fool of me," she persisted harshly. " Not at this stage."

" No, no," he said restlessly. " How could I do that? Don't be absurd. Everything's all right between us."

" Then answer my question," she said fiercely. " What are you going to do about this—this doll that Eva has flung at your head? "

" Don't, mother," he broke in uncomfortably. " Don't make such a fuss."

His lofty manner was gone: again he looked at her, muttering under his breath.

But she was not to be put off. She was resolved to terminate the issue once for all, to seize this infatuation, to crush it, annihilate it, before it could flourish and destroy her.

" For the last time will you tell me," she exclaimed grimly, " are you going to give her up? "

He was cornered; yes, he was completely cornered. She was so unreasonable, unamenable to compromise; it was hopeless to attempt to explain Rose's love for him, Mr. Tully's generous interest in him, amounting actually to an offer to finance him in a practice—all the glorious prospects for his future. How could she be made to understand this? He could foresee so clearly her conduct should he reveal his plans; she was so queer she would make a scene, a disturbance, an outrage of some sort.

Suddenly he raised his eyes, which had fixed glumly on the carpet, and he looked at her—that old ingenuous expression of his boyhood.

" There's some sense in what you say, mother," he declared slowly. " I suppose I am rather young to think of these things. Perhaps in a year or two——" He broke off, still smiling at her diffidently.

There was a pause. For a long time she gazed at him with secret intensity.

" You'll stop all this nonsense? " she demanded slowly. " Give her up—let nobody come between us? "

He affected to hesitate, then all at once he said frankly:

" All right, mother. Have it your way."

There was another silence during which she fathomed once more the depths of his dark brown eyes. Then she sighed; her set lips relaxed. He was Peter, her son, her own flesh and blood. He could not lie to her. She had won.

" You've given me your word, Peter," she said quietly. " And, after all, it's only your duty and my right."

" Yes, mother," he said.

She laid her hand on his arm.

" You've got to promise me another thing before I go out of this room," she said slowly. " It's only just that you should do so."

He gave her a doubtful wavering smile; then, still looking at him fixedly, she drew a deep breath.

" I want you to apply for that post in North Staffordshire. We've got to make our start some time, and the sooner it's made the better."

There was another pause, electric with the almost breathless silence. Then his eyes fell.

" Of course I will! " he said at length, picking at the arm of his chair. " As if you couldn't trust me."

" You've given me your word on these two points," she said in a low voice.

His eyes moved restlessly, evading the intensity of her look.

" That's right," he said quickly. " I've promised."

He might have been a boy, called suddenly to her knee for some transgression. And now, indeed, he was as suddenly forgiven. Her impassive face broke, her emotion welling through that mask of ice; a slow tear welled into her eye and ran down her pale cheek.

" I knew you would do the right thing by me, Peter," she said in a moving tone, stung by a pang for having doubted his loyalty to her. " I knew it, my son."

Before she left he had written his application for the Staffordshire post. She had a premonition about that application—the strange certainty that it would be successful. She posted it, indeed, with her own hand, on her way back to Flowers Street.

XXX

SHE went upon her holiday with a feeling of hard-won victory. In a sense she did not wish to go: she was too busy looking ahead, her mind too active managing in advance their new establishment. But her arrangements had been made, both at the office and with Miss Tweedy; she had, too, a sort of reactionary elation from her success; she submitted, therefore, with a preordained acquiescence to the circumstances which took her back to Doune.

Though nothing had been heard from Stafford, she had nevertheless that definite intuition—optimistic perhaps, yet understandable in her present mood; and, even if he did not get that post, there were others—yes, he was certain of obtaining an assistantship when he terminated his appointment at the end of April. And so she went off cheerfully from St. Enoch's Station. Actually, too, Peter had come to see her off. He it was, indeed, who had encouraged her to go; and now, as the train rushed through the same cuttings which she had traversed five years previously, she saw again that last look upon his face: constrained, almost apologetic. It soothed her to recall that look. He had so clearly come back to her. He was a good boy, her Peter, amenable to reason; and she had made him see the folly of his recent attitude. At twenty-three, indeed, to contemplate an attachment like that! Yes, he had come back to her. Of that she had no doubt. None. Once she had doubted Frank. Ah; if she had but taken his word. If only through that bitter lesson, she would never question the word and loyalty of her son.

Doune, she noted when she arrived, was greatly changed—rows of new bungalow houses ranged around the station—but Miss

Tweedy was not changed. It gave her quite a rush of feeling to see the slight, still drooping figure after all these years. And Miss Tweedy was, in her own particular fashion, equally delighted to see Lucy.

" You know," said she, laying down a plate of the memorable buns and placing her bony white hand upon the sharp angle of her hip, " I can't help but admit that it's agreeable to see you again. It's not often I take to a visitor like I did to yourself. But take to you I did. And I've never forgotten you. Many's the time I've wondered about you—yes, wondered if any harm had come over you." Lucy, in the easy chair, her hands clasped round her knees, looked up at Miss Tweedy and smiled.

" I don't look as if much had gone wrong with me."

Miss Tweedy shook her head slowly and laid a spoon gently upon its saucer.

" You're a changed woman," she said sympathetically. " Ah, yes, you've altered sadly. You've had your struggle, my woman, thinks I to myself when I opened the door to you this very day—and a hard struggle too, or I'm far cheated." And Miss Tweedy pulled down the corner of her mouth and shook her head again, as though on this point at least there was no deceiving her.

" It's all over now, anyway," returned Lucy.

" Yes—you're older," said Miss Tweedy in her weak voice, " and thinner about the face—much thinner."

" You're not very stout yourself, Miss Tweedy," said Lucy mildly.

" Me," rejoined Miss Tweedy, with a short sniff. " I'm away to a shadow. I don't eat enough to keep a sparrow alive. I can't do it. I've been delicate from my birth. That boy of yours," she resumed. " He didn't look a very strong young man neithers, from what I mind of him. Faddy on his food, wasn't he? "

" He's all right now. Look for yourself. I've just put his photograph out in my bedroom."

" I did take a look at him," said Miss Tweedy, with calm omniscience. " Bit of a masher, I can see. You've done a lot for that young man. I hope you don't get your thanks all in the one box." She paused—moved to the door. " I'll bring in your tea now. You'll be needing it after your journey. Tiring things, trains! Yes, quite so."

She departed gently, came back in a few moments with the teapot and, placing this upon the table, she nodded significantly to Lucy, remarked: " The best tea! " Then she slipped her fragile form from the room.

That night Lucy went to bed early and slept soundly. Next morning she awoke refreshed, and went out immediately after breakfast. It had rained heavily during the night, but now a fresh breeze blew from the sea, briskening her steps as it swept along the main street of the town. She stopped at the post-office and sent off a card to Peter—no coloured atrocity, but a quiet view of the front, worded discreetly. " Any news from S.? " she wrote thereon—a card which could appear without discredit upon his breakfast-table. Then, appeased, forcing her mind outside the circle of her contemplation, she sent off another card—mildly humorous, this one—to Miss Tinto. This terminated the full extent of her correspondence.

Turning, she went down the street, now battling pleasantly against the wind which, despite Miss Tweedy's assertion, made her feel vigorous and almost youthful. Outside a fruiterer's shop, the vivid red of a basket of apples caught her eye. She paused—she had always liked apples immensely; it was a long time since she had tasted them. On an impulse, she went into the shop and bought some of the ripe fruit.

At the front, fresh and blustery, to escape the gale's full force she entered a small wooden shelter which, since her last visit, had been built opposite the rocks where she had been accustomed to sit. She was alone, protected yet in the open, facing the lashing, restless water which at intervals threw up high clouds of spray that fell in a glistening froth almost at her feet. She ate one apple meditatively, enjoying the treat. Presently she ate the other, placed the husks in the empty bag, crushed this into a ball, then looked out again towards the sea.

And now—what had she to do? She was, ostensibly, upon a holi-day—which inferred in some sense the pursuit of pleasure. She ought to have had resources to enable her to overcome the disagreeable influence of the weather; but she had no such resources. The avenues of enjoyment open to her were limited. For a moment she considered the possibilities of a walk, then reflected that, from the very nature of her occupation, she was tired of walking. Besides, she had not much desire to take a walk alone in this high wind. She might have bought herself a magazine or a paper. But she had little inclination to read and no curiosity towards the affairs of the world. What did it concern her whether Consols rose or fell a fraction, or a new pre-sident had been established in Peru? She admitted her apathy to be peculiar, yet could not overcome it. That was how she had become. The years of endeavour had shaped her to this end.

Her mood altered. She became aware of herself suddenly as a solitary, middle-aged woman sitting in a windy shelter upon a deserted beach, a woman with few friends, a woman looked upon askance by those who knew her. A woman with a pale face, a thickening figure, and hands coarsened by the housework they had known. Inevitably her thoughts swung back to the holiday which she had spent here with Peter five years ago, and ardently she recap-tured its happy memories as she gazed out at the rough grey water of the bathing-pool. She saw him, in her mind's eye, diving from the spring-board in the sunshine. She smiled to herself at the recollection of his eagerness for her praise: how, when he emerged, dripping, he had demanded always her verdict upon the straightness of his plunge. Her face brightened with a distant gleam as she traced their progress through these pleasant days, giving free rein to her thoughts, indulging her reverie without stint.

At last she recollected herself with a start which was almost a shiver. She felt cold. She sighed, got up, and, moving her stiff limbs, went back to her lodgings. That evening, pursuing her illusion, she walked along to the entertainers. Here, with a start almost comical, she perceived that the elegant Val Pinkerton no longer held sway upon that narrow wooden platform. Yes; he was gone—his refined, dress-coated troupe supplanted by a younger and more brazen band, who wore the unashamed garb of pierrots and rattled their wooden collecting-boxes with relentless urgency.

She stared at them for a moment with a face as wooden as their boxes. A girl with a short skirt, her dunce-like cap tilted to a provocative angle, shook her tassels and a waggish forefinger as she sang saucily of " Molly O'Morgan! Molly O'Morgan with her little organ— the Irish-Italian girl." Vulgar nonsense. The swift and heedless flight of the modern age! The memory of Val Pinkerton, " vocalist," tall, red-sashed, hand over heart, ravished by the tenderness of his own rendering, rose up before Lucy with a contrasting dignity; she saw herself with Peter, seated within the enclosure, faces upturned, hanging delightedly upon the song. What was it again? " Daisy, Daisy, give me your answer, do."

Abruptly she turned. She was making a fool of herself, a maudlin, sentimental fool. No one took any notice of her. Children frisked about the grass whilst their elders stood sedately listening or strolled up and down in pairs. She was in the crowd, but somehow not of it. The wind had quietened with the fall of the evening, and as she walked the music faded to a whisper on the breeze and was lost finally in the endless murmur of the waves. She returned in the gathering dusk. She passed the frontage of the Grand Hotel with hardly a glance: she had not yet achieved the entry of this resplendent establishment, nor, indeed, did she now desire this; all she demanded was that neat house with the brass nameplate—anywhere, so long as she was with her son.

When she got back, Miss Tweedy was in the passage: she had the landlady's adept facility for instantaneous appearance, seeming, indeed, upon such occasions to issue mysteriously from the ground; and, looking at Lucy, she said:

" You're pale to-night, Mrs. Moore."

" I'm tired, I think," returned Lucy.

" It's the air," said Miss Tweedy wisely; " takes it out of you the first day."

" Yes—it must be the air."

" Turned chilly, too, it has."

" Yes, it has."

They looked at each other across the passage; an expression that admitted Lucy to equality of state, both in condition and degree, flickered over Miss Tweedy's face.

" The hot bottle's in your bed, anyway," said she oracularly. " So it's ready for you when you're ready for it."

So Lucy went to bed.

The next few days passed in a quiet fashion. Yet, stirred by this holiday so long protracted, her spirits returned; there flowed through her an unusual sense of well-being. She read and walked a little, but mostly she liked to sit in the shelter by the rocks. The weather continued broken; nevertheless, the air was tonic, briny, and infused in her unconsciously something of its keenness and its strength.

She had no word from Peter, but this was not unexpected; he was at the best a poor correspondent; still, when a week had passed she began to count the days remaining before her return. Her eagerness intensified; schemes for the future turned continually in her mind; happily she realised that now, indeed, the real reward of her achievement was at hand.

Upon the second last day of her visit she left her lodgings, after breakfast, and submitted herself to the bluster of the persistent wind with a feeling of persistent elation.

With reawakened zest she felt it good to be alive, felt the invigorating stimulation of life reopening after her cramped endeavour of the past five years. She relished the walk through the pleasant town, fresh with scrubbed doorsteps and dripping windows, bustling with the high activity of the morning, enjoyed the sending of her daily postcard, intimating on this occasion, and in case he should find time to meet her, the hour of her return upon the following day.

She did not set out for her favourite seat beneath the rocks, but, swinging back into the breeze, she tramped briskly along the front. Her mood demanded movement. And the reason of her mood, her briskness, her elation—it was clear, quite clear. She did not deny it. She was returning to her son.

She walked so far that she made herself late for lunch, and, hurrying, her cheeks whipped by the wind, she came up the steps smartly into Miss Tweedy's house. In the hall she took breath, hung up her coat, placed her umbrella in the stand, then, as she turned, Miss Tweedy emerged from another room. The landlady smiled over her tray.

" You look better," she said critically, " much better." Then, pausing, she added: " There's a letter for you on the mantelpiece—a fine fat one by the feel of it."

Lucy's eyes leaped—now only one person would write to her—and she smiled back at Miss Tweedy. A letter from Peter: good news of his post: it was an exciting thought.

" Fine! " she exclaimed, with such a word as Peter himself might have used. " It's the one I'm expecting." And she moved quickly into her room.

The letter, as Miss Tweedy had indicated, was on the mantelpiece. And it was from Peter. She would, in her own phrase, have known his neat hand anywhere; and as she balanced the letter on her palm, tantalising herself, she had a swift memory of those letters he used to send her from his school. Lovely letters, ingenuous, violet-inked, breathing of his affection for her, his enduring loyalty.

And here was another letter testifying to that same loyalty.

She was glad: she admitted now that faint uneasiness which she had felt at his silence during the past fortnight.

Her eyes sparkled; there was in her face an eagerness, something of a sublime tenderness, as she opened the envelope and took out the written sheet. Smiling, she began to read.

Then suddenly the light was extinguished from her face, which stiffened, stricken to a strange distortion. The blood drained from her skin, leaving it, not white, but grey—a sickly greyish tinge. A word in that letter, leaping towards her, not one word, but a string of words, not words but understanding. It came like a flash, the searing knowledge—in one frightful devastating gleam, a flash swifter, more illuminating, than any lightning stroke.

No cry escaped her—she was petrified to silence—but the hand which held the paper clenched, then shook as with the onset of a palsy.

Rose's name was in that letter, repeated and repeated amidst those words of weak conciliation which danced before her frantic eyes. Rose's name.

He had gone off with Rose. He had accepted the partnership which Rose's father had bought for him in London.

He had deserted her—his mother.

A dreadful coldness assailed her, like a pang of dissolution, and the fearful blackness of despair closed over her like death. Motionless she stood, then all at once she shivered. Her body felt dead; but her mind was not dead; it was alive, seething with the anguish of her thoughts—a ferment of feverish thoughts in which everything was revealed. She had been away—conveniently out of the way. They had connived deliberately behind her back; she had been set aside, humiliated, abased. But the humiliation was nothing. The abasement was nothing. He was gone—her son—married. After her years of toil, her abject self-denial, after her struggle, her pinching, her fierce and bitter sacrifices for him, after everything that she had suffered and endured, he had abandoned her. He had used her, deceived her, and cast her aside. She had surmounted obstacles of almost inconceivable difficulty in order to deliver him into the arms of another woman. It was torture—torture unbearable.

Dazed by the anguish of her soul, she sank weakly into a chair. The letter fluttered out of her hand.

BOOK III

I

NINE months later Lucy sat in the kitchen of her house in Flowers Street. The room was little changed, drab and unfurnished as before, the curtains dingier perhaps, the grimy windows in greater need of cleaning, the patch of damp upon the ceiling furred with a darker spreading mildew. Had she at any time foreseen herself within a room like this? Never! Yet what did they matter now—such trivialities of dust and disarray? Not one whit did they disturb her. Lately she had not troubled about the flat, so fixedly absorbed was she by matters of a far, far greater consequence. That dreadful day at Doune: then she had felt her life was over—ruined, shattered, destroyed. What a fool she had been, what a blind, incredible fool! She could smile now at these puny writhings of her obscured and so misguided mind. A woman with her head lowered to the earth seeking bright pebbles on a shore of infinite illusion, stooping madly for happiness amongst the wrack spewed up from a cold sea of bitterness—that was what she had been. Not even bright pebbles had she discovered, but ashes, only ashes, which wildly she had cast upon her hair; even the taste of those ashes had been in her mouth, with all the soft and mawkish savour of unfulfilment.

Yet in a sense those futile wanderings had been, perhaps, part of the divine pattern—the means to bring her at last to this: a lingering smile played over her introspective face as she considered her present happiness. She did not deserve it, yet miraculously she had achieved it—it was hers—unbelievably hers.

For some moments she sat reflectively at her table: she had just finished her lunch, for, free of the necessity of racing home at one, she had reverted to that later meal at four o'clock. Then absently, without recollection, apparently, of that frightful missive which had struck her down at Doune, she picked up a letter that lay beside her plate and scanned it in a manner quite remote. Yet this, too, was from her son, dated the previous day and stamped with an address in Maida Vale, London.

" MY DEAREST MOTHER," it smoothly ran,—" I was indeed pleased to have your note and to know that all is well with you. We ourselves are both very fit and happy. Everything is going

362

satisfactorily with the partnership. You will be delighted to hear that I have collected a new patient in the person of a titled lady—think of that! You may have heard of her: Lady Macarthy is the name. Half-guinea fees she pays us—could you believe it! So you see that your son is not doing so badly. Some day you'll find him in Harley Street. Yes, I'm determined—and that at not too remote a date. Believe me, it will not be for want of trying if I'm not famous one day. In the meantime we must be patient (no pun intended, my dear). I am still longing to have you down near to us, but actually it is difficult at the moment. Of course, I hate to think of you still working, but every penny I can make goes into the practice, and you will agree that it is essential for us to consolidate our position. Rosie's dad has been ever so good—he was down again last week—bless the man, he can't keep away from us. Really he is exceptionally kind, but of course we can't expect him to do everything. Still, the day is not far off when you'll be down here too and we'll be near each other. It can't come too quickly for me—then I'll be able to settle something really handsome on you to make you independent for life. That's what you'd like, I know.

" Rosie sends her fondest love, and so too do I.

" Your devoted son

" PETER."

She read it through quite calmly. It was typical of his letters to her now—a fair example of those epistles that reached her on an average once a week, and to which she could reply soberly, with an equal regularity. Yes, a loving, devoted letter, full of glowing promises. Those promises! Doubtless he believed them—but did she? Was she unjust? She did not know: yet dimly she conceived that in another ten years' time he might perhaps be making these identical pledges. And it was strange that her thought caused her no bitterness. Strange, indeed, was this new tolerance—she had never been a tolerant woman.

Again her thoughts flew back. Nine months ago, could she have surveyed so calmly and dispassionately these primly written words? Let her now recognise her past travail as the puny writhings of a misguided mind, but still they had a wincing memory: that return from Doune—she could never forget it—never! Nor would she forget the anguish, the bitterness, and the turmoil of her mind. Coming back to her house, so empty, so utterly deserted—even now a shiver ran through her at the thought—she had been like a woman distracted. Downstairs, the Maitlands had friends—a party with boisterous music thumped from the piano, singing of choruses, and a wild dancing of reels. She knew these hilarious parties of old, but then, as she paced restlessly about, the din rising to her ears had driven her frantic. So, too, had the utter loneliness of her house. Alone, deserted, forsaken so smugly after those years of supreme oblation, caged by bare walls, reminded at every fierce turn of her pacings of the struggle made, the offering rejected—she could not stand it. Desperately she had rushed out, striving to sink the turmoil of her mind in the rushing turmoil of the streets. Saturday night in Young Street—was it life or was it madness? Lights flaring, the pavements seething, garish with sound and colour; beshawled women arm in arm, roistering, laughing; a press of people surging forward like a babbling army pursuing pleasure; whores standing at street corners, alert, waiting, offering themselves to men; pallid children, deformed and uncouth, begging, playing, fighting; the trams racketing along, the public-houses wide open, more laughter, shouts, singing, the brawling of drunken men: all had swum before her like a mazy dream, a whirling nightmare of which she was the central rooted figure.

Rooted or wandering, it was the same; she was not of that careless army; she was lost, a woman with a lost faith. Bitterly she had regretted everything in her life. She had regretted even her virtue. Why hadn't she torn some happiness from life? She had a body— a better and more vital body than these cheap strumpets parading their doubtful charms; she had feeling. But she had stifled it all, pent up everything. Why had she bound herself within the narrow limits of respectability, scraping, pinching, denying herself everything—and all for nothing? It was her own doing. By the manner of her life she had mocked herself. Violently she wanted to escape, to hurl herself into some mad distraction, or into an eternal forgetfulness. What compensations were hers for those long years of sacrifice? Her eyes filled with burning tears at the memory of all that she had done. And now she was abandoned like a discarded mistress, useless, in circumstances of unalterable wretchedness: never could she see herself in a position of dependence in her son's house, accepting, as it were, the scraps of his affection. No! The star to which she had pinned her loyalty was quenched; the idol that she had raised lay shattered at her feet. Everything had been sacrificed; and sacrificed to folly and fatuity.

So she had roamed the crazy streets, returning late at night to her house, back into a quiet which startled her. Yet, for all that quiet, she could not sleep; she had tossed the whole night through. Next day—Sunday—she lay in bed exhausted, staring at nothing, without even a thought of church, hearing the heavy seconds pass.

On Monday she had dragged herself to the office. She would go; it was her livelihood; she would be dependent on nobody—entering the room numb, indifferent, yet dreading the inevitable scene: the covert glances, the sympathy which she did not desire, and under that sympathy the latent air: " I told you so "; " You were warned and you gave no heed." That had been a dagger in her side, keen anguish to her pride—she who had boasted so valiantly of what she would do when her son was through.

Then, the situation confronted with a set face, off to the slums. Back to that round of detestable and degrading work, and now no loyalty to enkindle her. On and on, that senseless drudgery, the slavery of life. It had begun all over again.

Those postcards, too, which showered upon her from the honey-moon pair on their tour of Brittany. How they loved Brittany, with its quaintness—that was Rose's phrase—and its wonderful cooking —that was her son's. Already they made mention of a second visit. The cards kept coming every day, peace-offerings, tokens of devotion —bright colours, women in caps and sabots, smacks in the glow of sunset—" Isn't this a nice scene, mother? "—pretty pictures; but, to her, lancinating reminders of her loss: abroad, enjoying them-selves, these two, and she here, left like a piece of refuse, yes, like the paper and orange-peel which littered Flowers Street. A crushing depression settled upon her, a cloud upon her brow which darkened and seemed steadily to deepen.

She ought no doubt to have accepted the situation in the tradi-tional manner: a sweet impulse of forgiveness, a moving letter to the happy pair, the gentle suggestion of a tiny weekly stipend, wistful memories mingled with a sentimental vision of herself as she might like to be in future years, white-haired, in a corner seat, dandling an infant on her knee. But that was not in Lucy. At the thought, a cold pricking of revulsion flowed through her. Grimly she felt that she had been cheated, defrauded of her right; and no palliative, no weak anticipation of a miserable and neglected retirement could wipe out the stinging injustice or the bitterness of her defeat. Her life seemed worthless and empty—empty, moreover, of all hope.

The days dragged on, and as the week drew in she too drew within herself the more. Saturday came, then again Sunday, with a reminder of its duty. Indifferently, wearily, moved only by habit, she had set out for church, but not, inevitably, for St. Patrick's. There she was known, and, shrinking instinctively from the rain of questions which, unreasonably in this new sensitiveness, she feared might fall upon her, she went instead to a distant parish, to the Church of St. Mary's, a small church set in a silent square that lay curiously remote amongst a welter of busy streets. Vaguely she had heard of it: the church or its priest—one or the other, she was not sure, nor did she care. It was to escape recognition that she went. But her motives were of little consequence, the manner of her going as naught beside the manner of her return. She had gone—that alone mattered. Bowed beneath her insufferable burden, racked by the pain within her, moved by that indefinite and intolerable craving—a force that was almost spent—she had entered the church.

There it was that the miracle had happened; for surely it was a miracle. She at least could entertain no doubts. Even now, as she sat at her disordered table, her face lit up at the memory. Yes, the hand which guided her life had guided her towards this. She knew it. She was utterly convinced.

She remained seated for some moments, a faint smile transcending her pale face, then she rose, put her son's letter with the others— a dusty pile upon the mantelpiece—and, gathering together her things, went quietly out of the house.

She reached the office at half-past four, went to her table, sat down, and began to check her bag. Then she made up her book. Finally she turned to Miss Tinto.

" Is Mr. Rattray in his room? " she demanded calmly.

Miss Tinto paused in her writing and looked reflectively along her nose towards the ledger. It was an odd remark—the orbits of Lucy and of Mr. Rattray did not usually intersect.

" Yes, he's upstairs," she answered at length, without turning her head. " I heard him go up before you came in."

" Thank you," answered Lucy. She rose and went out of the room.

Now Miss Tinto's head did turn; she surveyed the closed door with eyes popping with astonishment.

In five minutes Lucy came back, slowly, and immediately Miss Tinto spoke.

" Was he in? " she enquired discreetly; but it was an indirect demand for more positive information.

" Yes." Lucy paused, then added without alteration of her tranquilly indifferent tone: " I've just given in my notice."

Miss Tinto gasped; she turned her whole person and confronted the other with a majestic interest.

" You're going down—to London? " she exclaimed, " That's fine! You're going down to your boy at last."

Lucy looked at her for a moment.

" No, I'm not doing that," she said at length. " But I'm leaving here in a month's time." She moved to her table, stacked her books, then moved again to the door. " I think I'll go now," she added. " I've finished everything."

" But what will you do? " exclaimed Miss Tinto; and only a frightful curiosity straining within her proper bosom induced that wholly importunate enquiry.

" I've got other plans," said Lucy vaguely. Then she nodded, said good night, and left the office.

Other plans! Again Miss Tinto stared; mentally she was still staring when Dandie—delayed by a failure of the tram service—entered the room.

He was in an indifferent humour, and, impaling his hat cussedly upon a peg, he exclaimed disgustedly:

" The worst tram-cars in Europe; whenever you're in a hurry they break down on you for spite. Then it's push, push, push, when you try to get on to them. The women are worse than the men—shoppers they call themselves. Perfect gadabouts. And me that didn't sleep well. A piano going all night next door. Thump, thump, thump. Stops all of a sudden, then goes on again. I'll buy a firework and stick it under their window. Where's your Government? "

But Miss Tinto gave no heed to his tirade; her news, simmering within her, could not be retained.

" She's leaving," she remarked, with an imposing movement of her head towards the vacant table. " Given in her notice to-night."

Dandie lifted his head sharply, and after a pause slewed round.

" You don't say! " He curled his bandy legs round his chair inquisitively—each a living symbol of interrogation. Then, his spleen not yet evaporated, he added: " Going to that marvellous son of hers? "

" No! " A wealth of innuendo was behind the syllable.

" Then what—what's she after? "

" God knows," answered Miss Tinto slowly. She did not often invoke the deity, but now there was a terrific portent in her manner; and in the same fashion she added: " And God knows what will happen to her. She's her own worst enemy, poor thing. I'm heart sorry for her.

" Sorry for her? She's not sorry for herself. She's walking on air these days."

" On air? "

" You know—up in the clouds."

" There's a look on her face sometimes—what's the reason of it all? "

There was a silence. Dandie scratched his head with the butt of his pen and remarked dispassionately, dropping each word slowly, with a supreme knowingness:

" You know she's got religion now, don't you? "

Miss Tinto slightly inclined her head.

" Well——" guardedly, she said.

" It is religion she's got," persisted Dandie. " I've seen it before. There was a woman at a tent meeting I was once at. I went in for the fun of the thing, but fun! Cor! You should have seen how it took her. And a man I once knew—Gilmour was his name—ay, that was it—Gilmour. A heavy boozer he was in his day. But when he got

367

converted—a Salvation Army meeting at the Gorbals did for him—
do you know, he went about smashing every bottle of whisky he
saw. He would walk into a pub and lay about the bar with his stick.
They jailed him for it at last—and, crivens, high time and all it was,
too." He paused. " But the women get it the worst. And I'm telling
you that's what she *has* got. You can tell the signs a mile away. Ay,
Catholic or no Catholic. They can get it like anybody else. So it
would seem, anyway."

" Such a disappointment she's had," murmured Miss Tinto.

" That's it, don't you see? " shot out the inexorable Dandie.
" She was ripe for it. It was just inevitable."

" Inevitable? "

" Give a woman like her a big enough drop and she'll fall for
religion. It's the same the world over. Oh, I had a great old argument
with her the other day about the whole business. But she near took
the nose off me."

" But what on earth is she going to do? "

" She knows all right. if you don't," answered Dandie sagely.
" Believe me, she's a woman that knows her own mind." He swung
back to his table with a grin. " So long as she doesn't start smashing
the whisky bottles! " But Miss Tinto gave no answering smile.
Instead, she frowned and shook her head slowly, uncomprehendingly,
as though it might be a bad business—a bad business for somebody.

II

LUCY went towards the tramway station quite quickly, like a
woman with a fixed objective, she who, a few months ago, dragging
herself about, had so abjectly considered that there was nothing
for which she might live. It was indeed miraculous. And as such she
recognised the magnitude of the blessing bestowed on her, the magnitude of the change which she knew to have overswept her life.

Let Miss Tinto frown and wonder; let Dandie grin as sneeringly
as he chose. She did not care. If this sweet ardour which now thrilled
her served merely to excite their ridicule, it was to her a matter of
complete indifference. She was happy, happier than she had ever
been; and how could they comprehend this happiness—this great
inward joy at which she herself had scarcely ceased to marvel? But
it was hers none the less, a glowing, tender flame before which all
else paled to insignificance; the leaping flame which she had always
sought, which she had always found elusive—hers it was at last.
That was the reason of her new serenity and her air of quiet purpose.

At Kelvinbank she descended from her tram-car and began to traverse the familiar route towards Flowers Street. Amidst these fusty streets which once had caused her such high aversion her face was devoid of all repugnance. When she reached home, she prepared her tea and made an adequate meal. Then, without delay, she rose, washed her face and hands, tidied her hair, and again went out.

Upon the landing her eye fell for an instant upon the neighbouring door which, newly shorn of its name-plate, mutely proclaimed the Finches' departure. Yes, inevitably that short idyll had worn to its end: Bessie with gushing eyes had returned to her mother; and John discovered some bland haven with his bottle. Could more patent evidence be shown of the folly of earthly vanities?

As she went down the stairs, a suppressed sigh came from Lucy's lips. She was sorry for Bessie. Once she, too, had been like that—mistaken, straining to express a single drop of happiness from what held merely emptiness.

Outside, as she slipped through the gathering darkness, avoiding by design the main, well-lighted thoroughfares, she was touched by a transient recollection of those days when she had striven to capture the fleeting satisfactions of the world, when lights and crowds and shop windows had interested her, when she had been bound even by the petty vanities of dress. Had there once been a zibelline in which she had postured before her mirror, demanding of Netta " if she would do "? Had there been a time when she had sat down to sate herself with cream cakes? Cream cakes, indeed! The memories seemed unsubstantial and shadowy—far, far away. Yes, in this wondrous happiness which had come to her those trivialities had become remote, her only feeling a vague remorse that she had once so foolishly indulged herself.

Now she had almost reached Garnet Square, and with an ease born of familiarity she followed the short though devious course of an ill-lit alley and came out into the open opposite the Church of St. Mary's. The sudden freshness in her escape from that confined and tortuous way she felt always to be symbolic: like the great, the miraculous release which had befallen her upon the occasion of her first visit to the church. And again, as she passed through the narrow Gothic porch, she thought of that sublime spiritual experience which then had come to her. How, indeed, could she forget it. In one great sweep, like a torrent released, it had rushed over her, a flash, a lightning stroke of grace, a pure inward glow of a blinding light and it was done, the whole current of her life diverted, the very suddenness of her liberation dazzling. Nothing short of a miracle had compassed it! And to think that all her life she had been chasing phantoms whilst this—the great, the only reality—had escaped her.

Nine months ago it had happened, upon that Sunday—oh, blessed,

blessed day!—in this same dark and dingy church. Upon her knees, half concealed behind a pillar, she had essayed to utter a prayer—mechanically, almost heedlessly, too crushed by her misery to raise even that formal earnestness which customarily marked her devotions. Perhaps it was that she had never been devout, moved merely by usage and what she knew to be her duty. And on this day at least surely she was too stricken to find the energy for prayer. So spent was she, her being seemed like a cord tautly drawn that soon unendurably must snap.

Then suddenly she had lifted her head. Then, indeed, that cord had snapped and, amongst the echoing vibrations of its sundering she looked directly into His face. His face! She had started. Sideways and downwards that face was turned, and from beneath the drooping lids the eyes gazed towards her with a calm yet anguished recognition. Instantly a strange stab of pain transfixed her, and she sank down into the shadow of the pillar. But she could not remove her eyes. They were bound irrevocably to those tranquil sorrowful eyes which seemed to sorrow because of her, which for her seemed clouded by a sad reproach. Then she began to feel herself trembling, for the face held everything that now she herself could feel. Suffering stamped its every lineament: the brow pierced and bleeding, the cheeks sunken and exsanguine, the lips half parted to reveal the thirsting tongue. The frightful agony of a tortured and abandoned death was seared upon those riven features. But the face was not dead. It was animate, lifting her upwards with that strange compelling power, mingling pity with pain, strength with weakness, sternness with compassion. Suddenly she felt faint, and strove desperately to collect herself, to lower her eyes. It was only a crucifix fixed to the pillar above her head: the face of Jesus as He had hung upon the cross: nothing she had not known, nothing she had not seen a thousand times before. Large and lifelike it might be; yet it was nothing more than wood and plaster and paint. But her haunted eyes would not fall. Oh, she had often seen that face of the suffering Christ, but never, never like this.

It was so close to her, actual and living, with breath upon the tortured lips, and sweat upon the anguished brow; with eyes awaiting her, it seemed, understanding her misery, offering her mercy and peace and love. All her life Jesus had been awaiting her, patient and long-suffering; and only now did she realise it. He had been waiting for this moment. Her surroundings grew hazy as from a mist, through which the figure took on a quality both luminous and transplendent. Jesus! Jesus! His face was shining towards her. Her Saviour, whom she had neglected and forsaken, was offering His love to her! Empty, cast down, deserted even as He had been, she was still His. He understood her; He was calling her: His eye enkindled by compassion,

His side bleeding for her, His lovely body flogged for her, His arms —extended upon this gibbet of a cross—opened wide to receive her. He too had suffered, and that suffering, omniscient eye saw all that she had borne. He it was who had proclaimed the worthlessness of all things but the love of God. Had He not so ordained the pattern of her destiny that she might come unto Him at last?

Suddenly in her ears came a ringing voice: " Seek ye first the Kingdom of God." Her face paled; she was overwhelmed; a melting tenderness ran through her. Oh, the sight of that transfigured face! —it was now too bright to be endured. Her heart throbbed to bursting with a strange ardour that welled out of her very sadness; it grew and grew until her poor body could no longer contain the swelling of that ardour; within her something dissolved; her spirit suddenly took wings and soared upwards towards the figure of Christ—her Saviour. Rushing upwards, upwards, upwards into His waiting arms, Oh, unexpected, unbelievable joy! In her ecstasy she felt the arms of her Redeemer softly enfolding her. Her head fell forward, and a fearful gush of tears streamed blindly from her eyes. She was on His breast, weeping for joy. Jesus, Son of the living God —the splendour of the Father—the brightness of eternal light—the desire of the eternal hills—He was hers, and she at last was His. Why had she never turned to Him before? She had walked through deserts of uselessness, outworn herself with a travail of futility. But now she had come to Him; now her soul had surged to sweet union with its Creator. It was the end for which she had been created. Beside that union life was nothing—death was nothing! Around her the voices of angels blended in a celestial harmony of happiness.

" Jesus! Jesus! " she murmured in ecstasy. " At last I have come to You. You are mine, and I am Yours for ever and for ever."

For a long time she remained upon her knees, rapt by the transport of her beatitude. She saw nothing of the Mass; heard nothing of the sermon. She observed no one, nor was she herself observed. Without her knowledge the church emptied of its impoverished congregation; she was alone.

Then at last slowly she stirred. Her face, like the face shining in her vision, was now transfigured. Could she have believed that, entering this church so wretchedly, she would leave it thus, consoled and at peace. Swiftly, fervently, she stooped and kissed the feet of the figure upon the cross.

So uplifted did she feel, that a lurking fear had haunted her that her happiness would not endure. The treasure seemed too precious to be hers. But her fear was groundless. Never had she embraced a cause that she did not pursue with a fervent intensity. It had endured; it was indeed hers; and it had grown daily, become the essence of her life. There was much for which she must make atonement: all her early coldness and negligence.

It was wonderful how richly and how rapidly her fervour had flowered, and with that flowering those deep interior roots of happiness had increased. She had returned to St. Mary's; and had again returned; made of the church a sweet refuge towards which she inevitably turned. There was no special virtue in this small and unpretentious chapel, but it was here that through the sublime goodness of her Creator she had found grace. Here then she came to pray, to offer up her work, her life, herself to God, to attend the Sacrifice of the Mass, to make her daily communions: those treasured moments when Jesus gave to her His Body, uniting Himself with her, now flooding her soul with that unbelievable ecstasy of joy. Never before had she realised the full significance of the Sacrament. In the past, when she had made her duties at Easter-time, to receive the Host and feel the tiny disc of wafer dissolve upon her tongue had been a solemn but not a moving or convincing moment. She accepted it as part of her belief; so she had been taught; but now—how different it was! This fusion with Jesus was real and actual, fanning her fervour, increasing the passion of her yearning—sweet repetition of that moment when in her vision He had compassed her with His loving arms.

But what could she do to show her love and gratitude in return? The very intensity of her ardour demanded that she do more, driving her onwards in sweetness towards a greater and still a greater sacrifice. She desired a closer and more binding union. All for Jesus—that was indeed the *motif* of her life, and it bore her forward like an irresistible tide.

Then suddenly revelation had come to her, one evening as she sat meditating within her own quiet room; so perhaps had the Annunciation come to Mary. It was so simple, so inevitable; presumptuous perhaps; to those who could not understand, merely ridiculous; but to her an inspiration of exceeding sweetness. To give herself entirely to God! It was that impulse of complete surrender which moved her. And what was there in her life to prevent her leaving the world? No; nothing existed which might restrain her; it was as though her entire life—that gradual shedding of all earthly faiths—had been a preparation towards this sublime end. At once she fell upon her knees and thanked Jesus for the thought. Slowly the resolution had firmed in her mind. From her confessor she sought advice and received it. Then quite calmly she had decided.

Nine months ago she had entered this church a wretched and disillusioned woman. Everything had failed her. But that was all behind her: now she had something which would never fail her. This, then, was the reason of her sudden step in determining her employment with Henderson & Shaw; and it was in part the reason of her attendance here upon this present evening.

When the service of Benediction was over, she remained kneeling, observing the priest as he left the altar and entered the sacristy. He it was who had helped her; and now she wished to speak with him.

It was Father John Talbot who had at this time the charge of the Church of St. Mary's in Garnet Square. Severe, assiduous, a man of unimpeachable sincerity, even his enemies could not impugn the intensity of his belief. This fierce faith had drawn him from his possessions—he was of a known landed family—into the Church; this same conviction it was which drove him still. A zealot working alone in his impoverished parish, fasting consistently, eating no meat, drinking only water, wearing always a hair-shirt, flagellating himself at midnight before the altar—he practised in secret every chastisement of the flesh. He was named a fool, a saint, a bigot, but never—his very presence precluded it—never a humbug.

Tall, thin, and erect, his cadaverous figure had a relentless and almost bitter urgency. He was dark, with a lean, pale face, a fine beak of a nose, pinched nostrils, lips like a seam, large, severe, slightly sunken eyes. That face, like his manner, never relaxed, but remained always grave, strict, inwardly absorbed, openly almost formidable. Now, disrobing in the sacristy—a room dim, subtly tinged with the aromatic odour of incense and warm wax, and quiet save for the movements of two altar-boys, shuffling out of their cassocks in the corner—he took off his cope, folded it, removed his surplice. Then, suddenly, there was a knock at the inner door—that door communicating with the church.

" Go out," said Talbot to the two boys, without turning his head. His voice was cold, austere, and they immediately obeyed him, leaving by the back way which gave immediate access to the yard. He finished smoothing the folded cope, put on his biretta, then advanced to the inner door and himself opened it.

" I was expecting you," he said at once. And, admitting Lucy to the sacristy, he paused, contemplating her seriously. " So you have made up your mind ? "

" Yes, father."

" You have considered everything that I told you ? "

" I have considered it."

" To give yourself up utterly——"

She gave an emphatic affirmative, and for a moment the two stood facing each other in silence. His face was sombre and still severe, but now, as in the past, she drew a strange comfort from that firmness.

" It's the one thing I'm set on," she murmured, after a moment, " I'm determined on it. Nothing else has any value to me. I couldn't give up the idea, and—and you advise it. I'm in your hands."

" You are in God's hands," he corrected her sternly. There was a pause; he did not ask her to sit down, but stiffly made the interview a penance for them both. " I've known you for nearly nine months," he said at length, " and I know something of your life. You are not young. It is only the remnant that you have to offer. Still, if you are prepared to endure hardship, to make complete submission——"

" I will—oh, I will!" she broke in.

" Then I am prepared to help you. I do consider that you have the vocation. That alone influences me. It has come to you late— but still, it is there." He paused, aloof, utterly detached, whilst she watched him with glowing eyes. " I have given the matter some thought," he resumed. " The Order of the Servants of God; I know it well. It is the most suitable to you. Already I have sent two postulants there, and they have done admirably."

" I thought you spoke of the Carmelites," she broke in quickly.

" It is too severe. You are not young enough to endure their discipline," he asserted dispassionately. " Besides, you must remember your position, your age. What have you to offer that might induce them to admit you? No, under these circumstances they would not accept you."

She flushed, but still maintained her gaze upon his face.

" This Order I speak of—the severities are not great, though for all purposes it is enclosed. The only disadvantage is that the mother-house is abroad—it is at Sentiens, near Brussels. You would be obliged to spend at least three years there—perhaps the remainder of your life. But probably when professed you would be sent back to one of the houses in this country."

" That's nothing," she advanced eagerly. " I want to get away— to get away from everything."

" It is not what you wish. If you take the veil, you must forget what you desire." He paused again. " I have already written to the Mother General; and there are certain formalities which you must yourself complete."

" Yes—anything."

" Certain certificates—of birth, of confirmation, a medical certificate, and a certificate of your husband's death. Finally, you will require two references. I, myself, naturally offer one of these, and the other "—he looked at her swiftly—" I suggest that Canon Moore supply you with that."

" I'll write at once," she assured him; then, after a moment, " How soon may I expect——"

" The Mother General will write to you. If you are accepted— perhaps a month; it will be in her hands."

A month! It was what she had hoped. At the thought, a strange insurgent ardour suffused her like an intoxication.

" You've been good to me, father," she murmured. " I want to thank you."

" It is nothing." His tone held almost a rebuke, deploring all human feeling. Then he was silent, a significant silence which terminated the short interview.

" Go in peace," he said, as she moved towards the door.

She was happy. Voluntarily she had made the step. These few moments of conversation, so restrained and unemotional, would lead her to the haven she desired. She went out into the church. Already in the falling light the echoing nave was blurred to a sombre monotone, relieved only by the waving red gleam of the sanctuary lamp. For a moment she knelt down, filled by a moving sense of gratitude. If only she might be accepted! She prayed that she might be acceptable to God as His servant; that all her coldness, her early indifference, might for forgotten. But she would be accepted. Already she felt her life shaped towards that one end.

The quiet, the solitude, and the darkness encompassed her. Rapt by an unseen vision, her eyes glowed towards the obscurity behind that flickering light; her body, suppliant, strained towards the blankness of the altar in a passion of surrender.

" All—all for Jesus! "—with her there could be no half-measures. Yes, she must give all. How blind were they who rejected the sweet beatitude of the love of God! It was everything. It was the light towards which that strange fusion of instincts—her soul—fluttering moth-like in the darkness, was drawn with a blind and irresistible yearning.

Strange, strange thought that she, Lucy Moore, should be actually upon the verge of entering a convent. Only she could understand the true meaning of that step. " All—all for Jesus! " That was it— she was giving herself to Him with all the passionate ardour of a bride!

III

FOLLOWING the advice of her spiritual adviser, she had written to Edward, and on the following Saturday she was astounded by the manner of his reply. No letter was that response, but, veritably, a visit, a personal visit from the Canon.

" I had to come, Lucy," he asserted without delay, rather breathlessly after a hurried greeting. " I am busy. I am exceedingly busy. I have a diocesan meeting at four, but I simply had to come." His manner had altered subtly in those last few years—his diffidence masked by dignity, his suavity merged towards a higher pomp.

" What's all this you're saying in your letter ? " he went on, elevating his brows in genial reproof and pulling the written evidence from his pocket. " You're surely not serious? "

" Perfectly serious," she assured him, observing him calmly as he seated himself in the rocker, now the only secure seat in her back room. She was surprised at his call, but not dismayed by it. The days when the poverty of her house had drawn a blush of shame to her cheek were no longer here. Nay, she now embraced this poverty—the poverty preached by Christ.

" But you cannot be in earnest, my dear Lucy," protested the Canon, fanning his face with the letter—he had ascended the stairs too quickly, and lately his liver had been rather turgid—" or at least you are not fully aware of what—excuse me—you are contemplating. Do you know what it means—the hardship of it all? "

" It's no greater hardship than I've been used to. The Rule has been explained to me. Besides, I offer the hardship to God." She was tranquil—tranquil and remote.

" Very laudable indeed." He looked at her indulgently. " But honestly, Lucy, at your time of life you must not dream of it."

Time of life! Did he imply some aberrant impulse by that suggestive phrase? And she was only forty-two. Frowning, she made as though to speak; but he hurriedly went on.

" Now I want to say a few things to you. You've had a very stiff time lately, my dear. But the way you've come through it does you credit. Peter's marriage, almost a runaway match—well, it was a surprise even to me. So young, too! But there—it's only the natural law. What does St. Paul say: ' Better to marry than to burn '—you'd have had to lose him some day in any case. Sooner or later—what does it matter? And it's not so very soon. In Spain, now "—he flashed backwards a reminiscent eye—" in Spain they marry very young. They mature quickly, especially the women. Why, I've seen them married at fourteen. Besides, such a splendid match he's made. A fine Catholic girl—yes, a lovely girl—lovely "—he let the adjective slip seductively over his tongue—" and wealthy, too—what a start for the boy in that fine London practice. He writes me that he's getting on splendidly—actually attending the nobility, the pushing young sprig. In a few months or so he'll be able to provide for you. You've done a great deal for him—yes, of course you have—but you'll get it all back if you're patient." He leaned back and threw out his soft white hand. " Pax vobiscum ! " His air said plainly: There ! what cause for regret is there in that ?

" I don't think the question of what is past comes into this," she said with quite astounding mildness. " It's the future I'm concerned with."

" Yes, yes, my dear. But a natural resentment, a pique, might cause you to rush into some step like this. I mean, the marriage behind your back, so to speak. Though, goodness knows, I had no hand in it."

She shook her head slowly, offering her unanswerable argument.

" You don't know me, Edward, even yet! This means everything to me now. I've found happiness, inexpressible happiness, in our Lord."

Ironic fact; yet the prelate shied at her words like a startled horse; then along his fine nose he considered her dubiously.

" Yes, yes," he said again, this time soothingly. He paused. " Well, admitted that you want to go—have you considered the sacrifice?" He pursed his lips. " You can't give up the world so easily as you think."

She considered, with a faint indrawing of her lips, " the world ": the slums, this house, the drab drudgery of her life.

" I can give it up," she answered, more shortly than she meant. " And I will give it up."

" The life of the cloister, then," he persisted reasonably. " It's a life you must be moulded to gradually when you're young. You'll find, at your age—yes, you'll find humiliation there."

" Have I not found enough here? " she retorted, without bitter-ness. " Have I not found that life holds nothing but the love of God? "

" You can serve God outside, in the world," he suggested, flushing slightly. " We priests do that."

" It's all or nothing with me," she rejoined at once, firmly. " I've had the call."

He hummed and hawed behind his pressed finger-tips, thinking of those days when, so smartly dressed, so glowing and content, she had come to see him with her little son. How could he shake her from this—yes, this stupidity?

" What's taken you? " he said at length, studying her closely; then his long upper lip twitched with a sudden complacent humour; and, remembering that she had always liked his little anecdotes, he added: " You haven't had a vision, I hope—like the old lady that came to me the other day. Miss MacTara it was—you may remember her." He paused, moistened his lips in his best manner. " She's well-to-do, one of my best parishioners, and as pious as you could wish. ' Canon,' said she in a great flutter, ' I've had a blessed vision. God the Father and God the Son have I seen. After supper last night I saw them as plain as I'm looking at your reverence now.' ' Oh,' I said—I know her well, you understand, and she's fond of her wine in the evening. ' After supper, was it? And how much port did you have? ' ' Only two glasses, Canon. I never have more. Tell me, is it a miracle? ' ' Two glasses,' I replied. ' Go home, my dear good soul.

Have three glasses to-night, and no doubt you'll see the Blessed Trinity entirely.' "

He laughed benignantly at his own joke—most excellently related; but her face remained so unsmiling that gradually his merriment ran dry. There was a short pause whilst he looked at her askance, discomposed by the failure of his good intention.

" Be sensible now, Lucy," he declared at length in a conciliatory tone. " I haven't interfered with you ever; but now I'm a priest— I know all this from the inside, and I advise you strongly against it."

She looked at him sitting there, well-fed, plump of hand and cheek, smooth with good living and his own consequence, then swiftly her thoughts flew to Talbot's figure; gaunt, hungry, worn with its own intensity. Her brow creased. Did these two men profess the same faith? She knew, at any rate, the example which she wished to follow.

" Father Talbot tells me I have the vocation," she answered coldly. " He advises me to go."

His face flushed deeply.

" Talbot! " he exclaimed. " He's a zealot—a firebrand; the—the bishop has an eye on him. You mustn't count too much on what he says. We have a duty to life and to ourselves." He paused, his sacerdotal suavity swiftly recovered, and went on with considered gravity: " No! It doesn't improve our prestige here to walk about in old clothes, with our heads shaved; we must be in keeping. Why, only yesterday I interested a man in religion over a game of golf——" He spoke with a certain satisfaction, and not without a certain authority—his handicap was now eighteen.

She looked at him directly, with eyes which seemed to pierce him.

" You of all people—you're really not trying to put me off devoting myself to the service of God! "

His flush, still lingering, rose quickly; he moved restlessly; really her bluntness was not in the best of taste.   .

" I only want to save you from being stupid You're rather obstinate—I won't say wrong-headed, but you do take the bit between your teeth. Every logical person will tell you as I do. Even Miss O'Regan thinks——" He dismissed the sentence with an explanatory shrug.

So he had discussed her with Miss O'Regan—with that pale custodian of his fleece-lined comfort! Again that feeling of bitter injustice flared up in her.

" I am as I am," she declared, swiftly, " and that's how God made me. But I would never discuss you behind your back. And, more than that, from the way you talk you would think I was going to the devil instead of to a convent."

Outraged, he drew back, hand raised—a figure almost apostolic.

" Lucy—Lucy," he protested, " that tongue of yours! "

She controlled herself, letting her hands fall into her lap.

" I'm sorry, Edward," she said firmly, yet professing her new humility by lowering her head. " But I am going. Nothing you can say will alter that. I am going to offer myself to Jesus! "

A long pause succeeded those last words, which seemed to come from the bottom of her soul.

" Well, well," he said, with a movement expressive of pained resignation—whether genuine or false it was impossible to tell— " you will go your own way. But don't say I didn't warn you." He looked round the room with the air of a man who has done his duty. There was a silence, then she raised her eyes.

" Can I give you a cup of tea? " she asked, quite mildly. " It would be no trouble at all."

" No, no," he interposed, rising. " I'm dining with the Archbishop after the meeting. I'll take nothing till then."

His duty done, he seemed anxious to get away.

They shook hands in the little hall, and he imparted a high solemnity to the puffy pressure of his fingers.

" Good-bye, Lucy; and God bless you. Perhaps, after all, you may be given the grace to succeed. For we are in God's hands—each and every one of us."

He seemed to darken her doorway, but, for all his increased bulk, he had a soft and fleshy tread as he went sedately down the stairs.

Quickly she closed the door after him and went back into the room. Edward warning against giving herself entirely to God! Could she have conceived a situation more farcical? But she was not moved to laughter. Instead, her lips firmed; her eyes softened and shone with their one-time lustre; nothing could separate her from the joy and glory of her surrender. It was simply—simply that he did not understand. She would go to Jesus despite him. Slowly her gaze became remote, and into the compass of her vision came the Christ figure, bleeding, pierced by five wounds, with arms extended towards her.

IV

She had known, inevitably, with all the conviction of that inner light, that she was going, but when word came definitely of her acceptance, she experienced a sudden gush of happiness. Bonne Mère Générale in a fine angular hand, and in English of surprising excellence, expressed herself as " much struck " by the terms of Lucy's letter and by the good Father Talbot's recommendation.

She was, therefore, despite madame's age, agreeable to receive her as *postulante* of the Order on the conditions specified. Thanks be to God! With the eye of faith Lucy saw the gates opening to her; opening to peace and the happiness of prayer.

Gladly and at once she began to make arrangements for her departure from an environment which for years had immeasurably oppressed her. She had a strange sense of freedom, a feeling of release, and an energy, a glowing energy, which came from that fire within. It was no hardship for her to think of quitting the country. She embraced it. " Leave all that thou hast and follow Me," the Master had commanded. And what indeed had she to leave?

She had arranged for the removal of her things, purchased by a dealer in the second-hand from her district—none else would have touched them—for the sum of forty-five shillings. Forty-five shillings —something at least towards her expenses. She must rely upon her son for the rest—a paltry sum which it was impossible for him to refuse her. Yet it was like her that she did not write him. In London she would explain herself. She had her own way of doing things. Yes, she had decided to make no stir about her going. Who, indeed, was there to care? Richard and Eva, Joe, Polly, even Edward? The event would not cause a ripple on the surface of their lives. So narrowed had her life become through circumstances of her own making that she felt already isolated, strangely detached. Father Talbot she did see several times, formal interviews whose very restraint seemed to fan the fire of her zeal. It gave her a momentary wrench to say good-bye to Miss Tinto, but to her other acquaintances she made her leave-taking casual, cheerful, giving no indication of her purpose. She wanted to give up her work; she was going south for a rest, for a holiday, for anything that came into her head. She desired no spectacular valediction. It was enough that she was going. And how gladly was she going!

And so, on the morning of the first day of March, she was in the train for London, a pale-faced, plainly dressed, middle-aged woman with a steadfast eye and a faintly furrowed forehead, the battered trunk that had been her son's—could she then have foretold its present use?—packed with a few things and bestowed upon the rack above her. In her gloved hand was her ticket, in her purse something short of three pounds, and in her heart, passionately treasured, the priceless possession of the love of God.

Perhaps from her eagerness the journey seemed to her lengthy beyond her imagining. She had travelled little—never, in fact, although Frank had one time toyed in his indeterminate fashion with the idea of a Continental trip, had she been out of Scotland. She had brought no lunch; she desired no papers; she had no wish for conversation. She simply sat quite still in her corner of the compartment, silent, absorbed by secret meditation, filled by a thrilling exaltation.

At Crewe she had a cup of tea and a bun, a hurried meal partaken of standing in the refreshment-room.

At Euston, attained at last at six, she got out upon the crowded platform and immediately summoned a porter, who, in turn, summoned a cab. Amidst the bustle she was quite calm, and she had her plan quite calmly in her head. She was not going to her son's. No. She harboured neither rancour nor resentment, she had now no jealousy of Rosie, but still she would not intrude herself upon them. She went instead to a small private hotel in Gower Street, highly recommended by Miss Tinto, who, on a memorable visit with her sister, had found it " decent and reasonable." Here, though she had given no notice of her arrival, she experienced no difficulty. Quiet and contained, undismayed by the rattle of the streets and the strange experience of entering a strange hotel, she obtained her room with a factitious appearance of experience. Then she went down at once to telephone her son. His name was in the book, and his number, she found it easily, and without delay she rang up that number. And it was he who immediately answered in a voice brisk, pleasant, definitely professional and expectant; but when she announced herself and her whereabouts, the voice flattened out in a manner almost ludicrous. After a long, astounded silence, it came back, rather huskily:

" What—what on earth are you doing here? "

" Come and see me," she returned; " I'll tell you then." There was a potent pause; she could see him overwhelmed by astonishment.

" But you'd better come here, mother "; and another pause. " Why didn't you say you were coming? Yes—you must come over." Her lips smiled faintly into the mouthpiece.

" I'll expect you some time this evening," she said. Then, she put down the receiver and came out of the box.

Half an hour later he arrived, effusive, dismayed, concealing the one by the exercise of the other. And now in her room they faced each other—he lounging upon the bed, she upright upon the single cane-bottomed chair which the apartment contained—both affected by the memory of all that had passed since their last meeting.

" You can't mean it, mother," he said for the third time, still rather breathless and put out. " Really, it's the biggest shock I've had since——" He broke off and began to pick at the thin red quilt. " I don't see why you couldn't have let me know."

" Did you let me know? " she asked him, with a faint, wry smile.

He flushed deeply, his head still down, his fingers still picking at the quilt.

" Rose wants you to come out," he asserted uncomfortably.

" Indeed she does. It was the last thing she said to me before I came over." He paused, suddenly aggrieved. " Such a mix-up it is, your dashing down like this. And this idea at your time of life—I never heard anything like it. What on earth will people think? "

She looked at him tranquilly, even compassionately. It was natural that he should be engaged by the trivialities of existence. Despite her composure, it stirred her deeply to see him again. All the intimacies of their life together rose up to confront her. He had altered so little: his manner, his very smile, the same, tinged by the same diffident, unconscious charm. She still loved him; but now, of course, her fondness, her whole outlook, was different. She saw things in their proper focus—the minutiæ of existence now relegated to insignificance before the main and eternal purpose of salvation. Her eyes smiled at him. Had she once flogged herself on in a frantic effort to achieve temporal gratification from his success? Amazing folly! No wonder she had been punished. At this moment she saw, acutely, the justice of the punishment she had endured, and, with a sublime realisation, she accepted it as the instrument of her deliverance to grace.

" I don't like to think of your burying yourself away there," he again protested. " It's not very creditable to me."

" I know how you feel, my son," she said slowly, and as she spoke her short figure attained majestic stature, " but I am going for all that."

" Come and stay with us and think it over. I tell you Rose wants you to come."

" What use is it? " she returned, with a queer, unrecognised hostility. " Rose will never see me again. I'm going immediately— to-morrow or the day after."

He raised his eyes, half appealing, half aggrieved.

" You don't blame me for anything? It was only natural."

" I blame you for nothing. You don't understand how happy I am."

" I wanted to do so much for you," he explained dejectedly. " You know what I wrote. It was only a matter of time. I'd do anything for you."

" There are some things I require," she replied, calmly controlling the situation. " The cost is trifling."

His eye suddenly humid, the possessive instinct overcome by the thought of her departure, he again protested his willingness to help her. In the rush of his feeling his habitual meanness was swamped; he demanded detail, produced his pocket-book, emotionally handed over some notes.

" Get everything you want," he declared feelingly. " It's the least I can do for you." He had all the Moore softness in moments of crisis, making his donation with a sort of sublime largesse; drawing from it, indeed, the soothing sense of a duty adequately performed. Nine months ago she would have repudiated this gift scornfully, but now she accepted the money without comment or compunction. It was not really for her, but for God. And, touched more by this composure than by any demonstration of affection, affected now by a sudden tenderness towards her, he made more protestations, promises, exclamations of regret. But her self-command was great. He had the strange feeling that she was eternally remote from him. As he rose to leave he said, unhappily:

" I'll come and see you to-morrow." Again she smiled at him, and kissed him.

When he had gone, she sat for a moment thinking, then, rising, she put away the money he had given her and went downstairs. There she entered the comfortable, maroon-papered dining-room and began the plain though excellent meal which already was being served. She enjoyed it, but, seated in a quiet corner, she gave no attention to the others in the room. Her eyes, already schooling themselves, it seemed, to meekness and meditation, remained fixed upon the greyish tablecloth. And, immediately she had finished, she arose.

It was not yet eight o'clock, and, impelled by the force within her, she put on her hat and coat, made an enquiry at the office, and went out of the hotel. The streets pulsed with life: they were like great veins through which ran a constant vital stream. Hansoms and taxis dashed along. People were going to dine—to the theatres. A private car flashed past. She saw the glint of a white shirt, the gleam of a bare shoulder. Often in the past she had entertained a glowing anticipation of her first visit to London—she had talked it over first with Frank and then, a long time afterwards, with Peter: a little dinner it was to be, at the Trocadero—they had decided to be smart—with perhaps a little wine; a good play to enthral them or make them laugh; then supper somewhere in Soho for the real Bohemian savour—yes, she had planned it all.

But now all that was gone—ashes in her mouth, unwanted, unregretted. Had she been offered that programme so long ago desired, she would have coldly turned away her head. That was nothing—nothing to what she now possessed. As she walked along she had a longing—a sweet longing that only she could understand. Not during the whole of that day had she had the consolation of a visit to the church, and there was a craving in her heart which cried out to be appeased. She was obliged again to enquire her way, but after some searching she discovered and entered the church to which she had been directed. There she knelt down and signed herself with a sigh of happiness.

It was late when she returned to the hotel, and, fatigued from her journey, she slept soundly—a dreamless sleep of happiness. On the next morning she rose early. She had those necessities of clothing to obtain, and, after breakfast, taking the Mother Superior's list and the money Peter had given her, she went out.

It was difficult; she tried four shops without success: eyebrows were raised at the coarse material and plain pattern of the garments she desired. But the raising of an eyebrow was nothing to her now, and at last, after much searching—searching which in her eager mood became a veritable pleasure—she came upon a quiet shop in the Edgware Road where they had what she required: a modest black serge dress reaching from neck to ankle, some rough underclothing of a fabric guaranteed eternal, woollen stockings, cotton sheets, and a pair of harsh blankets. The total cost was little enough —the prices were as modest as the establishment—and she could be trusted to secure good value, if not for her own, at least for Jesus' sake. Later in the day the purchases arrived at the hotel, where she bestowed them carefully in her trunk.

Again, that evening, her son came over to see her, and for an hour they sat together in her small bedroom. It was a curious interview, marked on his side by a curious constraint. Once more she felt the sweep of her affection for him: it could never pass, this love; but now it was an emotion recollected rather than experienced, a feeling still recognised, yet recognised from afar, outspanned by the upward soaring of her spirit. Yet she was concerned by his distress. For he had now had leisure to consider the position, and he was afflicted by the irrevocability of the parting. His selfishness was not proof against that strain of inherited sentiment, nor crass enough to withstand the visible imminence of her departure. Had this happened at a distance—had she left directly from Glasgow—all would have been different. He had the happy faculty—so common in the gentle egoist—of inhibiting those matters outside his actual sphere of contact. His marriage, for example, effected in her absence, displayed this tendency in full. Then he had simply banished from his mind the awkward thought of her and her distress. But here—to have the unhappy situation brought home to him by her actual presence in this small bedroom—*that* evoked a lively, though perhaps a transient, misery.

He persisted in demanding if he had given her money enough; wished, indeed, to offer her more. Here at least was plain evidence of his sincerity! But she almost smiled: of what use to her was money now? He would discharge her small obligation to the Order —that she averred to be sufficient recompense for anything that she had done for him. Strangely, these efforts, once to her so desperate, became, in retrospect, remote and even petty. When endured, they had appeared unforgettable, searing as the pangs of childbirth;

yet, like those pangs, they had faded now vaguely into a curious in significance.

But he was very emotional, his eyes filling with tears as he demanded why she was leaving him. Again and again he went over it: he had been making plans for her future; he had meant to do this, and intended to do that; there was, above everything, as she had fully known, always a home for her in his home; even Rose had said——

Yes, though she comforted him, he was vastly upset. No matter that she indicated the visible evidence of her happiness, his dejection deepened. The years dropped from them, back, it seemed to her, to the days of his childhood in Ardfillan. Actually as he took his leave he was almost blubbering—manifestly a grief so boyish it drew from her a mild, compassionate smile. When he had at last departed, she sat thinking of those days, her eyes steady, that faint reminiscent smile still upon her parted lips. She felt, somehow, as though that was how she wished to take farewell of him. And so it was.

He had promised to drive her to Victoria on the following morning. But her intuition had been right; when morning came, a telephone message reached her that he was detained upon a case and would meet her at the station. But he was not at the station: it was no fault of his; he could not leave his case. And in a sense she was glad. All along she had wished her departure to be quiet and unpretentious. No false assumption of renunciation—no melodramatic leave-taking, no monstrous pretence of sentiment upon the threshold of the cloister. The very thought filled her with contempt. Her feeling was within—the love of God; to give herself to God: that was the motive, the force which drove her with a passionate intensity towards this step. And now the last barrier was down, the last earthly obstacle surmounted, the whistle of the speed-gathering engine like a trumpet-blast, shrilling the praise of God.

Seated in her compartment, she directed her eyes out of the window, whilst the gay Kentish countryside—prettier than any picture—spun past her rapt and shining gaze. Silently her lips formed the aspiration: " Blessed be God." The very wheels echoed and re-echoed that unspoken hosanna. " Blessed be God "; " Blessed be God "; " Blessed be God "! It swelled within her like a diapason, and from her ascended with soundless ecstasy to the bright blue cupola of the sky.

Yes; God was indeed good to her, even in these minor matters which she had so disdained. In spite of herself, she had dreaded the crossing, but, Dover reached by its chalky cutting, she found the sea flat, and untroubled as a windless pond. All things went well with her. God sat upon His throne within His templed heaven and smiled upon her with benign omnipotence.

The steady throbbing of the even boat replaced the thunder of the wheels, but to her the rhythm was the same. She was going forward—forward to the ultimate object of her being.

This was the spirit of her journey—a happiness, rushing, ardent, soft: a beating within her breast as of the beating of wings. At Calais she passed through the Customs quickly—her baggage was marked for examination at Brussels—and she entered the *rapide* quite untroubled by the strangeness of the scene or the difficulty of the language. It was all made so easy for her by that divine hand. The train started; again the wheels began their triumphant song. A quick excitement stirred in her, not at the novelty of the landscape: the flat grey country with its long white roads and lines of poplars passed before her like a dream: but at the prospect of her journey's end. An elation it was almost, a vivid thirsting eagerness. And to think that nine months ago she had thought her life ended. She almost laughed—laughed aloud. Nothing in that life of hers—and it all flashed before her like the fleeting landscape—had ever been like this. How could it be so? Her affections for her husband and for her son—how could those equal this present love for Jesus? And it was, in truth, to give herself to Jesus that she was in this train. Rushing nearer and nearer to Him.

At Tournai her flimsy ticket, now a fragment, was clipped again. Later she ate the sandwiches she had brought from the hotel. An Englishwoman seated opposite began a desultory conversation. Lucy made answer, smiling even at the other's remarks; but her manner, though agreeable, was detached. How could it be otherwise? They ran through Lille, Baisieux, and Blandain. Did she feel tired? Her back might ache a little; perhaps her eyes were hot and gritty; but, her spirit alert, she was hardly conscious of fatigue. She was aware always of that increasing sensation of approach, and at length, as the level rays of the sun pierced the umbered haze and slanted over a tumbled chaos of roofs and spires, the train slowed and entered the station. She was in Brussels.

At once she stepped out upon the platform, where for a moment she stood, splitting the moving stream of people by her immobility. Then suddenly her eyes lit up; she observed two nuns standing close to the barrier, and they, apparently, though how she knew not, observed her. She moved; so, too, did they; intuitively a flash of recognition passed with arrow swiftness between them; they advanced and met each other. Oh, happy—oh, thrilling encounter, preordained from her nativity.

" You are from England? " said the shorter of the two nuns, smiling and nodding her head. She spoke admirable English— another example, on top of this well-timed meeting, of the beneficent encouraging providence.

" Very soon," said the other nun also in English, but this time defectively and, with difficulty, by an accompanying inclination of her head, she indicated her meaning—that the train was up to time.

" It was good of you to meet me," murmured Lucy. If she had entertained vaguely some misgivings as to her arrival unaccompanied in this foreign city, now she deplored them by her gratitude.

" It is nothing," said the first; " we were so instructed." She paused, then, by way of introduction, she indicated her companion. " Bonne Mère Marie Emmanuel, Mistress of *Novitiat*; and I—I am Sister Joséphine, Mistress of *Postulat.*"

Lucy smiled warmly in return.

" You speak English so well."

" It is nothing," said Sister Joséphine again. " We have some houses in England. Mère Générale speaks also very well."

" But we must not remain," broke in Mère Marie Emmanuel restively.

" No, no, we must not remain," agreed Sister Joséphine at once. " There is the baggage." She turned, rather consciously, and led the way to the *douane*. Here, whilst her truñk was being brought forward, Lucy had a moment to inspect the two nuns.

They wore the long dark outdoor cloak which, enveloping the habit, concealed the entire figure, and each wore, too, upon her head, the white casque and bandeau surmounted by the black veil of the Order. But here the resemblance ceased.

Sister Joséphine was of medium height, with a dull, muddy complexion, enlarged pores, a blunt nose, small green eyes, mobile, talking eyebrows, and a cheerful, alert, childish manner. Vaguely that manner seemed familiar to Lucy, but where she had met it she could not at the moment recollect.

Bonne Mère Marie Emmanuel, Mistress of Novices, was pale, tall, severe, blue-eyed, with thin, very dry lips, sharp canine teeth which declared themselves prominently on the rare occasions when she smiled, and a bearing so erect and impersonal as to be almost exalted. Towards her Sister Joséphine manifested seemingly an open and obsequious respect, not so much from any difference in rank, as from that deference—the unconscious tribute which a weaker nature pays to one stronger than itself.

Just now Joséphine was moving her hands and speaking very rapidly in French to the Officer of Customs, who, listening attentively, bowed and bowed again with great respect, and finally lifted his peaked cap stiffly with that same air of deference. Thereafter he made intricate scrawls with blue chalk on the unopened trunk, then yelled suddenly: " *Porteur !* "

In a moment a blue-bloused porter appeared and shouldered the case.

" It is very agreeable," said Joséphine, turning with an expression of great satisfaction. She spoke rapidly, volubly, yet deferentially to her companion, and as the three went down the platform she remarked to Lucy:

" The father of our Sister Claire. He is high—very high in the *douane*." She indicated a sublime altitude. " Our religious coming to Sentiens pay no duty. Truly, it is a great privilege."

They went out of the station into a large open square, and immediately entered a waiting cab. The porter was dismissed with a small white coin and a stiff bow from Marie Emmanuel; the door snapped shut; then the cab rolled off over the cobbles. Steadying herself against the swinging motion, Lucy kept her eyes down; from the opposite seat she felt the two nuns studying her with a naïve curiosity.

" You are fatigued ? " said Sister Joséphine suddenly. She was the talkative one.

" No, no," replied Lucy, looking up quickly. Such a sign of weakness she would not so early or so easily admit. " The crossing was very quiet." Unconsciously she found herself imitating the other's phraseology.

" The waves derange me also," said Sister Joséphine agreeably.

" That—it is terminated," remarked Marie Emmanuel abruptly. There was a short silence, then in low tones the two began to talk to each other in French.

Lucy had a warm impulse of friendliness towards those two women with whom she felt she would now be associated, but she had no wish to interrupt their conversation; and so she turned her eyes out of the small window of the dark closed cab. It was an animated street which they discovered, filled by open carriages and little trolley trams that seemed to hurtle themselves along with a gay velocity. Rows of cafés lined the pavements: she read the names—Café du Pays, Café Belgique, Café du Postillon: dozens of cafés, with men and women seated outside at little round tables. The people were not animated, but sat with a placid and inanimate content. Their drinks were before them on the glass-topped tables, but never did they seem to drink. They merely sat, and gazed, and took the air.

At length the cab turned out of the main street and ascended a hill, past the vague shapes of statues, a fountain, another square, a large edifice—was it a palace?—then into a quieter quarter, where long dark houses with iron grilles and lattice shutters stood silently, relieved by an occasional shop. What curious names: *Epicerie—Boulanger—Robes—Charcutier*—these were the words above the doors. Truly she was in a strange land.

Then on, across a narrow canal into the suburbs where the houses were detached: little cut-off houses with bright ornamental façades: on past some hoardings into a more open countryside. Here they

388

skirted suddenly a wood which, reaching away vaguely into the
gathering blackness, seemed large and tenebrous as a forest.

" *Forêt du Sentiens*," said Sister Joséphine. " We are nearly there";
and, withdrawing her hand from her cloak, she pointed towards
the summit of a gentle elevation upon the left. Lucy's eyes strained
through the narrow window. Against the dull opacity of the darkening sky she saw dimly the darker outlines of a building which lay
with outflung wings like a great bat cowering upon the hill. Her heart
leaped and beat rapidly. She was no longer *en route*; she was there—
at the end of her journey. As the cab crunched into the gravel drive
she felt a trembling suffuse her like a thrill of mingled hope and joy.
At last—at last she was there!

V

THE convent of Sentiens, mother house of the foundation, which
in the distance seemed to cower like a bat, had actually the appropriate form of a cross. The head of the cross, which fronted closely
the Rue de Camboix, from behind a high wrought-iron fence interwoven with clematis, was made up of the hall, " the parlours," with,
above, a few bedrooms designed for the occasional reception of guests
—all cheerful and open, exposing a pleasant creeper-grown façade
towards the quiet roadway. On either side of this entrance two arms
reached out behind high walls: the left holding the refectory, the
workroom, and the cells of the professed religious, together with a
narrow detached strip, the *Postulat*, set aside, as its name implied,
for the enclosure of postulants and—superimposed almost like an
afterthought—a long, low attic for the housing of the lay sisters;
the right arm, duplicate of the left in size, enclosing the cells, refectory, and workroom of the novices. Finally, receding at right angles
to those wings—occupying the narrow body of the cross—and
rearing its narrow spire far beyond the highest branches of an
adjacent copper beech, stood the church.

Separating, yet in a fashion uniting, these four main divisions of
the building, was a central stone-flagged courtyard with, in its
middle, a statue of St. Joseph, which directed a placid and perpetual
gaze through the windows of the convent kitchen immediately in
front. And, stretching down and backwards from the whole, surrounding the church but reaching far beyond it, was the garden—
a large, exquisite garden laid out in alleys and avenues by an arrangement of its trees. Fruit-trees these were in the main, plum and
cherry and peach, but there were others—lime and larch, privet and

laurel, with trailing roses woven and shaped around the arbours which graced the dazzling white stone walks.

A great high wall ran round the entire territory, and, as if this were not enough, nature in all its redundance had heaped up a further barricade—the forest of Sentiens which, approaching actually to the wall, supported it with a gloomy and impassable barrier. Thus the whole community was girded like a citadel—a fortress with a solitary but somewhat complicated means of access. To enter the citadel it was necessary to pull the rope-bell, to wait, to be inspected through the sliding grille, to be admitted by the slow lay sister who kept the porch, to enter the hall, and then, by virtue of the special key which opened the intervening doors, to traverse the chain of parlours. Then only did one stand upon the threshold of the cloister.

And now it was in one of those front parlours that Lucy sat—waiting. She was alone—Sister Joséphine, with Mother Marie Emmanuel, had gone to inform the Superior of her arrival—and as she waited her eyes travelled slowly round the small room. It was bare—a table covered with oilcloth, some hard chairs ranged with meticulous exactitude, a yellow porcelain stove with an angled iron funnel, a single picture: Jesus walking on the waters; that made up the complement of furnishings. But the bareness of the chamber was as nothing before its terrific and arresting cleanliness: the wooden floor shone like a mirror; the old stove gleamed with a dull lustre and its funnel glistened like a new top-hat; the table, the chairs, the very handle of the door, all were furbished with amazing solicitude. There had been a time when Lucy prided herself upon the spotless condition of her home, but never—no, never—had it been so utterly immaculate as this.

She was still marvelling when the door opened and an elderly woman came impressively into the room, followed by Joséphine and Marie Emmanuel. She was tall, stoutish, and voluminous from the fullness of her habit. Her face was white and full, her head thrust forwards, her brown, myopic eyes, reduced by thick steel spectacles to the size of beads, had a peering intensity, and her lower teeth, projecting and very yellow, gave to her a curious carping look, as though perpetually she rebuked the universe. Still, she made a commanding figure; and now she advanced towards Lucy, stretching out both her hands.

" Welcome ! " said she, with a peculiar gracious gravity.

Lucy rose; instinctively she knew herself to be in the presence of the Bonne Mère Générale, and, the focus of three frankly observant glances, she surrendered her hands. There was a pause.

" You are not young," continued Bonne Mère Générale, now so close to Lucy that each word was clothed with a faint odour from her teeth, " but the ways of God are wonderful with a soul. The worker entering the vineyard at the eleventh hour. Do you comprehend? It is God's blessing you have come." She was silent, then with a quick change of subject demanded:

" Are you fatigued? "

" No, mother." She knew this, instinctively, to be the form of her reply.

" Have you need of refreshment? "

" No, mother."

The Superior drew back, well satisfied, and let her chin fall on to her bosom.

" You have arrived at a good moment. Later to-night we could not have received you. You must have slept here—above the parlours. But now we are prepared. We shall receive you before prayers. You have not much time for recollection—still, it is favourable."

As she turned away, her gaze fell upon the two sisters, who immediately lowered their eyes respectfully.

" Sister Joséphine is your guardian now," she declared pleasantly, " for some weeks, perhaps—then after, in your novitiate, you must obey Bonne Mère Marie Emmanuel."

She nodded slowly, and swept towards the door, with the firmness of absolute autocracy; as she went out of the room, she said finally, without turning her head:

" Sister Joséphine has told me; I am pleased that your baggage has passed the *douane* without payment. It is for you a good omen."

The door closed behind her. For a moment no one spoke—as if the agitated atmosphere must first be permitted to subside after the passage of that august presence—then Sister Joséphine said pleasantly, as though addressing a child:

" Come—we will prepare you "; and, taking Lucy by the arm, she unlocked the door and led her into another smaller parlour. Sister Marie Emmanuel accompanied them in silence: it was a strict precept of the Rule that no religious remain alone with one not so professed—always there must be two: and again they stood waiting, until in a moment an old lay sister entered, bearing in her knotted hands some black net veils.

Whilst Lucy sat upright, with a heightened colour, there was quite a fuss over the choosing and the fitting of the veil. It was of a cheap stiff material—something of the fashion worn in the churches by peasant women of Italy—but its correct adjustment upon her hair was a matter of delicacy. She must wear it always in church, they told her, and she was given a little cardboard box in which, at all other times, she must keep it neatly folded.

Suddenly there came the loud pealing of a bell, and at this she was hurriedly approved. The lay sister took up the discarded veils, and at once disappeared.

" Rise! " said Sister Joséphine. Lucy got up. She felt suddenly perturbed.

" What must I do? " she enquired nervously.

" It is nothing," returned the other indulgently. " So simple for the *Postulat*—so different from the clothing. You will kneel at the *prie-dieu*, and we will sing the *Magnificat*—quite beautiful. Yes, it is easy for you."

She raised her finger encouragingly, then once more she took Lucy's arm, and, again accompanied by Marie Emmanuel—she it was who this time used her key—they went out of the room. Along another polished corridor they walked, and outside a double door they paused.

" It is the church," said Sister Joséphine impressively, conveying that stiff finger to her lips, which still smiled gently. She lowered her finger; they entered, at the back of the church. Lucy slowly raised her eyes, which, from her tiredness and a strange agitation, had been downcast at that moment. Then slowly those eyes became no longer perplexed, but filled instead with a light of tenderness. Her journey, the strangeness of the place, the formalities of " the parlours "—all were instantly forgotten. The beauty of the church was extreme. The interior was long and lofty, the walls lined by a darkly mellowed wood, the vaulted ceiling—painted and spangled like a distant sky—now almost invisible. Lit only by the candles on the altar, and a candle on either side of a *prie-dieu*, which was placed before the altar rail, the church seemed filled by a brooding and mysterious tranquillity.

The small altar was of white marble. It stood in a semicircle made by five stained-glass windows, now lifeless in the darkness, and seemed, surmounted by a large crucifix, to stand much higher than the five shallow marble steps which raised it from the level of the floor. The candles flickered and shed a soft radiance on the brass doors of the tabernacle, and on the pale masses of flowers which drooped submissively on either side. Against the walls, the Stations of the Cross showed vaguely, and dim, too, were the black figures of the nuns, kneeling in that silence, which is felt nowhere so intensely as in a convent church, a stillness which now flooded Lucy's heart with a delicious feeling of calm and joy.

At a sign she advanced, knelt upon the *prie-dieu*, striving to recollect herself and to say some prayer. But she could not. All her mind was filled by the rushing thought that at last she was here, amongst this community of holy women—she who had lived all her life in the world, and lived it so unworthily. Now she was offering herself, offering the remnant of that worthless existence, to her

Creator. What peace was here in this exquisite house of God, pity and mercy and peace for her! Stinging tears flowed into her eyes.

Then, as she knelt, there came suddenly the low note of the organ, which swelled slowly into a glorious rhapsody of sound. Louder and louder! The choir of voices began to sing: " *Veni Creator Spiritus.*" Dumbly she listened, her throat swelling. Then there came the *Magnificat*:

> " *Magnificat anima mea Dominum :*
> *Et exsultavit spiritus meus in Deo salutari meo.*"

They were singing for her—to welcome her in all her unworthiness Something was choking her—her soul magnifying the Lord, her spirit rejoicing in God her Saviour—within her breast the tearing rush of emotion was unbearable; tears flowed silently down her cheeks. Why had she been so blind? There was one thing in life: the love of God. She struck her breast fiercely: " God be merciful to me, a sinner. Sweet Jesus, let me love Thee more and more."

They were singing the *Te Deum*—

> " *Te Deum laudamus : te Dominum confitemur.*"

And in her own heart there was now an answering hymn of thanksgiving. God had accepted her. Her mind, fixed upon the future, was filled with an intensity of resolution. Lifted higher and higher she was by her exaltation. How easy it would be here to forget all the world and its littleness, to give herself, surrender herself, to Jesus. Jesus was here for her to love for ever.

The singing ended and silence fell—the silence of meditation. Then in a moment she felt a touch upon her arm. She looked up, and rose. With her head again lowered, she walked out of the church into the cloister.

Now, by virtue of her acceptance, and this simple ceremony, she was within the enclosure. It was the first step. She stood passive, whilst the same lay sister removed her veil and tied on the black net bonnet which she now must wear.

" You will not wait for prayers to-night," said Sister Joséphine authoritatively; " clearly you are too fatigued."

She led the way to a varnished door, above which was painted the word " *Postulat,*" and, throwing it open, disclosed a scrubbed wooden staircase.

They ascended this staircase in silence, and turned along a narrow passage broken by a row of doors. Around them was a quietude and that curious convent odour: a closed, warm odour, unique, indescribable. Their footsteps echoed quietly on the bare boards. Then Sister

Joséphine opened the second last door. Inside it was dark, but, fumbling for matches, within the small black cavern she lit a candle and revealed the tiny, bare room which contained solely a mattress, a small armoire bearing an ewer, and upon the wall a large crucifix.

" It is the cell," she said. " As *postulante* you are permitted a candle—one for the week. Not, however, when you are a novice. To be in bed by nine with candle extinguished—that is the rule. And the rule must be obeyed."

The last phrase fell from her lips like a solemn, oft-repeated canticle; she looked at Lucy compliantly.

" As I have explained, to-night you are fatigued. But to-morrow you will begin to learn." A shadow of a smile wavered over her flat features. She went to the door. " Blessed be God," she said. It was her good night. And Lucy answered, as she had been directed: " For ever."

The door closed gently. She was alone. Alone within her cell. So quickly had her desire been achieved that scarcely could she realise the actuality of her position. Her head throbbed painfully with her fatigue and the violence of the emotion which had traversed her. Yes, she felt utterly worn out; and, from habit, for a swift, ridiculous second her mind flew to the consideration of the solace of a cup of tea; that would have restored her. But the thought lingered only for an instant. What absurdity! She smiled faintly, went to the small window, and opened it. Immediately the rush of the sweet night air blew gratefully into her hot face. Sweet with the scents of earth and forest it was, fresh with the cool dampness of the dew. She stood for a moment gazing out into the absolute darkness, whilst behind her the flame of the candle wavered and threw strange gigantic shapes against the wall. Then, suddenly, out of the blackness, from that unseen forest beyond, came a pure and exquisite sound: a note of beauty, so unexpected, so sublime and passionate, that it seemed to spring from some source not of this earth. Spellbound she listened, while the liquid notes rose and fell in a joyous rapture, a rapture filled with some quality which was wild and free.

Lovely, oh, how lovely it was, this sudden trilling ecstasy! It was the song of the nightingale. And it came to her like the final recognition of her happiness.

With a full heart she turned from the window, undressed quickly, and got into bed. Yes, there was shelter here and abundant peace! Before she blew out the candle, the last object upon which her eyes rested was the crucifix upon the opposite wall.

VI

At half-past four in the morning the bell of the convent rang loudly. Lucy awoke with a start. It was still dark; heavy with the darkness of night; and her head was heavy, too, filled by the troubled unrealities of her sleep and the clanging resonance of that bell. Where was she? Her mind fumbled. She could not understand. Then across the haze of her perplexity came a knocking upon the door, and the words uttered insistently: " Blessed be God! Blessed be God!" Instantly she made answer: " For ever!" Then, listening, she heard the sound of footsteps go down the corridor, another knock, again the salutation : " Blessed be God " and again the answer: " For ever!"

What was she thinking of? To rise immediately, without a moment of reflection, was the first act of self-denial the day contained. This much she knew. And here she was, at the commencement of her postulation, disobedient to the first mandate of the rule! Abruptly she sprang up from the mattress and lit her candle. To wash and clothe herself in her new dress and bonnet was the work of a few moments. No mirror was in the room, and it was, perhaps, as well, for she made a queer outlandish figure in that long black gown and cap. Then there was the bed to make, the dirty water to empty out, the basin to make dry and cleanse, the cell to be put in a state of the most perfect tidiness. This she accomplished diligently.

At quarter-past five the bell rang again—this she knew was for the *Angelus*—and immediately thereafter she heard the sound of opening doors and the tramp of feet along the corridor. Emerging from her cell and following instinctively the last dark form now disappearing down the dim passage, she descended the stair and entered the dim church, where already the community had assembled. A half-light vaguely filled the church, making the still, kneeling forms like rows of shadows, but she made out her place, which was in the front seat amongst the other postulants. Thither she advanced, and there at once knelt down.

Instinctively she held herself erect, and pressed her face into her palms. The silence of the meditation which followed the morning prayers was like the hush within a sepulchre. No one moved; the stillness was absolute. Then, into this crepuscular dimness, came slowly the first faint crayons of the dawn—thin streaks of colour traced downwards from the stained windows of the apse. The silence, too, was pierced by the sounds of the breaking day: the flutings of many birds from the trees which encompassed the church.

Kneeling there, she had a sudden surge almost of giddiness in answer to the curious colours of the dawn: strangely buoyant, she felt her mind enlightened, her heart uplifted with a high expectancy.

Fervently she prayed for the grace to become as those saintly souls around her.

At half-past six the bell rang again, and the Mass began, said by a small, bent priest, a very aged man, tremulous of hand and slow of foot, with a thin piping voice which creaked in its upper octaves. The Mass from necessity was unhurried, and it was followed by the thanksgiving; then, at eight, the community arose in silence, and passed out of the church for breakfast.

Clinging to her own kind, Lucy re-entered the *Postulat*, and, with the other postulants, of whom there were five, followed Sister Joséphine to the refectory. It was a narrow room, with a long wooden table flanked on either side by benches—a bare and serious room; but already upon the table stood the breakfast—seven meticulously appointed bowls holding a dark liquid, and beside each bowl, disposed with equal exactitude, a portion of bread. There was a significant pause; then, after the grace had been said, Sister Joséphine seated herself at the head of the table, and on either side of her the postulants ranged themselves.

Lucy sat down in the vacant place, and, with the others, began the meal in silence. She was faint from the long and unaccustomed fast, yet she seemed, strangely, to have little appetite. The dark liquid in the bowl was not coffee, but a form of coffee substitute, unredeemed by any trace of sugar, and it had an acrid bitterness. Nor was the wedge of loaf bread as she had known it; dry, coarse, and sulphurous, it had substance but no savour. Still, she knew the sacrifices demanded of her, and was ardently prepared to make them. Ardently, therefore, she ground her way through the meal, taking her conduct from the others: keeping her eyes downwards, maintaining an unbroken silence.

At quarter-past eight the repast was over, and immediately everyone rose.

" You will wait," whispered Sister Joséphine to Lucy as the others filed out of the room; when they had gone, she added in a louder tone: " It is time now to acquire the duties."

Lucy looked up agreeably.

" I have done my room," she murmured to the other.

Sister Joséphine frowned.

" No, no—not like that," she said in a grieved voice. " Not ' my ' —never ' my.' That is not your cell. You have it only by the charity of the Order and the goodness of God. Nothing is to you. Everything is ' ours.' You must say always ' our cell.' "

Lucy flushed.

" I did not understand, sister," she explained in a low voice.

" Do not reply ! " exclaimed Joséphine quickly. " Except for you to demand a question, silence always is the rule. And the rule must be obeyed." She paused, and mildly preened herself. " Moreover, you must address your superior with all reverence. Your superior is above you by God. She must be to you like God. Understand always that lowliness must be acquired. It is the first thing."

Lucy bit her lip and looked down. She had been perfectly innocent of all wrong—her remark so simple, so entirely devoid of harm!

But Sister Joséphine went on, her manner free of all rancour, yet filled with an almost childish insistence.

" To know how to pray is not everything, and religious life is not to spend hours before the tabernacle," she remonstrated. " There are lessons of humility to be acquired. Remember what our blessed Lord said: ' You must become as a little child ! ' Yes, remember."

Lucy listened obediently, restraining the impulse which had so suddenly risen within her to exclaim: " I meant no harm ! " Submissively she made no sound; and when Sister Joséphine, with a last survey, drew out her key and led the way out of the refectory, she followed with lowered head. They traversed the corridor to its end, and, passing through two doors which Sister Joséphine unlocked, paused before some cupboards.

" Attend now, Lucy," said the mistress indulgently. " You are the handmaid of the Lord, and you must be agreeable to do the lowliest tasks. First, then, you will start to brush and to clean the *petit pays.*"

To brush and to clean ? Still on edge, Lucy started. Surely she was mistaken ? She had not come here to enact the part of servant: they had lay sisters, the peasant women of the country, who willingly attended to this class of work. When she could not pray she would sew, embroider, stitch the vestments to be used in the service of God: but this, surely——!

" Pick up the brush and the tin and the sand," said the mistress, calmly unlocking and opening the cupboard door, " and come quickly. Already we have delayed."

Lucy's eye clouded confusedly. The brush and the tin and the sand ! Yes, she had stooped and picked them up; they were in her hands now, and she was following Sister Joséphine to the unknown territory of the *petit pays*. What, she thought perplexedly, was this *petit pays* ?

Suddenly she flushed again—deeply and painfully—as the sister, arrested before a certain place, plainly indicated this to be the region of her duties. The *petit pays*. It was the euphemistic designation for the privies of the *Postulat* !

" You see," said the mistress pleasantly, " you will clean and clean. Moisten the sand—so; and sprinkle—so; then rub carefully. No dust to be left, and no sand either. It is not agreeable. Nothing forgotten or left lying about."

Stupidly, Lucy stared at the scene of her future labours; then, with a face still suffused by colour, she looked up for permission to speak.

" Yes ? " said the mistress.

" I must do this ? " said Lucy, in a low voice.

" You are so directed," returned the other complacently. " It is the will of God." Then she smiled her naïve and strangely empty smile, turned, and, with hands folded inside her sleeves, swept down the corridor.

" The will of God ! " Lucy stood quite still; then slowly she went down on her knees and began to clean out the closets: moistening the sand—so; and sprinkling it—so; and cleansing with slow and careful strokes. Had she not already laboured sufficiently in her life at undignified and menial tasks ? And this to her—her spirit exalted, burning with the love of God—was not merely menial; it was a degradation unutterable.

For a moment she worked on with a face curiously stiff; then, suddenly, a long sigh broke from her lips. She was wrong! Yes, of course she was wrong! She must do as she was instructed, submit unquestioningly to the rule. She did not see clearly now, but later she would understand. She was tired, confused by the strangeness of it all. But she had courage—courage and determination. " Blessed be Jesus! Blessed be His most Sacred Heart! "; then into herself she began the litany.

In silence she continued the task, and with an aching back worked on until noon. Then the bell which now controlled her rang out once more. She rose stiffly from her knees at the moment when Sister Joséphine appeared.

" You have finished? " enquired the sister pleasantly; it was a great concession for her to speak at all.

" Yes," answered Lucy with extreme submission.

Joséphine looked round, and as she gazed her small green eyes lost their amiability and clouded with displeasure.

" It is not well done," she said abruptly; " I am not pleased."

Lucy opened her lips to reply; then closed them firmly.

" Regard this here," continued the sister, bending down sharply, and pointing to a few adherent grains of the moist sand, which had concealed themselves in a crevice of the wooden skirting. " It is not perfect—and after what I have remarked! " She picked out the sand with her finger-nail, and rose, holding it up like something obscene. Then, as she cast it finally into a convenient oblivion, she declared emphatically: " The good God will not love you for that. Even if I am not here to observe, His eye is always upon you. Enough—you will understand again." And she turned away.

A grain of sand left unwittingly in a crack. To be rebuked for that . Was she dreaming?

Dumbly Lucy followed Sister Joséphine into the refectory, and stood waiting at the appointed place. Already the other postulants were there—returned from whatsoever their tasks might have been; but they neither spoke nor looked at her; and so her eyes fell downward too.

Grace over, they seated themselves; then a lay sister brought in a long enamelled platter, upon which reposed seven raw pickled herrings.

Sister Joséphine took the largest—an act of sacrifice, since they were so unpalatable—then one was given to each postulant, sent down on a coarse stoneware plate, with a portion of bread of the same size and quality as that served at breakfast. Lucy looked at the herring, lying limply in its own brine, soft and phosphorescent, so raw and oily that instantly it repelled her. She was hungry, but her gorge rose at the sight. This was not the sort of food she had been used to; nor, indeed, though she had prepared herself to face a hard and simple fare, the kind she had anticipated. Covertly, she observed that the others had begun to eat, and slowly, with an inward shudder, she took up her knife and fork. It was rank, repulsive—she could hardly tolerate it upon her tongue. To her, the sight, even, of the sodden flesh, sprayed, when suddenly she pierced the roe, by a milky exudate, was nauseating. Yet she forced herself to swallow it. If the others could eat it, then so, too, could she.

Looking up suddenly, Joséphine caught her eye, and, permitting herself to violate the silence, she observed encouragingly:

" It is good; yes. When old Sister Adrienne has the gall, she demands always a pickled herring."

No sound, but rather a thrill of appreciation, ran through the other postulants, who, despite their air of introspection, hung, nevertheless, upon the lightest gesture of the mistress. And now each vied with her neighbour, or so it seemed to Lucy, in the effort to win the appreciation of Joséphine, until at length upon each plate only the backbone of the fish remained, so scraped and polished that it glistened. At this the platter was once more slowly passed around the table, and the skeletons departed thereon; then each, revealing the double purpose of the bread, rubbed her plate until it shone.

After a pause, the plates so cleansed were handed to the head of the table, and each received a sufficient portion of bread pudding, brought silently by the same lay sister. Yet, in spite of the burnishing, the plate retained its odour—to eat that pudding was to taste again the acridity of the herring.

The pudding finished—and it was forbidden to ask for more—the plates were polished as before, and the last scrap of bread consumed. There came a pause; Sister Joséphine looked round and rose. Grace once more; then dinner was over.

With the mistress at the head, they filed in single order to the church, where a chapter from the *Imitation* was read aloud; then they filed out of the church into the garden—not the vast open sweep of garden, but a small, separate enclosure reserved exclusively to themselves. A deeper hush hung for a moment in the air, then Joséphine raised her finger, and instantly the veil of silence was rent: six voices speaking at once—bursting with the suppression of long hours. " *Deo gratias* " was the cry—and it came like a high hurrah—it was the recreation!

Lucy started at this sudden magpie chatter, but Joséphine smiled at her reassuringly.

" Come," she said after a moment, " it is permitted. Now you shall make friends." She turned towards the five others who, ranged in a little group, ceased the clacking of their tongues to gaze at Lucy ingenuously.

" Marguerite—Emilie—Thérèse," said the mistress, enunciating clearly and indicating the nearest three. Young women they were, all of medium height, and to Lucy of a strangely similar appearance —each with dark hair, darker eyes, and a pleasant sallow face now parted in a smile of greeting. " They are cousins, these, of a good Brussels family," remarked the sister, pursing her lips. " And here " —she pointed to the other two—" Gabrielle and Wilhelmine."

Gabrielle—tall, superior—inclined her head, and murmured a word in greeting, but Wilhelmine—a stolid, thick-set woman, with a peasant's face—stood squatly, with an open mouth, gazing obtusely.

" Wilhelmine is deaf, but with a good *dot*," said Joséphine gaily; " a *Flamande* from Steinach. Recently from her father's farm she has come—many, many cows, and cream." She nodded her head towards the other's bulk: " Plenty cream—yes, it is significant."

" *Réclame !* " said Thérèse, roguishly—she had caught the sister's gesture; " *une bonne affiche pour la ferme.*" And at the words there was a sudden bubbling of laughter.

The *Flamande* blinked her deep-set eyes, threw out her stubby chin, and grinned.

" I hear! " she bellowed, in her deep voice. " But take care! I am not yet slaughtered."

It was a great *divertissement*, which caused a fresh burst of hilarity, in which Joséphine herself joined. Then the group pressed round Lucy, smiling, chattering—overwhelming her with their voluble and incomprehensible prattle. However, in a moment she had relief, for Sister Joséphine began to speak, and, judging by her quick and fluent gestures, it seemed an animated description of some adventure. Quite a thrilling adventure it appeared. From time to time eyes were turned on Lucy, heads nodded, little murmurs of approval emitted. The word " *douane* " was repeated, and again repeated; then suddenly it dawned on her that Joséphine was relating her triumph at the Customs. The incident of that poor battered trunk passing the *douane* without fee was moving the entire convent to excitement, and a thrilling gratification.

" Truly it is *gentil*," said Emilie, " truly *gentil* of the father of Sister Claire."

Following the story there was a pause, but it was a short one; irrelevantly, Wilhelmine gave her deep laugh, and tossed her head like a frisky cow.

" I must run," she said playfully. " Oh! how I must run! "

Swinging round with another laugh, she began to run down the path towards the arbour, kicking up her heels and sawing her arms from side to side.

" Catch her up! " cried out Joséphine gaily. " Catch her for market! "

There was another ripple of laughter, a little chorus of badinage; then, with quite a girlish frolic of innocence, Thérèse, Emilie, Marguerite, followed more languidly by Gabrielle, started off in pursuit of the stout *Flamande*. With a lingering smile, the mistress followed their lively gambols; then she turned to Lucy.

" It is good for the heart to be gay," she declared brightly. " To be as the little children—that is how we must be." Here she broke off, observing Lucy's numb and wondering face. " You must not be too grave, too silent here," she remonstrated, and, indicating the furrow on Lucy's forehead, she added: " That must be wiped out. A good religious is always joyous. At the recreation one must laugh! Remember—here we are the little children of Jesus."

" It is difficult to laugh to order," said Lucy doubtfully, her eyes puckered by a strange perplexity; she had come here to pray and not to laugh—" especially," she added with great diffidence, " especially to laugh at nothing."

" No, no! " cried out Joséphine. " You must not indulge. You must do against yourself." Then suddenly she pressed her palms together, and threw up her eyes in a caricature of extreme piety. " This does not make a good religious! "

Lucy coloured, and there was a silence, broken occasionally by little trills of laughter from outside the arbour.

The sister observed her curiously; then she said kindly:

" In time you will become as they. It will be more easy when you can converse. And look—now I will give you something precious." She smiled, and withdrew her hand with slow solemnity from the pocket of her habit. " Here is the key of Paradise." It was, indeed, a key, attached to a small leather thong on which was stamped the word *Postulat*. " All postulants have this," explained Joséphine more seriously, " for all doors are locked. Now, when you make your duties, you can unlock yourself these doors. It is always in the left pocket. You comprehend? "

" Yes, sister "; and Lucy accepted the key.

But did she comprehend? Where had she seen a key like this before? She felt stupid, strangely confused. To force herself to smile, to keep always the " key in the left pocket," to serve God by picking a grain of sand from a crack in the floor of a water-closet—was this what she had expected? When she had surrendered herself so utterly to God, should not the pettiness of life be forgotten, abandoned, before the majesty of that sublime passion? Quickly she drew herself up, suppressing those unjust and quite unwarrantable thoughts. She would learn. Later she would understand.

The bell rang for the end of the recreation, and at its first note instantly those merry-making voices were stilled. Ranging themselves seriously once more in a long line, they re-entered the *Postulat* for spiritual reading.

The afternoon passed in slow progressive harmony: the bell methodical, the obedience implicit. To sit down and to rise up to enter the church and to leave it; to kneel for prayer, and then to cease to kneel; to meditate, then not to meditate—during the long, still hours these quiet actions were performed like a ritual. And ardently she set herself to follow that ritual. Always since her conversion she had liked long periods of solitude in which to develop that mysterious sense of her relationship to God. But now she would make the community life her own. For the love of God she would do it.

At Benediction the blaze of candles upon the altar glittered towards her—white tongues of flame—and amongst this glitter, held by the gilded monstrance, was the source of all her comfort—her consolation—a vision too shining to be endured. Here she felt assuagement come to her. Jesus was here for her—the Christ who had been crucified for her. With lowered head she abased herself. Who was she, indeed, to have dared for a moment criticise the rule? At peace, she came out of the church.

She swallowed her supper, a mess of unsweetened semolina, like an eager acceptance of a penance. No sacrifice was too great.

" I must remind you," whispered Joséphine lightly, as they went up the stairs after night prayers, " after church your veil—it was not neatly folded in its little box."

But to-morrow it would be folded—no sacrifice was too great.

At half-past eight she was in her cell—alone. A long sigh escaped her, a sigh filled with a thrill of relief. To have accomplished this day successfully, to have endured its strangeness and its tribulation, induced a reaction of overwhelming ease. It was all so new to her and so difficult, and the day itself had been interminable. Yes, she acknowledged now the difficulties; but she would overcome them. Never in her life had she admitted defeat. She would not do so now. She could hold on. For a moment she gazed out of her window into the hidden darkness: it was raining gently, and the soft dampness touched her cheek, and for that moment she was uplifted, so fresh and free it seemed beyond—outside. Then she undressed wearily and got into bed. In the pallor of her face her eyes looked big and dark. She blew out the candle, and lay down.

To-night there was no song from the nightingale, but, with a regular rise and fall, through the thin wall of the adjoining cell came the slow stertor of Wilhelmine's snoring.

VII

" AND when the holy Benedict," read out Emilie gently, " was praying in his cell, Satan appeared to him in horrible form and mockingly told him that he was going to visit his children at their work. The holy man was alarmed at this intelligence, and immediately sent an angel to warn the brothers to be upon their guard. No sooner, however, had the angel arrived upon the scene than by the power of the devil the wall which they were building suddenly gave way, killing in its fall a young novice. The monks were greatly distressed, not only at the loss of their labour, but also at the loss of their brother. One of them ran quickly to tell Benedict, who calmly bade them bring the boy to his cell. But the youth was so mangled and crushed that there was no way of carrying him except by placing the pieces in a sack. In this manner they brought him to the saint, who laid the pieces on the mat where he was accustomed to prostrate himself in prayer. Then Benedict, having dismissed them all and locked the door, implored God not to let His enemy triumph. Suddenly a terrific clap of thunder rent the air; the pieces drew together, and the dead youth leaped up sound and——"

The even voice of Emilie ran on within the common-room of the novitiate, where, under the eye of Marie Emmanuel, some twenty novices were congregated for spiritual reading. Amongst those novices, seated upon the last of the unbacked benches which surrounded the lectern, was Lucy. Yes; her period of postulancy was over, her dress discarded for the habit and white veil, her foot now set within the enclosure of the novitiate—all this achieved, consummated by her recent clothing. A great change!—a change which at that ceremony she had eagerly embraced.

In the *Postulat* she had been, in her own thought, " neither the one thing nor the other ": a thought which had constantly sustained her through those few months of postulation. " This is not the religious life," she had inwardly insisted, forcing herself the while to conform to those usages which seemed so perversely in conflict with her devotion. It was all the shaping of a pattern; a preparation for that life which she had so determinedly embraced; this she had fully recognised. Yet there was no doubt—it had been a period of difficulty, filled by recurrent reminders of her ineptitude. The day on which she had forgotten to cleanse the remote corners of her dustpan with the little stick kept particularly for the purpose; that dreadful moment when she had entered the church without her veil; that occasion when, in the garden, straying inadvertently upon a walk reserved exclusively for the professed religious, she had been driven back by the agitated command: " Go away! Go away! It is forbidden! "—these were but a few of the blunders of her inexperience.

But now the *Postulat* lay behind her—now she had the habit, the veil, the discipline, the book of the holy Rule—now she was advanced upon the way to her ultimate profession!

" The angels," went on the tranquil voice of Emilie, " conducted Benedict on his way; and angels also came out to meet him: the guardian angels of the poor deluded inhabitants. With joy unbounded they implored the blessed saint to drive out the spirits of darkness——" Though, with a stumbling acquaintance of the French tongue, she could follow adequately the clearly spoken words, unconsciously Lucy's attention began to waver—not that she questioned the miracles of the good St. Benedict! She did believe! It was a miracle, that—like the miracle of the loaves and fishes, the walking on the waters, the raising of Jairus' daughter. Yet, despite herself, she was thinking of the *culpe*. As in the *Postulat*, there were usages here, usages to which she must gently yield and come gently to understand. The *culpe*! Always after this reading the *culpe* took place, and to-day, which was Friday, there would be, not simply the ordinary *culpe*, but the *chapitre de culpes*, the open avowal upon the knees of the accumulated transgressions of the past week.

The *culpe*! Of course it was necessary: part of the Rule which now she accepted as the word of God: yet strangely she could not contemplate its near approach without an inward discomposure. In the chapel that morning she had been distracted by this same thought, turned from her prayers by the consideration of what was so obviously constituted for her good. That was not reasonable: nor was there any hardship in the *culpe* to warrant this strange objection. It was easy; simple; absurdly simple: a mere declaration of the trivial violations of the Rule. Yet somehow the very simplicity of this open court—that it was which so confused her. No sense of frightful ordeal, but the abashed feeling of a child before authority, something which seemed subversive of all the high nobility of her belief. Abruptly she shook herself: why was she thinking like this— again? She frowned. She must not so easily submit to these distractions.

" Benedict's countenance shone with a heavenly light, and the peasants, seeing this, gathered round him and listened awestruck to his——"

Here the bell clanged, and at its first imperative note Emilie stopped dead in the middle of the sentence, as though stricken by a thunderbolt. That was admirable: implicit obedience to the Rule: and Marie Emmanuel, observant as ever, rose from her straight-backed chair with a faint approving inclination of her head. Already the docile Emilie stood high in her good graces.

With the movement of the mistress, immediately the others had arisen, and now in silence they knelt before the statue of the Sacred Heart which rested upon a varnished bracket beside the lectern.

The *Veni Creator Spiritus* was repeated aloud.

> " *Veni Creator Spiritus,*
> *Mentes tuorum visita :*
> *Imple superna gratia*
> *Quæ tu creasti pectora.*"

After the " Amen " there came a short pause for recollection, then the mistress stood up and, followed in single file by the others— who ranged themselves scrupulously in order of seniority—entered the adjoining room. Already this had been prepared: a single large chair placed imposingly in the middle of the floor, and surrounding it a wide semicircle of smaller seats grouping like satellites around a planet.

Marching directly towards her throne, Marie Emmanuel occupied it impressively, whilst the novices—each standing before her appointed place—awaited the signal to be seated. A moment passed whilst she sent her glance over their faces, then her speaking eye ceded this consent. There was a quiet rustle, then again silence; once more all attention was bound to that central figure; once more, too, Lucy felt within her that restive uneasiness which she so deplored. Observing Marie Emmanuel—now considering impassively a note-book containing the record of all faults discovered during the previous week—she had a quick impulse to remove her eyes.

She loved Marie Emmanuel—she must love her and respect her— these things were implicit in this house of God. And yet, new as she was to the novitiate, actually she had been harassed by a vague unrest. Surely it was impossible, this presentiment. Here all were sisters within the arms of Jesus; all of necessity bound by their common love under this common roof, and with her whole heart she desired to give and to receive that love.

Why, then, had she this strange intuition that Marie Emmanuel and she were not in sympathy? In the *Postulat*, Joséphine had smiled with her reproofs, but this other, so impersonal, so exalted, she did not smile. No; her pale eyes, which observed everything, were cold, her manner detached, free from all human feeling, her presence rigid with a glacial impassivity. The very fashion in which she set herself to order this unimportant court breathed of a high severity. She recognised her duty and would not stint its execution. If a serpent must be slain, she would slay it, then grind the mangled corpse into the dust.

Now, with a characteristic gesture of her fine hands—already Lucy knew that gesture well—she straightened her casque and let her gaze dwell upon the first novice. It was the moment of the commencement of the *culpe*. A deeper expectant hush hung upon the air: the eagerness of those who liked it; the recoil of those to whom it was disagreeable: a bated anticipation of this trifling interlude cutting the monotone of life.

" Commence," said Marie Emmanuel briefly.

Instantly the first novice plumped upon her knees, so that the floor re-echoed with a hollow note beneath the impact of her heavy frame. Cheerful and composed, she rattled off her rote:

" By holy obedience I make my *culpe* of all the faults I have committed against the Rule, particularly "—she drew a quick breath—" in lacking in the spirit of poverty by breaking a needle whilst sewing."

The mistress closed her eyes, and seemed to reflect.

" You will say three paters," she declared unemotionally. " And in the future be careful of your needle. Those needles, they cost the community very dear."

The first novice bowed her head complaisantly, and commenced the penance, whilst the next, a young Italian—Assunta was her name—fell upon her knees before the mistress and began, quickly, nervously:

" By holy obedience I make my *culpe* of all the faults I have committed against the Rule, particularly—particularly," she stammered, " particularly in lacking in religious modesty by walking too hurriedly along the corridors." There was a pause—an awkward pause; Marie Emmanuel slowly opened her pale yet piercing eyes.

" Have you nothing more to tell? "

" No, *bonne mère*," answered Assunta, blushing painfully. " I cannot think."

" Try, please, to recollect," came the frigid answer.

" I—I cannot recollect, *ma bonne mère*," stammered the other; quickly her flush faded, leaving her not swarthy, but suddenly pale, ridiculously pale and flinching. Marie Emmanuel raised her eyes dispassionately to the ceiling, making the silence suddenly oppressive.

" In your armoire," she exclaimed icily, " on examining it yesterday, I have discovered your two handkerchiefs folded below your towel. That, you are well aware, is against order. Always you have been instructed to place the large articles beneath. The handkerchiefs must remain above the towel—not the towel above the handkerchiefs." She broke off, then added mordantly: " For that you will say three aves—*les bras en croix*—in refectory during the dinnerhour."

Despite herself, Lucy felt something turn within her, so paltry was the offence, so pitiful the mortification of the offender. She had marked this Sister Assunta before—a small, insignificant woman, pious and delicate, who seemed attuned sensitively to shrink beneath the slightest word of censure. Surely it was unjust, a mean and petty tyranny, to punish so weak a creature. Again that feeling which she so dreaded swept over her in a hot tide. And to place such emphasis upon the simple arrangement of two handkerchiefs, to make of the position of a towel a matter of such gravity—was it not grotesque? Could she indeed have believed it possible? Her lips drew in and her fingers tightened nervously. A heat was in her soul and a quivering, reborn shame. Yes, at the previous *culpes* there had been this abject and degrading shame. Why, why, why need there be this——? With a start she checked herself. She must not think like this; she must curb her too impetuous spirit; a sin it was, and a grievous one, to set her judgment against the authority placed above her by the will of God. She lowered her eyes. Slowly the *culpe* was working along the line towards her.

This one had been negligent of her office. Three aves.

The next had spoken to a professed nun. Only two aves—surely she was a favoured child.

Beyond was one who had broken the silence. Three paters and a homily.

The one after admitted to leaving food upon her plate. Yes, three glorias upon her knees for scales left on the back-bone of a herring.

And the next had been too reserved at the recreation. This was her own especial fault; not yet could she match the birdlike laughter and the twitterings that bespoke the pure of heart.

But oh, she must not think like this; it was bitter and wrong and contrary to the holy Rule! She lowered her eyes as the next novice fell upon her knees. It was Marguerite now, who had spilled water upon the floor of the corridor. Here the homily was long. Twenty francs had been expended the previous year upon varnishing these floors. And the water, it ate, veritably it consumed, the varnish.

The *culpe* worked down. Each had something to confess—a dreadful sin against humility it would have been to protest a perfect innocence: what presumption! Besides, as the Rule ordained that each must tell upon the other, it was wiser by far to tell upon oneself. Yet all the faults admitted, multiplied and magnified, weighed but a feather in the scale. It was all so meaningless—incomprehensible; a childish game of forfeits about nothing. What! was she thinking that again? Her brow furrowed with dismay; she bit her lips and murmured a silent prayer for succour. Small wonder that she dreaded the *culpes*, when they induced such rank iniquity as this. She must— she must conquer that wicked obstinacy of her spirit; submit patiently to the will of God.

Shortly it would be her turn. Next to her, Wilhelmine moved restlessly; her full, stolid face worked anxiously; with jaw dropped and eyes fixed in a fascinated stare upon Marie Emmanuel, she seemed keyed to a pitch of dull apprehension, like a placid cow menaced by some grave calamity. When she dropped on her knees she could scarcely articulate:

" By holy obedience I make my *culpe* of all the faults I have committed against the Rule, particularly—particularly——" She faltered and broke down; then her full bosom heaved, she swallowed, and stammered out: " I could not help it—this morning I have broken my *pot*."

There was a stiff silence.

" Why did you not inform me? " enquired Marie Emmanuel. With mouth wide open, Wilhelmine blinked her eyes in agitation, bovinely perturbed; her head rolled over sideways, stupidly.

" You are aware that all broken articles must be taken down and placed upon the side-table of the refectory," persisted the mistress in a sharper voice.

But Wilhelmine could stand no more; she began to slaver, to weep hysterically, drawing in great noisy gusts of air between her fearful sobs.

For a moment Marie Emmanuel contemplated her with an expressionless face; then she said frigidly:

" Raise yourself. Take your chair and sit in the corner of the room with your back to me—in order that I may not be obliged to see you."

Gasping, Wilhelmine heaved to her feet and dragged her chair to the far corner of the room, where, like a child disgraced, she sat down as she had been bidden. For long her lowing lamentations rent the air, but with a cold front Marie Emmanuel would not proceed until they had subsided.

And now it was Lucy's turn. Detachedly she had felt herself almost a spectator at the grotesque confusion of the *Flamande*, finding no edification in the disclosure that this fount of holiness had broken her chamber. She knelt down. What was she to say before this gathering? A thought came to her head—yes, she too had been reserved at the recreation—and with quite a rush of words she admitted her culpability, then waited for her penance. But she received no penance.

" Have you nothing more to tell? "

She started as with a sudden pang, and looked up to find Marie Emmanuel observing her judicially. Surely she was not—yes, it was she—being so addressed? She made no answer.

" Is it not your office of this week to attend to the wash-basins? " pursued the other.

Lucy's brows came together, and she slowly replied:

" Yes, *ma bonne mère*." It was her duty, and she had discharged it scrupulously; the basins were spotlessly clean

But the mistress persisted:

" To-day I have found two small portions of soap broken from the main piece and lying loose in the dish. That is against the Rule. In your book of office you will find that in such circumstances the main cake of soap must be removed and the broken portions placed in a piece of muslin until they are fully utilised. This you have not accomplished."

Lucy looked up. Was there a latent antagonism behind those pale eyes? Impossible. Fiercely she drove away the thought; and so she forced herself to say:

" No, *ma bonne mère*."

" You understand that the office of the week must be accomplished perfectly? "

A terrific desire: the fragment of soap against her eternal salvation: but she controlled herself.

" Yes, *ma bonne mère* "; and she lowered her head to receive her penance and a sharp rebuke. When she had said her paters she rose from her knees. She was the last. The *culpe* was over; she drew a long breath: yes, it was over—over until next week.

VIII

THE peach-trees of the convent garden had borne their blossoms and scattered them upon the grass like foam. Already the honeysuckle fronds had opened; already the rambling glycine sprayed its heliotrope across the arbours. The copper beech behind the church stood burnished to a deeper lustre, its drooping leaves caressed by the light and tender airs of early summer.

But the sweet languor of the season was distant to Lucy—distant as a dream. Nor did the mild air reach her as, sewing within the workroom of the novitiate, she sat absorbed by the concentration of her thoughts. With the change of season seemingly she, too, had changed, how much she did not know, for, as in the *Postulat*, no mirror was here, and the inspection of the body was not permitted by the Rule. Cloaked by the habit, her figure was invisible, yet she was thinner, much thinner, and her shoulders had a more rigid set. Her face seemed smaller, clasped by the white casque to a narrow compass; her eyes, by contrast, shadowed, her hands thin and strangely nervous in their actions.

She knew, of course, that she had lost flesh, but it was a fact recognised without regret. Perhaps the dietary, adequate and wholesome though this might be, had reduced her. The food was unaccustomed, foreign to her palate, and, swallowed only by an effort of her will, perhaps not fully assimilated. But she did not know this to be the cause; nor, indeed, did she care. Like the callouses which had come upon her knees, the state had been of gradual development, and to her it was of trifling importance. Indeed, she made it trifling. She would not think about her health, nor admit the consequences of her debility. Once or twice that light remark of Edward's had come to her mind, but she had sternly dismissed it. She *would* stand the life, despite his pompous precognition. This strange new nervousness, the sudden jumping of her heart when someone suddenly addressed her, those dizzy fits which left her with a queer ethereal buoyancy— she resolutely ignored them all.

No. She had more to think of than that. When they asked her how she felt, she replied that she was well, quite well, and she had an unconscious pride in the firmness of her reply. Yet it was not pride alone which moved her: it was her will, and a mind strung to a more vital tension than the petty considerations of food and health —a mind taut with an inward brooding which had for weeks afflicted her.

This struggle within herself—she could not free herself of it—of this perpetual conflict. She had prayed for peace, had fought and fought again. Yet always now there was in her a qualm of curious apprehension. Abandoned was her dream of saintly women, moving, madonna-like, with gentle breasts and faces, pure hands, and tongues of placid sweetness. Why had this been her conception of the religious life? They were women; what was it Joe had once said a long, long time ago?—" We're only human, aren't we? " Yes, they were all human here. But what a repressed humanity; so strange, a life apart, far removed from what she had expected. Its very strangeness awoke in her sometimes a sudden painful bewilderment. Why was she here, in a queer dress, amongst foreigners, aping their language, their prattle, their infantile ingenuousness? For the love of God. God had led her here, and here she would remain. That was the answer—an answer with which she fiercely strove to scatter her wretched uncertainty.

Yet she could not evade her fear. And it was Marie Emmanuel, her good mother, who loomed before her as the propagator of that fear.

Lately, with a strange nervous reaction, she felt as though a fierce antipathy had sprung into being between the mistress and herself: almost—almost a hatred. She shivered. That could not be. It was impossible in this house, where the love of God must infuse the relationships of all within. Yet how else could she account for this perpetual persecution? Persecution—that was indeed the word.

As her needle flew, she reviewed again, with a tireless introspection, the last few weeks, fastened once more on those bitter recollections, scourged herself with her own thoughts and the morbid re-enactment of her humiliations—all so petty that they cut and mortified by their very triviality. Even this week. The routine inspection of her cupboard—two handkerchiefs not folded with sufficient neatness. The inspection of her cell: an insignificant crease had remained upon her coverlet, one single drop of water spilled upon the floor. " *Ça mange le vernis !* "—thrust at her in a tone of unexampled bitterness.

For faults like those she must stand like a child, stand and be pilloried by the tongue of Marie Emmanuel. At the very name her lips drew together, and her needle flew faster. On that first evening at the station, when she had advanced smiling, she had felt instinctively the coldness of the mistress; but now that coldness seemed charged with a bitter antipathy. And she—how violently could she have returned that feeling! But she must not; she must conceal it; stifle it; stamp it out. Yet it was unjust, this persecution. Why should the joy and rapture of her prayer be pierced by the dagger thrusts of perpetual censure? Her brow furrowed at the thought.

Was it her imagining? But no, that could not be. She had this constant presentiment of disaster, the feeling that somehow she was singled out, apart. She was convinced that Marie Emmanuel hated her.

Even as she sat sewing, with lowered head, she seemed to feel those pale eyes fixed coldly upon her. In spite of herself, she looked up towards the head of the room, and instantly a wave of uneasiness passed over her, for the mistress was observing her calmly, seeming dispassionately to read her thoughts.

Quickly she bent her gaze upon the sewing, exasperated by her own apprehension. What had she to fear? She feared no one but God. Never in all her life had she lacked courage to hold her head erect. Unconsciously her posture stiffened.

Around her the other novices, some twenty or more seated on low benches before the long tables that filled the room, were stitching silently, unconscious of the turmoil in her mind. Suddenly she felt limp, her hand numb and tired; worn out; but she persisted in the work, which was the hemming of an altar cloth. It was nearly finished and at length she laid it in her lap and ceased to sew. Still silence; then:

" Is the piece finished? " It came from Marie Emmanuel across the stillness of the room.

" It is finished, *ma bonne mère*," answered Lucy, without meeting those eyes. Why did she not meet those eyes? Was it at last humility?

The mistress rose, and, approaching, inspected the work minutely.

" Tst! Tst! " She made a sharp clicking with her tongue, then she held up the cloth. Was it mere fancy, or did she hold it contemptuously? Then came the words: " How you have made it filthy! "; and to Lucy her intonation of the adjective was diabolic. *Sale !* A shudder ran through her; an answering demon ranged wildly in her breast. To accuse her of that! The cloth had been given to her dirty. The mistress knew that, and knew, too, that her hands were spotless.

" Do you not understand? " persisted Marie Emmanuel. " You have rendered this filthy."

Her lips formed to reply: " Yes, *ma bonne mère* "; then something within her broke; all her violent indignation rushed to her lips. No matter that the Rule prescribe the meek acceptance of all injustice, a placid atonement for faults that never were committed! She raised her eyes challengingly.

" Do you not understand? " she repeated slowly and distinctly. " The piece was filthy when I received it."

This frightful violation of the Rule! A sort of stupefied gasp arose from the other novices at the retort, and at the frightfulness of that retort. But Marie Emmanuel stood quite still. A faint, unreadable expression was on her pale lips. She ignored utterly the remark, but, folding the cloth gently, she said dispassionately:

" It is enough. Before the dinner you will kiss the feet, and during you will kneel in reparation—*les bras en croix.*"

Then she turned and moved back to her seat. Lucy held herself rigid; her thin face had a drawn whiteness; the giddiness which so often affected her swam about her head like a mist.

Why must she submit to this—this tyranny? was the question which burned within her mind. It was without reason, without justice. God did not want His world like this: so petty, so infantile.

Must she lower her brow to the dust and grovel there? Must she surrender everything that was she, draw out her spirit, empty herself of everything, to obtain this perfection that was dinned constantly in her ears? There must be power in the human soul—not the faded, bloodless ineptitude demanded of her here.

Cutting like a knife across her quivering introspection, the bell rang for the dinner—the bell which now ostensibly controlled her. She rose with the others, her face masklike, and joined them when, like children in a row, they filed behind the mistress into the refectory. Yes, she was in a stream now, moving slowly, but always with that stream, always controlled.

Grace was said; then they sat down upon one side of the long, narrow table, with their backs against the wall. But Lucy did not sit down. She stood with her eyes fixed on Marie Emmanuel, her face calm, shrouding that inner turbulence by a grim tautness of her enfeebled nerves. Never, to the utmost clenching of her will, would she reveal how much it tortured her to make this reparation.

And now the mistress made her little sign, and at that she moved forward slowly to perform the intolerable apology—to Marie Emmanuel or to God?

Her humour was surely gone, or she might have laughed. Yes, surely she must have laughed at the sight of herself on her knees, kissing the boots of these twenty women: kneeling, lowering her face to the ground, rising, walking forward one pace, kneeling again, lowering her lips once more—kissing those boots. Often as a girl she had played the childish game, chanted the childish song: " Kneel down, kiss the ground—kiss the ground—kiss the ground. Kneel down, kiss the ground—my fair lady! "

Well, to be as a little child—as Joséphine had once said: " The little toy of Jesus! " And why not? What boots, though. Big and small; smooth and cracked; some with the regulation prunella uppers and blue elastic sides; some patched and stitched by the hands of Sister Cordonnière; some bulbous with the ludicrous protrusion of a bunion; some rank with the odour of perspiring feet; but all—all pressed close together for chastity, all lapped closely by a black hem of skirt, all ready to be kissed by her. If Frank could see her now— he who had pressed those lips in love—or Peter, or even Edward, who might now be walking round a golf-course, or savouring a sweetbread and saying " Delicious! "—what would they think of her? They might laugh—it was so funny, this sight of her dragging round on her knees, a middle-aged woman crawling on the floor, pushing her head under the table, bumping that head, kissing the feet of these foreign women! Perhaps Jesus was laughing, too, at the very torture which racked her. He had died for her, and so, at the word of Marie Emmanuel, she must debase herself for Him.

At last it was over. Stumbling to her feet, she went to the middle of the floor and, with her back to the table, knelt down. She extended her arms—*les bras en croix*—as had been demanded of her, holding herself stiffly upright, with head thrown back. Now, in this attitude of mind and body, she must abandon herself to inward prayer. But could she pray? Behind her the muffled sounds of the meal began— the passing of plates, the faint clink of fork on china, the quiet scrape of Marie Emmanuel's chair, the rustle of the lay sister's habit. And all the time she knelt, with arms extended, trembling with the memory of that grotesque tyranny which embittered and poisoned her mind. And she was supposed to pray!

She was weak, and the fatigue of her position became insupportable. But she would not give in. She would show this Marie Emmanuel, she would show them all, how she could endure suffering. Had she not suffered in the world? That was why she had come to this place. But where was the mantle of péace with which she had hoped to enwrap her bruised spirit? Was this it: with *les bras en croix*, with the eyes of Marie Emmanuel fixed in vigilance upon her back?

Her hands began to feel like leaden weights; then slowly the feeling stole along her arms, which dragged downwards and pulled painfully upon her breasts. The ache became insufferable; she wanted to lower them. She felt exhaustion stealing upon her with the heavy rhythm of her heart. She must lower these lifeless leaden arms. But she would not relax. Not acquiescence, but an intensity of pride, held her motionless.

At last the dinner was over; there came the gentle backward scrape of benches, the quiet sound of a general uprising, the prayers after food; then the slow shuffling towards the door.

" It is enough."

The mistress stood beside her, dispassionately indicating that now she might rise to eat her dinner. For a single second Lucy maintained her posture; then her arms dropped downwards; in complete silence she rose. As Marie Emmanuel swept from the room, she went over to her place and sat down. The relief was exquisite; but she felt sick, her fingers so numb they fumbled woodenly with the knife and fork. The lay sister, a little hunchback woman with a withered russet face, brought in her dinner with a swift glance of sympathy. An immense desire flooded Lucy to speak to this simple peasant, in whom she discerned some lingering evidence of humanity. One word of sympathy. But, no. She could not; the Rule demanded silence at this hour.

And so she ate in silence, desolately, relaxed in this moment of solitude. It was meat she had to-day—an unusual treat for the community, but not, alas, for her—a slice of flesh, and it was horseflesh, singed merely upon its outer surfaces so that it still retained its first empurpled lividity. Cutting it very small, with slightly trembling fingers and half-averted eyes, she forced herself to eat it. Again this effort, this perpetual struggle, this dragging of an ever-lengthening chain. Unobserved, her air was distraught, her eyes puckered to their faint perplexity, her small face drawn, yet some-how scornful.

When she had finished, she glanced at the window, and saw that it was raining—a warm, leaf-washing shower, but heavy—heavy enough to have driven the novices from the garden. Rising, she forced herself to enter the common-room, where in wet weather the recreation hour was held.

Again that inward wrestling when she entered the clamorous room.

No one took notice of her as she came in—it was against the Rule to intimate, even by a belated greeting, the observance of a repara-tion; but she knew what she must do. She must talk and smile and laugh with the others, maintaining no memory of her humiliation, giving outward and visible sign that she harboured no rancour. As she sat down by the window, where a little group chattered and giggled—Thérèse, Wilhelmine, and Marguerite were amongst them—she felt the eye of the mistress narrowly watching her. But to-day, with head averted, she felt careless.

Outside, the rain came drumming down insistently, but, un-deterred, some lay sisters went on working in the garden, habits kilted, blue rumps in the air, sabots widely planted. Neither the rain nor the Rule affected them.

Suddenly a voice in her ear startled her.

" This will amuse the fingers "—it was a pleasant voice, from the novice beside her, who now placed upon her lap a cardboard box filled with string. Each had some little occupation for these wet recreation periods—the turning of used envelopes that they might be used again, the rolling and rearranging of snippets of cloth from the workroom, the knotting of cords from which the discipline was made—diverse occupations recommended by the Rule. And now Lucy, wanly returning her neighbour's smile, set herself to straighten out the tiny ends of twine with which this box was filled. Neatly disentangling string, unknotting it, smoothing it, rolling it into perfect little balls; that was her present task.

Around her the conversation ranged; words flew to and fro like shuttlecocks.

" We must make some verses of felicitation."

" But yes, the feast of the anniversary of the *bonne mère*."

" You will make some verses, Thérèse."

" But assuredly—for the *bonne mère*—it is understood."

A pause. Was it her embittered fancy, or were these remarks directed obsequiously to the ear of Marie Emmanuel, with but one desire—and that to please?

" Oh, look, *ma bonne mère*, the pretty colour! " said one, with much animation, holding up, with a kittenish gesture, a fragment of satin from her box.

Marie Emmanuel nodded her head gravely, and looked—but without much animation.

Suddenly Marguerite pointed to the floor with an air of joyous discovery.

" Oh, again, *ma bonne mère*, Sister Gabrielle has lost her garter! " It was the selvedge of tweed used in the community as a garter.

There was a general laugh, whilst Gabrielle blushed, and laughingly retrieved the small garter.

" It is clear it is not to you," said Thérèse to Wilhelmine, who sat next to her.

Wilhelmine's deep laugh welled up from her sonorous bosom. There was a short pause, whilst she went on with her task—the meticulous cutting of newspaper into squares, shaped with exactitude, for the love of God and its ultimate purpose in the *petit pays*. In her immediate coterie, this occupation had all along occasioned an open and ingenuous hilarity, and now Thérèse, reverting to the topic, declared roguishly to the others:

" You must not interrupt. You must allow her to proceed with *délicatesse*."

" She has wonderful address, has she not? "

" But yes, it is a quality."

There was a little titter.

" You will see," returned Wilhelmine, with a short guffaw: long, long ago had she recovered from her discomfiture of the *culpe*. " Later—you will see." She picked up a square of paper in her fat paw.

" Pray do not hold like that," remarked Thérèse primly. " It is altogether too significant."

There was a lively burst of laughter, to which even Marie Emmanuel, watchful and remote as ever, unbent her firm lips slightly. It was the natural humour, simple, understandable, permissible; to be like little children; to laugh and be joyous. But Lucy did not laugh. To her it was an odious vulgarity, and all that deep resentment seething within her rushed upwards in a sudden flare. Was this the measure of a human soul straining upwards to its Saviour?

Repelled, shaken, and confused, she still persisted in her own belief. She would go forward, hold on, win through. She set her teeth firmly.

So there she was, with her pale thin face, her worn and rigid frame, a figure of infinite pathos: disentangling the short string with fingers that fumbled and faintly twitched—like a symbol disentangling the short string of her life.

IX

WERE they watching her? She did not know. But she had always the strange and fascinated feeling that they were shadowing the secrets of her mind. Oppressed by the crowding movement of the communal life, she longed passionately for solitude. Yet never was she alone except during those hours of darkness in her cell when she lay stiffly staring into that amorphous darkness, striving to make luminous the unseen figure upon the cross fixed to the opposite wall. Only her fancy made that figure luminous during those sleepless nights, except when the moon swung a transient beam through the narrow grille and made the plaster Christ actual and blanched.

She slept little, and that a restless, intermittent sleep. Her flock mattress of the *Postulat* was gone, and she had now the usual bed of the religious—sacking, it was, loosely filled with straw. Marie Emmanuel had said one day, impersonal and exalted as ever:

" It is now two months since your clothing. You shall lie in the straw to-night, like our Blessed Lord in the manger."

It was right and fitting. What was good enough for the Saviour was too good for her. That was no sacrifice. But, though her spirit valiantly accepted the sacrifice, her body refused to cede itself to sleep upon that pallet. Moreover, they had lately changed her cell— again according to the Rule: to remain in any cell too long stamped it with the forbidden quality of possession—and she was not yet accustomed to that change. She craved for that sleep which still eluded her.

During those wakeful hours of darkness and deadly stillness, unrelieved even by the ticking of a clock, whilst she nervously awaited the first paling of the dawn, then it was that her tired brain fastened upon the threads of thought and wove from them the concept of espionage. Not merely the everlasting watching of Marie Emmanuel's omniscient eye, but an observation more reticent and secret, stretching beyond the enclosure of the novitiate. Little colloquies behind locked doors; Joséphine, Marie Emmanuel, and Bonne Mère Générale in earnest conversation; suddenly an illuminating glance flashed upon her by the Superior as she emerged from church. Was this merely her imagining? It must be so; and yet there was that concrete fact which could not be ignored: that strange interview!

It came one day at the recreation, and then, confronting her, Bonne Mère Générale had said:

" The community remark that you get thinner. Is it that you are ill? "

She at once denied the charge that she was ill.

" It is necessary to have health to follow the common Rule. No exceptions can be made. Health too feeble and a heart too haughty cannot make a good religious."

Was her heart haughty? She who made ignominious and causeless reparations upon her knees? She remained silent.

" I am told you are truly favoured in the matter of prayer, so surely our good Lord will give you grace to continue the life."

To continue the life! Those were the words which Lucy took back with her, which persisted uneasily, confronting her suddenly, especially at nights, with a burning intensity. They held, with torturing uncertainty, the threatening implication of her failure: she who had never failed, who could not now fail in this last vital enterprise. Though her present period was, in effect, probationary, she had never so regarded it, but from the first had taken the convent as her haven—a refuge permanent and ultimate.

And, unaccountably, although she found the life so strange, so rigorous and incomprehensible, with all the passionate intensity of her nature she willed violently to continue it. In an illuminating flash she remembered with what supreme assurance she had entered the convent; was she a creature of enfeebled will to lose her fortitude and her faith so easily? God had led her here in all His love for her; that was the rock to which she clung.

Despite her inward doubts and struggles, and the frightful toll exacted by these struggles, she was utterly determined to persist to the bitter end. It was a paradox; but it was she.

And now, like a deeper shadow overcasting all those other shadows, came this fear of failure which she must always guard against; that perhaps was why there grew on her this sense of universal vigilance. She it was who spied perpetually upon herself.

This insistent dread of the impending and unknown was like a thin, sustained note plucked from her overstrung nerves. It droned in her ears and mingled with the singing silence. She became keyed unconsciously to a tense anxiety, her thin face listening, drawn, attuned to a strained expectancy. A fine network of wrinkles grew into the corners of her dark eyes, and spasms of an uncontrollable tic frequently affected her lax cheek. Sometimes, when she walked, she had the strange sensation of treading upon cushions of air— a light and almost buoyant progress which ended in a wave of giddiness. Yet she went on, moulding herself to this shape by the exercise of her will, sustained through everything by the burning purpose of her love.

She was doing it for Jesus. Jesus, her dear Lord, who had, for her, been scourged and crowned with thorns and crucified to an anguished death. Why, when He had suffered so for her, should she refuse to suffer thus for Him? " All for Jesus! All for the love of Him "—that was the eternal purpose of her soul. Immured within her cell during those long dark hours, she was consumed by this love. Like a tongue of flame it was, leaping inside her. Often, too, in the sombre blackness, she saw vividly the Sacred Heart of Jesus surrounded by leaping, answering, passionate flames—loving her, awaiting her adoration. Before that vision she wished to leap from her straw and fall upon her knees, offering herself body and soul to Jesus. Restrained only by the mandate of this Rule, she waited in wide-eyed eagerness till the first clangour of the morning bell should permit her to arise and go to him. " Blessed be God. For ever."

Then, in the darkness, she hurriedly arose, nervously habited her wasted body, and hastened to the church, where, before the actuality of God, she humbly prostrated herself in adoration.

There, in the dim chapel, making pale the steady candle-flames, she saw again around the tabernacle thin tongues of fire. Thus, she knew, the Holy Ghost had come upon the Apostles, thus the blaze had leaped from many a martyr's pyre—in flames like that, each a devouring symbol which kindled the ardour of her spirit and lifted her upwards in an ecstasy of love.

True, at nights, in her snatches of sleep, she was distressed often by a frightful dream: a wild incitement—flames rising at her behest— the convent burning as an offering to God. And she would awaken in an icy, dripping sweat of horror. That, of course, was but a nightmare—a phantasy without reason or relation to her love for Christ.

" Blessed be God."

" For ever."

How often had she made that fervent answer? Only for a few short months—yet to her those months were vast—each a wide desert of time. The peaches were ripe now in the mellow garden, hanging large and luscious, bursting with their own juice, exhaling a subtle perfume under the warm sun. It was pleasant to admire for a moment, during recreation, the fruits of the good God's bounty, to observe the lay sisters as they plucked those fruits, with coarse yet gentle hands, then packed the big flat panniers for market. But naturally no more than observation was permitted. Already they had heard that story related, and again related—as it had been through the years, to the exclamations and little shrugs of horror— of the novice, not a professed religious—that was unthinkable!— not in this Order—that was absurd!—but a novice of some other

Order—perhaps a Carmelite; yes, it might indeed be a Carmelite—who had fallen to the twin-headed monster of disobedience and gluttony. She it was who, coveting a nectarine in the garden of her enclosure, had, with incredible folly, abandoned her virtue to pluck it secretly and to greedily consume it.—A little cry of consternation from Thérèse!—But one did not trifle with the good God. No! There had been a stone within that nectarine. And the novice, in all the hurry of her hidden gluttony, had swallowed that stone, and so embarrassed her gorge that she had choked herself.

Another little outburst of awe and terror!

" *Ma bonne mère*——"

" *Moi, je ne*——"

But, lovely as they were, Lucy had no desire for these fruits. Perhaps she had been different once—a long time ago; the thought of a peach might then have wooed her pleasantly; now she did not care. Still, she loved the garden, entering it always, at the recreation, with a sense of strange relief. There, too, she had lately been favoured by a strange and unexpected companionship, which made her more eagerly anticipate that single hour spent beneath those sweetly burdened trees.

It was Sister Adrienne who had spoken to her—old Sister Adrienne, who had worn the habit of the Order for close on sixty of those eighty years of life that lay so placidly behind her. A shrivelled, wispy form and a toothless, puckered face had Adrienne, an eye rheumy and ringed like a dove's, yet somehow clear and gentle as her smile. Saying an interminable rosary which dangled from her sleeve, she tottered about the garden in the hours of sunshine. And one day she had stumbled and, when Lucy had assisted her, suddenly she had spoken. Only by virtue of her age—she was the oldest of the community—had she the privilege to address a novice.

" It is my sixtieth anniversary on the feast of the Twelve Holy Martyrs," she had said unexpectedly. " Is it not remarkable ? "

The gentle simplicity of her manner had drawn a wry smile from Lucy's impassive face.

" Thereon, if you are good," continued Adrienne, " you shall have coffee to dinner and a little *gâteau glacé*." Already Lucy knew about this little cake for each: for days it had been the joyful subject of discussion at the recreation of novices.

" I must felicitate you," she said awkwardly.

Adrienne had smiled again without reply, and, tucking her nodding head into her breast, had wandered off along the path. But next day she returned and again had speech with Lucy.

" I remarked you yesterday," she said. " Did you not felicitate me upon my anniversary, which comes on the feast of the Twelve Holy Martyrs? Accept, then, this little picture for your missal."

She proffered a small gilded card bearing a painting of the Infant Jesus, and, as she gazed at it, slowly Lucy's eyes moistened.

" It is too kind," she stammered, moved beyond her understanding at this trifling act of human kindness.

" It is the Baby Jesus," said the other, and her old head went nodding on. " So sweet—so gentle. How blessed the Virgin, to be mother to a Child like that. You are pleased? "

" Yes, I am pleased," said Lucy in a low voice.

" To hold in the arms that Baby," went on Adrienne. " Truly I am envious of the good Mother."

Lucy could not help herself. A sudden rush of emotion tore at her breast; she gave a short, suppressed sob. A veil was rent, and suddenly she saw herself nursing her infant son upon the shore at Ardfillan. Overwhelmed by a mingling emotion, indescribable, a pain that ravaged her being, that yearning which was the essence of her life sweeping across her in a spiritual orgasm, she stood unconsciously clutching the card. Then, without a word, she began stiffly to walk away. The old nun observed her with mild, regretful eyes, then stirred herself slowly:

" *Je vais la suivre,*" she mumbled. " *Je vais la suivre.*"

It was a strange and fitful companionship that followed—one not strictly according to the Rule; yet at this moment in her life Adrienne's friendship—if it could be called a friendship—was like a reprieve, a sudden intervention in the face of approaching disaster. She seemed to cling, almost, to the old woman; and she tried to draw from her something of that tranquillity which now so desperately she craved.

Sixty years a professed religious! Surely to plumb the depths of this old woman's heart was to solve for ever the eternal enigma which beset her. And she pressed Adrienne towards that revelation.

" Yes, sixty years on the feast of the Twelve Holy Martyrs I shall have worn the habit."

" And you have great happiness—great contentment now? " pressed Lucy.

" It is happiness to bask my old bones in the sun," replied Adrienne complacently; " and, moreover, there is my anniversary, which approaches on the feast of the Twelve Holy Martyrs! You understand! "

" But——"

" Ah, I entered with great fervour," mumbled the old woman reminiscently. " Still I remember. And how my poor mother wept at my clothing—in effect she was not agreeable to that. But after— this fervour—I do not know." She paused, and a fly crawled unmolested over her gentle, drowsy face.

" You see," she resumed, " in this life you make yourself to do—

do all the time. I have read some time of a great saint—I forget where; now I so easily forget—who not once in his life as religious has the blessing of real fervour, and has prayed for this all the time. But in spite of that he goes on and on, making himself to do what he does not wish for the good God. He says, ' I believe.' Then he must believe. It is the faith. It is understandable." Again she paused dreamily. " Myself, I am not a saint, but so it is with me."

Lucy gazed at her anxiously.

" But the reward, sister," she murmured, " when you die."

" I do not wish to die," answered Adrienne with unusual briskness, so that the fly started and flew off her nose as at the distasteful thought. " Myself, I find life very agreeable—to bask my old bones in the sun. It is sufficient at present. And there are memories so sweet."

Her smile was tinged with those memories as her mind—the mind of the very aged—flew easily to her distant childhood.

" At my home in Liège, it was agreeable. There was the fig-tree in the corner of the court where I would play. Once I was taken to the great fair—for a fortnight the gipsies came—and their children received instruction. It was a blue dress I wore, and my hair had many curls. ' *Mon petit chou frisé* '—thus my papa addressed me always." She rambled on gently for a moment; then Lucy, with a growing perplexity, demanded:

" But surely—surely you desire to be with our Lord ? "

There was a long silence, then slowly the old nun declared:

" It is very curious. Yes, it is very curious: at one time in Italy— where I have spent many years in our Order—an incident takes place. In retirement from age there was the Archbishop—a man very old, very saintly. Suddenly he becomes ill. What takes place ? He does not exclaim: ' I am old. I believe. Let me die for the great happiness of being with God.' No, no! He demands a doctor and specialists. An operation is decided. Yes, he agrees to get himself better. He recovers. And he is pleased—so pleased; and there is much prayer in thanksgiving. It is curious, is it not? "

The bell rang for the end of the recreation, and with a baffling dis-arrangement of her mind Lucy went towards the church—to pray for her place in that heaven which Adrienne had no urgency to achieve.

She did not obtain from the old nun the solution which now so restlessly she sought, yet she found a soothing tranquillity in her society. She became strangely, immensely devoted to her. To escape at the recreation from the piercing eye of the mistress, from that eternal: " Oh, *ma bonne mère* "; " Look, *ma bonne mère*, regard the first chestnut "; " Has not the pony grown so rapidly ? ": it was unutterable relief.

When a rebuke from Marie Emmanuel set her quivering and on edge, when that weary suspense overhung her like a pall, she would force herself to think of that aged, stoic face. It was a singular solace. Unconsciously the knowledge that she could speak to Adrienne at the recreation seemed to tide her over, to strengthen her endurance. Old Adrienne became unconsciously the antidote to Marie Emmanuel. But for the almost miraculous comfort of this assuagement she felt she must have lost herself in a morass of hatred. For Marie Emmanuel's dislike seemed to increase, between them that silent antipathy to grow. Still she constrained herself in brooding introspection to suffer and obey. She would go on. She would make herself go on.

Then came the eve of the feast of the Twelve Holy Martyrs. Because of the great occasion of the morning's anniversary she had talked with Adrienne something longer than usual. The old woman had given her another picture, and, when the bell rang, a faint smile lingered on Lucy's lips as she traversed the garden, holding the card loosely in her hand. Then, all at once, she felt upon her the fixed gaze of Marie Emmanuel. Instantly the smile faded from her face and she placed the card hastily within her pocket. No word was spoken. Yet she shivered, lowered her head, as though a sudden wind had struck her. It was nothing, she told herself—nothing! Still, the memory of that look persisted uneasily through the afternoon. Again, without seeing, she felt those eyes upon her in a coldly speculative gaze, and again she shivered. All her dislike for the other returned with a torturing insistency, and would not be denied. It was true, then! With all the force of her enfeebled nature she hated and despised Marie Emmanuel. Yet this she could not, must not admit. She must love her and submit to her. To turn the other cheek was now the precept which governed her life. In a rushing turbulence of mind and spirit she entered the church for evening prayers. She must conquer this feeling of revolt. She must—must submit.

With a straining intensity she fixed her eyes upon the glinting tabernacle, praying silently, with a vibrant intensity. Oh, how she prayed! She prayed for grace to continue—for a sign, perhaps, some sign of mercy and peace.

She came out of the church uplifted, her eyes humid and still lit with an afterglow of fervour. Now she was braced with greater fortitude to face the restless night.

Last of all the novices to leave the chapel, she did not immediately ascend the stairs, but made to advance along the corridor towards a small side door which it was her nightly duty to secure: a simple task, and one of many assigned to the novitiate. But, before she could proceed, a figure moving from the shadow at the foot of the staircase abruptly detained her. It was Marie Emmanuel.

" A moment, if you please," said the mistress in a low voice.

Lucy started. The Rule proclaimed a universal silence following the night prayers, a resolution broken rarely and that with circumspection upon the gravest circumstance. Astonishment tinged her rising apprehension as she paused, facing the other in the dim corridor. The dimness of that corridor was contained, and echoed, it seemed, with silence.

" I omitted to inform you," continued Marie Emmanuel in her cold, precise tones, " of what you must know before to-morrow." She paused, erect, a figure dim and shrouded, almost inhuman in that light. Then she said coldly: " It concerns Sister Adrienne."

Lucy felt her heart contract. Was this the sign she had demanded ? She grew chilled, and her limbs turned suddenly listless.

" I have observed," went on the other, frigid as a judge, " that you are much together at the hour of recreation. It is not just, such intimacy. To Sister Adrienne are the privileges of the aged, but they are not to you. You understand ? "

Did she understand ? The strained pallor of her face gleaming in the dimness of that passageway answered the question without speech. It was, then, as she had expected. With a rushing intuition she perceived that once again she stood on the verge of humiliation, injustice, and rebuke. Again and again—would it never cease ? Suddenly the tic started in her cheek, but she remained motionless, making no reply.

" To become a good religious," came the voice once more, " it is necessary to abandon all."

And the voice held no annoyance, only a frigid authority. Yet again Lucy made no reply.

" Do you understand ? " demanded the mistress finally, with her slow and measured tone. Then, expectantly, she paused.

Lucy stirred. It was the moment: not the sign that she had prayed for, something different, better ! And now, as though she had awaited it, alone with this woman who had so abased her, she grasped it fiercely. Her heart, that had been contracted, suddenly expanded. Her thin nostrils dilated, her pale lips compressed into a rigid line, as she demanded with a cutting disdain:

" Am I permitted to speak ? "

The mistress inclined slightly her half-averted head.

" You understand that Sister Adrienne first addressed me ? "

" It is no difference."

" And if she again addresses me, what must I do ? "

The words flew back across the gloomy stillness of the hall.

" As you are instructed. Make no reply."

They looked at each other, and into Lucy's eyes there flowed the fierce light of battle. She was a woman with a soul, not a cringing, spineless weakling that would grovel and lick the dust and fawn obeisantly, crying " *Oh, pardon, ma bovne mère* " for a nameless fault that never had existed. A sudden bitter nausea transfused her veins like fire. She was the equal of this white and barren creature. Yes, more than her equal. Despite her worn and beaten body, she was stronger—better than she. By Christ, she was. Stronger and better than she. She had known the ecstasies of love and the pangs of labour. She was no blenched virgin venting long-penned repression in this causeless spleen. She was a woman, and she was not afraid. Her head reared like an angry horse, her thin and haggard face was transfigured, as she confronted Marie Emmanuel with a menacing air.

" Do you recognise," she exclaimed in a loud, full tone, " that for three months you have made my life a misery ? "

" What misery ? " The exclamation was spontaneous, accompanied by a swift and surreptitious glance.

" Unspeakable misery. And all for nothing."

The words came with a furious rush. " You have set yourself out to deride me and to lower me to nothing."

Marie Emmanuel's eyelids fluttered faintly. She had turned strangely pale.

" It is so," she answered slowly, " but only for your good—for your benefit."

" My benefit ! " cried Lucy. She made a violent gesture of repudiation, and, as she moved her arm, involuntarily Marie Emmanuel moved backwards towards the staircase.

" It is not right," she exclaimed immoderately, her voice strangely shrinking. " You do not conduct yourself reasonably."

A frightful joy suffused Lucy's breast. She saw that discomposure, and it filled her with a bursting exultation.

" You see what I am," she declared passionately; " I have submitted. And all the time I am stronger than you."

Marie Emmanuel's face turned livid in the shadow of the hall.

" It is against God to speak like that," she exclaimed in a strained voice. " To-morrow you must make reparation."

" Reparation ! " A bitter exasperation swept her, flooded her suddenly with a cold disgust. " It is not yet to-morrow," she said scornfully. She stared at the other, who now leaned against the shadowed wall. Virtue had gone out of her, and in its place there remained only contempt.

" It is late," said the mistress hesitatingly; " it is time to retire."

For a moment the two women looked at each other in silence, then slowly Marie Emmanuel lowered her eyes, turned, and began to ascend the stairs.

With clenched hands and a quivering lip, Lucy observed her go.

"I can't," she thought to herself, "I can't stand it." Then, with a gesture of fierce despair, she turned, as though from habit, to the door. But she did not fasten the door. Instead, she opened it and stood with heaving breast gazing into the sweet, mysterious beauty of the night. Before her was the garden, lapped by the radiance of a lucid moon. Behind her, in the enclosure, that warren of cells, the pettiness and misery. Her heart beat loudly in her ears as, standing on the threshold, she held her hot face towards the tender invocation of the night, with head thrown backwards towards the sky, her body arched in the darkness, vibrant and intense, with all the tautness of a drawn bow. Then suddenly that bow relaxed. She started. The door slammed behind her. Trembling, she rushed into the freedom of the air.

X

THE garden engulfed her like a cool, unfathomable sea. The moment she rushed from that doorway she was absorbed, detached from reality, enclosed by the vast opaque billows which slid silently around her. Withdrawn by instinct, compelled now as by some force beyond, she ran crouching, heedless of her course, rushing only to escape.

Upon the grass, drenched with dew and stained by still shadows from the trees, her feet were soundless. Her bent figure swam through the ghostly light, itself a moving, unsubstantial shade which followed no path and left no trace.

But where was she going? Running—running with a quick, sobbing breath, running to nowhere. Enclosed by the impassable barrier which circled the grounds, whither could she escape?

Shaken and confused, the very movement of her flight touched her with a rising fear. Girded by the wall, the forest, and the night, trapped under the vault of the dispassionate sky, she was like a minnow quivering its tiny, frighted way through vast, uncharted oceans whose cold abysmal depths were pierced by neither light nor understanding.

Abruptly she halted in her course, panting, stricken by despair. Where was she going? What was she doing here? She, Lucy Moore, alone in this vast, incomprehensible enclosure, alone, shut away, at this hour, in the heart of a strange land. She clutched her drooping bosom and threw back her head. The moon, like a pale host set in the dark monstrance of the infinite, gleamed towards her without comfort. The stars were but a tarnished dust of gilt sprinkled randomly. For the rest, nothing but darkness in that sombre sky, a darkness beneath which she was submerged and nothing.

Stupidly she raised her hand to her brow, striving to think, overcome by the scent of the ripe fruit which hung in the quiet air like the fume of a languorous wine. Around her the garden now took shape under her wondering eyes: the trees still as statuettes, the pale flowers standing motionless, like lovely coral fronds. Such loveliness and stillness linked and laid out before her within this peaceful place. Yes—with knitted brows she remembered—she had come here for peace. Her face contorted, and in the contemplation of that thought all the new-found beauty of the garden dissolved and was lost to her.

The intolerable memory ran through her with a rising bitterness, and again her brows drew downwards, wincingly as from an arid pain. It was for love of God that she had come here—to offer herself entirely to Him. Not to God so much as to Jesus—Jesus the Saviour, crucified for love of her. Jesus was God—the Son and the Father together with the Holy Ghost, all in one. A mystery securely incomprehensible, so firm and safe she gave it now no thought, but blundered onwards towards her love of Christ. That had drawn her hither, compelling her to the sweet pain of sacrifice and utter abandonment. But to what end? Her hands clenched together and her eyes drew fiercely towards the faint amorphous outline of the convent sprawling shapeless and gloomy in the darkness. In that warren peopled by pale creatures who moved machine-like to the pealing of a bell—there it was that she had laboured to learn the fatuous rote, to crush the virtue from her soul, to spend the essence of her love on nothing. Cramped by the pettiness, ground by the discipline, she had grovelled and kissed boots when all her spirit strained upwards in that soaring of her love. God had made her a woman with a soul which was His soul. To abase that soul was to abase God. She would fight, and fight to the end; she would suffer; she would die; but no longer would she lower her head. So she had always been, and so she would remain.

A swift scorn mingled with her bitter anger. Were they women there within those narrow cells, or neutral beings that walked like shadows—sterile virgins who need not fight for chastity? Fiercely she embraced the memory of her life. Worn as it now must be, her body had at least fulfilled its function; her womb had burgeoned, her turgid breasts acknowledged the suckling's lips. Whatever she might be, she was a woman who had loved and worked and battled onwards fiercely all her life.

A sudden revulsion of feeling took her, and, turning, she looked about her with a straining eye. She must do something. She could not stand still weakly and let the futile rush of circumstance submerge her. Never had she done that! And Jesus was on her side, conscious of her love, watching her even now as she stood reaching out towards Him. A faint smile warmed her set face.

" Jesus," she whispered suddenly, involuntarily, " Help me ! " She lowered her head swiftly and stood stiffly, as though listening. Then, with a sudden uplifting of her voice, which split the quiescence of the night like a meteor soaring across that dull canopy above, she called loudly:

" Jesus ! Jesus ! Help me now ! I came here for love of You."

Again she waited, listening, her eye remote and wildly glinting. But there was no answer from the aimless, brooding sky.

Restlessly she stirred, and moved her cold limbs, whilst a vague return of that first fear laid a dank finger on her brow. She began to walk slowly and stiffly from under the trees. Then, suddenly, the moon went out behind a cloud, and all the garden sank instantly into obscurity. Unconsciously she quickened her pace to the impulse of this piercing blackness which now so utterly surrounded her. Her body, worn by the rigours it had borne, was bent forwards. Her legs moved fumblingly. Her arms hung limply by her side. In her head there was a throbbing pulse. Dazedly she asked herself why Jesus did not help her. A moment ago she had entreated His aid. Even a sign ! And she had been plunged into darkness. That was the answer. Had He not been like this Himself once in a Garden that was named Gethsemane: crying aloud like her for succour ? But His suffering had not passed. Nor did hers pass. A frightful mental anguish suddenly assailed her like a cruel wind, under which her mind plunged and tossed like a ship stricken by a hurricane. Was the suffering of Christ like her own suffering—all for nothing ?

Why was she here ? This darkness was not a garden, but a universe through which she staggered blindly. Her love for her husband, for her son, for Jesus—it was the same love repeated—senselessly repeated. She trembled. Her rushing tenderness towards the Infant Saviour was but the same tenderness which had flooded her when her infant son lay within her arms. The smile of the Baby Jesus was the smile of her own child, her love for one the love for both. And Frank ! She saw again those pale, waxen hands folded in death, and the vague, mysterious image of his face. But it was not his face. It was the face of Christ. And the body was Christ's body as, drooping, it had been borne by the holy women from the cross to be placed within the tomb. The same limp, exsanguine human form.

A low, inarticulate cry burst from her lips. And all her thoughts were inarticulate, too, whirling amongst uncertainty and doubt. But madly, amidst the unutterable chaos, those three loves united and made themselves mysteriously a trinity that was one. Rising out of her ! Her woman's body was the fount of all love, springing from the earth from which everything arose, into which everything must pass and be assumed again to dust.

She pressed her hands tightly across her eyes and sobbed aloud. She trembled and moved faster, like a quarry hunted by unseen hounds. Had she come to this place to lose her faith? It was impossible! Fiercely she fought against the thought. Jesus had died to save her. He had kindled in her the fire of His love: the love for His burning heart. Those flames leaping around the tabernacle—let that be the vision of an exalted mind!—the fact remained that Jesus was there—the Baby Jesus, as old Adrienne had said—so sweet a thought: bound body and soul into the substance of the Sacrament. That wafer was the Godhead—not bread, but God. Could she adore bread, prostrate herself, a pagan, before a disc of bread? It was Jesus, her sweet Jesus, who was there—whom she absorbed into her loving breast when, kneeling at the altar rail, the host dissolved upon her tongue. Would she deny her dear Lord whom she so passionately loved? He was there by virtue of a miracle. A miracle of the divine love for her. But what was a miracle? It was a word; letters of the alphabet linked together. But were there other alphabets and other letters, other creeds, other miracles, other gods, and throughout this vast, immeasurable universe other worlds whirling through space, where creatures prostrated themselves, maybe, before the symbols of their faith, in all oblivion of the name of Christ?

What in the name of God was coming to her? Was she going mad? She moaned, and in a frenzy fell upon her knees. " Jesus! Jesus! " she cried out. " Your noble brow pierced by thorns; Your lovely face dripping with sweat and blood. I love You! I love You! Help my unbelief." Passionately she beat her breast and lifted up her head. Nothing to show in that dumb sky whether her voice was heard or lost for ever in the infinite. Was she lost too, then? Suffused by hopelessness, abandoned. Her figure sagged listlessly, her eye lit with a light of wildness.

Her belief was nonsense—idiot's talk. There could be no God! Christ was a man. There never were and never could be miracles. The saintly Benedict with his holy sack expressed a fatuous mythology.

That place in there, with a key to turn every door, was but a madhouse. That key! Now she remembered! The key at Blandford. And that empty look, that smiling childishness upon those faces— it was the same look that marked Miss Hocking's senseless face.

So it was all for nothing—the tearing of paper—a tragic essay in futility! She shivered. As from a long way off she seemed to hear the ringing of a bell, a queer, insistent tolling—not a message of peace, but of alarm. Was it a bell, or merely the ringing within her ears? Was it from that asylum where, with bell and key, her life had moved so uselessly, controlled by the swing of the one and the turn of the other? The sound went on—on—on—soaring through the night. Then into the darkness faint points of light appeared and moved uncertainly, wandering and elusive as distant wildfire. Fascinated, she stared, then all at once she stumbled to her feet. The lights converged towards her, swinging like bells to the sound of those other distant bells. She was terrified. She had deserted God—denied Him! Was she now beset by devils who came rushing to torment her? Her dry throat constricted upon her feeble cry.

Turning, she made as though to run, but somehow she could not. She tried, then tried again, with inexpressible anguish, to move her numb and rooted figure. But she was petrified to immobility. She made a last convulsive effort; she fought, struggled, thrust the devilish lights away from her; then her stiff form relaxed, and she fell feebly to the ground, into the deeper darkness of her swoon.

There she was found by those who had been seeking her with lanterns, and thus they bore her back to the convent.

XI

WHEN she awoke she felt the warm morning sunshine striking upon her face, streaming over her coverlet, an experience so unusual and unreal that instantly she closed her eyes. But in a moment she reopened them. A large man in a frock coat was standing beside the bed. His beard was long and squarely trimmed; pince-nez balanced themselves upon his long and serious nose. But he was not serious: with one hand thrust into his breast, he was smiling.

" You have slept well," he said in an encouraging tone. " Yes, undoubtedly you feel better."

Her stiff face did not smile, nor did she reply, but again her swollen eyelids drooped. Though she felt drowsy, she was not asleep. Vaguely she heard voices; a conversation very polite and formal; the dignified departure of the doctor. Yes, she supposed it was the doctor. Beyond the *curé*, no other man was admitted to the cloister. Here she sharply opened her eyes once more and looked around. They fell at once upon the old sister *infirmière*, who nodded and smiled agreeably from over the high brass rail which formed the foot of the bed. But she was not in the infirmary, nor was she in her cell. The bed wherein she lay at once precluded that; *un grand lit* it was, so large and soft after her pallet of straw, that she seemed not to be on any surface, but to float enveloped by a cloud. And the room? The room was too pleasant, too open, the furnishings too lavish!

A Brussels rug upon the polished floor, curtains of yellow lace upon the window, actually a small swing mirror upon the chest of drawers, and, on the mantelpiece, flowers—red flowers of paper, half-poppy, half-rose, clustered closely in a yellow vase; yes, it was no room that she could remember.

And where was her habit? Quietly she let her eyes fall upon the chair by her bedside. It was empty, quite empty. So they had taken away her habit, and placed her in this strange elaborate room, meeting her frightful disobedience of the Rule with smiles, and kindness, and the stout, amicable apothecary with his thick square beard. Yes, now she knew where she was. They had put her out; she was outside the cloister in a bedroom above the parlours.

Again her eyes closed. But she could not think. She had, indeed, no wish to think. Her body ached, as though it had been flogged with heavy rods; her head was buoyant; her eyelids thick and drowsy. Some liquid was held to her lips in a bowl. She drank. A fly buzzed over the window-pane. Again she slept.

It was high afternoon when she awoke, and the sun now spread a soft, bright square upon the pattern of the rug beside the door. She was alone in the room—perhaps she had been awakened by the quiet closing of the door as the old *infirmière* went out—and, flat upon her back, for a long time she was still, thinking of nothing. Dimly she recollected her frightful experience in the garden, but without sense of time, without acuteness, like something terrible yet vague, like a storm which had ravaged and almost destroyed her but now was gone. No, she did not wish to think.

She was weak, very weak. It was strange. An effort to raise her hand from the coverlet; a still greater effort for her to raise her head from the pillow.

Then suddenly she became aware that she was not alone in the bedroom, and her eyes widened with a wondering enquiry. A curious old woman was facing her, a woman with a face so thin and worn and wrinkled as to be almost ludicrous, with drab grey hair, cut short like a boy's, and large, dark eyes staring from gaunt sockets. And the hands of the woman were like the face, bony, incredibly emaciated. Unconsciously Lucy lifted her own hand, and simultaneously the movement was effected by that other. She recoiled painfully—almost in fear. It was she herself, her reflection in the mirror carelessly left tilted by the sister *infirmière*, that she observed.

Stunned, she lay back, staring away from her image towards the ceiling. Such a little grey rat of a woman—this actually was what she had become! She was not yet forty-five. And only yesterday she had been a young and careless creature, quick with the eagerness of life, waiting in that glorious sunshine at her gate—for Frank. And now? No tears came to those large, dark eyes which fixed themselves so stiffly upon the ceiling; but they dulled and grew distant; and the pale lips of the face drew downwards with an infinite pathos. How ordinary, and yet how strange her life had been. Nothing unusual; just humdrum. Yes, that was the word—humdrum. Working for something which never came; reaching out her hand towards the infinite!

She lowered her eyes slowly. The door had opened softly, and now there entered Bonne Mère Générale, old Sister Infirmière, and finally, incredibly, the Mistress of Novices. Incredibly, too, they all were smiling; they entered amidst a perfect wreath of smiles.

" So, so, you are awake," said Bonne Mère Générale, advancing to the edge of the bed. " Already you look refreshed." Her small, pugnacious chin retreated as, almost playfully, she turned her head and demanded of the *infirmière*: " *Monsieur le docteur* is satisfied? "

" But yes, Bonne Mère Générale," answered the old woman obsequiously. " Perfectly. Already I have explained——"

Bonne Mère Générale put up her hand.

" He does not come again? " It was more a declaration than a question.

" But no, Bonne Mère Générale. He reports confidence in me. He remarks——"

The Superior turned her broad back.

" You see," she remarked to Lucy, pursing her lips pleasantly, " it is not serious for you. A little malaise. Some little fever in the head. Nothing "—she waved her hand—" nothing at all."

" Already she has the air more tranquil," advanced Marie Emmanuel with a white smile. " It is so agreeable."

" Truly my cordial is remarkable," put in the little *infirmière*. " *Monsieur le docteur* himself remarks it to be very extracted. High praise from him, I assure you, *ma* Bonne Mère Générale."

" You must have all that is required," declared Bonne Mère blandly. " There is *bouillon* for you, and wine, and egg with milk. Then we must not forget the so extracted cordial of Sister Marthe."

The three smiled at the little joke.

" Some fruit might be agreeable," murmured Marie Emmanuel with a regal air. " So refreshing—so cool, I imagine."

Lucy's eyes puckered. What lay behind all this? Could this be the woman who had forced her through the degradation of the past six months—now suggesting that she have fruit?

" Decidedly," averred the Superior. " Some fruit would be agreeable." She paused, then rose. " It shall be done. And now we must not fatigue your patient, Sister." They moved to the door. No mention of her deplorable delinquency; no mention of punishment; no direct question; nothing but indulgent friendliness.

They retired smiling, in perfect amity and order. She had not opened her lips during the entire interview.

She lay back weakly, wonderingly. Why, after such severity, this present pampering? What were they going to do with her? And again, what was to become of her?

Sister Marthe returned silently upon her prunella boots, bearing triumphantly a blue delf plate heaped with fruit. Plums and nectarines were there, with peaches and some vivid mulberries empurpled almost by their dusted bloom. She placed the plate on the chair beside the bed and remarked:

" There it will be to your hand when you desire it."

Lucy followed the other's movements slowly with her heavy eyes, then slowly she demanded:

" How long have I been here? " Her voice sounded cracked and reedy in her ears. Marthe inclined her head appraisingly towards the heaped blue plate.

" Only one day," she exclaimed cheerfully. " It is not much."

There was a pause; then across the silence of the room Lucy's voice came back:

" What is to happen—with me? "

But the *infirmière* pretended not to hear. Her soft feet nosed gently over the floor towards the armoire and, still with her head inclined, she measured into a worn spoon a darkish liquid from a long-necked bottle.

" Come," she declared, turning again. " It is time for your medicament."

It was syrupy, the medicine, yet tinctured with a bitter warmth; and afterwards a cup of soup was swallowed. Then there was silence, broken by a stray tapping upon the window-pane from a shoot of clematis. A passive hush, in which she too was static. Her body motionless, her emaciated hands flat upon the coverlet; her eyes once more directed into a distance that was remote and absolute. Tip-tap-tip, went the tedious tapping on the pane. Then silence. Away, far off, there came a faint murmur of singing; outside, the ivy fluttered its glistening scales; slowly the patch of sunlight drifted round and upwards, losing its brilliance as it mounted the grey wall, and fading finally into wells of wavering twilight. Before the last thin gleam was gone the drug had lulled her into sleep.

It was a dreamless sleep; a merciful oblivion into which she sank without resistance. So long without an adequate repose, she lay motionless, extended, breathing lightly, nor did she wake again until Sister Marthe touched her upon the shoulder. Unbelieving, she considered the rising sun; the night, lately so long and full of torment, had passed her in a flash.

" You are too kind to me," she said to the *infirmière*, a faint quiver moving across her lips.

433

" Soon you will be well," returned the other, nodding her head eagerly. " My cordial. You understand. It is specific."

A wan smile trembled on Lucy's lips. She did indeed feel better. Her head was heavy, but through her body returning currents of vitality began to stir like thin streams of sap within a parched tree. But how weak she was! As she drank her chocolate—so thick and strong—her trembling hand with difficulty supported the cup. And still her mind was numb, paralysed by a weight of doubt.

All morning she lay in this inertia, then at noon the door swung open to admit again those visitors of the previous day.

Once more she was complimented upon her improvement, then with a gesture the Superior dismissed the old *infirmière*.

" You look much recovered," she declared, standing close to the edge of the bed. She paused, then in a light, agreeable tone, with a quick nodding of her head, added: " Soon you shall be fit to travel."

Lucy's eyes did not leave the other's face. It was what she had expected; it was inevitable. Yet somehow her passive and enfeebled spirit stiffened at the words. They were getting rid of her: pleasantly, all without fuss. That, indeed, or so it seemed to her, was the reason of this attentiveness, those too agreeable smiles.

" So I am going, then? " she said slowly.

" It is so much better for your health," exclaimed the other volubly. She turned to Marie Emmanuel. " It is clear that we regret the step greatly." She shrugged her shoulders in justification. " But with health so enfeebled—what would you? "

" That is so," said Marie Emmanuel. " What would you? "

During the short silence that slow wave of bitterness welled up in Lucy's breast. With a calm, set face she declared distinctly:

" I was well when I entered the community. There was my medical certificate."

" Perhaps the age? " suggested Marie Emmanuel with infinite tact. " That was against you."

" It is you who are against me," returned Lucy in a low voice, " and everything that is here. I entered wishing to raise myself to God, and always you have thrust me down—dragged me back into something mean and paltry. You have robbed me of everything! "

" Still you do not understand," gasped the other. " It is the Rule—that perfect submission. Only to allow you to acquire it have I been severe. It is you who have estranged yourself. So different. Bonne Mère Générale is aware——"

She broke off and threw out her hands in vindication.

" Now it is not significant," said the Superior evenly, with her eyes on Lucy. " It is a great tribulation to the community that you are not convenable, but nevertheless the affair is terminated. And now you must be calm to think of your return."

Lucy compressed her pale lips. Still no excuses, no recriminations; it was assumed from the outset that she was in the wrong; simply the matter was not to be discussed. And they wanted to be rid of her—that she clearly perceived. Well, she had now no wish to remain!

" You need have no fear," she said with a dignity strangely pathetic. " I shall write to my son at once."

" Already I have written," answered Bonne Mère Générale quietly. " He should receive that letter to-day, your good son."

They had done even that—written to her son in terms of which she was ignorant, and must still remain ignorant. The same injustice, chafing her in the same way, causing the old resentment to rise within her!

Deliberately she controlled the tremulous twitching of her cheek. " A letter is not enough," she said calmly. " You must wire. Wire that I arrive to-morrow."

" No! No! It is impossible," they expostulated together. " It is too soon. In another week perhaps."

" I do not wish to remain here," she answered with a slow intensity which cost her dear. " Here it is hateful to me."

" But you are still too—too fatigued! "

" I will not remain here," she repeated again, firmly, imperatively; and in all her weakness she strove desperately for an outward calm and quietude. She would not betray herself. Yet with a rising agitation she exclaimed:

" If you do not wire that I arrive to-morrow evening, I shall go of my own accord."

They stared at her in the silence of misgiving; each looked at the other, then back again to her.

" You must remain tranquil," said one soothingly at length. " You know we cannot detain you. But it is not possible."

" It is possible," reiterated Lucy with set lips. " To-morrow morning I shall leave."

There was a long abashed silence.

" Well, if you desire it," said the Superior at last, with a protesting shrug. " But, truly, it is not reasonable."

She made no answer; nor did she move. But she closed her eyes, as though she must efface their hateful presence from her sight. For a long time after they had gone she lay still, her thin, veined hands motionless upon the counterpane, her cheek turned sideways towards the window, white and twisted. But for all her stillness a passionate shame was in her. A phrase of Frank's, long forgotten, flashed into her mind. Yes, for all her pretence of dignity, they had " chucked her out." She was chucked out! Her lip twitched. She was not suitable to them. She had entered this house bursting with the fervour of the love of God, with one passionate desire: to be the bride of Jesus. And now, her love refused, her fervour rejected, her soul emptied, the jilted bride of Jesus, she was going back—to what? Worn and stripped and empty as she was, devoid of everything, she was still conscious of a strange outreaching of her soul.

Outside, the sunshine lingered amongst the trees, and the flowers were ringed by the humming bees; and something beyond beckoned vaguely through the hazy distance. Perhaps for her there was still something? Without moving, her cheek still pressed sideways into the pillow and without sound, her heart flowed over, and she wept.

XII

THE following morning, which she had decided to be the morning of her going, broke fresh and clear. A brisk breeze fluttered the spray of clematis against the window-pane, and, beyond, she could see the trees whisking in a wind which sent the leaves of the copper beech soaring like startled swallows against the immobile sky. And it was colder. At one breath the summer had turned to autumn.

She had awakened early, and for a long time she remained in thought. Then at eight o'clock she rose slowly—even cautiously. She stumbled and swayed at odd moments. But it behoved her to be careful, lest under the curious eyes of Marthe she should betray the dreadful weakness that assailed her. It was incredible, that weakness: a struggle to hold her head upright upon her limp neck, an effort to keep those hands from trembling as she dressed.

It was the black dress which she had worn in the *Postulat* that she assumed, but now, too large upon her meagre frame, it hung loosely in folds like a coat upon a scarecrow. Never had that dress been prepossessing, but now, pinned and tucked and tightened upon her by the old *infirmière*, it had an air both ludicrous and tragic.

As she rose with a swimming head from lacing her boots, suddenly she saw herself in the mirror. What a spectacle, she thought weakly! The dragged-in skirt, that comical pouching of the bodice, the hat falling askew upon the cropped head. And it was she—she who once had been elegant, fastidious: Frank had even called her beautiful!

" Do you feel all right now you are risen? " old Marthe was asking her solicitously.

She turned. " Perfectly," she answered in a low voice.

" Then let us descend," said the other.

They went down to the parlour, where already Marie Emmanuel

and Joséphine were awaiting her. These two, once instructed to receive her, had now apparently been detailed for her departure.

Bonne Mère Générale was not present, but occupied at this hour with her devotions.

Her trunk was also in that parlour, open, with all her clothing—everything which she had brought in—laid out meticulously. And she was obliged to remain whilst an inventory was made before her eyes. Nothing, it was demonstrated, had been retained. All that she had brought was here and was now surrendered. Even the money, to the last sou, was accounted for; more than sufficient for her fare, it had been. Her ticket was taken, the cab ordered, everything done. It was just! And she had used the word " robbed "!

At last the trunk was packed and, because the lock, yielding finally, was broken, they corded it down with rope. It was secure, they said, but as the leather case, wherein were all her goods, stood upon its end in the prim parlour, it had an air almost like her own: worn and bedraggled by its batterings and journeying.

They waited, the three—for the old *infirmière* had slipped out without speaking—facing each other across the round, oilcloth-covered table. There was no excitement, no tension, no sense of the unusual. Nothing could disturb the inexorable movements of the machine which had accepted her, engulfed her, and which now disgorged her. It went on and on and on.

" Bonne Mère Générale regrets that she is occupied," said Marie Emmanuel for the second time. " In effect, she is not agreeable to your going so soon, but she cannot detain you."

The bell clanged, but it came faintly, as from a distance.

" The wire has been dispatched this morning," remarked Marie Emmanuel once more.

Outside, the swishing of dry leaves made sudden intermittent little gushes of sound.

" This package," said Joséphine, indicating a neat parcel before her, " it is a very good luncheon for you." She smiled: " Sandwiches and *paté*—yes, even sausage. All specially made ready for you."

Still loading her with these temporal benefits, these little attentions and smiles, when here it was that everything had been stolen from her.

Suddenly she raised her head.

" If it is permitted, I should like to take good-bye of Sister Adrienne."

At once the two religious looked at each other deprecatingly; Marie Emmanuel was silent, but at length Joséphine smiled her expressionless smile:

" But that is not possible, I fear," she said. " Early on the morning of her anniversary the good sister was found unconscious. A stroke of the brain—and she has since died." She smiled very gaily. " Yes, there is great joy in heaven. They are welcoming another saint."

So that was how old Adrienne had spent her anniversary—without her little *tasse* of coffee and her *gâteau glacé*. A great sadness came over Lucy with a sudden sense of loss. To her Adrienne alone in this place of unreality had seemed actual and human. And her passing was greeted with a childish, ingenuous smile: a smile at those golden gates opening for the old woman who had not wished to leave the sunshine of the earth. It was too fantastic.

There was the crunch of a wheel upon the drive.

" The cab awaits," said Marie Emmanuel, rising. " I shall send the driver for the baggage."

They followed her outside: the same closed cab, the same old coachman in the same faded bluish coat buttoned to his neck, touching his glazed hat, disappearing into the porch, reappearing bowed beneath her trunk, heaving that trunk upon the box. And in the air was that nip of autumn which she had always loved.

Marie Emmanuel turned the brass-ringed handle and opened the door.

" We shall accompany you to the station."

Lucy's eyes followed her movements.

" No," she said evenly, " I prefer to go alone."

The other woman observed her closely. There was a short, stiff silence.

" But we are instructed," put in Joséphine, her small eyes creased out by the sunshine and her discomposure.

" I am no longer instructed," answered Lucy. " Now I am myself."

She got into the cab, pulled the door behind her. Through the small glass panel she saw the two faces turned towards her with uncomprehending, faintly discouraged eyes. Then the coachman whipped up the horse, and those faces receded backwards from her sight.

It was finished, then—so quietly, so dispassionately, she might have been returning from a simple visit instead of concluding the most desperate experience of her life.

The cab rattled on. At first she looked neither to right nor to left, but kept her bent gaze upon the jolting floor. Then slowly she raised her head and with an impassive face gazed on to the busy street. Full of women was this roadway, women and girls hurrying back to breakfast from the laceworks of Sentiens, laughing, talking, gesticulating, clattering their sabots with a rude energy. How happy they looked, and how careless. The air rang with their loud, cheerful voices. Once she had set out in life like that, with the same energy, the same purpose.

She entered the outskirts of Brussels, going back—back the

same way she had come. Here there was greater quietude and an empty thoroughfare—merely a boy washing the window of a *charcuterie*, a concierge in a green baize apron polishing the brasses of his doorway, a little blue *gendarme* waiting at a street-corner, all so casual and matter of fact.

Then into Brussels. Again the trams, the traffic, shops opening, cafés already open, some topers incredibly early at their bocks. How restless her eye was! A mirror for everything. Yes, it was merely a mirror. She perceived only with the surface of her mind—those quick passing reflections were the light and shadows fluttering upon the surface of a pool. Beneath the fleeting images lay a dull obscurity. She was in the square: vast, full of writhing statuary; pigeons strutting on the pedestals; horses drooping limp necks before dejected fiacres.

Then came the station—the train—the compartment with its sulphurous smell and seats of figured velvet.

Now she had started upon her return; through that same country-side. The neat square fields, peasants bent within those fields, the unwavering canals, the thin lines of poplars plunging like plumes before the wind. She had traversed this land before, filled then by a thrilling ecstasy, her heart leaping to the beating of the wheels. And whither had the ecstasy led her? To a mad scene within a walled-in garden, where reason had almost left her! She shivered and shut her mind against the thought. And now she was going back! It was so foolish, this return.

A sense of abject futility suddenly invaded her All her life—what had it been but a blind reaching towards futility? On and on, striving for something that was never achieved. And she had struggled so hard, with all her forces, striving with both her hands to mould fate, for this egregious result. Everything she had done had been deliberate, firm. She was no shuttlecock; nothing was accidental; everything had come from within, from herself! And this raddled, ridiculous creature was the issue of it all—this beaten retreat the immutable conclusion of her destiny.

But was it the end? And was she defeated? Unconsciously she held her head to that familiar attitude of listening—listening to the thunder of the wheels and the note which rose insistently and throbbing as before. The same wheels, the same note—yes, and she the same woman! That was why to her the note was different. " On and on," it said to her. " On and on—on and on! "—urging her forward—farther, farther.

Straightening herself, she lowered the window and let the flying air rush full against her face. That was better. The wind, stinging against her brow, cleared it of its furrow, infused a tonic strength into her listless body. That wind, flailing the plunging poplars, casting a silver sheen upon the quivering willows, was better—better than the listless air which had recently enclosed her. Now she would do something!

No, she was not defeated. Something rose up within her at the thought. The past was finished and must be forgotten. She had the future; always she had the future. How muddled her head was, and how baffling the problem. She was actually stupid—yes, stupid and inarticulate. She could not think now, but later she would puzzle the whole thing out.

Her strength gathered. Instinctively she knew that something was reaching out to her. It was a conviction, a happy premonition. And she forgot her aching head, her exhausted body, her sorry clothing, her wretched predicament. She forgot them all, and was filled by a strange content.

Tournai—Blaudain—Baisieux—Lille—they swept past her in turn. Then she was at Calais, passing the curious inspection of the Customs, boarding the steamer that lay against the quay. And now her eye, directed outside the harbour, perceived the restless movement of the grey sea and the racing of the smoky clouds. She saw that the crossing would be rough. Strangely, this thought, which once would have moved her to the greatest dread, gave her no qualms. Her fibre had toughened since those days when she had quailed before a ruffled sea. Now she knew that she would be ill. It was inevitable, and she accepted it.

When the packet left the pier, she did not go below, but stood by the bulwark rail steadying herself against the sudden lurchings of the deck. It was bad—a dreadful crossing. The vessel jumped and pounded into the heavy seas, battered by the vast bulks of water which burst against its bow and hull. Like her own life, that passage —she and the ship were one. Staggering under every blow, yet rising, impelled by that inner force which drove them both, moving forward against those savage waves. On and on! The wind twanged through the rigging like a flight of whistling bolts; the flying spray stung her pale cheeks; a wave, cresting the bow, lapped the vertiginous decks and spilled itself gently towards her feet. A cold sickness assailed her: no physical nausea, but an inward deathly weakness.

She gripped the rail tightly and held herself rigid whilst the great masses of water rolled and raced beneath. Her hat was askew, her long loose dress flapping like a sail, her face blue with cold, her teeth tightly set.

A stewardess hurrying past, her figure trimmed against the gale, paused suddenly. Her eyes rested for a moment on Lucy.

" Come down—come down below," she said, and then she added: " Madam."

Madam—strange bedraggled creature to merit such a title—turned her wind-battered head.

" I'm better here, I think," she answered dazedly.

" But you look ill. Would you like some brandy? "

The stewardess awaited no answer, but went at once and brought a small glass of brandy. Still clutching the rail, Lucy drank the brandy. She thanked the stewardess, paid her fumblingly out of her foreign money.

It warmed her within, the liquor, glowing like a warm core within her chilled body. Yes, she was very cold. The cutting wind pierced her inadequate clothing, and lacerated her thin frame, which shivered as with a rigor. Her teeth chattered; her pinched features, drained of what blood they had, set with a frozen rigidity. A sharp stitch nipped her side.

Yet mercifully she conquered her sickness. She would not give in, but held firm to that rail, letting the biting wind chill the nausea until finally it left her.

Like the ship, she gallantly won through. They had said she was not fit to endure the journey; and she had endured it. She was here in England—home; and, after the torture of those Channel seas, the flat tranquillity of Dover harbour was peace indeed. Out of that shattering blast a feeble reaction stirred within her body—that stirring of that sanguine, inexhaustible courage. She had her fortitude!

It was not far to the boat-train, but somehow her legs did not now belong to her. She had a queer pain in her eyes and in her side.

" Nothing to declare? " Nothing—nothing but her fortitude! Where was the platform? She must follow the crowd. She would never get to that train. Yet, somehow, she achieved it. Actually she was now within the compartment, though in her stupidity she had chosen a smoker filled with men, laughing, talking noisily. No matter: she would not change now. It was not worth while. She was near the end of her long journey.

Still, it was warm, very warm. Her hands and forehead glowed and throbbed, though her feet were still icy. Her face felt flushed. Surreptitiously she pressed her cheek against the cool window.

The train rushed on through the mellow evening. Strangely, the wind had dropped, and gauzy veils of mist crept quietly into the hollows of the land. And some of that mist crept quietly into her mind, drifting in, then out again, in little swirling eddies. Travelling all day—that was what had tired her. Only a little fatigued. Someone was looking at her, asking if she would like the window down. She nodded her head. That was better—the cool breeze of the train's passage, sweetly fragrant with autumnal scents; the tang of dried leaves, a whiff of wood smoke, the bite of the early frost. No matter about her feet, nor that tiny stitch within her side; the sharp nip braced her. And how she had always loved that subtle fragrance of this season. On and on; rushing forward; linked not now to the ship, but to the train. Her head throbbing in sympathy. Still, she must now be nearly there, and Peter would meet her at the station. Her own—he at least was something left to her, something tangible, real, amongst all her recent unrealities. Hazily she considered the wire she had sent to him: her wire, for its wording had devolved entirely upon her. So short she had made it—already the letter had acquainted him with everything: " Arrive seven-thirty Victoria Mother." A wan smile trembled on her lips as she considered the sending of that wire: not so much a caprice as a challenge; a banner unfurled in the face of destiny. He would understand, and know that she was not defeated. Yes, her son knew that she would never admit to failure— she was bruised and battered, a tattered remnant of herself, but she was not defeated. And she had come back to him. Rushing memories of tenderness swept over her. That so familiar, teasing smile upon his face.

" You're not a bad-looking little woman, mother."

Arm in arm along the front at Doune on just such a night as this. Sitting together at the entertainers', close together in the dusk, and Val Pinkerton singing for them:

> " Daisy, Daisy . . . I'm just crazy,
> All for the love of you."

She smiled again faintly. Perhaps she had been hard, unyielding. In obstinacy she had battered her head against that stern wall of inevitability. But now she would accept the unalterable, accept Rose, accept everything—now.

The engine whistled an answering blast, and with a scrunch of brakes the train slowed into Victoria. She was home—or nearly home—at last!

She let the compartment empty of her fellow-passengers before she got out. Then, on the platform, she stood waiting. Her eyes had a bright and almost feverish light; she felt her heart throbbing painfully. Was it her heart, or that stabbing pain within her side? " A running pain " Peter had called it when he was a little boy come back to her, flushed from racing at rounders. And now her face was flushed, too, as she walked slowly down the platform.

The crowd was thinning, and she could see more clearly, but, although she strained her eyes, she could not discern his figure. But the train was early. Perhaps he was detained. She had no fear that he would not come. She could wait—only for a few moments—until he came. She would walk up and down—it was easier that way.

And so, slowly, uncertainly, she began to walk up and down—a little grey rat of a woman huddled in her ridiculous clothes. Walking up and down the station platform—waiting.

XIII

SHE walked up and down that platform for an hour. She might have set out alone for her son's house; but a sort of powerlessness prevented her. She was dazed, bereft suddenly of the final vestige of her strength. With no English money in her pocket, no consciousness of the passage of time, no power to move from this inertia which kept her swinging like a pendulum, with simply the faith that he would come, she waited.

But he could not come. He was away. Even as she waited, the letter of Bonne Mère Générale was following him to Brittany, whither he had gone upon his holiday with Rosie—yes, they had always said they would return!—to recapture the rapture of their first visit. And the wire, that wire of her own composition—so definite, so positive, she had known it must bring him to the station? Opened by his partner, who knew nothing of its significance—who was, moreover, rushed by double work—it had occasioned merely the passing thought: " She'll come on to his house," a message to the maid within that empty house, a vague expectation on the maid's part that someone might arrive. And that was all.

The situation was of her making, the blame entirely her own. She should have remained at Sentiens until she was stronger; until she had heard from him; until all arrangements had been made for her return. But that was not she! And so she had come; she was here; waiting. " On and on," those wheels had said. But really it was impossible for her legs to go on much further. They dragged and stumbled weakly under her; they did not belong to her, but wavered numbly beneath the light ethereal substance of her body. Her body was airy now, and might have floated but for that stabbing pain in her side which became a chain—each breath she took forging a new link—that weighted her and bound her to reality.

She must do something; that at last was certain, piercing her numbed consciousness as from afar. She could not remain here for ever, walking back and forwards so aimlessly upon this unending platform.

Vaguely she perceived a policeman standing beside a pillar watching her. He had been there for a long time: for minutes or hours or centuries he had been observing her with a curious concentrated suspicion. Then suddenly she felt worse, unutterably limp and faint. She thought hurriedly of her dizzy turns. This was another coming on. She would be all right, but she must do something—she must have assistance. She approached that policeman, opened her lips to speak, stammered, struggled with all her forces to speak. Was she speaking? She did not know. His round red face above the bright buttons of his tunic swam before her vision. What would he think? Would he smell upon her breath that brandy the stewardess had given her? Would he imagine she—Lucy Moore—— Then all at once she solved the difficulty for him, and for herself, by sinking down into unconsciousness at his feet.

There was a crowd, of course, a crowd as if by magic: a sympathetic crowd, who knew wisely that she had fainted, and demanded that she be given air. But, curiously, she did not recover from that faint.

There was then an ambulance: a white motor ambulance that swung like a grey ghost into the dimness of the vaulted station.

She was in that ambulance, lying upon her back, like an odd lay figure. Her eyes were open and faintly wondering; advancing and receding above her through the mists were two figures—the policeman, a man who wore a long white coat.

Hoot—hoot! Hoot—hoot! Something in her ears—something warm crackling in her side—and a roaring, rushing noise! She gave it up and weakly closed her eyes. From her dry lips came quick and shallow breaths.

" She breathes queer, don't she? " said the policeman at length.

The white-coated man nodded his head.

" These old women—what makes them get about on their own beats me."

" Yes, asking for trouble it is."

A pause.

" St. Thomas's your mate's taking us."

" That's right, mate."

Into the courtyard of the hospital; and still she was detached, still a lay figure, now lying limply upon a stretcher. It was all happening so quickly—a cataract of speed; she tried to lift up her hand to protest. But there was no power in her hand. The cataract still swept her forward. On and on through vast, interminable corridors; being wheeled through labyrinths of corridors. Lights and faces.

Tap-tap, tap-tap, over that really serious pain. Worse it was now, quite serious and bad. Was it toothache? It was in her side, yet so like—yes, she remembered—so like the tearing pang of those teeth coming out. " We'll take four out for a start! "—and her deliberate voice: " How much without the anæsthetic? " Lying back calmly in that red plush chair. She felt the pangs again. Then the big, smiling face of the dentist bending over her. But this was not his face; another, younger face smiling encouragingly; then the sharp prick of a needle in her arm, and herself trying to smile back, trying to speak, trying to tell them who she was—about her son.

Pain—more pain: each stabbing pain her own breath. And, finally, dark smoky clouds and grey seas rolling over her, rolling her into a blessed oblivion.

"Fulminating," said the house physician at the foot of the bed. "And no reaction."

"When we bathed her," said the sister, "frightful, it was—the emaciation."

"Better inform the relatives."

"There's nothing. No markings on the clothing. No bag, no letters, only some Belgian money in the pocket of the dress. And such a dress!"

He looked towards the bed.

"I'll let the police know, then."

"Yes."

"And screens!" As he moved away he glanced at her significantly. "An apical pneumonia and that constitution!"

And so the screens were put round No. 7. These were the white curtains which danced and fluttered occasionally before her clouded eyes: white curtains like those she had hung upon the windows of her house in Ardfillan. And hands parted those curtains; faces peeped at her—Peter's face. His laughing face was there, flushed from running as he came in from school. And she was back sometimes, rambling on Ardmore Point. Those picnics to the fishing-pool and to the shore. Farther back now: she was seated upon that shore suckling her infant son. The sun shone; the tang of sea wrack drifted to her nostrils; and, looking upwards from her lap, Peter's baby face smiled at her—laughing, a trickle of milk running from the corner of his mouth.

And then dim consciousness returned, wherein she heard a low bubbling beside her bed and felt someone giving her to drink. How thirsty she was. Her cracked lips were burning, her tongue dry and swollen with a feverish thirst. She tried to wipe her lips, but her hands, it seemed, were bloated to a size enormous, and to the heaviness of lead. And through it all her breath was so entangled, so difficult—caught in a web, a forest of crushing undergrowth through which she toiled and chased it pantingly. Panting, panting——

Then all at once she slipped back again. More faces peering from behind those parted curtains. Frank's face: calm and with that curious mocking smile; Anna's, taunting, sneering, reviling her; Netta's, ruddy and open; Dave Bowie's face, mild and laughing; faces of her childhood, too, all those early faces, distant, floating, forming now a ring which spun around her dizzily. Then came another interval of painful consciousness. Where was she? So weak, so filled with this burning and this anguish! Was she—was she dying? No! That couldn't be. She wasn't finished with things yet. Only forty-five. She wasn't beaten. Her head was still up. On and on. The wheels were racing madly forward—on and on!

Back again to that delirious dreaming. No faces now, but, instead, a light—a dazzling light which bathed her—so bright for her weak eyes. It glowed and glowed like the halo of a Christ. No, it was not that—Christ's halo was never so bright. It was sunlight—the burnished sunlight falling across the shining sea, and through it bright motes went flickering up like butterflies. She was back, back at the beginning; she was at her window looking out, waiting, raising her hand to shade her eyes against that light.

It flooded her whole being, that light, with final, blinding intensity.

Then all at once went out.

Suddenly, upon her, rushing, came the last eternal darkness.

It was upon the evening following her admission that she died. No resistance—no reaction—it was quite inevitable.

They took her to the mortuary. There, upon that thick stone slab, which once had been a vision of her nightmare fancy, they laid her.

The night was gentle, quiet with the late autumnal stillness she had loved. And into the silent crypt a grey mist rolled from the moving river, weaving mysteriously about her figure lying wasted, naked, stripped of everything, upon that slab.

Fixed in the rigid mask of death, the face was meaningless. The eyes were closed, the lips pale and faintly parted, the hands, translucent upon the breast, crossed with final impotence. And the vapours, rising more thickly from the water and the earth, enshrouded her.

THE END